Patrick Gale

was born on the Isle of Wight in 1962. He spent his infancy in Wandsworth Prison, which his father governed, then grew up in Winchester. He now lives on a farm near Land's End.

Praise for *The Facts of Life*:

'Brilliant. Vastly readable.'

Marie Claire

'Deftly characterised, deeply involving and relevant.'

The Times

'Patrick Gale offers us so much more than facts in this extraordinary blockbuster of a novel. Its exploration of family ties and tyranny is encompassed within a deft narrative. Much like the late Ivy Compton-Burnett, Gale presents us with a family saga which both questions and defies present day morality. Always fluent, Gale manages to be both brutal and witty. His analysis of the family tree is rooted in compassion and insight and expounded resoundingly well.'

Time Out

'A subtle, enthralling work, it envelops the bare necessities of living and dying with an evocative sense of social history and prevailing prejudices. Well written, unerringly true and very moving, the book reveals Gale to be an unabashed romantic and a novelist of increasing accomplishment.'

Scotland on Sunday

'A monumental feat of imagination, achingly true and beautiful. I'd be hard pressed to recall the last time a novel so totally captivated me.'

ead Maupin

Also by Patrick Gale

THE AERODYNAMICS OF PORK

KANSAS IN AUGUST

EASE

FACING THE TANK

LITTLE BITS OF BABY

THE CAT SANCTUARY

CAESAR'S WIFE (NOVELLA)

DANGEROUS PLEASURES (STORIES)

TREE SURGERY FOR BEGINNERS

ROUGH MUSIC

Patrick Gale

The Facts of Life

Flamingo
An Imprint of HarperCollins*Publishers*

Flamingo
An Imprint of HarperCollins*Publishers*
77–85 Fulham Palace Road,
Hammersmith, London W6 8JB

Flamingo® is a registered trademark of
HarperCollins*Publishers* Ltd

www.fireandwater.com

Published by Flamingo 1996
9 8 7 6 5

First published in Great Britain by
Flamingo 1995

This novel is entirely a work of fiction.
The names, characters and incidents portrayed in it are
the work of the author's imagination. Any resemblance
to actual persons, living or dead, events or localities is
entirely coincidental.

Author photograph by Aidan Hicks

ISBN 0 00 654768 0

Typeset in Monotype Apollo by
Palimpsest Book Production Limited,
Polmont, Stirlingshire

Printed in Great Britain by
Clays Ltd, St Ives plc

For Tom Wakefield, whose friendship shelters

I am ill because of wounds to the soul, to the deep emotional
self
And the wounds to the soul take a long, long time, only time
can help
and patience, and a certain difficult repentance
long, difficult repentance, realisation of life's mistake, and the
freeing oneself
from the endless repetition of the mistake
which mankind at large has chosen to sanctify.

D.H. Lawrence, *Healing*

Author's Note

Warmest thanks

to Pippy Ennion, the Curé d'Arsenal, Dr Frank Heibert, Jonathan Dove, Madge, Patrick, Simon, and to everyone at Bethany, for letting me plunder their memories and expertise.

To Michael and Moira, for all those frosty weekends in Norfolk.

To Jonathan Warner and Charlotte Windsor, for their patience.

To Alan Hollinghurst and Barry Goodman for their rigorous proof-reading.

And to Fingal, for the walks on the beach.

P.G.
1.7.94

PART I

1

She heard him before she saw him. She was on her round of Godiva Ward, checking on the children, listening to coughs, peering into pinched, white faces, tapping and listening at scrawny chests, when the sound of piano-playing reached her from the day room. There was an old grand piano there, half hidden by potted palms, one of several vestiges of the hospital's former grandeur as a superior hotel. It was rarely tuned and suffered from sea air, being surrounded by so many open windows. Someone accompanied the carols on it at Christmas, the children played musical statues to it at birthday parties and occasionally a charitable local artiste would subject them to a recital of pieces with evocative titles like *War March of the Priests, Rustle of Spring* or *Moscow Bells*. Pub-style sing-songs were, of course, out of the question, given the ragged state of most inmates' lungs, but patients chancing on the venerable instrument for the first time sometimes lifted the lid out of curiosity to pick out a melody with one erratic finger. Vera Lynn songs were popular – *White Cliffs of Dover* and *We'll Meet Again* – but Sally had noticed that it was the older, less overtly morale-boosting songs that people thumped out time and again – *Smoke Gets in Your Eyes* or *You've Got me Crying Again*.

The music this morning was serious stuff, played sitting down, and with both hands. She knew little of proper music – her father always switched the radio off when a concert was broadcast – but she recognised a waltz when she heard one. Gentle, lilting, ineffably sad, the sound made her pause as she was questioning a nurse about one of the more pathetic, long-stay patients.

'Brahms,' said the nurse, who had also cocked her head to listen. 'It's probably all he knows.'

'Who?'

'Edward the Gerry. Funny that. Edward.' The nurse tried the name out in her mouth like an alien sweet. 'It's not a Jewish name at all, when you think about it,' she added. 'More English, really. But you can tell he is. Jewish, I mean. Tell at a glance. But then I can always spot them.'

'When did he arrive?'

'Last week. They transferred him from that military hospital at Horton Down.'

'Is he Forces, then?'

'Only just. He'd only started his basic training when he was diagnosed. How he got through his medical is anyone's guess. I suppose they were less fussy towards the end. Like I say, he's German. He was in that internment camp at Westmarket, on the racecourse, and he reckons that's where he contracted it. Pretty rough down there by all accounts. Criminal really. I mean, it's not as though he was likely to be a spy, but I suppose they couldn't be too careful.'

No-one in the hospital referred to tuberculosis by its proper name or even its abbreviation. Even now that there was a cure and a vaccine, there was still a sense of it being a *dirty* disease. 'It' was quite sufficient, in any case, because few patients were brought in for any other illness.

'Isn't Horton Down closed now?' Sally pursued.

'He was one of the last patients.' The nurse dropped her voice. 'I think they'd rather forgotten about him, poor lad.'

She saw him for the first time the next day. Unlike the children's ward, where a dormitory had been imposed on what had once been a huge, ground floor saloon, the men's and women's wards afforded patients more privacy. Long wings were flung out on either side of the main body of the building. The bedrooms, forty in all, now sleeping two or three apiece, were ranged along their seaward sides. The incongruously well-appointed bathrooms across each corridor faced inland. A broad balcony linked the bedrooms along the front of the building and, during the conversion to a hospital, this had been scantily glassed over so as to afford a bracing promenade. Here those patients too weak to take even gentle exercise in the windswept grounds were expected to take the air for hours at a time. Swathed in dressing-gowns and blankets, they lay in tidy ranks on wooden reclining chairs, gossiping quietly, reading, playing cards or staring mournfully out to sea and gulping the salt air like so many beached fish. A trellis partition, painted an unpleasantly acidic green, which stretched half-way across the floor at the promenade's middle, was intended to indicate where the men's ward ended and the women's began but did little to prevent fraternisation between the sexes.

Beside the trellis, on the men's side, crouched an imposing radiogram, its wood bleached by the sun. It was turned on after breakfast and only silenced after the evening meal. It was tuned to *Worker's Playtime* when Sally emerged from the landing. She was struck afresh by the resemblance of the scene about her to the deck of some liner, tourist class. She had never been on a cruise, but she had seen them in plenty of films and during the war she had worked briefly on a hospital ship pressed into service from the Cunard Line.

A young nurse approached her, rubber soles squeaking on blood-red linoleum.

'Can I help you, Miss?'

Most nurses found it hard to call another woman Doctor.

'Yes. I'm looking for Edward Pepper.'

'He's up at the end there.'

'The one on his own, writing at the table?'

'That's the one.'

He looked far younger than she had expected. He was thin, but he had thick black hair which curled slightly and the sea air from the open windows all around him had touched his pale cheeks with a surprisingly deep pink. He worked intently at a pad of paper with a ruler and pencil. His forearms and wrists, off which he had pushed his dressing-gown sleeves, were thickly furred. As she drew closer, she saw that he was writing music. She stopped at his elbow.

'Mr Pepper?'

'Yes?'

As he looked up, his eyes ran over her and his lips parted slightly.

'I'm Dr Banks.'

'Are you another specialist?'

'Nothing so exalted, I'm afraid. I'm somewhere between houseman and consultant. We've been chronically understaffed since the war and the hierarchy's crumbled rather in the effort to get things done. Can I sit down?'

'Of course.'

She took the other chair and opened his file.

'How are you feeling today?'

'Better. A little tired.'

'You're one of the lucky ones. We got hold of you in time.'

'So everyone keeps telling me. How much longer will I have to stay here?'

'Two or three weeks.'

He sagged with disappointment.

'That long?'

'The virus has left you very weak. You feel tired and you've only just got up. It'll be some time before you're as strong as you used to be, Mr Pepper. You must know that. Your left lung is permanently damaged. A touch of bronchitis that would have other men reaching for cough mixture will probably lay you up in bed struggling for air. For now you need rest, good clean air, nutritious meals and just enough exercise to strengthen your cardiovascular system. Have you been taking walks?'

'I walk for an hour after lunch. Round and round.'

'Good.'

'It is extremely dull.'

'But you aren't letting the boredom get you down.'

She indicated the pad of paper on his table which he had covered in lines and little marks.

'No.'

'Can I ask what you're working on?'

'It's a string quartet.'

'Oh.' Her mind went blank for a moment, then all she could

picture was the three old women sawing away in the foyer of the Grand in Rexbridge, where her mother liked to go for tea on special occasions. 'Do you play?' she asked.

'No. I write. Well. I try to.' He smiled to himself. His eyes were sleepy and slightly hooded, the skin of the eyelids darker than his pale brow.

'Wasn't that you playing the piano yesterday?'

'Yes. It's very out of tune.'

'It's all we've got. Play all you like. It's a treat for the others. Presumably there wasn't a piano for you at Horton Down.'

'No.' His face hardened. 'There was nothing.' For the first time his choice of words sounded foreign, a little too precise – like a spy in a film. His light accent was entirely English; a parson's or a solicitor's. 'I couldn't even get proper paper. At least this is large enough but . . .'

'But what?'

'Well. I have to draw in my own lines to make up the staves and it gets confusing because they overlap with the lines already printed. You see? I need proper score paper with the staves already printed in.'

'Would a stationer sell that? There's one down the road, in Wenborough.'

'No. You have to go to a music shop. I mean, one would have to. I didn't intend that you should . . .'

She pushed back her chair, closing his file.

'Let me see what I can do,' she told him. 'But I can't make promises. And don't tell anyone, or I'll end up running errands for the lot of you.'

As he said his thanks, she could feel him reassessing her as all the men there did. Seeing a white coat and stethoscope, tidy brown hair and un-made-up face, their first reaction said spinster. When she healed or calmed them, dealt with their pains and assumed responsibility for their helplessness, they looked at her again and their second reaction said mother. Generally they saw the nurses as angels of mercy, the doctors as angels of death. The female patients, inured to such nonsense from the cradle, were more tolerant of her status but also more shy.

She found a music shop on her next free afternoon when

she rode on her motorbike into Rexbridge to find new slippers for her father's birthday. They had only five books of score paper left, handsome things with green marbled covers and black spines. She was unsure how many he would need, so she squandered her money and bought all five. She had to haggle slightly – the assistant sensed her ignorance and tried to ask a stupid price – and still it was more than she could afford. Money was short – the hospital paid her meagrely – and she had decided to be quite brisk about presenting him with a receipt and asking for her money back. But instead, she surprised herself by telling him to repay her by taking her to a concert once he was discharged.

'Yes,' he said, as they laughed, both startled at her boldness. 'Yes. I will. I should enjoy that. But you must let me give you the money too.'

As for so many women, the war had brought her a spell of social freedom, and with peace came a disappointing return to convention and what was suddenly declared to be a woman's proper sphere. She had returned to her parents' house because they lived conveniently close to the hospital, it was cheaper than living on her own and because reasoning with them as to why she should do otherwise was too daunting a prospect.

Sally's father had been laid off from work as a mechanic when she was still a child. A hoist had given way and a lorry engine had fallen on him, crushing his pelvis. He could still hobble about, with two sticks, but going back to his old work was out of the question. He kept himself in beer money by fixing small household appliances – toasters, alarm clocks, gramophones – which he dismembered across the kitchen table. The compensation settlement from his employers had been derisory and her mother was forced out to work at a canning factory where she put in long shifts, sickened by glue fumes as she stuck labels on cans of the rich local produce – apple slices, pears in syrup, rhubarb, peas and beans. Her father had got Sally ready for school, washed, fed and dressed her. When her mother was on night shifts, Sally would not see her for days on end, going about the little terraced house on tiptoe for fear of waking the short-tempered breadwinner. When she worked during the day, her mother would return exhausted and fractious and, more often than not, would nod off in her chair half-way through Sally's account of events at school.

Sally did well, very well by her parents' standards. She won a place at Rexbridge Grammar School – entailing long walks and bus journeys and even earlier rising – and there caught the attention of one of the school's governors. Dr Pertwee, the formidable unmarried daughter of a famous suffragette, singled Sally out as one who could go far. Heedless, it seemed, of what the child herself might want, much less the child's parents, she used her influence to find her scholarships, thinking this would stop her parents resenting any stretching out of Sally's education. She encouraged her interest in science and she coached her, in person, for a place at Rexbridge's medical school.

Since he had played a mother's role, Sally underestimated and overlooked her father, as her friends did their mothers. When he relinquished his sticks for a wheelchair, she found she ceased to even think of him as a man.

She was always torn, however, dreadfully torn, between the antithetical worlds education and her family represented for her. She frequently went straight to Dr Pertwee's rooms in Rexbridge after school. Dr Pertwee served her nutritious sandwiches, fruit and milk like any mother and pressed her through her homework but she also encouraged Sally to discuss subjects like death, politics, religion and marriage that were tacitly accepted as undiscussable at home. Dr Pertwee lent her books outside the school syllabus, and taught her the facts of life in the same calm fashion she used to explain the reproductive systems of horse chestnuts and crested newts. She gave her tea out of bone china cups so fine Sally saw the light through them, and took her on weekend excursions to examine Greek vases and doomy Pre-Raphaelite paintings in the Sadlerian Museum. Sally harboured the curious images and forbidden subjects, the crustless sandwiches and perfumed tea like things stolen and therefore unsharable. What else could she do with them? They sat as awkwardly on her home life as a mink cape would on her narrow, bony shoulders.

For better or worse, her home life was still the one she was born with and demanded a kind of genetic loyalty. She was as keen to please her parents as any child and as eager for their love. With the onset of adolescence and her mother's hasty lessons in how to wear the uncomfortable belt that held her Dr White's towels in place, she longed to emulate her mother's poise and savvy. She knew enough to suspect that her mother's chic was a cheap thing, worked up from images of Gloria Grahame and Lana Turner, but at the age when everything about her own body appalled her, she sensed too that her mother's way of inhabiting a dress or lighting a cigarette might, in certain circumstances, prove a stronger currency than Dr Pertwee's unsensuous wit and desiccated culture. Looking back on those days, Sally was astonished that the two women had never met. Sally's mother had no time to waste at school open days or prize-givings, even had she wanted to attend them, and Dr Pertwee was hardly going to join her mother for a darts match. Sally dared not suggest they invite her for a Sunday lunch, the way they sometimes did her parents' relatives, for fear of creating extra work for them to complain about.

In becoming her friend and patroness, however, and in opening Sally's eyes to a wider realm of possibilities than her parents' outlook dared encompass, Dr Pertwee alienated her from her home. As she grew towards school leaving age, Sally found her parents increasingly prudish and ignorant, while their pride in her achievements was tempered by an almost superstitious fear of what they took for arrogance and ambition. Around her sixteenth birthday, she finally raised the subject with Dr Pertwee during one of the discussions Sally no longer found so daring.

'I don't mean to upset you, Sally,' Dr Pertwee said. 'I would never *ever* aim to *supplant* your mother. But you must see that a sapling sometimes needs to be transplanted a little way off from the parent tree if it is to grow to its full potential. Would you rather I saw less of you?'

'No!' Sally exclaimed. 'Of course not,' and the heat of her denial made her accept that whatever changes Dr Pertwee had wrought within her were as irreversible as if the perfumed tea and cucumber sandwiches had been the tools of bewitchment.

* * *

Sally had not quite qualified as a doctor when war broke out, but staff shortages were acute. She served her houseman years in the Red Cross. First in London amid the horrible thrill of the Blitz, then on the hospital ship in the Mediterranean, then in a military hospital in Kent. From there she was transferred to the old isolation hospital on the East Anglian coast at Wenborough, a few miles' motorbike ride from her childhood home.

Her mother had spent the war working at a munitions factory on the other side of Rexbridge. The pay had been far better than her wages at the canning plant and, Sally guessed, her social life had improved commensurately. Evacuated from Hackney, her sister-in-law had moved in, with children, for the duration, and had been happy to keep Sally's father company. Her mother stayed in digs with her new 'girlfriends' and used petrol rationing as the perfect excuse to cadge a lift home with a gentleman friend only every third weekend. This she did with a headful of new songs and a suitcase crammed with black market trophies. Now she was back at home to an unsatisfactory husband, who could never take her dancing, and a tedious, poorly-paid job packing sugar beet. The advent of peace saw mother and daughter picking up the pieces in a domestic game whose rules no longer suited them.

Edward Pepper asked Sally out to a concert in Rexbridge chapel just four days after the hospital had discharged him. He telephoned her at work. They had talked inconsequentially enough several times since their first encounter, but she had discounted his promise to take her out as mere politeness. Standing in a corner of the crowded staff room, she blushed at his proposition. She accepted quickly, almost curtly.

'If I come on my bike, I can get in at about quarter to,' she said. 'Shall I meet you at the concert or somewhere else?'

'Neither,' he laughed. 'I'll pick you up. I'm borrowing a friend's car. What's your address?'

As she told him, she felt afresh the difference in their ages.

'What are you all tarted up for?' her mother asked her over tea.

'I'm going to a concert. A friend's taking me.'

'Which friend?' her mother asked. 'One of the nurses, is it?'

'What kind of concert?' added her father and was silenced with a slap on his arm from his wife, who reiterated, 'Which friend?'

'Edward. Edward Pepper. You don't know him. I met him at the hospital.'

'Oh. Is he another doctor, then?'

'No, he's . . . erm . . . Well. I'm not sure what he does, really. He writes music.' Feeling a little light-headed, Sally took a slice of stale dripping cake.

'So he's a patient, then,' her mother perceived.

'Was. He's one of the lucky ones.'

'Eh, Sal, he didn't have TB, did he?' her father asked.

'Do you know what you're doing?' her mother added, frowning.

'Of *course* I know what I'm doing.' Sally dropped the last piece of cake on her plate with a clunk. Her mother was staring at her, eyebrows raised. 'I'm a grown woman, Mum.'

'I was wondering when you'd notice.'

'What's that supposed to mean?'

'You're not getting any younger, that's what. How old's this man of yours?'

'He's not a "man of mine". Mum, for pity's sake, we're just going to a concert together.'

Her father snorted, whether at her naïveté or poor taste in entertainment it was hard to say. Her mother merely kept her eyebrows raised and took another, deliberate, sip of tea.

'I bought him some notebooks for his music and I suggested we go to a concert,' Sally explained.

'So you threw yourself at him!'

Sally pushed back her chair as her mother laughed.

'I can't sit here explaining all evening,' she said. 'He'll be here any minute and I've got to polish my shoes.'

'Which are you wearing?'

'The black.'

'Don't you think the blue'd go better with that dress?'

'I'm wearing the black.'

'Suit yourself.'
'They match my bag.'
'Suit yourself.'
A car pulled up outside the terrace; a rare enough occurrence to silence everyone and send her mother scurrying to the window to peer around the curtain. Sally glanced at the clock.
'Oh God! That'll be him. Let him in, would you, Mum? While I do my shoes. Please?'
'He's a kike!' her mother exclaimed, turning back from the window. 'He's a bloody kike and you're a cradle snatcher!'
The revelation that he was German, thought Sally, could wait for another occasion. If one should arise, that was. As her mother walked, hair-fluffing, into the hall, Sally dived into the kitchen and rubbed fiercely at each shoe with a tea towel. She could hear Edward's voice.
'Hello. I'm Edward Pepper. You must be Sally's mother.'
He said it too precisely, of course.
'He sounds like a bloody spy!' Sally hissed under her breath and stopped to dab a little vanilla essence behind each ear. Edward was ushered into the front room where he was joined by Sally and her father. Sally made formal introductions then her father started to ask why they were wasting money going to a concert and she herded Edward back into the hall, out of the front door and into the waiting Wolseley.
'Don't wait up,' she told her father. 'I've got my key.'
They drew away with a jolt and Sally found herself glowering out of the window.
'Doctor?' he asked at last and she saw he was smiling quizzically at her.
'I'm sorry,' she said. 'My parents are hell.'
'Yes,' he sighed. 'That is, they all are. You look so different,' he added.
'Do I say thank you?'
'Yes. I mean, you look most elegant out of uniform.'
'Thank you, then. You look better out of pyjamas!'
'And you smell delicious. Like . . . like freshly baked biscuits.'

'It's vanilla essence,' she confessed. 'I don't have any scent. Nothing nice anyway.'

'You must wear it always,' he laughed. 'It suits you.'

She smiled, looking down at her hands then out of the window, uncertain how to take this. She disliked ambiguity.

She would have liked to have said, 'Look, they were starting to make a fuss because they think we're courting.' But contented herself with, 'It's a nice car.'

'It's my old tutor's. He hardly ever uses it. In fact he can scarcely drive. He bought it in the hope that his students would take him on outings but they tend to borrow it and leave him behind.'

'Oh. Poor man.'

'Not really. He has a private income and a good life.'

She smiled to herself at this literal interpretation.

'Which college were you at?' she asked.

'Tompion. But only for two years. Then the war came and I was interned. I never finished my degree.'

His colour had returned and his black hair had regained its glossiness but he was still painfully thin. Perhaps he had always been thin? Perhaps he had been underfed as a child? Sally wanted to know.

'Tell me about all that,' she said. 'You've told me nothing really. Tell me about yourself.'

'No,' he said, firmly. 'Not yet. I'd rather not. Would you mind?'

'No,' she said and reassured him with a smile, even as her own assurance was jolted.

2

Edward watched her throughout the concert. He had chosen it for its accessibility, sensing her ignorance. *Eine Kleine Nachtmusik*, a middle period Mozart Piano Sonata and, after the interval, the *Trout Quintet*. Austrian music. Music he had missed through the years of patriotic self-censorship when every other concert seemed to be of Elgar, Vaughan Williams, Parry and Purcell. It was easy to watch her because they were sitting in the back row of the Tompion Chapel choir stalls and she was leaning forward for a better view. She looked – he sought a suitably English phrase – fresh as paint. Not fresh as a daisy – that comparison was only fit, for white-socked children or a newly-laundered shirt. Paint suggested something of her glow, her sweet, unthreatening face, her flawless complexion. She was older than him by a few years, certainly older than several of the hospital nurses and many of the eager girls his friends entertained around Rexbridge, but there was an abundant healthiness to her, an energy, that left the others grey by comparison and made Edward feel ten years her senior. After the months in hospital, in basic training, in internment and the grim years before that, she seemed to offer his life a freshness that dared him to lower his guard at last, to feel again.

He looked at the nape of her neck, where lines of down curled beneath darker hair, where the skin was still pink from having been scrubbed. He smelled, through the music, a faint waft of vanilla – evocative with unwitting cruelty – and he found the very look of her released memories he had not dared to recall for a long time. He breathed in the perfume, and there was his mother, humming to herself, cheeks pink with effort, as she tried to roll out biscuit dough while reading a textbook at the same time. There was Miriam, his sister, catching his eyes in her looking-glass with her mischievous glance as, lips pinching hairpins, she curled thick hair high on her head before her first adult dance.

He had not cried once since they had hurried him on to the boat for England, as he begged them, *begged* them to come too. Miriam had been coughing when he left. She had probably been tubercular as well. Once again he prayed she had been lucky; that the disease had taken her before the cattle trucks could. For a moment these thoughts, combined with the Mozart, were almost too much for him. He wanted to sob aloud, to break through the polite Viennese spell cast by the piano. Feverishly he distanced himself with an old trick, learned at boarding-school. The music was just music. He systematically reduced it back to a neutral code, stilling his spirits by forcing his mind's eye to trace a composer's scribbled notes on an imaginary score.

During the interval, tea and biscuits were served from a trestle table outside the vestry door – that pervasive British tea, brewed strong as German coffee then drowned in milk as though for an infant's softer taste. Sally bought some, laughing at Edward's squeamishness. She made him warm his hands, at least, on her cup before they walked around the shadowy interior of the chapel, which she had never visited before. She said nothing about the music and he thought it best not to press her. When the Schubert was finished, however, and they were caught up in the small crowd pressing to leave by the narrow door, she touched him hesitantly on the back and said,

'Thank you. That was special.'

'Worth the trouble of tracking down those music books for me?'

'Definitely.'

They emerged into the quadrangle, where concert-goers were standing around exclaiming at the clarity of the stars in well-rounded tones, confident of their unchallenged place in the scheme of things.

'Would you like to hear some more?' he asked. He knew

at once, from her silence, that he had pressed too far too soon.

'Edward,' she said, when they had walked a few yards. 'You're very young. You're what, twenty? Twenty-one?'

'I'm twenty-four,' he told her, piqued.

'Twenty-four. Sorry. Well you're twenty-four and I'm . . . I'm not that young. Edward, when you're young you want one thing and then you get a bit older and you want another. People's needs change and . . . Sorry. I'm being presumptuous.' She laughed nervously. 'Listen to me. You only asked if I wanted to hear more music. Sorry. I –'

He stopped her as they passed under the arch to the street, with a gentle pressure on her elbow.

'And how old are *you* exactly?'

'Edward!'

'Well?'

'I'm twenty-seven.'

'So you're old enough to know your own mind.'

'Yes.'

'And to do exactly as you please.'

'Yes. I suppose so, although living with Mum and Dad makes it a bit –'

'Sally.' It was his first use of her Christian name. 'Do you want to come out with me again?'

'Yes,' she told him. 'Very much.' And she kissed him lightly, on the cheek.

'*Gut*,' he said and laughed. She laughed too, and tucked a hand over his arm. 'Now,' he said, 'What about some dinner? You must be starving. We could eat in there over the road at the Sadler Arms. I'll pay.'

'Erm. Edward?' She held back, abashed by something. He knew many English girls could not go to pubs, but assumed the Sadler Arms, as more of an inn, was slightly more acceptable.

'What is it?'

'I had tea before you picked me up.'

'Yes. Tea. But –'

'Tea, Edward, as in Spam and eggs and mushrooms followed by bread and butter and a fat slice of stale dripping cake.'

'Oh.'

'Well don't look crestfallen,' she laughed. 'Think of the money I've just saved you. Let's go to the pub and you can buy me a bottle of stout and I'll watch you eat a plate of sandwiches.'

'Two plates, I think. I am very hungry.'

She chuckled softly.

'What is it?' he asked.

'You hardly ever sound German,' she told him, stopping to turn to him in the light from somebody's downstairs window. 'And then, hardly at all. But when you do –'

'What?'

'I like it *very* much.'

She drank her bottle of stout sitting in a corner of the saloon bar where other women drank ostentatiously respectable glasses of sherry or well-watered whisky. Then she shared his second round of ham sandwiches.

'So you eat pork, then?' she asked, direct as ever.

'Yes,' he said. 'There are times now when I forget to be Jewish at all.'

He could tell she was curious, so he told her a sensitively edited version of his life, that he was born and raised in Tübingen to two university lecturers who were more atheist than Jewish. He told her that they had sent him to boarding-school in England in the fond belief that the English in 1936 were less bigoted than the Germans, and that the English public school system was the best in the civilised world. He told her his parents had died but not when or how. He made no mention of Miriam.

Had he known then how unrooted her own upbringing had left her, he might have been more open with her, sensing in her a kindred spirit. He had not seen his family for ten years. Wrenched away from Tübingen at fourteen he had been forced to replace them with a less stable 'family' of teachers, other boys and distant, if well-meaning, kindred contacts. Unlike most young men, he had been deprived of the opportunity to reassess his childhood and criticise his upbringing, and thereby gain a truer sense of maturity than a merely biological one. The break with his first thirteen years was so complete and communication with home so patchy before it was broken off altogether, that his childhood memories remained enshrined, untested by time. He might have come to see his mother's absent-minded studiousness as a mask for frustration and rage, his father's iconoclastic gaiety, a front for despair. He would surely have argued with Miriam over her choice of boyfriends or with his father over his cowardice in the face of petty officialdom at the university. In the months before they packed him off to England – with all their cruel-kind lies about coming to visit before long – the façade had begun to crack in places. He had overheard acrid political arguments between his father and his more orthodox, more overtly Jewish grandfather, in which his grandfather's warnings began to dent the sarcasm with which his father armoured his fears. He had caught Miriam crying and not believed her when she said that she and her boyfriend Lorenz had merely had a 'silly argument about nothing'. With a child's acuity, he had detected the mounting panic behind all the tearful farewells. The grim realities of boarding at Barrowcester and the difficulty of loving the family acquaintance who took him to London in the holidays, forced him to focus all his warmer sentiments back on his absent family, and begin the process by which thoughts of his early years became fixed beneath an unyielding sugar-frosting of nostalgia.

His internment in 1940, along with other enemy aliens, and his eventual hospitalisation, had provided a neat physical expression of his abiding secret sense of immaturity which isolated him from his fellows. He was not interned for long, not shipped off to Canada or Australia like some unfortunates, since he had an eminent Rexbridge tutor to manoeuvre with the authorities on his behalf. The sense of an inexorable bureaucracy reducing human lives to numbers and personalities to mere nationality gave him, he later saw, a bitter taste of what would have been his fate in Tübingen. The eventual discovery of what befell his parents, the discovery that his grandfather's fears were not paranoia but grounded in a political reality, isolated Edward more than ever. Given refuge by his former tutor and encouraged by him to take his composition seriously, he felt all the more marooned between lives, stuck with a false name. Neither student nor soldier, he had evaded historical destiny only to be washed up in a provincial backwater, as powerless to move as a misdirected parcel. Even when he was eventually allowed to take action and sign up to fight, he was frustrated by a disease which, yet again, stigmatised him and set him apart. Someone had to give him the impetus to enter life and start living it from the inside. This girl, this woman, had not passed by with an uncommitted smile like all the others, but had boldly reached out and pulled him in by the hand. Small wonder, then, if he was anxious not to frighten her into letting go of him by telling too much too soon.

He drove her carefully home. She made him stop at the top of her parents' street so that the car would not wake everyone and she let him kiss her once, twice, three times on her slightly parted lips. She seemed a little unsteady as she walked away. She stopped to raise her hand to him as she opened the front door. Her white glove shone in the yellowish light from their hall.

Back at his former tutor's house, where he rented a room he stepped quietly into the kitchen to make himself some cocoa. There was a small bottle of vanilla essence amongst a cluster of greasy spice packets in the drawer beside the stove. He unscrewed the sticky lid and took a deep sniff. It was not the same at all.

3

Dr Pertwee's wilfully unromantic version of the facts of life had more to do with population control and the economics of female servitude than with technique. Sally received more detailed but scarcely more applicable sexual instruction at medical school and even there textbook and lecturer sought to preserve her perceived modesty with Latin terms, and studiously skirted any reference to pleasure. The gynaecological diagrams even left out those parts that were not directly germane to childbirth or urination so that she had to go to an ethnological study of African tattooing and ritual mutilation to find a name for her clitoris. She knew there was pleasure, naturally. Such things filtered down. Throughout her girlhood she went to the cinema, she overheard gossip on buses. There were, after all, whole industries dependent on what Dr Pertwee called romance, as differentiated from marriage. But nobody thought to instruct Sally in the less academic minutiae of the subject and she never thought to ask. Boys of her own age-group seemed hopelessly immature while the older ones, on whom she had occasional crushes, hopelessly threatening. For the most part, sex was a source of fascination but she knew instinctively to be wary of it as of a dangerous tide. As a teenager she had been consumed with the thirst to learn and escape, too busy fulfilling Dr Pertwee's grand design to fritter precious evenings fumbling with spotty youths. Dr Pertwee drew her as far away from her contemporaries as from her parents. At that stage and until Sally had turned twenty-two, her mother appeared to approve of the tidy path she was treading.

'My Sally's a good girl,' she would boast to other mothers, whose daughters she called sluts and minxes behind their backs. And when a friend of hers from the factory had insinuated, over tea and gossip, that Sally was missing out on life, she countered, 'You save yourself, girl. Don't make the mistake I made; save yourself until you find a bloke that's really *worth* it. If none of them comes up to scratch, think what you'll have spared yourself!'

She changed her tune after the war. Just as she returned from her months with the munitions factory women with a brassier, more defiant air, so Sally seemed to cross some invisible boundary, transformed overnight from her mother's good girl into her unweddable daughter.

On her posting to the hospital ship, Sally met a young officer. He also came from East Anglia – their first conversation inevitably drifted from chart-reading to homesickness. He had a fiancée in Norwich who, he confided, was pregnant and he would have to marry on his next visit home. He sought Sally out often to talk with her – earnest talk, for which she scarcely felt herself equipped, about love, marriage, the war and life back home.

The men and women on board fraternised compulsively: uprooted from their backgrounds, their tastes and class were masked by uniforms. All social niceties were swept aside by the atrocious wounds of the men brought on board and the daily possibility of being 'accidentally' torpedoed out of the water. Sally discovered that by voicing opinions which in Dr Pertwee's rooms were commonplace, she swiftly gained a reputation for being left-wing, if not exactly communist, and somehow 'fast'. The effect was giddying.

There were often parties – anything to relieve the tension – and at one such her officer friend plucked up the courage to ask her to dance. They danced through three songs in a row, went out on deck to cool down and, surprised by lust (she was, at least), went by discreet, separate routes to his cabin. His lovemaking was fast and hurt her, but he was apologetic when he realised she had been a virgin. This momentous event turned to farce when they tried to wash the blood off his sheets, then realised they had no way of getting the things dry again. They ended up stuffing them out of a porthole amid jokes about burials at sea. Sally was uncertain whether she had enjoyed the experience at all and was dogged for days afterwards by a fear of pregnancy. He found his mysterious way to quantities of black market condoms however, and she would visit his cabin at least once a week. The sex remained hasty and was never entirely without pain but, when the time came for her to be shipped back to England, she thought she was beginning to see what all the fuss was about.

Since then there had been nobody in her life, unless she counted Gordon Graeme, the hospital's senior registrar, who seemed to regard it as a grave discourtesy not to press his unwelcome hands and innuendi on any personable female who came his way. Living with her parents precluded anything beyond heartfelt courtship or extreme subterfuge, and long hours at the hospital and the motorbike rides there and back left her too exhausted for either. Until now.

After the concert, she and Edward saw each other almost every day. She began to lie to her parents, pretending that she was spending an evening with colleagues or old friends rather than have them know how often she saw him. She found they did not talk much. Instead they *did* things. They went to plays, to concerts, of course, and to the Sadlerian and Rexbridge Museums. They took long walks, breaking the companionable silence only to talk of what they saw, not of what they felt. Sally was not sure what she was feeling just yet.

She made up for lost years by reawakening in herself a keen appetite for the cinema. They saw anything, everything, from *Tarzan* to *Henry V*. Through the university film club they saw German films, and he would translate for her in whispers the grosser phrases the subtitler had censored. The foreign films were shown in a church hall but the trashier English and American things they enjoyed from the double courtship seats at the rear of the Rexbridge Majestic. They would hold hands in the darkness, fingers restlessly interlacing. He would wrap an arm across her seat-back and explore her shoulder or the side of her neck with his fingertips until the skin grew unbearably sensitised and she had to take his hand to make him stop for a while. They exchanged chaste kisses but went no further. Each was waiting for the other to make the first move; Edward, because she was older and he was shy, Sally, because only when he made a move would she decide whether she wanted him to. One evening, though, during a piece of historical hokum called *The Reprieve*, he seemed to come to a decision.

'I should catch my bus,' she said, glancing at her watch. She had left her bike at home for her father to tinker with that night and the film had been a long one.

'I'll drive you home later,' he replied. 'Come back with me first.'

'Won't Thomas be there?'

'Probably. But I'd like you to meet him. I should like him to meet you.'

Thomas was Edward's former tutor. *In loco parentis* before Edward was hospitalised, he had encouraged Edward to return to Rexbridge and, when he could not persuade him to finish his degree, had offered him two rooms to rent in his house and found him an undemanding job with a bookseller. When the owner had bought and priced any books brought in, Edward had to place them on the appropriate shelves. Otherwise he spent his days sitting peaceably behind the counter, and so could combine the work easily with labouring at a score. Few customers actually wanted to buy; most of them were indigent students, hoping to sell.

Thomas's house was an elegant early Victorian building, with railings at the front and a wrought iron gate. Sally smelled jasmine as they walked up the path. The hall floor shone with polish as did various pieces of antique furniture. A grandfather clock was striking ten as she checked her reflection in a looking glass that hung over a delicate table. For the first time with Edward she felt a pang of insecurity. Compared with all this, Dr Pertwee's rooms seemed Bohemian. Edward was used to such elegance, born to it, for all she knew. He was in his element. There was a cultured male cough from a half-open door across the hall. She pulled her cardigan straight, knowing, as she had when she bought it, that its shade of pink was somehow wrong. Even more than at Edward's brief encounter with her parents, she felt her age.

'Edward, *mein Schön*?'

'Thomas.'

Edward touched her shoulder reassuringly and led her to the open door.

Thomas was, she guessed, in his fifties. He had silvery hair swept back off a square, intelligent face. As he rose from his armchair by the fireplace, she saw that he had been sitting, cat-like, with a leg curled under him. He advanced to shake her hand, taking off his tortoise-shell reading glasses and searching her face intently, even as his smile said 'friend'.

'Thomas, I've brought Sally home to meet you. Dr Sally Banks, Professor Thomas Hickey.'

'How do you do,' Thomas said. 'Do sit down.' He waved her to the other armchair. 'Let me offer you a glass of something, young lady. Whisky? Brandy? I've some rather good port open.'

'Port would be lovely.'

'Edward, fetch us all a glass of port.'

As Professor Hickey sat, he curled his leg up again.

'I wish I were as supple as that,' she said.

'Raja yoga,' he replied. 'I picked it up in India years ago and now I suppose it's made me something of a crank.' He seemed pleased that she had noticed. 'What has Edward been doing with his evening? Something improving, I hope?'

'Not terribly,' she confessed. '*The Reprieve*.'

'Margaret Lockwood?'

'No, that new girl. The blonde. Myra Tey? No. Toye. Myra Toye. Still, it was better than the last film we saw.'

'Which was?'

'*Humoresque*,' said Edward, handing them their glasses. 'Isaac Stern played the violin on the soundtrack.'

Thomas shrugged as though to ask what could be so awful in that.

'Joan Crawford was the star,' she explained. 'She was a society woman married to a long-suffering violinist.'

'Oh,' said Thomas, in mock disapproval. 'Inexplicable

actress, really. So entirely false. And I find her hair unnerving. It puts one in mind of steel wool.'

The port was delicious. Sally sipped. Her head filled with its rich fumes and she noticed that, despite its sedate atmosphere, the room was filled with furniture and artefacts from the Far East. The prints she could see from her chair were of a distinctly pornographic nature. Sally saw Thomas watching her and smiled, nervously.

'It's a lovely room,' she said.

'Thank you.'

There was a pause in which they all sipped, then Edward piped up.

'Sally's the doctor who looked after me at the chest hospital, Thomas.'

'Ah.' Thomas widened pale blue eyes. 'So you're the one responsible for his miraculous recovery.'

'Well hardly,' Sally said. 'He was well on the mend when I first saw him. I only wish we'd got him away from that army hospital earlier, then he'd have been out and about much sooner. From what I can see, the treatment he got there was basic in the extreme; there were days when he saw no-one but orderlies.'

Thomas raised his eyebrows and shrugged, as though the reason for this neglect were tiresomely familiar to both of them – which irritated her, because it wasn't. At least, not to her.

'Sally very kindly tracked me down some manuscript paper,' Edward went on.

'I'd found him drawing in all the lines himself!' she laughed.

Thomas shook his head and tutted. A large black cat emerged, purring, from a hiding-place beneath the sofa and sprang on to his lap. It settled as he stroked it, and stared at Sally over his knees with gooseberry eyes.

'I was working on the quartet,' Edward added. 'Hardly anyone came in to the shop today and I've nearly finished the third movement.'

'We all expect great things of Edward,' Thomas told Sally. 'Great things.' He spoke pointedly but with the same, soft delivery. He spoke almost as though Edward were an infant prodigy, not a young man a few years her junior. It sounded like a challenge.

'Leave,' she told herself. 'Leave Edward all to him and run away.'

'Tell me more,' she asked instead.

'As you'll have gathered, I couldn't persuade him to finish his degree – and on reflection I think he made the right decision – but I think it's vital we all save him from London. London is death to creative talent in anyone but writers. He needs tranquillity.' There was another pause. Thomas looked down to fondle the cat's ears. Edward caught Sally's eye and winked. She simply stared back. For a moment he seemed utterly strange to her.

'Do you know much about music?' Thomas asked her.

'I'm a doctor.'

'Yes, but –'

'No. I don't know a thing.'

'I'm sure Edward will soon change all that.' Thomas smiled. The interview was over – he was releasing her back into plain conversation.

'He's doing his best,' she said. 'But I seem to like everything. I'm afraid I'm too undiscerning. My ear lacks taste.'

'On the contrary, your musical palate is unjaded; far happier for when you come to hear something Edward has written.'

She grinned across at Edward.

'What's his music like?' she asked.

'Like nothing you'll have heard in your *life*!' Thomas said and laughed aloud. The cat, plainly used to the noise, slowly closed its eyes. 'Tell me,' Thomas asked, 'I'm most curious. Didn't Edward say your name was Banks?'

'That's right.'

'So you must be Alice Pertwee's disciple.'

'Oh. I'd hardly say I was that. She took me in hand, though. What do you call a patron's patronee?'

'A project?'

'Yes.' Sally smiled, determined to show him she was undaunted. 'I was her project. Do you know her, then?'

'The Great Sexologist? To be sure. We've often found ourselves on the same committee. Rarely in agreement, mind you, but she's of that generation that doesn't hold such things against one. I know about you because she discussed your case once in a talk I heard her give on the social benefits of education to the less fortunate.'

'Well,' Sally looked with brief anger at her port glass then back full in Thomas's face. 'That puts me squarely in my place.'

'Yes,' he went on, with perfect equanimity, 'I suppose it does. Have you taken young Edward to meet her yet?'

'Not yet.'

'Well you must, you must. She's an institution and you clearly have an entrée. She won't be with us forever. I'd heard she was planning to leave Rexbridge altogether.'

'Doesn't she have an old house way out in the fens?'

'Yes. An extraordinary place by all accounts, but she doesn't seem to have lived there for years. Has she never taken you there?'

'No,' said Sally thoughtfully, 'I always visit her in her rooms. But if the state of those is anything to go by, she's probably let the house fall down.'

They sat on for a while, chatting, until it became clear that Thomas regarded himself as a chaperon – whether for Edward or Sally was unclear. At last he squinted at his watch in the lamplight, grunted, pushed the cat off his lap and said, firmly, 'Well, young man, I think it's time you drove this musical innocent home.'

They stood. Edward, well-trained, took the port glasses out to the kitchen, where Sally heard him giving them a perfunctory rinse under a tap. Thomas led her out to the hall, pausing on the way to straighten an old ink drawing of an Indian couple engaged in impossibly flexible coitus, their faces untouched by desire.

'It's done on rice paper,' he said. 'Part of a set. I'm very much afraid something's got inside the glass and is eating at it.'

'They seem so calm,' she said.

'Only to the unpractised view.' He pointed. 'Look at how wide her eyes are open and, there, how his fingers are flexed in ecstasy.'

They moved on. Edward went out to start the Wolseley.

'It's so very kind of you to lend Edward your car,' she told Thomas.

'I can't think why I bought the thing,' he said. 'I never go out of town really and if I *have* to, I go by train so that I can read on the way. It's nice to see it in use.'

'We must have an outing one day.'

'Yes,' he said, with no great enthusiasm. 'Did you have a coat? It's turned rather cold and that cardigan doesn't look very warm.'

'Er. No.'

'I believe there's a rug on the back seat.'

'Thanks.'

He touched the small of her back lightly, steering her on to the path.

'It was lovely to meet you,' he said quietly. 'I'm so glad.'

There was a sadness in the cast of his face, however, that made her doubt his sincerity.

4

Edward met Sally's patron the following Sunday afternoon. They had been out to her parents' for a very tense and largely silent lunch of roast mutton and had excused themselves at the first opportunity. Heavy with two kinds of potato and steamed pudding, they drove back into town for a much needed walk beside the Rex. Sally had warned him that Dr Pertwee made sandwiches for their Sunday teas together. Punctuality was another custom of hers, so they arrived promptly at four-thirty.

Thomas had filled him in on the old woman's history. High-born, she had qualified in medicine, then shocked even her suffragette mother by advocating birth control for unmarried women and publishing two pioneering sex education manuals, euphemistically titled, *A Husband's Love* and *Things A Wife Should Know*. That she knew so much without the blessing of marriage had earned her the title of 'That Pertwee Woman' for a season or two, a situation not helped by her open liaison with a notoriously unprincipled Dublin playwright. Nevertheless, the books sold in their thousands and the gratitude of countless readers won her a kind of honour. With the mantle of middle age, she assumed respectability, channelling the profits from her books into work among unmarried or abandoned mothers – who would otherwise have fallen into the punishing hands of the Church Army, lunatic asylums or their parents – and the foundation of girls' grammar schools in Rexbridge and Islington. It was to one of these that Sally had won a scholarship and so come under Dr Pertwee's protective interest.

Edward was expecting a formidable, tall amazon in high-buttoned black, with an iron-grey coiffure and commanding manner. He was taken aback therefore when the door was opened by a tiny creature in a pale yellow twinset and pearls, with hair like spun sugar, delicate, fluttering hands and a powdery, fluting voice. Edward was no strong-man but he felt he could have lifted her up with one arm. If she commanded attention, he felt, it must be through subterfuge rather than head-on confrontation.

'Come in, come in, Sally dear.' She kissed Sally's cheek. 'And you must be Edward. How do you do.' She gave Edward a rheumatoid hand which resembled a canary's claw and, instead of shaking, let him hold her fingers while she led him into her chaotic bedsitting room. A kettle was boiling on a gas ring and the table had been laid for tea, with a large plate of crustless sandwiches. The books and papers, which must have previously occupied the table, had been slung on to a heap which already engulfed the desk and was spilling on to the floor. The bread crusts were scattered on the windowsill, where sparrows and a starling were laying them waste. The mantelshelf was fringed with bills and invitations, weighted with an assortment of glass candlesticks.

'Sit,' she pleaded. 'Do sit, both of you. You're both so huge there's no room to move about!'

They sat at the table; the sofa was taken up by an open suitcase and an assortment of hats, the armchair by a typewriter, resting on a rough-hewn plank that bridged the arm-rests. Dr Pertwee snatched the kettle from the ring and filled a teapot, shielding her hand from a scalding in the steam by wearing what looked like an old rugger sock.

'How are your parents?' she asked, joining them at the table.

'All right,' Sally said. 'Dad gets ever more immobile. He just sits listening to the radio all day, I think, unless we find him something to mend. His mates come in now and then and sit with him, filling the place up with smoke. I got him a wheelchair but he doesn't like using it. Twenty years on and he still can't admit he's a cripple.'

'What about *her*? Tea, Edward?'

'Thank you.' Edward took his tea, relieved that it was both weak and Chinese.

'Mum ought to be stopping work by now,' Sally continued. 'I pay most of the housekeeping bills – but I think she'd miss seeing the "girls" every day, and she dreads the thought of being stuck at home with him.'

'And what do they make of you, Edward?' Dr Pertwee turned her cool gaze on him and he saw that she had extraordinary bottle-green eyes.

'Oh. Well.' He chuckled, still uncertain of how much leeway he was allowed in discussing Sally's parents with other people, having barely discussed them with her. 'They gave me lunch today. A proper Sunday lunch.' He glanced respectfully at the sandwiches, which Dr Pertwee promptly passed him. He took two. 'They didn't talk much. I think they disapproved when I said I only work in the bookshop to make ends meet – not as a proper career. And they aren't altogether happy with my being German, I suspect.'

'But you don't *sound* German,' Dr Pertwee protested.

'I think that makes it worse – as though I'm trying to deceive people. And then, of course, I'm Jewish.'

'Really?' The old woman was the soul of discretion. She reminded him of the headmaster's wife at Barrowcester. 'Do you know Simon Stern at Tompion?'

'No.'

'No reason why you should, of course. He's a mathematician. Have another sandwich, do.'

'Thank you.'

'I think their real problem is with me being older, actually,' Sally put in.

'You're not,' Edward protested. 'Not much.'

'Three years,' Sally said.

'My dear,' Dr Pertwee cut in, 'Your age is immaterial. She's probably jealous. After all, your poor father has been, shall we say, *hors de combat* for so long . . . In any case, the only reason for taking an *older* man as a partner is economic. With your earnings, pitiful though you might think them, and your qualifications, you have freedom of choice. I've always said that if *I* had ever married, I would have taken a man at least ten years younger than me.'

'Why's that?' Edward asked her.

'Biology, dear,' she said and he saw Sally smile at his naïveté. 'Men may keep their looks and fertility longer but their – how can I put it delicately? – their *potential* rarely outlasts a woman's. Now tell me, Edward. Do you have your own lodgings?'

'Not exactly, Doctor. I rent a bedroom from my old tutor. Professor Hickey. I think you know him.'

'But of course. We are old sparring partners.' She mutely offered the sandwiches to Sally, who declined with a smile and a headshake. 'So you have little – how shall I put it? – *independence* to offer one another. I thought that might be the case.'

The doorbell interrupted Dr Pertwee's train of thought. She glanced at her watch.

'Oh blast. That'll be my taxi to the station. I'm off up to London for the night – another ghastly committee. I really don't know why I can't say no. My mother was so very *good* at it. Even in retirement one isn't safe. I shall have to cultivate a deceptive veneer of senility. Odd shoes, perhaps, or a tendency to drool.' She hurried over to the sofa, threw a book on top of the clothes in her suitcase and slammed the lid shut with surprising vigour. Edward stood, followed by Sally.

'We mustn't keep you, Doctor,' he said.

'Nonsense, dear. Nonsense.' She fussed, pulling on a lightweight cream coat and tying a silk scarf loosely about her neck. At the gesture he could suddenly see that in her day she had been extremely attractive. Even in age, some of her movements had an actress's poise – she was used to being watched. 'I'm so sorry to be rushing off like this,' she added. 'But I insist you stay quietly and enjoy yourselves. Eat and drink anything you can find and light the gas stove if it gets cold.' The doorbell rang again. 'Yes. Coming!' she fluted.

'But –' Sally began.

'There are towels in the bathroom and clean sheets on the bed. I've got the key so just pull the door shut when you leave. Now. I must fly. Bye-bye, dear.' She presented her cheek for Sally's bemused kiss then held out her hand again for Edward to clasp. 'Such a pleasure meeting you,' she said, and left, closing the door firmly behind her.

They stood, waiting and amazed, until they heard her taxi shudder away down the street, then they tumbled, laughing, on to the mattress.

'A bed!' Sally gasped. 'A *bed*! She's given us a *bed*!'

She kissed him greedily then he rolled them over and kissed her back, small nuzzling kisses around the mouth, down on to her long neck and up behind an ear. She was wearing vanilla essence again.

'Do you think we can?' he asked, his face in her hair, unable to meet her eyes in case she was outraged.

'There'd be hell to pay if we didn't,' she chuckled. 'I think she'd have doubts about your – how can I put it delicately? – your *potential*!'

They laughed and writhed, kissed, rolled apart a little to stare, thought of something else funny, then kissed again, snorting with amusement. Slowly, with the unbuttoning of shirts, slipping off of belts and shoes and tense, gasping release of bra clasp and suspender fastenings, the prolonged frustration of the previous weeks came to possess them. Smiles fell away into bitten lips, laughter into a kind of astonishment. Slowly, intently, and with the occasional hoarse mutter and misplaced elbow, they made love. On one of his recent fortnightly visits to the barber, Edward had shyly accepted, with fresh understanding, the enigmatic offer of 'something for Sir's weekend?' He had been fearful since, lest this prove presumptuous on his part, but no less afraid of being without them should such a heaven-sent opportunity arise. Sally cried out when he thrust into her, prompting the first of several apologies, and he kissed away a tear forced out across her cheek.

Compared with Sally, he was a sexual neophyte, if not quite a virgin. There had been girls while he was a student – sheltered daughters of academics or bolder, but heavily chaperoned students at the few women's colleges. None of them, however, had gone further than teasing and flirting, stirring him to such fever pitches of frustration that he was often tempted to seek relief elsewhere. At the end of a drunken celebration following the completion of first year exams, he had ended up in a brothel on the edge of town. It was not the red plush sin palace of his teenage imaginings but a drably respectable private house, where gentlemen were expected to await the next available lady's pleasure in a far from cosy parlour full of crude knick-knacks and seaside souvenirs. After a numbing wait, a tired older woman led him to a back bedroom where he was shut in with a girl so young and evidently frightened that what little ardour was left him drained away and he fled in disgusted confusion. In his second year, when word from even friends of his family dried up altogether and Europe began her slow, reluctant manoeuvring into war, he found himself increasingly ostracized. Awkwardness was caused first by his Jewishness, and then his nationality. Even invitations to tea dried up and he spent hours of refuge from this tacit rejection alone in the college library or labouring compulsively at the piano. The internment camp, where he had to sleep in a crowded impromptu barracks, rank with the smells of underwashed clothes and frustrated male, crowded his libido into silence much as boarding-school had. There were women there who doled out the sloppy overcooked food, some of them quite young and friendly, but he regarded them as coldly as if they had been so many automata. It was only later, when he fell ill, that his sex drive came surging back – almost as a symptom, it seemed, of the disease. The mere memory of a nurse's black stockinged leg or downy neck as she rearranged his bedclothes or took his temperature could work him into hot spontaneous spasms of desire. Sally's unexpected arrival at his work table on the hospital promenade and her direct, encouraging smile, had been as warm bread to the starved.

Spent, he held her, panting, in his arms. Then he tiptoed across to draw the curtains, turn on a light and bring back a glass of water and the rest of the sandwiches. Seeing her curled there, soft, dark hair wonderfully awry, cheeks flushed, lips swollen as if with crying, he found himself unable to stop talking.

'It was strange having Sunday lunch with your parents today,' he began.

'How so?'

'It made me think. It was ten years ago when I last ate with mine. They're dead, of course. In the war. I'm sorry I've taken so long to tell you much of this. I just didn't feel ready and then, well . . . We weren't orthodox Jews or anything. At least, my grandparents were, on my father's side. We had to go to them for Seder and so on, and there were some fights because they wanted me to go to a different school with other Jews, not the *Gymnasium* with the sons of my parents' friends. But my parents were totally irreligious. They were intellectuals and socialists, which was probably worse for them; getting them onto two black-lists instead of just the one. They knew what was coming. They couldn't not, with so many of their colleagues losing their jobs and homes. Actually, I think most people knew; it's just that they couldn't bear to admit it. It's all very easy to say we should pack up and move in such circumstances, quite another thing to do it. Doing it is an admission of fear. They were passionate anglophiles. They had always planned to send me to school in England anyway, or so they said. It simply became an imperative instead of a choice for them, I suppose.'

'Where did they send you?'

'Tathams at Barrowcester. Do you know the school?'

'Do I look as if I would?'

'It was torture there. Unrelenting torture. I had no idea that small boys could be so cruel. Well, I did, but I had always been immune to it. In the *Gymnasium* in Tübingen, I was one of the strong ones. In Barrowcester, I was suddenly the outsider, the German, the Jew with the comical accent. My name was changed in a hopeless effort to disguise my otherness.'

'Really?'

'Eli Pfefferberg to Edward Pepper. But no-one was fooled, of course, from the moment I opened my little mouth, and I kept making matters worse by forgetting to answer when my new name was called.'

'How old were you?'

'Too young. Even eighteen would have been too young for such treatment.'

'Couldn't you leave?' She brushed his cheek with the back of her hand, frowning, concerned. Edward shook his head.

'There was nowhere I could go. I knew enough to know that I couldn't go home to Germany. There were only distant contacts of my parents in Manchester – which wasn't too far from Barrowcester – and a second cousin in London, Isaac. He was a lawyer. Unmarried. No sense of humour and an unmarried sister who had even less. Rosa. She could curdle milk with a smile. It was bad enough having to stay with them in the holidays without turning up unannounced mid-term. I learned to become invisible. I copied the others' accents, picked up their slang and their little aggressions. I learned to bully. And I spent hours hiding away in the music rooms. There was a Jewish music teacher. A Mancunian. We were allies. He saved my life by insisting I took extra lessons and be given time off the rugger. When I got a scholarship to Tompion I could hardly believe it. It was so civilised there, so understanding, so liberal. At least on the surface. Maybe they're all Jew-haters underneath, but they don't throw your books in the urinals or beat you up on the playing field. But then the war started and I was interned. Isaac visited me occasionally, and did his best to get me let out, and dear Thomas managed it, of course . . .' He broke off, staring across the rumpled bedding to their tangle of discarded clothes.

'What is it?' she asked. 'What's wrong?'

He breathed quickly, shallowly. For a moment a thick fist of grief threatened to break through his accustomed control.

If I cry now, he thought, *if I let it all out now, I'll terrify her.*

She reached out to touch his neck and pull him down beside her again, but he held back. He sensed she was on the verge of offering him pity, treating him as a patient just when she had honoured him as a man. He fought back the urge to weep, forcing his mind to focus instead on the extraordinary fact of their new, naked closeness.

'Nothing,' he told her. 'It's nothing. I'm sorry.' He gently cupped her breasts in his hands, amazed at the rapidity with which he was permitted a gesture so intimate. 'I shouldn't have started talking about it. This should have been special for you, for both of us.'

'Don't be daft. It was special.'

She laid her hands on his, encouraging him.

'But I've spoilt it all.'

'No you haven't. Anyway.' She slid a hand between his legs and he felt himself stir at her touch. 'We can do it again.' She smiled up at him at the sweet simplicity of this truth, her pale face warm in the lamplight across the sheets. Edward lay back on the bank of crushed pillows, and caressed the skin over her ribs with the back of his hand.

'I know,' he sighed, astounded, his mouth curling up into a private smile. 'I know.'

5

Sally rode her motorbike home through the network of dykes and waterways in a fury. The sun was dazzling but there was a water-cooled wind which stung her face into a grimace. In her anger she had left without her helmet and didn't care. Occasionally her hair blew across her face and she smacked it savagely out of the way. Gordon Graeme had called her up to his office after her rounds and placidly informed her that the doctor she had replaced had at last returned from serving his country and wanted his old job back.

'But I thought you said he'd resigned.'

'Well so I did. But it seems he only felt it was his duty to sign up, as he was still of an age to serve. Now that he wants to return, I can't very well refuse him.'

'I hate to sound selfish, but what about me?'

'My dear Miss Banks.' Like the nurses, he always called her Miss, never Doctor. 'You are young and relatively inexperienced. I'm sure you'll agree that your time here has been valuable. Now you can find something else.'

'Just like that, I suppose.'

'I can give you references.'

'This place is understaffed, though. Surely I could stay on to relieve the burden?'

'This place, as you so quaintly put it, is also underfunded. We could only afford to keep you on a junior nurse's salary – which I'm sure you'd be loath to accept.'

'Of course.'

'Even setting aside the future of the hospital, which you know is by no means certain now, you must see that we have to give Dr Grismby priority. Quite apart from it having been his job in the first place, quite apart from the debt of patriotism we owe him –'

'Debt of . . . ?'

Graeme held up a liver-spotted hand.

'If you would just let me finish?'

'Of course, Sir. I'm sorry.'

'Quite apart, as I say, from these considerations, it would be something of a risk to invest too much of the hospital's funds in training you further. You are not yet thirty, after all. For all we know, you may still want to get married, have children and so on . . .'

Sally ran his words through her mind again and grunted with irritation as she dismounted. She unlocked the door into the narrow passage at the side of her parents' house and rammed the bike against the dustbins. A dustbin lid fell off with a clatter. She stooped to replace it, wrinkling her nose at the smell of rotting fish coming from a bloodied newspaper bundle inside. She heard her mother's low voice from the kitchen window. Clutching her white coat bundled to her chest, Sally leaned against the cold brick wall behind her and waited to calm down. She absorbed the familiar scene about her. The yard, weeds springing up bright between paving stones. The washing line which she and a neighbouring girl used to unhook to skip on, on the rare mornings when it was empty. Her mother's bicycle, set against the concrete coal bunker, an old black Raleigh, with a thin, red, trim, elegant, curving centre bar and a bell that rang out one clear 'ping' instead of the more common, spring-powered jangle. Beyond lay a mean patch of garden, where a gardenless family friend, Ida Totteridge, was allowed to grow vegetables in return for a half-share of the produce. The runner beans were in flower already; the one vegetable which Ida always planted in excess. The far end of the plot was still disfigured by the mud-covered Anderson shelter, which no-one had the strength to dismantle. Ida grew marrows and sweet peas, trailing off its sides and top in gaudy confusion.

Calm again, Sally let herself in at the kitchen door. Her father was in his chair, hidden behind the *Daily Express*.

Undeterred, her mother was talking to him, her hair in a protective pink net. On the way home, she had stopped off at her friend Queenie's to have it done for the weekend; a fortnightly ritual. It was coiled and curled and more thoroughly blonde than it had been at breakfast. The sweet-harsh smell of setting lotion mingled with the room's customary tobacco clouds.

'Hello, Mum. Hello, Dad,' she sighed.

'Hello, love,' said her mother, breaking the flow of her address.

'Hair looks nice,' Sally added, setting the kettle on the stove and laying out three precious lamb chops in the grill.

'Thanks love. You should let Queenie fix yours up a bit. It would look nice with a perm. Give it a bit of body.'

'I told you, I like it natural. Lamb tonight. I did a trade with Alice.'

'Which is she?'

'The nurse whose Dad has the butcher's out at Three Holes.'

'That's nice. Dad?' Her mother flapped a hand against her father's *Express*.

'What?' he mumbled, lowering the paper a fraction.

'Lamb tonight.'

'That's good.' He continued reading.

Her mother took out her powder compact and checked her hair with a critical wrinkling of brows. She powdered her nose for good measure then slipped the compact away.

'That *bloody* Graeme,' Sally snapped, rubbing margarine on the chops then replacing the grill pan with a clatter.

'Sally!' Her mother stubbed out a cigarette. She took exception to swearing about the house.

'I'm losing the job.'

Her father's paper came down at the news.

'You've what?'

'You heard,' her mother said, then added, to Sally, 'What did you do, love?'

'I didn't *do* anything. It's just like you at Mosley's last year. They're bringing back the bloke I replaced and doing me out of a job. I thought the danger of that was long past.'

'Well, love, it was *his* job.'

'Not any more it wasn't. Anyway, he had resigned. It seems he's changed his mind and we aren't to hold it against him because he's such a bloody brave soldier and we owe him a "debt of patriotism". And because he's a man.'

'And what do they owe *you* I'd like to know?'

'Precious little, it seems. I've got till August then that's it. Graeme says he'll give me references.'

'There. You see? Something'll come up. Maybe in Rexbridge.'

Her father stopped listening, sensing a lessening of crisis, and returned to his newspaper.

'Anyway,' her mother went on. 'How are things *viz Edvard*?' She laughed at her own mimicry.

'You know he doesn't have an accent.' Sally turned back to check the chops. 'They're fine,' she muttered.

'Has he, er . . . made his intentions clear, then?'

'Not exactly, no. That wouldn't solve anything right now, anyway.'

'Sorry I spoke.'

'You think just the way Graeme does. You think marriage is all I live for. I've got a career.'

'Not after August you haven't. What's he worth then, anyway, your fine young kike?'

'Don't call him that.'

'Well he is one, isn't he? It's a perfectly friendly word. No pork chops when *Edvard* comes around, eh Dad?' Her mother laughed to herself again. Sally chose to ignore her.

'He's probably worth less than me,' she admitted. 'I haven't asked. We don't talk about things like that.'

Her mother lit another cigarette and watched Sally turn the chops.

'Ida's left us a potato salad in the meat safe,' she said. Sally took down the bowl of salad and set it out on the table along with knives, forks and pickle. The kettle came to the boil. She spooned tea into the pot.

'Hasn't sold any symphonies yet then?' her mother asked.

'No. No, he hasn't.' Sally grabbed the kettle, scalded her hand and swore.

'Temper temper,' her mother said, coolly. 'I'll say one thing for him, though: he's very good looking. You've got taste, girl. *Very* good looking. Nice hands, too.' She glanced at her husband, slouched, fat and rumpled, in his chair and narrowed her eyes. 'Very choice.'

6

The day had been unnaturally quiet. A cold mist at dawn had cleared slowly through the morning to reveal an unseasonal pall of cloud which hung low and heavy. Sightseers stayed away, the locals went, muted, about their business and any sounds there were – birdsong, the arrival and departure of trains, screeching bicycle brakes or the slamming of car doors – carried on the leaden atmosphere with uncomfortable clarity.

Miss Murphy, the bookseller, was already in the shop when Edward arrived. Unpacking two dusty cardboard boxes of Kipling's complete works and a nearly new sequence of Angela Thirkell's Trollope sequels, she was fractious. She snapped at him twice, once for over-sugaring her coffee, once for miscataloguing Mrs Gaskell under M. She then apologised, declared herself 'out of sorts and good for nothing' and went across to the Sadler Arms for a restorative glass of sherry, excusing herself for the rest of the day.

'It's a dead day, Mr Pepper,' she said, as she pulled on her cardigan. 'Early closing *and* this weather. Close early, too, if you've a mind to.'

No sooner had the bell finished jangling with her closing of the door than he climbed up to the shelf she couldn't reach and took his manuscript from its hiding-place. There was only the final movement to finish. It was to be the focal point of the quartet. He had been carrying the germs of the movement in his system weeks before he had even begun to think about the other, more sombre three. It was a presto, full of fever, of insane gaiety and furious syncopation. The melody was wilfully simple, its rhythm, a distillation of dance music he had heard at weddings as a child. It was lush, exotic – a parody verging on what, in later life, he would learn to call camp. He wrote all day, hour upon hour, pausing only when his bladder was bursting or his pen ran dry. And when he did break off, he whistled the melodies aloud, shielding his mind from interruption. If a customer had appeared, the door bell, let alone the effort of finding words and lending assistance would have broken his train of thought altogether. As it was, when the quadrangle clock in St Francis chimed the half hour after five, he realised, to his own astonishment, that he was on the final page.

Then the door bell was set flying on its spring. Edward glanced up, profoundly irritated. It was Sally, helmet over one arm, cheeks flushed with a touch of sun, brow creased into the look of anxiety with which she seemed to approach their every encounter. She looked around and, seeing him, relaxed into an open smile.

'Hello,' she said. 'I'm early, I know. I was through by about four and staying at home seemed a waste. It's going to be such a beautiful evening! It's crystal clear now the cloud has lifted, and all the buildings have that kind of glow.' She stopped her raptures and remained just inside the door, a hand still holding it ajar expectantly. 'Hello?' she said again.

'I've been working on the last movement,' he told her. 'I'd almost finished it.'

'I'll go away for a few minutes,' she said and turned back onto the street. The bell jangled again and she was gone as suddenly as she had appeared.

'Wait,' Edward called. 'Don't go.' He stood and hurried to see if he could catch her but, although there were several women walking along the pavement, none of them looked like her. He had not noticed what she was wearing, his gaze having been drawn intensely as ever to her face. He returned to his chair behind the counter. There had been no hurt in her tone, no hint of umbrage. She had absented herself delicately, to make as few ripples as possible in his pool of thought.

Edward stared at the clusters of semiquavers on the page before him. For a few minutes, his mind was aglitter with images of her. Sally on the sunshiny street, hands clasped behind her back as she strolled, stooping slightly to peer into shop windows, or wrinkling her eyes as she stared up at a trio of swifts that wheeled, whistling, round an old college wall. He thought of her and could only see the page as a system of repetitious dots, circles and inclines. Then the compelling sounds re-entered his head and pushed her image back into darkness. He started to write again. The tendons in his hand grew tight with the effort to put the notes down fast enough. The telephone rang and he managed to ignore it, letting it clatter on as though it were someone else's concern. He finished the last recapitulation of the main subject, hesitated, frowned, his stare searching the furrowed grain of the battered counter-top. Then, from nowhere, he found a strange, new chord and the makings of a short, unforeseen coda, slower than the presto, chilly and unsettling. The effect was that of a frame of unexpected irony being clamped around the image of hectic dancing; of a withdrawal from a joyful dream, revealing a cruel truth.

His father had hoped he would prove a classicist or an historian. His mother had cherished hopes he might combine the two and go into archaeology like her. He found Greek and Latin easier than other boys, perhaps because she had started him on them early as a kind of game. Her letters to him at Barrowcester – letters he kept in an old shoebox and never dared re-read – always contained a paragraph in Latin in which she mischievously wrote about the bullies or sadistic teachers he had described to her, secure in her assumption that no-one but her son would bother to translate them. When he left Tübingen, he was already a keen pianist but such were the attitudes at home and at the *Gymnasium* that no-one had encouraged him to consider music as a career or even contemplated the idea. Music was an accomplishment, not an end in itself. Jews had for too long provided entertainers and fiddlers for *goyim* celebrations and, looking back, he realised his mother felt an ambition for him to prove himself in a less racially typical field. It was his grandmother who encouraged his music. Whenever the two families met for dinner, she would steer him to the piano and make him play Mendelssohn – always Mendelssohn – to keep the political bickering at bay.

Certain of the *Lieder ohne Worte* were now a kind of emotional shorthand for him. So precise were their associations that he had only to hear a few bars to picture the rich gilt and cluttered mahogany of the room his grandmother liked to call the salon. At Barrowcester he had played the piano eagerly, since it provided an escape from the school's brutal society, and he found sympathy in his teacher, who he suspected was no less bullied by the other staff. The first few pieces he wrote there he wrote in secret, and then only in his last year.

He began to write short piano pieces and settings for over-wrought poetry at about the time that he started to suspect his letters home were going unread. There was a boy – Jarvis – whose father held a diplomatic post in Berlin. The post was no more, Edward suspected, than junior consul, but his letters were full of sinister news – about book burnings, shattered shop windows, the selective discrediting of eminent Jewish figures – and Jarvis passed the information on, with a harsh relish. After two months had gone by during which neither Edward nor Isaac had received replies to letters home, Edward stopped writing. His secret music became his one-way correspondence and a channel for his hope and dread.

Relaxed by his tutor's good wine and sympathetic conversation one evening during his first year at Tompion, he confessed as much. Thomas insisted he play some of his compositions and, after listening, insisted, too, that he make time to continue.

The ending took him by surprise. He stopped, eyes flicking back and forth across the last two pages, as though a glance could confirm the integrity of what was before him. His writing hand twitched and was wracked with a sudden cramp. He let his pen fall and shook the ache from his fingers and wrist. He yawned nervously and stretched. The door bell sounded again and a perfectly bald man in a crumpled linen jacket came in.

'Are you still open?' he asked, a hand touching his bow tie.

'Er. Yes. We are,' Edward told him. 'For a few more minutes.'

'I'm looking for a nice edition of *In Memoriam*,' the man said. 'For a special friend.'

'I'm not certain we have one. There are certainly some copies of the collected works. You'll find all the poetry upstairs.'

'Thank you.'

The man gave a neat smile and walked slowly up the narrow stairs, tugging on the greasy rope which hung there by way of a rail.

Edward shut the manuscript book and waited. When Sally came in again, he was ready for her. He jumped up from behind the counter and took her in his arms.

'I've finished!' he laughed. 'It's all done!' He kissed her. She slipped cool hands inside his jacket, where his back was hot. She didn't kiss him in return. Rather, she clasped him to her and laid her head on his shoulder, her face turned aside from his. The gesture was at once an embrace and a reprimand. She had her back to the stairs and missed the bald man's soft-footed descent. Edward met his startled glance apologetically and had to push Sally gently from him.

'Sorry,' he said, to both of them.

'Don't mind me,' the bald man said.

Flustered, Sally turned.

'Dr Banks, I presume.' The bald man laughed with unpleasantly triumphant recognition and shook her hand. He waved a copy of *In Memoriam* by way of explaining his presence. 'Last time I saw you, you were just plain Miss. Well, Miss, anyway – *never* plain!'

'Goodness, Dr Waltham. I don't think you know Edward Pepper.'

The bald man smiled and shook Edward's hand.

'Ah, you found a copy,' Edward said, taking the book. 'I'll wrap it for you.' He furled it in tight brown paper, sealed it with string and exchanged it for Dr Waltham's coins.

'Dr Waltham's an old friend of Dr Pertwee's,' Sally explained. 'I used to meet him at her rooms sometimes, after classes with her.'

'And how is your dear, er, Pygmalia?' Dr Waltham asked.

Edward saw Sally flinch at the faint snobbishness in his tone.

'Fine,' she said. 'I think. I'm afraid she likes to tire herself out.'

'She always did,' said Dr Waltham. 'Well. I won't keep you both. Goodbye.'

He had barely turned the corner when Sally sprang forward and shot the bolts on the door.

'Hateful man!' she spat. 'Always so soft-spoken and bloody self-satisfied.'

'He was rather smooth.'

'Smooth? He's got a personality of mink. Always harping on about Dr Pertwee as my Pygmalia, whatever that's supposed to mean, with that suggestive smirk, and always reminding me how common I am.'

'Sally!'

'I am. Bloody common. And there's nothing I can do about it. Why should I *want* to do anything?'

She changed the sign in the window to read Closed and pulled down the blind left over from black-out regulations. She turned, hands behind her back, shoulders rounded. Her eyes shone with anger. He had never seen her like this. He slid a hand into his pocket to mask his erection.

'Kiss me,' she said. 'Right here.'

As he walked over, she glanced down at his trouser fly.

'Never mind that,' she said.

Obediently he took his hand from his pocket and cupped her face in his palms. He kissed her slowly, his hips pressing hers. She kissed the side of his neck. He buried his nose into her hair.

'Let's go upstairs,' she said. 'We can lie down up there.'

'The concert,' he mumbled, as he led the way. 'We should get there in time to get good seats. The acoustic's so bad in St Francis.'

'Never mind the acoustic,' she said, as they reached the little room where the poetry and plays were shelved. 'Kiss me.'

He held her against a bookcase, kissing her again, caressing her breasts. She was wearing what Miriam and his mother would have called a courting dress, a pale blue thing with buttons, that unfastened easily from the front. It was a garment whose name he had not understood till recently. Since he had met Sally, he had started to look more closely at women in the street and behind shop counters, noticing their clothes. He was becoming an expert on fastenings. He slid with her to the dusty floor, clumsily tearing off his jacket and shirt. He rubbed his cheek against her petticoat, feeling the firm material of her bra beneath its whispering smoothness. Taken unawares, he had no condoms with him. Instead, she pleasured him with her hands, running cold fingers around his buttocks and balls, rubbing at his penis with untender haste. When he slid an uncertain hand inside her knickers she froze for a while and stopped touching him, such was her concentration on her pleasure. He came in three spasmodic splashes across her thighs and the floorboards. They chuckled as he wiped up the mess with pages torn from an undistinguished edition of Matthew Arnold.

The bells struck again in St Francis and he remembered the concert.

'Forget the concert,' she sighed, kissing his nose, making him lie down again. 'No more concerts. Not for a while. Take me dancing.'

'Dancing?'

'You'd think I'd suggested some impossible sexual feat!' she said.

'But I can't dance.'

'Believe me, you've got a sense of rhythm and two strongish arms; you can dance.'

'Where?'

'There's a charity do on at the Empire Rooms, for the Red Cross or something. The nurses were talking about it. There's a band from London. It might be fun.'

They went to a great gaudy room rank with saxophones and shandy, hair oil and a cocktail of cheap scents, and he found he could dance. He could not move like the men from the local air force base, perhaps, or the arrogant young shopboys, who manipulated their women like so many sides of beef, but he did better than walking round the room and turning at the corners – the charge Miriam had always levelled at him.

So began what he came to see as Sally's half of their mutual seduction. He had paraded for her the jewels of his weighty cultural education – paintings, polyphony, symphonic rapture and harmonic introspection. Now she showed him different riches, ones she had discovered by instinct. She began to talk more of her mother than of Dr Pertwee. 'Mum says this,' she would say, or 'My mother always says that . . .', and he detected the unfolding of an interior power struggle.

She taught him dance steps, the names of band leaders and the ingredients of lethal, highly coloured drinks. His ears were opened to the intoxicating qualities of dance music. As he went about his business in the shop, he found the melodies to enviably simple love songs circling his mind, at once banal and beautiful in their frankness of purpose.

He and Sally began to take trips, to the north coast, to London, to Brighton, and stay in hotels, posing, unconvincingly, as husband and wife with the aid of a pair of brass curtain rings. Occasionally, Dr Pertwee's deathless discretion again set her rooms at their amorous disposal.

'*You go to my head,*' he crooned over a new delivery of old anatomical textbooks, '*Like a sip of sparkling Burgundy brew and I find the very mention of you, like the kicker in a Julep or two.*' The words were like a passport to a territory from which he had previously been barred.

Then, one night, as he was driving her home, Sally made him stop at the side of the road in the pitch black of open fenland. She wanted them to talk, she said. They never seemed to have the time to talk properly.

'But we never stop talking,' he insisted, happily, 'Hardly ever.'

'Oh yes. We talk about Things; songs, films, symphony orchestras, people, your work, my work but –' she broke off, searching for words. He listened to her breathing. They had been at a party in the gardens at Tompion earlier. She had been drinking Pimms, and her breath smelled rich and sweet in the car's air of mouldering leather. She was slightly drunk, they both were. He had discovered that her emotions were not always directly available to her – she needed alcohol or a crisis to set them free.

She went on, 'But we never seem to talk about us.'

'Well?' He heard himself sounding German. 'Talk.'

'Where are we going, Edward? What do we want?'

'What do you want?' He touched her arm.

'No,' she said firmly, turning in her seat. 'No. You say what *you* want for once.'

'Me? I . . . I want *you*, my darling.'

'Yes but *how* do you want me? Sometimes I feel so unsure of you.'

'Sally!' He was amazed. 'Why?'

'Because I do all the wanting. I do all the suggesting. Sometimes I feel it's only *my* needs that keep our – that keep this going.' She laughed drily. 'If it hadn't been for me, it wouldn't ever even have started. You're so . . . so self-contained.'

'No I'm not.'

'Yes you *are*, Edward!'

'I love being with you! I love you!'

'Yes but you're not *in* love with me, are you?'

'I . . . I think I am.'

'Exactly! It's all a bloody intellectual process for you. You have to think before you know what you feel. You'd miss me if I disappeared but you wouldn't go to pieces.'

'Sally, I –' He struggled for words. Suddenly she seemed to be attacking him where his defences were weakest. He felt too terrified to open his mouth lest his words condemn him.

'Go on,' she prompted. 'Edward, please. Tell me what you want.'

'I want us to be together always,' he said. 'I want never to lose you. I want . . . Sally. I think that we should get married.'

She waited a second or two then asked with quiet determination, 'Do you really *want* that?'

'Yes.' He laughed with relief at the sudden simplicity of the ambition. 'Yes. Yes, I do!'

'Well?'

'Well what?'

'Ask me how *I* feel about it.'

'Hmm? Oh. Yes. Sally. Doctor Banks. Will you consent to be my wife?'

'I'll think about it.'

'How *can* you?' He clutched her shoulders and turned her towards him. Not knowing whether she was joking or serious was torture to him. 'Sally?'

'What?'

'Say yes. *Please* say yes?'

'That's more like it! Emotion. Real emotion!'

'Well?'

'Now I feel *wanted*, Edward.'

'Sally for God's sake!' If she didn't answer his proposal, he thought he would burst.

'Oh don't be absurd, Edward.' She looked down and stroked the evening bag on her lap. 'Of *course* I'll marry you.'

They kissed, laughing in surprise and pure pleasure. She encouraged him to unbutton her blouse and he began to stroke her, but the difficulty of bypassing the gear and brake levers held him back, and he drew away, caressing her hands thoughtfully.

'There are things I haven't told you,' he said.

'Yes?' She coughed in her effort to assume seriousness. 'Tell me now, then.'

'It's about my parents.'

'Yes.'

'They didn't just die in the war. It wasn't just a bombing raid or something like that. They were transported to a work camp and a while later they were shot.'

'Oh no!'

'Isaac told me. He had all kinds of contacts and he knew within weeks of the news getting out. He came to the internment camp to tell me.'

Sally squeezed his thumb in her palm.

'They were mad not to have sent Miriam with me. She'd just got engaged – well, as good as – to a town councillor, a gentile with a cousin in the army. They thought he'd protect her. Poor fools.'

'Who was Miriam?'

'My sister.'

'You never said you had a sister.'

'Didn't I? Yes. Miriam.'

'She survived, then?'

'Yes. No. We don't know. They were all sent to one place, then separated. Isaac went over as soon as he was allowed to, last year. I was too ill to go. There were lists. Terrible, long lists of names like garbled telephone directories. He traced my parents but not Miriam. He tried looking under her fiancé's name too, in case they'd got married in a rush to save her. Perhaps she was moved on somewhere.' Edward lifted Sally's hand and kissed it solemnly. The well of words was drying up finally. 'I don't know where she is,' he said. 'Isaac gave some money to a friend to keep looking for us.'

'Surely, if she survived, she'd have contacted you by now?'

'That's what I'd have thought but . . . her name hasn't been found anywhere.'

'Now that you're better, now that you're free to travel, wouldn't you like to go and find out?'

'There's nothing I'd hate more,' he sighed. 'But I suppose I shall have to. Isaac died, you see. Three months ago. The things he saw there, the stories he heard . . . It was as though he was shocked to death. He was a quiet, scholarly man; very legalistic, very dried-up – he had no imagination whatever. Rosa said that he began to have terrible dreams that made him cry out. And not just at night, either. He would nod off at his desk, after lunch, and she'd hear him shout and mumble.'

'How did he die?'

'A stroke. I suppose it was what is called a merciful release. Funny.'

'What?'

'He left me half his money. He was quite rich. But I don't get a penny until I'm thirty. That was his way of trying to force me to finish my studies.'

'Were you close to Miriam?'

'She was older but she was like a twin. We weren't identical, although sometimes it felt as though we shared a mind. But, she did all the things I didn't. She danced. She made people laugh. She was good at languages.' He fell silent, remembering, then returned Sally's hand to her lap and restarted the car.

When they reached her parents' house, he wanted to come in to ask her father's permission, but she laughed at him for being old-fashioned and Bavarian. They kissed and kissed and he got as far as undoing her blouse again, before a passing neighbour flustered her and she pulled back to tidy herself.

'You'll have to go, you know,' she said suddenly, frowning. 'You'll have to go and find out about Miriam sooner or later. I couldn't bear us to be married and happy, and for you not to know about her.'

Edward only nodded, relieved he had told her yet perturbed at how swiftly his revelation was assuming a shape and force between them.

Once she was lost to view, he drove back into Rexbridge and walked around the deserted streets, hunting for jewellers. Through a heavily barred window, he saw the ring he wanted and could not possibly afford. By rights, she should have his mother's wedding ring, but that was irrevocably gone. Walking back to the car he was ambushed by a sense of loss, of the cruel interruption the war had brought to the comforting continuity of family life. He could not take Sally to meet his parents and Miriam. He had no home. He had no parents.

The scent of the car's interior already bore a strong erotic charge in his mind after the frustrating, over-stimulated hours they spent there. When he parked outside Thomas's house and leaned forward, cooling his forehead, on the steering wheel, the scent of leather and a lingering trace of vanilla entered his thoughts and turned his grief to bewildering lust.

7

'You *what*?'

Sally's mother was crouched on the end of her bed, her toes separated with wads of cotton wool while she coated their nails with varnish.

'Not "pink",' she would exclaim to anyone who commented. 'It's *cerise d'amour*.'

'You what?' she asked again.

'You heard,' Sally said.

'He *never*!'

'Well thanks a lot.'

'He took his time, though, didn't he?'

'Not really.'

Sally fiddled with the brass doorknob, which was loose. Struck by a terrible thought, her mother paused a moment, varnish-brush in mid-stroke.

'He hasn't put one in your oven, has he?'

'What if he had? What difference would it make?'

'He'd be marrying you for the wrong reasons, that's what.'

'Since when were you so romantic?'

'Who mentioned romance? Marriage is hard enough when you start off on the *right* footing. You didn't throw yourself at him, did you? Didn't go cheapening yourself?'

'Of course not,' Sally lied. 'He just asked me.'

'And you said yes straight away? Well of course you did. Can't go calling their bluff at your age. Christ Almighty! Married at last! Well come here and have a kiss.'

Sally came forward and stooped to the bed. She expected the usual, cursory, don't-spoil-my-hair peck and was surprised by a hug that was actually tender. Then her mother quickly retreated into more characteristic gruffness.

'And now you've made me cry! Give me one of those hankies quick before I wreck my face.'

Sally reached for a handkerchief from the pile of ironing her mother had left on the bedside chair. Her mother took it with muttered thanks and dabbed at her eyes, which had already been pink and watery from an over-zealous application of cold cream. Then, seeing to the last of her nail-painting, she said, 'You were always such a *dry* little girl. You weren't one for dolls or princesses. No ribbons in your hair. And you never cried.'

'I must have done.'

'Well not while *I* was around.'

'I had you for an example.'

'I always tried to look nice for you, you know?'

'I used to think your nails *grew* that colour.'

Sally joined her mother on the bed although still kept at a distance by her careful labour.

'Was I a disappointment to you?' she asked cautiously.

'No. Not really.' Her mother stopped to consider then continued her work.

'Well,' she said, casually hurtful, 'if I'm honest, I wanted a boy. I knew I couldn't have any more after you.'

'You never said,' Sally sighed.

'Complications in the birth, they told me. You'd understand, of course. Back then we never thought to ask for details. Anyway –' she finished her nails briskly and screwed brush back into bottle '– you were the best of both worlds; brave as a boy, cunning as a girl.'

'Cunning?'

'You got your way. You always did. I admired that.'

'Oh.'

'So. Is he going to come and ask your dad's permission?'

'Certainly not!'

'Why not?'

'In case you hadn't noticed, I turned eighteen several years ago. I don't need permission. Your blessing would be nice, though.'

'Oh,' her mother snorted. 'That. Well, I wish you well, of course I do. Marriage is no joyride – especially if you've a will on you like you have. At least he's young. That way he'll respect you and you can get him well trained. Well don't go looking all old-fashioned! If you want wine and roses, you stay single, you know that. Marriage is a kind of business proposal when you get down to it.' She carefully stretched out her legs before her to give her handiwork a critical once-over.

Sally looked about the room, this temple to her parents' own marriage. There were so few clues. The big heart-shaped mirror over the pink-skirted dressing-table. Their wedding photograph. Sally's christening photograph. China souvenirs from their honeymoon in Scarborough, meticulously dusted. Nothing much. The ugly, heavy wardrobe and matching chest of drawers, the big divan bed and the his-and-her chamber pots not quite tucked out of sight suggested some of the profound lack of romance at which her mother hinted. Their wedding photograph, in which her father was still upstanding, a lithe, fit young man, younger than his daughter was now, gave more positive proof of disappointment. Her mother caught her looking at it.

'No,' she said, 'That picture's a lie. That's not the man I married. The man I married is sitting downstairs. That dreamboat in the natty suit and shiny shoes was a man I dreamt up and carried in my head. I hope you know him well, your Edward.'

'I do.'

'I mean really well. Men change, girl. They grow up slower than women.'

'You must have had some good times with him.'

'Oh. Yes. Good times.' Her mother leant against the headboard and snorted at her recollections. 'I suppose he made me feel safe, which was nice. And he was taller than me then, before his accident. And he was a good dancer, when he'd had a few, which makes it all the sadder I suppose.' She looked at her hands again, her hard, worker's hands with their incongruously lacquered nails, and sighed to herself. 'So,' she said, 'Have you set a date?'

'Not yet,' Sally told her, 'But I don't see much point in a long engagement.'

'No. I bet you don't.'

'What do you mean by that?'

'Oh you know, Madam. You know.'

Sally surprised herself by blushing and had to pretend to blow her nose. Her mother went on regardless of the confusion she had caused. 'Where will you live? You can't live here.'

'We might have to, Mum, to start with.'

Her mother began to protest but Sally cut her short.

'We'd pay you rent. Proper rent.'

'Well I don't know. You might end up like that Perkins lot up the street and never move out.'

'Don't be silly. Anyway, we'll probably find somewhere in Rexbridge.'

'You'd better go and have a word with the parson tomorrow evening. Fix up the banns and everything.'

'Oh I'm not sure we'll get married in church.'

'Because he's Jewish? We brought you up C of E, my girl, and we're paying. So you get married in church.'

'But we never *go* to church!' Sally protested.

'So? We're English and your father and I got married in church, and you can do the same. C of E.' Her mother wrinkled her nose. 'You don't want one of those poky registry office jobs like some old tart with a divorce on her. You want a bit of charm, girl. A bit of dignity. There'll be time enough for the other.'

'Well I'm going to wear cream, I warn you.'

Her mother sat up sharply.

'I thought you said you weren't in the club?'

'I'm not, but I can't wear white at my age.'

'At your age, at your age. You're only twenty-seven.'

'A moment ago you were carrying on as though I was forty.'

Her mother pointed a warning finger.

'You wear cream and it's over my dead body. I don't want all the neighbours getting ideas. We'll take you round to Ida's sister. She can do you something simple with a little veil. You can always shorten the sleeves and get it dyed later. I'll pay.'

'Where's all this money come from suddenly?'

'It's my money. I earned it. You don't have a daughter and not put something by just in case. Daughters cost. It's a fact of life. Now. Go to bed and get some sleep. I'm exhausted and you look as if you could do with some too. Have you told your dad?'

'Yes. He was asleep by the stove with the radio on. I told him when I came in.'

'What did he say?'

They looked at each other and started to chuckle at the thought.

'You know what he's like. He said "Oh," and asked me what Edward did again, as if I hadn't told him already a hundred times, and then he said, "Well you'd better tell your mother." I know he wasn't any wilder about me seeing Edward than you were, but I had expected a little more enthusiasm.'

'Oh he'll be pleased. In his way. When it sinks in.' Her hair wrapped in chiffon, her mother had already climbed into bed and was tugging the covers up around her. She sometimes claimed that sleep was the one pleasure that never disappointed. Sleep and Gordon's gin.

'Put the top light off on your way out, there's a love,' she murmured sleepily.

Sally crossed the cramped room with its loudly ticking alarm clock and bedroom smells of night cream and talcum powder. As she reached for the light switch, her mother made soft, pettish little settling noises as she snuggled into her pillows and Sally knew that even now, after so many years of hard practicality and cruel disappointment, her mother threw aside her khaki slacks and work gloves in her dreams to become some headstrong character from the films she loved, with a palatially draped bedroom suite, dour but loving Scottish servants and an embarrassment of impatient suitors.

8

The punt slid under a bridge. Sally dropped her head back on the cushions, steadying her blue straw hat with one hand. She gazed up at the clammy stones then, as they emerged, at a clutch of day-trippers who were staring at them. A red-haired woman took a photograph then turned immediately away, as though the seizing of the picture had rendered the actual beauty of the scene insignificant. Edward was punting proficiently, with a steady rhythm and minimal splashing. He was in cricket whites and had taken off his jacket to reveal a white shirt that – fetchingly, Sally thought – looked two sizes too large. He had rolled up his sleeves to keep them dry and now she could see the tendons flex in his forearms as he pushed and pulled on the glistening pole.

Impatient with holding the thing in place, she slipped off her hat and dropped it in her lap. She ran her fingers through her hot hair then, shutting her eyes against the sun, let a hand trail in the water. The Rex smelt faintly rotten, unless it was the odour of exposed mud at the base of its banks. There had been no rain for weeks and the river flowed slowly, deep on its bed. As they drifted past a college where the lawns were being mown, the sweet scent of cut grass washed over her and made her open her eyes.

Thomas sat before her, in front of Edward. Despite the heat, he had persisted in wearing both jacket and tie and his face was pink and shiny in the shadow of his panama. The picnic he had brought with him was packed in a basket between their feet. When they had first set out, he had kept up a stream of pronouncements and mordant witticisms. It was as though his position – wobbling in a damp punt, in a holiday setting far from his usual academic context – threatened to render him anonymous, so he strove to impose his superiority on the weed, the ducks and the idling passers-by. Then they passed a punt full of young men who mimicked his manner and roared with impudent laughter. With a faint pout, he fell silent, merely casting over his shoulder a look that could have bored holes in their boat timbers.

Pitying him, Sally drew him out afresh, asking how Rexbridge had changed since his undergraduate days. She assumed, correctly, that he had spent the best part of his life in largely unchanged circumstances, attached to the same, distinguished college. He had served as an air raid patrolman during the war, which had entailed his finally learning to ride a bicycle. He snorted dismissively when she suggested that the Home Guard might have been more amusing, then went on to question her closely about her work and responsibilities. Edward played no part in the conversation. When she addressed him, he would smile and give a short reply before returning to his labour. His assumption of the punt-pole appeared to make him at once a party and an outsider to their society, like a cabby or a gondolier.

Thomas had yet to congratulate them on their engagement. On first acquaintance, she would have mistaken this for a calculated discourtesy, but now that she had known him several weeks she suspected that Edward had simply not yet told him. This suspicion was confirmed when they were sliding through the ragged edge of town. Thomas said that he was planning to take a trip to Tuscany in the late autumn and hoped that Edward would come with him. Edward said nothing but blushed hotly when Sally threw him an angry glance.

He steered them in to the bank where some poplars marked the edge of a field. A family was picnicking noisily a hundred yards away on the opposite side of the river. One of the children was climbing a tree that hung out over the water. Sally looked at his baggy shorts and muddy feet and was startled by a sudden access of broody warmth. She had often pictured herself as married, complete with shadowy husband and roses around the door, but motherhood had never formed a part of the fantasy. There were no love songs about childbirth or motherhood, none, certainly, to which one could dance.

Even allowing for rationing, Thomas's picnic showed that eye for luxury at which selfish bachelors excel. There was none of the starchy mass which recent austerity had made a wifely virtue, just formal islands of flavour, enticing and rare. Sitting cross-legged on one corner of the rug, he delighted in revealing the network of more or less corrupt contacts through whom he had come by the ingredients – a rector's wife, to whose daughters he taught Latin, a butcher's boy he had once surprised in an act of public indecency.

'And these,' he crowed, producing a small, napkin-lined tin of *petits fours* as the coffee heated on a little oil burner, 'come from Didier.'

'From whom?'

'The college's new sous-chef. He's from Alsace, poor boy, and very young to be away from home and no-one in common room bothers to speak to him at all when he's carving, much less in French.'

Thomas's explanation tailed off as he sank his teeth into one of Didier's small confections and assumed an expression worthy of St Teresa. Edward caught Sally's eye and grinned but she looked back at him flatly and said, 'Edward, why don't you rinse these plates and glasses in the river, then it won't make such a mess of the basket when I put them back?'

Edward dutifully took a handful of picnic things down to the water's edge. Sally leaned back on the rug, resting on one elbow, and watched. Thomas watching him go. For the first time it occurred to her that he might be nervous left alone in her company. It would pay, she decided, to be direct.

'Thomas?'

'Mmh?' Thomas had closed his eyes again and was pretending to sun himself.

'Edward hasn't told you our news, has he?'

'Er. No?' There was a slight quaver to his voice, which he

promptly mastered. 'But I think I can guess.' He opened his eyes. 'Congratulations,' he said.

'Thanks.'

She glanced towards the river. Edward had walked along the bank and was crouching down to talk to the little boy and his older sisters, who had rowed across from the family party.

'You don't approve of me, do you?' she asked. 'I mean, as a wife for Edward. You'd rather he fell in love with some don's daughter. Someone with a plummier accent.'

'My dear woman, you couldn't be more wrong! I can think of nothing worse for him.' He looked full at her. Shaded by his hat brim, his eyes searched her face. 'You're strong. You'll protect him.'

'What on earth from?'

'Well.' He shrugged, and poured three cups of coffee. 'Cream?' he asked.

'No, thank you. I take mine black.'

'There you are.'

'What from, Thomas?' she persisted.

'Himself, largely. He's spoken of his family, I take it?'

'He said they were dead.'

'Yes.' He stirred two spoonfuls of thick brown crystals into his cup, raised it and sipped. 'Terrible to be so alone and so . . . so unsure. He –' Thomas broke off.

'Yes?'

'If I have any disapproval,' he said at last, 'It's with the marital institution, not with his choice of mate.'

'Oh.' Sally thought a moment, taking this in.

'And now, if you'll excuse me, doctor, I really must have a smoke.'

Before she could exclaim that she was inured to pipe smoke, he was up and striding away from her, busy with his tobacco pouch, parting a way through the cows that had drifted over to graze nearby.

Sally drained her coffee, relishing it to the bitter dregs. She looked in one direction and then the other at the two men – they could not have been further removed from her earlier life. As she formed the thought, it struck her with the force of a revelation, that her life had altered irreversibly. Her wedding day and its attendant rituals were, in a sense, a sentimental irrelevancy. The wedding was for the world, for her mother. Sally felt it was now, not then, that a part of her life was over and a new one begun.

She lay back, head on her hands, and watched a white cloud unravel on an eggshell sky. She felt full – with good food, of course, but also with possibility. She felt tired as well. The week had been no more exhausting than usual – a daily round of chest-tapping, medication, fretful children and adults respectful of authority, frightened of pain. Whereas previously she would have returned from work, eaten her tea then collapsed on the sofa with a library book or the radio, however, she had now the added labour – however bewitching – of a love life. She had become an athlete of sleep, adept now at snatching intense restorative catnaps in a vacant hospital consulting room.

Lulled by the sun, doped with wine, she let her eyelids close and drifted off into a heavy doze during which she could hear the afternoon progressing around her but was too somnolent to sit up and re-enter it. She heard Edward return and sip his tepid coffee. She heard him tentatively say, 'Hello? Sally?' but she failed to respond. He snorted – either from disappointment or affection – and packed away the picnic things.

'Sally?' he asked again more persistently. 'Where's Thomas?'

And still she could not answer. She felt him lie with a resigned sigh on the rug beside her, smelled the faint tang of his sweat and listened to the soothing rustle of him turning the pages to find his place in a novel. He had read a few pages when Thomas came back. The two of them spoke softly for fear of waking her.

'I say.'

'What?'

'Congratulations. Sally told me the good news. You are a chump to have kept so quiet. Made me feel a fool. I hate surprises.'

'Sorry.'

'I'm . . . I'm very glad, *mein Lieber*.'

'Thank you, Thomas.'

'Have you set a date?'

'Well, Sally's job finishes in August.'

'Good. Long engagements are pointless. Where will you live?'

'We'll find somewhere. Thomas?'

'Yes?'

'Would you – I'm not sure how you say it in English – give me away?'

Thomas gave a soft, affectionate chuckle.

'Be your best man, you mean, your *Trauzeuge*? I'd be delighted, you fool. You could use the college chapel, if you liked. No-one around in August and anyway, I'm sure you've the right. The chaplain's – er – he's very sympathetic.'

'I'd better ask Sally.'

'Yes.'

Edward patted Sally's hand as he spoke. His touch freed her as from a charm, and she felt able to stretch and sit up. Blinking, she looked at the two men.

'Sorry,' she said. 'Nodded off.'

'Sleeping Beauty,' said Thomas and kissed her hand, rather ostentatiously she thought.

'I suppose we should be getting home,' she said. 'Doesn't the punt have to be back by four?'

On the way home, Thomas suddenly burst out with another round of congratulations.

'I've had an idea,' he added. 'I'm going to give you the car as a wedding present. How's that?'

Amidst their delighted protestations that it was far too generous and surely he used it some time and what about emergencies and so on, Sally had her second revelation of the day. Thomas had insisted they change places going back so that she should have the view. She could see the ever so subtly beseeching way he was watching Edward's exertions with the punt pole. Tenderness welled up from the base of her spine, bursting out in an almost painful smile. She smiled at the uselessly clever, lonely man before her and thought, 'You love him.'

She sensed that the sad grin he gave her back expressed the closest approximation he would dare to an affirmation. Thomas, she resolved, should have a place in their married life.

9

The good weather continued through the week and they found themselves on a second excursion the following weekend. This time Dr Pertwee was the instigator. Sally had sent her a letter, announcing their engagement, and she had responded at once with an invitation to lunch in her rooms on Saturday. Her congratulations were heartfelt, even a little tearful. She gave them sherry then served up a characteristically bitty lunch of Spam, egg salad, pickled beetroot slices and a Stilton so strong it was nearly mobile.

'I have some news too,' she announced, handing out frugal third shares of a tinned treacle pudding she had heated inside the kettle. 'Not,' she laughed, 'I hasten to add, another engagement. No. I'm going away. I've decided the time has come.'

'What fun,' Sally said, 'A holiday?'

'In a way,' Dr Pertwee told her. 'But a long one. I'm retiring.'

'Forgive me,' Edward put in, 'But I thought you already had.'

'I'm retiring, young man, from the *world*.'

Neither Sally nor Edward knew quite what to say. Sally stood to take the kettle and set about making them a pot of tea.

'Properly speaking,' Dr Pertwee went on, 'I'm retiring from the vexatious world of men. I'm joining the women at Corry.'

'The island?' asked Edward.

'That's right. You remember, don't you, Sally? Off the

Dorset coast. That rather saintly woman from St Maud's went there – Professor Carson. Bridget Carson.'

Sally returned to the table with tea and cups.

'But I thought you were an agnostic,' she said, frowning.

'So I am, dear. And so I shall continue, barring miracles. But that doesn't seem to be a problem with them. Corry is a very unorthodox community – not like a nunnery at all. One of their number penned a tract prescribing division by gender as the cure for all society's modern ills. And they house a Buddhist and a Communist vegetarian. Not in the same room, though,' she chuckled. 'No, I shan't be becoming a Bride of Christ at my great age. The Mother Superior, Lady Agnes Bowers, wrote to me out of the blue this week. One of the sisters has been gathered, it seems, to the Great Dormitory in the Sky, so they now have a rather nice vacant room with a view of the sea. My name was put forward by several of the women, including the saintly Professor Carson.'

'Will you be happy there?' Sally asked, still uncertain.

'Could you pour, dear?' their hostess asked Edward. 'My old wrists can't handle that pot when it's full.' She turned her face towards Sally, although concentrating her gaze on a crumb she was chasing off the tablecloth with the side of her palm. 'Well happiness was ever a moot point. I should certainly be happier there than in some ghastly rest home. I know I could crumble away contentedly on my own – plenty of people here seem to – but the peace would be most beneficial and I could learn to keep bees, which is something that has always fascinated me. Apiculture is the island's principal source of income, you know,' she told Edward, like some benign geography tutor. 'There'll be a kind of liberation in leaving all my books and business behind and making a late, fresh start in a new, more practical world. I suppose the communal meals with some pious creature reading aloud from improving texts might take a little getting used to, but I usually read when I eat alone and it would be better than the din of everyone chattering at once, the way I fear a group of educated women might tend to. So,' she sipped her tea, 'I've told them yes and I shall be taking up residence – bag and baggage – at the end of August. Which sadly means I shall have to miss witnessing your first months of wedded bliss.' She pulled a comical-sad face at Edward, who smiled back at her.

'I'll miss you,' Sally said slowly. 'I've always thought of you as my second mother.'

Edward glanced at her, wanting to take her hand. He wished, guiltily, it were her real mother who was moving away so completely.

'I would hope that by now, I'd become a sort of friend as well,' Dr Pertwee replied.

Too moved to speak, Sally merely smiled and kissed her cheek. Her eyes were large with tears. He saw that Dr Pertwee was determined not to let Sally make her mawkish. Her tone was bracing.

'Anyway, you can come and *see* me.' She patted Sally's hand then thought to reach out and touch Edward's arm as well. 'You can *both* come and see me, you poor, untried young people. We have an open day once a year, or twice. I forget. Now, Edward, were you serious in your offer of taking the old crone for an outing in your marital motor?'

'I certainly was. Where would you like to go?' he asked.

'Ely?' Sally suggested.

'That would be nice, dear, but then we'd be forced to endure evensong and I was rather thinking I might pay my last respects to The Roundel.'

'But of course,' Edward told her. 'Where is it?'

'You drive out past Mildenhall towards Methwold. It's near St Oswald's church. Down some tiny roads. I'll know the way when I see it.'

In the Wolseley, Dr Pertwee sat up in front beside Edward, fluttering her hands in excitement as they passed old, familiar sights or new, surprising ones, and calling out comments to Sally in her soft tones.

The house was unlike anything Edward had ever seen, though he said at once that it reminded him of a cathedral chapter house. Its twelve sides gave it an almost circular appearance. Its small red bricks and pantiled roof were the only concessions to vernacular fenland style. A small hillock raised it slightly above the astonishing flatness round about, and a thickly overgrown walled garden shielded its lower windows from public gaze and winter winds. Not that there could ever be much public in such an eerie, isolated spot. The nearby village comprised no more than six houses and a church. The nearest building was a huge brick barn which looked older than anything else there.

'Sally, if you don't mind.' Dr Pertwee took a large iron key from her bag. 'The lock's a little stiff. You may have to jiggle it.'

Sally jumped out, unlocked the gates and Edward drove in. Brambles dragged cruelly along the car's painted flanks. What had been a steep gravel drive was almost buried beneath weeds and moss. He ground to a halt rather than battle on.

'When were you last here?' he asked, astonished.

'Oh,' the old woman said airily, waving a hand, 'Years ago, now. It was with Bridget Carson. I remember her car was very new and she was most concerned about it overheating so we drove at a snail's pace. It must have been at least five years before the war, anyway: Let's leave the car down here and walk up.'

Sally rejoined them and she and Edward walked up the hillock with Dr Pertwee between them, shielding her from the vicious lashing of thorny stems.

'You're right to talk of chapter houses,' Dr Pertwee said. 'The chapter house at Wells was said to be the inspiration, along with the Medici chapel in Florence because the designers had recently completed the Grand Tour. Personally I have always subscribed to its complete originality. The architects were women, you see, so people have always been at pains to dismiss the whole project as somehow derivative. My five-times-great aunt and her unmarried niece they were. Women designing buildings was unheard of then. It's pretty rare now. Men usually build in squares, of course. Assertive squares and self-important rectangles. Domes and circles have always had a suspect, popish and distinctly female air to them – one thinks of the Radcliffe Camera, and the follies at Stowe – all very well, but hardly suitable for home and family. Even the British Library's circle is contained and mastered by rectangles – and St Paul's *and* St Peter's – like inspiration brought to heel by rationality.'

They climbed up a short flight of steps to reach the front door. This was built into a gothic arch to echo the mossy, gothic windows let into the walls at even intervals. Dr Pertwee produced a second key from her bag and, with a helping push from Edward's shoulder, let them in.

A small panelled lobby led to a surprising galleried hall which reached up to the second storey's painted dome. Rooms led off the hall, at equidistant points, like slices of a cake. Their arrangement was echoed in the lower-ceilinged rooms above and by the store-rooms, kitchen and larders in the basement. The circularity was not entirely fanciful. Two single women, who had spent the greater part of their fortune on building costs, could not afford much in the way of staff or fuel. So, the interconnecting rooms followed the course of the sun. A breakfast room led to a morning room to a sitting room to a dining room to a study. Only one fire at a time would have to be made up, its hot coals preceding the inhabitants in a lidded brass bucket on their quiet daily passage through the succession of chambers. Rooms dictated the pattern of their day as strictly as the motions of sun and moon did the hours of worship in a convent. A housemaid's labour was halved at every turn, with cunningly disguised storage areas for linen, candles, fuel and cleaning equipment. A dumb waiter brought food by the directest route from the kitchen to a tiny servery off the dining room. The enlightened architects had even thought to let large, low windows into the kitchen quarters to give their staff an equal share in the view of the garden.

Dr Pertwee explained that she had not lived in the place for over fifteen years and that some distant cousins had long since made inroads into her stocks of furniture. What remained – some of it beautiful, if battered – was dusty and cobwebbed. There was a sweet smell of damp everywhere and a chill, despite the warmth outside. But the spirit of the place survived; inspired and invigorating.

Edward was enchanted, as he had never been by the grand country houses to which Thomas had taken him in the surrounding counties. Dr Pertwee opened an old steamer trunk that had been left in the hall, and began to lift out the antiquated dresses it contained to show Sally. The women laughed and gasped over the old fabrics, holding up their beaded and glistening surfaces like so many precious relics.

Edward left them and climbed the narrow flight of stairs that curved up to the floor above. Despite the overgrown shrubs outside, the house was intensely sunny. Light spilled into the hall from a grimy lantern window at the dome's apex. Clearly rain did too; there were greenish damp patches on the surrounding plasterwork and what appeared to be ferns growing on some of the lantern's glazing bars. He walked around the gallery, smiling at the crudely painted cherubs and clouds overhead and peering through open doors into sparsely furnished bedrooms. He investigated a bathroom whose massive fittings, including a free-standing, claw-footed bath, appeared to date from before the Great War. He played a few, wheezing bars of a Lutheran chorale on a harmonium that stood, incongruously, on the other side of the room, then he turned to walk around the gallery. He looked down on the women and ran a curious finger along the thick handrail of the balustrade, revealing a rich mahogany gloss beneath the dust.

The last bedroom, the same off-square shape as the others only narrower, contained a spartan child's bed with a rudimentary cast-iron frame. Edward sat on it. The springs complained and the yellowing ticking of the mattress felt clammily cold beneath his hands. Sally's voice exclaimed over something, and was followed by Dr Pertwee's, lower and persistent. He rose and was about to join them again when he saw that the pretty Gothic window had been spoilt by iron bars, rammed into the window frame on the outside.

Suddenly he felt the presence of Miriam, more strongly than he had in years. He stumbled back on to the mattress, oppressed by successive impulses of grief and a bleak unmanning fear. It was as though he could feel his sister's mind within his own. She was alive. All at once, he knew she was alive somewhere, and he had an overwhelming, hideous sense that she was suffering. He shut his eyes tight as if trying to rid them of painful dust. He forced himself to concentrate on real things, on the chill of the mattress, the undisturbed smell of the room, the clattering of birds in the ivy outside, and gradually the palpable sense of her slipped away from him. He reopened his eyes and, blinking, looked afresh at the room, like a man who had woken with a start but had yet to perceive what had roused him.

Sally's voice, laughing, was coming along the gallery.

'Edward? Guess what? Edward? Where are you hiding, silly?' She appeared in the doorway and saw in an instant that something was wrong.

Her voice quickened, 'Edward, what is it?'

'Nothing. I . . . I just got a bit breathless, that's all. I think it's the cold and the dust.'

He stood, taking her offered hands. 'I'm fine. Honestly Doctor.' He smiled at her, kissed her worried pout. 'Let's go down. This house is bizarre.'

'This house is ours.'

'*What*?'

'This house is yours.' Dr Pertwee had climbed the stairs to meet them.

'Don't look so shocked, Edward!' Sally laughed.

'Or properly speaking, this house is *hers*,' Dr Pertwee continued. 'Shall we go outside and see just how bad the garden's got? You see, Edward,' she said as they left the house, 'The Roundel has always belonged to women. The idea was that it should pass into the hands of the first daughter of each generation, with priority being given to any that remained unmarried. Both my brothers were killed back in 1917, so I've no family to leave it to.'

'You mentioned cousins,' said Edward, as they passed out through the jungle of tree-high tangles that had once been a rose garden. Dr Pertwee pulled a long face.

'My aunt had a depressingly respectable son who sired a clutch of depressingly respectable children. They are amply provided for by their father and I feel they are less than kin to me.' She paused for a moment to dead-head a spray of browning blooms. 'They live in Surrey,' she added, as though this explained everything.

'But it's yours,' he said, looking up at the weathered bricks, the cracked windowsills. 'Surely you still have some need of it?' What had seemed a charmingly battered folly was acquiring by the minute a high flavour of onerous responsibility.

'On the contrary, dear boy, I shall be glad to rid myself of such a heavy burden. Property can make one feel profoundly guilty. This poor garden!' She tut-tutted and vainly tucked a fistful of clematis back into the branches of an old, dead apple tree. The knotted hank of foliage and dark pink flowers swung back into Edward's path before he could pass. He ducked beneath it. Dr Pertwee was leading them down the hillock, on the opposite side from the entrance to the house. They emerged from the jungle into long grass. It reached the old woman's waist but she walked on regardless, trampling a path in which he and Sally could follow.

'I shall be able to rest content in my retirement in the knowledge that two young, vigorous people are living here. You don't have to transform the place. You don't have to become its slaves. Just enjoy it. Love it. I've neglected it so.'

'But surely,' Edward called after her from the rear. 'Surely you could sell it? A place of such historic interest . . . It must be valuable.'

'I don't *want* to sell it,' Dr Pertwee countered. 'Property out here is worth nothing and besides, I think there was something in the term of my unmarried aunt's will that forbade me to put the place on the market. My solicitor could tell you.' She stopped and turned to face him. 'Don't you *want* Sally to inherit all this? And your daughters?' she asked, waving a hand at the garden as she fixed him with her quizzical stare.

'Oh yes. Of course,' he stammered. 'It's only that your kindness . . . I should say . . . I'm most embarrassed, Doctor.'

A bewitching smile broke out on her wrinkled face. She told him, as though it were the easiest thing in the world, 'Well *don't* be.'

As they walked on, Sally reached blindly behind her, took his hand and squeezed it with controlled excitement.

The garden was not circular, as had at first appeared. At the road side it was rounded, following the line of the hillock and the house, but to the rear it stretched away to meet a stream that ran beneath a group of trees; rustling poplar and trailing willow. Beneath the surface, wigs of emerald weed shook in the current. Sally sighed with open pleasure and sat on the bank. Edward spread his jacket, inside-out, on the grass and helped Dr Pertwee lower herself to sit on it. He sat a few feet from them both, his back against a willow trunk. On the other side of the stream a few more trees clustered, then the garden gave way to drifting acres of fenland crops. The first two fields, Dr Pertwee explained, belonged to The Roundel and were let out to a local farmer for a nominal rent. The view would never be spoilt.

'Of course, I shall have to go through the motions of adopting you,' she told Sally. 'In the event of the cousins kicking up a stink. I don't think they will, though. As I say, they live in Surrey. A place like this would be anathema to them. Too many draughts. Too much dust. Too old too, probably.'

'What would your parents say to that, Sally?' Edward asked.

Sally had taken off her shoes and was dipping her white feet in the water. Roused from her child-like absorption, she turned, wrinkling her eyes against the sunlight.

'Mum would understand. She's a realistic soul.'

'And your father?' Dr Pertwee asked.

'He'd do as she told him.'

'So,' Dr Pertwee told Edward, after a thoughtful pause, 'you'll be gaining not one mother, but two.'

On the drive back into town, there was little conversation, but occasionally Edward would look at Dr Pertwee or catch Sally's eye in the rear-view mirror and would be given a comfortable smile in return. It was as though they both felt the need to reassure him.

'All will be well now,' their smiles told him. 'We have everything under control.'

When they arrived back at Dr Pertwee's rooms, he stepped out to open the car door but sensed that Sally wanted to lead her back inside without him, so as to enjoy a moment of private thanks.

As Edward drove her back to Wenborough, he asked, 'How will we manage to live?'

'Way out there, you mean?' She laughed at his simplicity.

'Yes.'

'Oh. I'll find something. I've convinced Bastard Graeme to do the decent thing and make enquiries among his GP contacts. There should be several out there somewhere. If we're lucky there'll be an old one with a comfy rural practice, looking to retire.'

'But what about me?'

'You?' She laughed again. 'Well you, *mein Lieber*, are going to leave your bookshop and beaver away in perfect peace at becoming a celebrated composer.'

10

Their wedding day dawned to thundery showers and proved just as awkward as Edward had secretly feared. Sally's mother had her way, predictably. The marriage was in church and the bride wore dazzling white. The complication even fastidious Thomas had overlooked was Edward's being a Jew. Thomas had successfully wangled them a wedding in Tompion college chapel and the chaplain insisted on having the couple in for some religious instruction. Once he discovered that Sally was a doctor of medicine, not a specialist in botany or Old Norse, he evidently thought better of issuing the groom with his usual pamphlet on godly procreation. Sally and Edward had already laughed over a copy lent them by one of Edward's contemporaries who had married while still a student. The chaplain got his own back, however, when Edward mentioned his Jewishness, first by urging Edward to be baptised and when that failed, prompting him to admit that his Jewishness meant little to him in religious terms and that he no longer practised. It was all one to Edward, or so he thought; but, after a boisterous evening on the town, he spent his last night under Thomas's roof tossing and turning through drunken, morbid dreams in which long-faced relatives accused him of denouncing faith and family.

'Do we mean so little to you?' his mother asked. 'It's not the religion, it's the *principle*.'

'The boy throws us out with the garbage,' his grandmother spat, 'to marry *what*? A penniless *Schickse*. A bloodletter in petticoats!'

That the figures in his dreams were all now dead did little to comfort him.

Having feared the congregation would all be on Sally's side he was surprised to see, through the painful mist of his hangover, how many friends turned out to support him. He and Sally had not sent out formal invitations, but Thomas had taken his position as best man seriously and been busy on Edward's behalf.

The social gulf was all too visible. With his foreign ear, Edward could hear all the more acutely the difference in accents. On one side, the women wore larger, louder hats, made larger, louder gestures to catch one another's attention and necks were craned to peer at unfamiliar fan vaulting and stained glass. The professors' wives and recent graduates on the other side contented themselves with quiet smiles and the occasional discreet murmur as they peered over prayerbooks, and out of eye-corners at the bride's people.

Deprived of the chance to impose a humiliating baptism on the groom, the chaplain had pointedly chosen as his lesson a passage from St Paul's letter to the Corinthians, concerning the spiritual problems posed by marriage to a heathen. Glancing sideways, Sally caught an unmistakable smirk of triumph on her mother's face. When at last they were taking their vows and she was in a position to meet Edward's eye, she tried to communicate the aching urge she felt to take him far away. Unbeknown to her, he felt exactly the same, seeing her serious and uncomfortable in the virginal white that had been forced upon her by older, cynical hands.

At the reception – tea, sandwiches and starchy wedding cake in a large, first floor room across the quadrangle from the chapel – social divisions were crudely emphasised again. Sally introduced her mother to Thomas, her father to the Master of Tompion, her cousin who had once played the violin to a friend of Edward's who still did; but conversation froze in each instance. Her mother, father and cousin soon scurried back to the rowdy camp her family had established around a great aunt on a window seat. Hip flasks circulated. Cups of tea acquired an oily sheen of brandy. Dr Pertwee effectively established a rival court from an armchair on the other side of the room, following a painfully awkward discussion with Sally's parents, in which she said, with disarming candour, that she hoped they didn't think her wedding present of The Roundel was intended to upstage any of their own gifts.

'It's all right,' Edward murmured, squeezing Sally's hand. 'Just think, it's your last day as theirs. Tomorrow's your first day as *mine*!'

She felt obscurely disappointed at this fleeting reference to her as property but grinned it off. She had been to numerous weddings over the last fifteen years – everything from formal village church affairs with page boy and bridesmaids, to hastily witnessed unions in registry offices and shipboard hospitals, but only now did she understand. The reception speech saw about gaining sons and daughters was a lie as well as a cliché. The wedding ceremony isolated the new couple, excluding the families and social baggage they had spent their young lives acquiring. We are sufficient to ourselves, the vows implied, we will thrive without any of you. But the slow sentimentality of the parting irked her. In China, Thomas had told her, the bride's family went into mourning. She became dead to them as soon she entered a different household. That was calling a spade a spade.

'I want to run away,' she thought. 'Now,' as Edward steered an old woman towards her. She was wearing black, and an unseasonal fur collar that matched her heavy, unplucked eyebrows. Her hand, when Sally took it, was all bone and loose skin. She gave off a strange sweet smell, an unhappy blend of mothball and tuberose.

'Darling, this is Rosa. Rosa Holzer. A cousin of my mother's, you remember? She and Isaac used to have me to stay in London during the school holidays.'

'My dear,' said Rosa. Behind her smile, her gimlet eyes searched Sally's face as they might look for cracks in cut-price porcelain.

'Hello. How kind of you to come all this way.'

'It was nothing,' Rosa said, her smile dropping, and Sally believed her. She sipped her tea, looked dourly about the room, her fat lower lip protruding in disapproval.

Sally muttered some courtesy about having met so few of Edward's family. 'That's because there are so few left to meet.'

Rosa's expression, as she turned back, was hostile as a suddenly drawn knife. 'Why did you make him do it?' she demanded. 'Are you so very Christian?'

Sally gasped.

'I'd happily not have got married in church at all,' she stammered, 'My mother –'

'So,' the old woman cut in. 'You could have gone to a synagogue. You could have respected his dead family – may their memory be blessed. Our wedding ceremony is so beautiful but you chose this . . . this humiliation.'

'Now Rosa, really,' Edward protested. 'I haven't set foot in a synagogue since you last took me when I was a boy.'

'And you expect me to be *impressed* by that? Look at you. With a name like Edward. That's what you call yourself still? Edward? Edward *Pepper*?'

As her voice rose in mockery of an English accent, other guests – Sally's mother, Dr Pertwee, Thomas – turned to see what was happening. Rosa glowered back at them all.

'His name is Eli,' she told them, succinctly. 'Eli Pfefferberg.'

Sally's mother flinched as at an obscenity and turned quickly away. Rosa's voice dropped. 'No good can come of it,' she pronounced, thrusting her empty teacup into Sally's protesting hands with a rattle.

'So, you're a doctor, my dear?' she mocked, looking Sally up and down. 'Your mother must be proud. But even *you* can't raise the dead.'

She turned on her heel.

'Rosa!' Edward said, raising his voice. 'Rosa, please!'

More heads turned as she stalked from the room. The cup began to shake in Sally's hands. Edward took it from her and led her to a window recess as nervous conversation burst out all around them.

'Ssh,' he told her. 'She's not herself. Don't worry. She's still not over Isaac's death. He was all she had. I'll make sure people realise. God Sally, I'm sorry! I should never have invited her. The stupid crone.'

The distress in his face was not entirely compassionate however.

'She cursed us,' Sally said, managing to laugh. 'She came in here like the uninvited fairy at the christening, and she *cursed* us!'

11

For their honeymoon they took Thomas's car – it would always be 'Thomas's car' – and drove east. They spent their wedding night in a profoundly uncomfortable bed and breakfast on the outskirts of Ipswich. This was not in their plan but night was falling and they found they could wait no longer, so they stopped at the first place they saw, only to find a creaking bed, paper-thin walls and a landlord whose expression alone would have pickled onions. Every time they tried to do more than hold hands, the bed's clattering betrayal sent them off into lust-stifling giggles. They finally managed to make love as man and wife, some time after midnight, leaning against a chest of drawers in the one corner of the room with trustworthy floorboards.

'Funny,' Sally said over breakfast, as they devoured the limp bacon and glistening eggs set before them by the landlord – whose face implied he had stayed awake as long as they had – 'funny. We've done this so many times before and yet, simply because of that little ceremony yesterday, we're now above disapproval.' She held out her hand to admire her simple ring. 'He probably thinks this is just another curtain ring, but now, I don't care.'

They drove on to the Suffolk coast and spent two nights in a hotel on the Aldeburgh sea-front. Their room overlooked a stretch of shingle beach where the fishermen hauled their boats clear of the water on old motorised winches. Catches were sold on the spot, out of ramshackle huts black with creosote and patched with roofing felt and squares of tin. Edward left the windows open so they could roll around on their wonderfully silent bed and hear the waves break and drag through the shingle. For hour upon hour they rejoiced in their new, sanctioned rights to one another. They ventured out once or twice, to walk by the sea or visit the hotel restaurant, but they felt vulnerable in their new status, soft and newly hatched, and they soon slipped back to their room out of the public eye.

At night they sat entwined in darkness on the window seat with the quilt around them. His torso hot against her back, his breath on her neck, they watched as the beach was taken over by the scavenging, lovemaking and territorial disputes of countless cats that seemed to melt away with the return of daylight.

They had to return home cruelly soon for Edward to return to the last weeks of his duties in the bookshop and Sally to oversee as much redecoration of The Roundel as her parents were able to pay for. They had been driven out to their daughter's new home just once, when Sally could persuade them into Thomas's car. Her father thought it was a ruin, and her mother declared it creepy but, after a lifetime of paying rent, they were impressed that she had become a property owner through a simple act of generosity. Behind their eagerness to have the place decorated and furnished lay a discreetly conveyed fear that a fairy godmother so plainly capricious in her dealings with the material world might suddenly change her mind.

In fact, the fairy godmother was relieved to have one less thing to tidy up before her departure from society. As The Roundel filled with the eye-watering smells of paint and putty, the date approached for Dr Pertwee's installation on Corry and her rooms became a turmoil of book and paper. Miss Murphy, the bookseller, was summoned to make a bid for a small landscape of volumes, and was deeply impressed that such a distinguished authoress counted her young employee as one of her friends. Just three Sundays after their wedding, Edward and Sally rose at dawn and drove Dr Pertwee to Dorset, along with the small trunk of possessions to which she had miraculously managed to reduce the clutter of a long and fruitful life. Men being forbidden on the island outside

Visitor's Day and the harvest celebration, Edward helped a fisherman load the trunk on to his boat, took the liberty of planting a formal kiss on the old woman's cheek, gave Sally's arm a squeeze, then stood on the quay to wave them off.

The two monastic islands, Corry and Whelm, female and male, loomed up out of a dazzling, millpond sea. Sitting beside Sally in the bows of the little boat, Dr Pertwee patted her hand and sighed with mock homesickness.

'Oh well. If push comes to shove, at least it's not too far for me to swim,' she joked. 'Or I could always steal a boat.'

Corry had a grove of pine trees reaching almost to its sandy shore, which was protected by great boulders, their undersides greeny-purple with weed, their tops mussel-crusted. By the time the boat pulled in, a deputation of women had gathered on the sands to greet them. Sally was astonished to see two of the stronger ones stride, fully dressed, into the water to seize the painter and tug the craft through the surf, their skirts swirling, blackened, about them in the brine. Not all were nuns. At least, not all were dressed in habits. Several contented themselves with stout brogues and serviceable tweeds that would not have raised a second glance at a point-to-point. Dr Pertwee had fallen silent. Sally wondered if she were nervous. A tall, thin nun, benefiting from all the flattering elegance of the wimple, stepped forward.

'Welcome, Alice. Welcome to Corry,' she said and kissed the new arrival's cheek before hugging her warmly. Sally suddenly realised she had never before heard Dr Pertwee addressed by her girlish Christian name.

The others drew, smiling, around, touched Dr Pertwee's back or shoulder, then briefly clasped her hand. There was a sudden, tremendous sense of transition, of, quite literally, passing over to the other side. Introductions were briefly made. The two women with wet skirts took the trunk from the fisherman, who remained respectfully in his boat, and the crowd began to wind up through the wood towards the abbey.

Dr Pertwee broke away from the Mother Superior, to clasp Sally's hand again and murmur wryly, 'My *dear*! With all these pine trees and soft-spoken, shady women, I feel quite as though we'd crossed the Styx!' She dropped her voice to a satirical whisper, 'Though I suspect they keep cats instead of a three-headed dog.'

Sally was not to know that the same thought had occurred to Edward. Waiting on the quay among sunburned holiday-makers who were taking photographs of each other with the crowded harbour as backdrop, he watched his new bride borne inexorably out to sea and felt the sense of her loss as a wrenching in the pit of his stomach. She looked back over her shoulder and smiled at him a few times, then she seemed intent on a conversation with Dr Pertwee and did not turn again. Her face became indistinct as the boat grew ever smaller. When he could stand it no longer, he tore himself away from the sight to explore the sea-front until her return.

He had a cup of strong, milky tea in a drab café, where the air was thick with cigarette smoke and bacon fumes, then walked by gift shops encrusted with vivid clusters of buckets and spades and little patriotic flags for sandcastles. Even outside, the air was unpleasantly sweetened with smells of toffee, candy-floss, frying onions and hot children. He sought refuge in a second-hand bookshop. He was casting a half-hearted professional eye over their stock when he was delighted to find a first edition of *A Husband's Love* by one Alice Pertwee. Smiling, he leaned against the dusty shelves and read the contentious opening page:

> If the husbands of our nation were less inclined to take the pleasures of the marriage bed for granted and their wives were less afraid of a little instruction in the god-given pleasures of the flesh, there would be a substantial drop in the number of sour faces encountered across the nation's breakfast tables and a concomitant fall in incidences of prostitution, adultery, divorce and syphilis.

Then he fainted. For the second time since his introduction to The Roundel, he sensed Miriam's presence. Again he felt her anguish, but this time it was joined with stabs of real, physical pain as though a small, feminine boot were treading on his outstretched neck. He smelled an indescribable human foetor – a stench of unwashed bodies, excrement, putrefaction. Then, unmistakably, he heard his sister's voice turned against him in anger.

'Here! Sir?'

'Are you all right young man?'

'He's coming round.'

'Open that window, Cyril!'

He regained consciousness to a trio of worried faces.

'I'm so sorry,' he said, fighting off a wave of nausea. 'I must have fainted.'

'Shouldn't read such strong stuff at your age,' the proprietor laughed, retrieving Dr Pertwee's book from where Edward had let it fall. 'Are you sure you're all right?'

'Yes. I think I just need air.'

'Well there's no shortage of *that* here,' the second man told him.

'You were shouting the place down,' said the woman. 'Screaming and moaning! We thought someone was being attacked, didn't we, Cyril? Then we found you on the floor here having a turn. You should be more careful.'

His cheeks hot with embarrassment, Edward thanked them all profusely and paid for *A Husband's Love*. He pressed it into Sally's hands when she returned, a little tearful, from Corry. She was overjoyed and began to read it immediately in the car, turning pages, rapt, beginning conversations she allowed to wither as the text stole her attention. He told her nothing of what had happened. He did not see how he could even begin to explain, and feared where his words might lead.

12

Having paid for basic redecoration and repairs, the Bankses' generosity understandably petered out after buying the young couple a bed, sofa, table and chairs. Edward had a few sticks of furniture picked up in junk shops and Rexbridge market over the years, but there was certainly not enough to furnish every room. Much of what they discovered under Dr Pertwee's dustsheets was mouldy beyond redemption. One of the new things they learned on moving in together, however, was their shared loathing of the clutter that had filled the houses of their childhoods. So, to Mrs Banks's horror, they happily *emphasised* the strange house's emptiness. There was one room with nothing in it but a bed, the next just contained a wardrobe, while another had nothing in it at all. Edward claimed he sometimes lay on its floor 'to think'. 'All it needs is a straitjacket,' Mrs Banks quipped.

The only room Edward avoided was the sad little bedroom with the barred window and iron bedstead. He said nothing of this to Sally, but he could not forget the strange sensation that had overcome him the first time he had entered it. The room spoke to him of Miriam. It unsettled him to wake in the night and remember that it waited for him through a low door only feet away from his marriage bed, a small, chill cell of doubt.

When they found that Edward's piano would not fit through any of the internal doors, they emptied the high-domed central hall to leave it there in glorious isolation with only a small sofa and standard lamp for company. The furnishing was completed with mirrors and abundant sunlight.

'I love the light,' Sally exclaimed on one of their first mornings, walking from room to room in her dressing gown. 'I love the way it bounces around here with nothing to get in its way. It gets everywhere!'

After the torture of spending the first weeks of wedlock in the Bankses' cottage – which was almost worse than not being married at all, they were afforded so little privacy – there were pleasures in the simple fact of their sharing an isolated house. There were obvious ones, touched on during their honeymoon, like uninterrupted, unlimited intimacy and being able to walk around stark naked. Then there were other, less obvious pleasures, ones unlooked-for. They found themselves together at times of day – breakfast, teatime, the dead of night – that they had rarely shared. Edward found Sally's culinary skills stretched no further than grilling chops and scrambling eggs but, for a man whose life had always been run by women of the nurturing-nourishing kind, this was oddly reassuring. It confirmed Sally's otherness from his family in his mind. After a few brave disasters in the kitchen, she abandoned the struggle and they started to learn together, working their way, recipe by recipe, through a cookery book given as a wedding present. That this meant starting on soups and progressing through eggs and cheese to poultry via fish was no bad thing since the earlier recipes were also among the cheapest in the book to make.

In their previous brief weekends away, even during their honeymoon, Sally had managed to keep a part of herself undisclosed out of a sweetly old-fashioned desire, Edward assumed, to sustain some romantic illusion of feminine perfection. But now that they shared the same antiquated bathroom day in, day out, the illusion was crumbling. He grew to know her smells – many of which, since they now shared a diet, were amusingly identical to his. He encountered and recorded as precious shards of knowledge, her favourite soap, her shampoo, the space above the bathroom cabinet where she hid a razor. He teased her delightedly when, in a fit of ostensible altruism, she bought him a shaving brush and foaming stick to change his old, monastic habit of using a meagre lather of Lifebuoy. 'It's what Dad uses,' she explained.

On her birthday he went shopping in Rexbridge, sniffing at countless scent bottles until his head was spinning and his nostrils raw. At last he frittered precious savings on a bottle of something floral and French which delighted her. When he related the difficulty of his quest and confessed that she had been bewitching him with mere vanilla essence at a fraction of the price, she seemed utterly charmed. However delicious, the new scent was perplexing on her skin, as if it were not entirely her lying beside him, only a near-perfect, over-ambitious replica.

'You sniff me like a *dog!*' she protested, playfully cuffing the side of his head as he ran his inquisitive nose across the side of her neck. But she divined what was disturbing him and began to wear vanilla again when she was alone with him, happy to save the French concoction for her sorties alone into the world outside, stepping into the alien aroma as into a protective shell.

Sally had tracked down the local GP and found that he had an invalid wife and badly needed someone to take over from him on a regular basis, but had so far been unable to persuade anyone to work somewhere so remote and for so little pay. He was a kind, careworn man, tormented by his fractious spouse, and initially Sally felt he would be taking bread from his own mouth to feed her. She hardened her heart, however, reminding herself that she now had a husband to support, and did not let on that the pay would be riches after her scant salary at the hospital.

In the evenings, they worked in the garden by the last of the sunlight. The fenland sky hung huge around them, with few interruptions – no hills or trees and no tall buildings save the tower of St Oswald's down the road. Town skies were a mere overhead strip compared with this dome which stretched to the far horizon. Even after the sun had set, the sky retained a glow strong enough to light the end of their labours. Neither had gardened before. Edward's childhood home in Tübingen had been inside a great, dark mansion block without so much as a balcony. For flowers and greenery, the family had taken walks in the public parks around the castle and ramparts, where all but the daisies were tidied tantalisingly out of reach. Sally's gardening experience stopped at growing mustard and cress seeds in a hollowed-out potato half. The space behind the Bankses' house had always been consecrated to precious vegetables, coaxed from the soil by Ida Totteridge and thus forbidden territory to her. Edward found a stash of garden tools in the heterogeneous disorder beneath the kitchen staircase. He oiled the secateurs and took them and a saw to be sharpened by the knife grinder in Rexbridge market. Then he and Sally set to work taming the small jungle that surrounded them. Roses that had become whippy trees were reduced to unpromising stumps. The Virginia creeper and jasmine that had engulfed one side of the house were hacked back from windows and carefully teased away from the roof and gutters. The ivy on the other side was killed off altogether, as it seemed to be damaging the masonry. The work was slow. Defeated by hunger and encroaching darkness, they retired each evening, bloody, mud-smeared, their skin burning and itchy with drying plant juices, and when they began again it seemed as though the previous day's work had been undone by foliage creeping in the night.

Gradually old forms re-emerged. A stagnant pond with a broken statue at its centre. Rope-shaped terracotta edging surrounded what was now recognisable as a rose garden. A sundial. There was a rosemary bush tall as Sally's shoulders and a colony of chives that had become a miniature lawn. Two curls of wrought iron were all that remained of a long-rotten garden bench. Edward spent a short-tempered day teasing out the old bolts and fitting the frames with new wood. They placed the bench down by the river and when one of her new mothers gave her a big bag of daffodil bulbs in gratitude for an easy delivery, Sally waded across the water to plant them in the bank on the other side. Edward took an old scythe to the long grass and, watching his rhythmic motion, his trousers streaked with grass juices and his shirt plastered to the sweating skin beneath, Sally ached for love of him and suddenly realised how badly she wanted to bear his child. She laughed at herself and later turned the moment to high comedy in one of her regular bulletins to Dr Pertwee.

'We're quite the new Adam and Eve,' she wrote. 'It's a good

thing I have *A Husband's Love* to keep my feet firmly on the ground amid all this honest toil and newly-turned earth.'

Left alone in the cavernous hall after Sally drove off to work in the mornings, Edward started to make preliminary sketches for an opera. It had begun life as a symphony. Great blocks of sound in his head, which he had to scribble down in a rush before they evaporated. Then he found that strings, wind and brass were not enough. He wanted voices. He wrote pages of wordless singing – a rhapsodic soprano and a chorus – well before he came up with a suitable subject for the opera. He wracked his brains but it seemed that every story – King David, the Fall of Troy, Mary Queen of Scots – had been done before. Finally, he put it to Thomas, who came over for lunch one day when Sally was at the surgery.

'A subject for a libretto. A *new* subject. That's hard.' Thomas pondered. He walked over to the kitchen window, chewing on a lamb chop he had taken between finger and thumb. He turned, leaning against the old belfast sink, and stared at Edward for a moment. His eyes twinkled.

'Job,' he said. 'Do the Book of Job.'

'Vaughan Williams.'

'That's just a ballet.'

'No soprano role,' Edward pointed out.

'He had daughters, a wife – his sons were probably married. Besides, the gender of the comforters isn't specified! Lucifer too, perhaps? The Shining One as coloratura soprano – or perhaps that would be a little much . . .'

All that afternoon, while Sally was visiting children with measles and mothers with morning sickness, Edward sat, hunched over her school Bible at the kitchen table, reading the Book of Job. He scarcely knew Sunday school stories, let alone the more obscure passages. But as he read, he understood Thomas's faintly mischievous smile as he made his suggestion. The tale of the man stripped of happiness, caught in a torrent of distresses, who yet praises God, could not have been more ironically apposite for a post-war German Jew. Sadly it could not have been less operatic either. Something in the tale held him however. Perhaps it was the shock of finding words familiar from *The Messiah* – *'I know that my Redeemer liveth'* – nestling like a jewel at the story's leprous centre.

He would begin his task by expanding the opening sentences, to establish Job's massive wealth, glory and earthly happiness. He decided to focus on the daughters, whom the text specifically named as Jemima, Keziah and Kerenhappuch, while leaving the sons as anonymous as the slaughtered sheep and servants. The opera could open with Job a kind of Lear, lapping up the adoration of the three girls – a convenient soprano-mezzo-contralto trio, with Kerenhappuch inevitably the contralto. It would end with a subtly altered reprise, but now the resurrected three would be giving their praise to their heavenly father, not their earthly one. It would become both cautionary tale and consolation.

Thomas's intention in his suggestion might also have been therapeutic. Reading and re-reading the text over the weeks that followed unlocked memories of Edward's boyhood, happy memories, of his mother, grandmother and sister. Suddenly his dream life grew crowded as a family album.

Aware how harshly secretive he must have appeared in the past, he found himself telling Sally everything there was to know about his childhood. Encouraged by her interest, he allowed himself to feel Jewish for the first time since he left his homeland. He allowed himself to be German. Sally found frames for some battered photographs he had of his parents and Miriam and he arranged them on the piano lid like so many witnesses to his new pleasures. He even taught her some Yiddish words and phrases and laughed at her Saxon difficulty in mastering them. With this final laying of the ghosts that had troubled him, it seemed that the seal was being set on his unalloyed happiness.

13

Edward's first string quartet, *In Memory of Lost Parents*, received its premiere at a concert in the hall at Tompion. An ensemble formed by some near contemporaries of his had wanted something new to sandwich between a Beethoven Rasumovsky and the Schubert *Quartettsatz*. Tipped off by Thomas, they had approached Edward. His piece was not easy to learn, and there were only three weeks in which to practise, but the musicians seemed confident.

It was the sort of concert Edward might well have taken Sally to anyway, but this time she felt as anxious as if she herself were expected to perform. It was an unusually formal affair, since the university chancellor was to be present and the Master of Tompion had invited some of the concert-goers for dinner afterwards.

Sally wore an old hand-me-down of her mother's in midnight blue crushed velvet and black, elbow-length gloves. She had to sit with Edward in the front row, within bowing distance of the chancellor. She was introduced to his wife by Thomas during the interval but her mind was entirely on Edward, who was so nervous he had wandered off to stare balefully at the portraits around the panelled walls. Thomas tapped her elbow and pointed out two former college men who had come down to review the concert for *The Times* and some highbrow arts quarterly.

Edward had never played her any of his music properly. Once or twice, when she had begged him, he had started, but each time, abashed, he played the buffoon, breaking off, after a few impenetrable wanderings on the keyboard, into a jokey rendition of a Glenn Miller dance number or some corny Ivor Novello hit. Once he had mocked her ignorance, slyly launching into a delicious piece and only telling her after she had exclaimed at its loveliness and his genius, that it was by Mozart. She had eavesdropped, of course, sitting in a room off the gallery, and keeping very still for as long as she could bear. On his own, however, he never seemed to play anything through, contenting himself with snatches and chords in between scribbling, making noises more like the piano tuner who called in once a month and drove her half-mad with his nagging repetitions.

They resumed their seats and the quartet returned to the platform. As the applause died down – even she could tell that the Beethoven had been excellently played – she reached over to touch Edward's hand. He smiled at her but returned her hand to her lap as though she were an overly demonstrative child. Someone coughed. The four bows were raised in expectation and, with them, the four players' eyebrows.

With the first chords she honestly thought there had been some mistake. Someone was playing the wrong piece, perhaps, or had their music upside down. But the strident cacophony continued its angry way and was met with the same complacent welcome as had greeted the Beethoven, only now it was punctuated by the occasional gathered brow or fine-minded wrinkling around the eyes at a particularly startling harmony. Sally realised, with a sickening finality, that she hated her husband's music. Perhaps hate was too emotive a word for something she felt she altogether failed to understand. The sounds he had written had no discernible melody, no comforting sonority. He had composed in an entirely alien language and she felt a mounting panic that he would expect her to understand it simply by virtue of their being in love.

With each successive movement, her hopes were raised then dashed on hearing more of the same. When he glanced at her, she smiled reassuringly back, but she felt that a crude wedge had been driven between them. The last movement came as a relief. She seized on its demonic gaiety and whistlable tune as something she could enthuse about later, but as the room filled with polite applause and the musicians took their bows, faces shining from effort, she knew she would always have to lie to him.

Bird-watching she could have handled, or a sudden bizarre demand in bed, a consuming interest in cacti or Victorian industrial architecture, but this music that was so central to his very being she knew she could never appreciate, never honestly admit to liking. When the concert was over, she clasped his arm as he received congratulations and she smiled proudly, in spite of the splinter of iron in her soul.

14

After an exceptionally mild December, the first frosts had come, filling the garden with browned and twisted foliage. Under torrential rain, part of the dome had begun to leak again. Until they could persuade the glazier back to remedy his shoddy repair work, a tin bucket noisily caught the drips in the hall. Eyes smoked pink by a comfortless fire of damp wood, they had retired early in an effort to stay warm.

Mrs Banks had been admitted to hospital for a series of cancer tests. The young-old woman had a horror of illness and was the sort to keep quiet about a pain for weeks rather than face the grim prospect that her body might be about to turn against her. When the telephone suddenly rang out in the darkness, Sally started as though a gun had gone off and rushed from the bedroom to reach it, tugging her dressing gown about her as she went, convinced it was bad news about her mother.

Edward's work on *Job* was progressing well by now. Just before the ringing shattered their peace, she had been asking him about it and he had felt her recoil from his unglamorous choice of story. He had also felt her discreet dismay at the prospect of him undertaking such a large-scale work with no commission, not even advance promise of a performance.

'Shouldn't you stick to smaller, cheaper things to start with?' she had asked, but she had gone to the telephone before he could answer, leaving him turning this unattractive piece of common sense indignantly over in his mind.

She must see that he could only write what he was moved to write? He would not, could not tailor his art to fit a household economy. He heard Sally talking in the hall, heard her steps on the uncarpeted stairs. As she circled the landing back to the bedroom, he was thinking scornfully to himself that if Brahms were still alive he would doubtless be working for the BBC composing incidental music for radio plays.

Sally pushed open the door and stood, a well-wrapped silhouette, against the light from the landing. He couldn't make out her face. Her voice was hesitant, perplexed.

'Edward? It's a call from London. I didn't quite understand, he had such an accent. Someone called Ivan? Ivan Airingson?'

'Aaronson,' Edward corrected her, jumping out of bed and pulling a jersey over his pyjamas for warmth. 'A friend of Rosa and Isaac's. You remember Rosa, surely? At the wedding?'

'How could I forget?'

'I'll go and speak to him.'

'Edward,' she stopped him, a warning hand on his arm. 'Darling. He thinks they've found a woman who might be your sister. Edward?'

He hurried past her, ignoring her protest. The hall floor was freezing beneath his bare feet. He took refuge on the rug by the piano.

'Ja, Ivan? Wie geht's?'

He noticed the bucket was full of rain water and needed emptying. By the time the conversation was over, Sally had come downstairs and was hunched up, worried, on the sofa, her knees tucked up before her. The water had started to trickle down the bucket's edge. When he hung up, she simply held out her hands to him. He took them and she pulled him into a tight embrace. He heard himself sobbing as she ran feverish fingers across his back and up through his hair as though searching for the source of his hurt.

'You must go,' she said at last. 'Where is she?'

'Paris. In the suburbs,' he said, thinking how innocuous that sounded. 'I don't think I could face it.' A tear ran down over his upper lip with a little shock of salt.

'You must. She's your *sister*, Edward. Don't be childish. You *must* go!'

'We can't possibly afford it.'

'No. But Thomas can,' she said simply. 'He'd pay your fare. You know he would.'

It was impossible to sleep. He lay for hours with Sally curled in seemingly heartless slumber beside him. Repeatedly he started when it seemed to him that the low door to the barred room beside theirs had suddenly swung open in the blackness, releasing unimaginable horrors.

Far from being happily laid to rest by Sally's redeeming love and the honouring of new family ties, the unquiet dead were thrusting back their tomb-lids. The nightmare had begun, or rather, the unquiet dream that had started years before was now becoming a reality, rattling forth from his subconscious to cavort in baldest sunlight. Shut his eyes, clamp tight his mouth, halt his own progress as he might, the evil continued unstoppably around him. And so, the following day, he found himself back in the quiet, glistening *chic* of Thomas's study, pushing aside friendly enquiries about the opera's progress with a blunt request for money.

15

He had been in England for over a decade without leaving. He had grown used to her great tracts of uncultivated countryside which reeked of immobile privilege, her bland unvarying food and the pervasive insincerity of good manners. It was only as the ferry juddered out through the drizzle on to a brown, untrustworthy sea that he appreciated how efficient a shelter England had been for him. However much her natives strove against it – with their incomprehensible traditions, private languages and cheerfully confessed mistrust of all that was foreign – he had become a party to the island's mentality.

The Continent, of which his English hosts spoke as a place of inefficiency, bad smells, worse water and insidious, dangerous seductiveness, embraced him like a neglected but forgiving friend. He had forgotten the frank odours, good and bad, of crude cigarettes and bodies, the nakedly assessing stares, the sudden shifts from shrugging unconcern to *bonhomie*. Waiting to board the train to Paris, he made an instinctive, fetishistic collection of the most Continental things he could find: a packet of Gauloises, a paper-wrapped sandwich of crisp French bread and garlic sausage, a buttery pastry oozing crème patissière and a magazine dripping scandal.

The cigarettes were a mistake, of course. His lungs were in a better state when he had last smoked and one drag left him wet-eyed and helplessly coughing. The other self-indulgences were all too soon exhausted and he had a long journey on the stopping train from Calais to Paris, then across the city and out into the grimy suburb to a hospital which held a woman who might be his sister. A long journey in which to think and to worry.

He had known there was a network of more or less unofficial Jewish agencies operating across Europe. Ironically, the effects of Nazi propaganda had made a reality of malicious lies, although the Jewish purpose was not world domination but the innocent desire to keep in touch. Built from the remains of large, now splintered families and numerous Resistance cells, and wringing what grudging co-operation they could from post-war governments keen to sweep the recent horrors aside, these agencies went about the Sisyphean task of tracing survivors and putting them in touch with lost family. Ivan Aaronson did a certain amount of research for them at the British and German ends – under the cover of his import/export business. It was Ivan who had come to Edward's internment camp to confirm that Edward's parents had been traced to their end. Ivan himself was free to come and go, having taken out British citizenship, like Isaac, some time before in the early thirties.

'But we can't find Miriam,' he had confessed, wizened brow wrinkling further with distress at his own helplessness. 'They don't keep all families together, you see. She may have been separated for another purpose.'

'She may have got married,' Edward suggested, clutching at straws. 'She was seeing a . . . a *goy* when she last wrote to me. Lorenz's family were rich, well connected – he may have helped her.'

'Maybe,' Ivan said. 'Maybe.'

But no record of a marriage was traced. Or of a death. And with the war and its bombings many such records had gone up in smoke, reducing personal histories to chaos.

Someone who might be Miriam had at last been found in a psychiatric hospital. By a long, drawn-out process as complicated as the demonic bureaucracy which had engulfed her to start with, a tattoo on her arm had been traced to those given at one of the camps. Records still existed to show who had died there and who had lived to tell the tale. Some of the survivors had obsessively retentive memories for names and family details of fellow inmates; details they intoned, rehearsed, perfected as a puny defence against the systematic destruction of all else that made them human. Those who, like the woman who might be Miriam, were too ill to speak, had to be presented to a succession of hopeful, dreading families. Edward's family was one of the last possibilities in her case. With both parents dead, the search for her family had not been widespread, until someone, a former colleague of his mother's from Tübingen now working in Versailles, remembered the boy sent away to England and Ivan was contacted.

'We are not certain she is your Miriam,' Ivan told him on the telephone, 'She . . . Apparently she is not responsive.'

Time and again since then, Edward's mind had examined the phrase, wondering just what degree of horror the cool words 'not responsive' might veil.

The slow train shuddered into another drab suburban station with another pompous name honouring another long-forgotten battlefield. Crossing the short platform, Edward turned up his collar against the drizzle. He was the only passenger to get off. Pale faces stared out at him with bored impudence as the carriages were dragged out again. He summoned his schoolboy French to ask for directions from a station official, but had to ask a passing man a few streets later because his unpractised ear had only retained a third of what it heard.

The hospital was not unlike a French school, with a small courtyard dotted with some sad trees and a bench or two. There were a few cars parked there. One could tell at a second glance that this was a human scrapheap, not an institution where lives were fought for and heroic recoveries made. This was a place where lost causes were fed, clothed, maintained to no purpose but the satisfying of medical and ethical honour. Sure enough, a small brass plaque by the entrance confessed with Gallic candour that this was *La Retraite St Martin de Tours, Hôpital des Incurables*.

The place was strangely quiet. As a blue-robed nurse-nun hybrid led him up several flights of stairs and along a long corridor, Edward entertained the fantasy that his sister might be the sole patient; helpless queen bee of a near-deserted hive. He had braced himself for moans, wracked coughing, the clatter of hysterically rejected bed pans, but found instead a silence broken only by the occasional mournful sneeze or murmur. He might have been in a scrupulously hygienic library. By way of a meagre concession to the season, a few Christmas decorations had been set up. A scrawny tree was hung with a few faded Christmas cards. Some irregularly cut paper stars had been pinned to patient's doors in unconscious parody of backstage tradition.

'*Regardez, Madame. Il y'a quelqu'un,*' said the nurse, breezing into a small room and tidying the bed with a few practised twitches of her small hands. '*Votre frère, je crois.*'

She left them alone. There were bars on the window. Edward instinctively walked over to touch their cold metal before turning to look back at the bed. His first reaction was of tremendous relief mixed with irritation. He had come all this way, suffered all this anxiety, for nothing!

Miriam was slender and had long, brown hair, glossy and ringleted. The woman in the bed had a clumsy crop, and her hair was shot through with grey. She was also immensely fat, her eyes reduced to two black dimples in a complexion of slack, off-white dough, her mouth a girlish rosebud on an old face.

'Er. *Pardonnez-moi, Madame,*' he muttered. '*Je ne veux pas vous déranger. On avait tort.*'

He threw her a desperate smile and turned to go, but his hand had scarcely touched the door handle than he became aware of a hoarse, effortful sound coming from the bed. He turned to find the gross, immobile face contorted by an attempt to speak. As her mouth worked and brows furrowed, the little, sunken eyes turned on his, beseeching as a dog's. She lifted a great, pale arm, like something from a butcher's window, to reach out, then let it fall on the blankets as if the inappropriately delicate hand at its end were too heavy to raise. He glimpsed the tattooed digits on her tender underarm skin. They had blurred slightly like writing splashed with tears. She might only have been asking for a bedpan but he turned back swiftly and took the seemingly proffered hand in his.

'*Ehh,*' she kept wheezing. '*Ehh –. Ehh –.*'

Then he saw it. For a moment, when she frowned with concentration, there was a flash of Miriam's pretty crossness, a small petulance no sooner recognised than smothered in fat.

'Miriam?' he asked. '*Meine Liebe*?'

'Ehh –. Ehh –.'

'Eli,' he prompted her and a nervous laugh burst from him. 'Eli. I must have changed a lot. I can hardly speak German any more, I'm so out of practice.'

Now she sank back on her pillows with a relieved sigh, as though beaten to the solution of a brainteaser, and released the only words he would hear her say. It was a shock hearing his childhood name given its German pronunciation again.

'*Eli*,' she said then, with an unmistakably sarcastic turn to her lips, she added, '*Bruderlein*.'

She gave a slight return of pressure on his hand and answered his stare for a moment with – perhaps he was being fanciful? – something like affection. Then it was as though the familiar face had slipped away from his reach, back beneath the surface of an impenetrably gloomy pool. Once again he was in a room with an unrecognisable, somnolent, grossly fat stranger. The difference was that now he knew his sister was trapped inside her somewhere. No. Not trapped. Hiding.

He kissed the pale hand, noticing for the first time that the top joint of her ring finger had been cut off. Her rings had gone. She used to wear two. He tried to hide his disgust. He looked back at her face. It was hard now to believe she had spoken at all. Had he imagined it, unable to face the alternative?

'What did they *do*?' The doctor, a faded young man, who hid his bad teeth with an unsmiling manner, scornfully ground out his cigarette in a full ashtray. Smoke wreathed about the bronze Christ that hung, lifeless, on a crucifix on his cluttered desk. 'Believe me, you wouldn't want to know, Monsieur.'

'But I just asked you. *Je vous en prie*.'

'In her case we can only guess at the half of it. She spoke so little in the early days, and then only in German. I have never heard her speak. If you look beneath her hairline you'll find evidence of . . . of surgery.'

The steely word sounded doubly cold in French. Edward

stared. Discomfited, the doctor picked at a dog-eared file before looking up again.

'I'm quite sure she was a healthy woman. Had she been sick in any way, she would have been killed. All the sick ones were. In that camp they were conducting experiments and for the, er, results to be accurate they would have needed healthy specimens to start with. As a scientific control, you understand.'

'But how did she end up here? Can she walk?'

'With assistance. But her muscles have wasted badly since her arrival. I think she was found on a train.' He glanced through the file for confirmation.

'A train?' Edward stammered.

'Yes. In the Gare du Nord,' the doctor confirmed. 'Without a ticket. She was asleep in the goods van. She had clearly been living rough for some time. Her only identification was the tattoo and that's by no means infallible since it is blurred.'

'I saw. On her left arm.'

'She may have tried to burn it off. Not all were tattooed. The system broke down towards the end, when they started to speed things up. She must have been in the earlier intake. The nuns took her in here. Her details were passed on to the authorities and I suppose the rest was done by your Jewish friends. She's been here for a year now. No. It's longer than that. Nearly two.'

Edward thought of the hours, weeks, spent in that small room, pictured her again as the heavily sleeping, still centre of the hospital's daily fussing.

'Has she . . . Has she changed much since she's been here?'

'I've only been here for a year, so I can't say precisely. She will walk, after a fashion, if led and supported, but with so many cases like hers, you know . . .'

The doctor's voice petered out and he shrugged. He held out a packet of cigarettes to Edward, who declined. Taking one himself, the doctor tapped it on the desk before setting it to his lips. The gesture, one could see, was habitual, like the way he shook the matchbox before opening it. Edward observed the small ritual, the shabby office, the man's unwashed shirt collar and imagined the ignominious exam results, the cheese-paring, the disappointment turned crusty with use. He understood that the man was less a doctor than a kind of under-gardener, whose undemanding, tedious task was the tending of so many unregarded, vegetable lives.

'So she's no worse,' Edward said.

'And no better. She eats. She shits. She sleeps. Did she respond to you? Say anything? Try to move?'

Edward saw now what he had to do.

'No,' he lied. 'I held her hand. Talked to her. Said her name. Nothing. But it's definitely her. Her name is Miriam Pfefferberg. At least, that's her maiden name.' The doctor frowned and Edward realised his rusty French was at fault. 'I mean,' he explained, 'her name when she was a girl. It's been eleven years. For all I know she was married in between.' Exhaling smoke with a sigh, the doctor made a scribbled note in the file before him. Edward stood.

'Thank you for all you've done,' he said. The doctor shrugged again. He didn't stand. 'I've got some business in town now,' Edward told him. 'I'll be back tomorrow. To see her.'

The doctor did not see him out. The institution seemed to function on a skeleton staff. There were no nuns in sight, but Edward waited in the corridor, on the pretext of running himself a glass of water at a sink, until he was quite sure that he was unobserved. Then he slipped back to Miriam's room and closed the door behind him.

In his brief absence, his lie to the doctor had been made fact. The fat woman in the bed did not register his sudden reappearance. As he approached her narrow mattress, she continued to stare at the ceiling from her off-white pillows, with no hint of intelligence behind her stare. She continued to breathe slowly and evenly through her open mouth, giving no more sense of an urgent will to live than did the sleek inertia of a closed sea anemone or the remorseless, slow rippling of an upturned slug.

Edward stood over her, daring her lifeless eyes to brighten again, turn on his, daring her to laugh from the tension of sustaining such a convincing charade. He thought of Sally and their new home. Could he take Miriam – this creature that had once been Miriam – back to The Roundel? Install her in a bedroom? She would have to have the little one with the bars on the window, of course. Could he devote himself to her unrewarding care?

He touched the slack skin of her cheek, half expecting his fingers to leave an imprint, the texture was so waxy. How could she stare for so long and not blink? He imagined her left untended, her eyeballs, cheeks, hair, slowly coated in the silent dust of neglect. Someone cut her nails regularly at least, or they would be clattering claws by now. He took her left hand and turned it to read the blurred figures with which the skin on her arm was punctured. She might have been living like a vagabond when the nuns took her in but, after years of inactivity and regular washing, her palms were soft and uncalloused as a duchess's. The hair was a shock. Miriam had always worn it pulled back into a long plait or coiled on her head. Not content with cropping it, the nuns had brushed it into a kind of *Struwwelpeter* mop about her scalp making a fat face fatter. But so many years had passed since he had last seen her that it was possible she had changed her style herself. They had let her eyebrows grow as bushy as Rosa Holzer's, so that they threatened to meet in the middle, and no-one had bothered to pluck the hairs from the little discoloration above her lip. In effect, the nuns had let her grow more like a nun.

As he began to slide the pillow out from under her head, he promised himself he would stop at the least sign of struggle. He held her head for a moment to prevent it falling back with a jolt, and found her hair dry and brittle beneath his grasp. Then, standing so that he was invisible from the little window in the door, he lowered the pillow over her unseeing eyes. He held it fast for what seemed like five minutes, emptying his mind, by a huge effort of will, of everything but the need to listen for footsteps outside. She did not flinch. She made no sound. Influenced by images of Othello and the Princes in the Tower, Edward had always imagined smothering as a violent, operatic act, requiring strength and a fearful resolution. In the event, her body was so still that the action felt peculiarly redundant, as though she had been dead long before he began.

Sure he had held it there long enough, he began to lift the pillow off her, then was startled at a sudden movement in one of her hands. He gasped, but before he could uncover her face again, her hand had swept up and tugged the pillow down against it, urging him to continue. Her fingers spread out like a murderous spider, squeezing the down and linen so hard that a crude outline of her profile became visible. With a groan that must certainly have been audible outside, he lunged back onto the pillow with all his body's weight, one hand on either side of her face. Tears coursed down his cheeks, dripping onto the bed and running ticklishly beneath his shirt collar. Or were they drops of sweat? He looked up at the wall as he continued to press downwards, and saw the crucifix over the headboard. From nowhere a childish tune came into his head, a Schubert tune, from a sugared childhood:

> Sah ein Knàb ein Roslein stehn, Roslein auf der Heiden,
> War so jung und morgen shon,
> Lief er schnell, es nah zu sehn . . .

It circled so persistently and with such clarity that afterwards he would never be able to decide if he had been singing it aloud or merely mouthing the maddening thing in his mind. All he knew was that when he reached the end, he could safely take the pillow from her face.

> Roslein Roslein Roslein rot.

The melody was childishly sure of itself, the words, despite dark hints at a violation, unruffled as a Sunday picnic in June.

> Roslein auf der Heiden.

It was done. He looked down and saw that her hand had fallen away to her side. The deed was his alone now. As he began to lift the pillow to put it back behind her head, there were sudden footsteps in the corridor and the rattle of a trolley. Thoughtlessly, Edward dived under the bed, knocking his brow painfully on the metal bedframe. He crouched as close to the wall as he could. He found he was still clutching the pillow but it was too late to return it to the bed. Instead, he tossed it quickly from him to make it look as though it had merely tumbled from the mattress.

The door handle rattled, the door opened and two stout ankles appeared, couched in unexpectedly florid shoes. An orderly, therefore, not a nun.

'Chérie? Tu veux de la soupe, chérie?'

Two more feet came in. Men's feet.

'Elle dort,' said the man roughly. *'On la laisse. En tout cas, la grosse n'en a besoin. Viens, alors. Moi, j'ai faim.'*

Edward winced at the realisation that one of them might stoop to pick up the pillow and find him cowering there like a wicked child. But they turned and left the room, the woman already continuing some story about *Jacquot et sa sale connasse de mère*. He waited, acutely aware of his own painfully accelerated breathing, then crawled out and stood. He dared to turn back to the bed. It was true. She might have been asleep. In her very fatness she seemed healthy and comfortable, haunted as he still was by newsreel footage of those the Nazis had reduced to starveling revenants.

Leaving the hospital without being seen was surprisingly simple. He waited until the corridor was clear, made for the staircase and left the building. Except for the occasional shout or laugh from a patient, the place could have been deserted, the orderlies all at lunch, the nuns all at prayer. No bells rang. No-one ran after him.

He boarded the train unhindered. On the way back into the city, passengers met his eye and he gazed straight back at them. He felt no guilt, so firmly was he convinced that what he had done was right. The woman in the bed, the stranger, presented such a pathetic change from the Miriam he loved, that it might, ironically, have felt like murder, motiveless murder. But it did not. In place of guilt, he felt sorrow, a distant rumble of it like far-off thunder. He had done his mourning for her long ago, in the unbearable ache of her unexplained absence, as the welter of unspeakable possibilities became crudely probable with the progression of the war. Now his feelings were out of synchrony with events.

Finding her carcase in the hospital bed, he had felt a staggering wave of recognition, not of her face but of her fate; the crazy-paving logic of the war-tossed.

'Of course! *This* is what they would have done to her. *This* is where she would have ended up.'

Why Paris? Had she *known* where she was going or merely boarded train after train, rattling around Europe like some large forgotten parcel, living off God knows what, until someone thought to apprehend her? Or had she, perhaps, felt some dim, glamorous prompting in what remained of her brain? She had been touched, perhaps, by a dusty memory of obedient childhood hours spent walking the Louvre, disobediently returning the bold, enquiring stares of Frenchmen behind her mother's back, itching to slip away from the dead weight of archaeology to go window-shopping for elegant fripperies in the Faubourg St Honoré?

Edward sought to fill the remainder of the day with harmless tourism. He found a cheap hotel overlooking the Donjon and took a long, scalding bath. In a café nearby, he ate a late lunch afloat on three tall glasses of strong beer. Fortified, he went shopping for Sally. She cherished notions about the unequalled luxury of French underwear – notions doubtless caught from her mother and too many romantic films. Driven away from specialist lingerie shops by their oppressive femininity and requirement of a more sophisticated French vocabulary, he braved the bewildering variety on display in a department store. A motherly creature with a silver crucifix hung against her black blouse helped him choose a selection of slippery articles in ivory and black. She summoned a second, younger assistant, whom he confirmed was roughly Sally's size, and held the things against her for him to admire.

Clutching his purchases, he drifted into a dark church to draw breath but found it noisy with the work of stonemasons repairing the chancel. Back on the streets he spent an hour trying to find a synagogue, but the few people he asked shrugged, ignored his limping French altogether or gave him a hostile stare.

On an impulse he bought himself a cheap ticket to a performance that evening of *Phèdre*. He went in tribute to Miriam, who had loved Racine. The scenery was shoddy, the costumes unconvincing and the wigs had seen better days. It was a shock to discover that he had grown so used to the relaxed, English style of performance that the high French manner now seemed absurdly stiff and unnatural. Somewhere, unnoticed, however, the spell of the old words worked. The solemnity of the language in the face of turbulent emotions and barely speakable revelations created a small, still space he found soothing. The grandeur and decorum were a firm shoulder on which he could lean and feel safe.

The following morning, he was meticulous as any cold-blooded murderer in his return to the hospital. He laid no suspicious trail by checking out of his hotel, but left his bag unpacked and paid for another night he had no intention of spending there. He bought flowers. Wasteful flowers for the corpse. He ate a pastry on the train – a coffee *religieuse*. Arriving at the hospital he made straight for Miriam's room but was headed off by a nun who led him gently to the same, chain-smoking doctor.

'For once one can honestly say she died in her sleep, Monsieur.'

'How?'

Edward found himself nonsensically suspicious, as though she had been killed twice over. The doctor sighed.

'Heart attack, we assume.'

'Did she have a weak heart? You said she was in perfect health.'

'Not to our knowledge but – after what she must have been through . . . Of course, if Monsieur wanted an autopsy . . .' He caught Edward's eye and raised an eyebrow.

'No. No. Of course not.'

Edward deflected the look with a careworn gesture, running a hand through his hair. There was a disturbing air of complicity in the doctor's expression. For a few mad moments, Edward entertained the fantasy that the staff were well aware that he had – how did one best put it? – helped his sister on her way, but that this was a common occurrence in the establishment, scarcely noteworthy. Then he looked up at the doctor again and saw that, no, of course, his face, his sighs, even his manner of offering Edward the tenuous companionship of a cigarette, were merely the furthest he dared go to suggesting that they both knew she could only be happier in her decease.

Edward signed forms. Of course, he had to deal with her body now – it had not occurred to him before. He bought a bouquet of white lilies for the nursing staff on Miriam's ward and a crazily expensive bottle of whisky for the doctor. He arranged for his sister to be cremated as swiftly as possible. He would take her ashes home with him, completing her life's restless trajectory by making her last resting place a country she had never known, whose language she had never mastered. He sent a telegram to Sally, saying why he would be delayed, trying to convey, as best he could in terse telegrammese, that this did not constitute a crisis.

He used the hotel room for another night after all. He took to his bed with a bottle of cheap wine and lay for hours in the darkness, waiting for the storm to break over his head and coming to understand, with the ponderous clarity of the wilfully drunk, that it had passed him by.

When he was a small boy, Miriam had tried to help him overcome his horror of storms by counting the seconds that elapsed between lightning flash and thunderclap.

'Every second is a kilometre,' she explained, crouching on his bed. 'Three. Four. Five. Six. You see? It's already further away. We're quite safe.'

But usually it seemed to Edward that the longer wait only made the ensuing blast sound louder. And he could never quite believe that the last was indeed the last. During the war, hiding in air raid shelters from his countrymen's bombs, he had sometimes longed for the spectacular, swift death of a direct hit. Anything to free him from the horrific game of trying to guess whether the hellish onslaught were moving slowly away or bearing inexorably closer.

16

Sally had always thought that writers exaggerated but while Edward was away, she truly did ache for him. No other verb would do. Waking in the night to an empty bed or seeing his piano with the lid down and the keyboard hidden, she felt his absence as a sporadic dull pain in her groin and her lower back that only his touch would cure. Without him The Roundel seemed too large and empty.

Twelfth Night had arrived, so she dragged the Christmas tree out into the garden wearing her oven gloves, heaped it with the strands of holly from around the house and set fire to the brittle leaves. As the swift flames roared and died, leaving her cheeks hot, the evening shadows seemed thicker, threatening winter more than ever about her. The ritual had failed, leaving her comfortless.

She hurried back into the house and busied herself sweeping up pine needles. She wrote a letter to Dr Pertwee. She washed her hair and made an omelette. She heard inexplicable noises, left lights and radio on for comfort and had trouble sleeping. Had she still been working at a hospital, she would have volunteered for night shifts to fill the void with work but Richards, the doctor she now worked for, still retained the principal loyalty of his country patients and if they had emergencies in the night they sent for him.

Her mother's tests had proved positive and she was being kept in hospital for a hysterectomy. Sally rode the motorbike over to Rexbridge every day to visit her, once taking her father in the sidecar. Her mother took badly to illness and surgery horrified her, but she masked her fear with social brio, sporting a succession of bed-jackets and scarves and repairing her make-up at frequent intervals. From among the other patients, she had gathered slavish admirers around her bed. These were mainly sad, impressionable women but a few men pulled on their dressing gowns and found their way to her from other wards, following some sexual magnetic north to bask in her harsh treatment of them. Her admirers left her tributes – fruit, chocolates, magazines – much of which she used as barter to win over newcomers. She pointedly sent Sally away with a pile of *Good Housekeeping*.

Unable to sleep, Sally sat up in bed with the magazines, driving away night thoughts with brightly coloured blasts of housewifery and sentiment. The stories – of naughty boys, errant husbands, untrustworthy ex-schoolfriends and culinary disasters made good – were mawkish and unconvincing. The large-print caption beside each introductory picture often made it needless to read on.

'She asked him to marry her,' she read. *'The man who had loved her forever. He asked no questions. Not then. Not later . . .'*

After glancing longingly through the fashion pages and demoralising herself with cookery articles, Sally concentrated on the advertisements. These provided an editorial of their own, at once chastening, flattering and envy-fostering. Faces beamed out at her, eyes twinkled knowingly, rhymes jingled their carefully plotted way into her memory – *Fortune Chocolates make the heart grow fonder. Sentinel Hygienic Towels. So soft, so safe, so secure. The cup that satisfies. Medilax laxative pellets encourage smiling cheerfulness by keeping the person free from the depressing poisons of constipation. It's a dream! It's a Harella! Faces turned towards her with wonder and admiration and the faintest hint of envy as she sailed in dazzling them all with the pride and confidence of her beauty. Protect your child from Deadly Diphtheria.*

When she finally slept, her head swam with a fever of brand names. Slimma Slacks. Stillmore Suet Pudding. Lux. Plasticene. Rinso. Lavvo. Propax. Carlox Tooth Powder. Vinola Baby Soap and Nell Gwynne Marmalade. She had terrible, insecure dreams in which women in indiscreet furs showed her *How to Distemper a Small Room* and an insufferably perky couple called the Young-Marrieds urged her to give her husband plenty of Vitamins A and D. The next morning she threw the magazines in the dustbin as if they were a source of virulent infection.

She realised she was pregnant on the same day Edward's telegram arrived from Paris. Knowing nothing of her sister-in-law, she could scarcely be expected to grieve for her, but her emotions see-sawed as her delight at what was happening inside her weighed against her compassion for Edward.

She had half-decided not to tell him, until she was doubly certain, not to excite him needlessly in what she assumed to be his present state. But as she rode her bike about the area, receiving the occasional wave from a patient, as she shopped in the market, meeting the flirtatious banter of stallholders with a deflecting smile, her happiness worked up to a pitch where she felt people could tell its source just by looking. Her first bout of morning sickness dampened her ardour somewhat, as did the cold realisation that when she was forced to give up work they would have financial worries, unless Edward managed to sell something or drum up a commission. At their wedding reception, Thomas's 'sympathetic' chaplain had murmured something about commissioning an anthem or some canticles. She resolved to be more of a Lady Macbeth, and lean on her diffident husband to follow through on opportunities.

Edward came home two nights later. A battering wind had blown up during the afternoon. It rattled window panes and filled The Roundel with thin, whispering sighs. He had rung from Dover, so she was ready for him. Towelling herself after a bath, she could hear the car's engine a mile away, even through the noise of the wind. From an upstairs window she saw the small cones of light from the headlamps swing this way and that as he crossed the bridge over the dyke and turned on to the perfectly straight road that stretched along a precipitous poplar-fringed bank next to the water.

He slammed the door against the wind, dropped his suitcase and turned to her. His cheeks were cold to her kiss. He half pushed, half carried her to the hall sofa where she tumbled, pulling him with her. Under his questing hands, her dressing gown soon fell open so that her naked flesh, still warm and slightly damp from the hot water, was chafed by the thick, hard textures of male clothes – tweed, drill, the buckle of his belt, the bruising toecaps of his shoes – all still chilly from the night air.

'I'm sorry, darling,' she tried to say. 'Poor Miriam. I'm so very sorry.'

But his lips chewed away her words. The hot insistence of his tongue overturned her train of thought. His unshaven jawline felt like sandpaper and as he rubbed it with heedless cruelty against her, an image from one of her mother's magazines popped up unbidden in her mind of a tearful girl with vividly scarlet cheeks, clutching a bar of Knight's Castille and sobbing, 'Now I can kiss goodbye to Stubble Trouble!'

Sally flinched, relaxed then stiffened again as, silencing her with a deeply penetrating kiss, he thrust enquiring fingers between her unprotected thighs. She had expected tears not passion and her head swarmed with words she wanted to voice, thoughts that impeded pleasure. For the first time, she found their desire out of joint. For the first time she found his need far fiercer than hers. For the first time she submitted her body rather than giving it. As he hammered painfully into her, his eyes were closed, viewing some dark, interior world, and when he came, it was not with his usual surprised shout of triumph. His entire body jerking spasmodically, he bit his lip then gave a series of rasping gasps as though the release were no delirious outburst, but something torn painfully from his guts.

Pressed between his clothes and the thick, discarded mat of the dressing gown, her limbs shone with sweat. As he rolled to lie beside her, to relieve her of his weight, she shivered at the chill of sudden exposure and picked at the towelling to pull the gown around her again. He spoke at last. His first words since his return.

'I could hardly tell it was her. Just her eyes, maybe, or the bushiness of her hair. We always had the same thick hair –' He broke off. Bit his lip again. He was staring up at the dome.

'What?' she prompted. 'Tell me.'

He turned to look at her.

'Do you mind if I don't? Not yet, at least?'

She smiled weakly.

'Don't be daft. Of course I don't.'

And he never did tell her.

Unwrapping the exquisite but slightly tight underwear he had brought her, Sally noticed another, smaller parcel in his suitcase. It was carefully done up, like a selection of pastries, and her heart jumped for a moment in infantile anticipation of a further treat. Then she realised from the startled way he pulled a shirt out to hide it, that the folded paper contained her sister-in-law's incinerated remains.

In the weeks, then months that followed, the subject of Miriam slipped back into the mire of his secrecy as completely as if she had never been mentioned. He had no photographs, no mementoes. All that Sally knew was her name and the colour of her hair and eyes. Trying to imagine the woman, she could only picture a feminised Edward in a quiet, floral frock; a disquieting image she hastily dropped.

17

From the night of his return, Edward felt sickeningly disoriented. It seemed impossible that so little had changed in his brief absence. He was now irrevocably different from the young man who had nervously taken Ivan's telephone call. His unavowable secret had changed the expression on the face that met his gaze in the looking-glass as profoundly as any livid scar.

Acts of violence produced a reaction – a gun's report, the smack of colliding skin and bone, blood, bruises, cries of pain or horrified gasps – but his, seemingly, had produced nothing. The body – he could not think of it as his sister – had been destroyed; no questions asked, no accusations levelled. A tasteful helping of its cinders had accompanied him, passportless, home.

Had he found The Roundel now as weirdly warped as the sets from *The Cabinet of Dr Caligari* it would have been more comforting than the sweet normality which greeted him. Only the harsh onset of January and the charred remains of the Christmas decorations accorded with his mood. The house was as still, the landscape as desolate, his wife as lovely as when he had left them.

His work-in-progress lay untouched on the piano top, challenging him to continue it seamlessly. But he felt compelled to break away from the passage he had been writing, developing instead the theme for Lucifer. Aged years in a matter of days, he reapproached the work with a new professional realism, promptly reducing its status in his mind from grand opera to staged church cantata.

Even the arrival of snow, coating the mutilated rose-bushes, piling thick against the door, blocking out the light from the dome, was not alteration enough.

He found himself seeking to effect a more dramatic change by making greater demands on Sally. He would take her often now, abruptly, in the kitchen, the bathroom, the larder – anywhere but in the smothering confines of their bed. He was wilfully inconsiderate in the hope, perhaps, of producing an indignant reaction, but he provoked nothing in her beyond mute acquiescence, tempered occasionally with a wry, wincing smile.

In the end it was she who heralded the change to his life, with the staggering announcement of her pregnancy.

'Are you sure?' he asked.

She told him precisely how she could be sure and it struck him how easily women could pretend to be pregnant since the proof all lay in areas from which ignorance and fearful disgust kept men at a long arm's length.

When his happy surprise had subsided and he had drawn her on to his lap on the piano stool, she ran a fingertip softly across his brow and down his cheek and said, carefully, 'If it's . . . If it's a girl, I think we should call her Miriam.'

His embrace froze for a second then he hugged her anew to hide his true feelings behind a mute show of approval.

Citing a passage from *A Husband's Love*, she said her pregnancy should not be affected by their lovemaking, but he found himself awed by the thought of the little thing within her, and was possessed by irrational fears that his entry would somehow damage it, causing it to deform or bleed away. He even woke terrified from a dream once, in which it had bitten his penis clean off at the fleshy base. Sally tried to comfort him.

'It's perfectly safe,' she urged. 'You're not *that* big!'

He knew she was laughing at him. He could hear the chuckle behind her words.

Change bred change. Despite her protest that the prospect of a baby need not affect her working ability and that they would 'manage somehow', he began looking for work that was better paid and which he could combine more naturally with composition than his previous job in the bookshop. Thomas made discreet enquiries around the colleges but found that none of the choirmasters or organists was on the verge of leaving. Besides, Edward was loath now to take work so far from home. Depressed at the prospect of someone saying yes, he began to offer his services around local schools as a piano and singing teacher.

The answer came, indirectly, from Miriam. As a sop to his devout grandparents' memory – 'alleviating the curse', Sally called it – Edward contacted Rosa Holzer about a proper disposal for Miriam's ashes. Having berated him for his sinful ignorance in having his sister cremated, and sighed that she did not know where the world was heading, Rosa agreed to organise a small memorial service at her local synagogue followed by a late lunch at her new house in Golders Green. She was plainly flattered to have been consulted.

They travelled up in the train, with the mortal remains in Sally's bag between them. Some fifteen people attended. Edward had not realised that so many friends of the family had survived the war and were living in London. His eyes remained dry throughout the service and, oddly, it was Sally who shed tears. She blamed it on the haunting singing of the cantor, who she said had a voice to wake the dead. Edward had become hopelessly christianised by his boarding-school years and found himself as confused as her in the turbulent sea of Hebrew prayers.

There was a flower bed to one side of the gloomy cemetery where the ashes were used to fertilise a camellia Rosa had bought for the occasion. Its glossy foliage looked alien against the frosted London soil and was already thick with flower buds for the spring.

'It's a Williamsiae,' Rosa assured them. 'Such a lovely, feminine pink.'

Sally had been nervous of meeting the witch-like woman again, but her blurting out about her pregnancy and her hope for a daughter she could call Miriam worked on the old woman's features like a charm. The news even drew out a smile and an almost earthy chuckle from among the sighs that came as naturally to Frau Holzer as breathing.

Sally later joked that she felt the curse on the marriage was modified if not exactly lifted; a long, enchanted sleep, perhaps, instead of certain death. But it was for Edward to fear the old woman's influence, for she telephoned the morning following the ceremony with ambiguous good news.

'Jerry Liebermann. You must have talked with him, Eli. The big fat man with the handsome son about your age. Heini, he's called. No? Well he talked to *you* . . . So. *Now* you remember!'

Edward remembered a man who claimed to have been at school with his father in Berlin, who had left Germany in the early thirties and who was now a major force in the British film industry. He had seemed more interested in Sally than in Edward, persisting in embarrassing her with his bullying flirtation – 'But your figure, the way you walk; don't tell me you've never acted. Of *course* you've acted! I've seen you in something. *April in Venis? The Moon in June*?'

'He wants to try you out as a composer,' Rosa said with satisfaction.

'A composer?'

'That's what you *do* now isn't it?'

'Yes, but what does he want with my music? A wedding march? A requiem mass?'

'Here's his number, Eli.' Rosa would not even acknowledge his artistic qualms. 'Take it. You've a wife and child to support now. Offers like this don't grow on trees.'

Edward made the call. He did not wait for Sally's return from work so he could ask her advice. He rang. He committed himself. Half an hour of music was required that could be chopped and edited later. An introduction and finale. A march. A waltz. A polka. And some 'horse music and train music' as Jerry Liebermann put it. The film was an adaptation of *Anna Karenina*, to be called *Desire* and to star a young actress called Myra Toye. Edward and Sally had seen her in a few films already, and, in his opinion, she was more suited to modelling bathing costumes than personifying complex adulterous passion.

'Very romantic. Very Russian,' Jerry enthused. 'We've got all the best boys on it. Rosa tells me you write plinky plonky music. Stravinsky stuff. We won't be needing that here. One note of that and you're out. Except maybe in the train bit. Give us a really blistering chord for the death. No, Teddy – I can call you Teddy, can't I?'

'Well, actually –'

'Great. Teddy? We need Tchaikovsky really, only the real thing's been used to death already. Maybe throw in a touch of Rachmaninoff. Now don't say no. You can do it blindfold. And *don't* pretend you don't need the money, 'cause I saw the state of your suit and I bet it's your best and only. Am I right?'

When Sally came home for lunch that afternoon, she paused just inside the front door, surprised at the delicious harmonies and soaring melodies flooding from Edward's fingers. When he told her the news she laughed and kissed him, happy as he had seemed on hearing of the baby. The money Jerry offered, it was true, was spectacular compared to anything either of them had ever dreamed of earning. She recalled the flirtatious little man with his bizarre accent – half cockney, half German – his sombre, painfully respectful teenage son – 'Shake hands with the lady, Heini. Show her you're a gentleman' – his chauffeur, cigars and pinkie ring.

Edward watched her joy and welcomed the sense that two swift telephone calls had corrupted him utterly. Here was the absolute change he needed. Here was the outward show of rot he deserved. No tortured chords for the sister-smotherer but a slow professional suicide by sweetness and facility, candied harmonies, corrupt, forgettable pastiche. All day, all week, undemanding, flashy melodies poured from his pen at a speed he would never have believed possible. He pilfered shamelessly from Russian symphonies, opera and ballet scores. He borrowed whole chord progressions, changed two notes to disguise a stolen eight-bar theme.

Rosa Holzer and Jerry Liebermann had snatched his soul as Miriam's due. Playing through a gaudy ballroom waltz, to which Sally was already humming along on the landing, he knew himself reborn: Edward Pepper, the Fleapit Faust.

18

With the progression of her pregnancy, Sally felt herself increasingly a stranger among familiar faces. She had heard, times beyond numbering, how the gestation of her child was a woman's most beautiful time. Now that she knew the truth first-hand, she spat upon the saying.

On her bad days, which were many, she was a seething, distended bag of hormones. She cried easily, over mere trifles. Her hair was greasy. Spots appeared on her forehead. She developed a craving for raw celery, a vegetable she had always avoided, even when cooked. She would devour whole heads of it at one furtive go, jealously munching over the kitchen sink, gums sore with the stuff's lingering stringiness, tongue bathed in a green, mineral spittle. She had back-ache, an inside-out belly button and the unpredictable wind of an incontinent ninety-year-old. The scientist in her regarded these developments with a certain horrified fascination but knew that only the perverse would call her beautiful.

She passed swiftly through a phase – inspired by her reading of Dr Pertwee – of encouraging Edward to make love to her despite her condition. Now she colluded in his squeamishness. She saw his boyish shock when she undressed her scary hugeness. Where once his love had encompassed her from scalp to toenail, now it shrunk to three small circles, shone discretely on to her face and hands, as though the rest of her were temporarily absent. Leaving the house for the studios – which he had to do increasingly, for all Jerry Liebermann's initial promises – Edward bent carefully to kiss her lips, hands in his pockets or tucked behind his back, like a boy playing bob-the-apple. It made her feel like an old-fashioned doll, her face made of china and the rest, if one stripped away the clothes and cotton wig, a sausage of faded pink cloth, lumpily stuffed, not intended for even a loved one's scrutiny.

Reluctantly, she relinquished her work for Dr Richards. There was a possibility he might still have a job for her when the baby was old enough to be left with someone, but he was too busy to do without help for long. Besides, they were not yet sure enough of Edward's new earning power to even think of hiring a nanny or a nurse. She became fearful of riding the motorbike and allowed her fears to be worked upon by her mother's reiterated suggestion that women on both sides of the family were prone to miscarriages and going into labour prematurely. She stayed in. Appalled at her extravagance with Edward's new money, she approached a shop in Rexbridge which made deliveries.

Needless to say, her mother and father had been thrilled at the news. They came over a few times, when one of her mother's admirers of either sex could be prevailed upon to act as chauffeur. She was making the most of being under strict doctor's orders to take things easy for a while. They smiled at Sally with a kind of unconditional, subtly cannibalistic pleasure, making her feel less an intelligent woman, more a side of beef. In her ever more substantial presence, her mother abandoned the role of queen bee for that of mother hen and clucked, actually clucked, around Sally with cushions, magazines and cups of tea. Her father merely sat, but his tired old face, which for so long had seemed set like an unsuccessful milk shape, in a permanent expression of depressive apprehension, was now unnaturally creased up into a no less fixed proud smile. Whenever she swayed up out of her chair, he raised his hands in an Italianate gesture of admiration towards her bulging midriff, as if surprised afresh at this biological wonder. It irritated Sally beyond measure that, after years of striving, with slide rule, exam paper and stethoscope, to add their approval to Dr Pertwee's, she should find their highest, most heartfelt accolade ultimately bestowed on something she could have done a decade ago, without a single qualification; something as passive as lying on her back under an appropriate man at an appropriate time. She kept their visits to a minimum by pretending Edward was working from home far more than he was, and needed peace.

The truth was that he was often having to spend the night away, in cramped studio digs. Smaller, swifter projects than the *Anna Karenina* film were also being pushed his way.

She pestered him for details of the famous people he encountered, genuinely fascinated, but he dismissed her curiosity. As her own life was diminished however, she found it hard to suppress the impulse to live vicariously through his. She had been unable to hide her delight at the newly tuneful music he was writing. She saw too late that her pleasure goaded him, betraying as it did the wifely insincerity of her support for the 'serious' work she had heard previously. His melodies entered her brain and she found herself singing them even as she strove to make no remarks in their favour. He kept her questions at bay, wounding her as he was wounded, and so her curiosity quickened into a lively envy that burned in her gut whenever he left her side to enter his life elsewhere.

With the speed of a fairy's swishing wand on a soap poster, he became a busy man, Sally, a housewife. This, too, was a galling source of pleasure to her parents. Not only were they impressed at Edward's new connection with the glamorous world of cinema in a way they had never been by the mere fact of his being a composer and pianist, but her mother's every comment implied that Sally was now in her rightful place. Her mother had worked all these years only from necessity, it seemed, never gaining one ounce of pleasure from the independence granted her. She managed somehow to imply that Sally's transformation from white-coated medic to heavily expectant *Hausfrau* was a step *up* woman's evolutionary ladder, like the acquisition of a second car, a washing machine or a son at a fee-paying school.

In her letters to Dr Pertwee, Sally tried at first to maintain a cheerful front. She laughed at herself, blustered away her doubts and suspicions with a gabbling, newsy tone. This cracked, in time, shortly after one of Edward's longer absences, and she began to fire off shorter letters, biliously truthful about the frustration she was feeling. In her letters back from Corry, Dr Pertwee judiciously held back from discussing any cracks that were appearing in the love's young dream but urged her not to waste her time, not to vegetate. Sally could hardly clean the house more than she did: with so little furniture, attic to basement housework was the labour of less than a day, and every stick of woodwork already shone with fragrant polish. She filled her other days with books. She began to work her way through the mildewed gardening encyclopedia Edward had unearthed beneath some seed boxes in the cellar storeroom. Breathing its sickly-sweet scent, she acquainted herself with every plant in the garden, and memorised the elegant Latin name for each, the way she had familiarised herself with muscles, bones and arteries as a medical student. Choysia ternata. Iris foetidissima. Lilium Candidium. She drove the names into her head by making an effort to 'greet' plants with their full names as she walked in the garden after breakfast. She cultivated a taste for novels, too, something she had always regarded as a waste of time but which now, with hours of leisure heavy on her conscience, she passionately understood. Slumped on the sofa, a cushion behind her aching back and a rug about her for warmth, she devoured whatever the library van had to offer – Mary Webb, Stella Gibbons, Rumer Godden, Ngaio Marsh, snobbish but oddly addictive Angela Thirkell. She read more from compulsion than pleasure, tossing one book aside and beginning another with barely a pause to digest what she had just finished. She swept dispassionately through other women's courtships, marriages, adulteries and trials of strength, pausing to smile only at the rare mentions of pregnancy, as from one sufferer to her fellow.

When Edward did work from home, she kept out of his way. Resisting the temptation to sit in the hall and listen, for fear of angering him, she borrowed the car to drive cautiously to market or to her parents, pottered in the garden as best the baby would allow or simply stayed in bed with a book. Despite her mother's gift of needles and wool, she declined to learn to knit; some principles, she assured Dr Pertwee, remained sacred.

Whether he worked from home or the studios, Edward

seemed to be always one step from exhaustion these days. His face began to crease from strain – a little trench appearing on either side of his mouth and a frown between his brows. He fell into a deep sleep often before he had kissed her goodnight, sometimes even before she had come to bed herself. Restless and uncomfortable with her size, she sat up beside his slow-breathing body, reading, stopping occasionally to stare at him. She loved his face when it slept. It acquired an openness, an expression of calm trust it no longer wore in waking hours. Usually he lay there still and silent, but sometimes a dream disturbed the pool of his slumbers and he would twitch and mutter like a hound hunting in its sleep. Once, lost to her in a nightmare, he even wept. He made no sound beyond twitching the bedclothes, but when she turned to him in the moonlight she watched in appalled fascination as three tears welled up, distinct as those in a Disney cartoon, and ran in quick succession down his bony cheek.

19

As Edward stressed in vain in the face of Sally's shopgirl curiosity, the studios were anything but glamorous. The initial thrill had lasted a week, maybe two, then he discovered they were actually a factory, perhaps shabbier and more ramshackle than most. Avenues of Nissen huts, cavernous sound stages and ad hoc mobile dressing rooms were linked overhead by a sparse canopy of telephone wires, stout, rusting pipes and haphazard swags of electric cable. The kitsch pomposity of the porter's lodge – a thatched, Tudorbethan affair designed to summon up the same sense of anticipation as a grand entry to a stately home – raised expectations that were entirely false, for one passed swiftly into a labyrinth of unloved industrial buildings without ever arriving at anything one could truly call a front or main entrance. There was not even a façade. The country house theme was taken up just once elsewhere, in the commissariat. The seventeen-forties' elegance of this oak-panelled dining room was as bogus as any ballroom or boudoir concocted in the scenery docks around it, its phoneyness heightened by the knowledge that, barely a decade before, it had been an indoor swimming pool where starlets disported for the entertainment of press and producers.

Musical soundtracks were recorded in a room like a cinema with all the seats taken out. The players – a ragged orchestra of hard-boiled professionals one suspected could play anything from Bach to Berlin with studied lack of discrimination – were ranged out across the floor. Edward conducted them from a podium while the relevant scene was projected on to a big screen behind them. They watched his baton, he watched the movie and, in a sound-proof cabin below the screen, a team of sound technicians recorded the noises he drew from them.

An actress's face loomed, lower lip trembling with desire, eyes glistening with droplets artfully administered seconds before. Edward would time a crescendo to the invisible beating of her heart, synchronise the peak of a 'cello's soaring theme to the second when she held her breath and wiped away a sham tear. The timing had to be perfect, as well as the performance. He came to know every magnified inch of Myra Toye's face, every inflection of her voice – so well that she began regularly to enter his dreams as he lay beside his wife. On some days they might spend an hour providing the melodic background to mere minutes of her latest film.

'Background?' Jerry Liebermann protested, waving a hand at the orchestra, 'This, Teddy, is the icing on the cake. This can make or break us.'

And often it was true. Edward knew that his music masked lamentable deficiencies in the acting.

'No. Don't ask me. I can't, you silly brute. I simply can't!' Miss Toye would jabber, shaking her beautifully gloved hands and covering her face, unable to hide the fact that she had been shooting all day, every day, for weeks, and was so tired she could hardly stand, much less emote on demand. Yet once Edward had counterpointed her words with a haunting, ironic echo of *Vronsky's Theme*, played adagio on an unaccompanied oboe d'amore, her drab performance was burnished to a semblance of glory.

A film buff from boyhood, he was fascinated to be gaining an insider's view of the film-maker's craft. For all his self-disgust, he could not restrain a certain proud excitement. Yet every week he received fresh evidence that what he had taken for artistry was rank manipulation. He saw now that the men and women whose art he had worshipped were actually artless performers, blessed with a certain voice or physiognomy. Invariably shorter and less glamorous than they appeared on screen. They were recreated in an image worthy of their public's fond delusions by a small army of gifted technical specialists. These would never be famous – no laudatory retrospective seasons awaited make-up artists and costumiers – yet all would still be working long after implication in a child rape case or a doomed sortie to Hollywood had rendered one of the stars yesterday's face.

The performers who endured were the grotesque and self-mocking, the buck-toothed and overly tall, content to degrade themselves playing shrewish wives in preposterous hats, alcoholic spies and back-street abortionists with shaking hands and broken reading glasses. Fame, it seemed, always assigned the godlike a shorter contact with the public's devotion. Edward did not always recognise film stars in the commissariat, so deflated did they seem in the flesh. The men, in particular, seemed less than heroic, even downright seedy, when not shot from below with the right lighting. But there were some who were so determined to maintain their screen persona and be always instantly recognisable – spinning manically from a joke with canteen staff, to cadging cigarettes from cameramen, to a touching recollection of the names of wives and children they would never meet – that he could almost *smell* their time burning out. Occasionally he spotted a former star whose face was still known to him. The lucky ones, who had married well and escaped, were usually seen stepping from a producer's Daimler, lapped in shielding furs. The commoner, less fortunate, appeared gamely in thankless supporting roles or, sadder still, were found haunting the sound stages, stricken shadows of their former selves, with memories for the names of wives and children intact, bravely hiding the fact that they were there to audition alongside newcomers.

While many of the scene-builders and technicians were cockney, an extraordinary number of the behind-camera staff were former refugees from Germany, Russia and eastern Europe, some Jewish, some political. If one added to that the mongrel background of most of the performers, the upper-middle-class drawing-room scenes the collaborators so meticulously fashioned were small teamwork masterpieces of socio-economic guesswork. Some of the emigrés had merely transferred from one studio to another, hastily translating technical vocabulary as they went along, but many had adapted their skills as well as their unpronounceable names. Tables at the commissariat in lunch breaks could assume the air of smoky academic common rooms. At least two of the men now called upon to direct forgettable froth on celluloid had been prominent theatre directors in their former countries. A lecturer in chemistry from Prague now headed the film processing laboratory, one set designer was a highly qualified Viennese art historian and the dwarfish woman regularly credited as *Gowns by Sylvia* was rumoured to have held a chair in fine arts somewhere in the Balkans. When the time first came for Edward's name to appear in a film's credits – a quota quickie called *Angela and the Men* – Jerry Liebermann took him on one side.

'Edward Pepper,' he murmured. 'Forgive me if I say so, Teddy, but it sounds too English, even if that *was* the idea all along. Now Teddy Pepper would be fine for a band leader, but we need something with more class. What did your mother call you?'

So it was that, writing with a full orchestra, a massive public and a sizeable salary at his disposal, Edward was once more known as Eli Pfefferberg. Meanwhile, he continued to work at his opera with no commission and no audience, under an anglicised name that was meant to win him friends and influence in his xenophobic adoptive country.

In the last week of his labours on *Desire*, Miss Toye singled Edward out as he walked along a corridor with the percussionists who were helping him approximate the sound of St Petersburg church bells. She was already working on something else and seemed to be dressed as Amelia Earhart, the chin straps of her flying helmet flapping against her luminous, heart-shaped face. Thickly made-up for the cameras, her expression was bright as a poster.

'Teddy!' she cried. 'It is Teddy, isn't it? Darling, the music for Anna's first waltz! I had it whirling round and round my head for days since I heard it. I dance like a pregnant mare but you had me positively floating. You're a perfect genius. It's not your real work, is it?'

'I'm sorry?'

'You can do this stuff standing on your head,' she said gesturing at the industry around them, 'So it probably doesn't make you very proud. Not like a proper string quartet. But plebs like me think it's perfect.'

'Well. I . . .' he stammered.

'And how's your clever wife?'

Astonished that she had divined so swiftly what Sally apparently could not, much less that she had troubled to find out that he was married, he shyly told her that Sally was expecting a baby very soon. For days afterwards she would throw him a sporty grin if they passed or call out across the lunch tables.

'Not long to D-Day now, Teddy!'

She never expected a reply, turning away before he could have given one. As a newcomer, keen to pass unnoticed until he was sure of his status, Edward found her public show of interest faintly alarming but succumbed in spite of himself to the enviable caress of her patronage. Newcomer or no, he was shrewd enough to sense that she was the current studio queen, she was young enough to last and her favour could only work to his advantage.

Sure enough, he was hired for her Amelia Earhart film, *Reach for the Stars*, and then for a cheap, unexpectedly triumphant quota quickie she was contractually obliged to make after that – a screw-ball comedy called *She Lied*. In common with many of the men at the studio, he came to find that regular proximity dulled her glamour, but it was soon replaced with a touching sense of her vulnerability, whose charm was infinitely longer lasting. It was known throughout the lots, though nowhere else, that she was involved with Jerry Liebermann, who had a hold over her that was a greater source of conjecture than the liaison itself – producer-actress affairs being almost institutionalised.

Edward did not find her especially attractive, at least not when she was being her public self, painted, bright and effortlessly energetic. She had another side, however, a haunting, bruised quality, so far invisible in her performances. It showed only occasionally, when she was exhausted by retakes of the same inane snatch of dialogue, for instance, and turned aside from cameras, lights and make-up crew for a few moments to regather her forces.

There was a dog in *She Lied*, a highly trained mongrel bitch, stage name of Bunny, who accompanied her character throughout the film, even into bed and bath, the gimmick being that this dog was the only living being to whom the heroine always told the truth. Apparently viewing the mutt as unfair competition, Miss Toye complained about it and its handler at every opportunity. It soiled her clothes, she said, and made her sneeze. It stole her best moments and was unpredictable as a child. In an effort at least to form a workable bond with the creature, she insisted on taking it with her everywhere for the few weeks of shooting, surly as an impatient young mother. Returning from lunch one day, Edward saw her walking the animal ahead of him along a pathway past the carpentry shops. The dog began to limp then let out a whine and sat firmly down, raising a front leg from the ground. Myra snorted with impatience at first and tugged on its lead then, seeing it was genuinely hurt, she knelt on the dirty, shaving-strewn path, heedless of the damage she might be doing her slacks, and set about teasing a splinter from its paw. It growled with the pain and yelped a couple of times. She soothed it, caressing its ears, then carried on. The splinter was clearly deeply driven for, as Edward approached, she was still working at it. He was astonished to see how little she reacted when the animal sank its teeth into her left wrist. She barely glanced around as he reached her side, saying only, 'Take the lead, will you, in case she tries to run.'

Edward did as she asked, watching in appalled fascination. The dog gave one more growl as she pulled the splinter free, then it sniffed suspiciously at the evidence she offered it. There was blood on the back of her wrists, welling from clearly visible toothmarks.

'Your wrist . . .' he began.

'I know,' she muttered, rubbing it carelessly. 'Continuity will murder me. Got a hanky?'

'Of course.'

He passed her the handkerchief from his breast pocket from which she improvised a bandage.

'If they give me any trouble, Bunny, you're cat food,' she muttered, taking back the lead.

'Doesn't it hurt?' he asked.

'Not really. I – I broke it rather badly when I was a girl and some of the nerves were damaged. Thanks, Teddy. Christ! Now we're late.'

Listening to gossip in the commissariat later, Edward heard how her broken wrist was no childhood accident but the brutal work of her first husband. She never returned the handkerchief and he pictured her maid puzzling over its mysterious initial. He began to watch out for her, half-consciously waiting for other unguarded moments when he might catch another glimpse of this sincerer incarnation. He sensed that, like him, she was distorting herself to make a living, swept along by a process beyond her control. In a moment of rash naïveté, he began to convey this to Sally. Shame cut short his explanation however, leaving her merely to laugh at him, 'And you accuse *me* of being star-struck!'

One night he worked late with the sound editor in the dubbing lab until long after the hour when the studios were usually deserted. Leaving his colleague to finish splicing the sequences they had edited, Edward walked to call the lift. Someone had left its downstairs door open, however, so when he pressed the button a distant bell rang to summon the night porter. Before the porter clanged the door shut and sent the lift motor back into trundling motion, Edward heard voices coming from an office further along the dingy corridor. He heard Jerry Liebermann's unmistakable drawl then, after the sound of breaking glass, Myra Toye, raising her voice to something near a yell and using vowels and colourful epithets that were a far cry from her ladylike screen image.

'Go suck it yourself!' she shouted. 'Or find yourself some little slut from the chorus.'

'At least they're not stuck-up,' Jerry Liebermann yelled back.

The office door opened, suddenly increasing the argument's volume and clarity. Deeply embarrassed, Edward hunched around to face the lift door.

'Come on,' he muttered, frantic to be out of the way as

Myra put in her parting shot, 'They're not fussy about size either.'

The office door slammed just as the lift arrived. Thanking his stars, Edward darted in and pressed G. Footsteps patted along the landing linoleum.

'Hold the door. Hold the door,' she called out.

Edward held the door back with his arm and Myra Toye, adored by millions, ran in past him. She was in her stockinged feet, clutching her high heels. Her dress was disarranged and entirely unzipped at the back. The celebrated blonde hair was askew and her mascara had run.

'Thanks, Teddy,' she said, stooping to pull on her shoes as he released the door. She tidied her hair, using the lift's control panel as a mirror. 'You heard, didn't you?' she asked, rubbing her eyes and cheeks clean with a handkerchief which she then stuffed into her thin gold slip of a bag.

'Sorry,' he said. 'I couldn't very well help it.'

Along with a trace of alcohol, she had brought an extraordinarily rank smell of sex into the lift's confining space. Edward pictured her frail body crushed against a desk by Jerry Liebermann's swarthy bulk, thought of the cigar still burning in Jerry's lips as he pounded away. He found this unpleasantly exciting.

'Everybody knows, don't they?' she asked.

'Miss Toye, I –'

'Don't they?' She brought an edge of steel back to her voice. Edward nodded. She sighed.

'That's it,' she said. 'I'm through with him. I'm going to marry again. Someone better. Do you know Julius?'

'No,' Edward said. 'I don't, actually.'

'Julius is sweet,' she said. 'Really sweet. I want a church wedding and a nice house with a garden and I'm going to have babies. I want babies and fuck the figure.' The lift reached the ground floor with a jolt. The door opened and Edward reached to slide back the outer one but she held on to Edward's sleeve, gently detaining him. 'Is yours born yet?' she asked.

'Mine?' he blurted. 'Er. No Sally isn't due for another month.'

'You're a lucky boy, though,' she said.

She was playing the older woman, a role she knew to perfection.

'I . . . I know,' he said.

She stroked the side of his face then, quite suddenly, cupped his chin in her slightly pudgy, childish hand and kissed him, lips apart. He felt the brief touch of her teeth against his. He flailed his hand to swing back the outer door, anxious lest they be borne upstairs to the wrath of Jerry Liebermann. The clatter of the gate startled her and she pulled back.

'Sorry,' she said. She tried to laugh. 'Sorry.' She hurried past him into the shabby-grand foyer that led to the commissariat and out to the car park.

'Wait,' he said.

'What?' She paused, suddenly nervous.

'Your dress.' He reached out and pulled up the zipper on the back of her dress so that the sheath of black velvet once more hugged her contours as the designer had intended.

'Thanks,' she said. 'Thanks, Teddy.' She smiled sweetly and walked on down the corridor, calling a greeting through the porter's cubbyhole as she went. Edward waited, so that the night porter would not think they were together and wondered why she bothered to dress up in such finery when everyone knew that she only had a short drive home to a studio bungalow.

He had worked so late he had intended to sleep in the studio trailer he sometimes used, but the encounter had unnerved him and filled him with a kind of panic to be back in bed beside Sally.

Driving through the dark, he fancied, time and again, that the car was filled with the cat-house smell that had clung about him in the left. He wound down the window until he felt chilled, then closed it – only to have the scent creep back. Finally, aware that his behaviour was entirely irrational, he stopped the car and darted into a strangely busy roadside convenience on the outskirts of Colchester to scrub at his hands and face until they smelled only of pink municipal soap, blameless as an alderman's chain.

20

What her mother maddeningly referred to as Pop-the-Cork Time was upon Sally sooner than expected.

The day continued the pattern of that summer, being hot, with no breath of wind from the fens to stir the pollen-laden air that hung around The Roundel like a bad mood.

Edward was at home, thrashing out a score for a period drama starring Myra Toye's principal rival. The film was about an adulterous duchess who drove her wretchedly well-intentioned husband to suicide and her lover to a violent death before making a spectacular repentance and dying, an exemplary nurse, in a fever hospital she had set up in the Belgian Congo. He had reached the Congolese section and the house was filled with his noisy experimentation with various ethnic percussion instruments a studio researcher had tracked down for him. This, and his thuds in the deeper range of the piano, had driven Sally outside.

They had spent some of his new earnings on a pair of reclining wooden chairs, delivered from Heals the previous week. She dragged one down to the stream – which the lack of rain had reduced to a lethargic trickle – and made herself a kind of bower half in, half out of the willow tree's shade. Ensconced there with cushions and a jug of lemonade, she soon gave up her attempt to begin a new Elizabeth Taylor novel. Hoisting up the skirt of her maternity dress to let her legs brown, she thrust her dark glasses back on the bridge of her nose and settled back to do nothing. Edward's noises came to her across the grass now and then, as did the occasional cries of birds and small, animal splashing on the water's edge.

Then she dozed off. In the two hours or so she must have been asleep, she dreamed, repeatedly it seemed, that she was being harangued by her unborn child for misdemeanours she could not recall committing.

Something woke her. She barely had time to glance at her watch and find that half the morning had slipped by before she felt a contraction around her uterus. She had felt a curious, niggling tightness over the last few days but the midwife had dismissed these as mere muscle flexing.

'She's just practising,' she said.

The midwife always referred to Sally's body in the feminine third person singular, as though pregnancy had sundered it from her personality, giving it a bizarre independence. As the delivery day drew near, there was a truth in this grammatical quirk, for Sally felt herself increasingly at the mercy of her own flesh; ruled by all-powerful biological imperatives.

For a moment Sally interpreted the contraction as another of her body's rehearsals for the real thing. Then she realised that the ache in her lower back was inflamed beyond its usual dullness. As the muscles relaxed, she shifted on the chair to rearrange the cushions and felt a stickiness between her legs. Frowning, she flicked up her skirt and dabbed inside her drawers with her fingers, unable to see over her belly. They came up with a trace of the bloody mucus midwives referred to, with almost veterinary zeal, as 'a show'. She glanced at her watch again, automatically, so that she could time the interval before her next contraction, then lay back on the cushions to wait. A faint breeze stirred the lime green strands of the willow about her head, then all was still again.

'My time is on me,' she said aloud and tried to chuckle.

She had rehearsed this moment so often in her mind during the monotonous unemployment of past months that she felt no panic, only a simple recognition of symptoms and swift recollection of how she must react.

The next contraction came in twenty minutes, and the one after that. Was it her imagination that made them seem progressively stronger? She had been unable to decide whether to have the baby at home or in hospital. The Roundel was so lovely and peaceful, even with Edward's rattling and

Congolese bells. She loathed maternity wards for the way they seemed to cap the indignity of pregnancy with a male-dominated conspiracy to steal from the mothers any moment of charm or intimacy that might make the whole ordeal worthwhile. The practicalities of needing to allow exhausted patients some precious sleep meant that their miraculous creations were corralled to bawl their new-born lungs out in a separate room, like so many calves in a veal pen. They were even tagged like cattle, and one still heard tales of them being muddled up or even wilfully exchanged. Obstetricians bullied, other mothers criticised and scaremongered, older children sulked in the visitor's area, terrified babies wailed for the moist security they had lost; motherhood could scarcely have a less welcoming base camp.

Another contraction. Sally checked her watch. Twenty minutes again.

She trusted the time-honoured skills of a midwife more than the surgical steel and book-lore of any male specialist, and yet, to have her first child at home was, perhaps, a temptation to fate? What could go wrong? Sally began to list in her mind the grisly possibilities, but was cut short by another contraction. She knew, this being her first delivery, that this stage could last for anything up to fifteen hours. If something began to go wrong, there was always Edward and the car. In her indecision and fear, she had already packed a bag, just in case.

She noticed that her face was bathed in sweat, and she wiped it on her sleeve. Gingerly she lowered her feet to the grass and hoisted herself upright. Then she supported herself on the willow's trunk for a few minutes, summoning up the strength to cross the hot expanse of garden which now seemed so much longer in the high noon sun.

On seeing her, Edward broke off from playing a passage through at the piano and jumped up. She dropped her eyes to follow his stare and saw that there was a trace of blood, along with the patches of sweat, down the front of her dress. She explained.

'But it's not due for two more weeks,' he protested.

'Due or not, it's on its way.'

'You're sure?'

'Of course I'm sure!' she snapped.

He didn't take chivalric control as she had hoped he might. He merely dithered. Hearing his voice on the telephone to the midwife as she hauled herself upstairs, she began to wonder whether a maternity ward might not be a wise option after all. But once she was flat on her back between cool, garden-scented sheets, all resolve left her save the determination to stay still, rest and gather what powers lay at her command.

The midwife came, soothingly joked that this was going to be one very impatient baby, and sighed at Sally's decision to have the delivery at home. Sally knew she was pleased at a pregnant doctor's reliance upon a midwife's competence. She timed the contractions and felt briskly around Sally's nether regions, placing expert hands on the unborn child as though to assure it, too, of her knowledgeable presence.

'Now,' she said, as Edward hovered in the bedroom doorway, 'I've just got Mrs Storey to help though hers over at Digby's Farm then I'll be getting my breath back at home when you need me. It's her fifth, so it shouldn't take long. Get Mr Pepper to call me out when your contractions are coming every five minutes or so. It shouldn't be for, oh,' she glanced at the watch that dangled upside down on her bosom, 'at least another ten hours or so. Call me sooner if the pain gets bad or you think something's going wrong and you're frightened. Don't look so *worried* my love! You're not ill. Thousands of women go through this every day and live to tell the tale.'

Sally smiled obediently, wondering how thousands of women could face going through this more than once and not demand superior living conditions, a state maternity allowance and festivals in their honour. She never usually thought much about religion, except fleetingly at Christmas, but now she found herself thinking about Jesus; and the archetypical God with flowing beard and voice of thunder. She was astonished that the pair of them had got away with ruling the roost for so long while the woman who had gone through childbirth to make it all possible allowed herself to be relegated to the puppet role of Carnival Queen. Edward came back from seeing the midwife off and asked her nervously what she was giggling about. She started to tell him but a contraction scrambled her thoughts and she sent him instead to fetch some lunch and to heave the radio upstairs for her.

She dozed for a while after lunch, finding the contractions barely woke her. The ripple would run through her lower body, like a wave turning in on itself. She would half open her eyes, hear a few minutes of Edward's music coming from below, then slip back to sleep. She woke at last at dusk with an urgent need to pee. She had made him bring her a pot but he had left it coyly hidden beneath the bed so that it was out of her immediate reach. She threw back the sheet and slowly swung her legs off the mattress. She had assisted at births so often in the course of her work, that she felt she knew the best and worst of it, knew too the astonishing variety between one woman's experience and another's.

Reaching for the pot, she was just congratulating herself on being one of the lucky ones, when a fresh, savage contraction knocked her, gasping, on to all fours. Somehow she used the pot as soon as she could, unable to tell whether the hot liquid splashing below her came from bladder or womb or both. She was barely back on the bed before another contraction came. She scrabbled on the bedside table for the handbell Edward had left her and rang it hard.

'Edward?' she called out, feeling doubly vulnerable at the fear she heard in her thin voice. 'Edward, my waters have broken.'

Another contraction gripped her before he had even made it upstairs.

She knew now that the agonies in store would be beyond anything she had experienced to date. Like everyone, she carried a scale of pain in her head, with notches carved by each new experience from the cradle on. Nappy rash, teething, stinging nettles, burns, the first splinter, the first grazed knee, the first scalding splash from a kettle, the first bee sting; any sensation more painful than its predecessors merited a new notch. She had suffered terribly from impacted wisdom teeth at medical school, had known the sudden, white-hot pain up the side of her face and, in the weeks before a dentist could operate, had learned to fear its unpredictable return. This new pain, which made her yelp, then almost laugh with surprise at its brain-clearing force, redefined her sense of suffering. Toothache was a mere itch by comparison; the only similarity was the pain's spasmodic nature and her lack of faith that it would ever be over.

During the hours that followed, Sally not only lost all track of time but also all feelings of impending intimacy, all welling sense of mother-love. Instead, she was gripped by a single caustic desire to have the baby ripped from her by the swiftest means possible – anything to bring the pain to an end.

21

'You're not serious!'

Sally's face shone with sweat as she stared incredulously up at him. One of her thighs had ridden clear of the sheet and it, too, glistened in the lamplight.

'Don't worry,' he said. 'Her husband said he'd send one of the boys over to Digby's Farm to see what was keeping her. Mrs Storey must be, er, having complications. But listen, I've called the ambulance and –'

He broke off as a fresh spasm seized her frame and she snatched instinctively at his wrist as though it could somehow ward off the pain. By a huge effort, she drew enough breath to gasp instructions to him.

'It's too late for that,' she hissed between her teeth. 'God! Listen. We'll just have to manage. Get towels. All the towels you can, and string and scissors.'

'Scissors!?'

'Yes. And we'll –' Again she had to stop for a contraction. She tugged back the bottom of the sheet as she raised both knees and pressed down with her feet, grimacing. Her fingernails drove hard into his skin and she let out a yell. Edward had never been present at a birth. His mind raced with scenes from films; maids sprinting, white-faced, pursued by a mistress's tortured screams and a house-keeper's barked instructions.

'What about hot water?' he asked, remembering.

She managed a laugh.

'That's for later,' she said. 'When we need to wash the little bugger. You'll need some now, though. Give your hands and forearms a good scrub with disinfectant and soap before you come back up. Oh and bring a pudding basin and the meths bottle.'

Cursing the midwife, Mrs Storey and the ambulance service, Edward raced off to do as she said. He lathered up his hands at the kitchen sink and scrubbed at them with the vegetable brush before rinsing them off in scalding water made milky with disinfectant. Humming under his breath, he found meths, pudding basin and scissors. He finally tracked down a ball of string in the cluttered drawer of the kitchen table, tugging it free of old knives, candle ends and seed catalogues. He swore, realising his hands were now dirty and would have to be washed afresh. Tugging an armful of towels from the airing cupboard, he found he was shaking.

When he got back to the bedroom, Sally was sitting up, clutching her knees, her head forward. He picked two fallen pillows from the floor and packed them behind her back and shoulders along with the ones from the other side of the bed. She sighed her thanks. Edward pulled up a chair beside her. As she lay back, she let him wipe the sweat from her face and arms with a towel.

'Spread one of the others under my legs,' she said. 'Better make that two; we don't want to ruin the mattress. What can you see down there? Besides the obvious.'

Edward looked.

'There's a bulge!' he gasped.

'Well of course there's a bulge.'

'No, I mean another one.'

Sally gave a glottal shout and threw her head forward, bracing herself once more against her knees. She forced herself to breathe as she did so, great deep breaths, dragged out raw through jagged edges. For a few seconds, as the contraction continued, he saw the lips of her vulva part and something round and dark and glistening briefly unveiled.

'I think –' he began. 'I think –'

But her contraction stopped and it slid back inside.

'What?' she gasped. He looked up at her. From his position, crouched at the foot of the bed between her feet, her body seemed a magnificent, powerful thing. Panting, hair plastered in rats' tails across her forehead, eyes and teeth brilliant against a complexion flushed with blood, taut with effort, she might have pronounced a curse and turned him to stone.

'I think I saw its head,' he admitted.

'Thank Christ,' she sighed.

'What?'

'Not breech,' she muttered enigmatically before flinging herself forwards again to strain against her own body's strength.

Labour and delivery; everyday use devalued the two words' currency leaving them to sound neutrally euphemistic, but now that they were being enacted before him, Edward saw their rigorous precision. It was a warm evening and, even with a window open, the relentless cycle of Sally's savage contractions and brief, panting moments of respite seemed to rob the room, the entire house, of air. Before long, Edward imagined he felt her every hoarse breath on his face and with her sharp, whooping sucks on the stale atmosphere, he felt suffocated. The sheer concentration of her being on this single act of expulsion made her the heaving centre of the house, queen of the anthill. He strained his ear for the sound of the midwife's car or the ambulance bell but heard only Sally.

'*Now!*' she bellowed. 'No. Don't come up here. Stay down there and – Jesus! – I – I need you to take its head. You must be able to by now.' She stopped talking to snatch a few quick pants then gabbled in her effort to communicate in the short time left her. 'Just steady it. Don't pull and don't twist. Stop it coming too fast or it could burst a vessel.'

Startled into action, Edward wiped his hands on the towel and reached out for the smeary dome that was now recognisable as a wizened head. He saw, with a shock, that Sally had suddenly shat herself. Without stopping to think, he used a flannel to roll the big, firm turd clear of the baby's face, then wrapped it in the cloth and tossed it quickly through the open window.

The baby's head was hot, slithery with blood, mucus and God knows what else. Taking it gently in his hands he could hardly believe Sally could stretch so wide without tearing.

And there were still the shoulders to come. Or had she torn? It was impossible to tell where the blood was coming from. He marvelled that she could do this and live. Perhaps it would kill her. He had made her pregnant and now she was going to die.

'The cord!' she yelled suddenly.

'What?'

'Umbilical cord.'

Edward looked back at the emerging form.

'Oh God! I – I think it's around its neck.'

'Don't panic. Ease it round over the head.'

'But it looks so tight.'

'Gently. It'll give. Gently. Oh God.'

Wincing, Edward slipped his forefinger behind the pulsating cord. After two failed attempts, when it slid from his quivering grasp, he managed to move it around to the other side of the head. The tension in it relaxed.

'It's coming. Oh God, it's coming!' he murmured.

Suddenly Sally gave out a full-throated scream as though her very innards were being torn out.

'It's coming!' he encouraged her. 'Push, Sally. Push. Oh God in Heaven!'

Glistening like a pink frog, a whole new life was emerging from his wife's insides and into his no less slithery arms. The sight was utterly surreal to him. Neither uplifting, nor abhorrent, it was so far removed from anything he had seen before that he watched in pure bewilderment. For a few seconds the child seemed lifeless, then a minute working of its mouth prompted Edward to wipe its face with a clean corner of a towel. Instructed by Sally, he cleared the tiny nostrils and prised his fingers between the lips to release a thick gobbet of mucus and was rewarded by a thin wail.

'It's a girl,' he said. 'A girl.'

Sally let out a sob and held out her hands. Still hunched in her tangle of sheets, with raised knees, she clutched the minute creature to her heaving chest and released a low moan that turned into a sigh. She looked up at him, weeping with happiness, pain, and relief.

'The house,' she said. 'A girl for the house!'

'Shall I get that hot water now?' he asked over the noise of the baby's crying. She nodded. He left them, fetched another towel and filled the biggest saucepan he could find with hot water. When he carried it carefully back into the room she told him to set it on the bedside table, then made him snip two lengths of string into the pudding basin and pour the meths over them, dropping the scissors in to soak as well.

'Here. Hold her for me,' she said and he held the baby while she dipped a towel in the water and gently washed the baby's wrinkled limbs with languorous, careful gestures. 'Now,' she said, when the baby was dried and furled in another towel, 'The cord.'

The umbilical cord had stopped pulsating now. Under Sally's supervision he tied string tightly around it in two places but he hesitated with the scissors.

'Won't it hurt?' he asked.

'Here.'

Sally took them from him and snipped cleanly through the meaty vessel between the two knots of string, tucking the short length still attached to the baby away inside the towel, and muttering something about a dressing.

'What about, er . . . ?' Edward held up the other length, the root of which was still hidden inside his wife. The cut end was seeping slightly onto his fingers. She smiled at his ignorance.

'No,' she said. 'Don't pull. All that'll come out on its own in a while. Oh, Edward. Darling.' She began to cry again. 'Sit by me a little. Sit by *us*!'

Edward wiped his hands on the towel and walked around to the other side of the bed, where he clambered up. For what seemed like the first time in months, he put his arm about her shoulders and she leant back against him. His nostrils caught the strong mineral scent of her drying sweat and blood.

'Hello,' she said to the bundle in the towel. 'Hello. Oh look, darling. Look! She's here. Miriam's arrived! Miriam. Miriam. Miriam. It suits her. Don't you think. Miriam. *Miriam*.'

Their reverie was interrupted by the arrival of the midwife, who congratulated him on his handiwork then shepherded him from the room while she fussed back and forth with blood-soaked towels and set about tidying Sally. She was followed shortly afterwards by ambulancemen, who carried sedated mother and sleeping child from the house on a stretcher.

Left alone with the hot night and his wife's deserted house, Edward poured himself a large whisky, took out the address book and twice began to dial her parents' number to give them the news. Twice, however, he set the receiver back in its cradle, unable to rid his mind of Sally's tone as she repeated, in a dreamy incantation, the name of his dead sister.

22

After the brisk spring evening outside, the theatre's air felt uncomfortably warm and it was rendered heavier still with expensive scent and alcohol. Not counting a grim Christmas spent at her parents' house, it was Edward and Sally's second proper excursion since Miriam's birth the previous summer. People yawned, coughed, burrowed in handbags and jacket pockets for pastilles and handkerchiefs, some even fanned their programmes slowly against glowing cheeks yet nothing could detract from the power of the sounds welling up from stage and pit.

Following a blood-chilling orchestral evocation of a sea storm, the scene had just changed to an East Anglian tavern interior. Fishwives huddled around a fire, their menfolk sulked over pints and argued over women, the storm howled at intervals whenever someone new crashed in from outside. Suddenly the villagers' worries found a focus in loathing and mistrust for a drunken fisherman who did not belong among them. Just when Edward was expecting a straightforward choral expression of dislike, composer and librettist surprised him by having someone start an old-fashioned round in a well-meaning effort to dispel a dangerous atmosphere. Character after character joined in the vigorous, catchy tune with a kind of desperation until chorus and orchestra caused the sound to surge up to meet another burst of storm music as the door once more flew fatefully open. The handling of the material was almost cornily melodramatic – the musical equivalent of the broad, wide-eyed gestures of an old silent film – and yet it succeeded brilliantly. The aggressive rhythms, the huge crescendi and piling of texture on texture were utterly seductive. Edward glanced at Sally and found that even she, who he had long since guessed found modern music difficult to enjoy, was sitting forward in her seat, mouth slightly agape in her excitement. Irritated, he stared at her openly, only to irritate himself further as the music held her so raptly attentive that she did not notice his gaze.

The première of *Job* in Tompion College chapel, their only previous excursion, had been an unmitigated disaster. Encouraged by Thomas's enthusiasm for the little he had heard and by an offer from the university's operatic society to stage Edward's next work, he had pressed on to finish the piece. Working was not easy. When Miriam cried, the sound could not be escaped anywhere in the house and Sally's efforts to silence her only added to the distraction. Sometimes, guiltily, he was driven to lie to her. He would ring from the studio, saying he and the orchestra had to work too late to make it worth his while coming home, then he would work alone through much of the night, piecing together his cantata in the relative bliss of a soundproofed rehearsal room. Once he found he had broken the back of the task he laboured on like a man possessed, dodging out of his less urgent film responsibilities. Often, if he were at home, he would obligingly take Miriam a bottle when her cries woke him in the night. If she refused to go back to sleep after a feed, he would sit up with her, working on the score at the table where Sally changed the baby's nappies.

From the day *Job* was finished to the evening of its performance was a brief idyll which Edward now looked back to as a lurid false dawn. He remembered penning the last chords and hurrying out past the terrace, where Miriam lay gurgling in her pram. He remembered Sally calling up to him from where she was gardening on the other side of the stream.

'Down here!'

He remembered triumphantly waving the manuscript and her waving smilingly back, hands black with peaty earth. He had paddled across, heedless of soaked shoes and trousers and her half-angry shout, to seize her and seal his deliverance with a stolen kiss. He remembered the scene with the unsparing exactitude of a man reliving a mountaineering accident or car crash.

'If I had placed my feet here instead of there . . . If I had turned the wheel thus instead of so . . . If I had stayed, wise-cowardly, at home . . .'

For those days of celebration and hectic preparation had indeed seemed a deliverance, not only from the task he and Thomas had set themselves, or from the lingering fear that his prostituting himself at the studios represented an irreversible downward step, but also from dread.

He had begun living as one under a curse, his dead sister's hand heavy on his shoulder, her condemning shadow thick across the empty page before him. He was haunted by her image, fancying time and again that he saw her amid the familiar faces around him, sitting in the third row of violas, quietly spooning soup into her fat face in a corner of the commissariat, watching him, soberly dressed amid a flurry of suggestively spangled chorines. And now it was as if the curse had lifted; he had served out a terrible penance and, with the careful wording of a dedicatory page in her loving memory, consigned her to oblivious rest.

Job was not what the university singers had expected. Used to Sullivan and Donizetti, they had planned to be adventurous, but not *this* adventurous. They were game in their attempt, polite as missionaries facing the nightmarishly inedible. The counter-tenor was excellent as Lucifer, as was the baritone singing Job – even though he was much too young and had a controlled perfection of tone that smacked more of English church polyphony than Old Testament rage. Job's daughters, however, were tall and hearty as county tennis champions. They sang flat whenever Edward persuaded them to drop their winsome smiles and, in lieu of the decadent luxury he had envisaged, the society's costume mistress decked them out in matching outfits of a drab curtain material which could never have been attractive, even when new. The orchestral players were hopelessly lax about turning up for rehearsals, thinking rowing practice or an essay crisis sufficient excuse. Occasionally they seemed to understand Edward's meaning and produced an approximation of the sound he had sought, but in the performance they were hopelessly ragged, and Lucifer's triumphant bergamask was no more threatening than an amateur marching band.

On the evening of the performance, the chill in the chapel affected the audience's concentration as badly as it did the singers' tuning and the applause was more grateful than heartfelt. Edward and Thomas were not summoned for a last curtain call, since the first one was barely over before audience members had started re-tying scarves and stamping life back into numbed feet. Fulsome praise from the chaplain stung like the harshest criticism since he alone saw fit to offer it, and the celebratory dinner laid on at Thomas's house soon degenerated into a bibulous, self-pitying wake. Sally knew better than to enthuse.

'It deserved better,' she pronounced carefully. 'Nothing could succeed in that cold, and those stupid rugger players shouting outside in that quiet bit didn't help much.'

'Ghastly,' Thomas had said. 'The most humiliating experience of my life. Never again. Never.'

His words fell on Edward's ears like an unanswerable accusation. They did not speak for days afterwards and when he eventually wrote to Edward, enclosing a belated, not unkind review of the piece from the *Rexbridge Chronicle*, it was without apology. The cantata's corpse lay unburied between them, unregarded, undiscussed. The strain of this estrangement told on Edward's nerves for, after weeks of respite, he found the memory of his sister returning to haunt the periphery of his conscious and sleeping thoughts, like a resurgent stain on a newly whitewashed wall. He had the ill-fated score bound and placed it on a high shelf before throwing himself into the overdue task of composing music for a new spy thriller, set on board a transcontinental express.

His cantata's failure was all the more galling for his continuing success as a screen composer. Jerry Liebermann – who naturally had not found time to attend the performance, but had sent a telegram and asked keenly after the work's reception – felt that his protégé had learnt a painful lesson and had now rid his system of any ambition to become a 'proper' composer. He commiserated indignantly, but his relief was plain.

Myra Toye made overt the depressing truth that Jerry had left unspoken.

'Heard about your lousy première, Teddy,' she said wryly. 'I suppose this means you're stuck with us after all.'

This jibe hurt him in a way she had never intended. More than anyone, more than Thomas, more, he guiltily accepted, than Sally, she had always seemed to be the one who understood the dreadful artistic compromise he was making. He had felt she had faith in him. Now he saw that he had laid too deep an interpretation on their sketchy exchanges, that she had been remembering to mention *Job* as she remembered to mention a cameraman's prize roses. Even had it not been mere politeness, a show of interest, she too had now given him up for lost.

Eventually, relations with Thomas approached their former, comfortable level. Edward had been sure that his gift of these tickets to see a revival of *Peter Grimes* was meant only in generosity.

'Sally hasn't been getting out nearly enough and I think it's frustrating her hugely,' Thomas had said. 'A night on the town will do her good. Do you think you could find a babysitter who can stay the night?'

Now that his nose was being so thoroughly rubbed in another young man's genius, however, Edward was not so confident of Thomas's kindness.

'*Home?*' yelled the chorus, as Grimes dragged his new apprentice out into the storm with him, '*Do you call that home?*' The orchestral tempest brought the first act to a sudden blaring close and the audience to a frenzy of applause and cheering. Edward's hands remained on his knees. He stared at them. They might have been made of lead. As the chatter swelled around him, he stood, badly in need of an interval drink.

'Say what you like,' a skinny redhead behind him protested to his companion. 'I had goosebumps. My hair was on end. Thrilling. Say what you like.'

Sally remained in her seat, studying the cast list. Realising he was waiting for her, she shut the programme and slipped it into her handbag. Her eyes were shining. Tactful though she might try to be later, she couldn't hide the music's immediate effect on her.

'Well?' she asked, playing for time. 'What did you think?'

To his astonishment, Edward found himself on the brink of tears. There was a pricking in his eyes and his lips felt full and heavy. He shrugged, hardly daring to open, his mouth.

'I –' he began. 'What about you?'

'Wonderful. You know what a coward I am. I mean, coming up to London and going out to dinner and everything's lovely but, well, frankly, I was dreading the opera and –' She broke off, laughing at herself. 'It's such a surprise. It's like some incredible *film*!' She squeezed his arm tenderly. 'Thank you.'

'Why thank me?' he heard his tone freeze over. It seemed to be beyond his control.

'Well, I . . .' She faltered. Surprised at him. Embarrassed. 'I suppose it's dear old Thomas we should thank but it's made nicer having you here to share it with.'

'You don't think I'd have bought us tickets for *this*?'

'Well wouldn't you?'

'I'd have taken you to Mozart. *Così* or *Figaro*. Something – something purer for you to start with.'

'Don't be so bloody patronising,' she laughed. 'I told you. I'm loving it. What's *wrong* with you suddenly?'

'Nothing.'

'Honestly, Edward, there's no point making comparisons with *Job*. Even an ignoramus like me can see the aims are totally different.'

'Who said anything about making comparisons. I'm not comparing. Are you?'

'I do believe you're jealous!' she said. 'Poor darling. I hadn't thought. How *awful*!' And then she made the mistake of laughing at him.

He did not slap her particularly hard, but there were some steps ahead of them and he caught her off balance so that she tumbled backwards. A woman in a red dress darted forward to catch Sally's shoulders and her male companion seized Edward firmly by the arm, holding him back and exclaiming something indignantly chivalrous. Edward stopped struggling and, feeling him relax, the man let him go. The crowd which had gathered briefly around the ugly little scene passed on, murmuring disapproval, but Edward only had eyes for Sally.

'Christ! I'm sorry,' he said.

She stared at him for a moment then gave a little snort and stood, saying, 'So am I. Let's get out of here. People are staring.'

She let them skip the last two acts so that he could buy her dinner early. She thawed with the second glass of wine and chatted lovingly about Miriam, the things she would like to do to The Roundel once they had the money and what Dr Pertwee had said in her latest letter. He admired the brightness of her eyes in the candlelight and drank in the warmth of her forgiveness, but as she slept in the car beside him on the way home, he kept remembering the look of horrified surprise she had thrown him in the second before his slapping hand had made contact with her cheek. It was a look in which he could read just how fast he was falling. And how far.

23

Edward had warned Sally that the party to celebrate the completion of *Desire* would be nothing very glamorous – drinks, canapés, a few speeches, a few famous names – but she had seemed quite excited on receiving Jerry Liebermann's personal invitation, immobile as she had become in the social mire of young motherhood. On the evening however, she suddenly cried off. Their usual babysitter, a sensible girl from a neighbouring farm, had already arrived but Miriam was found to have developed a temperature and Sally was scared of leaving her.

As he drove to the studios alone, Edward worked himself up into a rage. Miriam was forever having slight temperatures. In his opinion babies' colds and minor fevers were necessary to the development of their immune systems, and he saw no reason to make such a fuss. He had bought Sally a new dress for the party, picked out the previous week and, when he said it seemed a shame to have gone to so much expense, her brisk dismissal of his present wounded him.

'It's just a dress,' she said. 'I can dress up for you *any* time. We don't need to go out for me to do that.'

He knew he was being unreasonable, that of course the baby must come first, but he could not help feeling that Miriam had been coming first for rather too long now and was in danger of assuming a permanent supremacy.

Sally had, it struck him, made no great effort to lose the weight pregnancy had forced her to gain and, now that she was no longer working, she spent less and less effort on her appearance. At pains to see that Miriam never left the house looking anything less than a diminutive princess, she sometimes neglected to brush her own hair or teeth in the morning. She slouched about the house in her gardening slacks and seemd to have developed an objection to putting anything on her face but soap and water, so that she often looked drawn and tired. His view of her appearance was not helped by the inevitable comparisons he drew with the women about the studio – even *Gowns By Sylvia*, who was built like a shot-putter, was always turned out to her best advantage.

Sally had already put on the new dress when she slipped across the landing to take a last look at Miriam. Her whole manner seemed to rebel against its understated elegance, and remembering this as he drove, Edward reflected vindictively that it was sometimes a pity she was not more her mother's daughter.

Once at the party, his anger was initially overlaid with excitement at the praise Jerry Liebermann and his colleagues lavished on the *Desire* score, topped up with more anger that she was not there to hear it. He drank several strong drinks in quick succession, then stood glowering from the sidelines as dancing began. Still sufficiently sensitive to know that his mood could be doing nothing to enhance the gathering, he took another drink and pushed out through the commissariat doors and on to the terrace. Cooler air sobered him slightly and he was wondering whether he should telephone Sally to apologise for having left with so perfunctory and bad-tempered a farewell, when the star of *Desire* came out too. Looking like a vestal virgin, with complicated hair and tasteful white and silver drapery, Myra Toye slipped a cigarette between her lips then swore with deadly clarity as her lighter failed to produce a flame. She saw him and walked over.

'Teddy!' she said. 'How nice. Light this for me, would you?'

'Sorry,' he said. 'I don't smoke any more.'

'Course you don't,' she said quickly. 'Half a lung or something ghastly, isn't it? Liebermann told me.' A couple walking back inside stopped and the man struck a match for her and left her the box. Expertly fabricating delight, she asked a few quick questions about his family, ignoring the fact that the girl on his arm was plainly not his wife, then released them both with a smile.

'Doesn't bother you or anything, does it?' she asked Edward, exhaling a small cumulus about them.

'No,' he said. 'Not really.'

'Walk with me, would you. I was feeling stifled in there.'

They walked along the terrace's length to where its brief elegance gave way to a grim series of avenues between the high scenery docks.

'Sir Julius is very nice,' he said.

She only snorted in reply. By way of a public announcement that her liaison with Jerry Liebermann was now categorically over, she had arrived on the arm of her new fiancé who, to Liebermann's interest, had mooted the possibility of investing in a film or two.

'He's not as thick as he looks,' she said at last. 'He can talk ancient Greek.' She sighed. 'Somehow I'd thought he'd be easier to manage though.' When Edward had last seen him, the young man had been hobnobbing with her friends from the make-up and hair departments – Myra's Boys as they were known.

'Who *is*?' he asked moodily, thinking of Sally and her recalcitrance. Myra seemed to read his mind.

'You too?' She turned in surprise. 'I meant to ask you, darling. How's the bouncing baby? D-Day was months ago wasn't it?'

On any other evening he would have acted like the matchbox man and fawned in gratitude for her unnecessary interest in the mundane details of his life, but tonight a madness stole over him.

'You don't have to do all that stuff on my account, you know,' he said.

For a second she froze at the breach in protocol, then she relaxed, her voice dropping down an octave, discarding its customary brightness en route.

'Thank Christ for that,' she said and continued walking.

'But the baby's fine,' he said. 'A girl. Miriam. Sally was meant to come tonight but the baby had a temperature.'

'Ah,' she said. 'I see. So what's it like, then, marriage?'

'I thought this was going to be your second time around.'

'My first time didn't count. I was so young my mother all but sold me to him. Now the prospect scares the hell out of me.'

'It's odd,' he said. 'I didn't realise two people could live so close and know each other so little. Sometimes I might not be Sally's husband at all.'

It was a lie. He knew it for a lie and yet it nicely expressed the bitter bravado he was feeling. Myra's perfume reminded him of that distant night when she had kissed him in the lift. It excited him like a bold caress. He made an effort to control himself, aware how drunk he was and how risky it was to be talking like this. He drummed up a polite enquiry about where she and her fiancé would be setting up home, but she stopped him with a kind of sneer.

'Drop it. Just drop it. You don't have to do all that stuff either.'

'Sorry,' he muttered.

'And kiss me,' she added.

'What?'

'No one can see us. Come on. Kiss me.'

If he had excused himself right then, pleaded drunkenness, pleaded anything, he might have escaped with only her transitory disdain, but he kissed her and knew from the way the blood surged into his groin at the feel of her fingernails on his backside that only she had the power now to stop what she had set in motion. She led him by the hands into the shadows then through a great opening into a scenery dock. Stumbling in the semi-darkness, he followed her through a Grecian temple to a mock-up of a lorry cab. She made him climb into the driver's seat then she slid up beside him.

'Put your hands on the wheel,' she said, unbuttoning his fly, 'and keep them there. Sammy was hours fixing this hair.'

Painfully swollen, his penis was doubled up inside his underwear. Eyes growing accustomed to the gloom, he watched in disbelief as she slid cool fingers around it and set it free. She kissed him once more, probing so deeply with her little tongue that he feared he might come in her hand, then she bent down into his lap and took him in her mouth. He sat rigid in the driver's seat, peering out through the windscreen, petrified lest someone – Max Hirsch, Jerry Liebermann, anybody – appear before him with something similar on their minds. The assurance with which Myra led him to the cab told him it was a well-established trysting place.

Fighting the urge to grasp her head in his palms to bring the sweet torture to an end, he came with no warning. He felt the climax purely in his penis and testicles, much the way he did whenever Sally and he had made love first thing in the morning when he was tense with the need to urinate and too embarrassed to tell her. Myra swallowed everything he pumped into her. She buttoned him away again then sat up and made him hold burning matches in the air while she repaired her lipstick. Then she lit herself another cigarette. The flare of the matches flattered her preposterous glamour, not a hair displaced.

'Er. Thank you,' he mumbled.

'That's all right,' she said. 'I gave you for nothing what that stoat Liebermann thought was his for the asking. Toye's Law: Those who ask don't get.' Then she slipped down from the cab ably as a Land Girl, leaving him to follow after a discreet interval.

He sat on feeling light-headed. He knew he should also feel guilt, but the encounter had been too impersonal for that. He felt no closer to Myra now than if she had stumbled against him in the lunch queue or brushed past him in the sound studio corridor. Keeping all his clothes on, not even touching her after the preliminary kisses and surrendering himself entirely to her control: it was as though she had answered a passing need in them both for a transgression that left no traces. Her perfume lingered in the air around him but there was none of that feral muskiness that had seemed to cling to him after their encounter in the lift. Perhaps *that* smell had not been hers at all but Jerry Liebermann's. More appalled at that possibility than by what he had just done, he rejoined the party.

In swift succession he registered her dancing cheek to cheek with her fiancé, eyes blissfully closed, then found the crowd abuzz with people looking for him. Apparently he had no sooner left the room than Sally called to leave a message about Miriam.

'I looked and looked, Sir,' the porter said. 'Couldn't find you anywhere.'

'I . . . er . . . I slipped up to my office,' Edward explained. 'I'd forgotten some notes I left there.'

'I tried there too,' the porter insisted maddeningly.

'Really?' Edward stammered. 'I must have missed you by seconds.'

He drove home like a madman. He was terrified at his inability to hold the car on a straight course and all too aware that the apparent clarity in his head was a dangerous deception wrought by adrenalin. Inevitably he made guilty pacts with fate.

'Never again. Spare her and I'll never do it again.'

When he had to swing out of the path of an oncoming lorry, startled by a furious blare from its horn, he even honoured the Hebraic teachings of his grandmother, considering the possibility of offering himself in poor exchange.

The Roundel was silent when he arrived and his footsteps rang out as he ran upstairs to their bedroom. Sally was dozing in bed, an open novel slipping from her hands. She woke slowly, smiled to see him there and yawned.

'Oh it's you!' she said fondly. 'I hope you didn't rush.'

'Of course I rushed. I got your message about Miriam.'

'But I said not to rush home on her account,' she said, laughing. 'She's fine. Her temperature dropped back down and I didn't want you to worry.' She kissed his cheek.

'I drove like a bank robber.'

'I'm so sorry. Poor darling. Kiss her goodnight and come to bed quickly. I got Richards over to look at her just in case. There's been some meningitis around and –' She yawned deeply as a cat. 'It's probably just a little cold. It was so silly of me to lose my nerve. Not like me at all. It was not having you around to calm me. Where *were* you? The porter man kept me hanging on for ages, and when I called again the person who answered said he was still out looking for you.'

'I went up to my office for a bit then I went outside for a walk. I had a headache. It wasn't much fun without you.'

'I'm sorry. God I'm tired.' She yawned again and stroked the lapels of his dinner jacket. 'This needs dry cleaning again. You're always spilling food on it or something. Wretch.'

He took the novel from her hands and pulled the bedding up around her shoulders, kissing her again, then slipped next door to kiss Miriam. Hearing her deep breathing, smelling her sweet, babyish warmth, he was disgusted that instead of delight at the child's good health, he felt only relief that his act of betrayal had gone undetected.

Once back at work among his colleagues, he could not ignore a persistent feeling of fear and suspicion, tortured by the possibility that someone might be about to accuse him. Unable to forget, unable to suppress a detestable hope for a repetition, he at once dreaded and longed to see Myra again. So publicly and so advantageously engaged, she was unlikely to grant him any indiscreet acknowledgement. Her actual reaction was worse than he could have imagined. When she passed him in a crowd of costume assistants on his way to the sound studios, he prepared a careful, non-committal smile only to have her look straight through him. Their coming together the night before had been so abrupt, so brutal even, that now he was left with the crazed sensation that it might never have happened at all but had been the product of alcohol and feverish fantasy.

Once more, Edward tapped his baton impatiently on the music stand.

'No,' he said and the players broke off raggedly. 'No,' he repeated. 'Again, please.'

Behind their window, the projectionists rewound the film, then one of the technicians wearily raised a thumb from inside the sound cabin. Raising his baton for silence, Edward tried to sound patient.

'I know the sudden rhythm change in bar twelve is difficult at that speed, but it's an *exact* reproduction of the sound a train makes as it goes over points. Think of that when you play and it makes sense. And if the strings mess it up, George can't coincide his blowing the whistle with the image on the screen. And if he can't do that then we must start again, and again until he can. All right?'

He glared at the 'cellists, convinced that two of them were laughing at him but caught only innocent attention on their faces. He could not believe the story had not leaked out. For all the names on the payroll, the studios were small as a village when it came to the dissemination and elaboration of gossip. The smallest secret – from a bust size to a birth mark – was soon uncovered, so he could not understand how his, large by any standards, was taking so long to become shaming common knowledge. Perhaps they really had been unobserved and he was to go unpunished?

Edward waved to the technicians. The red recording light came on and the film began to roll again. On the big screen before him giant numbers counted from five to one. He gave the upbeat and the string players began to scrub at their furious semiquavers as footage of a train's wheels and hammering pistons flashed overhead swiftly followed by the scarlet words *4.15 TO BUCHAREST*. There were more shots of wheels, then snaking track and flashing sleepers, then steam billowing white against a dusk sky and the gaping maw of an approaching tunnel, then a jet of steam from the whistle. George was still having trouble with his whistle and the sound came late. Edward stopped immediately, causing the orchestral train to derail messily around him.

'Sorry,' said George helplessly. 'I . . . Sorry, boys.'

'Again,' Edward sighed, with an exhausted flap of the hand to the technicians.

Again the film was rewound, again the red recording light came on, again the strings and percussion mimicked the furious clattering of a train and carriages over points. This time the string rhythms were perfectly articulated and George's whistle flawlessly synchronised, so they carried on well into the film's title sequence. Surprisingly they flew through a tricky passage Edward repeated later in the score for a murder scene, in which the brass players had to slide mutes in and out of their instruments to suggest the distorted blare of another train hooting as it flashed by in the darkness. Then Edward glanced across from them to give George the cue for another crucial whistle blow.

The blow came exactly on time and the players were

flummoxed to see Edward drop his baton on the floor, stagger off the podium and race around to where George was sitting. He stared hard in the faces of two women flautists and at George and they stared back, wondering what their offence could possibly have been this time. For a moment they thought he was going to wither them with sarcasm or throw a tantrum but instead, far more alarmingly, he seemed to crumple from within.

'Forgive me,' he stammered. 'For a second I thought – Forgive me.' Then, to everyone's amazement, he slumped into a vacant chair by the kettle drums.

'Sir?' the junior percussionist asked him. 'Sir? Are you all right?'

But Edward was examining his hands, lost in thought. Around him murmurs rose to open-voiced discussion. Hands touched his arms and shoulders, spread fingers passed back and forth before his eyes. A doctor was sent for and – a sure sign of crisis – the technicians emerged from their soundproof layer. A motherly viola player conjured up a cup of strong tea for him but she had to take it back, kindly tut-tutting, when he threatened to let it slop all over his lap. He wanted to thank her, to explain, but mustering words had suddenly become an overwhelming effort.

It was as though he were slithering into a waking dream that held him tight as a bog; to struggle would make things worse but if he relaxed, the panic in his gut might soon pass. He kept his eyes lowered, lest they betray him by showing him more substanceless horrors. A studio nurse arrived with a commissionaire and, as they led him from the room, he heard the woman with the tea say, 'Well, of *course* he was in a camp, poor love. In Poland somewhere, I think it was. It would take years to get over it. It's a wonder he's as sane as he is.'

24

When a studio car brought Edward home, Sally's heart turned over.

'He's been overworking,' she told Jerry Liebermann. 'Sometimes he's been so frantic to meet your deadlines that he's done without sleep altogether. No-one can keep that up for long. I insist he takes a complete rest.'

A doctor nominated by the studio's insurers drove out to The Roundel and concurred with her opinion. Edward was freed from contracts for two cheap war films and a lavish Shakespeare project. Jerry sent him flowers, as did the studio orchestra. Myra Toye actually sent flowers to Sally, a big bunch of yellow roses. The card, which Sally was obliged to show to her mother, her father, the Richardses and countless other fans in the coming weeks said, '*Take good care of him, Mrs Teddy. We need him back in one piece and* soon!! *Yrs. Myra Toye.*'

Edward was indeed tired. Sally made herself up a bed in a room on the other side of the gallery and moved Miriam's cot in with her so that they would not disturb him during the night. He slept whole days away. He was too tired to read and turned off the radio moments after he had turned it on, muttering about there being 'too many voices'. Even music seemed to disturb him, and repeatedly Sally found windows she had left open closed again, as though birdsong too was an insufferable stimulus. When Miriam was being affable, which was usually just after a feed, Sally took her in to visit him but he was uneasy holding her – often shaking his head and hiding his hands in wordless refusal.

Invariably the baby soon picked up on his tension and began to grizzle.

One day he seemed to feel stronger, for he dressed and came downstairs. Sally dared to imagine a steady recuperation, with him beginning to work again sporadically, clad in his fetching silk dressing gown, and her serving him small, eggy lunches on a tray. Although she knew they needed the money, a part of her enjoyed having him all to herself again.

The effort of staying upright, however, or even making conversation, soon proved too much for him and he became as immobile and withdrawn in an armchair as he had been in bed.

She shut the piano lid one day while she was dusting and it remained shut.

Meanwhile she was amazed at how her fascination with Miriam never seemed to lag. If anything, her needless panic over the baby's mysterious fever had made time with her all the more precious. She could watch her, play with her, hold her for hours. Since the birth she had felt no need of adult company beyond Edward's and with him away at work so much, would often spend days on end wrapped up in her daughter's emerging abilities. Fellow adults, particularly childless ones, only made her embarrassed at her preoccupation. Visitors no sooner arrived than she longed for them to be gone.

'I'm becoming quite bovine!' she wrote to Dr Pertwee. 'I'll never lose all the weight I put on, I move so little and I swear I move at half the speed I used to. My head seems fixed at forty-five degrees from the vertical I'm so obsessed with her. The other day I'd just given her a bath and I caught myself sucking at one of her little feet like some great, hungry cow. Reassure me. Can this be *natural*?'

She could not understand Edward's reluctance to hold their child. It seemed to her that if he only let that soft, vulnerable creature sink on to his lap, let her pull myopically at his jacket buttons, let those milky blue eyes fix on his, then all his secret pains would rise to the surface and evaporate in love. She began to find herself guiltily drawn to spend more time with Miriam and less with him. At the slightest sound from

Miriam, she dropped her novel and ran from his side with as much eagerness as concern.

When he began to have fits of crying she was appalled. She kissed him, held him to her, rocked him in her arms, begged him to tell her what the matter was. But he could never say or, if he spoke at all, it was only to mumble an apology and say it was nothing, nothing at all.

'But it must be. Don't be daft. Edward, I *love* you. You can tell me. What is it? What's wrong?'

At last her persistence would drive him from the room. If she pursued him, she felt brutal, if she stayed away, she felt callous. The sound of him weeping quietly in another room wrenched at her vitals as insistently as her baby's wailing. She knew she could never stand by and let Miriam cry and, at first, the same seemed to be true of Edward's pain. With Miriam, however, she could still the cries, offer milk or a comforting shoulder, rock her back to sleep or bring her down to play. With Edward, it seemed, her approaches were useless. After many failed attempts to comfort him, each one leaving her more depressed at her impotence than the one before, time gave her lessons in hardness. She found, to her disgust, that she could stare at his sob-distorted face across a room without flinching. If, midway through one of the many meals during which she provided most of the conversation, she looked up to see his eyes red with trickling brine, she could politely overlook it as one might somebody's runny nose. Her parents called a few times, bringing flowers and fruit, as to the conventionally sick, but she could tell they found the situation alarming and she saw the willingness with which they accepted her suggestion that they leave him in peace.

Sometimes she stirred at night, aching for his touch, his sleeping grasp on the underside of her breasts, the pacifying weight of his thigh between hers, the soft, slow stages by which their somnolent shifts beneath the bedclothes could warm into lovemaking. Then she felt the chaste confines of a single bed around her or heard Miriam making her muffled, sucking, baby sounds and remembered. Twice, maybe three times, she had tried to kiss him or run a hand across his neck with more than an everyday, nursing tenderness, but she felt herself rebuked at his stiffening, as though her touch chilled him to the marrow.

Gradually her compassion for him came to be coloured by irritation; a change insidious as the arrival of mildew on the dining room ceiling. He broke a plate on his slow progress about the kitchen and her angry words were out of all proportion to the event. When a heavy cold made him adenoidal, she became unreasonably disgusted at the noise he made by trying to munch toast and breathe at the same time.

'*Must* you do that?' she cried out, when she could bear it no longer. He stopped chewing, stared at her for a moment, replaced the piece of toast on his plate and, murmuring, 'Sorry,' left the room.

'Edward? Edward don't be silly,' she laughed. 'Come back.' She followed him to the door, but he had vanished into the fabric of the house as completely as any chastened child and she was left alone with the rays of heartless morning sunshine and his uneaten breakfast, an accidental ogress.

The day she finally came to accept the worst began with her losing her temper again. Miriam was fractious with the cutting of a tooth and had woken her repeatedly through the night. Pink and cross from boiling up nappies, Sally was carrying the steaming linen out to the garden to hang it when Miriam's cries rang out through the house again.

'Damn!' she swore as she opened the door. Edward was sitting in an armchair, hunched and sniffing. Even the way he sat made her angry, because she sensed he was trying to shrink from her view. More tired than her work as a doctor had ever made her, worried about how long the insurers would continue to pay his salary, and intensely frustrated suddenly with being the only one in the house who did any work, she snapped at him bitterly.

'Oh for Heaven's sake, why can't *you* shut her up for once?! You *are* her father, after all.'

He turned his sad, blank look on her as she stamped out to the washing line. He would not move, of course. Not to help, at least. He might slip into another room out of her way, go upstairs and lie on his bed to stare at the ceiling like some miserably captive ape, but help his wife? Take a small part in caring for his daughter, his own flesh and blood? Oh no. That was asking too much. Sally hung out the nappies, stabbing the fury out of her with clothespegs, until she was calm enough to be dismayed at the kinship in rage she was beginning to feel with her mother.

When she returned to the house he had, indeed, left his armchair and disappeared. Once again she was appalled that he was making her into someone best avoided. Miriam had stopped crying, which made Sally's burst of anger feel even more unjust. She climbed the stairs in any case, to make the beds, then froze in the doorway to her room, amazed. Edward was leaning tenderly over Miriam's cot, his hands lowered to rub her back to sleep. She had not known, until she felt this relief, how deeply his apparent rejection of the baby had wounded her. Then she took a few soft steps into the room to lay an apologetic hand on his shoulder and gaze down with him. He loved Miriam! Miriam would help him! All would be well!

But his hands were not stroking. He was holding a pillow over her little face and his hands were shaking with the effort of pressing down. Sally let out a kind of roar and ran at him, pushing him so hard he lurched to one side and fell, still clutching the pillow. Miriam writhed in the cot, bellowing and snatching at the air with angry fists. Sally picked her up and held her possessively to her shoulder. Edward was rising from where he had fallen. His teeth chattered.

'Get out!' she yelled. He raised a hand defensively. 'You! You – just get out!' Simply by running at him she was able to drive him from the room. She kicked the door shut with a bang and fumbled to turn the key in the lock, then she sat heavily on her bed and began to rock back and forth, calming herself as well as the hysterical baby. Slowly Miriam's cries lessened. Sally brought her down to lie in the crook of her arm. She stroked her cheek and Miriam suddenly yawned. Sally looked up to see the two of them in the old, stained looking-glass which leant beside the wardrobe waiting for someone to rehang it. The tableau they made might have been soothing in its domestic normality were her face not pinched with fear. She looked back to Miriam and stroked the baby's wispy hair.

Her surgical coats, boil-washed, ironed and redundant, hung on the back of the door. Her black medical bag crouched suggestively on a chair. With a supreme effort of will, she drew doctorly dispassion around her. Slowly her disorderly emotions – the fear, the dismay – fell away to leave rigid self-condemnation. What could she have been thinking of all these weeks? Edward was sick, not exhausted. It was pointless to rage at him for something so obviously beyond his control. It was she who had allowed their child's life to be endangered by not snapping out of her milkily sentimental delusion earlier to find him qualified help. Resolve allayed her terror. Her world had not quite collapsed. Her child would live. Marriages had weathered worse storms.

Miriam was sleeping now, weighing heavily against her mother's arms in her total relaxation. Sally listened to her baby's deep breathing and forced a sigh. Then she listened harder, reaching beyond the door. There was no sound from Edward. Was he crouching on the landing? Was he listening too, perhaps, an ear to the other side of the door? She frowned then murmured, 'Edward? Are you there?'

She stood and carefully settled Miriam back in her cot then let herself on to the landing, locking the door behind her and pocketing the key.

'Edward?'

She had looked in all the other bedrooms and was on her way back to the stairs, irrational fears mounting the quieter the house seemed to become, when she heard the clatter of metal against enamel and saw blood welling out over the lip of yellow linoleum which protruded below the bathroom door. He had not locked himself in but was slumped against the door so she had to lean on it with all her weight to force her way in. His safety razor lay open and bladeless in the bath. He had already cut his wrists and, as she came in, was hacking above one of his ankles in an effort to open the artery there. He was lying in a great pool of gore.

'No!' she gasped and ran at him, slipping on the blood. As she tried to seize his arms he lashed out at her with the blade.

It caught on the fabric of her blouse just nicking the skin of her forearm, then his wet fingers lost their grip on it and it fell into the blood. He stared at it for a moment, then held out his hands to her and gave out a single despairing wail which almost turned her stomach. His arms fell and his head dropped back against the door as his cry for help subsided into terrible sobs.

Sally ripped off her blouse, twisted it into a rudimentary rope and tied it so tightly about his bleeding calf that he yelped with the pain. Skidding in the blood which covered them both, she tugged a towel off the rail, slashed at it with nail scissors then, with strength born of desperation, ripped first one then another long strip from it. As she tied these with necessary brutality about his arms, she became so bloody that a casual observer could not have guessed which of them was the one in mortal danger.

'Come on,' she sobbed, manoeuvring his arms about her neck. 'Try to hold on. Try. *Please*, Edward!'

He made an effort to lock his hands behind her neck, failed with a small, boyish gasp, then hooked an elbow around instead. Trickles of his blood running down inside her petticoat and soaking into her bra, his breath – still sweet with breakfast coffee – warm against her shoulder, she managed to slide him out on to the landing. Half-pushing, half-swinging him along like some grotesque carnival puppet, she dragged him to the locked bedroom and laid him on the floor while she dashed inside for her medical bag. She began to thread a surgical needle, froze for a moment in indecision, then sprinted down to the telephone to call an ambulance first.

'There's severe blood loss,' she warned, and the maddeningly calm voice at the other end asked for his blood group, which she didn't know.

Edward passed out half-way through her stitching his first wrist. Somehow this made it easier for her. Silent, immobile, he seemed less human. She avoided looking at his face, concentrating her furious gaze on the few inches of outraged skin beneath her working fingers. In the bedroom behind her, Miriam began to cry, working herself up into tiny mountains of rage. As Sally stitched feverishly on, stopping from time to time to rub her hands free of blood and sweat on her skirt, the baby seemed to express with an almost operatic fervour the anguish her mother dared not voice.

She saved his life. Later, much later, when a hospital car dropped her and Miriam off, she found that word of the crisis had spread. Local women friends had been in and cleaned every trace of congealing blood from the bathroom. The landing floorboards had been scrubbed with carbolic, the towels and bathmat boiled and hung out to dry alongside the nappies. The offending blade had been set back inside the razor which had then been tidied thoughtfully away between the toothbrushes. There was a small steak and kidney pie on the kitchen table. Standing there with an overcoat and her scarf thrown on to hide her brown-stained petticoat and bra, Sally felt the irrational shame of a refugee plucked from the scene of undiscussable atrocities.

She fed Miriam, wolfed half the pie cold, straight from the dish, washed it down with a whisky then lay on the sofa with Miriam in her arms, following her into a profound and dreamless sleep. It was dark when the baby woke her again. She rang the hospital to check on Edward and heard that he was sedated and sleeping. She started to ring her parents then checked herself. She thought for a moment, glared at her watch, and called Thomas instead.

25

Sally swung the Morris off the road between the high walls. The porter recognised her as a regular visitor – the place had few enough of these – and waved her through.

'Thomas,' she began. 'This is so kind of you.'

Thomas pointed out a parking space in the crowded car park.

'Don't be an ass,' he said.

'I don't think I could have faced it on my own today.' Sally sensed that, as ever, her sincerity unsettled him. He was fiddling with the doorhandle, waiting for her to release him. 'Unto the breach, then,' she sighed and they opened their doors.

Every dark red brick in Rexbridge Psychiatric Hospital betrayed the fact that it had once been called an asylum. Or worse. It was as though, building for so many blind people, the architect had produced an edifice devoid of the details that humanised such utilitarian structures. There were no fanciful touches. The best efforts of the hospital's gardener, who had produced the usual expanses of lawn, rosebed and gloomy shrubbery, did little to mask the joyless brutality of the place. Sally was inured to institutions and had visited this one many times already since Edward's transfer from the general hospital, but she could not help stiffening as they turned from the car towards the entrance. Thomas touched her elbow briefly, in reassurance – or perhaps to reassure himself – and let out a nervous cough.

There were no bars, but the ward's windows only opened at the top, well out of reach, and to leave by its double set of doors, one had to pass by a muscular, all-seeing duty nurse at a raised desk. Sally also knew that, as in the old isolation hospital, all personal belongings and clothes were surrendered to the nurses' safekeeping on arrival so that even if anyone did escape, their ill-tailored, hospital-issue pyjamas would brand them a patient not a person. These were the sick, the threatening, the embarrassing, the tidied-away, the impossible. Once again Edward was one of them.

This was not some low-grade Hollywood shocker, however. There were no wide-eyed ravers, no dismal chatterers and her feminine presence caused no lustful commotion. Sally and Thomas might have been shadows for all the interest their arrival caused and the faces they passed were not frightening, just ineffably sad. Two men played cards in slow motion. A third sat staring at a blank point on the lemon yellow wall, trying on expressions as a frivolous shopper with time on her hands might experiment with hats.

Edward sat limply in a chair beside his carefully made bed. There were now glistening scars on his wrists where Sally's stitches had been taken out. He mournfully returned her kiss but the gesture seemed unfelt, automatic as sneezing or catching a ball. She hugged him, then, feeling tears begin to prick her eyes, busied herself picking the dead flowers from a metal vase and replacing them with some she had picked in the garden earlier. The petals were still wet with dew. Thomas fetched two more chairs and the three of them sat in a cramped circle.

Sally found herself prattling on about the garden, Miriam's emerging teeth and tastes in food, and her attempt to redecorate one of the spare rooms as a nursery. She tried in vain to elicit from him whether he thought a design of ducks more suitable for a frieze, or one of flowers. Then she passed on encouraging messages from the studio.

'Jerry says they're missing you. Apparently the music Wexel wrote for the Falstaff film is all wrong and they've had to commission yet another composer. They're way over budget and about a month behind schedule. But you know how Jerry likes to moan. And he says even Myra Toye's been asking after you, or Myra St Teath as she must be by now. I read all about her wedding in a silly magazine Mum brought over. She thought you might like it but I forgot to bring it in . . .' She ran out of words and cleared her throat nervously. After a pause, Thomas asked the question she had been skirting.

'So. How are you feeling, Edward?'

Edward shrugged.

'Oh. All right,' he said, which was patently untrue. His hair was too long but he made no attempt to brush it from his eyes. His voice, robbed of animation, was little more than a stage whisper. He gulped heavily as though the very action of speaking had caused him pain. Sally made a mental note to check what levels of medication he was being kept on.

'Let me get you another book,' she said, reaching for the copy of *Our Mutual Friend* which seemed to have been on his bedside table for weeks. 'This must be driving you mad.'

He smiled faintly, perhaps at the unintentional clumsiness in her choice of words, and picked the book up to hold it in his lap like a pet.

'No,' he said, quieter than ever. 'I'm still reading it. Off and on. It – takes me out of myself.'

The effort of producing such a long sentence seemed to exhaust him. He was saved from speaking further by the arrival of a nurse at Sally's elbow.

'Dr Waltham will see you now,' he said. 'Do you know the way?'

Sally turned, puzzled.

'Dr Waltham? I thought Dr Caldecott –'

'He's away on a conference. Dr Waltham is taking over his patients in the meanwhile.'

Sally had not seen Dr Waltham since their awkward meeting long before, when he had caught her and Edward kissing in the bookshop. She muttered this to Thomas as they walked along the corridor to his office.

'I doubt whether anyone has ever kissed Ernest Waltham since he was out of nappies,' Thomas said. 'And even then, one suspects he lacked a mother's love.'

If Waltham remembered the incident, the memory was adding to the piquancy of the encounter, lending it the quality

– pleasing to him, no doubt – of the grim, told-you-so climax of a cautionary tale.

'To be frank with you,' he told her, once the social niceties were out of the way, 'I believe we need to try something stronger than the drugs.'

'Stronger?' Sally objected, thinking of how vague Edward was already. 'But surely –?'

'All they can do is maintain him in his present state which, as you've just seen for yourself, is scarcely satisfactory. It's been first aid, so far, little more than that. But if we are to proceed with electro-convulsive therapy, we shall need your signed permission.'

'No!'

Dr Waltham registered glassy surprise.

'Your reaction seems remarkably vehement.'

Sally glanced to Thomas, seeking his support.

'There's no proof that ECT works,' she told him.

'On the contrary –'

'Thomas they want to electrocute him!'

'Now really, Miss Banks.'

'It's Dr,' she said, 'and my name is Pepper now.'

'Of course. Forgive me. Now really you must see that we have little option. A patient has been entrusted to us for curing to the best of our ability.' He pushed a form of consent across the desktop to her. 'With the most developed of our techniques.'

'Yes but *you* must see!' Sally gasped, pushing back her chair to stand. Thomas glanced from her to Waltham, unsure. 'You must see you're asking me to allow you to try out a technique nobody really understands. ECT's hardly comparable with medication. You're asking me to let you fry his brains.'

'Now *really*.'

'Yes you are. Effectively. I want him well, himself, not permanently addled.'

'Which is precisely why ECT is the answer. In some depressive cases it has a remarkably stimulating effect.'

'Well of course it's stimulating, sticking that kind of voltage through the most finely-tuned organ in the body! The organ we know the least about! And what about the *other* depressive cases? For pity's sake, Thomas, say something.'

Thomas opened and shut his mouth, clearly worried but just as clearly at a loss for words.

'He's a composer, not a bricklayer,' she pursued, exasperated, turning back to Waltham. 'What happens if you do this to him and he can't read music any more? Hmm?'

'What happens if we *don't* do this to him?' Waltham countered. 'He vegetates. He becomes institutionalised. Precious little difference between a bricklayer and Beethoven then. What you're suggesting is highly unlikely in any case.'

'But possible.'

'Well . . .'

'Why else would you need my consent?'

'There's always an element of risk, as in any surgical operation.'

'How great a risk?' Thomas asked at last.

'Minimal,' Waltham told him, relieved to have a man to deal with.

'And there's no other option?' Thomas asked.

'Yes,' said Sally. 'He could come home with me. Now.'

'With all due respect,' Waltham said, showing her none, 'it was in *your* care, Doctor, that he nearly succeeded in killing himself.'

'How dare you!' Sally said, but the fight was leaving her and she sank back into her chair. Thomas rebuked Waltham.

'That was hardly necessary,' he said, then caught Sally's eye and said in a kinder tone, 'I hate to say this, dear girl, but –'

'What?' she asked.

'You're not the specialist here.'

'No,' she sighed. 'No. I'm just the wife.'

She reached for the form and tried to read it but her eyes were merely scanning the words and the legalistic sentences assumed no meaning for her.

'How many times will you have to – do it to him?' she asked, picturing electrodes, teeth clamped hard on a plastic bit, pyjamas loose around convulsion-wracked limbs.

'Once a week for a trial period.' Waltham's tone was

warmer, almost seductive, as he sniffed approaching surrender. She looked up and he held out a pen. 'We may not know precisely why it works,' he added, 'but it's not as though these things aren't done under strict clinical conditions. He'll be under constant observation. The treatment will be closely monitored. Any changes, good or bad, will be recorded and acted upon.'

'Yes yes,' she said, impatient now, and she took the pen.

She paused, searching his face for something she could trust. Would she, she wondered, react so emotively if the patient in question were but a patient. She looked from Waltham back to Thomas. He set his jaw and gave a barely perceptible nod. He was urging her to be brave.

As she signed, she felt both men subside into their chairs slightly with relief. For a moment it was as though it were she, the troublesome wife, and not Edward, who was being handed over to have an errant mind brought crudely to heel.

26

The little boat which ferried them out from the Dorset coast was filled with visiting relatives. It was Corry's annual Visitor's Day, an opportunity for dominant culture briefly to assert its mob superiority over the eccentric. Only one couple – a comfortable parson and his harassed-looking wife, whose nervous hands strayed repeatedly to touch the silver cross round her neck, as though even such plain adornment were too ostentatious – seemed likely family for a nun. The others – parents, married sisters, grown-up children – were stirring up the kind of camaraderie among themselves that implied a shared adversity. The way they brightly swopped holiday plans and public gossip with strangers was a way of making plain to one another that nuns, for them, represented the outmoded and unnatural. The women they were visiting on Corry – their daughters, sisters, mothers, whatever – had turned their back on everything these, their survivors, represented, on family, procreation, domesticity, social achievement. The facts of life, in short. The colourful boatload, with its potted plants, knitting, family snaps, tins of cake and chatter of politics and film stars, was a worldly, see-what-you-missed delegation. Women were wearing their prettiest dresses in much the same way that Sally persisted in carrying armfuls of flowers from The Roundel's garden to adorn Edward's hospital ward – behind the cheering display nestled a small thorn, an unconscious sting, to remind the visited of their rightful place.

Miriam dropped the rattle she had been shaking onto the deck with one of her inappropriately triumphant laughs.

Having stooped to return it to her hot little grasp, Sally tickled the tempting mound of her child's belly. Looking up to see their progress, she surprised a faintly covetous smile on the tired face of the parson's wife and guessed that this woman, after all, had also been nun-thwarted, deprived of the compensation of grandchildren.

Dr Pertwee was waiting well away from the flurry of her sisters on the shore. Sally found her on a rock, deep in conversation with a plump, lively Indian woman whom she recognised from Dr Pertwee's letters as Miss Bannerjee. Larger than her friend, Miss Bannerjee was furled in a vivid, gold-trimmed sari which flapped in the sea breeze. Even by her bird-like standards, Dr Pertwee had become shockingly thin. Her cheeks had sunk and there were dark stains beneath her eyes. The pair greeted Sally before paying brief, obligatory homage to Miriam.

'She looks so wise,' Miss Bannerjee laughed, as the baby devoured her with a stare from beneath her frilly sun hat, 'and so important. Like an imperial dignitary on a tedious mission.'

Then Miss Bannerjee's visitors arrived and Sally and Dr Pertwee were left alone together.

So much had passed between them in their recent letters that they said nothing at first. It was as though their physical selves needed time to catch up with the alterations made on paper during their long separation. When they did speak, walking slowly along the shoreline, well behind the boisterous crowd, it was deliberately of practicalities – Sally's journey, how long she could spare, Miriam's needs, the older Bankses' health – and not of emotions. Edward was not mentioned until they had visited Dr Pertwee's spartan room to fill Miriam's bottle and collect a picnic the old woman had amassed on the sly to spare them the hectic intrusiveness of a communal meal in the dining hall.

'Here, my dear, you take the things and let me carry this divine creature.'

'Are you sure you can manage? She already weighs a ton.'

'You're worried I'll drop her?'

'No.'

Sally smiled and passed her baby into Dr Pertwee's confident grasp, noting how huge she suddenly looked in the little woman's arms. As they left the room, she spotted the small photograph of Miriam she had posted with a letter. It was tucked into a dusty, framed picture of herself, aged about twelve, all hair and travelling teeth. She felt once again the queer ambiguity of being a daughter-elect.

Dr Pertwee led her down a spiral staircase, out of a low door, and through a walled herb and vegetable garden whose air hummed with bees from the community's hives. Several landed on the old woman's sleeve and Sally noted with surprise how calmly she brushed them off, unstung. They passed out onto a narrow headland, bristling with gorse and a few stunted pine trees and down to a tiny, sheltered beach.

'My secret place,' Dr Pertwee announced, as they settled into a natural sofa where tussocks of coarse grass and stout cushions formed by decades-old sea pinks sank into the sand. Hungry from all the fresh air and an early start, Sally dug in the bag and uncovered a clutch of roast chicken legs. Holding her food with one hand, Dr Pertwee twitched up her skirt a little with the other to let the sun onto her legs. She caught Sally noticing how skeletal they had become and leaned back with a sigh.

'I'm ill, you know, my dear,' she said.

'Yes,' said Sally. 'I'd guessed.'

'A year, they've given me. Six months to a year. It's really of no consequence. Ah the sun, the *sun*! It feels so good on old bones. I suppose it's because they're so much nearer the surface than plump-fleshed young ones.'

Sally stared out at the gentle waves for a moment. She was perturbed at how little pain the news had caused her – no more than a brief chill, as at a momentary clouding of the summer warmth. Had the dreadful months of Edward's suffering left her with such a hard crust? Perhaps it was simply that her friend's tranquillity was infectious.

'God,' she said. 'I'm so sorry.'

'Don't be. No point.'

'But can't I do something? Don't you want to see someone besides the doctor here? I could find you a specialist or –'

Dr Pertwee silenced her with a gentle touch on the forearm and a deep, kind look from her bottle green eyes as she shook her head.

'Listen, dear, I don't *want* to be kept alive. And for what it's worth, I've already ascertained that the dispensary here has a healthy stock of morphine.'

'Oh. Well. Good.'

Sally managed a smile and took Miriam back into her arms to let her suck at her bottle while her companion poured them each a glass tumbler of tart, slightly warm white wine with a homemade label on it. She admired the way the sun caught the faint down where the baby's pale hair began.

'A pity *he* isn't here to share this,' Dr Pertwee said. Sally caught her eye and looked back to Miriam but her daughter pulled back from the bottle with a miniature grimace and stared at her too, as if to say, 'Well?'

Sally sighed, wiped Miriam's mouth with a handkerchief and set her on the sand between her knees. She drew together some largish pebbles for her to play with. Miriam grasped one with both hands, laughed, dropped it, grasped another, laughed, dropped that. She seemed to be weighing them, divining against some mysterious scale which was the best, which was most quintessentially pebble. Occasionally one of the small waves broke with a slight crash and Miriam would start, threatening to lose her balance in the effort to face the source of the noise.

'I wish I knew what to do,' Sally began. 'It's so unlike me to be so indecisive. At first I was so scared. I only told them about him trying to kill himself. I didn't like to say anything about him hitting me or going for Miriam like that. I mean, Thomas knows, of course, and you, but I thought if I told Ernest Waltham he'd be. Oh. I don't know. I'm rambling aren't I?'

Dr Pertwee smiled kindly.

'Yes. Go back to when you were scared.'

'I was scared. Being on my own back in the house, just me and Miriam, I felt so safe. But when I went to see him he seemed so harmless, and desperate. I suppose, if I'm honest, I feel I've failed him. Thomas keeps saying the specialists know what they're doing and I should trust them, but in a way I still think of Edward as my patient as well as my lover.'

'You haven't failed him in love.'

'Haven't I? Well I've failed him as a doctor. I managed to get Mum to take Miriam for a day last week and I spent an afternoon in the medical faculty library. I read up on ECT. It seems it affects memory. Some researchers claim it can wipe out whole tracts of memories. Well I may not be a specialist, but even I can see that he needs to come to terms with whatever's in his past if he's to be well again, not lose it altogether. I think memories could be the key. They've tried drugs on him. They've tried vitamins. I know depression can be purely chemical and I know it's sacrilege for a doctor to say so, but in this case I think their approach is just too bloody scientific. When someone cries, you don't say shut up, have a pill, you try to find out why they're crying, surely?'

'And aren't they trying?'

'Oh I think Caldecott tries to talk to him, but you know how cold Waltham is.'

'A human fish.'

'Caldecott's pretty feeble too, anyway. The ward's so crowded that no-one can get proper attention. And the other thing I can't stand is Mum's attitude. She manages to imply that it was somehow my fault. She can't bear people knowing. I found out she's been telling them he's gone to Hollywood for a bit. She seems to think I should have soldiered nobly on in private, cured him with sex or better cooking or something.'

Dr Pertwee chuckled. Sally went on.

'And last week she was daring to say we should never have had Miriam, that it could be genetic. I *hate* leaving Miriam with her, even this young. I can't bear the thought of what she might pick up.'

'You didn't pick up much.'

'I picked up more than you suppose,' Sally said with a grin. 'The apples don't fall so far from the tree. Anyway, I had you to counteract her. And why are you laughing? It's not funny.'

Dr Pertwee opened her penknife and began to peel a pear. Its juice ran over her gnarled fingers and plopped into sudden dimples in the sand. She stopped laughing but made no response until she had cut off a slice and eaten it thoughtfully.

'We survive,' she said at last. 'It's the harshest lesson of all; worse than sickness, worse than losing the one you love – and believe me, dear girl, I've lost *plenty* one way or another. I don't know how we do it, but we survive. Compared to the perfected simplicity of the lower animals, man seems expressly designed to suffer, punish his fellows and destroy himself. He's been given faculties to make every bad thing worse by analysing it and comparing it with the bad things that went before. Worst of all, he remembers so acutely that he can relive any suffering he might be in danger of forgetting. But he survives. Exhausting really, but there it is. It will be a relief to stop, frankly. Oh Sally Banks you are a sweet fool, but no-one could ever change your mind for you. Anyway, I can see, beneath all this hand-wringing, that it's already firmly made up. Now *please* don't cry. I said *don't*! Oh hell. Here. Use mine.'

Sally's handkerchief was too damp with milk to be of much use. She took Dr Pertwee's with mumbled thanks and blew her nose. Miriam looked up at her mother briefly then returned happily to clicking her pebbles.

'I don't *want* you to die,' Sally said at last.

'Well thank you *very* much. I moan about what hell life has been and you say you want me to have more of it. Such selfishness!'

'Sorry. But you know what I'm trying to say.'

'Yes,' the older woman said quietly. 'And thank you.'

'What did you mean just then about me making up my mind?'

Dr Pertwee busied herself peeling another pear.

'You're going to take him away from the doctors and try to care for him at home,' she said.

'But I never –'

'And it's going to be hell, but gradually it'll get better and then you'll hardly notice you're suffering at all.' She held out a chunk of dripping fruit for Sally to take and watched her bite into its delicious, sun-warmed flesh. 'You're a sweet fool,' she said again, suddenly serious, 'but you'll live.'

27

The room was yellow. Edward knew every detail of it like an overly familiar text. The high windows with their flaking paint and unpeopled view of brickwork, tree and sky. The fire precaution notice and accompanying, padlocked extinguisher. He read the patterns of clouds without further understanding. He strove to learn the language of the old radiators, annotating in his head their vocabulary of clicks and gurgles as though it might impart some secret purpose of the institution that housed him. Yet a pattern in their sounds no sooner began to emerge, filling him with an urgent desire to write it down or rouse one of his fellows to tell him, than it dissolved before the wavering light of his comprehension.

At first he was kept heavily sedated. He would wake, allow himself to be led, shuffling, to bathroom and dining room but, whether eating, bathing, or simply sitting in a chair beside his bed, he did not mentally enter the scene around him. The drugs made him neither elated nor depressed. Rather, they seemed to suppress his emotional and mental life altogether. This state, in which he was reduced to a kind of walking plant, registering sun on his skin or a draught on his ankles but little more, was as welcome after his recent turmoil as sleep after labour. To be sure that he was taking them, the nurses liked to place the drugs straight onto his tongue. Their fears of subterfuge were groundless; when the pill trolley was wheeled to the end of his bed he began to salivate on cue.

People talked to him. The patient in the next bed lay stroking his pillow and poured out melancholy, circular monologues about the hopelessness of trying to communicate with others. Edward learned to avoid the man's eye and so evade the unwanted confidences. Other patients needed little encouragement to leave him in peace, cast, as each was, as the lead in his own drama, which left the staff. A nurse led him repeatedly to a room with a large, stuffed fish, where a man with a kind face and a tweedy suit sat back in a leather armchair and asked him questions.

'Does my pipe bother you?'

'Do you dream?'

'What does this image suggest to you?'

He had a manner which inspired confidence and, ordinarily, Edward might have liked to talk with him. Even when the doctor's words made sense, however, Edward found his encounters with him unreal. The one-way conversations were as impossible to enter as dreams in which he was mouthless, doomed to observe. This did not bother Edward especially. He was beyond bother.

Sally came to see him, as did Thomas. Sometimes they came separately, sometimes together. When Thomas came alone, he sat in silence, close to the bed, and held Edward's hand. Often he did this without meeting Edward's eye. Edward felt Thomas's caress and Sally's bright words the same way he felt the sunlight on his skin. And Sally's needy hugs and Thomas's sad, loving gaze. All were welcome sensations, but he could only receive them passively. Sometimes his inability to stir himself sufficiently in response caused a terrible panic to boil up inside him, a feeling he could only counteract by lying quite still and closing his eyes. He dreaded decisions being made about his welfare in his hearing, as though he were no more than a corpse. As the weeks went by, however, he would occasionally hear a mumbling voice responding to his visitors' and doctor's enquiries and realise that it was his, but he no sooner heard it than he slipped back into watchful wordlessness, discomfited as a man sunk in mortification after obeying a sudden compulsion to call out to an actor on a cinema screen.

There was no clock in the ward and Edward's watch had vanished with his clothes. For the first time in his life, he lost all track of the passage of time. He knew day from night and that his days were divided up by more or less indistinguishable meals, heralded by a gurgling in his stomach, but to tell whether it was Monday or Friday, the twelfth or the thirty-first, was beyond him. He had a birthday, marked by cards, a cake and a new pair of slippers. This gave him a date to seize on briefly, but he soon lost it again and did not especially care. Sometimes he seemed to miss a day. Sometimes it seemed he had no sooner fallen asleep than it was time to rise again. He had been liberated from numbers as utterly as he had been liberated from bother.

Then the comfortable doctor was replaced by one whose shining pate, fat hands and penetrating, sarcastic gaze were dimly familiar to him. He explained that he was going to treat Edward's brain with electric shocks sufficiently strong to send him into convulsions.

'Don't be afraid,' he said. 'There is no cause. These shocks will heal you and the process will be quite painless. Think of it as a necessary but controlled violence, like shaking out the creases from a sheet.'

He explained it as though it were the most ordinary thing in the world and Edward believed him.

'I have your wife's consent,' the fat doctor added. 'Have you any questions?'

The merest hint of a smile twitched the corners of his lips, as though he were well aware of the unlikelihood of Edward's mustering any response, much less anything so assertive as a question. Sure enough, Edward merely shook his head.

The shocks did hurt. He was led to a treatment room where he had to lie on a couch. Nurses tied his arms and ankles down and made him bite on a plastic spatula. A wet substance was smeared on his temples before something not unlike a pair of the bakelite studio headphones was slipped over them. Then followed an instant of shattering pain which, invariably, caused him to black out. When he came round, his arms and legs were untied and the apparatus had been wheeled away. He ached all over, his tongue felt far too large for his mouth, his head, as though it might float grotesquely off his shoulders. The strange thing was that the memory of lying down, of the electrodes and the brief, outrageous pain was wiped out afresh with each treatment. Each time he was led back to the treatment room he felt a gnawing sense of recognition which flared into sudden, sickening *déjà-vu* for the brief instant of the electric shock, only to be smothered again by the shock's after-effect. He found he began to reach for words and be unable to find them, even if he wanted only to think them, not to speak them aloud. It seemed as though the ice that held him over the abyss were being methodically melted from below, but to express his fears aloud was increasingly beyond him.

As the strength of his night-time medication was reduced, he began to dream again or, at least, to recall his dreams for a few confused minutes on waking. He had a recurring nightmare in which he was pursuing someone or something through a set of empty rooms. The rooms opened out into each other to form a circle but, although he tugged each door open, he would find it firmly closed again when he returned to it. He knew it was vitally important for him to maintain his pursuit. If he stopped, not only would the doors become impossible to open but he would cease to be the hunter and become the prey. And yet, even as he persisted he felt the doors inexorably stiffen until he was having to squeeze through little more than a crack and his quarry's progress grew louder behind him.

'I dream now,' he managed to tell Dr Caldecott, the man with the stuffed fish.

'And what precisely do you dream about?'

'I . . . I . . .' Edward stumbled. 'Trains.'

'Trains?' From the doctor's frown it was clear he expected more than this.

'Trains,' Edward repeated and retreated back into silence.

Superficially his dreams had nothing to do with trains, it was true, but now it seemed to him that in allowing the word to rise unbidden to his lips, he had somehow blundered on to the very essence of his nightmare horror and there was no more to be said.

Even as the treatment fogged his recent memories, they seemed to revive images from the distant past. Inspired perhaps by similarities of institutional life, the same smells, the same long corridors, the same all-powerful, all-male routines, he began to recall his schooldays in minute, even insane detail. His English schooldays. He remembered timetables exactly: Latin before breakfast, double Maths on Saturday morning, divinity on Sunday night. He remembered the brutalities disguised in sports clothes, depths of hypocrisy plumbed in order to escape senseless punishment. He remembered hard little fists, relentlessly vindictive tongues, the stripping away of privacy, the pervasiveness of sarcasm, the difficult ambiguities of friendship. Now his personality was submerged by what? Fear. Medication. Electric currents. Back then he had learnt to submerge it voluntarily, learnt to suppress the characteristics most likely to attract derision or violence and, crucially, to offer mimicry as a kind of pacifying homage to the boys most likely to cause him harm. Letting his eyes stare, without seeing, at a few feet of yellow wall or clouded sky, Edward found himself trapped by remorseless memory in an environment where he lived in daily fear of exposure.

When Sally burst into the ward early one evening, pursued by an angrily remonstrating nurse, threw a coat about him and led him to the door, she unwittingly offered the eleventh hour reprieve every child in boarding-school prayed for.

'We're going home,' she said.

'Please,' he told her, tightly holding her hand. 'Yes.'

28

Sally had retrieved Edward – she thought of it as a kind of rescue – without discussing the matter with Thomas, her parents, anyone. What she was doing made her so nervous that, if she allowed someone to dissuade her, she could never again find the necessary resolve. Waltham was furious of course, threatening her that having once discharged her husband, she could not have him readmitted, but she found that his anger only stoked up her determination. Once she had Edward in the car, however, and was driving home, the enormity of what she had done dawned on her. She kept glancing across at him, fretful lest he fling open his door while they were moving or become violent, but he merely sat hugging himself and staring with a kind of greed through the dusk at the passing countryside. She had taken the precaution of chatting with a show of professional curiosity with a nurse during previous visits so she knew exactly what medication he was on. If all else failed, she could always approach Dr Richards to prescribe him some.

She drove back to The Roundel via her parents' house, leaving Edward in the car while she darted in to collect Miriam. Miriam stirred sleepily as Sally transferred her from her bed to a carrycot, but she was dead to the world within minutes of their returning to the Wolseley. Edward said nothing but he watched his sleeping child for a few minutes before turning back to face the road. Sally took her straight to bed as soon as they were home, leaving Edward walking in the garden. She turned from switching off the light to find him standing in the doorway. She gasped.

'You made me jump,' she said.

'I'm sorry,' he murmured. 'Is . . . is she asleep?'

'Yes.'

Sally smiled and touched his chest, gently pushing him back onto the landing as she half-closed the door. To her surprise, Edward took her hand in both of his and pressed it. Then, hesitantly, he put his arms around her and drew her to him. Their movements felt as awkward as those of inexperienced dancers. He smelled strong, feral. She hugged him back, pressing her nose into the base of his neck and breathing deeply against his skin, which was still cold from the car.

'I'm sorry,' he said again.

'No,' she replied.

He sighed heavily into her hair, once, twice, and then he began to cry. But this was not like his crying before. Then it had seemed like the expression of an anguish he could not express with words, now it had lost the edge of desperation. Now his sobs felt like the uncoiling of more straightforward, pent-up emotion. Whereas before she had found his tears alienated her, this time she found they gave access to a direct communication. Within seconds, she was crying too, for him, for her, for Miriam, for Dr Pertwee. Leaning against him, she sobbed with relief, heaving up the griefs and tensions that had been choking her. Clinging together in the darkness, they staggered, leant against the wall and eventually slumped to the chilly floor where they sat, clinging, pawing, stroking one another as they fell slowly silent. Sally felt an insidious quickening of her flesh, a kind of sweet inability to get close enough to him, then recognised the under-rehearsed sensation as desire. She turned her head slightly and planted a stealthy kiss on the skin below his ear. Then she realised his teeth were chattering and came to her senses.

'My God,' she said. 'You're still in those pyjamas! You're freezing. I'll run you a bath.'

He began the night in the room adjoining hers, pyjamas buttoned up to his neck, blankets pulled up to his chin. The sudden change of scene and withdrawal from sleeping tablets made him restless, however. Several times in the night she woke to hear him pacing about the landing or saw light in the crack beneath their interconnecting door. In the early hours of the morning he crept into her room and slipped with an apologetic mumble into her bed. They did not make love, although several times she felt his erection press her thigh, merely lay close, loin to buttocks, knee to knee-back, his chest against her shoulders, his arm heavy below her breasts. It was as if separation had begun to alter their shapes and they needed to mould themselves to one another afresh.

She found he liked to shadow her about the house and garden, mutely offering tentative help with her tasks. It was only with Miriam that he held back, for all Sally's encouragement, but as she fed her, changed her clothes, brushed her emerging curls, he watched intently. Once, when Miriam tossed a toy aside and laughed her laugh of triumph, he looked as though he were about to smile. On one occasion, he spent longer than usual in the bathroom. Suddenly uneasy, Sally ran along the landing and called out to him. Emerging, he nearly smiled again, but contented himself with a sort of snort as he caught the relief in her expression.

'When I think of what they might have done to him,' she told Thomas, as they watched at a window while Edward pegged out nappies to dry, 'it makes me seethe. I mean, I know he was withdrawn, but I'm sure half that speechlessness was drug-induced.'

She had no fond belief in the healing power of her love, not now, but she trusted to a peaceful atmosphere, and time. Without her forcing him, he began to offer up shy fragments of conversation; simple discussions of food, flowers, weather. She brought Thomas over often, persuading him to stay overnight, in the hope that his presence might stimulate Edward too.

Her abiding fear was that the electro-convulsive therapy had somehow damaged his musical abilities. When she wrote to the studio insurers to say that he was out of hospital and should soon be available again for work it was with a certain superstitious dread at the hopeful deceit in her statement. Days later, Jerry rang in great excitement to say that Edward's score for *4.15 To Bucharest* had been nominated for an Oscar.

'Don't worry about the money. We'll fly the pair of you out there for the ceremony, just in case. What do you say?'

'Oh Jerry, that's so exciting!' she enthused, genuinely pleased, but at the same time tense at the prospect of having her hand forced. 'I'm sure he'll be thrilled. He's asleep now or I'd call him to the phone.'

'So you'll both come to Hollywood?'

'Jerry we can't. Not really. I just don't think he's up to it yet. Soon, I'm sure, but not just yet.'

Jerry had made understanding noises and said of course someone else could collect the award for Edward if he won, but she heard behind his words the rustle of fading contracts and impatient ticking of financial clocks. Edward still tended to turn radio programmes off when there was too much talking, but he had begun to listen to records, sitting close to the radiogram on a stool and scrutinising sleeve notes intently.

He won the Oscar. Jerry rang from California in the middle of the night. She woke Edward to tell him the amazing news but he seemed singularly unimpressed. The studio sent newspaper photographers to picture an actor dressed as a postman delivering the statuette. Edward smiled obediently for the cameras, clutching the thing while Sally stood proudly beside him, Miriam in her arms, and he said a few words to the local newspapermen. Sally's parents were tremendously proud and Thomas had champagne delivered 'to wet young Oscar's head' but after the fuss had died down, Edward climbed the ladder in his study to set the thing on a high shelf along with the bound manuscript of *Job*. Sally had begun to fret seriously about money, and was convinced the studio would not pay his salary indefinitely, so the award came as a huge relief, since even *in absentia* Edward could be seen to be earning his keep. When an American studio rang to enquire about his contractual situation she referred them to Jerry Liebermann, secure in the knowledge that the enquiry would raise Edward's value.

Then, one day, she was tugging dirty sheets off the bed when she was surprised by the sound of the piano. She walked onto the landing and looked down. Miriam was strapped into her high chair, her hands patting vaguely at the toys before her but her gaze concentrated entirely on her father. Edward was sitting at the keyboard. He played a few simple chords, then a cadence or two. Although the piano needed tuning, he seemed to be relishing the simple harmonic progressions, the resolution of one chord in the more open texture of the one that followed. Miriam banged the tray before her and let out a delighted shout. Edward looked up at her and smiled, truly smiled. Then he walked into his study, came back with a lapful of music books, riffled roughly through them, selected something, dumped the rest on the floor with a bang and began to play. It was a sweet, trilling melody with a burbling accompaniment in the left hand. Miriam shouted again and tossed a teddy towards the piano. Spotting Sally leaning on the landing balustrade, Edward looked up as he continued playing.

'Wouldn't you know it!' he laughed, 'she likes Clementi, of all things!'

After weeks of cracked mumbling, it was a shock to hear him using his full voice. Sally smiled encouragement but said nothing, frightened he might stop, but he played solidly for over an hour. It was as though his musical language and interest in his daughter had burst simultaneously through a soft wall in his mind like a flashing spring of new water. He tried piece after piece, testing Miriam's reactions, although her gurgles and shouts were probably as much a reaction to her father's sudden vivacity as to the harmonies he was producing.

After dealing with the washing, Sally threw open the door to the garden and began to sweep the steps in the wintry sunshine. Behind her, Edward continued to play, Miriam to shout, oblivious of the arrival of the postman. He brought an electricity bill and a late holiday postcard from her parents, who were already back from visiting friends at Hastings. There was also a thin envelope with a Dorset postmark. Frowning at the unfamiliar writing, her heart telling her in advance of its contents, Sally tore the letter out and sat on the steps to read the news of her old friend and second mother's death.

29

Sally swore on discovering she had left her umbrella behind when dropping off Miriam with her father. She switched off the wind-screen wiper and peered out across Westmarket's broad main street to the imposing entrance of the Grand Hotel. The torrential rain showed no sign of slackening up. She turned up her raincoat collar, tucking the tails of her headscarf well down inside it, braced herself, and opened the car door. Her coat was drenched almost to blackness before she could even cross the road and she arrived in the hotel lobby as inelegant and crossly shuddering as a waterlogged cat. Above the quiet chink-chinking of tea things in the dining room, a violin played sentimental melodies. Sensing the eyes of staff and guests on her, as they padded about the thickly carpeted lobby, Sally shook as much rain as she could from her coat, untied her clammy scarf and ran a comb through her hair. She looked about her.

Miss Bannerjee was reading the *Telegraph* on a corner sofa, her legs stretched out before her. She wore shiny, bright-buckled patent leather sandals, merely a few inches in length. The newspaper almost hid her; it was only a tell-tale flash of canary yellow silk, as she smacked the wrinkle from a page, which caught Sally's eye and stopped her walking straight past.

'Miss Bannerjee?'

The paper was lowered and Miss Bannerjee's eyes were at once wide with concern.

'But you're soaked. I'll get us more tea. Waiter! Another pot please. And brandy. My guest must have a shot of brandy. With perhaps a splash of Stone's ginger wine.'

A brief fight with the waiter ensued, in which he insisted that such things could not be served at such a time. Miss Bannerjee won the day by raising a voice as shrill as her clothing was exotic and invoking the cause of Medicinal Purposes.

Warmed with brandy, her coat and scarf despatched to the hotel's bowels for drying, Sally sat back in an armchair to face the executor of Dr Pertwee's estate.

'Your letter mentioned the will,' she said. 'I've been so worried about it, I didn't like to tell my husband. Is there some problem about The Roundel?'

'Absolutely none. The legal papers confirming Alice's adoption of you and the deeds to the house are still in the safekeeping of her bankers in Rexbridge. They merely await your collection. As she had expected, her relatives in Surrey kicked up something of a stink. They came to Corry for the funeral and when they saw that you weren't there and then heard the terms of the will, which stipulates that your daughter is to inherit the house after you, they had you down as something of a gold-digger –'

'But I couldn't possibly have got there!' Sally protested. 'I explained at the time; my husband –'

Miss Bannerjee raised both her small palms to calm her, clattering silver bracelets on her wrists.

'Of course you couldn't. And I made it quite clear to them. Anyway, as Alice had predicted, they seemed perfectly pacified with her legacy of jewellery – far more valuable than the house and much less bothersome to maintain. However there was one thing she wanted held back for you.'

'But she'd given me so much already,' Sally sighed. She had no use for valuable jewellery and dreaded anything which might further antagonise the mysterious Surrey cousins.

Muttering to herself, Miss Bannerjee heaved a big, old-fashioned leather brief-case on to the sofa beside her and thrust an arm through its brass-studded maw. She groped for a moment then raised her eyebrows and brought out something wrapped in royal blue spotted silk.

'There,' she said, placing it with a clunk on the table between them. She poured them more tea. 'From Alice. A final legacy.'

Sally lifted the bundle to her side of the table. It was surprisingly heavy. She unknotted the silk and folded it back to reveal a layer of yellowed newspaper. Peeling that aside she found a carved stone figure. It was female, with sharply conical breasts and an exaggerated lap, broad enough to bear up twins, or even a grown man. The hair was wound up underneath a crude crown, the eyes were inscrutable slits and the full mouth was pulled back in what could have been a smile, could have been a growl. The stone was icy to the touch. Sally shivered involuntarily.

'Oh,' she said.

'She's no beauty, certainly,' said Miss Bannerjee, 'but there's a vigour to her. I'm afraid I couldn't resist taking a closer look on the train here.'

'I've never seen her before.'

'Alice had been keeping her in storage. She brought her out – perhaps with a view to ensuring she reached you – and had her on her bedside table throughout her last illness. She's an Anglian princess. Or a goddess, perhaps. She was dug up in the peat during excavations to build The Roundel apparently. So she really belongs in the house. Look at the strength of those arms! Blessings in one hand and cruel destruction in the other, I should say. Alice's family had always kept her quiet in case the place was invaded by bossy archaeologists. The Surrey cousins made no mention of her during their scavenging, so I can only assume that even they don't know of her existence.'

Sally set the figure back on the table to look at her for a moment then felt compelled to pick her up again, feel her small density, chill and weighty in her hands. Repelled as she was, she could not help admiring the passive force with which the carving asserted its ancient identity over the scene of genteel cake-slaughter.

'I've no doubt that she's worth a great deal to a museum or a specialist buyer,' Miss Bannerjee added firmly, 'but Alice was adamant that she shouldn't be sold.'

'But of course,' Sally agreed. 'I wonder what she's called.'

'Oh, deities are far more potent when they're nameless. Think of the tremendous difference in his worldly standing when Jehovah became simply God! That was cheating, really; using a generic mopped up the too-specific opposition.'

'Whatever shall I do with her?'

'Shut her in a broom cupboard? Honour her with flowers? It really doesn't matter. She's only a lump of stone.'

'Yes,' Sally laughed. 'Of course she is.'

But even though she knew Miss Bannerjee's words to be entirely rational, she couldn't help registering a shaft of discomfort at their flippancy. She noticed too the insistence with which they each acknowledged the statue's gender; she was firmly a She, not an It.

Sally began the drive home with the statue, furled in its wrappings again, on the passenger seat beside her. Then she found herself unnerved by the way it rocked whenever she turned a corner, so she stuffed it into a pocket of her coat. Hidden in layers of cloth, it rested between her thighs.

The rain, which had barely stopped for three days, remained insistent. Whenever a car or van turned into her path, she would drop well back to avoid the great wash of spray sent up over her windscreen. The Wolseley was a venerable machine whose wiper could barely clear the water before the screen was awash once more. Twice the rain became so torrential that she was forced to pull over, unable to see the road ahead. She passed through Rexbridge, fighting down the temptation to take shelter in Thomas's comfortable house, and set out, instead, towards her parents' cottage at Wenborough. She was barely into the fringes of the fens when she found the road ahead blocked by the surreal sight of a policeman in waders, vainly trying to shelter under a black umbrella. He flagged her down and she cranked down her window.

'Sorry, Miss,' he shouted through the downpour. 'You'll have to find another route. The road up ahead's blocked.'

'What with?'

'Flood. It's the high spring tides. Sedwich Dyke's burst its bank.'

'No!'

'Where are you trying to get to, Miss? You don't want to go too far in this. That car doesn't look like it could handle much.'

'Not far,' she lied, winding up her window. 'I'll find another route, maybe via Methwold. Thank you, Officer.'

She stopped at the next hamlet: There was a telephone kiosk marooned in a great brown puddle. Her feet were soaked as she dashed across. She fumbled with her change purse as she dialled with numb fingers. She rang The Roundel first, to reassure Edward that she was coming. This was the first time she had left him alone for more than an hour since his return. There was a pair of milk churns on a slate shelf beside the kiosk. She could barely hear the ringing tone above the din of the water drumming on their lids. She let it ring and ring. He didn't answer. Praying he had not been foolish enough to venture out on her motorbike in the wet, she hung up and dialled her parents to explain that she would be later than arranged in picking up Miriam. She could not get through. The operator calmly assured her that a line was down and that normal service would be resumed as soon as possible.

30

The chord circled in the air, a pure, naked triad made to vibrate with a new keenness by the addition of a single dissonance. Holding it in place with the *sostenuto* pedal, Edward scratched on the manuscript with his pen, the tip of his tongue brushing his upper lip in his concentration. Then, holding the pen in his teeth, he played swiftly through the last four lines he had written and saw at once how they could be improved. Just as he began to write again, the telephone rang. He frowned, hesitated a moment, but managed to ignore its insistent interruption. The terrific wind blew a bedroom window open and set it flapping on its hinges. He knew the rain would be coming in now and staining the floor, but he managed to ignore that too. The seemingly impossible was happening: he was working again.

It had happened, like so many of the recent alterations in his behaviour, in slow, blurred degrees, perceptible only with hind-sight. At first he had merely played the piano. In his schooldays, his piano teacher never trusted him to practise enough during the holidays and forbade him to play anything in the first days of a new term but meticulous Bach and page upon page of studies. Remembering this, Edward had spent the days following his rediscovery of the piano working on his technique with the guarded determination of an athlete recovering from painful injury. Deep in a box of music he found his dog-eared copy of Hanon's *The Virtuoso Pianist* and began to play daily once through its merciless system of finger-stretching exercises, scales and arpeggios. He permitted himself no flaws, punishing each mistake by returning to the beginning of the study in hand. His teacher would have been proud of him.

'You don't mind?' Edward asked Sally. 'It isn't driving you crazy?'

She shook her head, but was unable, as she encouraged him, to prevent a fleeting smile at his ironic choice of words.

For he had been crazy. He saw that now. Thomas and Sally called it 'severe depression'. Thomas found him books and poems by fellow sufferers, as though by recognising his symptoms in literature, Edward might place them in some demystifying, historical perspective. As though a man with skin erupted in deadly buboes might be comforted to read *Journal of the Plague Year*. They called it depression and Edward was content to let them. They could not know of the waking dreams he had suffered, the unspeakable fears that had pursued him. His recovery was still in progress and he shied away from society, uncertain still of how he might behave. He was, however, far enough recovered to be aware of the depths of irrationality he had plumbed. Waking to look around his bedroom without its contents seeming to condemn and threaten him, he felt he could begin to regard what had happened as something slipping away from him into the past, a separate thing, his breakdown. Waking in the darkness, however, from one of the nightmares that still seeped from within him, sour juices from an unhealing sore, he was afraid lest such blessed mornings represented only a brief, fool's dawn in a night without end.

As well as the Hanon studies, he taught himself the *Goldberg Variations* again. He had not played them since his teens and was daunted to realise how strong his technique must have been then and how flabby it had become in the interim. He dissected and reassembled them, one variation at a time, marvelling at the games Bach played, crossing hands, inverting melodies, interweaving three or four lines at a time, spinning sonic illusions in the listener's mind from the web on the page. He was forcing himself to play through one of the movements towards the end of the set, with a metronome clicking in his ear, when the telephone rang. For weeks, Sally had been answering it, protecting him from the outside world with words like 'resting' and 'studying', but she was pushing Miriam's pram around the garden and Edward was at once so relaxed and preoccupied that he answered without thinking. It was Jerry Liebermann.

'Teddy! Good to hear your voice!'

Edward hesitated a moment. Fat, rich, cigar-thickened, the sound conjured up in an instant an environment he had fled and barely contemplated since. He pictured Jerry at his sham-Louis Quinze desk in his sham-Rococo office, where the latest from his stable of starlets was languidly checking her seams in a mirror. Jerry's voice cut in on his imaginings.

'So the Oscar-winner's back in the land of the living.'

'Er, yes. I think so.'

'You *think* so? Same wicked sense of humour.' Jerry chuckled richly. 'We've missed you, you know. Listen, Teds, are you ready to work? I'll tell you why. I've got a project. Something new. Very daring. Very . . . modern. But the music's going to be an integral part. You heard of Schnitzler?'

'I've heard of Schnitzler.'

'Well that's one better than me. Anyway, it's an adaptation from Schnitzler, but modern dress. Very sexy. And like I say, the music is going to be very up front. We're even calling it *Theme and Variations*.'

'Hmm.'

'Nice, isn't it? *Classy*. But we need the kind of score people talk about afterwards, something they can play on the radio, and only you will do. What do you say? We miss you, Teds. Don't disappoint us.'

So Edward found himself working again. But this time Sally intervened and insisted he work from home until it was absolutely necessary to visit the studio.

'And even then,' she told Jerry, 'if he's not up to it, he's coming straight home.'

They celebrated with the bottle of champagne Thomas had sent in honour of the Oscar. This led to them making love again for the first time since Miriam's birth. And since Edward's encounter with Myra . . . He was so nervous he came almost immediately.

'Honestly,' she assured him. 'It doesn't matter. Really.'

But he could sense her frustration and when they woke the next morning to find that, by some miracle, Miriam was content to gurgle to herself in her cot, he managed to hold back for a little longer.

'It's like learning all over again,' he explained, frantic now at the thought of what he had imperilled and so nearly lost. 'I love you so much. You know that, don't you?'

'I know that.'

'Hold me.'

'Ssh. I'm here.'

The renewed lovemaking, faintly alarming at first for one whose life had been temporarily rearranged so as to be as unexciting as possible, began to irradiate Edward's uneventful days with a kind of glow. His experiences with Myra, buried behind the wall of his breakdown and its treatments, now seemed aberrations, almost a part of his illness. He looked at Sally, at The Roundel, at music with a new fascination. The lovemaking altered entirely his reaction to his child, too. Watchful respect tinged with fear lest he do something wrong was swept away by little surges of physical delight in her presence. Emboldened by Sally, he carried her around with him until impatience made her fractious. He showed her how to bang the piano keys, and sat by her high chair encouraging her – to Sally's irritation – to clink her spoon against her bowl or clap her little food-smeared hands together in wild, spontaneous rhythms. He made Sally show him how to wash her and change her nappies, astonished at the huge turds such a tiny animal could produce. He even tried to annotate musically the noises she made, weaving them into his score for *Theme and Variations* as a personal memento. Whenever Sally had to go out, even briefly, she still took Miriam with her rather than leave her alone with him. This was never discussed. He remembered enough to understand her motives perfectly, however, and connived in the pretence that it was because he needed peace and quiet to work.

Sally moved back into his bed permanently, establishing Miriam's nursery in the room next door. He woke from a nightmare one night to find her arms about him.

'You were screaming,' she said. 'I was frightened.'

'There's something I should tell you,' he heard himself begin. 'Something I've done.'

'Yes?'

Her kind, expectant face in the lamplight was so utterly reassuring that he only just pulled back in time from a spontaneous confession. He could not tell her about Myra. It meant nothing and would only hurt her needlessly. He had to tell her something, though. She was waiting. He wanted instead to explain about his sister but, just as he had found himself explaining away a nightmare as being about 'trains', so he now found himself owning up instead to a long forgotten crime he had committed at school. There had been a boy, a third son, Wykeham Minimus, a weakling whom everybody teased as a matter of course, a matter of honour even. As a fellow victim, Edward had won a small measure of valuable esteem in his oppressors' eyes by a piece of inspired cruelty.

'It was quite straightforward really,' he told Sally, turning his face from the lamp's accusatory glare as he lay in her arms. 'He was known to be homesick and I had noticed that his voice was peculiarly bovine, especially when he was upset. So, one night when he was up late on bog duty –'

'*Bog* duty!?'

'Er. Yes. It was his night to clean all the lavatories. All the junior boys were meant to do it. There was a roster. But some were forced to do it more than others.'

Sally snorted with disgust. Edward went on.

'Anyway, while he was up late cleaning the lavatories, I took the photograph of his mother from the little frame beside his bed, tore it up and replaced it with a big picture of a cow from a condensed milk label. When he came to bed I made a mooing noise until he noticed the photograph frame. After that everyone did it to him all the time. Whenever he spoke, even in classes, they mooed.'

'How horrible.'

'Yes. He became extremely withdrawn. There were worse things. Done to other boys by other people. Arms were broken. Once someone was even killed, with a rifle – which was passed off as an accident, of course. But this was my thing. I don't know why I should suddenly have remembered it.'

'Do you want me to absolve you?'

Edward examined his conscience for a moment, thinking about Wykeham Minimus, then about his sister, puffed up, senseless. Then he thought of Myra, reapplying her lipstick by the light of a burning match.

'No,' he said. 'I was only young after all. I just wanted you to know.'

'Little boys are horrible.'

'Yes. Usually.'

He had finally managed to tell her about his sister that morning, before she left to meet Miss Bannerjee, forcing her to sit down and listen when she was hurrying about getting Miriam ready to go to her parents. He sat her on the sofa beside him and held her hands. He told her about the hospital, about how fat and simple-minded Miriam had become. He told her about her tattoo, the scar on her skull and what it signified. Tears sprang into her eyes and she held him to her, gently rocking him as she did their baby.

'I killed her,' he said.

'It was a heart attack,' she insisted. 'The doctor said so.'

'No. No,' he said, shaking his head but she silenced him, staring urgently, closely, into his face as if reassuring an irrationally frightened child.

'Edward you mustn't blame yourself. You *mustn't*! You're just feeling guilty because it was her and not you.'

'No. You don't –'

'Edward listen to me: it was beyond your control. You were not to blame. They sent you to safety, you didn't choose to go. You were only a boy, for Christ's sake. Just be glad she was set free. She must have suffered so dreadfully. Think what memories she must have been carrying inside her! The dreams! No-one should be kept alive in such a state. It was inhuman.'

'But I *killed* her!' he insisted.

'No, Edward. No.' She refused to believe him with such calmness that he was almost persuaded. 'But if you had, it would have been an act of kindness.'

'So,' he asked, thinking now of how Myra had led him so firmly into the dark by the hand. 'Do you absolve me?'

'Ssh. Don't be silly.' She held him again, avoiding his staring eyes and softly chuckling at her response to his previous confession. 'You didn't *do* anything. It was a heart attack. You might have wanted to put her out of her misery but, effectively, she killed herself.' She pulled back, looked at him and kissed him softly on the lips. 'I really must go,' she said gently. 'I've got to get there before Miss Bannerjee has to catch her train back to Dorset. I won't be too long. You're sure you'll be all right?'

'Sure.' He gave her a wry smile. 'I'll be fine.'

He was straining his eyes to read what he was writing in the gloom. He reached up to turn on the standard lamp. Nothing happened. He checked it was plugged in. It was. Irritated at the interruption, he tried the overhead light with no more success. He turned towards the kitchen stairs to check the fusebox but froze at the top of them, gasping. In the hours he had spent at the piano, listening to the heavy rain on the windows, the basement had filled with water. The murky brown tide reached almost to the kitchen ceiling. A bizarre assortment of displaced articles floated around the third step down and was mounting to the second even as he watched; corks, a cabbage leaf, the bread board. Amazed that he had heard nothing, Edward dashed across the hall and tugged open the front door, letting in a gust of rain and wind that almost blasted the door from his grasp.

The front steps, like the basement ones, were almost all submerged. The shrubberies on either side of the drive were nowhere to be seen. An already sparse landscape had vanished beneath the brown flood waters and their swirling cargo. In a dusk advanced by storm clouds, he could make out the barn roof and treetops and thought he could see people moving against the lowering sky on the tower of St Oswald's. A barge lit with hurricane lamps moved slowly across what had yesterday been a ploughed field.

'Hi!' he called out, waving his arms, 'Over here. Help!' But the wind snatched the words from his lips and he realised he was probably invisible in the gathering darkness. He watched in terrified fascination as a small wave unfurled from the skin of the flood and rushed towards the house, gaining bulk as it came. Edward cried out as it broke over the steps around him. He lost his balance, falling heavily backwards onto the drenched floor. Another wave was gathering as he scrambled back to his feet and ran to slam and bolt the door.

Spurred into sudden action, he raced around, seizing objects and furniture at random and carrying them up to the landing and bedrooms. Music, books, pictures, candlesticks, a mirror, an armchair, the standard lamp; the little they had amassed. Water began to lap over the top of the kitchen steps and under the front door, sending weird ripples through the rugs before he snatched them, dripping, out of harm's way. Gasping with the effort, he propped the piano up on books already ruined by water, one leg, and one book at a time, until it was nearly a foot clear of the great puddle that now covered the floor. Then, sweating from his labours despite the bitter cold and his soaked shoes, he retreated upstairs.

Huddled by a bedroom window, he found himself retracing the route between The Roundel and his parents-in-law, anxious for some memory of a gradient that would lift their house and his child clear of the flood. Wenborough was close to a canal. They would surely have taken early refuge on a passing boat. They would be fine. And Sally? Aware that he was beginning to whimper, he checked himself, roughly clearing his throat.

31

Sally had stopped twice more to try telephoning but now the line to The Roundel was also down. She had no option but to keep driving. For all she knew, the road behind was blocked by now and more policemen in waders would have been posted. It was getting dark and even with the headlamps on full she had to screw up her eyes and peer over the steering wheel like an old woman to see where she was going.

A part of her was excited by what was happening. As a local schoolgirl, she had been told time and again how the countryside of her birth had been won from the sea. Like many children before and since, she had marvelled at the thought of fish and whales swimming where she climbed trees, of seaweed uncoiling where wheat now waved. She had walked on the top of Sedwich Dyke with friends, peering down into the eerie depth of water it held back and tossing in stones to hear the hungry plopping sound as they were swallowed up in peaty blackness. She had imagined the excitement of climbing onto roofs to escape flood water, the fun of rowing past secretive neighbours' bedroom windows and peering in. And as an adult there were many times when she had scared herself witless on the way home from the chest hospital by imagining a great wall of water in inexorable pursuit of her motorbike.

At first it did not seem to be a real flood. She imagined Sedwich Dyke had burst and covered a road, but that the water had swiftly dispersed into the surrounding fields and waterways with no harm done. Then she twice drove the car through puddles which turned out to be deep as fords, and offered prayers as she felt the engine splutter. When she saw a terrified horse frantically pounding its bloodied way through a fence to vault out of a flooded field where ducks now swam, when she saw a family bicycling in the opposite direction, backs laden, faces white, a chill of comprehension made her shudder so badly it caused the car to swerve.

Many of the fenland roads were built from filled-in, redundant canals and so ran along high banks, along unnaturally straight routes. This was one such. When it joined another to make a T-junction, she had to scrabble for her torch and consult the map, briefly disoriented. She faced a decision. One fork led back to her parents' village and Miriam, the other, on to Edward and The Roundel. She flicked off the torch, tossed it aside and began to drive towards Wenborough then bumped to a halt, flung the car into noisy reverse and backed swiftly to the junction so as to turn and drive on to Edward. It was simply and unsentimentally decided. Miriam was with her parents. Edward was alone.

She was close now. She recognised the road and dared to drive a little faster. Then she hit what seemed at first to be another big puddle. She drove into it warily then slammed on the brakes as she felt the road dip deeper into the water ahead of her. She backed up a little, turned the wheel slightly to the left and started forwards again. Suddenly she seemed to be surrounded by water. The head-lamps gave her no help in finding where the road lay but merely confused her further by setting the surface water aglitter. Once more she had pointed the car the wrong way. Once more the bonnet lurched sickeningly downwards. She thrust her foot down on the brake. She cursed her stupidity. The road clearly bent somewhere around here. Why could she not remember it? She began to reverse, gently at first, then slamming her foot down wildly on the accelerator as the tyres lost their hold on the submerged turf and the car began to slide. Then water reached the exhaust pipe and the engine died. For two, maybe three seconds, as the rain clattered on the roof, she was paralysed with fear, then the car ploughed down the bank and crashed into a clump of trees beneath the water line.

Sally yelled as a sharp branch shattered the windscreen and

freezing water slammed onto her with the force of a punch. Somehow she found time to snatch a whooping breath before she was entirely submerged. She thrashed out of her seat and forced herself to open her eyes. The water was filthy, however, and night had fallen. She could see nothing. Beating out with her hands, thinking she might be able to swim out through the windscreen space, she found it blocked by branches. She felt her way back along the seat to first one door handle then the other. Both doors were wedged against something. One opened only slightly, the other not at all. She knew the rear window was too small to be worth smashing. Lungs burning in her effort to resist the urge to breathe, she returned to the front and began to force her way through the tree. The branches seemed to grow thicker and more tangled as she pushed on. Then her coat caught on something. She tugged it wildly before she realised Dr Pertwee's idol, still in her pocket, must have swung out in the water and locked itself into a fork. Trapped like a bird in lime, she stopped struggling. She dared to let out a few bubbles of breath, then released one, long, suicidal sigh.

Had she climbed sideways out of the tree rather than heading instinctively through it to the surface, she might have escaped. The rain stopped within hours and the flood grew no higher. When it subsided after only a day, Sally was found wrapped in branches and dislodged ivy, her bare feet dangling some fifteen feet above Thomas's wrecked Wolseley. Edward was shown the body only after it had been restored to dignity, but the farmer who had taken a ladder to retrieve it needed several whiskies to restore his nerve.

'She looked like a broken bird,' he told the barmaid in the Lamb and Flag, pale at the memory. 'She looked like she'd been blown up there by some great wind.'

32

Disparate, far-flung households had been made a temporary community by disaster, a community that was still in shock. Many of the people who cried openly during the brief, careful service at St Oswald's did so from a grief that was more than compassionate; Sally was only one of several claimed by the flood. A thirteen-year-old boy was drowned when he dived from a bedroom window to try to save his sister. A farmer in the land immediately below Sedwich Dyke was crushed by his own tractor under the first wave. A woman had broken her neck trying to gallop her horse to safety across the fields. As the waters subsided and the full extent of the damage to land, brick and inhabitants was laid bare, three of the oldest people on the parish register breathed their last, as though the effort to survive the dreadful night and the trauma of the scenes it left behind had knocked all the fight from their ancient frames.

Thomas had cajoled a rather good-looking cab-driver into bringing him all the way from Rexbridge and picking him up again from The Roundel later. The man swiftly sensed Thomas was not the kind of fare who liked to chat but from time to time he caught his eye in his rear view mirror and his own creased with a kind of amusement that might once have made Thomas blush. Thanking him for the tip, he called Thomas 'Guv'nor' with no trace of the customary sarcasm.

They had been held up by a delivery lorry and Thomas arrived late, slipping into a place just inside the door as Sally's pale, flower-laden coffin was borne towards the altar. He craned his neck to look past a pillar towards the principal mourners. As always, even after all this time and in so anti-erotic a setting, his heart turned over uncomfortably at the sight of Edward's high-boned face and the contrast between its pale complexion and the dark hair that curled above his ears and vulnerable nape. An only child, whose mother had died young, Thomas had once longed for younger brothers and sisters. At their most avowable, the feelings Edward inspired in him were those of an older brother eager to protect a weaker sibling, but he knew they had darker, more difficult roots.

To Edward's right, the Bankses sat stiffly, rendered incapable by grief of kneeling or standing. Sally's father had never been strong since his accident, but within his own reduced capacities, he had always seemed indomitable. Now both he and his wife were prematurely aged, plants robbed unnaturally of sap and sunlight. When she raised her veil to blow her nose, Sally's mother afforded a brief, shocking glimpse of a face left grey and defenceless, without rouge or purpose.

Thomas had telephoned Edward the previous night and asked if there was anything practical he could do for him, and was confronted with the impossible question, 'Thomas, how do I grieve? Where do I begin?'

Having shed so many tears, for reasons that now seemed obscure at best, Edward found himself unable to shed even one for the best – worst – reason imaginable. In one of her outbursts of hideous frankness, which Thomas already knew he would miss, Sally had said that the drawn-out agony of giving birth to Miriam had been so much greater than any pain she had ever felt that it had been hard to react to it. It seemed that Edward too now lacked the necessary vocabulary of outrage. Granted a reminder of joy just long enough for him to start fantasising about his future only to be faced with the brutal truncation of this happiness, he was punch-drunk. Compared to his shattered in-laws, however, he was already used to this sense of unreality. He knew better than to seek explanations. He could swim in the medium while they floundered. Overnight, he was the one who was strong, they the ones in need of constant watching and support.

The pallbearers stepped forward to hoist the coffin back on to their shoulders and Mrs Banks let out a harsh, seabird's cry which caused Edward to hunch his shoulders as though he had been struck. Then he seemed to steel himself and stood to help his stricken mother-in-law to her feet. Mr Banks seemed to have seized up from sitting still too long and could not manoeuvre the wheels of his chair so his wife, in turn, had to help him into the aisle. The three of them thus presented a small paradigm of frail human altruism. As they made their slow progress back towards the irrelevant sunshine, Thomas found his eyes fixed on his friend's downcast face. When Edward looked up suddenly, Thomas dropped his gaze down to the prayer book he was still clutching, unopened. Then he thought, with a kind of inappropriate amusement, *Bloody hell! I don't care,* and he looked up again and sent out a great mental beam of love. Edward looked around and spotted him as smartly as if Thomas had called his name. He gave a broken-down attempt at a smile and stepped away from the Bankses to grasp Thomas's hands in his. It was a gesture of quite uncharacteristic warmth and, disarmed by it, Thomas found himself just as uncharacteristically allowing Edward to draw him out of the crowd to walk with him behind the coffin. Edward continued to hold onto him. Thomas supposed the action was unconscious and gently tried to pull his hand back, but found Edward's grasp firm and intentional. As quiet improvisation on the organ gathered itself into a sombre Purcell march, Thomas gave Edward's hand a squeeze and felt momentarily very young and stupid.

People in crises do this, he thought. *Aeroplanes lose control, liners sink, buildings burn and crumble and the people within them abandon themselves to unwise fondlings and violent, unplanned embraces.*

Edward eventually let go of his hand but not until he had mutely steered Thomas to a position beside him at the grave's mouth. The priest intoned the sentences that were familiar as certain lines of Shakespeare – familiar to the point of being incomprehensible to the casual ear. Thomas kept his head bowed but found his eyes straying now to the black hairs on Edward's hands, now to an earthworm that had taken a wrong turning and begun to emerge high in a wall of the moist, black chasm before them.

'I'm so very sorry,' he told the Bankses as Edward unnecessarily reintroduced them. Mrs Banks could only stare at him and nod. 'She had so much to give us all,' he added fatuously. She looked ill. Wondering whether she were due for a second operation, he looked politely aside, casting a last glance into the grave and, for the first time since Edward rang him hysterically with the news, he felt his throat tighten and had to gulp away the possibility of tears.

He preferred not to be among the first to arrive at the house, so he dawdled in the churchyard while the others set off, Edward caught up in conversation with a rounded, effervescent Indian woman in a white sari. By the time he had finished reading the inscriptions on headstones, by the time the crowd had melted away and the sexton was arranging flowers and wreaths on the small mound of newly turned earth, his mind was made up. It was quite possibly a foolhardy course of action, but he knew he would regret not taking it for the rest of his days. He was going to ask Edward to live with him again. He would move out of the college house and buy himself somewhere larger, on the edge of town perhaps. He would find somewhere big enough for Edward's grand piano and hire a nanny to care for the child. His father's death had left him comfortably off. He could afford it. When they shared a house before, he had kept his desire penned in with a regime of spinsterly austerity designed, with unconscious masochism, to drive Edward from him. He had been at pains to treat him like a lodger. Now he would hem him round with unlodgerly luxury. Yet, he entertained no fond delusion that their relations would ever warm to anything more fleshly than friendship.

No. That was a lie. He did, frequently, usually in unguarded hours of the night, feed just such a fantasy. But at least he kept the fondness of the delusion well to the fore of his mind. More realistically, he suspected that a constant supply of creature comforts and kindness would make it harder for Edward to leave him a second time. And proximity was intimacy of a kind.

Thomas left the churchyard just as a florist's van drew up. The red-haired lad who jumped out saw in an instant that he had missed the funeral and swore roundly under his breath.

'I told her it was cutting things too fine,' he said, claiming Thomas as witness to his innocence. 'Her Ladyship wouldn't have none of it. Made me drive all the way from the bleeding studios because she wanted the note to be in her handwriting and not some local florist's.'

He was clutching a huge bouquet of white arum lilies arranged with strips of willow and what appeared to be long sprigs of rosemary.

'That's all right,' Thomas told him. 'I'm a friend of the family. I'll make sure they get to Mr Pepper.'

'It says Pfefferberg here,' the lad protested, frowning at the foreignness in his mouth.

'Same man. I'll give them to him myself.'

'Oh. Well. That's very kind of you, then. Sign here.'

Thomas signed.

'You needn't tell her you were too late,' he assured him.

'No,' said the lad and laughed. 'I suppose not. I charged her enough. See you then.'

He jumped back into his van, made a show of roaring the engine and tore away again. Thomas carried the flowers to Sally's grave and made space for them beside an evergreen cross, on which Sally's name was spelled out in silvered cardboard. There was an envelope in the bouquet, which he took to pass on to Edward. Half way up the lane to The Roundel, temptation got the better of him and he opened it to read the message. In large handwriting that would have disgraced a girl of twelve, was written, *'Teddy you poor poor darling!! If there's anything Julius and I can do, anything at all, just let me know.'*

It was signed *Myra*, then, in modest brackets, *(St Teath)* and there were three large kisses. Thomas thrust it back in the envelope and, as he walked, turned the name over in his mind for an instant like a half-forgotten scent. When he remembered that it was the name of an actress, not of anyone he knew personally, he folded the envelope up and pocketed it, resolved now not to pass it on.

The Roundel and its grounds bore signs of damage as

obvious as his friend's were hidden. The grass had been combed flat into strange patterns by the retreating water currents and streaked with sweetly pungent mud. In the flower beds only the huge deep-rooted old roses appeared to have emerged unscathed. Numerous plants had been torn out and swept to one side. Others lay broken, crushed, rotting. Someone had made half-hearted efforts to tidy up, but still objects that did not belong lay everywhere, carried from Heaven knows where: children's toys, a lavatory brush, sodden magazines, buttons, orange rind. The disorder was oddly comforting – a reminder that the recent natural violence had not been exaggerated in remembrance.

The strong, rivery smell grew even stronger as Thomas entered the house. The boiler had been turned up high and fires had been lit in every room in an effort to dry the old place out, adding heat and humidity to an atmosphere already thick with the mildewy stench of wet carpet and sodden wood. The place was crowded with funeral guests, the respectful murmurs of each combining in a chatter which only their mourning clothes held on the gloomy side of festive. Thomas guessed from the way many were looking around them like fascinated strangers that, apart from a few colleagues from the film studios, most of these were people Edward had never met. These were people Sally had worked with, people she had cured, school friends, cousins who couldn't make the wedding but who had crossed counties to see a relative put in a hole in the ground. The kitchen was full of steam and loud with the clatter of pans and china. Glad of something to occupy their thoughts, some women had organised tea. Thomas had barely set foot in the water-stained hall when a cup of strongly brewed Assam was thrust into his hand with a hunk of seed cake balanced on its saucer.

Mr and Mrs Banks were marooned on the sofa by the piano, his wheelchair folded away as though to prevent escape. Plates of cake and biscuits clustered with several cooling cups of tea on the low table before them, votive offerings laid out to appease the bereaved for whom no-one could find sufficient words. Women passing before them composed their faces into kind smiles, men limited themselves to awestruck nods;

attentions which isolated the couple still further. She had at last folded back her veil and her eyes flicked around the scene before her, the only living things in a face stony with tension. Thomas approached and managed a few sentences but even the need to react with nods and murmurs seemed to cause her and her husband pain, so he retreated, leaving his slice of seed cake – a confection he had never liked – on their impromptu altar.

He found Edward in the child's bedroom, watching her as she somehow managed to sleep through the social roar.

'We three,' Thomas thought as he saw Edward's expression soften on seeing who had come in. The young man held one hand spread, protective, on his daughter's back. 'We three alone.' The blood quickened in him. There was a tightness in his chest. When Edward had lodged with him he used to slip into his bedroom some mornings when he was taking his bath, to kneel on the hard, worn rug beside the narrow bed and press his face into the sheets to breathe in their faint trace of male musk. He would do that again. He would do more. He didn't care what people said. His gossiping students. The other fellows at Tompion. If he could be wife, husband, father, friend to the man before him, the world could go hang.

'Sorry,' Edward murmured. 'I was hiding.'

'Why not?' Thomas said, shutting the door behind him. He stood nearby for a moment, looking down at the sleeping child then walked over to the small, barred window to hide the emotions he felt sure were emblazoned on his face. Someone on the landing met a friend and singly failed to disguise their unseemly laughter as a cough.

'Well say something, Thomas,' Edward said. 'I can't believe *you're* at a loss for words.'

'Actually I . . . I think I probably am,' Thomas told him.

'Please. Try.'

'Well I . . .' Thomas turned back to the window, looked out at the water-scarred landscape. 'There's no blame,' he said at last.

'Where?'

'Here. In this. That's the beautiful strength of natural disasters, plagues, acts of God, whatever; they sweep all before them. They're inexorable. They leave no space for if-onlys. They're nobody's fault.'

'Except God's.'

'Oh. Him. Well even He isn't to blame. Not really. It's like a momentary lapse of concentration. A trace of His human side.'

Thomas stopped rambling. The preposterous image of a benignly bearded deity hung between them for a few seconds, then Edward stood abruptly and went to examine himself critically in the looking-glass. His voice had one of its rare moments of faintly Germanic inflection.

'Thomas, this is of no help whatsoever.'

'No. It isn't. Sorry.'

Thomas sat on the edge of the bed. After a moment, Edward came back and slumped beside him. His lack of tears was terrifying, a supreme exercise of control.

'I can't bear to lose Miriam too,' he said.

'Why should you?'

'Think, Thomas. She needs a mother. A woman to love her. They were talking about it last night. Miriam already has a bed at Sally's parents'. A drawer full of clothes. But Sally's mother is too old, really. I don't think she's well.' Almost absently, Edward took Thomas's hand again and pressed it between his. Thomas felt a tremendous urge to lift the other hand and stroke Edward's cheek. He had never felt so tempted by danger. With one touch he might destroy everything. He raised his other hand but found it reaching instead for the folded note in his pocket.

'Here,' he said. 'There was a late delivery of flowers at the church. Beautiful ones. Lilies. Rosemary for remembrance. This was with them.'

'Yes?' Edward took the note, releasing Thomas's hand. He held it unopened on his knees.

'It's really not a problem,' Thomas assured him. 'Of course Mrs Banks wants to help, and of course she'll want to have Miriam to stay occasionally, take her for walks and so on. But she's not strong or young enough to do it full time. All you need is a nanny. There are agencies. Reputable ones. So I'm told. Obviously you'd have to pay the woman you hired to live in, but money need not be a problem.'

'You really think so?' Edward's face lit up. The thought had clearly never occurred to him and he had been worrying himself into a state of needless turmoil. Thomas relished the advantage of wisdom. 'Would you help me?' Edward asked.

'Of *course* I'll help. Edward, you must realise I'd do anything –'

'And you think a nanny would be prepared to come and live out here? There's no question of my moving, you see.'

Thomas could only hesitate.

'Well . . . Well yes. Of course she would,' he said.

A handful of words like so many bullets had torn his dream to tawdry ribbons. Edward talked on, his mind entering a comfortable channel, about the legal impossibility of selling The Roundel, of how rooted he was there now, of how it now belonged to Miriam. Miriam woke at the excitement in his voice and he lifted her free of her bedding. Her eyes focused sleepily on Thomas, a hint of challenge in their stirring curiosity. Thomas stared back at her and, as he sensed the exclusivity of the bond between father and daughter, muttered automatic promises to seek recommendations among the wives of other senior fellows.

Together they walked out onto the landing and down the stairs to where there was soon a circle of admiring arms stretching out to caress the now boisterous child. When Mrs Banks had stirred from her sofa, seizing on a role, and taken Miriam from his arms, Edward opened the envelope and read the note. Thomas was perplexed to see two quite different emotions reflected on his face. First he blushed and began to fold the note away again then, seeing Thomas watching him, he smiled and displayed what seemed like manufactured amazement, showing the note to the people around him, avoiding Thomas's gaze.

'Myra Toye!' he exclaimed. 'Myra Toye and Sir Julius sent flowers and even wrote a letter with them. Look! Wasn't that kind?'

Thomas thought he seemed quite disproportionately pleased with what was surely a routine gesture from an assiduous professional, and felt a stab of jealousy. He fed Edward's pleasure, however, and with it his own disapproval, by explaining that she had insisted the florist deliver the flowers to the church himself, all the way from the studios, so that Edward should receive a note in her own hand. Others exclaimed, impressed, and asked to see the ordinary scrap of paper which, by the mere addition of a certain name, had been transformed for them into a thing of worth.

After another cup of tea and a second, this time inescapable, slice of seed cake, it was with a certain gratitude that Thomas saw the same, broad-shouldered cab-driver walk hesitantly through the front door. His sly, inquisitive smile as Thomas greeted him and suggested they stop off for a drink on their drive back into Rexbridge, suggested that, romantic disappointments notwithstanding, life would not be entirely without unexpected treats.

PART II

They reminded me of photographs of the victims of the Holocaust concentration camps at the end of the '39–'45 war. They were mostly in their middle twenties . . . I wanted some way of dignifying their deaths. I longed for music, poetry; something which would restore to them some of their human dignity.

Dr Anne Bailey, describing her
first encounter with AIDS in Uganda
THE PLAGUE, CHANNEL 4,
WORLD AIDS DAY, 1993

33

Edward had been failing to concentrate on his work all morning and when he heard tyres on gravel and looked up to see an unfamiliar car swing up the drive, he left the sequencer with a kind of relief and went out to meet it. Ordinarily he would have received such a person, if at all, at his flat in London. Over the years, he had kept the flat studiously impersonal, the kind of place one could lend to visiting colleagues or let out for a year with the minimum of preparation. Journalists eagerly agreed to meet him there only to be sent away disappointed by the lack of photographs, or mementoes. But this one, the biographer, with all the worrying Jamesian overtones her profession carried, had telephoned beseechingly once too often and had caught him, exhausted and uncaring, after a three-week European tour. Then his record company's publicist had joined forces with her and Edward's weakened resistance had crumbled. So here she was.

She was young, svelte, freshly dressed. Unaware that he was padding over the garden behind her, she took a pocket camera from her briefcase and snapped a few quick photographs of the house. When she heard him cough, she slipped the camera away, surreptitious as a thief. For a second he caught the frown on her unguarded face, then she looked up, turned a bright, almost friendly, smile upon him and came to shake his hand.

'Mr Pepper. What an honour. I'm Venetia. Venetia Peake.'

Her quick appraisal of his face was palpable, like the brisk strokes of a nurse's flannel.

'Come on in,' he told her. 'I'll make us some coffee.'

She seemed disappointed that they were heading away from The Roundel.

'I haven't lived in there for decades,' he explained. 'It's always belonged to women, and I was only ever a caretaker. My daughter lived there for a while, with a group of her friends in the late sixties. A commune of sorts, though rather half-hearted. She got married a few years ago and moved away, so my grandchildren use the place. They both live in London so it's quite peaceful here again.'

'Don't you ever get lonely?'

'I love to be alone.'

They arrived at the single storey studio whose modern bricks had almost disappeared beneath a cushion of clematis and rampaging jasmine. He smiled, waving her in. 'Besides,' he added, 'this place is a damned sight cheaper to heat.'

'Doesn't the river ever flood?'

She realised too late the gaffe she had just made.

'Frequently,' he told her, amused at her little discomfited pout. 'That's why I had them build this on a bank. Do you take milk?' She shook her head, pausing to note a slightly battered Oscar statuette doing duty as a doorstop.

'I thought you had two,' she said.

'I use the other as a paperweight,' he told her, gesturing towards his desk. She arranged herself on a sofa and took some files and a tape recorder from her bag. He served the coffee then sat across from her. Now that girls were wearing short skirts yet again, they had taken to sitting the way their grandmothers were taught to do, with ankles crossed and legs tucked chastely to the side. She had good legs. Nervous again, he tried to seize the initiative. 'So tell me. How's Myra?'

'Fine. Radiant. Hard at work on a fourth series. Do you watch it?'

'Afraid not.' He glanced around them in explanation. 'I don't watch anything.' The studio had always been a television-free zone. He occasionally sneaked an evening in front of the one his granddaughter had installed in The Roundel, but there was no need for this journalist to know that, not least because it was often Myra's old films that he watched.

'She says hello by the way,' Venetia Peake continued. 'Sends her love.'

Edward merely raised his eyebrows and nodded non-committal acceptance.

'So she knows we're going to talk?'

'Yes, but not how deeply.'

Edward stalled, unsettled by the threat of steel in her tone.

'I don't quite see what I can tell you,' he began. 'Myra and I saw each other at the studios of course, but I'm not sure there's much I can add to the anecdotes you'll already have.'

Ignoring his disclaimers, she clicked down the record button on her dictation machine and a little microphone popped out of it towards him.

'You don't mind?' she asked. He shrugged. 'Perhaps we should start with some photographs from around forty-eight and forty-nine. I want to be sure I've identified them right. Who's this?' Edward looked and smiled. It was Myra in aviator gear clowning with Howard Winks.

'He was a lighting man called Howard Winks. This was during *Reach for the Stars*. He died in a fire in fifty-seven. Bad heart.'

'And how about this?'

Edward looked again. Myra linking arms with two men in dark overcoats and hats.

'The one on the left is Sam Hirsch,' he told her. 'I recognise the one on the right but I can't remember his name. Jim? John?'

'James?' she prompted.

'That's it. James something. James McBean. He did make-up. Sam was hair.'

'Myra and her Boys, eh?'

'That sort of thing, yes.' Edward thought back, remembering raucous laughter and the hot, dark undertow of his jealousy. 'Myra with her Boys.'

She produced more photographs, six or seven. Two he could not place at all. In one, Myra was being kissed by someone, clearly unaware of the photographer.

'And what about this?'

Another of Myra. Myra curled in a chair in an outsize man's dressing gown and little else, one small foot caught in surprising detail against the dark fabric of the chair cover.

'Well that's just Myra.' He made to hand it back. 'Myra in a chair.'

'Yes,' she pursued, 'but where?'

He had known straight away. It had been his chair, his photograph, his London bachelor pad on a long, boozy Sunday afternoon. He remembered the brisk excursion to the nearest corner shop – trousers and coat tugged on to cover his nudity – to buy her cigarettes, and the return to the womby fug of his gas-fired rooms with their smell of body and tobacco. He looked up into Venetia Peake's unflinching gaze.

'I don't know.'

'How about this one then?'

She sounded almost like a policewoman. It was another picture of Myra, this time sprawled on a car rug amid the remains of a picnic, laughing as she added extra leaves to her already mussed-up hair.

'No idea,' Edward said, although he knew that the shadow cast in the inexpert snapshot was his own.

Venetia Peake watched him for a moment then opened another file.

'The thing is, Edward,' she said, her abrupt familiarity startling as an unwelcome proposal, 'That I seem to know more than you do. I've got some letters and things here. Rather a lot, so I won't bore you with the details, but they're all to her and they're all from you. To "Darling M from Hopeless E", to "My Darling", to "Sweetness", to "*Liebchen*", to "Cupcake" . . .'

'She *showed* you these?'

Venetia Peake merely shrugged.

'Let's just say they're all here. You can see them if you want. I have photocopies in my office in New York.' She held out the file full of old, crumpled scraps, scraps of a cherished and utterly private devotion, but he brushed it aside, blood racing, as he lurched to his feet and made for the bookcase.

'Here,' he said. 'Since you're evidently going to tell the story at least make sure you tell it with *both* sides fully documented.' He climbed on a ladder, scanned a high shelf and tugged out a thick pink tome called *Fond Remembered Loves*, bought in a second-hand shop with the sole purpose of providing an ironic hiding-place. 'Here,' he said, opening it and passing sheet by faded, crumpled sheet to Ms Peake who had come eagerly to the ladder's side. 'Letters from her. To "Dearest E". To "My Darling". To "Bunny". To "Mr Hotinsack".'

'Oh. Well. Thank you,' she stammered, turning greedily from one to the next. 'She said she never wrote any letters.'

'She forgot.'

'Of course, I already have her side of the story.'

He followed her back to the sofa.

'Let me guess,' he said bitterly. 'I besieged her with flowers and letters and she finally succumbed out of pity?'

'Well . . . Er . . . God, I never thought this could be so embarrassing.' She struggled back to composure. 'Yes. Something like that,' she said at last.

'There were no letters. No flowers. Not at first,' he said after thinking for a while. 'It started when she was drunk. She used to drink. Everyone did then but she drank more than everyone. I found her in the studio car park. She could hardly stand up and she was about to climb into her racer, the one St Teath gave her as a wedding present. Luckily for her she'd dropped the keys and couldn't find them or she'd have killed herself.'

'So what happened?' she asked, adjusting the volume on the tape recorder.

'Nothing much. It was raining. She was wet through, crying, hair everywhere. A real mess. I drove her back to London, to my place in Albert Hall Mansions. Ran her a bath. Lent her some pyjamas while her clothes dried. I put her to bed while I slept on the sofa.'

'And then?'

'And then she woke up in the middle of the night having a panic attack, screaming the place down. I went to calm her, explained where she was, what had happened then she . . . well . . . she had a rather winning way of saying thank you and ended up spending the weekend.' Edward found he was smiling despite himself.

'Then what?'

So Edward told her the whole sad, sweet, humiliating story of their affair. It was not the only liaison of his long widowerhood but the first and the last in which he had allowed himself to become involved to the point of pain. The telling of it, the long-forgotten sight of her childish handwriting and of the intensely evocative snapshots so mysteriously acquired, softened his rage. Venetia Peake's questions, her relentless interest, broke up the heartless flibbertigibbet image of Myra he had carefully constructed in his wrath, and expensively endorsed in prolonged psychotherapy.

His inquisitor made no allusion to his and Myra's having had anything but a professional relationship in the brief years of his marriage to Sally. Either she was being cunningly manipulative, or she was genuinely ignorant. In his initial outburst of rage and panic, he had assumed that Myra had not only handed over private letters for this young woman's cold perusal but had told her of their one adulterous encounter. Now that his vengefulness seemed cheap beside her delicacy, he wanted to unsay what he had said or at least take back some of the letters which showed her at her most sluttish and illiterate. Then he reflected that this was, after all, to be an authorized biography and that Myra would surely therefore have power of veto.

He softened slightly towards Venetia Peake too – but to say that he warmed to her would have been an exaggeration. He offered her a drink once the dictation machine and letters had been clicked away into her capacious bag and was touched to observe, from her evident relief, that she had been as apprehensive about the interview as he. She knew nothing whatever about music – although it seemed she came from a musical family – so they talked about America, where she had taken out citizenship after a brief, convenient marriage, and about his grandchildren.

'Are these them?' she asked, picking a photograph off the piano.

Edward nodded.

'Alison and Jamie. It's a bit out of date apparently but that seems to be the way I remember them.'

'He's so handsome,' she enthused politely. 'What does he do?'

'In the City,' he said and had to touch his brow to rub away a frown he felt forming there. 'She's in publishing.'

'Oh but I think I know her. That is, we've met once. She wouldn't remember. She's at Mallard and Rose isn't she?'

'Pharos, actually.'

'That's the one,' she bluffed. 'I get confused. You must be very proud of them both.'

Her tone was rather patronising, but he found himself nodding and feeling a small warmth of pride, if only in being a grandfather. Regretting his initial hostility, he showed her the hall and gallery of The Roundel. She presumed to peck him on the cheek before climbing into her car. Then, slightly drunk from a whisky on an empty stomach, he found himself waving her off as fondly as if she were a favourite niece.

Back in the studio, having abandoned all hope of useful work for the afternoon, he telephoned Miriam to warn her the journalist might track her down. However he learned from a halting conversation with her cleaning lady that, incongruous but true, Miriam was out at the hairdressers. He telephoned Pharos to ask Alison if she intended to come down at the weekend, but she was in a meeting and he had to trust a message to her arrogant male secretary. It was actually Jamie he most wanted to speak to, but he knew the boy found it awkward to receive personal calls at the office. He rang his flat instead and left a pointless and slightly garbled message on his machine beginning, 'Don't worry. It's only me –'

34

'No! No, I'm not ready.'

'Yes,' Jamie commanded and thrust home so hard that the man gasped as if he were being stabbed. 'Yes you are.'

'No.'

'Yes.' Another thrust. 'Come.'

'No.'

'Yes.'

'No.'

'Yes. Go on. you're coming.' Another thrust. Harder this time. 'I can tell. Come *now*!'

'No. Yes. No! Oh God!' The man arched his back and wrapped his thighs tight around Jamie's waist, pulling him towards him. As he came, with a series of dry sobs, the muscles in his arse seized and released Jamie's numb, bruised dick, seized and released it. For a moment, watching the man thrash and wince on the rug before him, Jamie wondered whether he could be bothered to come as well. But even as he made up his mind to pretend to, he felt the obscure mechanism in his loins thumping into motion of its own accord.

They had kissed already – against the side of a lorry, inside the porch, on the stairs – kisses between perfect strangers, conveying only hunger and curiosity. Now, as he spurted his juice into the man's insides, desire sated, he felt an old familiar yearning to kiss in tenderness, to be held, to be made to feel, however fraudulently, safe. He fought the feeling, roughly pressing a hand across the man's face, forcing his thumb between his teeth and on to the hot vulnerability of his tongue. The man sucked obediently, expressing Jamie's need on his behalf. Jamie watched him for a moment, until the beating in his chest subsided, then he pulled back his hand and let his dick slide out with a wet, suggestive plop. In the half light from the lamps along the riverside, he could see that the condom had slipped off. With a practised gesture, disguised as a further caress, he slipped two fingers inside and tweaked the thing out.

He began to stand but the man, eyes still closed, took him by the wrists. Jamie waited, making no reciprocation, until he was released again, then walked slowly to pull on some tracksuit bottoms. Taking a small, black towel from the neatly folded stash kept in the bathroom for just this purpose, he came back to clean his visitor. Wiping sweat and sperm from limbs that were lent a deathly pallor by the thin light, an effect heightened by the man's heavily corpseish stillness. He wiped the body longer than was strictly necessary, enjoying the slow ritual courtesy and the almost paternal feeling it invariably stirred in him.

At last he roused himself with a little, comical snort.

'What did you say your name was?' he asked.

'I didn't,' Jamie said. 'But it's Tony.'

'Well, thanks. Tony.'

He rose, lit a cigarette and began to wander around the eerily lit room, peering closely at things in the gloom. Walking near the windows his body was lit by the diffused glow of lights from outside, revealing a suggestion of belly.

'What's this?' he asked, picking up the idol that perched on Jamie's only bookcase.

'I inherited her from my grandmother. She's from an East Anglian burial barrow. A fertility goddess.' In three short sentences, Jamie realised, he had destroyed his carefully assembled image of tight-lipped machismo. The man chuckled.

'Whatever she is, I wouldn't want to meet her up a dark alley,' he said.

Jamie watched him replace the treasure and said, 'I . . . er . . . I'm afraid I've got to get to work early.'

With mumbled apologies, the man dressed and left. He behaved perfectly. He made no awkward overtures about leaving addresses or telephone numbers and he gave no name. He only spoiled the encounter's smooth completion by having to ring on the doorbell when he realised he had left his watch and wedding ring in an ashtray by the sofa.

Ever since he had started attending a gym after a summer with a leg in plaster caused him to put on weight, Jamie had checked himself religiously on the bathroom scales at night, charting his progress from slack-thighed wimp to urban olympian. This evening, stepping off the scales, he sensed it was a habit he would have to break if he was to retain his sanity. These things became obsessive, tedious even. For the fourth night in a row, instead of luxuriating in the pleasures of an unshared, unrumpled bed, he found himself fretting wakefully over complex mental indices of indulgence and retribution, teasing, circular lists of profit and loss, the nightmarish equations whereby risk might be calculated.

The twenty-five years of Jamie's life had been shaped by an impulse towards transgression in one form or another. Miriam, as his mother had always insisted her children call her, had brought him and his sister into the world in a haphazard commune, made up of fellow art school graduates she gathered about herself. Uncertain as to which of the group's floating male population was their father, she had proudly given them her surname. She had fed them on home-made bread and home-made cheese and encouraged them to run naked as savages and decorate their bodies with natural pigments. Seven-year-old Jamie had transgressed against this self-conscious paganism by winning a place at a Rexbridge college choir school, where he sang like an angel, wore a collar and tie and learned slabs of the Bible by rote. When Miriam finally put communal life behind her and married her accountant, she tried hard to become the kind of mother who liked having a privately educated choirboy for a son. Like her father, she became keen for Jamie to pursue his musical training and shed a little culture on her by association. Reliably disobedient, he changed direction again, taking Economics, Politics and Maths A-levels, giving up singing and skipping university to take a job with a Lloyd's syndicate. Now his contemporaries seemed to be falling over themselves in the rush to settle down and have babies and/or cats, so he remained petless and resolutely – even callously – single. His regular encounters with men he picked up in the street or the gym were lent an added spice by the knowledge that his settled colleagues, and even his stepfather, enviously pictured him playing the field with a fragrant address book of single women.

Appalled by Miriam's transformation following her marriage, equally wilful, though not, he suspected, quite as committed to the single state as he was, his older sister Alison was his only confidante. They lived on opposite sides of London but spoke every day and made a point of meeting once a week, if only for a sandwich and coffee. The morning after this latest adventure, they had time for complicated salads and a bottle of Chablis.

'But that's such a waste of perfectly good man!' Alison protested after the detailed account she claimed as her due.

'I've told you before. Twice is a mess, three times, a commitment.'

'But a married man is already committed elsewhere.'

'Allow me *some* principles,' Jamie insisted. 'I'm many nasty things, perhaps, but I'm not a homewrecker.'

'Not intentionally. But he probably went home and couldn't look his wife in the eye.'

'And that's *my* fault? It takes two.'

Alison reached across with her fork to help him finish his salad which he was starting to neglect. When he caught her eye she said, 'It's only rabbit food. And you know I hate waste. You should eat more yourself. You're looking skinny.'

'I'm not,' he insisted. 'I work out three times a week at least.'

'You're still looking skinny.'

Jamie laughed at the concerned enquiry in her gaze. He swopped their salad bowls so she could eat without stretching, then he topped up their glasses.

'I want to be a gay man,' she said.

'Ssh!' he chuckled. 'People are staring.'

'But I *do!*'

'Oh please. Not still? I thought working on the helpline might have cured that.'

'If you pick up some sexy married stranger in a late-night supermarket, it's all in an evening's entertainment. If a woman does that, she gets called a scrubber.'

'So does a man. Depends on his friends.'

'But you know what I mean. Sex is so *easy* for you.'

'What about that bloke in your office?'

She dropped her fork with a clatter and pushed the bowl to one side. Last time they had spoken, she had hotly denied anything had gone on between her and a younger colleague but now her reaction to Jamie's sudden question had betrayed her. She looked up, caught, smiled ruefully then looked down again and fell to pleating her napkin.

'That. Well that won't happen again. I'm sure of it. Anyway it's madness to sleep with colleagues.'

'Didn't stop you.'

'Stop it.'

'Scrubber.'

'Stop it,' she squeaked. 'Get us some coffee. I've an editorial meeting at three.'

He paid the bill while he was fetching the coffee – even following her recent managerial promotion, she earned almost half his salary – then halved what she owed him when she insisted on paying her way. He suspected Alison knew he did this and he was touched that she let him. She paid him back from time to time with small but satisfyingly dense parcels of the books she published. He usually kept these for a while, enjoying their crisp promise before giving them away, unread, to his secretary. His secretary was indefatigable but entirely undiscriminating in what she read, and it fascinated Alison to hear how fiercely the woman judged the latest Aldo MacInnes conundrum, say, against some piece of mass-market escapism.

'Guess who phoned me this morning,' Jamie said, munching the chocolate mint from her saucer before she could be tempted to change her mind about not wanting it. 'Regular as clockwork.'

'Miriam,' she said, then imitated their mother's voice with

deadly precision. 'Angel, Frank and I were wondering if you could find time for us this weekend.'

'She asked you too?'

Alison nodded.

'Are you going?' Jamie asked her.

'I said I'd let her know.'

'Oh dear. Me too.'

Brother and sister exchanged a guilty look. Miriam had staggered them several years before by marrying colourless, conscienceless, enthusiastic Francis, moving into his large Essex house and taking up sports to please him. Both children had been in the throes of leaving home in any case, and Miriam's eagerness that they should continue to have 'their' rooms in her well-appointed prison only speeded up the process. Francis had left his first wife for Miriam and the defection had still not been forgiven by his own children. The new pair rattled around in a house far too large for them – filling their spare time with tennis, swimming, golf and 'going for drives' – beleaguered by two sets of angry offspring who refused to play family unless spectacularly bribed.

Alison had a small box of her mother's old photographs which she and Jamie occasionally pored over, fascinated at the drunken images of boozy, druggy afternoons at The Roundel, everyone dressed in flares and the men indistinguishable with their beards and long hair. It was hard to understand the impulse behind Miriam's dogged attempt to transform herself from bread-baking, peace-marching, free-loving earth mother to an only slightly eccentric surburban matron with big hair and redundant four-wheel-drive. Or would have been, had not so many of her contemporaries abandoned hippy principles with equally gay abandon at about the same time.

'I'll go if you will.'

'Done,' Jamie agreed. 'I'll drive us. But I'm not playing tennis.'

'Absolutely not.'

'And we leave after Sunday lunch. Promptly.'

'I was telling Grandpa the other day, I suppose I could forgive it – I mean, we all want security, and there's nothing sadder than a hippy in middle age – if only she wouldn't try to involve us so. And that awful, hopeful way she has of saying "and do bring a friend, if you like".'

'She never says that to me,' said Jamie. He felt perplexingly stung by this.

'You never have a "friend" long enough for them to get invited.'

'She *knows* though, doesn't she?'

'Of course.' Alison glanced at her watch then held out her empty coffee cup to a passing waiter with a beseeching smile. 'But she doesn't like to think about it in case her reaction turns out to be at odds with what's left of her liberal sensibility. And he'd die of embarrassment. Sometimes I think he's like an Action Man. You know? Nothing down there but a fold of hygienic plastic.'

A thick-set, Danish-looking man with short, ash-blond hair, his suit jacket slung over one shoulder, strode by their table. The conversation stopped momentarily as both cast an appraising gaze at his rear. Jamie sighed minutely as they turned back to face each other. Alison's understanding was immediate.

'Hetero bottom,' she said. 'My gaydar's improving.'

'Your friends on that helpline are teaching you about more than the medical crisis,' Jamie clucked and they laughed. He reverted to the previous, perennial topic between them. 'But how can she *stand* him? He's such an Easy Listening sort of man.'

'At least he's rich. How did she stand Joey or Phil or Reefer or any of the rest of the Beards? Miriam's always had lousy taste in men.'

'Unlike us.'

She smiled at him sunnily across her cup. He loved her like this; strong, bony, alert. He liked to think people would look at them and know at once they were brother and sister. His grandfather had a framed photograph of his late wife looking up from her work in a flower bed at The Roundel, no-nonsense hair pulled off her face by a spotted scarf. Although Alison affected not to notice it, the resemblance between the two women was uncanny. She set her cup down, made leaving motions with her bag, and moaned, 'But I never *have* any men!'

'Only because you make no time for them.' Jamie left the wine bar with her. 'You fill your evenings with manuscripts, lame ducks and that fucking helpline.'

Alison peered dubiously at herself in a car window and worried some frizz back into her hair.

'Half the reason I took that on,' she explained, 'was in the forlorn hope of meeting somebody.'

'A lesbian-run, gay-manned sex problems helpline is hardly a likely hunting ground for *you*, sister.'

'What would you know, with your selfish life? Kiss.' He pulled her to him and kissed her on the lips. 'Now,' she added, 'change your gym and eat some steak or something. Sleep more, party less.'

'You're late for that meeting.'

'I'm serious, Jamie. I wish you would.'

'Yeah yeah.'

She gave him a brief, earnest look from under her fringe, kissed her fingers to him then turned the gesture into a frantic wave at a passing taxi which honked and pulled over. He watched her drive away, then turned back towards the office and his deskload of data about a recent petrochemicals disaster in Germany. For a few moments a chill hung about him, despite his walking on the street's sunny side. Then the Dane in the rumpled suit walked by with some colleagues, caught his eye and, falling behind his companions, smiled lazily at Jamie with the corner of his mouth.

35

'I'm sorry. This chair's taken.'

'Well could I borrow it till they get here?'

Alison placed a hand protectively on the chairback and faced the woman out.

'He'll be here any minute,' she said, unconsciously using the male pronoun as a weapon. 'He's just a bit late.'

The woman sighed crossly and turned her back to try elsewhere. Alison topped up her wine. She had almost finished the bottle already. She glanced at her watch, then carried on with her attempt to read a manuscript. The yacking, hooting voices around her were oppressive. Her eyes stung with smoke and, after a day with nothing to eat beyond some fashionably austere fish, the wine was turning rancid on her tongue. A knot formed in her stomach: her habitual quiet seething against the rudeness of Londoners, their casual discourtesies, slovenly insults.

Damn him! Where was he? At the meeting that afternoon she had stuck her neck out for him, defending him, against two outstanding interviewees, as the best in-house candidate for a vacant editorial post. Cynthia, the editorial director, whose loudly touted belief in feminist solidarity had a way of deserting her when dealing with female colleagues, had grilled her.

'Well why, exactly? Come on, Alison! You can't just say "Oh but he's good" without giving us chapter and verse! *Why* is he good? I mean, we all know he's pretty . . .' And she had used her just-one-of-the-girls manner to make everyone laugh and forget Alison's argument. Alison persevered. He had an eye, she said. He had spotted Petra Levy. 'Oh, and there was I thinking *you* had spotted Petra.' Cynthia fixed her with a mocking stare and Alison suddenly knew that Cynthia knew that the young man in question had already flattered Alison into bed. Wondering whether the decorative bastard had not perhaps already done the same with Cynthia, Alison had fought back, dropping hints to remind the board that at least two of their number were ex-Adonises of Cynthia's, whose worth, beyond a certain public-school prettiness, had taken considerably longer to prove itself. Embarrassed – they had long since settled for younger, more malleable women than Cynthia – the ex-Adonises began to agree with Alison. Cynthia pretended she had only been playing devil's advocate and Alison's candidate won the day. She broke the good news to him herself. He hugged her in full view of the office and they agreed to meet for a celebratory drink at six-thirty. It was now seven-fifteen.

'Hi?'

As he answered the telephone, she heard laughter in the background. He was already celebrating. At home. With friends. Having expected only his answering machine, she wanted to hang up without speaking but instead said, 'It's me. I'm at the wine bar. Remember?'

There was a second of quick thinking then he blurted, 'God I'm so sorry, Alison. Listen, I –'

'That's all right,' she said, thinking it wasn't. 'I've run into some old friends here. We were just wondering where you had got to, because they're treating me to dinner and you could have come along.'

He opted for what he gauged as disarming frankness.

'Do you know, I was so excited and, what with everyone ringing to congratulate me, I completely forgot!' She could picture him running a hand through his boyishly tousled hair, one shirt tail carefully untucked. 'Alison I'm a bastard. You must let me buy you an extra special lunch.'

'Yes,' she said shortly. 'You can. Bye.'

'Bye. See you tomorrow. And listen. I'm truly sorry.'

'Yes.'

Cynthia would have taken revenge, scuppered his first

big deal then pretended to rescue him from the mess, while spreading rumours that he could only get it up with women over fifty, but Alison feared this was yet another area in which she was not like Cynthia. She would probably end up paying for the proposed lunch, because he had managed to forget his wallet. She paid for the Beaujolais, carried out the rest of the bottle to give to a girl she had noticed camped outside, toyed with the idea of a taxi, then let prudence draw her inexorably on to the deep escalators at Holborn station.

As she rode out towards Mile End, she thought back to a conversation at Cynthia's Notting Hill house a few nights before. Cynthia had been holding forth about how she felt every fiction editor worth their salt should invest at least six months in psychotherapy. As the chatter progressed, revolving around Cynthia's extensive psychic safari, Alison realised that she was the only one at the table never to have consulted a therapist, analyst or some kind of life-healer, and made a mental pledge never to let Cynthia discover this.

Between courses, Alison stacked up the dirty plates and carried them out to where Cynthia was whirling up flambéed bananas for pudding.

'That was delicious,' she said of the stringily overcooked duck stew they had just finished. Rather than thank her for the kind insincerity, Cynthia offered one of her pieces of unsolicited constructive criticism.

'Your trouble, Alison,' she said, splashing some more whisky into the pan, 'is that you're a Good Child.'

Alison smiled, taking this as a kind of back-handed thank-you.

The following day, her friend Sandy, never one to stifle opinions she could share, also accused her of being a Good Child. Prompted by Alison's blank reaction, she lent her a paperback from her library of self-help books, *Know Yourself*. Alison read the relevant chapter with a shock of recognition. She was, it seemed, a textbook case – quiet scion of a noisy mother, an only daughter using goodness as a cement to hold together a home which could not with any accuracy be called broken since it had never been whole. She discovered at an early age that the world wanted her to be good – easy, compliant, no trouble. She also discovered that she had a *gift* for goodness. When Jamie went away to boarding school and she found herself spending long periods as the commune's only child, she deduced that, since children made demands, childish was the least convenient thing for her to be.

As if by some physical law, she and her brother expanded to fill contrary roles. He did exactly as he wanted, while she fulfilled the wants of others. She had tried to emulate Jamie from time to time, just as she now tried to emulate Cynthia; to be transgressive, as she did on most of the occasions when she slept with anyone. Time and again, however, she then discovered that what she took for transgression was merely what someone else required of her. The world, it seemed, was a checkerboard of conflicting wills and whenever she stepped bravely onto a black square, it turned white. She aspired to anger, a white-hot rage of will that would silence rooms and command respect, but found she merely became angry with herself. When, as on the telephone earlier, she required an apology from another, she could not bear the tension of waiting, and so supplied one herself.

She wondered how she would introduce herself at a first therapy session.

'My name is Alison Pepper. I am a disappointment to my mother; despite my having taken her name. I am twenty-seven. Sometimes I am so envious of my brother and step-siblings, with their money and their ease, that I must leave a room rather than commit an act of violence. I have a good job which often bores me and that in turn makes me feel guilty. Spoilt. I live alone. I dislike my face but have learned to live with it, unlike my mother. My life lacks motion. At times I feel I am not yet quite alive. I am still marking time.'

She could flash before her mind's gaze phases from her life so far, like so many brightly coloured educational cards. Her Commune Girlhood, Her Two-Month Summer of Subsidised Rebellion, Her University Years, The Dawn of Dissatisfaction. She had recently cut out and faxed Jamie an interview with several of their contemporaries, also children of middle-class communes. Apart from one, who had been imprisoned for rape, all had reacted to the revolutionary shapelessness of their early years by carving out young lives of supreme conformity. All lived in cities, all worked in offices, and none planned to continue the experiments of their parents. Alison pictured the pair of them, she, parcelled tidily away in her office at Pharos, on the fringes of Covent Garden, and Jamie, boxed more tidily still, in his dust-free, bookless office in the City.

She often wondered about Jamie. He might be seeing a therapist already. He kept his private life so private, was so selective, at least, in the version of his private life he revealed to her, that she could never have guessed at anything he chose not to tell her. She felt that he strove to obliterate the need for a private life at all. He worked and played obsessively. He watched a lot of television. If ever she felt threatened with self-pity, she had only to think of Jamie to feel better, for all the freedom of his love life, easy money and parental adoration he heedlessly received. Her envy of him was never lasting. Sometimes he seemed so tense with things unspoken she was astonished he did not crack. Perhaps he yet would. Cracking ran in the family, after all.

She left the brightly lit station for the walk home. Even so late, Mile End Road was busy with cars and lorries. Few of her friends or colleagues understood her decision to buy a terraced house on the edges of Bow, far from delicatessen, wine bar or bookshop, while they were settling amid the cosier hostilities of Kentish Town or Westbourne Grove. They accepted, however, her excuse that the East End was handier for driving out to The Roundel on a Friday night – weekend cottages were part of their vocabulary.

The house was pretty, even if it did look out over a succession of tower blocks. She had Bengalis on one side, West Indians on the other and an heroically camp Irish priest and his young 'lodger' two doors down. A superb, chaotic Indian restaurant, two markets and three Hawksmoor churches were all in easy walking distance. On weekends when she was forced to stay in town, she borrowed the priest's dog and took long, determined walks. If there was a park, muzak-free pub or unspoilt Dickensian backstreet, she had discovered it. She liked the area. At least, she was hell-bent on liking it.

When she wanted prettiness, there was always The Roundel. Bow was vigorously alive.

To a therapist she might have admitted that she chose to move there from a superstition that its rough energies might kickstart her life, its inconveniences produce an adventure. Several years on, the adventurousness remained resolutely an inconvenience and she had to throw a serious party, with a lot more than bowls of crisps on offer, to convince friends into visiting. The fickle editorial assistant had visited, but then, he was as ambitious as he was pretty. She gleaned a certain retrospective pleasure from contemplating the nightmarish tube voyage he must have taken to shave and change in Tooting Bec before returning to Pharos the morning after their night before. On dark, drizzle-swept nights she, too, found her decision to settle there hard to understand.

Tonight, however, was mild and clear. Above the sodium cloud of street lighting she could make out a faint dusting of stars. She slipped into a grocer's to buy milk and a pair of tights. As she turned off the Mile End Road into the rabbit run of narrow backstreets that made up a shortcut to her terrace, she became aware of the human sounds emanating from all the windows open to the night – the murmur of televisions, voices raised in anger, the punchy rhythm of dance music, a sudden peal of uncontrolled female laughter.

She stepped out into the road to pass a ragged pool of cats picking over the contents of a toppled restaurant dustbin. She had to pass through one of the rare sections of bomb-damaged land still untouched by developers or council after fifty years, a summer sanctuary for buddleia and butterflies. Where there had been mean houses backing onto a railway embankment there was now yard upon yard of corrugated iron fence held together as much by thick layers of record company posters as by its original bolts. The drifting population of the homeless had claimed this no man's land as their own. Travelling by on the train, one could see their make-shift shacks of planks, car bodywork, discarded curtains and polythene sheeting. By day there were few signs of life – she supposed they left early to take up begging positions around the City – but at night one could see firelight flickering beyond gaps in the fence.

She saw it now, as she passed by and she heard someone playing a guitar badly. She smiled to know that some buskers actually practised. A dog bounded up to the fence barking and she hurried on, reminded of her hunger by the harsh scent of cooking meat.

She slipped quickly through the dankly cavernous space under the railway lines, which was unnerving even on summer nights, and came to the isolated pub on the other side. The pub was inexplicably popular. Jamie said he had heard that some of the East End 'lads' among the City traders bought drugs there, but it seemed unlikely. As usual the pavement around it had been encroached upon by the drinkers' cars – fast-looking things, much waxed and improved-upon, which made Alison guiltily aware of how much she neglected her company car. She rarely washed it and used it so little during the week – preferring the tube because it allowed her to read – that she had been known to forget where she had parked it.

Two men emerged from the pub as she passed. Young men. Younger than her, she guessed. She smelled their strong cologne. They looked as pampered as their cars, groomed, waxed, careless. They were fraudulently dressed as American high school students from the late 'fifties – chinos, deck shoes and gaudy baseball jackets. As she passed, she thought they were commenting on a car, then realised it was her they were appraising. She made out something about her legs and a supposedly flattering mention of her tits before their words degenerated into mere roosterisms.

Alison was used to this. She knew she was not beautiful but that her scrawniness made her breasts seem larger than they were and that something about her, an air of vulnerability, of immaturity even, invited the comment of men who clammed up in the face of a real, womanly sexiness like Cynthia's.

Her defences rising, she clutched her bag more tightly and marched on, trying to speed up imperceptibly. She was not entirely sober, but she was more so than they.

'Hey!' one of them shouted. 'Hey! Cop a load of this, then!' She walked on, busily mapping out alternative routes to take should she have to break into a run. She must not look round.

'Oi!' called the other. 'Take a look!'

They chuckled. The second one had a slight huskiness to his voice, like Tony in the post room at work, which she had always found rather sweet. They could not have been more than eighteen or nineteen. Boys not men. She decided to humour them, stopped, sighed and looked over her shoulder.

It was clearly something they had rehearsed, a laddish routine. They were side by side, hands in their open flies and the second she turned they whipped out their beer-gorged pricks and started to pee towards her. Alison found herself freezing and staring like an idiot. It was only when she realised she was standing still and they were still walking towards her as they peed that she gasped, lurched back and began to run. They whooped and followed. She looked wildly about the street ahead of her but it was deserted – a tunnel of corrugated fence. Someone else left the pub and drove past her heedlessly.

They caught up with her easily. A hand seized her arm. Pulled off balance, she found herself clutching at a shoulder with her other hand to stop herself falling. Realising what she was doing, she tried to jump back, clawing out, and received a slap on her face. She had not realised a slap could hurt so. They pushed her hard up against the metal fence, face first. Regaining her breath, she tried to shout but a hand clamped brutally over her mouth. A huge hand, with a thick gold ring that dug into her chin. She tried to bite it but the bruising grip was so fierce that her lips and teeth were crushed into immobility. Another hand clutched at hers, another tugged down her skirt, scratching the skin on her thighs. They were laughing still. She could not believe they were laughing. The laughter of boys teasing a cat or burning a beetle. Then agony made her yell behind the muzzling fingers. Unable to get it up, the one who had been lunging at her was punishing her for his impotence by scrabbling vindictively with his hand.

'Stupid cunt,' he hissed. 'Stupid fucking cunt!'

There was a sudden commotion. Pressed against the fence she could see nothing. The man holding her cried out in pain and shock, releasing her hands from above her head.

'Shit! Tel! Wha –?!' the first man began. He started to pull away from her then pushed fiercely back into her spine. There was a dull crack, like a stick breaking and he let out a deafening roar into her ear. He rolled aside and fell against the fence in time to receive a massive punch to his jaw. Turning, Alison saw it was not from the second man, as she had expected, but a third, much taller than the others. The second man was twenty yards away already, poised for flight, calling nervously to his companion, who had now slumped, groaning, to the ground.

'Mike? Come *on*, for fuck's sakes. Jesus!'

He turned and ran.

'My bag,' Alison murmured to herself, rubbing her arms as the feeling returned to them. 'The wanker's got my bag.'

The fight had gone out of her entirely. She knew how these things went. She expected the attack to be continued, first by one man, then the second, then the third. But the third simply touched her shoulder and sprinted away. She tried to walk, then stumbled and stooped to readjust her torn clothes.

'Bitch,' she heard from behind her. 'Stupid cunt.'

She turned back to where he was lying. Carefully avoiding looking at his face, she parted his outstretched legs with two hacks from her toe, then delivered a quick, hard kick to his groin. She had thought he would squeal but he merely let out a kind of wheeze and doubled up. She calculated she had a good five minutes before he managed to follow her. She glanced both ways and decided to double back towards the Mile End Road in search of a minicab. She was only minutes from home but either of the other men might be lying in wait up ahead. She dared not face the pub in her present state.

Walking back, she feverishly rehearsed what had just happened, not to go over where she might have done something wrong, but to enumerate what she had been spared. They had abused her, clawed her, called her childish names. Her face was bruised. Her skirt was torn. But the man had not penetrated her. He had not dirtied her utterly. Not possessed her. And she was alive. She would get home, take a bath, call Sandy, then ring the police. She could give descriptions of near photographic accuracy. She knew two of them were called

Terry and Mike. She knew where they drank. She would see them sentenced.

'Hey!'

Her system still humming with adrenalin, she was swifter to react this time.

'Hey! Wait!'

She ran. Hard. She would never look around. Never.

'Your bag. I got your bag back for you!'

She turned. It was the taller one, the third man, his black coat flapping about his legs.

'Fuck off,' she warned. 'The police are coming.'

He was indeed clutching her bag. Turning to continue running, she made a rapid mental checklist of its contents. Wallet. Press-on towels. Diary. Lipstick. Chequebook. Paperback. Condoms. All replaceable. The manuscript. Damn! It was a particularly valuable one; the first draft of a new Judith Lamb she had bribed from someone in Lamb's agency by putting forward a modest proposal for one of his newcomers. Alison's secretary had not yet found time to photocopy the thing. She staggered panting to a halt and turned, pointing.

'Stop there.' He stopped. 'Move back below the light so I can see you.'

Breathless too, he took a few shambling steps back to stand beneath a streetlamp. He had short, untidy black hair, a gold earring and several days' growth of beard. A spotted handkerchief was tied at his neck. Beneath the coat his clothes were filthy. A far cry from the other two.

'Look,' he said. 'If you like I'll leave it down here for you then just piss off, all right?'

His accent sounded West Country. Or was he just another Londoner? She found it hard to tell. He was older than the others. Thirty. Maybe a little more.

'No. Stop. You . . . You weren't with them, were you?'

'Jesus! What planet are you from? Of course not. I broke the bastard's arm for you.'

She remembered the crack and felt slightly sickened, and at the same time excited.

'I chased the other one to those flats near the flyover. You know?'

'I know,' she said. 'Did he, er, put up much of a fight?'

'Look. Do you want the bag or don't you?'

'Yes. Sorry.'

She walked hesitantly over to him. He was very tall. Huge in fact. Despite the layer of grime, he didn't stink. He wasn't a wino. The grime, she now saw, was brick dust, making him almost swarthy in the face. He held out the bag and she took it, glancing to check for the manuscript.

'Look. I didn't take anything,' he said. 'All right?'

'No,' she tried to explain. 'I was only –'

'My pleasure.'

He turned on his heel and began to stride away. She scrabbled inside for her purse and found herself calling after him.

'Look. I'm sorry.'

He stopped.

'What?'

'You . . . You saved my life. Thank you.'

He shrugged.

'Here,' she went on. 'You must let me . . .'

She opened her wallet.

'I don't want your money,' he said.

'Well let me buy you a drink.'

'No. How far do you live?'

'Not far.'

'I'll walk you home, then.'

'But . . .'

'I'll walk you home. Come on.'

His tone was firm. Sober. She paused for a moment then began to walk beside him. She thought of leading him to a false address, to the priest's house perhaps, then took another look at his long, extraordinary face and decided to repay chivalry with trust. As they walked, the after-effects of the adrenalin began to make her shudder and she asked him questions to occupy her quivering jaw. He was from Plymouth, it transpired. Laid off at the naval docks, he had hitch-hiked to London and spent the previous two years working on building sites where the foremen weren't fussy about national insurance papers or bank accounts. When she told him she worked in publishing he confessed to having once enjoyed *North and South*. And he told her not to be such a patronising git when she voiced happy surprise.

'What will you do about, you know, back there?' he asked.

'Ring the police when I get in.'

'Why?'

'They tried to rape me. I saw their faces, their clothes. I heard their names. I could give good descriptions. I've even got a witness, now.'

'Oh no,' he shook his head.

'But surely?'

'Please,' he said, stopping to lay a huge, beseeching hand on her forearm. 'Don't call the police.'

'But I should. They might do it again.'

'They won't. Not after what I did to them.'

'It would make me feel safer.'

'I'll protect you.'

'Oh well, now I feel a *lot* safer.'

'I'll protect you,' he repeated, challenging her cynicism. She caught that expression in his eyes again. True. Sober. Lost for words, she turned and they continued on their way in companionable silence.

'Well,' she said, as they reached her door. 'Good night. Are you sure you won't let me give you something? The price of a pint at least?'

He shook his head.

'Don't drink much,' he said. 'And I've money of my own. In you go.'

He watched her turn her key in the lock and let herself in, something she had been trying to persuade taxi drivers to do for years. 'Goodnight,' she said, 'And thank you.'

She set a bath to run then walked briskly round the house drawing curtains. When she came to pull the ones at the front, she glanced down and saw him lying on the broken council-issue bench across the way from her house, gazing up at the sky. She stared for a moment, astonished, then twitched the curtain closed. Greatly though the Cynthia in her rebelled against it, his guarding presence did make her feel safer. It relaxed her to the point where she found it safe to cry. Weeping, she tore off her clothes and stuffed them all in the kitchen dustbin. Ignoring the telephone, which rang twice, she lay weeping in her richly scented bath until she could cry no more and the water began to cool. Wrapped in her dressing gown, preparing to tumble into bed, she looked out of the bedroom window again, assuming he would have gone by now. He was still there.

Though she often felt only half-alive, and was regarded by the more powerful women in her life as a sort of listless child, Alison had a powerful will when she found the courage to assert it. Occasionally a strong resolve formed in her mind and with it, an utter calm and clarity of vision. Sure of purpose, she would do what she had to do.

He stirred from slumber at her touch, blinked awake, then sat up, astonished to find her out on the pavement in her dressing gown.

'What? Oh! What is it?' he mumbled, rubbing his hair. 'What's wrong?'

'You can't sleep here,' she said. 'It's absurd.'

'I nodded off. You want me to move on, then?'

'No. But don't you have anywhere to go?'

'I lost the key to my bedsit chasing that wanker back there. I can get another one tomorrow, when the caretaker's in. It's not cold though. I'll be okay here.'

'No. You must come inside. Come on. I've got a spare room that I never use. I know that sounds disgustingly middle class, and I suppose it is, and I am.'

'But . . .' He sat back upright on the bench, looking at her, running a hand across his dusty hair and frowning with uncertainty. 'You don't know anything about me. You don't know who I am.'

'You saved my life. Come on. I'm still hot from my bath. I'll catch my death out here.'

She pulled gently on his sleeve and he stood, towering over her once more, stooping slightly as though his height shamed him.

Leaning out of his kitchen window to water his tubs of herbs, the priest saw her lead the huge man inside and smiled to himself. He tweaked off a sprig of rosemary, sniffed it, then, turning back into the sitting room held it out to his friend who was watching an old film on television.

'Here,' he said. 'Smell.'

36

'You did *what*?'

'I asked him in. Offered him the spare room. I couldn't leave him outside. He's been there three, no, four nights now. It's fun!'

Alison had no sooner begun to tell her story than she wished she had held her peace. Jamie was looking amazed and slightly prurient, Miriam stunned and disapproving and Francis, whose face could never be called expressive, simply looked shocked. The weekend had gone fairly well until this point, with everyone on their best behaviour. She had helped Miriam cook lunch, avoided teasing her about her unsuccessful but doubtless expensive new hairstyle and carefully parried her attempts at unnervingly intimate 'girl talk'. Relaxed by too much wine however, she had started to tell them all about Sam and, having started, had been unable to stop on account of their relentless interrogation. She had given them an edited version, made the attack sound like a simple, random mugging.

'Why didn't you just give him some money?' Francis asked.

'He doesn't *need* money,' she insisted. 'He gets building work. He has savings.'

'Typical scrounger,' Francis declared. 'These homeless people are all the same.'

'No! You don't understand,' Alison was appalled. 'You're not listening.'

'Let him get a flat,' Francis went on.

'She doesn't want him to,' Jamie put in playfully. 'She's taken a shine to him.'

'You shut up,' she snapped, patiently turning back to Francis. 'He's got a bedsit in some awful hostel,' she explained.

He shrugged brutally, pouring himself some more coffee.

'I don't know,' he sighed, tapping the back of Miriam's chair in passing. 'Your children.'

'But we get on, I like having him around and I've given him a key,' Alison continued, desperate not to let him rile her.

'Your idealism's great, Angel,' Miriam enthused. 'Just great. I think it's awful – all these people on the streets – but isn't it, well, a bit risky for you?'

Alison rounded on her.

'I told you. He's not homeless. I only *thought* he was because of how he looked and where I met him. He's not even on the dole.'

'No. But . . .'

'Oh *please*!'

'I mean,' Miriam went on, 'if he disappeared, you wouldn't know where to get hold of him.'

'So? He probably *will* disappear. I don't think he's really comfortable being back in a house. He goes on these huge, restless walks. To Epping Forest. Greenwich. All about the city. He hardly sleeps. I don't know how he finds the energy to work.'

She smiled across at Jamie, apologising with her eyes for not having told him before, in the privacy of his car.

'It makes me feel quite safe at night,' she said. 'Like having a big security guard in the place.'

Jamie merely raised an eyebrow at this as he sipped at his cup, teasing her over its gold-leafed brim. He forgave her. Alison stood and went to the French windows to look out at Francis's immaculate, mower-striped lawn. He threw a party out there every summer for his grateful clients. He hired staff, put up a marquee, Miriam wore a hat, people cried in bathrooms and there was always a fight over the 'children's' failure to attend.

'Honestly,' she said. 'I wish I'd never brought it up.' She knew Miriam would be throwing a look at Jamie behind her back; one of her 'is-everything-okay-really?' looks. 'If I'd wanted a normal lodger,' she added, 'I'd have advertised for one ages ago and ended up with some drip with a dying yucca, a soap allergy and a cash-flow problem.'

'I'm sorry, Angel.' Her mother's voice reached out at her across the room like a plucking finger. 'I didn't mean to get heavy. You tell her, Jamie. It's only that we never see you and I *worry.*'

'Well don't. All right?'

'Fine. Pardon my caring.'

The telephone rang. Mother and children looked studiously in opposite directions and listened to Francis answering it. Jamie helped himself to a chocolate from a box on the unplayed piano.

'Henchley Manor,' Francis announced pompously.

'Since when?' Jamie asked and Miriam shushed him conspiratorially, regaining lost ground at her husband's expense.

'It's for you.' Francis turned and held out the receiver. 'From America.'

'If it's that bloody woman again about . . .' Miriam fell silent as she reached him, finishing her sentence with an eloquent glare. She cleared her throat and pushed back her hair. 'Hello? . . . Yes, this is Miriam Deakins speaking . . . I thought I *told* you! . . . No. Absolutely no. I know nothing and I don't think there's anything more to find out.'

She dropped the receiver smartly back into its cradle. Francis touched her shoulder, bending his head towards her. She took his hand and squeezed it briefly. Alison watched, still fascinated, despite herself, by any evidence that might explain the mysterious dynamics of her mother's marriage.

'Who was it?' she asked, happy to deflect attention away from herself once more.

'That wretched Hollywood journalist again, Call-Me-Venetia.'

'Which?' Jamie asked, opening a colour supplement as he stifled a post-lunch yawn.

Miriam poured herself a brandy and flopped back on to the sofa. Francis came to stand behind her, rubbing her neck with a thick, proprietorial hand. Alison watched his unreadable expression and wondered, as she often had since her mother had married him, whether he found them all intimidating. She feared the depressing truth was that he found them merely stupid and wantonly irrational in their behaviour.

'The one writing the biography of Myra Toye,' Miriam explained. 'She spent hours at The Roundel with poor Dad. – almost an entire day, rooting through boxes and papers he'd stashed away. And now she keeps asking what *I* know. As if I'd know anything. The book's due out soon in any case. She's probably just pestering me for more information to help publicise it.'

'Why on earth would she ask you?' Alison asked.

'Did Grandpa know her then?' Jamie added, suddenly interested. Francis sighed histrionically, indicating that this was ground that had already been gone over thoroughly and had bored him the first time around. He left the room and turned on a satellite sports programme next door.

'No,' Miriam insisted, ignoring his departure. 'I'd have remembered. I mean, he knew her to chat to – like he knew Vivien Leigh and Margaret Lockwood. Poor Vivien came to the house several times before she died. She was always sweet to me. But that Toye creature wasn't a friend or anything. Silly tarty woman, she's become. Grotesque. Plastic surgery's obscene.'

'Oh I think she's good!' Jamie protested. 'And she hasn't had surgery. I read an interview. And it's amazing how she's got herself a second career so late on in life. She must be, what, sixty? Seventy? Grandpa's age, at least.'

'Eighty. She looks eighty,' Miriam insisted.

'Never. She'd pass for fifty-five in *Mulroney Park*. Her body's amazing.'

'You don't *watch* that trash?' his mother asked.

'Every week,' Jamie admitted. 'I'm completely hooked.'

'I'm going out for a bit,' Alison murmured. 'Come on dogs.'

She pushed open a French window and Miriam's nervy, overbred red setters slipped eagerly out with her, charging ahead in a clumsy race to pee on Francis's mock-Georgian urns and scuff up the perfection of his daisy-less lawn. Sunday weighed heavily on her as it always did there. She longed for proper countryside, unmanicured, bleak and windy. She thought with envy of her grandfather. Having made his feelings towards his son-in-law amicably clear at an early stage in the courtship, he lived happily on in his studio and his flat, spared these stifling weekends at his daughter's bogus manor, as if they were some meat from which he had a religious dispensation. Alison smiled to herself, thinking how little truck Sam would have with Francis and Miriam's pretensions.

The morning after the attack – she could not, would not think of it as rape – she was momentarily startled to find the huge man drinking tea in her kitchen. He was utterly calm and unsmiling, however, and his calm proved infectious.

'Hope I didn't wake you,' he said. 'I tend to get up with the sun.'

'No,' she said. 'Is that tea still drinkable?'

As answer, he poured her a mugful. She cupped it in her hands and sipped. Then she found her hands were shaking and she had to set it down.

'Hell,' she said, mopping scalded fingers with a tea towel. He furrowed his brow in sympathy.

'Bastards,' he muttered. 'They won't come after you again, though.'

'Maybe not,' she said. 'But they'll probably go after someone else. I really should go to the police.'

He sighed wearily.

'Yes,' he said. 'You should.'

'You'll come with me? You saw them, after all.'

'No,' he said. 'I said last night. I'll make myself scarce. Thanks for the tea and everything, though.' He pushed back his chair.

'No,' she said hurriedly, acutely aware now that the last thing she wanted was to be left alone, even in the banality of a weekday morning. 'Don't worry. I won't. There must be hundreds of people who look like them in any case. But why don't you want me to?'

He kept on out into the hall.

'No,' she said. 'Don't go. Please. Stay for a bit.'

'I can't answer questions,' he told her, suddenly angry, 'and it's not fair on you to expect you not to ask.'

'That's my problem. I won't ask.' She held open the kitchen door to him respectfully. 'Please?'

For what felt like a full minute, he seemed to read her face, registering what he saw there with minute alterations in his own, ironic expression.

'Please,' she said again and at last something in him relaxed and he walked past her back to the kitchen. His legs were so long that they stretched out right below the table when he sat and under the chairs on the other side. The leather on one of his boots had worn down so that a steel toecap shone dully through it.

'Good,' she told him, sitting too. 'I'm Alison.'

'I'm Sam,' he said.

'Suits you,' she said.

'So they tell me.'

For the first time, he smiled. It was a lovely, sexy smile, that dimpled his cheeks and made little creases around his eyes. Alison had grown up surrounded by men with unkempt beards and long hair, so she remained vulnerable to the charms of naked male grins. She feared he had shaved with one of the blunt disposable razors she used on her legs and hoped it had not hurt him.

'Do you want some breakfast?' she added. 'I can never face anything but there's bread and so on.'

'I'll grab a bacon sandwich in a caff on my way in,' he said. 'I should go.' He glanced at the kitchen clock. 'I'm going to be late.'

'Where are you working? Sorry. That's a question, isn't it?'

'The new hospital,' he said. 'Where the glue factory used to be.'

'I should leave too,' she told him. 'We can go together.'

'You'll be all right going out?'

'I don't know,' she admitted. 'But I'd rather be in the office than out here on my own. I can get a taxi home if I'm going to be late. And I've too many things to get done today. I'll go to pieces later, when there's time. It's okay. That's a joke. Here, take the spare key,' she said impulsively. 'I often have to work late and I don't want you waiting out there on that bench.'

He took the key and looked at it in the palm of his hand, puzzled.

'Are you sure you know what you're doing here?' he asked.

'Not really.' She reached for her bag of still unread manuscript. 'But it feels right.'

'But you don't know me or anything about me.'

'You're Sam. I trust you.'

'I've already got a place to live at the hostel.'

'But do you like it there?'

Sam paused a moment, then snorted.

'It's bloody horrible. Sarajevo under siege.'

'So stay here. There's nothing worth stealing anyway, I've been burgled so often. Not that I think you would.'

'I wouldn't. But still . . .' He hesitated.

'Come on,' she said. 'Or we'll both be late.'

As they parted company outside the tube station, he plucked, quite unselfconsciously, at her jacket sleeve, holding her back by him.

'I might not come back tonight,' he said. 'It's . . . I . . . I can't explain but –'

'It's all right,' she assured him, light-headed from risk and an empty stomach. 'Keep the key in case.'

But he had come back. And the night after that. He came home reddish-grey with building dust, leaving a faint tang of sweat behind him in the kitchen while he paused for a cup of tea before taking a shower and falling into a deep sleep in a chair or on the sofa. He usually woke again after a couple of hours, half-way through the evening. He shaved with a noisy, battery-powered razor he carried in one of the deep pockets of his coat. Apart from the odd finger-print, he moved through her small household leaving remarkably few traces, fastidious as a large but graceful cat, comforting, in his strongly felt presence, as a dog.

'But he's a *man*!' the Cynthia within said when she caught her mind tidying him away in this emasculating fashion. 'He must have appetites, needs. He'll soon start making demands.' But Sam seemed more self-contained and less demanding than any man or woman she had ever met. He let slip certain pieces of information. He had a savings account where he stored his wages for safekeeping. He owned no clothes other than the ones he stood up in and a second set of shirt, socks and underwear, which he carried screwed up in another pocket of his coat. A precious spare pair of jeans was retrieved from the hostel. He had a blue shirt and a red one, and was scrupulous in washing each set of clothes with a bar of soap on the night he took it off. Alison envied him the simplicity of this system, being tyrannised herself by a large wardrobe, much of it bought for momentary psychological comfort rather than long-term physical necessity, and much of it deemed unwearable. He asked her no questions about herself, which was strangely liberating, allowing her to exist for him just as she appeared, there, then, simply. He was keenly aware of his surroundings, however, and openly curious about things he found lying about the house. Books, mainly, and house-plants and compact discs. He regularly listened to whatever disc she left in the player, content to play it over and over until she changed it. And she knew he had occasionally looked at the manuscripts she brought home because, turning their pages at her office desk, she had found signs of his work-dusty touch on their pages.

'Has he been doing time?' Sandy asked when Alison described the quiet charm of living with him.

'Of course not,' Alison told her. 'I'm not a total fool.'

But it was only as she denied it that she saw that he probably *had* been in prison. It would explain his reluctance to have her involve him with the police – especially if he were still on parole – and his inability to find a better job. It would explain his tough self-sufficiency, and the armour of discretion he wore over his emotions, much as going to boarding school had done to Jamie. She felt foolish at having taken for unworldliness the symptoms of institutional abuse. In her weaker moments, she also felt shame at the prurience with which she now imagined the extent of his criminality. She felt fear, too. He had already showed himself to be violent, albeit in a good cause, and she wondered how long it would be before she witnessed that violence again. She determined not to tell him her assumptions about his recent past. If there was any purpose in their paths crossing, it was that she could discreetly help him to make a fresh start. She pictured Miriam and Francis's horror if she had hinted at any of these suspicions.

She reached the bench at the far end of her stepfather's garden and sat squarely, glaring across the lawn at his fatuous house and waiting for her anger to evaporate in the still air. It soon would; she had always been reliably even tempered, quick to speak her rage – which she seldom did – quick to forgive. The dogs slumped to the grass on either side of her legs, faithful without encouragement. She petted one, rubbing its long, silky ears between her fingers and scratching its chest. It was as far removed from Amos, the scruffy adopted stray of her childhood as 'Henchley Manor' was from The Roundel. It was so maddeningly typical that Miriam, who had given open house to any number of more or less criminal men throughout her youth and had even conceived children by two of them, should now react towards her daughter's simple act of grateful hospitality with querulous alarm. There was always the possibility, of course, that a mother's intuition had prompted her to guess that the hospitality was not quite so simple as Alison would have it appear.

At a fierce two-finger whistle, Alison looked up to see Jamie waving to her from the terrace. The dogs bounded away towards him. He bent to pet them then looked back to her, tapped his watch, jerked his head towards his car and grinned. She held up a thumb in agreement and stood.

'So do I get to meet him?' he asked as he swung the car up on to the Bow fly-over. 'Mr Strong-and-Silent?'

'Jamie, he's just my lodger, all right?'

'If you say so.' He grinned across at her and accelerated through some lights as they were turning red. He allowed the music to swell up between them for a few moments; listening religiously to the entire Top Forty every Sunday evening was one of his eternal teenage habits. He would still be wearing jeans and baseball boots in his fifties, she sensed, and, damn him, he would still have the figure to get away with them. 'But I do want to meet him,' he added. 'Can I?'

'Of course you can,' she sighed, weary of his teasing and

wondering, with a trace of apprehension, what he and Sam would make of one another.

'He won't run away or anything?'

'Jamie!'

'I'll be good,' he assured her. 'Promise.'

He turned up the radio for a song they both liked and wound down his window to take a better look at the pale torso of a cyclist who had stopped to peel off his Lycra top at the roadside.

Sam wasn't there, however. Adept at reading her house's atmospheres, Alison could tell it was empty as soon as she crossed the threshold. She laughed the disappointment off, telling Jamie her lodger must have heard him coming, but after he had driven off, excusing himself for some, urgent, unspecified assignation, she examined the house more carefully. She saw that Sam had taken the previous day's shirt with him, although it would still be damp. The spare jeans were gone, and a loaf of bread, and a pint of milk. She knew then that he might not be coming back, knew too with a spasm like the shivers that heralded an infection, that she wanted him.

Alison was not a woman to lose control. She sank to the point of sitting on his tidily made bed, touching his pillow and moping like a lovelorn teenager, then checked herself on the safer side of folly. She spent the evening reading manuscripts and the next few days gathering information on the coming season's fiction titles for a sales conference, and putting in extra hours doling out advice and calm on the helpline.

Sam came back on the Thursday night, just as she was preparing for bed. She was unreasonably glad and could not help letting it show and when, four days later, he disappeared again, she was unreasonably miserable. Sitting at the kitchen table over the remains of a bottle of wine, she forced herself to draw up her emotional accounts, listing Sam's good and bad points in two conflicting columns. She was happier having him around occasionally, she concluded, than not having him around at all. She kept the L-word at bay by emphasising to herself the absurdity of attempting to build a romance upon a one-sided interest in a man who had restructured his whole life so as to keep it clean of domestic intimacy. When he returned, she tried cultivating the stoic self-sufficiency of the sailor's wife. It worked.

During a long evening of reading while Sam ploughed a deliberate furrow through all her Mahler symphonies, he twisted around on the sofa beside her so as to stretch his legs out over a neighbouring armchair and rest his head in her lap. At first she found she could only pretend to read, every cell of her being focused on the sensation of his body warmth against hers. Her hand tensed with the temptation to caress rather than merely hold. Then, forced to reread a paragraph her eyes had only scanned, she found herself drawn back into the story and her body became as relaxed as his. The second time this happened, she found it the most natural thing in the world to throw a sisterly arm across his chest and continue reading as though his unexpected gesture of affection were no more than a restless cat's passing bid for attention.

As though secure in her sexual neutrality, he began to stay for longer stretches, disappearing less often. He even planted some autumn crocus bulbs in her patch of untended garden and built a makeshift barbecue with some stolen bricks and an oven shelf retrieved from a skip. She decided the time had come when he could safely be introduced to her brother.

37

Jamie did not normally go on marches. He never had, in fact, since he had been of an age to choose not to. He was not a political animal. He resented, perhaps, dim memories of hours spent on protests for peace, marches against racism and smoke-ins for the legalisation of cannabis in a scratchy, home-made papoose as a baby and then on various bearded men's shoulders as a small boy. In some ways, Alison had taken up where Miriam had left off. She relished playing her brother's conscience, cajoling him, hectoring him to pull on some sensible walking shoes and take to the streets in support of this or that beleaguered cause. Sometimes he had almost gone as far as joining her but had been diverted on the way by a challenging glance or casual smile.

'Something came up,' he would tell her later.

'I bet it did,' she would jeer, but she never stopped trying. He suspected that she preferred him to be a backslider as it reinforced her own, strong, sisterly role.

For once, however, she had caught him at a good time. Or rather, a bad one. He usually enjoyed his work, relishing its combination of austerity and glamour. He gained a dubious thrill from the occasional reminders that the dry pages of five, six, even seven digit figures he spent his days laconically juggling on his computer screen represented lifetimes of personal savings – gambled in a game where there was no moderation, where the losses and gains were regularly of a size to cripple or corrupt. He loved the ugly scenes when some hot-cheeked Name or other burst in to protest at an especially cutting demand for money, as though Jamie and his colleagues had hoodwinked them, disguising a casino as a building society.

'There is always a high element of risk, Sir,' the members' agent told them. 'We *deal* in risk, Madam. No syndicate ever promises a sure return.'

His own money was paid each month into a high interest account or used to purchase unit trusts. Francis sniffed out the best deals for him – something Jamie never told Alison lest she pour scorn on his duplicity. He enjoyed the vertiginous, glossy surfaces of the building where he worked, especially when its hypocrisy was punctured by his recognition of some crisp-suited executive, spotted on a previous evening at a more openly louche establishment.

Recently his work had begun to lose its charm, however. His previous boss, a sweetly crusty, ex-cavalry type, with fly-away eyebrows and a pipe had retired to amuse himself with a rare breeds farm in Hampshire. There had been three candidates for his position, of which Jamie's least favourite had proved successful. Nick Godfreys had made his fortune writing computer software while still a schoolboy, and had become the youngest Name in Lloyd's history. He did not need to work and everyone suspected he had bought into the syndicate only because it amused him to make a better job of caring for his own money than Jamie and his colleagues could. He had the sex appeal of a newt but, because of his self-made wealth and extreme youth, the tabloids had elected him a people's hero and, by extension, a worthy sex symbol. They tirelessly ran stories charting his on-off engagements to a succession of aristocrats' and government ministers' daughters, their inexplicable, laddish affection for 'Naughty Nick' increased, if anything, every time he successfully sued them for libel. Somewhere after his second million, Godfreys had, rather greedily, Jamie thought, claimed Jesus for his own personal saviour. Unconvincingly jocular with most of his colleagues, he made no attempt whatever to conceal his distaste for Jamie. Jamie's job was secure, for the moment at least, but, in the name of financial expediency, Godfreys had swiftly begun to make life uncomfortable for him, and Jamie could no longer risk the slightest infringement of office policy.

Lunch hours were curtailed, telephone calls logged, workloads increased and the secretarial staff halved, forcing him to share his secretary with four colleagues. Four times, Godfreys had carefully humiliated him by querying his calculations in full hearing of the others. With comforting reliability, Old Eyebrows had been dimmer than any of them.

The morning Alison telephoned – even *receiving* a personal call was now an infringement of the new order's code – Godfreys had just walked through the office handing out invitations to an engagement ball he was throwing at his house outside Westmarket.

'You don't have a girlie, do you, James?' he asked in an insinuating manner as he dropped a stiff, white envelope on to Jamie's blotter.

'Not at the moment, no,' Jamie told him. 'Why?'

'Well try to rustle one up to bring with you, will you? Someone pretty enough to fool people? Not that bull dyke you brought to the last Christmas party. People talk, you know, and it upsets me.'

Jamie felt his face burn as Godfreys walked on. He caught his secretary smirking at him. Then Alison called to insist he come on that year's Gay Pride march.

'Just this once,' she wheedled. 'It's more important now than ever, Jamie.'

'But why are *you* going?' he asked her, a hand over the mouthpiece as Godfreys strolled by again.

'Solidarity,' she said. 'And pride. My friends make me proud, but you don't, and I'm fed up going on your behalf year after year.'

'Okay,' he said quietly. 'I'll come.'

'It's not rabidly political in any case,' she swept on. 'There's even a gay Tory group from Wimbledon and – *What?!*'

'I said I'll come.' He glanced across at his secretary, challenging her to smirk. 'I'll come,' he repeated, and felt himself committed.

Crossing town on the Piccadilly Line, he stopped reading the overhead posters and looked about the carriage, noticing something strange happening. He never rode the Underground without spotting at least one or two gay people, either by some obvious piece of subculture uniform or by a covert glance or discreetly clasped magazine or novel, but always they were in a minority of two or three per carriage. Now the social chemistry of the train was changing visibly. More and more noticeably gay groups were climbing on board – lesbian couples with toddlers holding their hands, hip young politicos with sideburns and fierce-sloganned tee-shirts, chattering groups with picnic baskets, a big leather guy who looked as though he could break your neck with one slap of his palm, but paraded his humour and soft heart by bringing along his dalmatian in a matching leather jerkin and red bandanna. As they neared Leicester Square, the straight people on board were gradually being eased into the minority. Some of them enjoyed the free cabaret and murmured to each other or smiled their approval, others looked distinctly unnerved and Jamie realised that moments like this one probably rearranged far more people's perceptions than the actual march.

The concentration of gays and lesbians when he emerged onto the pavement was still more dizzying, even though they were streets away from the assembly point. A bunch of young women growled down St Martin's Lane on Harley Davidsons and were greeted with whoops and whistles by some appreciative elder sisters who were climbing down from a Welsh coach. Jamie counted ten same-sex couples openly holding hands. A policewoman held up the traffic to let another chunk of the crowd cross the road. She smiled when a lesbian blew her a kiss and Jamie felt an impulse to laugh out loud. The long, excited queue for a cashpoint machine on the Strand might have been calculated revenge for years of tediously boy-girl advertising imagery plugged by the banks. The only woman in a skirt was dressed like Annie Oakley and looked as if she could have lassooed a prize bull, never mind a bullock, with one hand. She caught Jamie admiring her and raised an unplucked eyebrow before snatching her wad of cash and striding on southwards.

Alison was just where she said she would be, with her friends by the Embankment Garden bandstand. One of them blew a whistle to get his attention, then Alison waved and came over to meet him. She had on a big pink tee-shirt which introduced herself as REGRETTABLY HETERO – presumably the sexual equivalent of holiday insurance on such an occasion. She ran the last few yards between them and threw her arms about him.

'I'm so glad,' she said.

'Me too,' he admitted. 'I think. It's weird. How's it feel to be in the minority for once? Oh. I forgot,' he added as they approached her little gang. 'You immerse yourself all the time anyway.'

'That's right,' she sighed, caressing one of his biceps quizzically. 'My life is a Uranian festival.'

He felt unusually protective towards her as she said this, and slipped an arm across her shoulders.

As they came to greet him, he recognised some of her friends from her last birthday party in Bow. There was Sandy, who ran the helpline, Sean and Nick, who were so very married it would be no surprise to find one of them pregnant, Belgian Agnes and the thin one with the glasses. The thin one was pushing a man in a wheelchair who was skeletal and obviously very sick. Jamie instinctively averted his eyes. He looked over to where a tall man in a crimson shirt was coming across the grass from the ice cream van, his fingers twined around a clutch of cornets. Melted ice cream ran in streaks across his sunburnt hands. He looked like a Michelangelo angel who had been given a haircut with blunt nail scissors.

'And Jamie, I don't think you've met Guy,' Alison pointedly introduced him to the man in the wheelchair. Jamie shook his hand, which felt like paper-covered bone. 'And this is his buddy, Steve.'

'We've met before,' said Steve.

''Course we have,' said Jamie. 'Hi.'

He shook Steve's hand too, then glanced back, irritated to find he had lost sight of the man in the red shirt.

'And this, after all these weeks, is Sam. Sam, here's my brother, Jamie.'

Jamie turned and managed to hide his surprise. Sam wasn't ready to be introduced, occupied as he was with handing out ice cream cones without dropping any. He gave Jamie a grunt as he licked the backs of his hands clean.

'Didn't you want one?' Alison asked.

'Dropped it,' he said. 'Someone's dog's got it.'

'Oh but –'

'No. no. This'll do me.' He indicated his sticky hands.

An abrupt surge of whistling and banshee whoops warned them that the march was setting off. The column of demonstrators stretched from Hungerford Bridge to Temple Station and there were still ribbons of people hurrying to join it from all directions. Leaving the gardens, Jamie was confronted with crowd barriers blocking off the pavement from the road. The nearest opening was guarded by a bullet-headed man with a walkie-talkie and clipboard. Steve pushed Guy past him, followed by Agnes, Billy, Jamie, Sean and Nick. The bullet-headed man blocked the way, however, confronted with Alison and Sam.

'What are you?' he asked, as though this were the most ordinary question.

'I'm *sorry*?' Alison replied, laughing.

'Put her down as a gay man,' Nick called out. 'Make her day.'

'What are you?' the steward repeated, undrawn by their good humour and choosing to ignore Alison's tee-shirt.

'Well . . .' Alison hesitated, glancing uncertainly at Sam, who was starting to scowl dangerously. Jamie remembered that Sam had broken someone's arm with impunity. 'We're here with friends. *Gay* friends.'

'I must ask you to join the group of supporters at the back of the march,' the steward told them.

'But that's daft!' Alison insisted. 'We came to be with them, not to be segregated.'

'What is this, a camp?' asked someone in the queue that was pressing up behind her and there was a guffaw at the unintentional pun.

'Oh just tell him you're a dyke,' someone else muttered.

'It's quite simple,' the steward continued. 'Are you Lesbian, Gay, Bisexual or Other?'

Sam pushed to one side and began to unhook a section of crowd barrier.

'Hey! You can't do that!' the steward protested.

Lifting the barrier clear as though it were so much balsa wood, Sam threw him a look of innocent puzzlement. With a cheer and a few mutters of Nazi and Silly Cow, the people behind him – men, women and children – swept through the new space. Sam and Alison slipped through with them. Belgian Agnes clapped. Seething now, although Sandy was protesting that the steward was probably some kind of political performance artist, Alison pointedly led them all to march under the first banner she could find that least described any of them – Kent Sapphic Gardening Collective. A serene woman in African batik handed them each a flower.

As they were sucked into the tide of people, Sam tried to push his sprig of sweet-william into a buttonhole on his shirt but dropped it. Jamie picked it up before anybody could squash it.

'Here,' he said. 'I'll do it.'

'Oh. Ta.'

They stood still for a few seconds, but none of the horticultural sapphists complained or bumped into them – instead they walked neatly around, bearing Alison and the others away with them. Jamie reached up. Sam was a full head taller than him, he realised; six foot four at least. Fiddling to pull the stem through a buttonhole high on his chest, Jamie felt the rustle of hair beneath the hot shirt fabric. He glanced past Sam's shoulder and saw Alison watching them to see why they had dropped behind. Still walking, she smiled, waved and turned back to take a turn pushing Guy's wheelchair.

'What's wrong with him, do you reckon?' Sam asked as they continued, surrounded now by the London Transport SM Group, several of whom were chained to friends.

'The usual,' Jamie said.

'Thought so. Is he a friend of yours?'

'I've never met him before today,' Jamie lied.

Their section of the march was passing under Hungerford Bridge now.

'Give us an O!' somebody called.

'Oh!' people shouted.

'Give us an*other* O!'

'Oh!'

'Give us an*other* O!'

'Oh!'

'And what does it spell?'

The was a flutter of anticipatory laughter before about a hundred people yelled, 'OOOOOH!!' making the most of the booming acoustic overhead. Some scaffolders waved from their workplace on the bridge far out over the water and received another, ever so slightly ironic 'oooh' in return. Sam glanced at Jamie and snorted. Jamie quickly followed suit, as though in agreement.

'Oh I know. They're not with us. *We*'re not like that.'

Jamie noted how Sam's cheek dimpled, and let his eyes flick down to where the man's big, worn hands were swinging at his sides. He wondered how Alison had contained herself in the same house as him at night. Perhaps she hadn't. Perhaps she was already deeply in love and had forborne as yet from telling Jamie out of the usual misplaced concern that bachelors are saddened rather than encouraged to hear of the connubial joys of others. Or maybe. Just maybe, Sam had wanted to come on the march for reasons of his own . . .

'Alison tells me you're a builder,' Jamie said and promptly wished he had thought of some less crass opening gambit. Sam snorted again, and this time Jamie had the impression it was at him.

'Yes,' he said. 'I'm a naval fitter by trade. But that's about as much use as knowing how to shoe horses, maybe even less. How about you?'

'Oh I'm er . . .'

'City gent, is it?'

'Not really.' Jamie hesitated. His immediate impulse, well practised, was to lie. He usually said his name was Greg or Tony and that he worked for a landscape gardener or the Forestry Commission – something outdoorsy – but Sam had met him in context, knew his bloody sister. 'Actually I'm in a Lloyd's insurance syndicate. It's reinsurance mostly.'

'And is it interesting?' Sam clearly had his doubts.

'Well. It was.' Jamie felt himself going off his career choice rapidly.

'Do you have to wear a suit and tie?'

'Every day.'

'I'd hate that.' Sam laughed to himself. Jamie had the queer sensation of being the shy one who was being expertly encouraged to reveal himself instead of, as usual, being the drawer-out. He was about to change tack when Sam bounded aside, in answer to a hoarse shout, to exchange quick pleasantries with three ragged-looking women and their scrawny dog. A Harrods tour bus crawled by chock full of stunned overseas visitors. Marchers played up shamelessly for the cameras inside. A drag queen with a reporter's notebook came by. She was surprisingly chic and restrained in an excellent, heavily up-scaled copy of a Chanel suit, and wore a beauty queen sash that read Fashion Police. She looked Jamie over and clicked her pen against the tip of her tongue.

'Somebody didn't make an effort today,' she sighed. '*Il faut souffrir*, honey.'

Laughing, Alison beckoned Jamie to come forward to join her. He was on his way, pushing back among the lady gardeners when Sam reappeared at his side and offered a swig from a can of luke-warm lager someone had given him. It seemed like a challenge, so Jamie accepted it.

'So how are things in Bow?' he asked. 'You must have settled in well if she persuaded you to come to this.'

Sam wiped his mouth on the back of his hand. He frowned.

'Yeah, well I'm not . . . you know . . .'

Jamie knew.

'No. No, of course not. I knew that,' he said abruptly. Sam's earring was on the right, of course, which nervous hetero men always thought less riskily ambiguous. Any self-respecting queer would have paid for an artfully artless haircut rather than sport one that was so unmistakably home-made. Hoping he had not made a fool of himself, or betrayed more than a brotherly interest, Jamie walked faster, drawing Sam with him. They caught up with Alison and the rest just as they were passing a nostalgic Margaret Thatcher impersonator in a royal blue tailored outfit and imperious wig. 'She' had clambered on top of a stack of beer crates to harangue the marchers down a spangled megaphone as they came off the Lambeth end of Westminster Bridge.

'There is *no* alternative,' she enunciated in an eerie approximation of the familiar hectoring tones. 'We will never surrender to sexual terrorism. In the words of Saint Francis . . .'

Jamie watched Alison also accept a swig of Sam's lager, tried to picture the two of them sweatily naked, candlelit, and found it all too easy to see how well they would fit together. He cast the image from his mind, gave them his mental blessing and began to chat to the others, scanning the men in the crowd around him from the shelter of Nick and Sean's coupledom, using their quasi-parental air as a foil for his own availability. This nonchalance was a defence mechanism learnt early amid the brutally shifting loyalties of the playground, then honed in clubs and bars since his late teens: appear to brush him off before anyone notices that he brushed you off first. His gaze could find no purchase elsewhere, however, and kept sliding back to Sam.

The march began to move through increasingly residential streets towards Kennington. There were fewer and fewer spectators, just scowling men in traffic jams and little groups at bus shelters who tried to look invisible.

'Why *are* we doing this?' Nick asked suddenly. 'Someone remind me. I mean, why really? Is sex so important?'

'It's not about sex,' said Sean.

'Isn't it?' Jamie asked, only half-concentrating because the rest of his mind was wondering whether a big-thighed man walking on his own with a rucksack over one shoulder was interesting, foreign or merely friendless.

'It's about freedom,' Sean went on decisively. 'The inalienable right to *be*. About saying we're here, we're uncategorisable and we're not going away just to suit somebody's economic policy.'

'I think a lot of us just come because it's an excuse for a fun day out,' Nick suggested and threw a mischievous glance at Jamie. Jamie grinned back because Nick was so sweet and untroubled. He didn't fancy him – Nick was too puppyishly winning for his taste – but Jamie could see how he could be good to come home to, to wake up to. If one wanted that sort of thing. Sean hardly seemed to notice Nick was there, which was perhaps what had held them together so long; devoted compliance on one side and a kind of tender oversight on the other. When Jamie tried to picture himself as settled with someone – which he did no more seriously than when he fantasised about having a baby to push around the park or handing in his notice to take up singing professionally – it was inevitably with Nick and Sean's marriage as a model.

The park was full of people by the time their section of the march arrived, and after queuing for twenty minutes to shuffle past the volunteers with begging buckets at the gates, Jamie felt overcome by sudden fatigue and was quite content to sit on the grass with the picnic things while the others headed off to explore the disco tent, bar and countless food and trinket stalls. Alison flopped down beside him and lay on her side, watching Sam saunter off between Nick and Sean. It was one of those moments when Jamie enjoyed the sense of her being his negative image, her hair dark where his was blond, her skin pale where his was olive, her limbs soft where his were gym-hardened.

'I'm glad you came,' she said.

'So am I,' he told her, though in truth he was beginning to find the crowd enervating and the event – now that the march had finished – unfocused.

'So what do you think?'

'Well the sheer number of people who've turned up is amazing but I –'

'No,' she laughed at him. 'I mean about Sam.'

'Oh.' He screwed up his eyes against the sun, wishing he had brought his dark glasses. 'He's great. He's lovely.'

'You think so? But he's so *tall*!'

'So? Think what you could do with those legs.' He broke off to regard her quizzically. 'Have you had him yet?'

'Jamie! I don't regard every man I meet in a sexual light.'

'Pinocchio!'

'Well I don't. I'm not like you.'

'Since when?'

She slapped his thigh with the back of her hand then pushed her sunglasses further up her nose to hide her expression, but her nose was shiny with the heat and they slowly started slipping down again.

'All right,' she said, after stopping to watch two old women stroll by arm in arm. 'So I *did* want him. But I don't think he's interested. Or he respects my space as a woman or something. Anyway, if something was going to happen it would have done by now, so there's no point my fretting about it. He's a nice bloke and it's nice to have him around and there's an end to it.'

'You can't just push sex away because it's beyond your control.'

'I can,' she said. 'I always have. Like chocolate or long, expensive holidays. If I put it out of my mind, it's gone. Life's too short to mope around pining for what you can't have.'

'But you pine all the same.'

'Not if I don't want to.'

'But that's so controlled!' he protested. 'I know you. You're not that cold.'

'I can be. Just like you putting people out on the pavement without letting them stay the night.'

'That's not cold,' he protested, 'it's just honest. Letting them stay the night *then* putting them out, *that's* cold.' He caught sight of Sam in the distance, shambling awkwardly through the mass of sprawling bodies on the grass. 'Well if you're *not* going to try any harder to get him,' he suggested quietly, 'maybe I will.'

He said it partly to see how she truly felt, partly because her admission that Sam had yet to make a move on her had excited him afresh.

'Fine,' she said with a shrug, not meeting his eye. 'I mean, it would be a dreadful waste of man if you didn't.' She was hurt and trying to hide it by playing the good sport. He knew her too well to be fooled.

'You don't want me to,' he said, then glanced back at Sam and added, 'do you really think I'd be so *mean*?'

'Honestly, he's all yours,' she insisted. 'If you can get him, that is.'

So she *was* still interested. Jamie slapped her knee playfully and looked away. He would back off, he decided, and let Sam decide the contest for them, *à la* Ivanhoe.

One by one, Sam and the others returned bearing, variously,

veggie-burgers, shirts, love beads and pamphlets. Nick was shyly clasping a book called *Cook Together, Stay Together*. Guy had bought a black baseball cap which proclaimed, OUR DEATHS YOUR SHAME. He told a brief, unexpectedly funny anecdote about having just run into – literally – an old PE mistress of his, then lapsed into exhausted silence, letting his cap talk for him.

Jamie let Alison hang some love beads around his neck and kiss his cheek, and wondered why she felt the need to make peace when they had not argued. He jumped up to buy some cheap black sunglasses from a passing vendor. Examining Guy safely from behind them, he realised he must once have been handsome. It was less that one could see traces of the handsomeness in his ravaged face than that he unconsciously retained the gestures and posture of a beauty, even in his decline. The group spread themselves on the grass around his wheelchair and the crowd, in turn, seemed to spread itself on the grass around the group.

After a few angry speeches, a raucous, all-woman rock band began to play on the stage – archly melancholic songs of heartache and betrayal. Beer cans flashed in the sun and little puffs of cannabis joined the scents of cigarettes and sunblock on the breezeless London air. Everywhere people were beginning to stretch out on the grass, exposing pale bellies and sunburned shoulders. As if this reminder of the interminable navel-gazings of his boyhood were not enough, Jamie found himself obliged to watch as Sam slowly unbuttoned his shirt to the waist then casually raised his head off the grass and onto Alison's lap so as to sunbathe and watch the stage at the same time. She, heedlessly lucky, stroked Sam's hair without even looking down at him.

Accepting defeat, Jamie excused himself, muttering about needing to take a leak. The queues for the temporary gents were long, however, and their chatter began to set his nerves on edge. He followed the example of some mustachioed Germans and peed in the crowded privacy of some municipal laurel bushes. Rather than pick his way back over the countless bodies to Alison and the others, he wandered for a while around the impromptu market that had been set up in the other half of the park. He drifted aimlessly past stall after stall of things he had no desire to buy and groups he had no desire to join and found his mood sliding uncontrollably from grey to blue. The more linked hands and puckered lips he saw, the more hugs he witnessed and wittily brazen declarations he found himself reading on passing chests, the more out of kilter he felt with the proceedings seething around him. Earlier, on the tube train and crossing Covent Garden, he had felt a certain subversive elation, but now that had evaporated, and in its place he felt no pride, no solidarity, only a dim anger and encrusting sense of isolation.

He had been walking back onto the main lawn where the others were lying, but impulsively he turned aside to a path and began to stride towards an exit and the first taxi that would take him home to the private security of his Battersea flat. Alison would understand. She'd be pleased that he had at least joined her on the march, been there for the important part. He would tell her he had begun to find the crowd overpowering. This was, after all, a part of the truth. He need not upset her pointlessly by voicing his political heresy. Or his sibling envy.

Reaching a park exit, where local children jostled with marchers in competition for service at two ice cream vans, he fancied he heard her calling his name, but pressed on.

Sam caught up with him at a zebra crossing. He had obviously been running and, in his eagerness to catch up with Jamie, had not planned what he was going to say once he did.

'Hi,' he panted. 'Are you going, then?'

'Er. Yes,' Jamie said. 'Looks like it.'

Sam furrowed his brow as though this were momentarily incomprehensible.

'But you didn't say goodbye.'

'No. Sorry. I'll ring Alison later, tell her.'

'I thought we were going to, you know, talk some more.'

'Oh.'

Once again, he had Jamie feeling uncharacteristically at a loss. Jamie was aroused by the suggestion that he was interested, yet shy in the humiliating face of a possible misunderstanding. From urban instinct, he had waved at a vacant taxi, which was now pulling over from the middle of the road, causing cars in the nearside lane to swerve, tooting, around it.

'I couldn't face much more of that crowd,' he explained.

'Where d'you live, then?'

'On the river,' Jamie told him. He glanced at the taxi, which had now reached the kerb ahead of them. The driver shouted something impatiently. 'I can wait for another one,' Jamie started to say.

'No I –'

Sam faltered. Jamie looked back into his face and was surprised by an expression he recognised from other faces, other times. He stared for a moment, startled, feeling his spirits quicken, then murmured, as he had said many times before, with a flicker of a smile he knew was infallible because he had watched it on himself in countless bar and lavatory mirrors, 'So let's go.'

38

The conductor, Peter Grenfell, slowly beat the last few bars. It was hard to see how such a quantity of strings playing simultaneously could produce so magically quiet and glassy a sound. He pointed to the harpist, drawing from her one last, funereal statement. The sound grew thinner, thinner, then faded into nothing. Grenfell left his plump, white hands in the air to a count of eight, holding the players' attention and the audience's rapt silence – he was a consummate showman – then let his arms fall to his sides. Applause surged up behind his back.

Alison slid to the edge of her seat, leaning on the worn velvet parapet of the box and clapped too. In the arena below the orchestra the few promenaders not already standing had leaped to their feet and, as Grenfell returned to the platform leading her grandfather triumphantly by the hand, a great cheer went up. Alison always loved this moment, could never quite believe it was her grandfather, *hers*, they were cheering. She stopped clapping for a while, looking down at the thin, familiar figure in the crumpled, dandyish clothes, then she lifted her hands to her mouth and added her voice to the crowd's. He still looked faintly aghast at the vigorous response his work could arouse. His darting eyes dancing over the players, his little gasp when a young woman in sandals thrust herself up onto the front of the stage to hand him a clutch of flowers, were not yet insincere with use. He was still, Alison knew, a little frightened of the public's enthusiasm. He had not always been famous. It was quite a recent phenomenon.

When she was a child he had still been primarily a film composer, well-known only among cognoscenti. He used to encourage her and Jamie to wander in and out of his studio in the garden, the space where he lived and worked beside the stream, away from the chaos Miriam had drawn about herself in The Roundel. The only music in the main house came from incessantly played rock and folk records and a guitar which one of the Beards used to twang of an evening when drugs and alcohol had left their ears too sensitive for anything louder.

The studio had been a place of enchantment and astonishing order to the children. It still was to Alison, now when her own life was little more orderly than her mother's had been. Back then, her grandfather would always make time to sit her on his lap at the piano to see if she had remembered what the notes were called – which she never had – and he would let her tap on bells and blow gingerly down strange foreign pipes which smelled of spice and made noises like mice or wood pigeons. Then, when her brother began to follow her, her grandfather discovered that Jamie *could* remember what the notes were called, *could* remember tunes, *could* sing. Slowly, bitterly, Alison had found herself ousted from pride of place, as her grandfather began to shush her or even send her from the studio the better to coax Jamie towards a place in the supreme orderliness of a choir school.

He had been respected, of course, ever since he had won his second Oscar, but as a girl Alison had never quite believed it when Miriam had clutched her hand and pointed to a strange, foreign-looking name during the title sequence for a film and said, 'Look, Angel! That's him. That's Gramps!'

His real fame came later, when Alison had escaped her mother's marriage by leaving home to read Comparative Literature at Sussex. It began quietly, with a modest but intensely fashionable Scottish revival of his second opera, *Jacob's Room*, which toured to several European music festivals before receiving the recognition of being welcomed into an English National Opera season. The work had been dismissed at its first unveiling at the 1963 Trenellion Festival as impressionistic to the point of being unstageable. The revival, twenty years on, was a hauntingly designed production, and the work's plangent repetitions and strings of ironically corrupted melody – his equivalent, it was authoritatively stated, of Woolf's prose evocations of memory – attracted an audience the London opera management had rarely seen before. These new enthusiasts were young, restless and fashion-conscious, people prepared to queue for admission to nightclubs.

Eager to cash in on the success, a record company signed Edward up and began speedily to issue trendily packaged recordings, not just of his 'serious' music – the chamber pieces, *Jacob's Room*, the two symphonies written in the early 'sixties – but of his film scores too. These, it was now perceived, were actually serious music disguised, out of commercial necessity, as something more frivolous. A bondslave to the cinema, he had yet managed to satisfy two masters simultaneously, for his *amour propre*. Played without interruption, the famous score to *4.15 to Bucharest* was revealed to be a symphonic set of variations on a disguised Balkan theme, the score to *Room with Yellow Paper*, a piano concerto, and that to *What Maisie Knew*, a sinfonia concertante for cor anglais and french horn. Selling unexpectedly well – albeit in the fire of envious references in the press to 'dubious facility' and 'sterile, crowd-pleasing architectonics', these in turn led to concerts, well attended by the same enraptured young crowd who had so unpredictably detected sympathetic chords in the dreamily pacifist *Jacob's Room*.

By the time Alison was asked to come for her second interview at Pharos, she found that a slipped-in reference to her now celebrated grandfather made all the difference to Cynthia and the board's perception of her.

All Edward's works had now been recorded and many were finding comfortable niches in the orchestral repertoire. Retired from the film studios for ever, he was entering an Indian summer. The piece played that evening – *Debate for Strings and Harp* – was one of several new works directly inspired by his delight at finally finding an audience, and such a young, open-minded one. Only the score of *Job* remained on a high shelf in his studio. He had meticulously destroyed all orchestral and vocal parts and, despite repeated overtures from the record company and a prominent opera producer, he refused to release the work from the outer darkness into which he had cast it. His mysterious insistence, of course, only fascinated the interested parties the more. Accounts of the work's long-distant Rexbridge première were tantalisingly thin on detail. Alison had looked at the score once in an inquisitive moment, brushing thick dust off its handsome, tooled cover. The stylised libretto by Thomas Hickey – the 'Uncle Thomas' her mother referred to with such fondness – had struck her, but the notes on the pages told her nothing.

The stage was suddenly aswarm with furniture movers and extra players as a larger orchestra assembled for a Mozart piano concerto. Violinists stepped aside, fiddles protectively clutched to their chests, to clear a path for the Steinway that was being trundled into their midst like a great black insect queen among lesser attendants. As Alison came down a staircase into one of the hall's entrance lobbies, she could hear applause for the soloist and returning conductor.

Her grandfather was waiting for her beneath a street lamp, on his own. One would never have guessed he had just been the centre of so much attention. He had perfected a technique for politely giving hangers-on and well-wishers the slip. Though he remained a softhearted prey to autograph-hunters and zealous student musicians, he had an unconscious way of looking not quite like his public self when going about his private business. Sitting at restaurant tables or in theatre seats beside him, Alison would often see people begin an approach, then halt a few yards away, their progress checked by an indiscernible wall of doubt and indecision. She smiled, looked down again and waved, a small, familiar squeeze of love in her chest. He was more father to her than any man had ever been.

His dress sense had stopped developing somewhere in the early 'seventies, so he favoured down-at-heel velvet jackets, full, white shirts and a series of richly coloured waistcoats. Fashionable now, all over again, these had become his trademark, worn on the concert platform in place of evening dress. Tonight's waistcoat was a glowing shade of plum that set off his sleek silver hair to advantage and made his dark eyes bright. She thought again how handsome, how ungrandfatherly he could look, and wished she could have known his wife.

'It was so *good*!' she exclaimed as she hurried over. Always precise in her admiration of fine writing, she remained lost for epithets to encompass the intangible pleasures of music. '*So* good!'

'Angel.'

In his mouth, the nickname was a courtly blessing, not the irritant her mother had made of it. He kissed her cheek and handed her his bouquet. She saw at once his disappointment that Jamie was not with her.

'Jamie sent his love,' she lied quickly. 'He couldn't make it after all. That creep he works for threw a load of extra paperwork at him just when he was about to leave the office. He was furious at having to miss seeing you.'

But it was she who was furious. Jamie knew how much his coming meant to his grandfather. He understood musical language. He was the more favoured of the two, probably because he was the less solicitous. And he had given his word. She had not seen him since the march, two days before, and each day her sense of injury gained in focus. First he had left the park without so much as a goodbye. It took no mastermind to deduce that he had left with Sam in tow. Sam's unexpected interest in him had been evident, to her at least, from the start and it irritated her that Jamie felt the need to slope off with him like a poacher. Then, when Saturday stretched into Sunday and there was no sign of Sam, and Jamie still didn't call, she found herself manipulated into feeling a jealous resentment she could not logically justify. Then Monday dawned and Sam had still not returned. He had vanished before, of course. She knew better than to expect any explanation. It was quite possible that the silence of one man and the nonappearance of the other were quite unrelated. Possible but, something told her, unlikely.

On the second night, a ghastly possibility had struck her – that Sam, of whom, after all, she knew so little, might have turned violent. Through her own misplaced sensitivity, she had let her brother disappear with a dangerous man. Jamie might be unconscious in hospital. He might even be lying on the floor of his flat, dead or dying. Her mother's words echoed sinisterly through her head: 'If he disappears, you wouldn't know where to get hold of him.'

Ashamed and worried in equal parts, she had swallowed her pride and called Jamie's office that afternoon. There was a long pause before the telephonist connected them.

'I was going to call you,' he said at once, without greeting.

'Sorry,' she said, flustered with relief at hearing his voice. 'I'll be quick. You're not meant to get personal calls in the office any more, are you?'

'Oh sod that,' he breathed. He sounded exhausted, strained. Burning to question him, she found herself only hastily checking he was coming to the concert and he gave her his promise.

'You vanished after the march,' she blurted at last.

'I know,' he said. 'You didn't worry? Something came up.'

'Ah,' she said and hung up moments later, blood boiling at his casual use of the time-honoured evasion even though she knew it was impossible for him to talk openly in his office. She was wounded that both men could so easily neglect her and irritated for having given herself occasion to *feel* so wounded.

Waving aside his disappointment with a sweet compliment about enjoying the rare opportunity it gave him to have her all to himself, her grandfather walked her to a small, expensive restaurant in a narrow lane off Gloucester Road. The management and cuisine were French, so he could rely on the waiters not to recognise him.

'So,' he said, after their wine had arrived. 'Tell. How's work?'

'Oh. All right,' she told him. 'I'm in Cynthia's good books at the moment because Aldo MacInnes is already looking like a certainty for the Booker shortlist and he's one of my babies.'

'That's good. Worth reading?'

'Not really. Well. Yes, of course it is, but I know what you like, and you wouldn't like Aldo.'

'Ah.'

'And it looks as though I may have got us the next Judith Lamb but there's no skill in that – even authors with a high moral tone have their price.'

He frowned for a second at the streak of bitterness in her voice.

'But you're happy there?'

'Yes,' she said. 'I suppose so.'

'You must come down for a weekend again soon. The house misses you.'

'I will. I was – I was busy this weekend and the weekend before that I was being dutiful in Essex.'

He raised an eyebrow as he tore a chunk off his roll. The territory of her mother's marriage was well mapped out between them so that much could be conveyed in shorthand.

'Oh he's not so awful when you're patient with him,' she said, taking as read his unspoken comment on his son-in-law. He only snorted in reply then sat back to make room for the arrival of soup. 'Why's she so angry about that writer asking questions about you and Myra Toye?'

He tasted his soup, salted it, then took another spoonful, pondering the question. His hand shook slightly as he replaced his spoon. When he answered, it was elliptically.

'Your mother's never really forgiven me for sending her away,' he sighed.

'When?'

'She was nine. No. She was ten.'

'But she liked her school,' Alison insisted. 'She always talks about it as if she did.'

'That's because she's since decided it was something of a status symbol to have been sent there. It was a very, very good school. Better than anything she found for you. I didn't want to send her away, but it wasn't much of a life for a little girl. She was only a baby when your grandmother died, not even a toddler yet.' He paused in tearing another piece off his roll and raised his brows, shrugging off his words in a way that yet failed to conceal lingering pain. Alison knew at once that these were memories with which he rarely tampered. 'She stopped crying for her long before I did,' he said. 'I was earning quite well by then, so I found a nanny. Molly.' He smiled to himself at the recollection. 'Molly,' he said again, enjoying the name's pillowy sound. 'Haven't thought of Molly in years. Very strong, devoutly Christian and an even worse cook than your grandmother. Anyway, Miriam adored her and I felt safe leaving them together for days on end. But eventually Molly's father was widowed and she had to go back to Somerset to look after him.'

'She must have been heartbroken,' Alison said dispassionately.

'Who? Molly?'

'No. Mother. Miriam.'

'She was. Molly was all the mother she'd known. There was Sally's mother, of course, but she wasn't well and couldn't see her that often. I've . . . I've never seen a child as *angry* as she was after that. All the sadness came out as a quite extraordinary spell of rage. She broke things. She took scissors to her dresses. She was sweet and clinging with me – it was all directed at *things* – but I got the message. I tried a couple of other nannies but Miriam's trust had gone and, I suppose, in a way, so had mine. I didn't want to hurt her again – how could I tell how long the next one might stay? I thought at least in a school she'd have a stable group about her. And I'd be sure she was getting a good education. I promised myself I'd make a special effort to be with her during her holidays. I told myself she'd have friends of her own age at last instead of some choked-up, ageing virgin. I bought her presents. Dolls. Dresses. Books. It was terrible.'

Alison finished her soup, watching him carefully. He had never talked with her like this before and she was not entirely sure she wanted to be the recipient of such confidences. Not right then.

'I'd had such a bad time away at school,' he continued. 'I'd always sworn no child of mine would go through that, but what option did I have?'

Alison shrugged supportively, then saw he was not looking to her for a reaction but was facing some jury of the mind.

'I drove her there,' he said. 'It was a beautiful place. Early Victorian I think – I've always been hopeless at knowing things like that. A park dotted with follies. A lake. Horses.

I decided maybe girls' boarding schools were not the same as boys' ones. Mine hadn't been like *this*! She seemed excited too at first, but then she found her way to a telephone and used to ring me up and cry. I spoke to the headmistress. Perhaps it wasn't working out? I said. Perhaps I should take Miriam away, but she said it was all perfectly normal and she'd soon settle down. And she was right. There weren't any more phone calls and I started getting little Sunday morning letters from her instead. Two sides, tidily written, perfectly cheerful, asking for money and so on. She made friends. She found she was good at art.' He paused and looked directly at Alison. 'I should never have done it.'

'But if she was happy . . . ?'

'Happy without me –' He broke off as a waiter took away their empty bowls and topped up their wine glasses. 'I pushed her away,' he continued, brushing his crumbs into a tidy heap on the tablecloth. 'I showed her she could thrive on her own. I made myself redundant. When she came home in the holidays I could see the school's effects. She was growing up. She was almost poised. She brought friends home to keep her company and she sat at the dinner table with them and *made* conversation to me. It was enough to curdle the blood.'

'Is that why you made such an effort with me and Jamie?' she asked and realised she had been too open, too obvious from the way he answered with only a cursory, wordless nod.

'Now she's decided I sent her away so I'd be freer to have affairs.' He curled his lips at the word. 'Probably some stupid self-help book she's been reading has put the idea into her head.'

'She doesn't, Grandpa. Honestly. Only the other day she said you hardly *knew* Myra Toye. She was quite angry at the suggestion you might –'

'What your mother believes,' he broke in, 'and what she says don't always tally. She's quite pathetically respectable in her way. It's all my fault. When she went to art school in London, I thought there might be hope for her. When she moved back home and brought all those hopeless, long-haired boys and chickens and looms and things, when she started that wretched market stall in Rexbridge, when she had you without getting married, I thought, yes, she'll be all right. I didn't fool myself we'd ever be close, but I thought at least she wasn't lost. I thought she'd at last have a life. An original life. Then when she stopped all that it was the triumph of education over nature. I'm not such a monster of self-centredness as to believe she married that . . . that amoral cipher of a man just to get back at me, but I can't help feeling I ended up with the daughter I paid for.'

Alison wondered what had drawn this unusual acrimony from him. She worried that it might be Jamie's neglect, hoped it was merely the result of one of her mother's fortnightly telephone calls. A different waiter brought their main courses – chicken for him, fish for her – which, to her relief, seemed to mark a change of subject. They slipped into habitual roles of *roué* and *ingénue*, comforting, because long since outgrown.

'And what about you?' he teased. 'Do *you* have affairs?'

'No,' she said and grinned down at her *Sole Véronique*. 'I don't think I'd know one of it hit me in the face.' At this juncture the role required a blush but she merely looked knowing. She had never been able to blush on cue the way Jamie could. She had read somewhere that this ability, along with the inability to pronounce one's Rs – a failure Jamie only lapsed back into when drunk – was an indication of rich sexual responsiveness. The information was absurd, but she felt nonetheless hurt by it. It was yet another little shard of genetic injustice, like her sloping shoulders, tendency to burn in the sun and inability to hold a melody – each of them inherited from her mother.

'You *should* at your age,' he said with that tactlessness to which the old are privileged.' 'Your first bloom has barely left you.'

'Nobody has *affairs* any more, except adulterers,' she pointed out.

'Alright, *sex* then,' he countered.

'Why does everyone think it so important?' she asked.

'It helps one grow. It reminds us we're alive.'

'But it's so time-consuming and upsetting. It gets in the way of everything.' She knew she was playing devil's advocate but she wanted to see what he would say.

'But that's half the point, surely?' he insisted. 'If affairs, sex, whatever, could be timetabled, they wouldn't be half so beneficial. Joan Crawford used to give her husbands timetables to make love to her – "5.30 feed children, 6.30 cocktails, 7.30 make love" – and look what became of her!'

'She became one of the highest earning women in America and lived to a ripe and rich old age,' Alison retorted, having caught a sneaking admiration for Joan Crawford from her friends at the helpline.

'A *monstrous* old age!' he laughed.

They talked on through puddings, dessert wine and a round of unwise, strong coffee. Then Alison remembered she had to work the next day and her grandfather paid the bill and called for a taxi. A lull followed as they waited and the atmosphere between them, cleared by good humour of family acrimony, became charged instead with nostalgia and regret.

'Tell me,' he said, 'since it's been an evening for honesty, do you think Jamie will ever marry?'

'No,' she said, adding, after a slight pause, 'never with a woman. Probably not with anyone.' Despite the absurdity, she held off from saying 'man' but she saw him wince.

'I suspected not,' he said. 'And what about you?'

She thought a moment, fingering her coffee spoon.

'I thought you were always telling us not to plot destinies.'

'I am. I do. But let's say, for once, you had the choice. Would you?'

'Not marriage,' she said cautiously. 'I don't really see the point. It seems to me the benefits are too unevenly distributed. But I'd like to *find* someone. Live with them. I don't know why I say that because I love my own company, I prefer it really. And I'm not lonely. Not what I think of as lonely. And I hardly ever meet couples who don't make me grateful to be single. But. Oh. I don't know. Why does anyone want to live with *anyone*? I know women who do it over and over. Cynthia's one of them. Serially domestic. And they never learn that they're happier single. I'd like to think it's conditioning and we could overcome the urge with logic and politics, but I'm afraid it might be biological. We're programmed to share, for better or worse.' She saw him smiling, the kindness of his gaze tinged with irony.

'Actually,' she said, 'I think half the trouble for me and Jamie is that we grew up with the ideal of your marriage.'

'But Sally was dead long before you were born.'

'So? We soon found out about her. Miriam told us. About how she fell in love with you even though you were her patient and Jewish and German and younger than she was. And then The Roundel and writing for films and how she pulled you through when everything was so awful –' She heard herself reach instinctively for her mother's euphemisms. 'Maybe it's just because it ended so tragically. Who knows? Maybe if she was still alive and we'd known her and seen you both together arguing and cooking and buying groceries, it would all be less romantic. But it was so perfect.'

'You think so?' He frowned minutely, then seemed to wipe the frown away with a nervous movement of his hand.

'Of course,' she insisted. 'I was always asking Miriam to tell me details over again. It was better than a fairy story. You loved each other. You supported each other. It set us a bewilderingly high standard. I can't really believe I'll find any relationship that comes up to scratch.'

'I'm sure you will,' he assured her. 'I just hope that when you do you'll have it for longer than we did.'

'Sorry,' she said. 'I'm tired and I've been drivelling.'

'No you haven't,' he said as the waiter approached to tell them of the cab's arrival. 'You're making perfect sense.' But there was something hasty in the way he stood that implied relief at the interruption of her outpouring. Of course, she told herself, he loved Sally still after all these years. The subject still caused him pain.

They passed out onto the pavement and she felt his hand come to rest protectively on the small of her back. He kissed her goodnight and she briefly resented the pity in his tenderness. Once she had told the cab driver to take her to Bow, she slid the pane of glass between them closed so as to be alone with the thoughts the old man had stirred up in her. The bunch of flowers on the seat beside her threatened to make her sneeze, so she tugged down one of the windows to dilute its scent with the warm, trafficky breeze from the Brompton Road. She realised that, for all the talk of living alone and romantic yearnings, neither of them had mentioned Sam. Whether this was delicacy on her grandfather's part or merely a septuagenarian's forgetfulness, she was grateful.

Woozily warm-hearted with wine, she dimly discerned that, through all the talk and, oddly, through her grandfather's anger, a stage had been reached in her spirit, a phase passed through. She knew that in all probability she was returning to an empty house but she was glad of it. She was no longer angry with Jamie and Sam, she knew, would go his own way whatever she said or did.

She sprawled back into a corner of the seat, yawned, fingered the bunch of flowers and yawned again. She would give her brother a few days then suggest lunch and a little placatory truth-telling.

39

Jamie's intentions, at least, had been good. Although Alison's tone when she called had given him every reason to dread the occasion, he had fully intended to come to the concert. He and his grandfather did not meet as often as Jamie would have liked, and he was as proud as she was to be a famous composer's heir. He also loved Edward deeply, but found the love hard to communicate and weighed down by respect for the old man. Ever since he had abandoned music for mammon, his love had been undercut by guilt. Although he would never have amounted to anything more glamorous as a singer than a jobbing professional, he could never see his grandfather without being aware that, in choosing Lloyd's, he had chosen the easy path.

Work, however, had not prevented him from going to the concert. He had returned home in good time and taken the unprecedented step of missing a session at the gym in order to shower and change. Dressing was a quick process. He knew men with complicated, expensive wardrobes divided into clothes for working, clothes for hunting love and a bewildering array of smart yet informal clothes for meeting the lover's family at weekends, should the hunt prove sufficiently successful. Jamie's own wardrobe was simplified by having never developed clothes of the third category beyond a dinner jacket and trousers, bought during the brief phase in his late teens when he had made a few appearances with a semi-professional chamber choir. The suit's only outings now were an annual excursion to Glyndebourne with his grandfather and occasional pretentious parties connected with his work, such as Nick Godfreys's forthcoming ball. Less vain than he was practical, when Jamie found something that suited him – a certain colour of shirt or cut of jeans – he bought several at once. His shirts were all white, black or blue. His work shirts, relegated to a special shelf in his wardrobe, came in a wide variety of stripes but he never, ever wore them except for work. This practice dated from his first day at Lloyd's when he vowed he would never allow its dubious influence to bleed into what he thought of as his *real* life.

Tonight he made a concession to culture and his grandfather by wearing his jeans with all the fly buttons done up and leaving his condoms at home. He shaved for the second time that day, dabbed on some cologne that Alison had given him and, with similar tact, made a last-minute exchange of his habitual cheap plastic watch for the silver one his grandfather had given him for his twenty-first birthday, which he rarely wore because he worried about losing it and the strap tweaked painfully at the fine hairs on his wrists. He checked his reflection in a space wiped clear on the steamed-up bathroom mirror, snatched his wallet and keys and headed out to the street.

He was shocked to see Sam leaning on the balustrade of Albert Bridge, plainly waiting for him. Sam spotted him before Jamie could change direction or dart out of sight into the park. Sam was wearing his coat, despite the residual warmth of the day, and as he walked briskly back from the bridge, it slapped about his legs. For one insane moment, Jamie was terrified. Sam's face was set like that of a man about to deliver a blow or sweep someone violently off their feet. He gave no smile in response to Jamie's nervous, 'Hi. Fancy seeing you!' but coldly asked, 'Going out?'

'No,' Jamie said.

'Good. Then you can buy me a drink. That poncey pub on the corner by your place'll do.'

Jamie had lied on impulse and the lie was no sooner uttered than he found himself borne along on another's implacable will.

He had brought Sam back with him from the march and they had made fairly unremarkable love. For all his experience,

Jamie retained a guarded romantic ideal – carefully hidden from his sister and friends – that somewhere out there lurked the Right Man and that, if ever they met, he would know, he would sense his rightness from the first, knee-trembling kiss. He knew from the way the first clumsy embrace began with them painfully clunking noses, that Sam was to be just another one-night stand. He regretted this because of the awkwardness it would inevitably cause with Alison. If he was to hurt her, as he surely had done, she would prefer to see it done for some long-term benefit, but that could not be helped. As one-night stands went, it was neither the dullest nor the most exciting.

After a few nervous pleasantries, they had said nothing to one another during the taxi ride back to the flat and Jamie could almost pretend that they had just met in the street or in a launderette. Sam took to staring out of the window. Glancing across at him, Jamie saw that he did so not from boredom but tension. When they arrived, his every movement was stiff, his fists were rigid and his jaw was clamped tight. Serving him a lager from the fridge, Jamie wondered if it were Sam's first time, but discounted the idea as preposterous in someone who must be nearly thirty. Sam stood by the big picture window which gave on to the balcony, gruffly admiring the view of the river.

'It must be good here when the lights come on on the bridge,' he said.

'Yes,' Jamie agreed. 'It is.'

He decided to move swiftly. In one deft movement, he took Sam's unfinished beer from his hand and made to kiss him but Sam reacted with no less sudden violence, shoving him from him and sending the lager can flying. For an instant, Jamie was frightened of what he might do next, then Sam seized his arm and pulled him back towards him. He was shaking.

'Sorry,' he muttered, as if in pain. 'Sorry. Try again. Quickly. Please.'

Confused, Jamie reached up around the bristly nape of his neck and kissed him again. Still shaking, Sam responded feverishly, almost with greed and Jamie decided it might be his first time after all. Their bodies bumped against the window, rattled a picture on the wall, and rocked the bookcase so that the idol fell heavily on to the carpet. This much *was* exciting.

It was exciting, too, to strip Sam's clothes from him item by item. Clunked noses or no, it was exciting to embrace someone so much taller than himself. But from the moment they tumbled, button-fumbling, on to Jamie's mattress, Sam appeared to lose his spirit as swiftly as he had found it. His dick was hard but so was his body, unyielding, stiff. Jamie made love to him easily enough, fucked him, in fact, but Sam didn't come, expressed no interest in doing so. All this left Jamie with the conviction that Sam had indeed been a virgin. He also feared the decision that Sam was no more than one-night-stand material had somehow been communicated with merciless clarity. Jamie had soothed his own unease by scribbling down his telephone number before making his customary, half-apologetic declaration about an early start the following morning. Remembering just in time that it was Sunday the next day, he hastily took his grandfather's name in vain, mumbling that he had agreed to drive out to visit him for lunch.

'Well, you know where you can get hold of me, don't you?' Sam had muttered, snatching the scrap of paper before slipping out into the night.

Sam had not telephoned, and Jamie certainly had not tried to contact *him*. He had spent Sunday lolling on the sofa in a newspaper sea, flicking between matinées that were not quite bad enough to abandon, and spent the evening at a peculiarly horrible all-male dinner party in an over-designed flat off Holland Park.

'What'll you have?' he asked in the pub, because Sam had pointedly sat down at a table without offering.

'Bitter.'

As he bought the drinks, Jamie felt a sudden wave of common sense. What was he *thinking* of? He returned to the table and, after they had each taken a gulp, offered the truth.

'Actually, I was on my way to meet Alison at the Albert Hall. A new piece by our grandfather's being played and –'

Sam stood, slopping the drinks.

'Well you should have said. You'd better go.'

'Well . . . No. Listen.'

'She'll be angry.'

'No she won't. Alison always understands.'

'If you say so.' Sam shrugged and sat down again. He drew a finger through the puddle he had made on the tabletop. 'Did you ring?' he asked. 'I didn't go back to her place, so I thought you might have.'

Jamie wondered whether to lie.

'No,' he said. 'To be brutally honest.'

When Sam spoke again, his voice was no longer sullen but coloured with vivid anger.

'Well I did,' he said. 'At least I tried. Why go through all that business with the phone number, then give me the wrong fucking one?'

'I didn't,' Jamie insisted, all innocence, then broke off when Sam confronted him with the crumpled paper. The number was right, in a way, but Jamie had scribbled a zero in such a way that it read as a six. 'My writing,' he said. 'Sorry.'

Sam merely stared at him in a way that withered the untruth and sent curls of tension through Jamie's stomach, then he drained off his pint, his adam's apple working at his shirt collar. He finished it without so much as a gasp and, standing, pointed at Jamie's barely touched lager.

'Same again?'

'Er. No. I'm okay, thanks.'

Jamie watched him stride to the bar. The man was acting like someone unhinged. Everyone knew – surely even wild cards like Sam – that a one-night stand remained just that unless the host gave some sign, like an invitation to stay the night, or stay to breakfast or return to supper. Everyone knew. There was an etiquette to these things, painfully learned. It was designed to make harsh truths less harsh. Rejection or, at least, non-involvement, was an axiom of the casual encounter, precisely to avoid misunderstanding like this one. Jamie did not want an involvement. Not even with a friend of his sister. Especially not with a friend of his sister. Not even if he looked like an angel with a New Brutalist haircut. Not even if he were tall enough to carry one around the room. He did not want an involvement and yet something kept him pinned to his seat, fingering his chilly glass and watching Sam stare the barman into serving him next. The way to the door was clear, there was still time to slip out, flag down a taxi and escape to the concert. He stayed.

When Sam returned, Jamie could see at a glance that the beer was already going to his head. His eyes were bright and slightly unfocused, his voice unnecessarily loud. A man and woman at a nearby table turned pale and lethally respectable stares their way. Sam raised his glass to them, threw Jamie a mocking smile then drank half his second pint.

'You just can't go doing that to people,' he said.

'Doing what?'

'You know what I mean. Not even animals behave like that.'

'Most animals pair for life,' Jamie quipped. 'Or die within the year.'

Sam merely paused, glass half-way to his lips and said softly, 'quite.'

The superior smile died on Jamie's lips.

'How often have you done that?' Sam asked him.

'What?'

'You want me to spell it out?'

'Go on.'

'You know. Picked someone up.'

'You picked *me* up,' Jamie insisted. This at least was true, but Sam reacted as if Jamie had thrown beer in his face. He turned sharply aside and seemed to make a great effort to calm himself. Once again Jamie had the sensation that he was about to lash out with the flat of his hand, but Sam merely exhaled heavily, forcing himself under control.

'Whatever,' he said, mouth tight with irritation. 'Just how often do you take someone home, ask them nothing about themselves, tell them nothing about *your*self, screw them like a whore then push them back on the street without even letting them stay the night!'

'Quite often.'

'How often?'

'Look, what is this?' Jamie protested. 'I don't need –'

'How often do you do it?'

'Two, maybe three times a week.' Jamie shrugged but felt the gesture for the hollow bravado it was. 'Sometimes more.' He would not be made to feel guilty. Hundreds of men behaved as he did. Thousands. It was one of the liberties the Pride march had been set up to defend. Sam watched him for a moment, no longer angry, it seemed, just appalled.

'Isn't that a waste of energy?' he asked. 'Can't be doing you much good.'

'What does good have to do with it? It's sexy. It's fun.'

Sam's timing of the brief pause before his disbelieving 'Really?' was devastating.

'I don't need this,' Jamie said, pushing aside his lager and standing.

'You're right.' Sam stood too and once again Jamie found himself towered over. 'We've talked enough.'

'But –'

'Come on.'

Out on the street, Sam put a hand on his elbow and steered him back towards the river, then moved his arm to place it heavily across Jamie's shoulders. For a moment, Jamie flinched, furious, afraid and embarrassed. People were looking at them. Then he relaxed slightly because he realised the situation was as out of his control as if he were being abducted at knife point. This was a man who could snap people's arms. He returned the insolence of passers-by, his stare lent boldness by Sam's height and force. Sam stopped unexpectedly at the corner flower stall.

'I know we've already had a drink, but it's not a real date unless you buy me flowers or chocolates,' he said, with no discernible break in his gravity.

Jamie laughed, beyond embarrassment now.

'What colour?'

'Blue,' Sam said, seriously. 'To match my eyes.' He turned to the bemused stall-holder, who was looking up at him as at some apparition, hands clutching nervously at his leather money-apron. 'He'll buy me some of those,' he told him, pointing to some electric blue delphiniums with black hearts. 'Three bunches.'

'*Four* bunches,' Jamie laughed. 'I'll buy four. No need to wrap them. Here.'

He thrust a note into the man's hands, took the dripping bunches and offered them to Sam, who accepted them with a ghost of a courteous gesture.

As Jamie let him into his block once more, he felt Sam's outspread hand on the tail of his spine. Urging him on, making second thoughts unthinkable, the hand felt hot through the fabric of his denim shirt. They made love again, more slowly than before, with the blinds still open to flood the sheets with evening sunshine off the river. This time it was Jamie who found himself naked while Sam was still dressed. As they kissed, Sam brought a hand up to his face, entering his mouth with fingers as well as tongue. He chewed the pads of Jamie's thumbs, raised Jamie's legs over his chest, pressing into his thighs and licked heavily at his heels and the soles of his feet. When they stopped, for a moment and, deeply breathing, looked one another in the eyes, it was as though Sam were seeing him, truly seeing him now, and Jamie had to turn his face aside as from a hot light. Sam irresistibly rolled him on to his side, on to his belly and, working his way down his back, nuzzled at his arse with nose, tongue then, wetly thrusting, with fingers.

Jamie stiffened.

'I told you,' he muttered. 'I don't.'

But Sam thrust in deeper, adding a third finger to the first two and Jamie found himself stretching out across the mattress, flattening himself away from the other's inescapable touch.

'You didn't,' Sam murmured, his breath suddenly hot in Jamie's ear. 'Now you do. Where d'you keep your stuff?'

And he fucked Jamie, who had only been fucked once before in his life, and had never forgotten or forgiven the man who had done it.

Sam fucked him watchfully, without abandon, so that Jamie felt at once ravished and, strangely, guarded from danger.

When Jamie came, he cried out so loudly that Sam laid thick fingers across his mouth.

Despite himself, Jamie subsided into a kind of faint afterwards, a powerless state of hearing, feeling, near-sleep. Only the abrupt sound of the front door closing restored power to his body, and he opened his eyes to find himself alone on the bed with the shocking blue of the scattered delphiniums their bodies had crushed.

40

Alison's secretary swung on his chair, a finger on the telephone's muting button.

'It's your brother,' he said laconically.

'I'll take it in there,' she told him, walking back to her office.

In the seconds between leaving one desk and reaching the other, anger boiled up within her.

The morning after the concert, her good will towards Jamie had been smothered in hang-over and she had dropped her friendly resolve to call him for an air-clearing lunch. Sam had been missing for days and she was more than ever sure, from her brother's continued silence, that it was somehow Jamie's fault. But Jamie's voice on the telephone sounded a faint imitation of his usual ebullient self, and her irritation was swept rudely aside by a fearful contraction in her gut.

'I've got to talk to you,' he said.

She agreed to meet him outside her office after work. She spent the rest of the day distracted from paying a querulous author his proper attention by the dread she had rarely dared entertain till now, that Jamie was going to tell her he had taken an HIV test.

She rehearsed in her mind what she would say if the news were bad, planned how they would make the magical best of whatever time was left him. She even astonished herself by deciding that, if he let her, she would abandon the office altogether, demoting herself to copy-editor status so that she could be with him when he became too sick to work. Perhaps he would leave work anyway, before the need arose, driven by a desire only to spend his time and precious energies on what was meaningful. She disliked the thought of him working in the City. She had retained from her years with the Beards a vestigial mistrust of the workings of money as fundamentally and infectiously damaging. Shamelessly, out of control, she projected and fantasised in exactly the pointless and harmful way she dissuaded callers to the helpline from doing. At around six, when she pushed through a crowd spewing out of the building's revolving doors, and found him hunched on the steps, suit rumpled, tie askew, the new shadows beneath his eyes and the sallowness to his normally olive skin did nothing to dispel her fears.

She hugged him tightly and, for once, he did not pull back but crumpled onto her. He looked dreadful. His breath smelled sour, as though he had drunk too much coffee or had forgotten to brush his teeth.

'Come on,' he said. 'I need a drink. Where isn't too vile around here?'

She led him to a wine bar, bought them a bottle she could ill afford and sat beside him at a dark corner table.

'So,' she said. 'Hit me with it.'

He breathed out heavily, gouging at drops of candle wax with a neglected fingernail.

'I haven't seen Sam in days,' he said. 'He hasn't rung or anything.'

This pole-axed her. Seeing that he was not ill after all, or not seriously, her fear for Jamie was displaced by the shock of how strong her feelings still were for Sam. The defences she had built against her desire for him were brittle, intellectual constructs, projections of will – not an emotional reality. She had been a fool, and now was hoist on the petard of her own feigned disinterest and assumed nobility. The chorus from one of Miriam's favourite Joni Mitchell songs jingled through her head – *Don't it always seem to go, that you don't know what you've got till it's gone*? She glanced back at Jamie, whose dishevelment was so gallingly fetching. Her anger at his selfishness returned with new vigour.

No more Good Child, she thought, telling him, 'You got me all worried just to tell me that?'

'What?' he blinked like one just roused from a doze. 'Why were you worried?'

'Never mind. Why should *I* know where he is?'

'He lives with you, for Christ's sake.'

'Sometimes.' She poured herself a generous top-up, resenting, now, that she had paid. She might as well enjoy her own bounty, she thought. 'He lives by his agenda, I live by mine,' she added, determined not to let his crestfallen act sway her from rigour. 'So. What happened? You jumped him and he turned out not to be jumpable? Don't tell me you've finally failed to seduce a straight?'

'Alison he isn't straight and he isn't gay.'

'He's confused, then,' she snapped.

'He's just himself. He just does what he feels like doing at the time.'

'Since when were you an authority?' she demanded. 'I thought you'd hardly seen him.'

'Why are you being so hard on me?'

'Me? Hard?'

'I'm sorry. I owe you an apology, don't I?'

'You owe me two,' she said, curtly. 'At least.'

'I'm sorry about the concert.'

'Don't apologise to me, apologise to Grandpa. I had a great time. It was fun to have him to myself for once. We had a good evening. The new piece was great. I think. You know how it is with me and music. But I liked it. Then he bought me dinner. But he was hurt at you not coming. I'm sure he was. Ring him up. Better still, drive down and *visit* him for once.'

'Yes, yes all right,' he said hastily. 'I will.'

'He really cares for you, you know, and you're always so off-hand with him.'

'I'm not.'

'You *are*, Jamie.'

'Well he . . . He doesn't like the way I've turned out.'

'How do you know?'

'I just do,' he said.

'How can you be sure if you've never discussed it with him?'

'Spare me. You may have dragged me on a Pride march

but I'm still English and I'm male. We don't talk about these things . . .' Jamie faltered. 'About Sam . . .' He faltered again. Alison glowered at him.

'You *did* seduce him, didn't you?'

Jamie nodded. He began a reflex-reaction sheepish grin, then thought better of it.

'You little bastard!' she cried out. 'He probably thought he was just coming back to your place for a couple of beers.'

'He knew exactly why he was coming back.'

'Oh I'm sure.'

'He did. You've got to believe me. It was his idea. He's sort of innocent, but he knows exactly what he wants.'

She regarded her brother coolly over her wine glass. He was shaken. He was actually talking, and with interest, about someone other than himself.

'And he wanted *you*?' she asked.

'Apparently.'

'I'd guessed, actually,' she lied dispassionately. 'When he first saw you . . .'

'He followed me. I'd had enough of the crowds and he just came after me. Promise you won't laugh.'

'I'm sure I won't.'

Jamie poured himself some more wine, gulped it, poured some more.

'That isn't water,' she told him.

'What do I owe you?'

'Don't be silly.' A Good Child, even in her rage, she suppressed the impulse to snatch the wallet he proffered so casually.

'It didn't work out too well,' he went on. 'I dunno. You know how I am.'

'I do,' she prompted.

'So I let him go –'

'Kicked him out.'

'Okay, so I kicked him out on the Saturday night, assuming that was it, that he'd got the message that I didn't want to take it any further. Then he turned up on my doorstep just as I was leaving for the concert on Monday.'

'Oh my God!' She felt spiteful laughter bubble up within her, all the more tart for his wounded expression.

'You said you wouldn't laugh,' he protested.

'You dropped him but he refused to be dropped then he came back for seconds so that he could drop *you*,' she said in triumph.

'That's not quite it.'

'That's *exactly* it.'

'It's not funny, Alison! Honestly. I haven't been able to think about anything else. I keep catching myself staring out of the window or waiting for the phone to ring.'

'So it's *you* who's been calling my number and leaving no message.'

'I thought he might be there.'

'Well he isn't. He hasn't been there since he left the house with me for the march on Saturday. God only knows where he is. His hostel probably.'

'Shit. Where's that, then?'

'Search me.'

'I really want to see him.'

'Evidently the feeling's not mutual.'

'You're enjoying this, aren't you?'

'It does have a certain pleasing irony,' she confessed. 'The biter bit.'

'Bitch.'

'Now now. You stole my beau, remember?'

'But he wasn't yours. You said he wasn't interested and that I could have a go.'

'Well I didn't mean it, *all right*?' she snapped. She was as shocked as he that she had suddenly blurted her true feelings, and only just managed to veil the awkwardness with a wry, 'Had you fooled for a moment, didn't I? So. Tell Momma,' she mocked on, thorns tightening around her heart. 'You're really truly smitten?'

'I dream about him,' he admitted. 'I keep seeing him in the street and finding it's just a lookalike, someone with his hair or his red shirt. It's as though I've been bitten by a vampire and gotten sick.'

'That's not funny.'

'But you know what I mean.'

'I've never been there,' she said grimly. 'But I read a lot of novels. You're in love.'

'But I *can't* be.'

'Why should *you* be immune?'

'Well *you* are.'

'I'm not immune,' she explained ruefully. 'I'm just naturally good at dodging the darts.'

'You *did* want him too, though. Didn't you?' he asked, touching her sleeve across the table in a way that riled her hugely.

'For a while,' she confessed, 'then I stopped. It's stopped hurting. But you already knew that. At least I sincerely hope you did.'

'Do you mind me . . . you know?'

'Would it make any difference if I did?'

'Alison, I –'

'James, *please*,' she protested with a bitter laugh. 'I was joking! Do stop casting me as the vengeful frustrated harpy! Why should I mind?' Even as she spoke the words, she saw again the truth in them and felt her face soften towards him. There had been many occasions, throughout their entwined lives, when she had needed to prove she was not the fierce older sister of his imaginings – when he had spilled modelling paint on her pink dress, when he had drawn pictures in the margins of her schoolbooks, when he had blabbed some secret of theirs to Miriam, when she had caught him, aged eight or nine, curled in an upstairs corner wrapped in one of the better-looking Beards' dirty workshirts, believing himself unobserved. Remembering these times, she saw his face lighten under her kinder gaze.

'Why should I be anything but happy for you?' she asked, adding, to dilute the sugar, 'And now you've got me sounding like Ol' Big Hair.'

'But I'm *not* happy,' he said. 'I'm fast becoming a wreck. It's only been a week and I swear I'm already losing weight. I've tried looking at other men and I don't feel a thing. I look like shit. I feel like someone in one of those unreadable Judith Lamb books you like.'

'Ah,' she said, mocking him, 'but I have your passport to Oz.'

She enjoyed smiling mysteriously. For a second his interest kindled then was quenched by doubt.

'How do you mean?' From his weary tone, he plainly thought she was teasing.

'I can't promise that he'll be interested back, but I'd imagine you'll stand a better chance if he sees you've gone to the trouble of tracking him down, and that you're prepared to make a public fool of yourself.' She turned the screw on his suffering. *As close to vengeful, frustrated harpy as I get,* she thought, wryly.

'But how do I find him?' he pleaded.

'I know which building site he's working on.'

She laughed as Jamie made to leave the wine bar on an immediate search. She had never seen him at the mercy of his emotions before. The spectacle had her utterly beguiled.

'He won't be there now, you prat,' she chuckled.

''Course not.' He sank sadly back to his chair. She stroked his hand, touched his cheek.

'He'll keep another night, surely?'

'You don't know what I'm going through.'

'Oh, for pity's sake, you're not the first.'

'Yes but –'

'Look.' She took a napkin from a glass on the table, found her pen and drew him a thumbnail sketch, showing how to find the hospital building site. 'It's not that far from Lloyd's,' she pointed out. 'You can walk there straight after work. You can even nip over in your lunch hour if you're truly so desperate.'

Jamie took the napkin and pored over it, then smiled his old, hunter's smile.

'Thanks,' he said, almost shyly. 'Thanks, Ali.'

'It's just a napkin,' she scoffed. 'You've still got the hard bit to do.'

But he was carefully folding the scarlet paper into his wallet, not listening. She raised her glass.

'Here's to true love,' she murmured, 'and the happy stability of the single state.'

They finished the bottle between them, lapsing via his guilty questions about the concert, into a rare wallow in reminiscences of the old, messy days, before Miriam had married. She recalled the times when he returned for the school holidays, slowly reacclimatising to the patchouli-scented, bead-fringed chaos where, as a pupil at a local day school, she had waited impatient months, the solitary child. He remembered the long heady days of their summer holidays when they had been left in charge of the commune's craft stall in Rexbridge market, unwisely judged mature enough to mind it on their own. Giggling at their gloomy corner table, long after their candle had burnt out and the other office workers had staggered off into the night, they indulged in the game of which they never tired – guessing, from an old group photograph Alison carried, talismanic, in her wallet, which of the Beards could have been their fathers.

Alone again, in a late tube train home, she watched a boy and girl who had remained standing even though the carriage was almost empty, so as to be able to lean against a glass partition and kiss. The wine began to have its usual depressive effect on her mood. She looked away and stared in the other direction. A much older couple, together some twenty-five or thirty years, she would guess, sat with great bags of shopping on their laps, intently discussing something. They were forever interrupting each other, their voices softly interleaving, the pacing of their phrases unconsciously worn to a perfect fit from years of proximity. Alison perceived a kind of deflated tenderness between them. The woman looked up and caught her staring, so she turned aside and read a short, dejected poem on a poster overhead, then fell to returning her reflection's look of hollow-eyed reproach.

Like one admitting at last to middle age, or the need for more sensible hair, she realised she had become one of those women who spent so much free time with homosexual men that she uprooted herself from the possibility of any but a vicarious fulfilment. Now that she had stooped to pandering for her brother and a man she had wanted for herself, her past denials of the pathetic truth were futile. She thought of taking out her address book to prove that she had plenty of heterosexual male friends, but knew in advance they would all be either married, hopeless or dull. She could not stop working at the helpline – for better or worse, the people there were her intimates. Forcing herself to list the options left her, she came up with only two: to make a vow to accept every social opportunity that came her way, however unpromising, or to step off the romantic treadmill altogether and convince herself that she was spoilt for straight men and that her happiness did not depend on the unforeseeable arrival of that elusive He. Both options seemed equally tragic, but the second at least preserved her pride and self-rule. Appalled at the pattern her life had assumed, she toyed with the idea of asking someone to recommend a psychotherapist. Therapy, Cynthia was forever saying, was like the Tarot; best approached when one had a single, burning issue to resolve. Women who prefer men who prefer men seemed as hot an issue as any.

The first thing she noticed when she let herself in was the lingering smell of burnt toast, the second was Sam's old coat, slung over the back of a kitchen chair. Music was coming from upstairs. Something bright, new and American her grandfather had given her, with a warning that it was banal, but which she liked playing as she drifted off to sleep. She found Sam flat out across the sofa, still dusty from the site, one arm thrown across his sleeping eyes against the glare from the lamp by which he had been reading. She stood watching him for a moment, wondering whether she was kind, or indeed right, to unleash on him the complications her brother would surely bring. Then she faded out the music, clicked off the lamp and retreated to her empty bed.

'This is my bed,' she told herself. 'My comfortable bed. My bed which I am *lucky* to have all to myself.'

She lay there, hands hugged for comfort between her thighs, and wondered, as she had often caught herself wondering that summer, whether she wanted a child, a new job or an uncomplicated lover and whether the three were, by their very natures, mutually exclusive. Perhaps, she thought, as she drifted off to sleep, it would be wisest to leave the visit to a therapist until she could make up her mind.

41

The site lay on the eastern perimeter of the City or the western fringe of the East End – depending on one's priorities – where banks and trading houses began to give way to lower-rent businesses and still lower-rent housing and the mixture of private and public domains was nicely reflected in a scattering of sinisterly stylish eighteenth century churches. The new hospital was rising from the derelict shells of a Victorian glue factory and a tannery, which had once added their distinctive stenches to the ripe London air. The design was clean and white, not so very different from the great new offices in Docklands. In order to help pay back some of the building costs, there was to be a shopping precinct under the hospital at street level, with restaurants and boutiques to tempt visitors away from their troubles and into debt. The ambulance and mortuary exits were to be placed considerately down a side street and the chimney outlet from the incinerator was cunningly designed so as to recycle valuable energy back into the heating system. The locals might have been grateful for the erection of this gleaming temple to health and commerce had two perfectly serviceable Victorian hospitals, admittedly without shopping precincts, not been closed down in the area the previous year. The same building contractor was due to move on to the older buildings once the new one was finished, to begin converting their unwieldy red-brick spaces into 'novelty' flat-office hybrids coyly dubbed *ateliers*.

Alison had been joking when she suggested Jamie would have time to visit the site in his lunch hour, but he had contemplated doing so in all seriousness. He had spent the night in a fever of erotic anticipation, the morning in turmoil at his inability to focus on the urgent work in hand. He had forgotten, however, that it was his secretary's birthday and had been forced to spend the lunch hour in liquid cheer with her and other colleagues. At last, at around four, he could bear it no longer and, pretending to have thrown up in the gents and be 'not feeling too hot', he sloped off early. He no longer needed Alison's rudimentary map, having already compared it with the *A to Z* and scorched the relevant details onto his memory. It took him nearly twenty minutes to reach the place, weaving across streams of pre-rush hour traffic, diving crossly through slow-moving clots of fellow pedestrians. He was panting slightly when he arrived.

Jostled by shoppers and schoolchildren, he stood his ground beside a bus shelter and scanned the network of scaffolding. It was definitely worth a resounding 'oooh' – icons of hackneyed homoerotic fantasy were everywhere. Scantily clad in cut-away shorts and heavy boots, three labourers heaved a pre-constructed window frame into place. A fourth, on the level above, his thick arms ending in grotesque padded gloves, his barrel chest spattered with mortar, carried a concrete block as lightly as if it were styrofoam. There were so many men at work that he had to force his eyes to search the site systematically, one level, one section, at a time. He wished he were in jeans and an old tee-shirt. Dressed in his suit, he felt like the Dirk Bogarde character in *Victim*. He remembered, with disgust, a conversation at Sunday night's Holland Park dinner party where his barrister host had rolled his eyes discussing the latest 'piece of rough' he claimed to have seduced. He tugged off his tie and rolled it into a pocket then slung his jacket over one shoulder. Now he felt like the Dirk Bogarde character on holiday.

At last he saw him. He had passed over him twice, not recognising him because he had shucked his coat and shirt, but his eye was suddenly drawn back to the grimy bandanna tied around Sam's neck. As he watched, Sam stopped in his work beside a cement mixer to pull off the piece of scarlet cloth and wipe his face with it. He wasn't tanned all over like the other builders – evidently it was rare for heat to overthrow his modesty – and once Jamie had spotted him, his paler skin made him easy to find again in the toing and froing high on the walkways that encompassed the bright, emerging walls. As Sam tied the bandanna back about his neck, he seemed to notice Jamie down on the pavement and froze for a moment. Jamie could wait no longer and raised an arm.

'Hi!' he shouted. 'Sam! Hi!'

At this distance it was hard to gauge Sam's expression but as his hands dropped back from his neck, he raised one of them in a kind of American Indian greeting, then glanced about him. Jamie tried to beckon him down to street level but Sam shook his head then pointed to the site office Portakabin and beckoned in turn. It was a test.

'Very well,' Jamie thought. As he began to cross the road, he glanced back up and saw that Sam had gone back to work.

'I've come to see, er, Sam,' he told the woman behind the rudimentary desk. She looked him up and down but betrayed no surprise. Her accent was breathily west-coast Irish. 'You'll need one of these, love,' she said, handing him a yellow hard hat. 'Sign the book,' she added, 'and don't keep him long.'

'I won't,' he said. 'But it's quite urgent.' As he signed, she slapped a yellow VISITOR sticker on his chest and consulted a grimy work book.

'He's on the fourth level,' she said. 'Out of the hut and use the lift. Stay by the gate when you get there, and I'll call him over to you. Don't get in anyone's way and mind your back, for Jesus' sake.'

'I will,' he grinned.

As he rode up in the rickety cage lift, her voice rang out over the Tannoy system.

'Visitor for Sam. Visitor for Sam now.'

Someone, who presumably hadn't seen the visitor's gender, let out a piercing wolf-whistle. Heart racing already, Jamie looked down at the stretching drop around him and felt his stomach fall away. The cage came to a halt with an abrupt lurch. He slid aside the safety barrier and stepped out, careful now not to look down through the planks that were supporting him over the void. There was no sign of Sam. Jamie waited a few minutes as he had been told to do, then saw that Sam was at the far end of the walkway, pointedly continuing to load cement blocks onto a hoist. Jamie called his name tentatively, then louder but his voice – now he even *sounded* like Dirk Bogarde – was drowned out by a sudden burst from a pneumatic pump or generator in the half-formed stairwell that plunged down to his right. Looking straight ahead, one hand groping along the horizontal scaffolding to his left, he walked gingerly over to join him.

'Sam?'

Sweat shone on his back, darkening the V of coarse, dark hair that curved down into his jeans at the base of his spine. As he heaved another block, a web of muscles worked across his back and shoulders like wings beneath the skin, and a single mole seemed to dart back and forth on the edge of one of his shoulder blades. Wishing more than ever that he was dressed for the occasion, Jamie took another step forward.

'Sam?'

Sam's tone was icy.

'What the *fuck* are you playing at?' he said, continuing to load blocks, as though no-one were talking to him.

'I came . . . I came to find you,' Jamie blurted out.

'Oh yeah? And how am I supposed to explain *you* away? A visit from my friendly local bank manager, maybe? A bloke asking me to move my BMW?'

Jamie had not thought of this, having seen the awkwardness only from his own viewpoint. He wished Sam would at least turn round to acknowledge him.

'You could say I was one of the architects,' he suggested weakly.

Sam withered him.

'Yes. Well. The architects keep their ties on.'

Jamie looked wretchedly down at his feet, saw through the planks below and had to steady himself against a scaffolding upright.

'I'm sorry,' he mumbled. 'I'll go away. Sorry.'

Now Sam looked over his shoulder. He raised an eyebrow, taking in Jamie's incongruous clothes.

'Like the hat,' he said.

Jamie let out a snort of nervous laughter. Sam yelled up to

the level above, 'Okay! Take her up!' and the hoist juddered into motion. He turned back to face Jamie, tugging off the bandanna again to wipe the gritty grime away from his eyes and brow. There was a flash of white dust across his hair which Jamie imagined brushing away with his fingertips. He suspected he was about to grovel. He was beyond caring.

'You shouldn't be up here,' Sam muttered, glancing about him again. 'It's dangerous. Let's get back over there.' He gave Jamie a push back towards the lift barrier.

'I'm sorry,' Jamie repeated and realised he had never wanted anything so much as he wanted this man beside him, even if only for a single night. Even two feet away, he could smell him. Sitting, dazed, at his desk the morning after their fateful second encounter, he had caught a whiff of his musk lingering on the back of one of his hands, and had felt as naked in the spasm of desire it triggered as if Sam had just materialised beside his computer terminal in nothing but a smile and a hard hat.

'So,' Sam said, wilfully unhelpful. 'What's up? Is Alison okay?'

'Yes. Yes, she's fine.' Jamie stammered with a twitch of irritation. 'I saw her last night.'

'Ah.'

Jamie knew he must speak now or never.

'Sam, I . . . I was in the neighbourhood,' how *wrong* that sounded, 'and I remembered Alison had said this was where you worked.'

'Yes?'

'Yes and . . . I wondered what you were doing this evening.'

Sam scratched the back of his neck, frowning. Surely he was doing this on purpose?

'Well, I'll knock off here at five then I suppose I'll find a bite to eat and crash out.'

'Sam, I'm asking you out.'

'You *are*?' He looked slightly amused at the idea. 'Ask me again. I don't think I caught it first time around.'

The lift arrived back at their level and two vast, slack-gutted men, one of them black, both stripped to the waist, came out and strode off down the walkway laughing at something. Jamie watched them, not daring to meet Sam's eyes.

'I'm asking you out. Will you come out with me?' he said.

'Okay.'

Jamie spun around, disbelieving. Sam was looking out over the site, pretending they weren't talking, although one corner of his mouth had curled up, dimpling, mocking him. 'I said okay,' he said and laughed bitterly. 'You've never had to *ask* before, have you? Jesus!'

'I have,' Jamie lied.

'Naa. Never.'

'I . . .' Jamie's defences were down. He had no shame. *If Alison could see me now,* he thought.

'But we've got to do it properly,' Sam went on.

'Of course,' Jamie blurted, not sure what he meant precisely but willing, at that moment, to agree to anything, anything in the conceivable repertoire of pleasures.

It turned out that Sam's requirements were endearingly conventional. As befitted a first, *proper* date, they met for dinner, then went dancing. Dinner was relatively easy, although Sam favoured a mouth-blistering Bengali curry, one mouthful of which left Jamie wondering if he would ever kiss, much less taste, again. As they ate, he watched his intake of Indian beer, wary of loosening his tongue and starting to prattle. Sam hardly spoke at first. He was obviously hungry, ordering with swift impatience and concentrating on the food once the dishes began to arrive. Jamie caught his eye now and then and smiled foolishly, to which Sam responded with shyly raised eyebrows and a diversionary offer of more naan or cooling raita. The restaurant was bustling and noisy with chatter and the sinuous wail of Bombay pop.

'So what are the people you work with like?' Jamie asked at last.

'All right,' said Sam. 'They're just blokes. You know.'

'Do you talk?'

'Not much. We don't all take our breaks at the same time. But yeah. We talk. Go to the canteen. Eat a bit. Read a paper. You know. I'm not really a builder.'

'I remember you saying. 'You trained as a fitter.'

'Yeah. Naval fitter. Devonport dockyards. My dad worked there too and my granddad.'

'Is your dad still alive?'

'Yeah. And my mum and my brother.' Sam frowned. 'At least, I think so. We don't talk much now. It's been a while.'

Jamie watched him dab up some sauce with a last piece of naan.

'Ali and I don't know who our father is, or even if we share the same one,' he said.

'Yeah. She said.' Sam licked scarlet juices from his fingers. 'Well I had a dad and a mum and I lived in a house and went to a school and had holidays at Torbay every year and I used to watch *Blue Peter* and *Jackanory* and I wanted to be a painter or a market gardener when I grew up.'

'Why are your telling me all this?' Jamie asked, perplexed at his hectoring manner.

'So you can see I'm just a bloke, not some fantasy of yours.' Sam looked up with searing directness. 'I know what your lot are like. Plumber. Garage attendant. Trucker. Construction worker. It's all just another fantasy. It's got nothing to do with me.'

'What do you mean, "my" lot?' Jamie asked, defensive lest his thoughts had betrayed themselves.

'You know,' Sam said impatiently.

'I'm no more a typical faggot than you're a builder,' Jamie insisted.

'You go out to bars and pick people up,' Sam said, lowering his tone. 'You said so yourself.'

'Oh. And straight men don't do that? I was talking about stereo-types. I hate disco music, I have no eye for interior design and ever since I first saw *The Wizard of Oz* I've found Judy Garland plain sinister.'

'But you don't play rugger or anything, do you?'

'What is this? Some kind of contest?' Jamie protested, half laughing at the absurdity of Sam's questions, but threatened nonetheless. 'Look. You don't have to prove anything. You already went to bed with me, remember? Twice. You obviously weren't used to it, but you still knew what you were doing.'

Sam scowled as a waiter came to take away their dishes, then his expression softened.

'Yeah,' he said. 'You're right. Sorry. I'm new to all this, that's all.'

'Well so am I.'

'No you're not.'

'Sam, I'm new to *this*!' Jamie indicated the two of them, the restaurant. 'I'm new to dating.'

Sam grinned suddenly then looked away. Watching the people at the neighbouring table pulling on their coats, he said, from the corner of his mouth. 'Well you're not doing badly for a beginner. Come on. Get some coffee then we're going dancing. I've heard of somewhere that's meant to be good.'

Jamie feared dancing might involve some chichi discotheque in the West End. He was not one of nature's dancers, loathed the way men camped around to dance music and tended to avoid such places in favour of bars, where he found he could get what he was after with less time-wasting or damage to the ear drums. If Sam were so very new to the game, Jamie found it hard to believe he would want them to dive into some sweaty-chested, laser-slashed hell-hole. Sam scoffed, however, at the very suggestion. He had somewhere much less banal in mind.

'But this is an all-women place!' Jamie protested, as Sam tugged him drunkenly off their bus as it pulled past a notoriously rough converted cinema, south of the river. 'And it's Country and Western night. Look at them all. We'll be lynched!'

'No we won't, you daft twat,' Sam said. 'Trust me. I know the bouncer. We used to live in the same hostel. She's a scaffolder's mate.'

Sure enough, the awesome, beefy-armed woman on the door waved them through, without them even being charged, and her benison also seemed to confer a kind of gender immunity status on them.

'I should warn you,' Jamie gabbled, eyeing the denim-shirted Elvis and Tab Hunter lookalikes, 'I really can't dance, and anyway you're far too tall for me. People will laugh.'

'Shut up and come here.' Sam towed him onto the dance floor, which shimmered beneath the ersatz starlight of a mirror ball. 'I can't dance either. We can just walk slowly and turn at corners.'

He pulled Jamie to him and, after jokily trying to rest his chin on the top of his head, bent down to kiss him as they shuffled slowly around the room, protected by pair after pair of urban cowgirls. After a while the ballads petered out in favour of slightly faster, line-dancing music, and there was a dancing instructor to hand who soon had them performing an approximation of the rudimentary steps necessary. Sam danced as seriously as he drank; as if it were less a pleasure than a test of strength. As he spun Jamie around in a two-step – his very height dictated he lead – pushing him away and tugging him back, Jamie caught his eye, then looked down at his feet or out at the less mismatched dancers beside them. Suddenly he felt a strange sensation churning in his chest.

'Stop!' he gasped to Sam, feeling as if he might burst.

'What?'

'Stop. We've got to stop. I think I'm . . . Come on.' He walked swiftly out of the sunken dance floor, unconsciously leading Sam by the hand.

'What is it? Eh?' Sam stood beside him, a small frown distorting his brows. He touched Jamie's chest then lifted his hand to tip Jamie's chin so that he met his worried gaze. '*What?*' he asked.

'Nothing. I . . . I was so breathless suddenly,' Jamie said. 'I thought I was getting a stitch.'

'You okay?'

'I'm fine. Sure. I'm fine,' he insisted, laughing and playfully punching Sam's hand aside before grasping him around the waist and pulling him close. 'I don't believe it, that's all,' he went on.

'Believe what?' Sam had to raise his voice above the music.

'That it's this easy. It *is* this easy, isn't it?' he asked. 'It really is!'

Sam looked away for a moment, grinning as at some sweet, private satisfaction. When he looked back, trying to compose his face, there was surprise there too, which gave Jamie some relief.

'Looks like it,' Sam said and it was immediately clear that they had reached that point when it was no longer bearable merely to dance cheek to cheek, thigh knocking thigh. 'Shall we go, then?' he added.

Although they fell to lovemaking within moments of stumbling through Jamie's front door, not even bothering to draw down blinds or switch lights on, it was not, this time, the climactic point of the evening. That came afterwards when, in the flattering glow spilled from the bathroom, they lay still on the mattress, a few feet apart – caressing with their eyes the bodies their limbs had exhausted, tabulating differences. Sam had patches of toughened skin where Jamie's was office smooth. Jamie's muscles were carefully nurtured all over. Sam used some more than others, so that his long legs were quite wiry compared with his strong arms and chest. Sam had a line of black hair running up across his navel and spreading out to envelop either nipple in an unexpectedly silky mat. Jamie had blond hair on his legs and forearms but, beyond a small fan of it below his belly button, his torso was furless as marble. Sam had said nothing, but the smoothness seemed to amuse and fascinate him by turns.

Jamie traced with a finger the outline of a tendon in Sam's neck to a small, semi-circular scar below his left ear.

'How d'you get this?' he asked.

Sam met his gaze.

'Fight,' he said simply. 'They had a broken glass.'

'You're lucky it wasn't worse.'

'It was bad enough.'

Jamie leaned over to brush his lips on the piece of puckered skin but Sam pushed him gently away. Then, as if to soften the discomfort he had caused, he asked, 'Well how d'you get that, then?' pointing, in turn, to the thin red scar some four inches long on Jamie's right calf.

'Skiing accident,' Jamie told him with a trace of pride. 'Eight years ago. In Germany. I swerved to avoid some idiot who was messing around, showing off to his children, and I left the run and hit some rocks. I came around just long enough to see the bone sticking out of my skin. Then I passed out again.'

He grinned, but Sam winced. Jamie reached to smooth his brow, brushing away this sympathetic memory of pain. Gently Sam took away his hand, kissing it briefly as he did so. Once again, he fell to examining Jamie.

'Tell me things,' Jamie said at last, growing restless, however flattered, at being treated like a work of not entirely accredited art.

'What like?' Sam gave a faint snort of derision.

'About your family.'

'No.'

'Why not?'

Sam shrugged.

'Boring,' he said. 'They don't matter anyway.'

'How about Plymouth? Do you miss it?'

'Sometimes. I never go back though.'

A cloud passed across his expression warning Jamie not to pursue the matter.

'Your turn,' Sam said.

'Ali's told you everything.'

'She's told me fuck all. I don't pry. Unlike some.'

'Well, I left home when I was little, in a way, because I went to boarding school. I wanted to be a singer. I was quite good, and kept it up until I was about sixteen. Used to live in a commune, but it all fell to pieces when we were teenagers and my mother married a jerk. Well, he's not so bad but he's wrong for her.'

'How can you tell?'

'I just know. She should have married a painter or a potter, but she chose an accountant. So I don't see much of her. Ali's all the family I care about really. And my grandfather. The composer.'

'I'd like to meet him.'

Jamie frowned, then stroked Sam's arm-hairs thoughtfully.

'You'll have to go gently with me,' he warned. 'I'm not very good at this.'

'How d'you know?'

'I just . . . I can tell. I'm . . . I suppose I'm too used to being on my own. I'm very . . . private. Anyway, you're not exactly a nest-maker.'

'Just because I pulled up my roots,' Sam teased him, 'doesn't mean I'm not looking to put them down again somewhere.'

'Oh God,' Jamie groaned. 'Kiss me.' Sam thrust a quick, slovenly kiss onto his lips. 'Properly,' Jamie told him.

Sam kissed him again, lingering. They rolled together, dragging stubbled jaw across stubbled jaw, groping with weary, restless hands. Jamie felt his dick swell again as he grasped Sam's leg between his thighs and rubbed himself slowly against his bony flank. Sleepily he pushed Sam's arm up across the pillow so that he could slide his nose into its hot, furred cavity. He breathed in deeply, then turned his face to Sam's, who bent down to meet him, lower lip loose, expectant. They kissed, chewed, kissed again then Sam pulled away, crouching over Jamie, and began to trace a hungry trail down the side of his tensed neck, across collarbones and down his torso towards his straining cock. Jamie was shocked that movements so timeworn could feel so new.

'Just . . .' he began, chuckling. 'Just . . .'

'What?' Sam looked up, eyes bright, a trail of spittle falling from his chin.

'Just don't go expecting me to have your babies right away, okay?'

42

Alison was sitting in a deck chair in The Roundel's garden, rereading a young author's first novel. She had bought it because it was funny and clever and beguilingly out of love with youth, but it needed work and would probably never repay in sales the labour she was putting into helping the woman tidy it. She smiled to herself at a passage then frowned and drove a pencil line through the sentence where the author had tried to stretch a joke out too far. This was the work she enjoyed most, not the endless meetings, not the intimate, therapeutic telephone calls from household names – *My husband's left me. My cat's sick. My computer's gone down* – nor the launch parties which, after all, were work and not parties at all. What she enjoyed was helping to bring a new novel to its best bloom, dissecting its filaments, tentatively suggesting subtle rearrangements, then quietly stepping back to let the author take all the praise, and sometimes blame, for what she had done. She was not a writer, had no desire to be, but she knew that her delight in the total transformation that could be made to a paragraph by a simple excision or realignment bore more than a touch of a true artist's pride. When she had been interviewed by a magazine as part of a last ditch campaign to find a way of devoting some column inches to an esteemed but notoriously unpublicisable authoress, she had compared her own work to that of a gardener whose judicious pruning and training showed the work of God the Mother off to best advantage. Invariably, as writers grew more successful, most became less and less willing to have their work properly edited, only to round on her in indignation when reviewers gleefully singled out an increasingly baggy style or sloppiness of grammar.

A breeze ruffled the papers in her lap. A cloud slid off the sun. She flexed her bare feet in the wet grass and lay back in her chair to enjoy the renewed warmth on her face and the dewy, early morning scents carried on the air. She had always loved The Roundel, but had come to appreciate it far more since moving to London and gathering points of comparison after a parochial youth. Miriam had seemed eager to dissociate herself entirely from the place once she had married.

'Too many memories, Angel,' she explained. 'And the damp is dreadful for poor Frank's back.'

Alison had insisted Jamie enjoy an equal share in the old house, urging him to come down at weekends, bring friends, throw parties. He did few of these, however, and a part of his sister's refreshed pleasure in the quirky building was proprietorial, based on her deeply cherished knowledge that, legally, the place was now hers until such time as her claim should be supplanted by her marriage or production of a female heir. She had quietly taken financial responsibility – paying council tax, fuel bills, having loose tiles replaced – and it was with considerable satisfaction that she whitewashed out the inept and gaudy murals that the Beards had perpetrated in the bathrooms. She had thrown out her mother's legacy of swivelling leatherette chairs, macramé pot-holders, orange lampshades and grungy sagbags – keeping just one of the latter for use by visiting dogs – and replaced it with the clutch of post-war Utility furniture with which her great grandparents had sparsely furnished the place. It was all stained by floodwater and her grandfather had long since relegated it to a store room in the cellar, blind to its enchantment in the minds of those too young to remember rationing or air raids.

Alison had raced around a supermarket then driven up late on Friday as she often did, preferring to go to bed exhausted and wake to a clear weekend in the fens, rather than spend half of Saturday queuing in traffic just to reach the motorway. The lights were already off in her grandfather's studio when she swung her car up the drive so she went to bed without greeting him. One of the charms of having him live on the doorstep was the ease with which he could be prevailed upon to slip in and turn on the boiler for her, so it was rare that she arrived to a house that was truly cold, for all Miriam's aspersions about damp. He was up now, though. He had been up long before her, as usual. Lying in a delicious weekend doze, too awake to dream again, too sleepy yet to move, she had pressed her cheek deep into her pile of lumpy old pillows and listened to the familiar, welcoming sounds of his piano-playing coming from the studio across the garden. This was always the time when she bizarrely found herself envying him his solitary, industrious life – bizarrely, because she knew the terrible cost at which that solitude and industry had been purchased.

She had tried to persuade Jamie to come down too and bring Sam with him, but he was still umming and erring about introducing Sam to their grandfather. She pointed out that nothing need be said about their relationship, that Sam could simply be introduced as a mutual friend, but Jamie was evasive and she knew better than to push it.

Love had crept up on them and taken them captive while they were too busy enjoying one another to notice its approach. She noticed however, unlove – as she liked to think of her single state – lending her the acuity of vision that pleasure had snatched from them. She could tell it was love and not infatuation. She had tasted infatuation's fizzy, egomaniacal savour often enough, knew it was marked by an excess of talk, the brain using verbal gush to paper over the cracks left by romance's shortcomings. Jamie and Sam never gushed, even by their repressed standards. Often they did not even talk. Jamie would meet her for their lunches as usual, and it was all she could do to get him to mention Sam by name. When he did, usually at her curious prompting, he became halting, inarticulate and would end by changing the subject with a shrug. The shrug, a gesture he had caught off Sam, was usually betrayed by a beatific smile.

Sam remained her lodger in name at least although, ironically, now that he spent fewer and fewer nights under her roof, he insisted on paying her proper rent. Guilt money, perhaps. He had left his hostel bedsit for good. Her spare room, in which he usually left no trace, began to bear signs of his continued tenancy. For Sam, monastic Sam of all people, began to *acquire* things – pieces of pottery, stones, bottles, a new shirt, a pair of soft suede boots – things stumbled on during his weekends with Jamie. Alison rarely saw them together. Jamie insisted on seeing her at lunchtime, so as to 'have her to himself', and Sam resisted her ever so slightly mocking suggestion that he might care to 'bring a friend back' to their sporadic, midweek suppers-in together.

On a few occasions, she had been insistent, and found herself going to a concert or a film with the two of them. Their combined good looks, their radiating sexiness, were as powerful about her as a sweet, head-turning perfume, and she enjoyed a certain reflected glamour in their company. She realised, however, that she still found it a bit overwhelming to see the happy pair together. Sam was becoming more desirable rather than less since he had passed so entirely out of reach. Any sensitivity he might have felt for her physical presence was eclipsed utterly now that he was fixed in a sentimental orbit around her brother. After too long in their company, she was left an envious, darkened star. They clearly had to make a painful effort not to lapse into mutual face-gazing, and she saw no reason wilfully to bring such suffering on herself. She preferred to infer the absent one's influence when alone with either, noting Sam's subtly improved, though no less brutal, haircut, or Jamie's suddenly ceasing to wear the cologne she had once given him. Despite the pain it caused her, such was her ability to live vicariously that she was able at times to register an intense pleasure at her brother's pairing-off. Wilfully unromantic though she strove to keep her outlook, she liked to feel she might one day have the option of romance laid before her. With so terminal a bachelor as he happily betrothed, the odds of such a thing occurring to her had surely improved.

During their lunches together, Jamie said nothing about Sam's past. Either he knew and was keeping it secret from her or he had not guessed. Or, indeed, her fearful suspicions were groundless and his criminal record consisted of nothing more sinister than a speeding ticket. After wrestling with her conscience on seeing how happy Jamie was, she decided to say nothing. If Sam *had* done time, he was making a spectacular new start, if not, speaking out would only make a fool of herself and an enemy of both of them.

She looked towards the studio, suddenly aware that the piano had stopped playing. Then she frowned, angry that thoughts of her brother's love-life should so distract her from her manuscript. Her grandfather was either rewriting what he had written or, as she suspected, had spotted her outside and had broken off to brew coffee. He persisted in a fantasy that his grandchildren's generation's ills all stemmed from neglecting to breakfast. It pleased her to sustain his delusion while she was down there, she who fuelled her office mornings with so many doughnuts, biscuits and cups of stewed coffee that some days she actually *needed* wine at lunchtime to slow herself down.

'You none of you eat breakfast any more,' he would exclaim. 'Cigarettes. A cup of tea. *This* is not breakfast. Forgive me if I sound like my mother but if you eat no breakfast, how can you get anything *done* in the mornings? Tea and cigarettes – ha! You, will amount to nothing and probably die young.'

Sure enough, the studio door opened and he appeared in weekend clothes – baggy, threadbare cords and an equally ancient polo shirt – bearing a coffee jug, mugs and a sheaf of virgin newspapers. She made as if to rise but he flapped her back down with a brusque gesture at her manuscript.

'Work,' he said, and kissed the top of her head in welcome.

'Hello,' she told him. 'What were you playing?'

'Secrets. I assume you've eaten nothing nutritious since yesterday lunchtime.'

She nodded, with a guilty smile, enjoying being made to feel about ten again.

'Thought so,' he growled and disappeared again, to return, minutes later, with a large plate of thick wholemeal toast spread with butter and marmalade. After setting it before her, he dug in his pockets to produce a banana and an apple as well.

'Grandpa, I can shop you know. I do eat sometimes.'

'I know. Silly food. Medallions of fish on vine leaves poached in some useless aromatic *vapeur*. Don't stop working. We can talk later. Eat.' He shook out the first of the newspapers and flicked with quick impatience through the news before settling with a small grunt on the weekend section. She poured them both coffee. They both took it black. Like most people who have spent years far from convenience stores, they had both learned to take coffee, tea and spirits unmixed so as to avoid the pangs of late night frustration when house supplies of milk or soda ran dry.

She worked on as he read, munching toast from one hand and brushing crumbs and butter drips off the page with the other, glancing up occasionally when he snorted or laughed to himself over something he had read. She ate the banana and the apple, almost without noticing, poured them each a second, even stronger, coffee, then worked on until she had finished.

'Done,' she said, slapping the pages onto the paving stone beside her and weighting them with her coffee mug.

'Already?' he asked.

'Short novel,' she explained. '*Pithy* is what I'll say in the blurb, otherwise people won't think they're getting enough pages for their money. Of course, her agent has no idea how good I think it is, or he'd have doubled the advance he asked for.'

'Has it always been like that?' he asked.

'Like what?' she replied, puzzled, upending the coffee jug in vain over her mug.

'Did Stendhal and George Eliot have agents and editors? Did they have all this politicking about money and advances.'

'Not exactly, but then they weren't *paid* nearly as much. Actually. Think about Byron. And Dickens! Authors have always been preoccupied with their earnings and now it's one of art's great disappointments; the Muses can't hold hands to dance any more because they're clutching calculators and the latest tax dodge handbooks.'

'The Muses didn't dance. That was the Graces.'

'Yes. Well . . .' Another chasm in her scrappy education

loomed. Her knowledge of Greek mythology was as thin as her familiarity with the Bible. 'You know what I mean.'

'Actually they *did,*' he laughed. 'Now that I think about it. Stravinsky and Diaghilev had them dance in *Apollon Musagète*. Or was it Balanchine by that stage?'

'Well of course I knew that. I was just humouring you,' she joked and he waved a paper at her. She chuckled, reaching for some news-free pages. It was a ritual of her weekend newspaper reading, along with the fact that she never bought the papers herself, that she begin with the weekend pages – restaurant reviews, gardening chores, shopping tips – then do the crossword, then skim through the news to see what she had been missing all week and only then, when she was feeling strong, turn to the book reviews to see how her authors had fared, if indeed, *any* had sprung to a literary editor's notice. She flicked idly and began to read a profile of a lovely actress Sandy had recently told her lived with another woman. The actress was shown beaming in her new, empty kitchen, and beaming, in different clothes, on the edge of her equally spacious, equally empty double bed. The piece focused on her ruthless dedication to self-development and her art.

'Boyfriends?!' Alison read. 'With the hours I keep, even my cats get impatient!'

The telephone rang. Alison groaned and began to get up, then realised it was the studio one. Her grandfather sighed heavily, folding the newspaper open at the page he was reading.

'Let it ring,' she urged him. 'Who'd want to bother you now?'

'Your mother,' he said grimly, stretching the small of his back with his hands as he rose.

'How can you tell?' she laughed, but he was unexpectedly grave.

'Because by now she'll have read this and so will most of her friends.'

He dropped the article he was reading onto her lap.

Instantly her eye was drawn to a familiar photograph of him and her grandmother, brave, ill-fated Sally, posing with baby Miriam on the steps of The Roundel, not fifteen paces from where Alison now sat. To the left, and much larger, was a glamorous picture of a film star, dressed in clothes of roughly the same late 'forties period. It took Alison a moment or two to recognise her, she seemed so podgily vulnerable compared to her more recent bitch-goddess image. Underneath was a photograph of a letter, unmistakably in her grandfather's sloping handwriting. It started 'Dearest Witch'.

She drove an eminent philosopher to distraction, the bold-type headlines exclaimed. Alison read on.

> She sat in bed with Auden, drinking cocoa and concocting obscene limericks, and she shattered the inhibitions and possibly the heart of Edward Pepper. See our exclusive preview serialisation of Venetia Peake's scandalously readable biography of the soap queen with a long and surprising past: *Miss Myra Toye.*

As her grandfather disappeared into the studio with the coffee pot, shutting the door behind him and silencing the telephone's shrill summons, Alison looked up briefly then began to read the extract. She was at once enthralled and mortified. As usual, having doubtless paid a fortune for the exclusive rights, the editor had felt free to gut the book and string only the choicest gobbets together, which did few favours to Ms Peake's thinnish prose but dragged one, breathless, straight to the heart of things and left one in a position to bluff having bought and read the actual book. Alison often wished the readers' reports she commissioned were half as efficacious.

> Myra's affair with Edward Pepper began in earnest when each was at their lowest ebb. Pepper, then known to filmgoers by his original, German-Jewish, name of Eli Pfefferberg, was nearing the pinnacle of his success as a composer of lush, unsettling movie scores. But he had become an automaton, married to his work in the few years since the horrific death of his wife in freak floods that swept in from the East Anglian coast of England. Abandoning his only daughter to a string of underqualified nannies, who by all accounts veered from the alcoholic to the downright sinister, he suppressed his considerable libido into an inhuman drive to achieve, but in so doing reduced himself to a husk of a man. Never exactly blessed in her private life,

Myra was still licking her wounds at being so publicly discarded by Sir Julius. The British studios, it seemed, were determined to punish her hubris in aspiring to snub them for her first, abortive Hollywood career. But publicly they allowed people to believe it was her indiscreet bid for homewrecker status that was causing them to neglect her. Since the second abortion, she had begun to drink heavily again, Scotch this time, any which way, which only provided another excuse for them to downgrade her casting value. Financially vulnerable after Marton [her accountant, ed.] had decamped to Argentina with the lion's share of her savings, she had no option but to take on some of the most unrewarding roles of her career – a Sioux squaw in *Blue Smoke*, the comic housekeeper in *Knock Knock My Lady*, the outwitted and discarded mistress in *Hell's Fury* and, perhaps most humiliating of all, as Margaret Lockwood's simple-minded mother in the kindly suppressed (and since lost) *Katie of Killarney*. This part, it was well known, had been stoutly rejected by Flora Robson. It required her to streak her hair with grey and wear merciless cosmetic dewlaps and a strap-on waist-thickener. Lockwood's memoir claims dismay at such casting of her contemporary, but it must surely have granted her some satisfaction as recompense for the notorious mink stole incident.

Composer and fading star were already known to one another – Myra had always been meticulous in her good, even hearty, relations with members of each film's technical crew. She had sent him flowers in hospital and a wreath on the death of his wife, but the acquaintance could still be described as no more than casual. After one too many days in the waist-thickener however, Myra drank more than even her iron constitution could take and passed out on a bench in the staff car park having, luckily, failed to locate her MG. Pepper found her, did the gentlemanly thing, and drove her back to the mansion block flat he had recently bought in London's Kensington. He put clean sheets on his bed, tucked her, still comatose, under the covers and went to sleep under a blanket on the put-you-up. Some time during the night, she woke up in a screaming alcoholic panic. He hurried in to reassure her and one thing led to the inevitable other. The encounter was unplanned and possibly an embarrassment come breakfast time, but Pepper had underestimated how parched he was for passion and she, during her recent succession of bruising involvements and disastrous marriage, was a sitting duck for the first man who displayed anything approaching old-world courtesy, much less tenderness. Pepper offered her both, in spades. It was a Friday night. She spent the weekend with him, disguising herself in his clothes and an old homburg on the rare occasions they left the flat to cat. He took to visiting her little house in Carlyle Square, but seems to have had some superstition about letting her visit The Roundel, his late wife's house in East Anglia (by now the legal property of his daughter Miriam, who was conveniently sent away to boarding school). They wrote letters to each other, little notes tucked under one another's wind-screen wipers, scribbled into scripts and orchestral scores. Surprised by passion, their enslavement appears to have been mutual . . .

Alison read on, through extracts from embarrassingly unguarded letters – *Dearest Ludo – Darling Witch – Your tender neck – Your wicked roving fingers – I want you so badly I could burst right here in front of everybody – I don't care!!! – Your bad bristles on my titties – Hang Larry and Vivien, come to me NOW!! – I can't wait another hour – See you outside the gates at four – On the sound stage at six – At the station at eight – In my bed as soon as poss!!!*

It was evident that there were far more details than the newspaper editor had seen fit to reproduce. He was concentrating on maximum humiliation for both parties, maximum entertainment value for his readers. There were repeated dot dot dots, then a large gap during which the affair underwent a violent offstage sea change.

The end, when it finally came, was predictably bitter, which makes it the more astonishing that they have succeeded in keeping the entire liaison a secret until now. Edward had restored her faith in herself as an attractive woman and he had gratified her old yearning to have her undertrained intellect taken seriously. But however unflattering, her gamble in taking the lead and allowing herself to be sent up so grotesquely in

Goodman's cheap horror production paid off. *Come Into My Parlour* proved hugely successful and gave her new bankability in the eyes of the moguls. Accordingly she came under pressure to produce a new beau for the press department. An otherworldly Jewish composer, even one on their payroll, was not a suitable candidate given the image they were intent on cultivating for her. In one of those ruthless snap decisions on which much of her extraordinary professional longevity rests, Myra made full use of the studio's bureaucratic apparatus to make herself suddenly and entirely inaccessible to Edward. She gave no explanation, possibly because she mistrusted her own ability to withstand his tears and angry recriminations in the flesh. His last letter to her was among the bitterest she would ever receive . . .

When it was clear that there was no more about her grandfather in the extract, Alison, puzzled, turned back to the first page to look once again at the old photographs there, at her grandmother, pale, fresh, essentially ordinary, and at the actress, her face no less ordinary but transformed by a dazzling smile, breasts like a life jacket and all-concealing studio make-up. The first photograph was an amateur snap, over-exposed, its subjects a trifle stiff with embarrassment, but it belonged undeniably to the real world. One could almost smell the after-scents of a Sunday roast, sweetly fatty on the air. Her grandmother's cardigan looked home-made and was unravelling at one of the cuffs. Her nails, if one could see them, would probably be chipped from gardening. The studio portrait, by contrast, had been touched up to the point where it had ceased to be a photograph and had become a kind of kitsch altar painting. Myra's skin was flawless, her eyes twinkled with latent tears, the hairs on her head appeared to have been individually curled and bleached by patient, white-gloved attendants. The image bore as little relation to blood-and-sweat feminine reality as an orthodox icon of the Blessed Virgin or a wigless department store mannequin.

Alison dropped the paper back on the heap. Her grandfather was rooted, in her mind at least, at The Roundel, in a clutter of strange instruments and keyboards, among roses, old coats and mildewy 'forties novels. It was as surprising to Alison that he could have passed freely from the fresh memory of one woman to the metropolitan bed of the other, as it was that Jamie had found true love. That the old man should be famous for music was only just – a natural reward for a life of inspired application – but that he should also be suddenly famous for sex shook her. She needed time to adjust to the idea. A part of her was even jealous on her grandmother's behalf.

She saw him framed in the studio's picture window, by the piano keyboard, telephone receiver in hand. Talking, he turned back into the room. He was agitated but hiding it. She could tell because he kept touching his free fingers to his temple, which he always did, unconsciously, at stressful moments. He hung up and stood there for a moment, watching the telephone as though waiting for it to ring again. Then he disappeared from view to emerge at the door with a fresh jug of coffee.

She found she could not face him at that moment. Turning aside with a vague wave, she hurried back into The Roundel and up to her room. She sat on the bed, then lay down and stared at the ceiling, her heart racing. This was the room, she had often heard, where he had taken refuge during the flood that had torn Sally from him. The change she felt in her view of him was no less violent than the one worked by the unnatural tides that had swept boats to the level of this room's sill and had dragged a car down the bank of the Rexbridge road.

That her grandfather had known great love and been more or less in celibate mourning for it ever since, was one of the simple certainties on which her life was founded – like the warmth of the sun or the sweetness of sugar. Now that she was forced to examine it, the myth was of a sentimental flimsiness she would not have accepted even in the most romantic of her company's fiction. She had always assumed the tragedy of Sally's loss had enriched his creativity, even though it overshadowed the possibility of his enjoying any other woman. To have this faith betrayed by so much casual Saturday journalese left her breathless, confused and angry. She had only told him half the truth in the restaurant the other night. Certainly she might have idealised his marriage – perhaps it was not so special to him, or perhaps it *was* and he was simply lonely afterwards. There was no law against widowers remarrying or finding consolation. What she did *not* idealise was her view of Sally. From her earliest girlhood there had been witnesses enough to give her a detailed portrait of her grandmother. The more she heard of Sally's feistiness and independence, the more she felt out of sympathy with her own chaotic and all too dependent mother. Sally's memory had usurped Miriam's place, and she had become a spectral surrogate parent, the kind of woman Alison hoped to be. Now she was forced to see her as a dead wife, nothing more, a pallid rival to a more potent heroine, her small, domestic achievements long since outrun by the grander ones of a surviving husband.

Alison walked to the bathroom and flushed the loo so as to acquire a pretext for her sudden withdrawal, then descended the stairs to rejoin her grandfather. Faced with a dilemma, she habitually asked herself what Sally would have done. In this case, she realised, Sally would have shrugged, not unlike Cynthia, and said, 'He's a man. Men's needs are simpler than ours and they're harder to deny. Besides,' this with the laugh Alison had never heard, 'being dead, I wasn't much use by that time.'

This revelation had brought her grandfather into a new focus. He had become less a grandparent – with all the sentimental castration the status implied – more a man.

'You've read it?' he said as he sat down beside her again.

'Yes,' she said. 'Had she?'

'And how. She's reacting out of all proportion. She started saying, "Don't worry, I'll pack a suitcase and drive up" as though there were some crisis on, like a death or a press siege.'

'Oh no!'

'It's all right. I put her off. I said you were here to answer the telephone and protect me. It's not as if it's in a tabloid anyway. When she goes to church tomorrow and finds she isn't mobbed she'll probably be disappointed and blame me for not hiring myself a press agent. I'm sorry if you feel I deceived you.'

Alison paused for a moment, to think. He *had* deceived her. It certainly felt that way.

'You didn't,' she said. 'Not really. You just held back the truth. May I ask why you told her anything, though? Couldn't you have just kept quiet? None of us need *ever* have known!' She heard a trace of anger enter her voice.

'To be honest, I wasn't sure just how detailed the book would be and I didn't want to do more damage than was necessary.' He looked at her benignly, mocking her caution, oblivious to her wrath. 'In fact, I did precious little. Miss Peake already had my letters. She was obviously a most determined researcher and she was plainly going to tell the story with or without my help. When she confronted me with what she knew, I thought the least I could do was make sure she gave a balanced account. Your mother thinks I should have kept quiet. She says it will cause "difficulties for poor Frank" though how, I can't imagine. Anyway, I'm not ashamed and I don't see why she should be, or you. It's all true. It happened. I'm actually rather proud about it.'

They laughed, he more than her. She fancied he was relieved at something. Perhaps there were still *more* embarrassing details the biographer had left out, though discretion hardly seemed to be her keynote.

'The record company will be thrilled,' she pointed out drily.

'Really? Yes. I suppose they will. Do you think I come out of it badly?'

Alison picked the paper up again and glanced at the relevant paragraphs.

'No,' she said. 'Sadly but not badly. Except for the nanny bit, but everyone will forgive you that as it's a period detail.'

'Well that bit's all exaggerated. Some friend of Miriam's probably told her something. Miriam's now saying, "But how *could* she? All the nannies were such *angels*!"'

He laughed at his own impersonation. Alison poured them both more coffee. She had already drunk too much. She could feel her hands wanting to shake. She forced herself to confront the unpalatable.

'Were you terribly hurt when it finished?' she said. 'She doesn't give any details here.'

He nodded and for a moment she thought he was not going to reply, then he sighed.

'I'd never been rejected before. Sally dying was pure loss. Senseless and altogether different. This was calculated. First rejection is hard at any age. And it was such a very physical thing. I think those always end in anger more than sorrow. The scales really do fall from your eyes and you wonder what on earth you saw in the person, and how you could possibly have degraded yourself so in front of others.'

'What did you say in the last letter? They don't quote it.'

'The last letter?'

'Yes. She says – Where is it?' Alison scanned the newsprint. 'Yes. She says "His last letter to her was among the bitterest she would ever receive . . ."'

He furrowed his brow, touched his temple.

'God. *I* can't remember. It was so long ago. Probably something very vindictive. I knew all her weak points by then.'

They sat for a while in thoughtful silence, listening to the lazy courtship of pigeons on The Roundel's roof. Then the telephone rang again, only this time it was hers.

'Hell,' she said, getting up. 'Now she's probably ringing to see whose side I'm going to be on.'

'Don't answer,' he suggested. 'Sometimes I don't answer for hours on end. I put a cushion over it.'

'I know,' she said firmly, patting his shoulder as she headed back to the house and feeling her anger at him threaten to rise again. 'It can be extremely irritating.'

The hall floor was cold under her feet.

'I'm coming, I'm coming,' she grumbled and snatched up the receiver, answering far more brusquely than she had intended. 'Yes? Hello?'

There was a static-filled pause, announcing a very long distance call, then a woman's voice, smoky, oddly familiar, asked, 'Now who's that?'

The accent was English but wore signs of American influence, like a deep, creasing tan.

'It's Alison,' Alison said. 'Alison Pepper.'

'Ah,' said the voice, then '*Ah!*' with fuller understanding. 'Are you a new wife, then, or what?'

'I'm sorry?' Alison laughed at the improbability of it.

'Is it possible for me to talk to Teddy?'

'*Teddy*?'

'Edward, then. I want to talk to Edward Pepper. May I?'

'But of course. I'm so sorry. You've come in on a different line. He's in the garden. Hang on. Who should I say is calling?'

'Just tell him Myra.'

'Oh,' Alison said sheepishly. 'Right!'

The call might as well have come from her dead grandmother it startled her so. She found herself setting down the receiver very carefully so as not to cause a clunk in the famously bejewelled ear. She stood staring at the phone for a second or two, debating whether to break off the connection in a feeble attempt to abort whatever process might be about to start. Then she remembered that her family's involvement with Myra Toye was now being read about in hairdressers' across the country. Again she thought of floods and their inexorability.

Her grandfather seemed equally shocked at the news and began to dither until she reminded him it was a call from the depths of the Californian night. She resisted the temptation to eavesdrop on such a topical reunion and flopped back into her chair pretending to read a scathing review of a new Domina Feraldi play. He returned very quickly, avoiding her impudently enquiring gaze, and began to read as well. When he broke the silence, it was without looking up from the article before him.

'I hung up,' he said. 'I didn't speak to her. If she calls again, which I don't suppose she will, but *if* she should, could you say I'm away or something?'

'Yes,' she promised him, confused and strangely disappointed. 'Of course I will.'

It was rare for him to show any Germanic severity *en famille*, but when he did, as now, it commanded her immediate respect, because it was in such contrast to his usual manner.

The subject of the affair was indefinitely closed between them. The time when she might have protested against his destruction of her last veil of innocence was past. She knew he expected her not to tell her mother about the call, and pledged him her silent allegiance, marvelling, as she did so, at the capacity of the human mind to feel pain decades after a wound's infliction. At least, when he had dishonoured Sally's memory, it was not for some casual flirtation. At least it was for something that had made him suffer. At least, in the cheapest sense, he had not got away with it.

43

Jamie's existence had been transformed. From the first tentative admission that he was in love, he felt as though an opaque layer had been peeled away, leaving its colours brighter, its every sensation more acute. Overnight his life fell into two discrete sections; the time before and the time since, and he was enabled to see now that the contentment he had felt before was no more than a pleasure in sustained control and stasis, as far removed from the real happiness he felt now as a boiled sweet from a blood orange. Lying awake at night in Sam's arms – for however happy, his sleep remained fitful – he felt the slow, warm fall and rise of the other's chest against his cheek and dared to register relief.

Beginning a slow colonisation of Jamie's flat and possessions, Sam had begun to investigate seams of Jamie's record collection, long neglected since the advent of compact discs, and had unearthed an album of Billie Holiday songs. He had only played it once before, declaring her voice 'miserable as fuck' and moving on to other things. Jamie kept returning to it, however, charmed afresh, despite the embarrassment of not remembering who the Julian was who had so keenly inscribed the sleeve in making the record a present. One song in particular began to speak to him, its lyrics – however cynically Holiday sang them – falling on his ear refreshed with new relevance. He found it pestering him at odd times of day.

'Just in time,' he sang in his mind, washing out the bath or riding the glass lift to a meeting at Lloyd's, 'I found you just in time.'

Once, after Sam had rung him at work from a call box to clarify some detail of their plans for the evening, his secretary had caught him humming the old melody out loud as he scanned the figures on his monitor. Where he would once have glowered the mocking smile off her face, he now found he could disarm her mockery by smiling easily back. She had a lover too. Not a builder, but a working man, a carpenter. She had shyly confessed over one too many birthday drinks, 'My dad thinks I should aim higher now that I work here. But it's no good, Jamie. I like the feel of his hands.'

The feel of his hands, Jamie thought, tossing his magazine back on to the waiting room table and reaching instead for the *Financial Times*. He made a dim attempt to read a report on the performance of a Swiss coffee and chocolate giant Francis had been recommending, then tried instead to summon up the feel of Sam's hands, their cuts, their dusty callouses, the unexpected softness of their palms as they brushed across his armpits or the nape of his neck, but all he could summon up was dread. Suddenly the receptionist was at his side, taking away his emptied coffee cup.

'Mr Pepper. Mr Pepper? Dr Penney will see you now.'

Jamie was never ill. It was something doctors always commented on, glancing over his notes. Once the usual childhood ailments and teenage vaccinations were out of the way, his only brushes with medicine had been for accidental damage – concussion after falling off his bicycle, a tetanus injection and stitches after an undramatic but messy brush with some barbed wire, and that nasty fracture sustained on a skiing holiday which had led to a short spell in a German hospital. He had colds like the next man, of course, hangovers, the rare crisis of food poisoning or 'flu, but he was never ill; not what he thought of as properly ill. He ate carefully, he took vitamins and he kept fit. This meant that the unease with which he faced his rare encounters with a doctor was accompanied by an inappropriate excitement at the novelty of the experience.

Not only had he found Sam just in time, he had dared, like a fool, to lower his guard, having found him, and feel safe, immune to his old bachelor fears. The mark might have been there for weeks, for all he knew. In his new reassurance, he had stopped his former obsessive monitoring of skin tone and weight gain. He only found the thing because he had caught athlete's foot after the two of them had been swimming in a public baths one weekend. Upending one foot and then the other to shake fungicide over them, he found a mark, below his toes, slightly larger than a fifty pence piece, raised a little above the surrounding skin, the colour of a recent blackberry stain. He could not tell if the soreness was caused by the athlete's foot which had made some of the skin between his toes crack. He tried to hide it from Sam but found he couldn't and thrust it out for his inspection in bed one evening.

'Was that there before?' he asked.

''Course,' Sam said. 'It's just a mole.'

'Are you sure?'

'Well I *think* it was there before. I quite like it.'

Jamie watched in alarm as Sam lowered his bristled chin to kiss the thing. While content to use condoms at Jamie's insistence, he seemed utterly without anxiety, either from ignorance or bravado. Jamie tried to take shelter beneath his lover's confidence but his own fear leaked through and chilled him by degrees.

'If you're so worried, take it to a doctor,' Sam said.

'But I'm never ill.'

'So? You're not ill now. But go if it makes you stop worrying. I hate you like this.'

Sam made it sound so simple, but to Jamie the very act of taking the blemish to someone qualified to pronounce on it gave his fear a fleshly dimension he would not countenance.

Then Fate took the initiative out of his hands. The syndicate was changing its employees' private health insurance arrangements and all personnel were required to have a health check with a doctor approved by the insurers – hence his visit to Dr Penney. This was, they had all been assured, purely a formality. Steeling himself, Jamie called at Dr Penney's well-appointed consulting rooms one lunch hour, allowed the first part of the examination to run its unruffled course then pulled off shoe and sock and asked, 'Should I be worried about this?'

Dr Penney frowned and prodded.

'Tender?' he asked.

'Yes. Rather.'

'And it's new?'

'Yes.'

'Mmm. It's only a mole but it's rather big. Probably nothing to worry about, but I think we should whisk it off just the same. Lie on the couch over there.'

And he and his nurse had removed the mole then and there under local anaesthetic, leaving Jamie with a neat row of stitches, a temporary limp and a tremendous sense of relief.

'Berk,' Sam jeered kindly when Jamie finally spoke the thought that had been going through his mind for weeks. 'Told you it was nothing. Now peel us another orange.'

Only days later, Dr Penney had telephoned the office to ask him to call back, 'on a matter of some urgency'.

'How're the stitches?' he asked, waving Jamie into his seat. He was a smartly dressed, irredeemably plain man and, Jamie thought, wryly, rather young to have power over life and death. He probably specialised in health insurance work because it paid well, was impersonal and strictly limited in the strains it could place upon his medical knowledge and social inhibitions.

'Fine,' Jamie told him. 'A bit sore, but they're holding. I've kept them out of water, like you said. I just wash round them with a flannel.'

'Good. Good.' Dr Penney opened a file then closed it again, as though fearful of revealing a second too early what lay hidden there. He evidently felt extremely uncomfortable about what he was about to say.

'Do you have a regular GP? I see these notes date from when you were still at school.'

'Not really. I'm never ill,' Jamie said.

'So I see. Right. Good. Well. The prognosis on the mole we removed was fine. Quite benign but probably just as well that we took it off, since it was getting large and causing you discomfort.' Dr Penney tidied one of his firmly ironed cuffs, patting the gold link, then met Jamie's eye again.

'Yes?' Jamie prompted him.

'But there's other news that's less good, I'm afraid.'

'Ah.'

'I'm afraid I'll have to refuse you for the health insurance and I don't think you'll be covered any longer by the former policy except for accidents and routine operations. Not for sickness.'

Jamie's mouth ran suddenly dry.

'Why not?' he croaked, knowing, as he asked, what he was about to hear, he had rehearsed the scene so often during his wakeful nights.

'Your blood showed evidence of a contact with the HIV virus. Now this doesn't mean you're sick. It doesn't even mean you have AIDS. As yet we know very little. There are no dangerous symptoms or anything. This simply means you've been in contact –'

'Please,' Jamie broke in, standing. 'Spare me the spiel.'

'I think you should speak to a counsellor. I can refer you –'

'Just . . . Just spell it out for me. Just once,' Jamie insisted. 'I'm HIV positive, aren't I?'

'Yes.'

'Which means, insofar as medicine has anything but deaths to go by, that at some stage, in the near or distant future, barring a miracle, I'll develop AIDS.'

'Not necessarily.'

'Oh come *on*! Probable. Say it's probable.'

Jamie pushed back his chair impatiently. Dr Penney stood too now, backing off slightly behind his desk, as though fearing Jamie might be about to hit him. Or bite him.

'Are you married?' Jamie asked him.

'Yes,' the doctor blurted.

'Children?'

'Two. Boy and a girl.' Dr Penney gestured spasmodically at a silver frame on a corner of his desk.

'Then I suspect,' Jamie told him, 'that I may be in a position to know far more about this subject than you.'

And he left.

He had not been back at his desk an hour – plunging with automatic efficiency into the streams of figures and risk appraisals – when Nick Godfreys arrived at his elbow asking if he might have a word in private. In his inner sanctum, which was furnished like a bright twelve-year-old's idea of how a senior executive's office should be, he assumed a sickening impersonation of man-to-manliness.

'Brian Penney just called me, Jamie,' he said, swivelling his chair. 'I can't say how sorry I am.'

'He *told* you?' Jamie felt suddenly clear-headed with rage.

'He was right to. As our medical adviser, he has to apprise me of anything that might endanger my staff. Look, I'm afraid we'll have to let you go. Obviously there's no need to work out your notice. You'll have the rest of this year's salary in full. And, er, I'll tell the others you've been headhunted.'

'Well thanks, Nick. That's big of you.'

'The least we can do,' Godfreys went on, impervious to the sarcasm. He shook his head, phonily rueful. 'I can't say how sorry I am. You've done some great work. We'll miss you. You'll be in my prayers.'

'That's it?' Jamie asked. 'I just stop. Now?'

Godfreys lowered his voice as though discreetly pointing out an unzipped trouser fly.

'I think it would be best,' he said.

Jamie left immediately, with no goodbyes and no explanations. There was nothing of his to clear from his desk that could not be slipped into his jacket pockets – a few pens, a chic calculator Miriam had given him as a starting-work present. It was mid-afternoon, so he had the unwonted experience of being able to sit on the train home. He held himself tightly in check, his mind watchfully numb, until he was able to lean the door to the flat firmly closed behind him. He slipped off his jacket then wandered across the flat removing tie, shirt, shoes, trousers, letting them lie where they fell, until, naked, he dropped heavily on to his bed and blocked out the daylight with the duvet and an armful of pillow.

He had never known the hard anguish of bereavement, but he cried now as for a friend's death. He shook with anger at the injustice of it all, moaned into the mattress, fell asleep, exhausted, the sheet below his face drenched with brine and snot, only to wake again, remember why he was there and begin to cry afresh. Trauma worked on him like a drug: the afternoon and early evening dissolved in spasms of shocked self-pity and merciful blanks of temporary obliteration.

When Sam arrived, grimy from work, and let himself in with the key he had only held for three weeks or so, he saw the discarded clothes and Jamie's sleeping form outlined by the bedding. He took a quick shower then slid into bed as well. Expecting a sleepily loving embrace, he found himself tugged instead into a kind of battle as Jamie, eyes half-glued with congealing tears, incoherently explained the situation. Desperate, confused, Jamie lashed out at him, tried to drive him away, with all the querulous urgency of a parent persuading a playful child away from a precipice.

'This isn't your problem,' he kept saying. 'There's no need to get involved. Just clear out. I don't need you. You're probably still fine. Just back out now. Go. Fuck off. It's not your problem.'

As Sam later tried to explain to Alison, an abiding problem of adult life was the embarrassment of choice. Able to do this, that or the other, one could rarely make a decision without the suspicion that one of the rejected choices might have proved happier.

'Then something narrows the choices,' he said. 'Or takes them away altogether, and suddenly it's all so simple. As simple as when you were a kid.'

With hindsight he liked to feel that his decision had been arrived at with an almost heroic sureness of purpose. In fact the process was longer and messier. There were days of arguing when they were together, worrying when they were apart and one purgatorial evening when Jamie locked him out and refused to answer the telephone. He spent the night wandering smugly curtained Chelsea streets and failing to sleep on benches and doorsteps, unable to understand Jamie's total rejection of him. After this dark night of the soul, Sam caught Jamie unawares in the thin morning light, returning from the newsagents with milk and orange juice. They confronted one another on the pavement, haggard with care and sleeplessness.

'She told you, didn't she?' Sam said, catching him by the

shoulder. 'She fucking told you what I did and that's why you don't want me around any more.'

'Alison? She's told me nothing.'

Jamie watched, bewildered, as Sam summoned up the words.

'I did time, all right? Two years.'

Jamie's mind reeled.

'Prison?' he asked, trying to take the information in.

'Yes. I did time,' Sam repeated. 'Not long.'

'What for?'

'GBH. There was no excuse. No reason. I was drunk.'

'Oh.' Jamie shifted his weight from one foot to another, confused by this unexpected intelligence and, even more, by how unimportant it had become. 'That doesn't matter, Sam,' he said slowly. 'That's not why I can't have you –'

But Sam cut in, pushing him hard on the chest with the flat of a hand in his frustration.

'Why does this have to be so *fucking* hard to say,' he groaned, turning aside and glowering at a woman passing with a baby-buggy.

'What?'

'I need you,' Sam insisted, looking back at him. 'Ask me to walk away now and you might as well expect me to chop off my own feet. I – I just don't have a choice.'

Loath as ever not to have the last word, Jamie drew breath to speak, then, as if frightened he might be swept off on another crying jag, shut his mouth again and fumblingly pulled Sam to him and held on hard.

44

The helpline was currently squeezed into a grim 'suite' of three tiny rooms in an office block left redundant and virtually unlettable by the onward sweep of new technology. The small organisation was constantly in danger of being moved on. It lurched from one ad-hoc lease and funding crisis to another, despite the desperate public need which the hours of meticulously logged calls would have made baldly apparent to any junior health minister or minor royal who cared to enquire. Though still officially existing to help with any enquiries of a sexual nature, from girls worried they were pregnant to cheating husbands in need of a discreet clap clinic, its work was increasingly AIDS-based. An already derisory government grant had just been halved following the production of highly suspect figures which, it was claimed, proved that any danger of an epidemic among respectable, white heterosexuals had been forestalled. The fact that most homosexuals, drug users, sex workers and African immigrants paid taxes too was, as usual, conveniently ignored. The helpline badly needed space so that London callers could hang up the telephone and come to be counselled face to face, but any such expansion would involve health and safety regulations and their consequent, impossible cost. In one room there were telephones, just five of them, ranged on a big trestle table along with a jumble of medical reference books, drug guides and directories of useful addresses and telephone numbers. The numbers most often passed on to callers were chalked on a blackboard under headings: Doctors, Hospitals, Law, Housing, Drugs. Volunteers had scribbled some inevitable graffiti up there too, the most enduring of which was a plaintive, 'Whatever happened to herpes?' The second room, wittily labelled RECOVERY in flowery writing with rabbits and bluebirds drawn around it, housed two old council-issue sofas, a coffee machine, an assortment of mugs and a bowl of goldfish Sandy had donated because she said pets were soothing and an office cat impractical.

Sandy was the volunteer coordinator, the fundraiser, the general secretary. Sandy *was* the helpline.

'I started it when both my flatmates died,' she used to joke. 'So I'd be sure of someone to talk to in the evenings.'

She and Alison were drinking coffee on the sofas, preparing to take over the telephones once the previous shift finished. Sandy was an ex-solicitor, an obsessive tennis fan who preferred talk to reading, and television to either. At first it had seemed that the two of them had nothing in common but free evenings and a need to help. Then a chance comment from a third party revealed that Sandy's real name was Harmony Rainbow and that she too was the disenchanted daughter of a commune – they needed no further common ground. Like Alison, Sandy had effected a reactionary escape into a professional career but she had found the constraints impossible and had rebelled in another direction, shaving her head, piercing her nose and becoming a full-time worker in the twilight world of charitably funded switchboards and support networks that was increasingly mopping up the messes the National Health Service and Social Services were forced to leave behind. She was lesbian with a cheerful frankness that left one no room for awkwardness or disapproval and she delighted in completing Alison's sexual education where Jamie's lunchtime confessionals had left off. She never tired of hearing Alison's more or less polite refusals to sleep with her and continued to make regular, cajoling proposals despite, or perhaps because of, an enviable erotic life.

'You'll never know until you've tried,' she'd say.

'I know, I know, and women do it better, but –'

'It could be just what your inexplicably unappreciated body has been waiting for.'

'I know.'

'So why not?'

'Sandy. I'm straight,' Alison would laugh at last. 'Totally. As a die. Sometimes people *know*, you know.'

Alison was flattered at the continuing attention, however, which had become such a cement in their odd, largely nocturnal friendship, and would miss it if it suddenly stopped. She enjoyed asking for details of Sandy's latest conquests with all the critical asperity of a discarded mistress. She also caught herself wondering if one *could* be so sure. Time and again she thought of Sam who, despite his commitment to her brother, seemed somehow to defy labelling. She had seen the way he gave men and women equal, cool appraisal. Once or twice, now that he was safely answered for, she had been sure she had caught him appraising her.

This evening Sandy was trying again.

'Oh go on. You *know* you'd enjoy it once you relaxed.'

'Are you *that* patient? Sandy, it isn't something you can just persuade people into, you know. I can't will my skin to change colour or my fingers to grow.'

'Yes but . . .' Sandy paused, glancing through the window in the door to where the others were still taking calls. 'Don't you ever wonder why you have all the free time to do things like this?'

'Because I make it.'

'Ah but –'

'Sandy please don't tell me that my having free evenings and no boyfriend means I'm a repressed lesbian; it's almost offensive.'

'But you *should* have a sex life.'

'Why? You sound like my grandfather now.'

'And he should know! You're an attractive woman.'

'So you're always saying, and that's very nice and can't I just enjoy being attractive without having someone paw my tender parts?'

'Now you *are* sounding repressed.'

'Oh *please*!' Alison scoffed, glancing at her watch and getting up from her tattered sofa to begin work.

'You seem to be doing all your loving vicariously,' Sandy pursued, calling over her shoulder as she gave the coffee mugs a quick rinse in their cubby hole of a washroom. 'You should listen to yourself. I asked you how you were a moment ago and instead of telling me about you, you went on about how nice it was that Sam had finally taken the plunge and moved in with Jamie, but how worried you were that Jamie had thrown in his job and you were sure he hadn't given you the real reason. Face it, Ali, you're becoming a fag hag.'

'I hate that expression. Anyway, he's my brother,' Alison said with a shrug. 'So's Sam, in a way. I care about them.'

'Yes, but it was you I asked after, not the plot of a soap opera. When does *your* life get to begin?'

Alison held open the door to the office.

'Enough, all right?'

'Sorry.' Sandy grinned. 'Am I coming on too strong, Angel?'

'Just a little. And don't call me that.'

She gave Sandy a playful smack on the stomach with the back of her hand and Sandy pretended to be winded. They pulled up chairs at the table alongside the other four volunteers, who cast grateful glances their way as they talked to their callers.

'Want me to stay on?' one man asked. 'There are just the two of you and things are pretty busy because of that documentary earlier.'

'We'll manage,' said Sandy. She was strict about allowing no-one to work more than three hours in a row, however hectic things were. 'Just unplug that phone would you, like a love? I can't think straight when they're all jangling in my ears –'

She broke off to answer the telephone beside her. The others left, chattering with relief, heading for an unwinding drink at the rough Irish pub across the way. Alison carefully unplugged the third telephone, so that all the calls were now being channelled furiously into just two. She took a deep breath, pulled over a pencil, pad and log book then picked up the receiver.

For the rest of the evening she received the usual dose of hard, sex-related reality in the shape of patient conversations with an HIV-positive mother of three on income support, and a teenager thrown out of home by a father who seemed to think his sexuality would somehow infect the household plumbing.

She took calls about needle-sharing facilities, from the profoundly worried well, from people who needed immediate hospitalisation, and one from an incredibly abusive Christian who sounded as though, in Sandy's books, she was having far too many quiet nights in. As always, by the time she turned the answering machine back on and bodily prised the receiver from Sandy's compulsive grip, sex had come again to seem an arena of bloody war and her single state, an unjustly lucky neutral zone.

45

Inspired by a morning of unheralded autumn sunshine, prompted, too, by the memory that Alison had begged for contributions to a big jumble sale in aid of the helpline, Jamie and Sam purged the flat. To mark the end of Jamie's life as an office animal, 'and to celebrate the beginning of the rest of it' as he put it, they went through cupboards and drawers. Jamie began by hurling all his striped cotton office shirts into a heap in the middle of the floor and after them, with only a moment's hesitation, his pinstriped suit. Sam tossed several books on reinsurance and economics after it, a tax guide, a bouquet of silk ties, which he pronounced 'poncey' and, ignoring Jamie's protests, the matt black calculator. Then the purge expanded into a total clear-out, filling bags and boxes with records, books, CDs, jerseys, mugs, a joke tea pot, a sickly African violet, three bottles of untouched cologne, assorted pornography, a hair dryer, a rolodex whose cards Jamie had never finished filling with addresses, a travel iron, an electronic phrasebook and an asparagus steamer. One by one they had snatched objects from shelves and out of corners, held them up to one another and, with Jamie laughing at their daring, condemned them before consigning them to oblivion. Jamie wondered if Sam felt he was expunging traces of predecessors. He stopped for a moment or two, watching Sam throw open a cupboard door revealing, with a kind of relish, another hoard of redundant items. It struck him that he had never had a boyfriend before, that his first would probably prove his last, and that some might find this sad.

'What?' Sam asked, catching him staring.

'Nothing.'

'You don't use telephone directories. Nobody does. Why do you keep them?'

'Security?' Jamie suggested, heaving up the first bag of things for the jumble sale to carry out to the car. Half-way downstairs a ripple of self-pity acute as a dizzy spell threatened to make him break down and cry, and he had to lean against the staircase wall to wait for it to pass.

He returned from the car to find Sam had cleared the mantelshelf of its clutter of postcards, announcements and invitations and put Sally's idol there instead. Jamie stopped in the doorway, looking at how the squat goddess now seemed to preside over the newly purified room. Sam paused in the act of tossing the cards one by one into the kitchen bin, briefly following Jamie's gaze.

'She looks better there,' he said.

'Yes,' Jamie agreed. 'It's more like her place now.'

'Jesus! Do you know *him*?' Sam exclaimed. Jamie looked over and found him holding out the gilt-edged invitation to Nick Godfreys's engagement ball.

'Of course,' he muttered darkly. 'He was the one that sacked me, wasn't he? Bin it.'

'No.' Sam fingered the piece of card. 'When you told me I never realised he was the Godfreys they're always writing about in the papers.'

'Bin it, Sam. All that's over and done with now.'

'Are you kidding?' Sam was incredulous.

'What's wrong?'

Sam laughed.

'I want to go.'

'You're not invited, berk. Anyway, he expected me to take a woman; the bastard actually said so. In front of everybody. I wouldn't be seen dead there. Even with both Liz Taylor and Myra Toye on my arms. Bin it.' He tried to take the card but Sam held it out of reach, smiling mischievously.

'Look,' he said, swinging away from Jamie's clutching hands. 'It says James Pepper and Friend. I'm your Friend. Let's go.'

'Now *you*'re kidding.'

'No I'm not.'

Once again Jamie lunged after the offensive card but Sam slipped it down inside his tee-shirt and grinned. Jamie had noticed he was always more playful at weekends, less remorselessly macho when freed from the dead weight of exhaustion and his workmates' potential ridicule. Out on the streets he became more guarded again, as though on the watch for people who might recognise him. He thrust a hand up inside Sam's shirt for the card but was tugged down onto the sofa instead. Sam gave him a brusque, toothpasty kiss.

'I do love you,' Jamie said, the statement still sufficiently unfamiliar on his lips to give him a piquant sense of risk.

'But I love you more,' Sam said simply, then held up the card to examine it again. 'I've never been to a posh git do before. I don't know any famous people. It'd be a laugh.'

'It'd be hell in a basket.'

'No it wouldn't.' Sam ruffled the hair at the nape of Jamie's neck with the stiff card, tickling him. 'Go on,' he murmured. 'You can hire me a suit. After all. Think of all those lovely people you didn't say a proper goodbye to.'

'Huh.'

'Are you ashamed of me?'

'Don't be stupid.'

'But I haven't met any of your friends.'

'I don't have any friends.'

'What about all those names and addresses we just threw out?'

'Exactly. We threw them out. If they were proper friends, I'd have kept them. I mean, I do *know* people. I could pick up the phone and get us asked out to dinner with a load of people but, well, I don't see the point when I can be with you.'

'You mean like *instead*?'

'Yes. No. Listen. Would you really like to go?'

Sam considered the invitation, sensing a serious proposition.

'Yeah,' he said at last, smiling to himself. 'Yeah.'

So they took Jamie's dinner suit to the dry cleaners and hired a second, longer-legged one for Sam. Unexpectedly he didn't look like a bouncer in it, but like some gaunt, dissident poet instead.

Sam drove them out towards Westmarket. Jamie had only recently discovered that Sam, though carless, had a driving licence and enjoyed indulging him at the wheel. Sam drove much as he made love; with an almost indignant concentration on the matter in hand. He manoeuvred with fast assurance and delighted in the car's speedy acceleration which allowed him to pull away from traffic lights before anyone else. When Jamie called him a 'Boy Racer' he merely grinned, taking the mockery as acknowledgement of something of which he was proud. He changed gear by making rapid swipes at the gear stick with the flat of his hand and soon became quite rapt in the business of driving. Conversations died on his lips as he concentrated on a piece of risky overtaking or enjoyed a sweep of steady acceleration up a hill. Jamie lay back in the passenger seat, sucking peppermints, discreetly watching the aggressive flicking of Sam's eyes across the road before them, and nursing a comforting hard-on. Occasionally Sam would swear at another driver under his breath and Jamie would smile to himself.

Nick Godfrey's house perched like a creamy wedding cake in a few acres of tidy parkland. There were big gates with octagonal lodges, a lake, old cedar trees, clean and fluffy sheep and a watchful family of horses. Some crucial element seemed to be missing, however, so the scene felt oddly two-dimensional, even temporary, like an elaborate film set. After showing their invitation to the security guards at a gatehouse, who handed it back with a yellow card to be placed inside the windscreen, Sam drove them through the park and Jamie found himself picturing the gigantic props and weights that held such extravagant scenery in position.

'Those sheep are probably rented for the evening,' he laughed.

They left the car to be parked in a field, and joined the throng that was mounting the shallow flight of steps into the Palladian portico. A few press photographers, carefully vetted, had been allowed this far. They jockeyed for position at the foot of the steps, calling out with bogus familiarity the first names of celebrities they recognised as their cameras flashed and whirred.

'Unreal,' Sam murmured.

'That's the whole idea,' said Jamie. 'They're probably hired along with the sheep.'

There were stylized braziers between the pillars, flaming from a cunningly concealed gas supply and the open doors had been lushly framed with a construction of foliage, fruit, flowers and gold silk swags.

Had Godfreys been standing in the hall to greet his guests, with his politically astute choice of fiancée at his side, there might have been some sense that this was his party, his house. But he was nowhere in sight. The crush of dark-suited men and glossily turned-out women allowed their coats to be taken by one lot of staff and accepted flutes of champagne from trays held by another. They then fanned out across the hall and into the sequence of grandiose, high-walled rooms, taking possession of the place as effortlessly as if it were a new nightclub just opened for their informed critique.

For all his bluster, Sam's frequent questions over the previous few days had revealed his nervousness at the prospect of a doorstep introduction, and he visibly relaxed as the two of them moved away from the phalanx of attentive staff. Jamie felt calmer too. Since Godfreys had not been at the door, and had invited such a mob, it was perfectly possible for them now to pass the entire evening without encountering him. His only concern was that, despite having already condemned it as 'rat's piss', Sam was putting away the champagne as though it were sweet and innocuous water.

Drawn by the sound of a jazz band, Sam led the way to the ballroom and seemed quite prepared to take to the floor on his own. Few people were dancing, the bulk of the guests forming a still sober, inhibited audience. Among those who were attempting to invent appropriate steps for the music's hectic pace, however, Jamie made out their host and his tall, blonde intended – the health minister's daughter. He managed to persuade Sam just in time that it might be wiser to watch from the candle-spotted shadows for a while.

Although the house was huge, the party took only a short

while to fill the available space. The upper floors were barred to the curious by a discreet silk rope in Tory blue. A sequence of large lower rooms with interconnecting double doors led from the ball-room at one corner of the building, to a dining room at another. The dining room boasted a vast buffet – glistening salmon, roast hams aglow with honey and mustard, daunting pies, cauldrons of salad, unapproachably perfect rafts of asparagus. Guests were free to serve themselves and eat at tables dotted around the room. In the saloons in between, guests talked, smoked, lolled carefully on sofas and gazed about them with nervous, hunted expressions. For those not yet hungry enough to raid the buffet, or too vain to be seen loading a plate, staff circulated with trays of tempting one-mouthful morsels. Whenever Sam found something he liked, he took several at once. Somebody somewhere was washing up constantly – glasses of champagne were not topped up, they were simply replaced. Flickering braziers like the ones in the portico marked the way across a lawn from some French windows to a silk-lined tent where more up-to-date dance music throbbed. Several men, any one of whom could have been a Government minister, boogied with sweaty ineptitude around younger women, who danced too well and were dressed too daringly to be their wives.

Jamie and Sam danced briefly, at the more crowded end of the tent, then returned to the house, disillusioned now that the party held no unexplored corners. They raided the buffet and sat, munching, at one end of a long sofa where a very young couple were strenuously kissing. Pausing mid-supper, Sam eyed the pair; the boy, pink-cheeked, neck straining in his formal collar, the girl, all red crushed velvet and tumbling, black hair, her lit cigarette held carefully out of singeing range. He snorted, gazed at the numerous pairs milling about them, then turned back to Jamie.

'When you get down to it, it's like bleeding Noah's Ark, isn't it? Boy girl. Girl boy. Boy girl. It's no different from a Friday night disco. If this lot had handbags, they'd be dancing round them.'

'Well he was hardly going to lay on lesbian soul,' Jamie said.

'That old guy's staring at us.'

'Which?'

'The one with the . . . Oh I don't know. *Him*.'

Sam pointed and Jamie tried to see who he meant.

'Which?'

'The only guy in the room with a woman his own age,' Sam said, exasperated. 'He's coming over now.'

Jamie saw a man slightly younger than his grandfather. He had short silver hair and his old-fashioned white tie and tails had been tailored for a younger man who had since shrunk. The woman with him was tall, unmade-up and, in her dingy floor length tent dress, looked priestly and aloof. The old man paused and quizzically stared with his head on one side, trying to place Jamie, who hesitantly lurched to his feet out of the sofa's depths. Suddenly the old man was smiling broadly.

'Hello?' Jamie asked.

'You don't remember me, do you?' The accent was German or Jewish, or both.

'Your face is familiar but . . .' Jamie shrugged in apology. 'I'm sorry. I'm lousy at faces.'

'Don't worry. It's the little stroke I had. Nobody recognises me any more. Heini Liebermann. Your grandfather used to work at my father's studios. We met at Teddy's sixtieth birthday party. Now, you remember that, I think.'

'But of course,' said Jamie, still uncertain, and shook the cold little hand that was proffered.

'You've grown up a lot since then. I hardly recognised *you*!'

'Really?' Jamie laughed. 'It seems like yesterday.' He had a recollection of The Roundel abuzz with merrier, less conventional guests than the ones around them now, its garden decked with Japanese lanterns, its riverbank rendered astonishingly dramatic by a few cheap barbecue flares. It seemed months since he had last seen or even spoken to his grandfather. He felt a pang of remorse and a sudden, sweet homesickness for the house of his boyhood.

'You've lost weight,' Heini Liebermann said, then, thawing, he added, 'Not really my sort of thing.' With an eloquent glance at the people laying waste the buffet, he explained,

'My famous goddaughter dragged me along. I've lost her in the crowd somewhere, she's such a serious worker-of-rooms, but then I ran into dear Beatrix.' He tapped the woman's elbow to attract her lost attention and chuckled. 'Beatrix is a Name,' he said. 'You've probably sent her demands for payment. Lost *heaps* of her husband's money, but you don't care, do you Beatrix? This is Edward Pepper's grandson, Beatrix. James. Beatrix Maxwell.'

'Good evening.' The woman extended a heavily ringed hand.

'Jamie threw away the promise of a singing career to work for bloody Godfreys,' Heini told her.

'Very sensible,' she said. 'If a little sad.'

'This is Sam,' said Jamie, clumsily gesturing to Sam, who was still sprawled on the sofa, watching the introductions.

'How do you do?' Heini said, with a slight, ironical bow to spare him the trouble of getting up.

'All right?' Sam replied.

'And what do *you* do?' Mrs Maxwell asked. Sam stood.

'I'm a builder,' he told her.

'A contractor?' asked Heini.

'No,' Sam said steadily. 'A builder.'

Jamie saw Mrs Maxwell's eyes widen with alarm and Heini's with interest. Her social training had clearly been long and comprehensive, however.

'And have you,' she asked, 'built anything I'd have visited?'

'Working on a new hospital,' Sam said.

'I think we should be getting some supper, Beatrix,' Heini cut in. 'You know how hungry you get. Perhaps, er, Sam would like some more?'

'Wouldn't say no.'

'James?' Heini turned to Jamie.

'No thanks.'

Sam winked at Jamie and walked with the curious pair back to the buffet. Jamie's cheeks burned. He raised his glass automatically to his lips but found it was empty. In a flash, a waitress was at his side with a tray, her deferential efficiency implying that his discomfiture was visible even across a crowded room. Following her murmured directions, he slipped away with his fresh glass to the cloakrooms to recover.

It was the first time his two lives had collided, and the experience left him mortified. He did not count Alison, since she already knew Sam, and he had always kept her squarely in both his lives at once. But he had introduced Sam to no-one. Sam had not even met Miriam or his grandfather. In this brief encounter with Heini Liebermann – who Jamie felt sure was an old closet case, hiding behind a statuesque woman of irreproachable finances – he had suddenly seen how the world would view them, Edward Pepper's grandson and his 'bit of rough'. When he was alone with Sam he scarcely noticed their social differences, or rather, he only noticed them so as to celebrate them. They provided, within the two men's intimacy, an equivalent of gender difference, a necessary friction. He had agreed to bring Sam to the ball in a spirit of impetuous transgression, but once there he had been forced guiltily to recognise his own inverted snobbery. Faced with the potentially disastrous collision between Sam and Beatrix Maxwell, he had frozen, socially incapable, and been shown up by the older, worldlier man's unflustered, uncalculating good manners.

He peed, splashed his face with cold water and was leaning against the sink to pluck up courage to go back into the fray when the door opened and an elegant blonde woman came in whom he thought he recognised. An actress, perhaps, or a newscaster.

'Christ, I'm sorry,' he began, startled. 'I didn't think to look at the sign –'

'No no,' she said. 'This *is* the gents but the ladies has a queue, as always, and I'm desperate.' She threw him a dazzling smile and he remembered she was on television in a morning programme Sam usually watched on days off work. She touched the thick silver hoops on her wrists.

'You wouldn't mind awfully guarding the door for me?' she pleaded, ruefully bargaining with his recognition and her fame.

'Of course,' he promised and, while she shut herself in

the loo, he leaned against the cloakroom door to protect her from further awkwardness. She emerged in a cloud of freshly squirted scent that swiftly filled the small room and tickled Jamie's nose.

'Thanks,' she said, washing her hands. 'Friend of the host?'

'No,' he said. 'Not really.'

'Me neither.'

Rapidly, expertly, she reapplied her lipstick then unscrewed a little compartment in one end of her silver lipstick holder and tapped out two tiny shards of dark brown gel.

'Want some?' she asked, holding them out in the palm of her hand.

'What is it?' she asked, suspiciously.

'Nothing much,' she said airily. 'Helps you dance. Makes the world a little friendlier.' She smiled again, showing her teeth, and the chunky silver chain at her neck caught the light. He hesitated only a moment. His experience of drugs was limited to dope offered him by various Beards behind Miriam's back, some speed he had once bought on a New Year's Eve to help him stay awake for an all-night party, and some Ecstasy Sam's scaffolder-bouncer friend had sold them recently, which had proved to be little more than overpriced aspirin. On the evidence of these, he did not seem especially susceptible.

'What the hell,' he said, loath to appear cowardly in the face of her generosity. 'Try anything once.'

'Under your tongue's the quickest way,' she said, as he took a piece of the glistening stuff. 'Like those little pink heart attack pills.'

In unison they opened their mouths and tucked the drug under their tongues, then, with a smile as mischievous as her previous two had been brittle, she opened the door and sailed out into the corridor, leaving Jamie to enjoy the envious stares of the men now queuing outside. He allowed himself to smirk impudently back at them then saw that one of his former colleagues, a dim public-school fraud, was at the back of the queue, adjusting a collapsed black tie.

'George?'

'Jamie! Good to see you, my old mate.' George shook his hand. 'Glad you could make it. How's life treating you?'

'Fine. Just fine,' Jamie said, hoping he wouldn't ask where he was working now.

'Just met your friend Sam, out there, with that old gambler Beatrix Maxwell.'

'Oh really?'

Jamie braced himself for the worst, expecting sarcasm or clumsy prurience, but was surprised by a look of unguarded amiability on George's puddingy face.

'Great bloke,' George said. 'Lovely sense of humour.'

Jamie passed on gratefully, charged up now with a desire to find Sam and make amends, introduce him to people. He had been behaving disgustingly, he now saw, by hiding Sam away in shady corners, dodging Godfreys and his friends like a fugitive, counting the hours till he could reasonably suggest they return home. Now his only wish was to show him off, but he could see neither Sam nor Heini Liebermann. He ran into Beatrix Maxwell, who told him, rather stiffly, that she had left them out in the portico and thought perhaps they were now walking in the garden. Jamie searched on but found only a succession of former colleagues and city contacts. The drug had begun to take effect, for these now seemed the most attractive men and women imaginable, sheeny and pantherine. He felt himself overflowing with remorse and affection at their blandly polite enquiries. The fire in the braziers, the golden pyramids of fruit, a dripping ice sculpture of a swan filled with ice cream, all started to glow before his eyes with a glamour they had not held before. He finally found Sam when the music now pounding from the disco tent drew him inexorably back across the lawn. Subject to the same narcotic spell which had transformed the other guests, Sam now loomed out of the dark like a very archangel and, overwhelmed with relief and lust, Jamie could not help but clutch at his chest, his arms, his hands. Sam laughed, pawing him back, assuming he had been drinking.

'You've made up for lost time. I thought *you* were driving us home, you bastard,' Sam said. 'What are you on? Where's your glass?'

'I dunno,' Jamie mumbled, his mouth turning to a pleasing jelly in his jaw and wanting only to kiss the lips that grinned before him and left his own feeling incomplete. 'Sam, I – I thought I'd lost you.'

'I went for a piss in the rose garden with old Heini. Lost him now. Did you know he knows Myra Toye as well? She had a fling with his dad too, apparently.'

'I'm sorry,' Jamie blurted. 'I should introduce you to people. I was too embarrassed.'

'No more than I was by you on the site that time.'

'Really? Really, Sam?'

Sam looked around them.

'Really,' he muttered.

'Sam I do love you.'

'Ssh.' Sam touched his fingertips to Jamie's lips. 'Come on and dance.'

The temperature in the tent had risen sharply and the air was humid with the odours of bodies, grass and split wine. Lovingly fashioned hairstyles were subsiding in the rhythmic mêlée. Zippers and buttons slipped open unregarded. Wet skin glowed in the dim, coloured lights. Joining in the dance was easy now for, under the influence of whatever Jamie had taken, it seemed as though the music had taken everybody over and even their wildest motions were in harmony. Everyone, he felt sure, joined him in having a little piece of sharp magic gel glowing under their tongues like a jewel; if they all opened their mouths, they would light up the night. It seemed, too, as though a tightly buttoned collection of sexless mannequins were transforming before Jamie's eyes into a pack of glorious animals in rut. Dancing, he began to feel himself grow more attractive, confident in his body again. He was clean, healthy, untouched by infection. Just as he wanted to reach out and caress Sam and all the men and women around him, so he felt their gazes stroking warm across his body.

All was well until, after a momentary break in the music because of a technical problem which drew brays and jeers from the crowd, something in the atmosphere began subtly to alter. At first Jamie was aware of a few, a very few, questioning glances cast his way. Then the glances came more frequently, and with them an unmistakable tut-tutting. He had quick glimpses of hideous faces, saw, from the corners of his eyes, bodies distorted with fury. The stares were not admiring, he saw that now, but fiercely disapproving. He grew breathless, the more so as Sam was so plainly still enjoying himself. His heart beat savagely in his chest and he saw even Sam turn a look of disgust upon him as though he had wet himself on the dancefloor or begun to bleed from some hideous wound. They knew. They all knew terrible, shameful things about him! Seizing his moment, his heart constricted in the grasp of invisible hands, Jamie staggered towards the tent's opening and into the relative cool outside. His tie, which had come undone in the dance, fell to the grass and somebody stamped it into the mud before his fingers could rescue it.

'What *is* it?' Sam shouted behind him, catching him up. 'What's wrong?' Even here there were harsh eyes upon him. The famous woman with the silver neck-chain whispered by and visibly recoiled at the sight of him. 'Jamie. Jamie, it's okay. I'm here.'

Jamie turned and saw at once the only benevolent figure in the entire crawling hell-scape, and he clung to Sam for dear life.

'Come on,' Sam laughed. 'Get your breath back. It was fun in there. Let's go back in.'

'No,' Jamie almost screamed. 'I can't! Please.'

'What's got into you, for fuck's sake? You *did* take something, didn't you?'

'Yes,' Jamie confessed through chattering teeth. 'Only a bit, though.'

'Berk.'

'I'm sorry.' Suddenly it seemed that he had ruined everything for everybody. 'I'm so sorry.' Sam's moving back a few inches threw Jamie into a panic. He clutched out wildly, wanting his height and warmth to protect him from the others.

'Hey!' Sam laughed, gaining some idea through his drunkenness of the irrational terrors that were besieging him. 'It's okay. Come here.' More openly affectionate than he had ever been in public, he pulled Jamie to him, kissing his forehead and stroking his hair as one might soothe a frightened child. But Jamie's nightmares were still closing in. Every passing Noah's Ark pair looked at him in scorn, hissing indignantly at the sorry spectacle. Worse still, a security guard was standing nearby, watching and muttering something about two defectives to be neutralised into his walkie-talkie. *Could* he really be saying something so appalling for all the crowd to hear? Now the guard was coming over, walkie-talkie whispering maliciously in his grasp. His tone managed to be simultaneously obsequious and threatening.

'Could I see your invitations, Sirs?'

Sam checked his pockets.

'Left it in the car, mate,' he said good-naturedly. Hearing Sam's accent, the guard's manner immediately frosted over.

'If you'd like to come with me quietly,' he said.

'Listen. We were properly invited,' Sam said. 'I told you. It's in the car.'

'Yish,' Jamie began, and found his mouth unable to work.

'James Pepper and Friend, it said.' Sam went on angrily. 'I'm the friend.'

'Oh yes sir. I could see that. Very friendly. Come along now.'

People were definitely stopping to stare now. The guard had made the mistake of taking Sam by the upper arm to steer him away. Sam shook furiously clear of him and pushed him away. The guard quickly pressed a button on his walkie-talkie that set a red light flashing, then tried to seize Sam again. Sam spun round and landed a powerful punch in his face, sending him staggering back against one of the marquee ropes.

'Come on, for fuck's sake!' he shouted, but Jamie couldn't run, couldn't cry out. All he could do was stare at the blood pouring from the security guard's nose and think of Sam behind bars and how this was all his fault, all of it, and that he deserved to be severely punished.

'Come *on*!' Sam urged.

For a moment, Jamie even imagined that the taking of the drug *was* the punishment, rather than the cause of it, and that everyone here, Sam included, had planned this, had sent the woman into the cloakroom after him, primed and falsely smiling. Then two more guards came running through the crowd and one shoved Sam's arms behind his back, tightening their hold when he struggled so that he cried out in pain. The other held Jamie by the upper arm. As they began to be led away, Jamie saw Nick Godfreys, white-faced, hurrying the minister's daughter away from the edge of the crowd. The utter lack of recognition in the glance he threw them was more chilling than any hallucination Jamie had suffered.

'Say something,' Sam shouted. 'For fuck's sake tell them who we *are*!'

But Jamie's mouth had turned so dry that his tongue was glued to his palate, and his teeth were chattering so furiously he feared he would bite into his lips if he even *tried* to speak.

Salvation came, surprisingly, in the tall, disapproving form of Beatrix Maxwell, who had thrown a dowdy knitted shawl about her gaunt shoulders. Tent dress billowing in the night breeze, she stepped out into their path.

'Stop,' she said, patrician as a vestal in the dancing light of a brazier. 'There's been some stupid mistake.'

'No mistake, Madam. Don't you worry. Just some gate-crashers.'

'But I *know* these people! Heini. You tell them.'

Heini caught up with her and his imperious manner, silvery hair and old-fashioned white tie and tails worked like a charm on the guards, who promptly released Sam and Jamie to talk with him. Then the one with the bleeding nose came back to apologise to Sam, a handkerchief clutched to his face.

'So sorry, Sir. I had no idea. No hard feelings, I hope.'

The three of them melted back into the crowd around the tent.

'Whatever did you tell them?' Mrs Maxwell asked.

'That my tall young friend here is a distinguished, if unconventional 'cellist.' She scoffed but Heini insisted, 'He looks the part. Now, these two are in no state to drive anywhere.' He turned to Jamie. 'I assume you came by car?' Jamie could only nod his head and wipe away the dribble from his lower lip with the back of his hand. Heini turned smartly back to Mrs Maxwell, betraying only a hint of disgust. 'Perhaps you could explain to Candida, if you see her, Beatrix? She's wearing green. I'll drive them to Edward's place. It isn't far. He won't mind.'

Miraculously sober, Heini took control, making Jamie feel more than ever like a disgraced delinquent as he retrieved their coats, then bundled him into the back of the Volkswagen, threw the tartan rug over him and drove them in silence to The Roundel. He seemed as familiar with the building as Jamie was. The studio was all in darkness so he led them straight into the main house, ignoring Sam's amazed questions and briskly finding Jamie a room with a made-up bed to fall into.

Lying beneath chilly sheets and weighed down by the two eider-downs Heini had thrown over him to stop his teeth chattering, Jamie was slightly soothed by the familiar surroundings and by the sudden withdrawal of stimuli – no more music, no more stares, no more strangers, only soft near-darkness and the clean smell of the sheets. He listened to the distant murmur of voices from the kitchen and waited impatiently for the effects of the drug to wear off. Sam eventually came to bed, too exhausted to do more than mutter, 'Alison's here and she says to say you're a berk. She says you can give me the guided tour in the morning.'

Jamie kept him awake however, nervously fingering Sam's chest hair and asking again and again, 'Who am I?' or 'Who did you say I was?' never quite believing Sam's patient, sleepy replies.

When, once too often, Jamie turned on the bedside light to stare fanatically at his own hands moving in the air before him or to jump up and examine the unfamiliar face in the dressing table mirror, Sam was forced to fling an arm and leg across his restless body, pinning him down until the natural anaesthetic of exhaustion took a hold on them both.

46

Assuming Alison to be too engrossed in the Sunday book supplements to mind, Heini Liebermann and her grandfather had allowed their conversation to lapse back into the soft, eager German she had interrupted earlier. There was a disarmed gentleness to her grandfather's voice when he spoke the language, as if the underused idiom of his youth had retained the intact imprint of his younger, untried self. He gestured when he spoke German, tapping the table for emphasis, uncoiling his hands to shape words he was perhaps no longer sure of choosing correctly. When he spoke English, his hands were still, his inflexion wearier and less musical.

The Munich café atmosphere so alien to The Roundel's kitchen was heightened by the sweet smoke of the little cheroots Heini had persuaded her grandfather to share with him – in spite of the way they made his lungs heave – and by the smell of the cripplingly strong coffee he had brewed. Heini had thrown a borrowed tweed jacket over his evening dress but otherwise it was easy to imagine that they had been up talking all night. She glanced at her watch and, judging the morning to be far enough advanced, poured a couple of mugs of tea and took them to the Boys, as she had taken to thinking of Sam and Jamie.

Their bedroom door was ajar and water was noisily running in the adjacent bathroom. She knocked.

'Brought you some tea,' she called out. 'Cover up. Woman coming in.'

Jamie stirred in the bed, mumbling, edged upright and clutched a pillow to his chest. Shocked at how bony he looked since she had last seen him naked, she passed him his tea and smiled. 'Could you draw the curtain again?' he muttered, wincing.

'No,' she said. 'You're down here so rarely. I'm not having you spend the whole day in bed.'

He sipped at his tea, crestfallen.

'Sam's in the bath,' he said, indicating the second mug. 'I'll drink that one too. He'll be hours. Are there any old clothes of mine down here still? If I have to get dressed in last night's I'll throw up.'

She opened the little wardrobe in the corner and tugged out some jeans and a frayed white shirt for him along with some Donald Duck boxer shorts Miriam had once made the mistake of giving him for Christmas. Then she stood, triumphantly, with her arms folded.

'Okay, okay,' he protested. 'I'll be out in a second.'

She went away to brush her teeth. As she walked back onto the landing, Jamie joined her, hair in spikes, stamping his way into some old, red plimsolls.

'Heini Liebermann's in the kitchen smoking cheroots with Grandpa,' she warned him.

'*That*'s what the smell is. Christ. Let's go in the garden, then. Is it warm enough?'

'It's fine.'

She saw him throw a quick look around him at the hall as they headed for the garden door. He scowled as though the house were a familiar enemy. She was glad to see him here again feeling as unsettled by his neglect of the place as she would by the estrangement of friends.

'I hear you made a spectacle of yourself last night,' she said, not intending to be as judgemental as she sounded.

'Don't ask. Godfreys's friends were nightmarish enough even without the chemical assistance.'

'You should be more careful taking drugs from strangers.'

'She was a TV personality for Christ's sake!'

'You shouldn't be taking drugs at all.'

'Hark at mother.' He nudged her playfully but she scowled. 'I know, I know,' he admitted. 'I could have died.'

'I'm envious as hell,' she laughed as she dropped the responsible pose. 'What was it like?'

'Fab at first. Then it started teaching me things about myself I didn't want to know. I mean, I never thought I was especially well adjusted but I did think I had the paranoia under control . . . I'm not sure it's stopped yet.' He peered around him and shivered. 'I'm still a bit wall-climby. And it feels weird being *here*. Sam got in a fight. All I could do was watch,' he went on. 'Heini saved our lives. They could have pressed charges. Imagine Miriam's face!'

'He's . . . He's never hit you, has he?'

'Sam? Don't be silly.' He threw her a mocking look as he walked on. 'His emotions are so boxed away most of the time. I think he lashes out because he can't cry.'

'I wonder if his parents beat him as a boy.'

'Hmm. God. Listen to the bleeding-heart liberals!'

They walked down to the stream together. Instinctively she led him into the cool chamber formed by the canopy of willow branches; a childhood refuge from grown-up curiosity. He stepped forward and gave her a tight but curiously formal hug, then backed off.

'There's no easy way to tell you this,' he said, and then he told her. He told her just the way she had always imagined he would, baldly and swiftly.

'How long have you known?' she asked.

'Since I lost my job.'

'I thought you left.'

'Godfreys sacked me,' he said quietly, watching for her reaction.

'But he can't do that!' she shouted.

'He did.' Jamie shrugged. 'He could always think of a reason if I bothered to press him.'

'But you could appeal through a tribunal.'

'Let's not talk about all that.'

'And how did he find out?' she pursued, dismayed at his apathy. 'The doctor must have told him. You could sue *him* for breach of confidence – at least get him struck off.'

'Alison, I don't want to talk about it.'

'And you went to his *party*!' she began indignantly. 'Sorry,' she added, more softly. She began to lean against the willow trunk then sank to the grass instead.

All her counselling training abandoned her, and she reacted in precisely the unhelpful way she always advised callers against. She cried. She responded as though he were already dying, weeping as much because she was losing him as because he was going. She cried for herself because in him she saw her own mortality – the casual ease with which she too might be snuffed out. He did not try to comfort her, just stood a few feet away, plaiting willow strands and waiting for her to recover. She was grateful for this. If he had hugged her again, however formally, it would have opened whole new pits of grief.

'Sorry,' she managed at last.

'That's all right.'

She was beginning to feel damp from the ground, so she stood and walked over to look at where the tips of trailing branches flickered in the stream's dark currents. She felt a sudden anger at his exclusion of her.

'Why did you take so long to tell me?' she asked. 'If you hadn't ended up here last night, how much longer would you have waited? Hmm? Sorry. Fuck. Forget I said any of that. How can I be so crass? Sorry.'

'You have to understand,' he murmured. 'I've been finding well people difficult to be around. Old people too. Poor Sam's been getting the –'

'But you're not *sick*,' she cut in, thinking. *Oh my God if you are you'd better tell me quickly.*

'Spare me the psychobabble,' he rounded on her. 'It's all right. I'm not being a victim. I'm not being negative. But I am being realistic.' He snorted, his tone softening. 'I've been doing a lot of maths recently, you know? I've been trying to work out when I last had unprotected sex and adding fifteen years to that to see how long I have. But then that's a best possible case scenario. The worst possible is more like eight or six years' incubation period, or less. This thing's been around all my sexual life! Then there are all the times I got a little carried away, or the condom broke, or I had mouth ulcers or a cut on my hand.'

'Oh Jamie.'

'Then Hilary was saying how they're now finding people who could only have caught it through oral sex – years after they told us oral sex was perfectly safe.'

'Jamie please!'

'Don't cry again. It doesn't help. *Don't.*'

'Sorry.'

He tugged fiercely at a willow branch, stripping it of leaves.

'I've been reading up on the subject,' he went on. 'Sam goes to the site and I go to the public library, finding out about what causes the virus to go into action. Wake up. Whatever they call it. And start fucking up the immune system. Alcohol's one thing. Well I drink plenty. Not to excess but I go out to pubs and I drink. Then there's protein. Apparently cum is full of protein and there are some researchers saying that while promiscuity *per se* doesn't do any harm – except of course putting you more often in the firing line – that multiple contacts with numerous different kinds of cum proteins might activate the virus. The only thing I haven't been doing wrong is becoming a vegan.' He chuckled. 'There's always someone worse off than yourself, eh? Vegans seem to be doomed. Apparently people in my condition *need* animal fat. Sod looking after my heart or worrying about cancer! I tell you,' he laughed now, 'I've been eating butter and cream with *everything* since I read that.'

'You know the test isn't a hundred per cent accurate,' she said.

'Thank you, Miss Helpline. I know. So I went for a second one. A proper one at a clinic with strict but motherly doctors and nice gay nurses in ACT UP badges.'

'And?'

'Bingo a second time. The health worker wanted to know if I could give her a list of my sexual partners. I nearly died laughing. I have to hand it to her, so did she. In fact, I think she only asked to break the ice, you know? Stir up a little nostalgia for syphilis. Sam went in too. Jesus he was calm! Either he's very brave or incredibly stupid. He went along as if it was a routine tetanus jab or a dental check-up.'

'Oh God.'

'Which reminds me. I've got to change my dentist because they checked up on their little blacklist and apparently mine is way up there with Mengele for political bloody incorrectness.'

'But what about Sam?'

'It's okay. He was negative. Twice now. We've both been very careful. I'm just amazed that he still wants to stick around.'

'Why?'

'I've been treating him like shit.'

She shrugged.

'He loves you, Jamie.'

'Yeah, but –'

'But what?'

'Nothing.'

He turned aside, pushing out through the willow canopy and back along the stream towards the studio to sit on an arm of the bench there. Alison went to sit beside him, astounded that he was still so unable to accept the fact of Sam's love. Suddenly time was shrinking around them, a fragile sand bar in an encroaching tide. She felt and knew better than to voice, that her time with him was now infinitely precious to her. Once again she thought about throwing in her job to be with him but all she said was, 'Now you've told me, you know you can pick up the phone and talk about it any time at all, don't you? Even at work.'

He avoided her eyes, staring down to pick at some moss on the bench wood.

'I know,' he said.

'What about Grandpa? Oh God and what about *her*?'

Jamie shook his head.

'Not until I'm strong enough to deal with it myself, and maybe not even then.'

'Don't they have a right to know?'

'Don't I have a right to *privacy*? No. I don't think they have any rights here.'

'But they'll find out sooner or later.'

'Yes,' he said firmly. 'But I'll face that when I come to it, okay? I don't even know if I can look the old man in the eye.'

'There's nothing to be ashamed of.'

'It's not shame,' he insisted, eyes tight with a momentary fury. 'It's so fucking *unfair*. That old bastard gets to survive the holocaust, marry a saint, live in this place, earn a fortune, write symphonies people actually listen to, even have an affair with a sex goddess. What do *I* get?'

'You get *him*.' Alison raised a hand to greet Sam, who had appeared at the side of the house and was sauntering down the garden towards them.

'Yes,' said Jamie drily. 'I've got him.'

Sam reached them, threw himself on to the bench between them and began enthusing about The Roundel.

'Some commune,' he teased them slowly, after praising its fanciful shape, its cunning brickwork, its pantiled roof. 'The way you go on about it, I'd pictured you two growing up in a sort of squat with no hot water and plastic sheets for windows. Your granddad's great, by the way.'

'You met him,' Jamie said levelly.

'Yeah. Heinrich just introduced us. But this *place*! You could open it to the public.'

'It's not that special,' Alison said.

'Let them be the judge of that,' he told her. 'Listen. *That* is not your average holiday cottage. What are you both doing living in London? You should live here. We could *all* live here.'

'I dunno,' Jamie began, suddenly harsh. 'It's hardly practical. We'd get bored in no time.'

As they walked back to the house to see Heini off in his taxi, Sam diverted the conversation to less emotive subjects, but his suggestion had lit a slow-burning fuse and Alison found herself picturing the three of them – four including her grandfather – forming a brief, golden ménage.

They waved Heini off from the top of the drive and Alison assumed for a moment that her grandfather would clap a hand on Jamie's shoulder and suggest he take them all to the pub for lunch. Then she realised that the very accident that had brought Jamie to The Roundel, and Sam to a forced introduction with her grandfather, now left the three men stranded in an impasse of unreadiness. Far from her expectations, relief at the departure of his guest left her grandfather icily angry; it was as though tactful Heini had taken all diplomacy with him.

'That was profoundly embarrassing,' he hissed. 'Heinrich is one of my oldest friends. He handled the situation with charm, of course, but it can only have been painful for him. I hope you are thoroughly ashamed of last night's *disgusting* display.'

Neither said anything. Jamie froze, his jaw set rebelliously. Sam was plainly too surprised to speak.

'Now I have a great deal of work to do,' her grandfather went on. 'I don't want to be disturbed.' And so saying, he stalked off to his studio.

'Yeah, well fuck you too,' Sam jeered after him.

'Shut up,' Jamie snapped coldly.

'Why? He said –'

'Just shut up. Come on. Let's get our stuff.'

Alison watched wretchedly as, Sam in confusion, Jamie in a quiet fury, they made a hasty departure. She began to intercede, suggest lunch at least, but was silenced by a glare from Jamie.

'Let's speak soon, okay?' she asked him.

'Sure,' he said brusquely. 'I'll ring you. Come on, Sam.'

Sam drove them away and Alison was left in turmoil. She was appalled that a member of her family should have reacted so badly just when Jamie was so vulnerable. She was also unsettled at her sympathy with her grandfather's indignation and embarrassment. Her grief at her failure to make peace rested uneasily alongside her irritation that her brother's departure marked her out as a member of the reactionary faction. She had already assumed that, after taking her into his confidence, Jamie would feel the need to withdraw from her a little, but she feared lest this ugly little scene provide grounds for a longer, deeper rift.

When she felt calm enough, she ignored her grandfather's request for peace. A BBC photographer was coming to take pictures of him 'at work' to publicise a forthcoming concert broadcast and she knew he would need help tidying the studio. He accepted her offer with a nod and she set about organising the chaos of CDs, concert programmes and unanswered correspondence that littered the place, among which she found piano concerti sent in for his magisterial advice, string quartets, and a piece for massed bassoons.

'Have they left?' was all he said.

'Yes,' she replied as neutrally as she could. 'They left right away.'

His ignorance of her grim new knowledge lent him a spurious youthful innocence beside her, even more than hearing him chatter in German. Thanks to AIDS, she had been to more funerals over the last two years than he had. This thought stoked up her anger at him afresh. He relied on his show of temper silencing her, but she was determined not to be cowed.

'Now that they've gone,' she asked casually as she stood above him on the ladder returning scores to the shelves, 'what did you think of Sam?'

'Do you want me to say something nice?'

'I thought you got on. He seemed to think you had.'

'Then he's dimmer than I imagined. I was being polite.'

'Just because he's working class –'

'That has nothing to do with it.'

'Granny was working class.'

'Sally was a doctor.'

'So? She got lucky.'

'There is no comparison.'

'Her mother was a factory hand,' she reminded him indignantly. 'Yours was a bloody professor. I'm sorry if the memory offends you but I think there's every comparison.'

Indignation made her voice waver. Coming soon after Jamie's revelation and the frantic protectiveness it aroused in her, her grandfather's lofty unconcern, his trivialisation of a relationship she knew to be crucial, outraged her. He made no reply to her outburst, but merely grunted.

For a few minutes they worked on wordlessly, Alison seething, he, humming an unplaceable tune under his breath. When the telephone rang, she made to answer it, but he gestured her away from it with a violent backward slash of his hand, as though it were a scorpion. They waited through six long rings before his machine took the call. There were the usual clicks then Myra Toye's unmistakably smoky tones emerged from the tinny loudspeaker. Her words were rambling, her tone angry and apologetic by turns. They each pretended to continue with what they had been doing but Alison could tell he was listening as acutely as she was.

'Teddy darling?' said the voice. 'Teddy are you there? It's me. Myra. Myra Toye. Who else? Ha! It's the middle of the night. I couldn't sleep and I started reading that fucking awful book. Christ I let her choose some unflattering pictures. And that awful one of me in your flat – you must have given them that. Do you hate me so very much? Sorry, darling, I'm a bit woozy. Found some pills somewhere that hadn't been flushed away with the rest. Yes I know I shouldn't, but I don't drink any more. Anyway. What? Oh. Yes. Do you? Do you hate me so much? I don't hate you. I mean, you must have realised the things I could have told her and didn't, like that time at the studio party for –'

'Stupid woman,' her grandfather hissed. He unplugged the machine, cutting off the famous voice mid-flow. Alison had come down the ladder again.

'I don't think it was pills,' she said. 'She sounded drunk. And so sad. Terribly sad. Poor woman. You'd never think that –'

'She's an actress, remember?' he said bitterly. 'She was probably sober as a judge and making the call while someone did her hair. And forget what she said. The book left out nothing. Nothing at all.' He coughed, abashed at his own petulance. 'I'll make us some coffee. Did you eat any breakfast? Do you want lunch?'

'Just coffee would be fine,' she said. 'Maybe some toast.'

She had been on the point of leaving him to stew in his sour memories and unjust opinions, but he suddenly seemed vulnerable, pottering about his kitchen opening and closing cupboard doors without finding what he wanted, touching his temple as though trying to remember something. She stayed on, reminded that his life was not quite the uncomplicated triumphant ascent Jamie would enviously have it.

47

Sandy was predictably appalled when Alison told her Godfreys had sacked Jamie and of the medical indiscretion which had led to his doing so. She was also revolted at Jamie's willingness to accept this as his proper lot, and went hotfoot to his flat to tell him so, dragging his embarrassed sister in her wake.

'I honestly don't care any more,' he explained to her. 'I was angry then, but things are turning out all right now.'

'Listen, you,' she retorted. 'You may be crippled with self-hatred and have juicy savings to rely on, but at least let me go for that shit of a doctor. Otherwise he'll only do it to someone else with a thinner financial cushion. He probably already has.'

So Jamie allowed her to resume solicitor status and proceed on his behalf. Her enquiries, however, revealed that during his relief over the mole analysis, he had signed a release form whose small print agreed to make all results of the medical examination available to both his employer and potential health insurers. There was some small satisfaction, however, in knowing that Dr Penney's name had been added to the helpline's medical and legal blacklist, and circulated to the compilers of others.

Protesting, in the face of Sam's concern, that he was not letting himself go now that he was married and settled down, Jamie stopped going to the gym and let his membership there lapse. Try as they both might to ignore it, he had lost weight and did not seem able to put it back on, at least, not with the kind of muscle that helped him blend in unregarded in the showers. He seemed to be sweating himself away into their marriage bed. When he woke in the night, brine running from every pore, he slipped out of bed, took a quick shower and returned to Sam's frightened but wordless embrace. They had clean sheets as often as guests in a luxury hotel and pretended it was done for pleasure and not from necessity. Jamie bought himself a metal and black leatherette construction called an abdominal board, on which he was supposed to perform daily sit-ups to preserve what remained of his washboard stomach, but the sit-ups made him breathless, which scared him. So he left the board out for show and made do with leisurely bike rides around Battersea Park or up to the King's Road.

Around the time that Sandy was trying to make a legal case for unfair dismissal or breach of confidentiality, Alison urged Jamie into attending an HIV support group on the basis that he had started to offload emotional problems on to Sam that could be more comfortably and usefully shouldered by other people in a similar position. Obedient and detached, he had gone to sit in a room lent by the local genito-urinary clinic, where a mainly male group was encouraged by a sweet-faced Welsh facilitator called Geraint to voice its angers and despairs. For the first few weeks, Jamie found himself paralysed by shyness. He saw several faces familiar to him from his old world of saunas and bars, and the sudden lurch from beer-blurred, stylised anonymity to the harshly lit, brutally sober particularity of saying things like, 'Good evening, I'm Rory and I'm *really* angry,' seemed intolerable.

Geraint knew his job well, however. Each week he caught Jamie's eye as he walked in, offered him a quiet smile of welcome and said, 'Hello there, Jamie,' just to show he'd remembered his name. Then, one-day, mid-way through a heated discussion of blame started by a woman infected by her bisexual husband, Geraint took advantage of a brief lull to turn to the corner where Jamie was growing dozy by the radiator and ask, 'So what about you, Jamie? We haven't heard from you in a while.'

'Me?'

'Yes. What do *you* think?'

Taken completely by surprise, Jamie blurted out all sorts of things he had not even realised he was feeling. He said he had not told his mother or his grandfather yet because he thought they would blame him and that maybe they'd be right.

'My grandfather's generation didn't sleep around and they're only just starting to die from natural causes.'

'Oh no?' someone piped up. 'How'd they catch so much syphilis, then?'

'What about TB?' someone else added. 'That was treated like a dirty disease.'

'Vivien Leigh died of that as late as the sixties,' the woman pointed out.

'You should blame your mother before she blames you,' a younger, American woman insisted. 'It was all that Free Love and drug-taking that gave you the space to live such a risky life.'

'But I don't care about how I was living,' Jamie cut back in again as the discussion turned into an unexpectedly angry session of recrimination and counter-recrimination. 'I don't regret a thing. Not a single fuck. I'd have them all again.'

'But you'd wear a condom this time, right?' Geraint asked. He was trying to lighten the tone but Jamie wouldn't let him.

'Maybe,' he said, shrugging. 'Maybe not.' This unleashed another storm of disagreement.

The next week he felt he couldn't go back. Alison was anxious that he still needed the group's so-called support, but he found there was less to offload on to Sam than there had been. He knew from various indigestible books he had borrowed from Alison that he was meant to be passing from shock to refusal to anger to depression and so on, before reaching acceptance, but all he felt, a lot of the time, was a kind of flatness. He had always imagined this was how he would feel in the minutes following the declaration of atomic war; the rooms and streets around him would be raucous with last minute sex, confessions of crime, love and hatred. Shops would be pointlessly looted and the air would buzz with the forging of frantic bargains with the various available deities, but Jamie had always anticipated that he would just sit quietly by the television, waiting for the first pictures and feeling sort of *flat*.

By slow degrees he stopped sitting around 'waiting to die', as Sam put it in an angry moment, and began making a conscious effort to get out and do things he had never done before. He joined the local library and began to devour novels so famous he was almost ashamed to be seen reading them in public. He took boats to see the huge silver shells of the Thames Barrier, to pant round the palm house at Kew and to sail through Docklands to Greenwich. He went greyhound racing, gave Sam four hundred pounds and made him place it all on fruitless bets. He sat, detached and observant, through afternoon screenings of punitive subtitled films and even persuaded Sam to sit through a new production of *King Lear,* which neither of them greatly enjoyed or entirely understood. He reached a point, however, when he felt he had exhausted the possibilities of at least the reasonable items on his mental list of Things To Do Before Sickness Sets In. All the discovery and self-improvement started to feel suspiciously like activities to ward off fear – cosmic waiting room syndrome. If he was truly to do as Geraint urged and live with the virus rather than wait for it to swallow his life away – live with it simply, contentedly even, as one might learn to live with a silver streak in one's hair or a new scar on one's cheek – he had to reenter daily life. But how? He stopped reading Jane Austen and forced himself to read new novels, harsh with realities. He read about psychotic killers, incest, cannibalism, insanity. He read novels about sick people, men with cancer, mothers with AIDS.

'The trouble is,' he tried to explain to Sam, 'they're all written for people who are well and feel bad about it. You know how they'll end before you begin.'

He preferred, he decided, novels that ended with a betrothal or a birth, and returned to his voyage through the works of Jane Austen, George Eliot and Mrs Gaskell. Unlike the rude health of others, which he still found hard to take on bad days, convincingly happy endings were not an insult. They had never seemed more important.

The last melancholy days of summer shaded into a dazzling autumn. Sam's work finished at the new hospital and he took Jamie to admire the gleaming building, lit up as the carpet fitters, painters and electricians worked through the night to meet the contractor's deadline. Sam followed a tip from some friends and moved to work on a new riverside housing estate in Wandsworth, which meant they would be granted more precious minutes in bed in the mornings. After a week of dramatic storms, the clocks went back, autumn hardened prematurely into winter and Jamie decided it was time to take a job again.

Rather than lose face by returning to the City now that his bridges with that area of his past had been so satisfactorily burned, he opted instead for working in the classical department of a big West End music shop. His early training had left him with a fairly broad musical knowledge and his former salary had allowed him to acquire enough experience of the best performers and recordings to bluff credibly where his knowledge wore thin. As Alison had found in applying to Pharos, the mere mention of his grandfather's name during the interview did the rest.

Work was now an entirely different experience. He could wear whatever he liked. He could drink tea in bed with Sam before he set out and admit to having done so once he got there – although such domestic details, however enviable, were tame compared with the adventures recounted by some of his colleagues. His personality was no longer split between his work self and the self he expressed elsewhere. He now felt he was truly himself most of the time. The only exceptions, jarring with the new, cautiously preserved equilibrium of his days, were encounters with his mother. To Alison's dismay, he now shunned his grandfather and The Roundel. Ironically, the memory of his grandfather's disgust remained a useful goad, spurring him on to rid his life of pretence and wasted social effort.

When Jamie told Alison that he and Sam had a regular, careful sex life still, he was being economical with the truth. For a while after Sam had tested negative, they had had no sex life at all.

'It didn't make any difference before,' Sam told the health worker. 'Why should it now?'

'Just be prepared,' she said. 'That's all. With some couples it's not a problem, with others, it's like a layer of permafrost slicing the bed in two.'

Sure enough, the frost descended that first evening. They had a romantic night in. Curled on the sofa together, the fridge full of beer for Sam and fruit juice for Jamie, they guzzled an Indian takeaway and quietly watched two horror videos in a row. One of Sam's closely guarded secrets was that, despite his bravado, scary films reduced him to vulnerable jelly. Nervous hand-clutching during the second, nastier film, led to reassuring fondling until, with the video pouring forth its shrieks and scenes of gore to an empty room, they were rolling around on top of the bed, trying to kiss and kick jeans off at the same time.

Then Sam found his cock deflating as swiftly and finally as if his mother had burst in from the balcony and threatened it with a rusty breadknife.

'Maybe it's just the beer,' Jamie suggested, trying not to add stage-fright to humiliation by peering at the cause of their frustration. 'It can happen to anyone.'

But it had never happened to him and it had never happened to Sam, however much he drank. It happened to Sam again, the next evening. Again he tried to ignore it, setting about pleasuring Jamie with his hand, in a kind of fury. The third time, Jamie stopped him, forcing him simply to lie close and cross in his arms. There was nothing to discuss. However near they lay, his condition had placed them in categories as radically discrete as separate cages. The abrupt refusal of his lover's body to penetrate his own, or even put itself in a position where it might be called upon to do so, made Jamie feel branded INFECTIOUS in a way no number of medical insurance rejections could have done.

'I want us to fuck so *badly*,' Sam groaned, at last beginning to break free of Jamie's restraining hug to run his fingers across his chest and down between his legs. He leaned over, encircled the base of Jamie's dick in finger and thumb then ran his tongue slowly up its shaft. Jamie shuddered, smiling despite himself.

'Go on,' Sam whispered. 'Fuck me. Just this once. Fuck me. I don't care.'

'No,' said Jamie, laughing but adamant.

'Why not? Just once.' Sam reached out with his mouth once more and, with a supreme effort, Jamie rolled aside, evading this most persuasive kiss.

'You know why not.'

Sam flopped back onto the pillows, tugging the duvet up around him with a wounded grunt.

'Fucking stupid test,' he said. 'Poxy thing. I don't know why you made me take it if this was going to happen.'

'You wanted to, remember? It was your idea. They're not even a hundred percent accurate.'

'I know.'

'So? Stop fretting. Maybe you're positive too and it just didn't show up yet.'

The bitterness in Jamie's tone silenced them both

The following Saturday morning, Sam confessed that, talking in terms of a mythical girlfriend, he had opened out to a man at work who had experienced similar problems with his wife because he had been terrified of making her pregnant again. They had resorted, apparently, to toys.

'*Toys?*' Jamie asked, picturing pink rabbits and water pistols.

'Oh, you *know*. *Toys!*' Sam tried to sound as though he used them all the time. 'At least then we could do *something*. Let's go shopping.'

And so, at that time of the weekend when other couples were browsing for new sofabeds or sensible shoes for the children, they had headed into Soho and braved the fluorescent-lit cellar of a marital aid shop. They picked, chuckling, over negligées edged in mock ostrich feather and packets of condoms flavoured with peppermint or tandoori chicken, then went on to garish displays whose very frankness silenced their chatter: vibrators, dildos, butt-plugs, harnesses, douche kits, uniforms, stimulant lubricants, whips and handcuffs. Jamie was amused and, beneath his amusement, guiltily excited.

'What d'you want, then?' he murmured, as Sam fingered a huge set of rubber genitalia that purported to be modelled on those of a famous porn star, down to their very veins, 'realistic' curly tufts of brown nylon hair and shifting, gelatinous balls. Sam raised the thing to his nose and sniffed its shaft judiciously, like a chef tasting a sauce.

'I dunno,' he said and set it back on the shelf. 'I can't be doing with all that bondage crap and as for the rest of it, well, it's all so *big*.'

'Just what I was thinking,' Jamie said. 'Would it make you feel a tad inadequate, or just left out of the party?' Sam shoved him in the ribs.

'Piss off,' he said. 'And it's all so . . .' He pulled a face. 'So *pink*.'

Just then Jamie saw a woman nestling a thick, dildo-shaped package into her basket amongst more innocuous weekly food shopping, and was inspired.

'Come on then,' he said. 'I've had a better idea.'

Back out on Berwick Street, Jamie led Sam along the market, past displays of cut-price underwear, naughty nighties, Christmas wrapping and cordless kettles, to a fruit and veg stall whose electric lights made its heaps of produce glow in the drizzle on their lush bed of emerald nylon turf.

'Yes,' he said, as the stallholder turned to serve him. 'I think this'll do nicely,' and he picked out a thick, gnarled carrot, some ten inches long. 'And these.' He selected two similarly generous courgettes and a wispy-tipped parsnip. 'Oh, and a pound of those nice fat grapes to eat afterwards. The black ones.'

The stallholder weighed up the grapes, rubbing her mittened hands for warmth as she eyed the scales.

She thinks we're just mild-mannered vegetarians, Jamie thought.

'What's this, then?' Sam reached down and held up a big green plantain.

'People chop them up and fry 'em,' she said. 'I think.'

'We'll take that too, then,' Sam said, having understood without even catching Jamie's eye.

'And my vegetable love did grow,' Jamie murmured, a hand thrust in his pocket, as they walked back to the tube, surprised to find himself as excited as he used to feel in the minutes before a first assignation.

They fell to experimenting on one another as soon as

they got home. Jamie gave top marks to the carrot, Sam, once he had got over a certain bashfulness, voted for the plantain. They spent a happy afternoon window-shopping on the King's Road like any other Saturday couple, but disgraced themselves in a superior supermarket by loudly scorning the display of outrageously expensive vegetables, intentionally picked during dwarfish immaturity.

That evening, as Sam was pleasuring Jamie with an unexpectedly erotic stick of frilly leaved celery still chilled from the fridge, his impotence left him as suddenly as it had arrived. Catching Jamie's look of greedy surprise as Sam stopped what he was doing to fumble on the bedside table for the tandoori chicken condoms, he mumbled that he didn't see why the celery should have all the fun. When he came, for the first time after days of frustrated non-participation, he slipped into a faint like sudden death. In the full minute before Sam's eyelids flickered open again, Jamie felt hot panic boil up within him.

48

Alison had always hated Christmas. Even more than her birthday, it was a celebration which never lived up to its promise and invariably left her wanting to cry tears of childish disappointment. It contained individual elements which pleased her. She liked its scents of spice, orange peel, warm red wine and pine needles. She liked giant, bank holiday crosswords, log fires, old films on television, snow, before it melted, and even the occasional present. Over the years, however, these elements had become so associated with family arguments, over-eating and the inevitable sense of personal failure that came with the death of each year, that the pleasure they brought came hand in glove with bitter melancholy. In the days of Miriam's commune, Christmas had always seen The Roundel invaded by strangers, noisy friends of friends. These interlopers had even less respect for a child's property and private space than the Beards did, so Alison and Jamie would find their beds taken over by queer-smelling adults, their toys broken or borrowed and even their clothing purloined by hostile visiting children. Aware from talk at school of how family Christmases were meant to be, they were forced, if they wanted rituals, to perform them for themselves. They gave each other Christmas stockings. They taught each other Christmas carols. Once they even built a crib in an uncultivated corner of the garden. When an invasion grew too hard to bear, they would escape to their grandfather's studio where, despite his scorning to celebrate the feast himself, he played them appropriate pieces of Bach and Berlioz on his record player and fed them festive gingerbread and biscuits, bought especially for them from a German delicatessen in Belsize Park.

When the commune disintegrated, its flimsy structure corroded by age, boredom and acrimony, and Miriam had married Francis, she began to take Christmas very seriously indeed, as though in compensation for years of pot luck. She shopped thoughtfully for presents, which she wrapped following hints from magazines – *Financial Times* pages offset with pink and silver silk ribbon was a recent coup. Resuscitating the craft skills that had helped stock the commune's market stall with knick-knacks, she wove her own holly wreath, twined ivy up the bannisters, painted her own cards for her nearest friends and was fiercely purist in her decoration of a large tree. She threw a punch and pies party for all Francis's friends and clients. She revived Christmas rituals even her children had never dreamed of, such as burning a fantastically adorned yule log out on the drive and insisting on a Germanic exchange of presents on Christmas Eve so that Christmas Day dawned for Alison as a ready-made anti-climax.

Every November, Alison and Jamie indulged in mutinous rumblings about how nice it would be to stay in London for once, and celebrate with friends of one's choice rather than relatives thrust upon one by Fate. Every year, however, having shown eagerly willing, the friends of their choice slipped guiltily back to their various family reunions, leaving brother and sister with no option but to do the same.

'It's only three days,' one of them would admit, resolve now undermined by fear at the prospect of Christmas alone in London. 'Four at the most. And she does make a special effort, I suppose. And if Grandpa can stick it, then we certainly can.'

This year, however, their grandfather was to join Heini Liebermann and some friends for a reindeer-free holiday in Marrakech. The frost between him and Jamie had, by unspoken common consent, been kept from Miriam. This was easily done since the two of them saw each other so rarely in any case. Edward claimed that Heini had been inviting him for years, but the implication was that he was leaving the way free for Jamie to enjoy Christmas without his disapproving presence. Assuming that, now there was Sam, Jamie would find a way of staying in London with him, Alison had begun to plot either to spend the holiday fielding festive angst on the helpline or helping dole out pudding and turkey at one of the temporary shelters set up for the army of homeless. Either way, she had figured, guilt would silence Miriam's protest, and imagined her response. 'You're so *good*, Angel. I really ought to do something like that too but you know how Frank is. Christmas means too much to him. He's so sentimental. We will *miss* you, though.'

Perhaps she would have to compromise, weakened by emotional blackmail into running up brownie points by going to the punch and pies party.

Then Jamie scuppered her plans. Meeting her for a drink after one of his late shifts at the record store, in a pub already rendered crustily yule-ish with tinsel and spray-on snow, he announced that he was going home for Christmas because he thought it was time Miriam met Sam.

'Reading between the lines,' he said, 'I think it's years since he had a proper family Christmas. His dad was usually at sea.'

'Isn't he the lucky one!' she exclaimed. 'Since when did *you* think it was such a great institution?' Then she realised it was since he began to wonder how many Christmases he had left. She could have bitten off her tongue. 'Have you told her yet?' she hurried on. 'She'll probably be impossible. And what about Francis? Oh God.'

'We always assume they'll react badly,' he said in the soft voice of a group facilitator. 'The least I can do is let them meet him once, give them the benefit of the doubt.'

She protested but he started to cough, a wet, wheezing cough.

'Are you taking something for that?' she asked, wincing as he fumbled for a handkerchief.

'It's okay,' he spluttered, eyes watering, as the spasm subsided. 'Caught it off someone in the shop. Every other customer is sneezing and snuffling. The smoke in here doesn't help. It gets to me more than it used to. Let's clear out of here. Oh. Sorry. You haven't finished your drink.'

'Yes I have. Come on.'

As they walked down Shaftesbury Avenue to the tube, she found she was covering for him, stopping repeatedly to gaze with confected interest in shop windows, shielding them both from the fact that he was having trouble keeping up. 'So you'll come?' he asked as they rode down the escalator.

'Yes,' she sighed. 'But maybe you shouldn't make too much of an issue of it. The three of us can turn up together as if Sam's just a mutual friend, then you can take it from there.'

'We'll see,' he said. 'Maybe.'

As things turned out, having advocated political cowardice, it was Alison who made their relationship an issue. Sam drove the three of them down in Jamie's car after she finished work on Christmas Eve. Miriam actually came out with the line, 'Hello Sam. I've heard so much about you,' then showed them to their rooms. Seeing she was putting her in a double bed and Sam and Jamie in a room with two singles, and being still slightly fuddled from festive-red wine drunk in Cynthia's office, Alison piped up that it was all one to her and the Boys would be far happier if she swapped with them. Miriam misunderstood, but only for a moment. Then, having said that was fine, perfectly fine, she covered her confusion by bustling off to put the finishing touches to dinner, leaving the three of them on the landing. Jamie gaped like a ten-year-old.

'Did I just do what I think I did?' Alison asked, stunned at herself. 'Do you mind?'

'Mind?' he gasped, 'I've been wondering how to do that since I was fifteen and you just came out and did it in seconds.'

'Maybe she knew already,' Sam suggested.

'I'm sure she knew,' Alison laughed. 'She just wasn't thinking when she planned the sleeping arrangements.'

'Well she looked pretty surprised to me,' Jamie said and his words seemed borne out by what happened next. Francis came out to greet them as they returned to the hall and he shepherded them away from the kitchen doorway for a fireside drink in the sitting room. When Miriam joined them, some twenty minutes later, her crackling laughter and tense smile could not disguise a fresh redness around her eyes.

It was so rare to see her mother tearful – the last time, she recalled, had been at the shooting of John Lennon – that Alison was filled with tenderness towards her, coloured a little by the excellent whisky sours Francis had mixed them all. She was glad that the Boys were being monopolised by man-talk about journey times and roadworks because it was easier to draw Miriam onto the sofa beside her.

'Happy Christmas,' she said.

'Happy Christmas, Angel. I'm so glad you all made it down.'

'Me too. Sandy had almost persuaded me to work for Crisis instead.'

'Those poor people,' Miriam sighed, sparing a thought for the homeless, then started, by association, appraising Sam, who had stood to warm his back at the fire. He was hardly recognisable as the man Alison had brought in from the street all those months before. Leaning against the richly decorated mantelshelf, wearing black jeans and a new, royal blue cord shirt over a gleaming white tee-shirt, he looked more like a model in a Christmas fashion spread than a builder who had done time. She watched him smile as his glass was refilled.

We have corrupted him, she thought, then saw the idea was as naive as it would be patronising to say they had 'saved' him.

'He seems very nice,' Miriam said.

'He is,' Alison confirmed then looked away, confused by an inappropriate spasm of desire. 'You'll see.'

'He doesn't seem very . . . well . . . you know.'

Alison grinned at her coyness.

'Neither does Jamie,' Alison said.

'No,' her mother sadly admitted. 'Neither he does.'

'It's okay, Mum. They're mad about each other.'

'Good. I'm glad,' Miriam said breathily, before making a palpable gear change back up into a more convivial mood. 'What *are* they finding to talk about?'

'It was roads. Now it's work. You know what Francis is like on the dignity of labour. He's probably saying he doesn't understand why so many people carry on being unemployed when someone as underqualified as Jamie could drop one job and pick up another so easily.'

'Being his usual sensitive self.'

Alison pricked up her ears.

'Do I detect a note of disenchantment?'

'No. Not really,' Miriam said, but then she turned back from studying the men and her eyes betrayed her. 'But you know how he can be.'

'The thing is, Sam,' Francis was saying, 'I can call you that, can't I? We don't stand on ceremony here.'

'Sure,' Sam nodded his assent.

'The thing is, my dad was a working man too, a plasterer, and so was my granddad. So I know what real work is. Now these two,' he indicated Jamie and Alison, 'they don't know the meaning of labour. I mean, have you ever come across two such pointless occupations as selling classical records –'

'CDs,' Jamie broke in.

'CDs. Whatever. And publishing highbrow novels which a fraction of the population read. Pointless. They could stop tomorrow and the world would still turn. But building, now *that's* a worthwhile trade for a man.'

'So what do you do, Francis?' Sam asked, adding the Christian name with a barely audible irony.

'Well now I'm an accountant, of course.'

'Of course.'

'But I *used* to work for my dad, in the holidays, even when I was a nipper. I replastered the guest bathrooms here myself actually.'

A kitchen timer went off in Miriam's pocket, breaking up the conversation to call them all to the dining room for a rich spread of duck soup, roast gammon and profiteroles. Crossing the hall, Alison snatched a moment with Sam and Jamie.

'She fancies him,' she told Jamie. 'I can tell.' Jamie cast his eyes to heaven. He was slightly drunk.

'I'll protect you,' he told Sam.

'And you're getting on well with Francis,' she added. 'No-one usually knows what to *say* to him.'

'He's all right,' Sam said. 'Quite funny really. Well . . . I thought I ought to make an effort, you know?' He paused as

Francis bustled past them with a bottle of claret he had left by the fire to take off its chill.

'Something rather special I've been saving up,' he said as he passed them, stroking the label.

'Smashing,' Sam said, adding in an undertone, when Alison caught his eye, 'Right-wing twat.' For a moment his face was too close. She was too aware of his chin. The fullness of his lower lip. His eye seemed to linger on her longer than was necessary.

Stop it, she thought. *Stop it at once*, and she slipped aside into the kitchen to see if she could help.

During dinner it was Miriam's turn to be charmed, sitting between Sam and Jamie while Alison sat by Francis.

'What do you *really* think about having these two share a bed under your roof?' she wanted to ask him. 'What would you be saying if Jamie was *your* only son and not hers?' For once, however, she found it hard to be angry with him. Sam's attempts, however cynical, had nonetheless humanised him in a way that Miriam's efforts had never succeeded in doing. Either from sensitivity or self-absorption, Francis managed to pass the whole meal without so much as a passing reference to her still being single even though Jamie, for better or worse, was hitched.

As glasses were raised and eyes sparkled, enlivened by candlelight, she kept thinking of her brother's secret, biding its time in the shadows, just out of sight. By the standards of their generation, Miriam and Francis probably thought they had passed the evening's stiff test of social attitudes with flying colours – a minor awkwardness here and there, a few tears shed in the kitchen, perhaps a few hot words exchanged out of sight between courses – and yet, compared to the test Jamie still had in store for them, being civil to a son's boyfriend was elementary as finger painting. This thought, too, softened Alison's heart towards them and, when the time came for opening presents over coffee and yet more alcohol, made it easier to accept their entirely unsuitable gift of a three-speed hairdryer with 'professional' diffuser, 'bodifying' attachments and hot curling set.

Sam had given her a bottle of Italian scent, which was probably far more than he could afford, given that he had been nowhere near a duty-free shop. Delighted, she squirted some on her wrists and was wreathed at once in a warm, jasmine cloud. Jamie was always cool and uninvolved about present buying so she guessed that Sam had chosen it on his own, and was doubly touched. By comparison, the book she had given him seemed a lordly, lazy choice. She crossed the room to kiss him, but he seemed flustered at the abruptness of the gesture and she realised it was the first time she had done more than touch him diffidently on the shoulder. Jamie had given her a new recording of *Gurrelieder* she had been hankering after. She turned to thank him but found he had suddenly fallen asleep, his head lolling towards Sam's shoulder on the sofa-back. Sam made as though to wake him but she shook her head. Francis chortled, tickled by the evident tenderness between the two men.

'Tired himself out selling symphonies to the undeserving rich,' he said, glancing at his watch as he stood. 'Ah well. Midnight beckons.' Miriam wandered off to fetch scarves and coats. Alison had been going to chicken out of church, thinking one could take duty too far, but she realised that the Boys might appreciate an hour alone on the sofa by the fire. She looked at Jamie dozing. Yet again he had won the fatted calf without even trying.

'See you at breakfast,' she told Sam as envy lent a twist to their parting.

They were no sooner in the back of Francis's Jaguar than her mother began voicing worries.

'I still don't understand why he threw in a perfectly good job at Lloyd's to become a sales assistant,' she said.

'Quality of life,' Alison improvised. 'He works with nicer people now. He can be himself. And the money's not so bad. After all he's already paid his mortgage off.'

'Yes but . . .'

'I don't think he'll do it forever, if that's what you're worried about. It's just a stop gap.'

'But I can't bear it if he becomes one of those pathetic thirty-something drop-outs.'

'Well you should know all about those!' Francis jeered from the front, ignored by Miriam.

'Not much danger of that,' Alison told her, crossing her fingers. There was a pause. Miriam glanced forward at Francis and saw that, despite the interjection, he was entirely focused on the business of driving in a straight line and watching out for policemen.

'We're talking about him again,' Miriam said ruefully. 'We never seem to talk about you, Angel.'

'No,' Alison agreed. 'Funny that.'

'How *are* things?'

'Things are fine.'

'Good. I'm so glad,' Miriam said, unable to suppress her true concern. 'And he looks terribly thin,' she went on. 'Has he been ill?'

'No,' Alison insisted and forced a sisterly smile. 'I think he's just been so happy, he's stopped eating for comfort. Unlike me.'

'You don't have to, you know. It's quite simple, Angel. I was reading about it the other day at the hairdresser's. You just have to ask yourself before you eat anything, "Now am I eating this from body hunger or soul hunger?" and if it's soul hunger, you drink a glass of water instead.'

For the rest of the short drive, Miriam was successfully diverted into diet chat before the Christmas ritual took over. On the drive home, she was overcome by exhaustion and wine and fell fast asleep on Alison's shoulder. Alison recognised that the time she had read of in self-help manuals had arrived – she had started mothering her mother.

Christmas Day dawned sunny and unchristmassy with not even a threat of frost, much less of snow. The effect was not helped by Alison's first glimpse of the morning being Miriam and Francis jogging across the garden in coordinating tracksuits, pursued by the dogs, Francis vociferously in the lead. She would not have minded so much if her mother's transformation had been successful. But her effort to keep up, in every sense, was too pathetically palpable and Alison turned aside from the window in revulsion. As always, having been made to open their presents the night before, the day felt as heavy and directionless as any bank holiday Monday. She had packed a bag full of little presents – some useful, some funny – and a pair of old rugger socks, so as to retaliate if Jamie and Sam had thought to surprise her with a stocking. But they hadn't, so she left the things tucked away in her case. She tried to snatch a quick coffee and orange juice in peace with the jumbo crossword, but soon had Miriam and Francis making a noisy and complicated breakfast around her, Francis steaming slightly despite the towel about his glistening neck.

'Happy Christmas, Angel,' Miriam said.

'Happy Christmas, Angel,' he echoed her, pleased at his tease. Miriam giggled and Alison somehow knew they had made love last night, or perhaps this morning. Francis did his best to irritate her into a good humour by leaning sweatily over her shoulder to supply unhelpful suggestions for the crossword. Then they were joined by the Boys.

All unwitting of the effect it might have, Sam was wearing an old speckled jersey of Jamie's, the only one that had survived from Miriam's knitting era.

'Suits you,' Miriam told him as she kissed both of them on the cheek, clasping her pain before it had time to sting, as a gardener might a nettle. Stirring sugar into his coffee – a new habit – Jamie looked drained, as though he had barely slept, and Sam had grey stains below pinched eyes.

'How did you sleep?' Alison murmured to him while Francis demonstrated a new electric slicing machine to Jamie.

'Not much,' he mumbled, picking sleep from an eye. 'Does it show?'

'Naa,' she assured him, unconvincingly. 'Not much. Maybe they'll go for a walk and you can collapse later. The party isn't till tomorrow so we've a day off.'

'Francis has had a great idea,' Miriam announced. 'It's so sunny, almost warm, so we thought we could take the bikes and ride out along the tow path and have lunch at the Old Swan.'

'Have you got enough bikes?' Alison asked, clutching at straws.

'Of course. Now that we've got the tandem.'

'You've bought a *tandem*?'

'We couldn't resist it,' Miriam confessed as though admitting a weakness for Sèvres.

'Well, I –' Sam began to demur, with a glance at Jamie, 'I don't know how.'

'Great idea,' Jamie cut in with a rebellious air. 'Let's.'

Alison caught Sam's eye. He shrugged. Breakfast trailed on. Francis and Miriam went upstairs to shower and change and Jamie insisted on watching the special Christmas episode of *Mulroney Park* he had taped the previous evening, even though he knew Miriam might be thrown into a bad mood at the sight of the soap's star, Myra Toye.

Alison had not ridden a bicycle in years and was slightly wobbly as they set out, Miriam and Francis resplendent on their new tandem in front, the Boys bringing up the rear and talking quietly, the two dogs bounding along beside them. She was on a nasty, small-wheeled thing designed for undemanding shopping and felt that her feet were having to churn the pedals faster than anyone else's. It was a beautiful day, however, the colours intense after recent rain. The towpath had been widened and carefully gravelled by a young offenders programme to provide a more convenient cycle track. The canal waters seemed devoid of life, poisoned by rainbow seepages from weekend pleasure boats. There was a charm in the sunlight glancing off the murky water, however, and in pursing an activity for all the world as any other happy family, past camel-coated and wax-jacketed dog-walkers offering self-conscious season's greetings, Alison began to find the whole thing funny.

'We look like people in an ad for yoghurt,' she shouted to Jamie.

'Tampons, more like,' he gasped back.

'No,' said Sam. 'Press-on towels with wings and a uniquely formulated stay-dry lining.'

'Children, really!' Miriam shouted playfully, and Alison thought it sad that her mother had become the kind of woman for whom the very mention of feminine hygiene constituted daring.

The unwonted exercise gave her a kind of euphoria and when Sam flew past and began to race Francis, despite

Miriam's protests from the rear of the tandem that they would exhaust the dogs, never mind her, Alison was surprised to find she was enjoying herself. They passed, whooping, under a red brick bridge and she turned back to share with Jamie her happy realisation that they might be about to get through a whole family Christmas without having to eat Brussels sprouts.

Jamie had stopped, though. He was breathless, the colour drained from his face.

'Jamie!' she shouted and swung clumsily back to him. 'What's wrong?'

He wiped his temples and forehead with a spotted handkerchief. They were beaded with sweat and his voice sounded high and strained.

'It's okay,' he said. 'I should never have stopped going to the gym. I'm so unfit.'

'But I thought you'd been biking to work each day.' Sam had ridden back to them. Miriam and Francis waited some twenty yards ahead, chatting, assuming a chain had come off.

'Only as far as the tube and I stopped that when it started getting too wet,' Jamie told her.

'What's up?' Sam asked, then saw Jamie's face and turned to Alison.

'It's okay,' he said. 'He's just worn out. I reckon it's 'flu coming on or something. There's a lot about. We'll go back so he can lie down. You go on with the others.'

'Are you sure?' she asked, feeling excluded.

'Honestly,' Jamie managed. 'Please. Take them on while we –' He paused for breath. 'It'll be easier without her fussing. Honestly.'

He turned back without waiting for her reply, as if faintly ashamed. He stood on his pedal, painfully forcing the wheels to turn again, and started back for the house. Sam threw her a look she could not read and set off alongside him. She clunked her bike around again and rode back to Francis and Miriam.

'Jamie doesn't feel too good,' she said. 'It looks like a nasty 'flu. They'll meet us back at the house later.'

'Probably overdid the cognac last night, more like,' Francis said. 'Remember how he passed out.'

'Oh shut up,' Miriam snapped and made the tandem lunge forward so that he barked a shin on a pedal.

They rode on to the pub and ordered lunch, but the brief illusion of family harmony had evaporated. Alison picked at her food, appetite dwindling in the over-rich steam rising off gravy and roast parsnips. Try as she might, she could not rid herself of her feeling of dread at the sight of Jamie's ill-concealed weakness. The memory of the Boys riding slowly back to the house haunted her – Sam's hand pushing with tender force at the small of Jamie's drooping back. Nobody ordered pudding and they left before finishing their coffees.

Francis strode off to his study as soon as they arrived home, muttering about a late report. Alison and Miriam walked upstairs, each trying to pretend to the other that they weren't hurrying. Miriam even went through the motions of slipping into her room on the way to hang up her jacket. Jamie was still dressed, flat out on the bed, staring at the ceiling. His breathing was laboured and his eyes shone with fever. Sam came through from the bathroom with a damp flannel to wipe his face.

'He's definitely going down with something,' he said.

'Poor Angel,' said Miriam, sitting on the edge of the bed. 'And at Christmas too.'

Alison reached through them to touch Jamie's forehead.

'Shit,' she exclaimed. 'You're on fire!'

'I'll get the thermometer,' Miriam said. 'Get into bed properly, Jamie. I'll bring up a tray. You'll need lots of cold fluids. I'll whizz up some nice lemonade in the blender.'

Alison gave up any pretence.

'Sam, you'll have to drive him to hospital.'

'What?' Miriam was incredulous. 'For 'flu?'

'It'll pass if we wait,' Sam said. 'He was as hot as this last night and this morning he was fine again. It comes and goes.'

'Sam, he needs to be in hospital. Look at him. Don't kid yourself.'

'I'll be fine,' Jamie murmured. 'Honestly.' His face was

awash with sweat again, darkening his hair where it ran off his brow. He began to wheeze, then couldn't stop as he tried to sit up.

'Do you know where to go?' Alison asked.

Sam nodded.

'Same place as we've been for the tests,' he said.

'Yes, but you'll need to go straight to the fifth floor. Say he's been coming to the clinic for check-ups, then they can bring up his notes from downstairs.'

'I'm sure this isn't necessary,' Miriam said as Sam half-rolled, half-tugged Jamie back onto his feet. Jamie's knees buckled like a drunkard's.

'Listen,' Alison told her. 'He's really sick. He needs oxygen. He needs drugs. They can put him on a Septrin drip. I think that's what they do. Sam, I'll call the ward for you and let them know you're on your way. They can have everything ready for him.'

Sam mumbled assent over his shoulder as he helped Jamie downstairs.

'Since when did *you* know so much about medicine?' Miriam asked, following them.

'Since I started telling adults the revised facts of life over the fucking phone,' Alison hissed, snatching up the landing telephone. 'Shit. Damn!' She slammed it down as she realised she had forgotten the all-important number. She tugged out her wallet and, hands shaking, fumbled a mess of notes, cards and receipts onto the highly polished table top and started scrabbling through them. Jamie's car revved up and pulled swiftly away, spitting gravel. She found the switchboard card of emergency numbers and punched out the one for the ward's direct line. After an intolerable wait, she got through. She could hear Motown carols in the background, *Santa Claus is Coming to Town*. The nurse was laughing as she picked up the receiver. The ward was evidently mid-way through a late Christmas lunch.

Miriam had slumped to the top step, a hand on the banisters, by the time Alison hung up.

'How long have you known?' she asked, quietly now.

'There's nothing to know. We don't know anything.'

'How long have you known he was sick?'

'He isn't. I mean. He wasn't. Not till now.' Her mother turned to look at her, her old-young face lined with new care, full of wet-eyed reproach.

'We didn't tell you because Jamie didn't want you to worry,' Alison explained.

'Ha!'

'Not before you needed to. Oh God.' Alison felt herself beginning to cry. 'He's got sick so *fast*, Mum! He should have had six years. More even. Some people don't have any symptoms for fifteen. Of course, we don't know when he got infected.'

'What are you talking about? I don't understand.'

'It doesn't matter.' She sniffed heavily, controlled her breathing, blew her nose. 'I couldn't tell you. It was up to him. He'll probably be pissed off as hell that you found out. Oh Mum. I'm so sorry.' Why was she apologising?

Miriam lurched suddenly on to her feet before Alison could hug her. She hurried downstairs, snatching up a coat in the hall. Her tone was brusque, as though she were late for a meeting and would brook no distractions from her purpose. The dogs bounded about her, expecting another walk and she had to shout over their barking.

'Frank, Jamie's had to go to hospital,' she called out. 'Francis!'

'What? Why?' Francis emerged bewildered from the study. It had been insensitivity, Alison realised, not tact, that sent him in there. The entire crisis had brewed up and broken around him, she realised now, without his even sensing it. Scornful, Miriam made no attempt to explain.

'I'm taking the Jag. The Merc needs petrol and we don't have time to faff about.'

'Wait. I'll come too. I'll drive you in.'

'No, you stay here,' she said. 'Dad was going to ring from Marrakech. For fuck's sake don't say a thing.'

'Well I have to say something.'

'Wish him merry Christmas and tell him we're having a lovely time,' she said, impatiently. 'But that we're all out on a long walk and I'll call him when we get back. Take his number at the villa. I've lost it. I'll call you from the hospital when we know something. Keys.' She held out her hand. He passed her the precious bundle with infuriating hesitancy and she snatched them. 'Come on, Angel.'

She drove them into town in silence, hands tight on the wheel, mouthing curses at every source of delay. Alison couldn't tell if Miriam was angry or frightened. She had not been so aware of her mother in years. The woman's presence seemed to envelop her, the force of her emotions clamorous.

The hospital's top floor was designed so that mysterious or highly infectious diseases could easily be isolated from the rest of the building. Even before the epidemic had been recognised as such, the administration had placed its AIDS cases there. As the epidemic swelled, the entire floor had been taken over. Rather than facing the humiliation and insomnia inflicted by an open ward, patients here had the privacy of individual rooms. Various charities and rich private donors – many on their deathbeds already – had paid for a stylish redecoration job, and supplied each room with a colour television and fridge. The corridors and sitting areas were now furnished with thickly cushioned sofas, so necessary for the chronically thin, and dotted with pretty potted ferns and palms. The few people sent to the floor with hepatitis B or contagious nasties picked up abroad now found themselves plunged into unexpected luxury, and would usually spend their first hours worrying that there had been some administrative error – that they had been booked onto a ward for paying patients and were already clocking up a bill.

Even without the physical differences, the fifth floor would have had an entirely different atmosphere from other hospital wards. Once the fierce realities of the syndrome became known in the nursing and medical profession, certain men and women, some but not all with a personal interest in the matter, stepped forward to dedicate themselves entirely to the new speciality which others were spurning in fear and disgust. As a result, nurses and doctors got to know patients intimately as they returned to the ward to fight off the successive infections and cancers to which they were now prey. Impersonal medicine was forced to socialize itself, relationships with patients became friendly, honest, even loving, and staff were obliged to unlearn all the rules of emotional boundary they had acquired in training and allow themselves to become involved. Now, when patients died, their carers demanded, and were granted, time to attend funerals, time to grieve.

Alison had been there plenty of times before; Jamie was far from being the first person she knew to fall sick. She noticed with fresh eyes, however, the differences in the ward from the grimmer parts of the building they had just passed through, and was grateful. There had indeed been a Christmas party. Those patients and visitors not sleeping off the effects of turkey and pudding were rowdily enjoying a broadcast of *The Sound of Music* in the day room.

The duty nurse led Alison and Miriam along a corridor hung with paper chains and glittering stars, still wearing his pink tissue paper crown from his lunchtime cracker. He confirmed Alison's fears that Jamie had succumbed to PCP, a pneumonia rare until the AIDS virus made it one of its party turns. Hearing the news, she found herself clutching her mother's hand, as much to remind herself this was truly happening as for any comfort the flesh and blood contact might give.

'We've put him down at the end here,' the nurse said. 'Where it's quiet. Don't expect much reaction, what with the drugs and the fever. His temperature's still sky high but we're bringing it down gradually. Don't worry,' he added, seeing Alison's expression. 'This is one of the ones we can beat now.' He held open the door. 'I'll be back in the day room if you need me.'

It was immediately noticeable that Jamie's was the first room on the corridor not hung with Christmas cards and decorations.

'Jesus,' Miriam gasped involuntarily on seeing him. He was wired up to a drip on one side and plugged into a ventilator on the other; by no stretch of the imagination a 'flu patient. Publicly acknowledged, the virus seemed to have gained ground with rapacity. A black rubber lung on the machine puffed and concertinaed in ghastly parody of the geriatric breathing it was supporting. Sam was sitting up by the pillows, beside a translucent bladder that was feeding into Jamie's sweaty body. He sprang up as they came in, face taut with nerves, and grasped both their hands with an odd formality, like a frightened husband welcoming midwives. Alison saw at once that he was one of those men in whom hospitals and sickness inspired a mortal terror.

'I think he's asleep now,' he said. 'He's shut his eyes anyway.'

He pulled over a spare chair so that Alison and Miriam could sit on either side of the bed, then found a stool and sat at the mattress's end. He had been holding one of Jamie's hands. Now he reached out to where one of Jamie's feet stood up, surprisingly big, beneath the sheet. Hesitantly, shy perhaps because Miriam was there, he touched the foot then slid his hand to rest on Jamie's ankle, giving the joint a slight squeeze. Alison saw her mother's eyes flick down to see what he was doing then flick away again.

The three of them sat there, symmetrically arranged as for a dinner party, boy, girl, boy, girl. No-one spoke, abashed and helpless in the presence of suffering, for nearly an hour. Now and then a burst of *The Sound of Music* reached them. Occasionally Miriam took a tissue from the night table and tenderly wiped Jamie's face. She had not seen the waste bag hooked on the other side of the table, and kept the used tissues crumpled in her lap. Twice the nurse came in to check Jamie's pulse and temperature, twice they refused his offer of tea. With nothing to counteract it or keep it in scale, the sound of Jamie's breathing swelled until it was a large, fifth presence in the room, pressing up against them, stealing the air mouthful by greedy mouthful.

At last, Miriam stood stiffly, scattering tissues to the floor and, in a librarian's whisper, said that she was going for a coffee after all and did either of them want one. Sam shook his head but Alison whispered that she was coming too. As they left, Sam stood to stretch his legs and moved to sit in Miriam's chair, nearer Jamie's hands. Alison glanced back from the door and saw him clasping one and leaning forward to murmur something.

'Do you think this place has a cigarette machine?' Miriam asked once they were outside.

'Down in the lobby, probably. I thought you gave up years ago.'

'I did.'

They rode down silently in the lift, avoiding the eyes of visitors who joined from other floors with their bags of library books, toys and nighties for washing. Miriam bought a packet of the mildest cigarettes in the machine and lit one at once. Alison took one too. They made no further comment on this emergency dereliction after years without nicotine. Halfway through, after they had slumped on a green nylon sofa in the smoker's section, Miriam said, 'That's better. Christ I needed that.' Then she started to weep, stopped almost immediately, apologised and lit a second cigarette from what remained of her first. Alison lit a second too, although she knew it would give her a headache. Abruptly, Miriam began to talk about her marriage.

To a casual listener, this would have sounded crassly self-centred, even irrelevant but, familiar with the diversionary tactics and codified grieving of callers to the helpline, Alison knew it was her mother's way of talking about Jamie.

'It's no good,' Miriam said. 'I can't leave him. Poor Francis. I've thought about it. I've thought about it often. But it's so *comfortable* there and I never have to worry about anything any more. Going to the supermarket is a kind of pleasure now. An outing. I'm like a woman on the telly now. I can buy whatever takes my fancy and stick it in my trolley. Anything. Anything at all. He hates me to worry. He says that's what he first wanted about me. All those sessions trying to sort out the commune's taxes for me and he was sitting there with his calculator thinking, "I can stop her worrying if only she'll let me". Did you know I never paid his bill? He's devoted to me. Poor Frank. He's so boring and conventional. I know I've tried to make myself like that too. A bit. Conventions are restful after trying so hard to be different.' She looked up sharply with a bitter laugh and caught Alison's eye through the smoke.

'What?' Alison asked.

'Some of his little habits . . . Like the way he hums to himself even when I'm in the room, and the way he closes doors too slowly – have you noticed that one? As if he's afraid of making a noise.'

Alison nodded slowly.

'Sometimes he makes me want to scream,' Miriam went on.

'So? Scream the house down.'

'Angel, I couldn't. Not now. Not ever. I'm too fucking *placid*. Too much stuff going into my system for much too long.'

'Have an affair then. Most wives do.' Alison hated herself for sounding so cool.

'It's not that easy, Angel. You make it sound like changing my hair or repainting the bedroom. I mean . . . there've been a few times I could have. I suppose. But it would be so humiliating to be turned down or discarded. I'm no chicken. Anyway, sex is so risky nowadays.'

'So? Wear a condom, don't floss your teeth before a date and don't let him come in your mouth.'

Alison drew in her breath sharply. The words had just slipped out of her but they left as strong a charge on the air about them as a brutal slap to the older woman's face. She was surprised people didn't turn to stare at the outbreak of violence.

'Listen to me,' Miriam sighed, letting Alison's retort pass and exhaling wearily. 'I suppose I should find a payphone and ring him.'

'Yes.'

Neither of them moved. Miriam stubbed out her cigarette. She offered Alison another and, when Alison shook her head, she crushed the packet viciously in one hand and tossed it into the coffee-streaked litter bin beside them. She stared for a few seconds after it. When she turned back, her eyes were tearful again.

'I do love you, you know. Both of you. Equally.'

'I know,' Alison said, mortified.

'No you don't. I'm so proud of you. Look.' She reached for her wallet. 'I carry this everywhere.' She produced a dog-eared photograph. Alison was shocked. She thought it one of the least flattering she had ever seen of herself.

She and Jamie were pictured side by side in front of the willow tree at The Roundel, wearing matching, pea-green, tie-dyed vests. She had no chin and a thick fringe. Jamie's hair covered his ears and his face looked slightly dirty, with its dark adolescent fluff and greasy nose. Alison marvelled at how much he had changed and was appalled that this poor, haphazard reproduction of their youth had become a memory their mother cherished. She wondered whether to counter it by producing her similarly grisly shot of Miriam and the Beards.

'I've been a lousy mother,' Miriam went on, fondly smoothing out the picture's creases with a thumb. Alison knew a good child should contradict her but she failed to.

'I suppose it was lacking any example to follow or something. All alone in the world. Huh! When I think about it, I had you so *young*. Eighteen!'

'I thought it was nineteen.'

'Eighteen, nineteen – something like that. Who's counting? I was still an art student. I was a child myself.'

'I know.'

'Little fool that I was. I mean,' she added hastily, 'I never regretted *having* you. I wanted you both so much. But still, I was very very young.'

'Yes.'

'If there wasn't Francis. I mean, if I still lived at The Roundel and everything, would it make a difference?'

'Don't be silly,' Alison protested, because it was true, of course. If Miriam were still drifting around in Indian cotton with home-hennaed hair, trying to sell candles, soap and inexpert little rugs, she might even love her. My mother the eccentric. My mum the old hippy.

They bought watery coffees and chocolate from some machines, embarrassed to bother the nurse having refused him twice already, and went back to join Sam's vigil. On the way, in the lift, Alison heard herself suggesting Miriam come up for lunch occasionally, or dinner and a play, like other people's provincial mothers.

'You could even stay the night,' she said. 'Brave London's fashionable East End. That would be fun. We could start having girls' nights out, if Francis could survive without you, that is.'

They walked back along the corridor sounding as easy together as office workers returning from a lunch hour on a park bench. When they opened the door they found a doctor and a new nurse busy at the bedside and saw Sam, leaning pale against the window, unable to do more than raise his eyebrows in greeting. Alison wondered whether all her bad Christmases had been rehearsals for this one. She handed Sam his coffee and snapped off a chunk of chocolate.

'No thanks,' he muttered.

'Eat,' she whispered, making him take it. 'You didn't eat lunch.' She reached up to rest a hand on his shoulder as he sadly munched.

She thought ahead to her return to the office. People would ask her how *her* Christmas had been. She realised she would have to lie. Anything for a quiet life.

'Fine,' she'd say. 'The usual. Mother, turkey, presents, telly. How about yours?'

49

In the unconsciously harsh language of tired nurses the world over, Jamie was not a good patient. He lacked the inner resources and ready passivity necessary for life as an invalid. The very word, invalid, with its connotations of low worth and non-participation, raised his defences. His was not one of those personalities that allowed itself to be overshadowed by an interesting malady. The very opposite of a hypochondriac, he would always deny an illness rather than let it take him to bed, staggering on through attacks of 'flu when his colleagues would call in sick. It had taken the advent of Sam in his life to persuade him even to take lie-ins, much less enjoy them.

At first, he was so spaced out with fever and pain and drugs that his experience of hospital was ungraspable as a dream. Familiar faces – Sam's, Alison's, Miriam's, Sandy's – floated in and out of the fish-eye view of his suppressed consciousness, their words boomily nonsensical. He was wiped, patted, squeezed, injected and occasionally led, in a vertiginous daze that was pure Hitchcock, to an echoing bathroom. Insofar as he was aware of his body at all, it seemed to have become all weeping eyes, giant lungs and gasping mouth; a primitive, unsuccessful fish. His intervals of serenity were marked by delicious sensations of floating or sinking his sleepy way through an infinite expanse of harmless water. Then, like a tide, the fever receded, leaving him beached in a hospital room with a grey view of rooftops and his mother crying softly in an armchair.

'A lot of help that is,' he said, and she jumped up as

though a corpse had spoken and ran into the corridor calling for a nurse.

His body was no longer burning up, his lungs no longer drowning in their own soup and his breath was once more his own, but the fever had left his body weaker than he would have thought it possible to be yet still live. The first few times he made his way down from the bed unassisted, his legs crumpled beneath him like a couple of straws. One of the male nurses – the camp, plain one as opposed to the cute, straight one – brought him a pair of walking sticks without having to be asked. Now Jamie could shuffle like an old man to his bathroom and review, with unflinching curiosity, his new face and body.

If he had been thin before Christmas, the New Year saw him skeletal. He turned his face this way and that in the merciless mirror. He now had the Montgomery Clift cheekbones he had always dreamed of, but the washboard stomach had been ousted by plate-rack ribs and a pelvis by Barbara Hepworth. His buttocks, once meatily pert, now drooped, wrinkled like tired balloons.

'They could use me to sell famine relief,' he told a plump Glaswegian nurse. 'My adam's apple's become my best feature.'

'And your hair,' she said. 'You've still got lovely hair.'

'Gee thanks. You can come again.'

'Look at it this way, sunshine,' she told him. 'For the first time in your life you can eat anything, absolutely anything you can keep down. Cheese. Cream. Chocolate. Cake. That sore patch in your mouth is a little bit of thrush, which we can knock on the head with Fluconazole. It's going to hurt a bit when you swallow, but you've got to try to eat all you can.'

His bodily weakness had sapped his appetite, however, and the drugs he was on had placed him within constant sniffing distance of nausea. However delicious and calorie-rich the food that was set before him, he had become like the Queen; unable ever to eat more than half.

No less active than usual, his brain took poorly to under-occupation, which left him angry and bored. Now that he was aware of his surroundings, he started treating the ward like a luxury hotel, leaving towels on the floor for the cleaners to pick up, purposely dropping food on his sheets so they had to be changed more often, complaining about the light, the dark, the heat, the cold, the noise, the mattress. He knew he was being a bad patient. He expected a stiff talking-to, expected the last-ditch summoning-up of some Ealing comedy gorgon in starched hat and squeaky shoes, but the nurses were used to such reactions and maddened him further by meeting his bad behaviour with pained sighs and resolute patience. In their experienced eyes, his frustration was a common, easily diagnosed symptom that would pass with no more medication than time. This it duly did, once he realised that his gracelessness, like a child's tantrums, was isolating him from small treats and tendernesses.

With her usual efficiency, unaware that he would see straight through it, Alison had worked out a visiting plan to ensure frequent stimulus for him, stave off depression and prevent visitor build-up. Miriam came to see him in the morning. Alison came in her lunch hour, Sandy came in the afternoon and Sam, freshly showered, appeared after work, ate supper with him and stayed, lying on the bed beside him, until Jamie fell asleep. Word spread by the usual mysterious channels, and surprise visitors began to appear too, not always entirely welcome, with their superstitiously generous bunches of flowers, their fearful, there-but-for-the-grace-of-God smiles and numbingly irrelevant observations.

After a few sharp rebukes, Miriam stopped crying on him and began to make herself useful, arranging and watering flowers, filling his little fridge with nutritious goodies – which he usually fed to other patients, the way he had distributed cake at choir school, to curry favour and ward off envy. She chatted to other morning visitors on her way up and down the corridor and made Jamie take exercise, walking slowly at his side, while he made his halting progress to the day room or the balcony, throwing him smiles of patient encouragement as though he were a valiant toddler again, leaning on his home-made pushcart. She tried to excuse

Francis's non-appearance, now saying he was dreadfully busy, now that he had a horror of hospitals.

'He sent a card,' Jamie silenced her. 'A card with horses on it. That's enough. I never wanted him to visit me when I was well, why should I start now?'

Miriam also started harping on about the Beards. No more sure than she had ever been which was his father, she nonetheless felt it her duty, as his mother, to give them all the chance of contacting him. He had no desire to hear from any of them, but encouraged her because the process of tracking them down gave her an occupation and Alison a source of amusement. Unfortunately the results of her research only depressed her. Two Beards had died of accidental overdoses and one in a sailing accident. One had become a successful Chicago restaurateur who sent Jamie a signed copy of his recipe book, and one had evaporated into the clouds of Tibetan Buddhism, leaving a trail of bad debts and a Californian indictment for mail fraud. Jamie said he hoped his father was the one who died at sea, because it was a romantic yet clean way to go, and they left the paternity hunt at that.

Miriam tried to teach him to paint. Amid the books and flowers and chocolates, someone had given him a sketch pad and a small set of watercolours. Jamie had no visual gift and quickly lost interest, but he soon found that the paints kept Miriam quiet. Ostensibly still teaching him by example, she executed little paintings of the view from his window, of bowls, of flowers, once, disastrously, of him. She rediscovered her old ability and soon, for all her shy protests, the nurses were pinning her work among the timetables on their noticeboard and circulating it among the other patients. She had to buy herself a second block of paper and became something of a ward celebrity.

Visiting in her lunch hours, Alison was often in too much of a rush to stay long, but she kept Jamie supplied with newspapers and magazines. She seemed anxious lest he lose touch with current affairs. He had never been so well informed to so little purpose. If she resented the extra time that Miriam spent with him, she hid it well. She never cried. Sometimes he wished she would, because he feared she was crying on Sam, who was less able to take it. The mask of resolute cheerfulness she wore in his presence fitted her ill. On several occasions it even drove him to behave badly with her, mounting displays of depression and unconstructive petulance so as to goad her into a more honest reaction.

Jamie had never felt that he and Sandy had much in common. He had always regarded her merely as an adjunct of his sister and was slightly perturbed when she began to call in without Alison, sometimes with friends, sometimes alone, always on the pretext of dropping in on the way to visiting somebody else. She made no attempt to hide what she was feeling. If she was in a bad mood, she dumped her feelings on his bed like so much heavy shopping, if her mood was high, she brought him ice creams in the shape of feet, trashy novels or spotted bandannas to wear in his pyjama pocket. She talked baldly about the progress of his ill health and made him do the same. He found they had more in common than he had imagined, and encouraged her in turn to regale him with details of her erotic conquests, finding he was as hungry for them as Alison had once been for his.

Sam's visits were entirely different from any of the others. He was obviously frightened by what was happening, and Jamie found that he was having to reassure his lover rather than vice versa. As far as possible, their evenings together in hospital began to mimic ordinary evenings together in the flat. Sam would pace around a bit, drinking beer from a can, then flop on the bed and, between hugs and kisses, recount the comforting banalities of his day. They would eat, then, often not talking at all, they would lie arm in arm to watch television. He never left before Jamie had fallen asleep, however long this took. Sometimes Jamie woke again as Sam pulled his arm out from beneath him and the sight of the stolid figure stealing from the darkened room filled him with an unspeakable regret. Once he teased Sam that he must be looking elsewhere for sex. Sam was as furious as he was scandalised, however, his anger frightening in so confined a space. Having conjured up the possibility, though, Jamie returned repeatedly to it when he could not sleep, wondering how he would react if Sam were unfaithful. He suspected he would feel a kind of release; it would make him officially invalid, relieved of normal social duties and responses. Alison confided that sometimes, after visiting the hospital, Sam came to spend the night back at her house in Bow. She said it was because he felt unhappy being in the flat on his own, but Jamie wondered if it were not Sam's way of removing himself from the temptation of having so discreet a love-nest at his disposal.

When he wasn't being visited, Jamie found it impossible to avoid encounters with others on the ward unless he pretended to be asleep – a pretence which frequently melted into the real thing.

'We have nothing in common but a medical affliction,' he told Alison. 'I don't see why we should all be expected to get on. It's Belsen up here, not a holiday camp, for Christ's sake!'

But gradually his curiosity and the social divisiveness of their common condition got the better of his reluctance. Several of the twenty or so patients were, like him, walking wounded, and would drift in and out of each other's rooms exchanging gossip, comparing symptoms and treatments, discussing visitors. Often they were accompanied by militant buddies or cheery but painfully tactful volunteers. One of these wore a badge saying POSITIVE, as though to assure patients he was one of them too and could be trusted. One of the more politically minded patients had even had HIV tattooed on his forearm. Relentlessly, Jamie found himself drawn into a kind of exclusive brotherhood founded on the ravages of an unexclusive virus.

For better or worse, this socialising slipped into all the spaces in his day when he was not being visited, emphasising the otherness, the healthiness of his visitors. When the two worlds overlapped, as when Sam arrived and froze in the doorway, finding him chatting to a patient whose body now displayed more purple lesion than healthy skin, or when his room was invaded by a shriekingly effeminate posse of two ex-waiters and a chorus boy during one of Miriam's tranquil painting sessions, he felt guilty as an outwitted adulterer. Of course there were women on the floor too, and even, briefly, a pitifully undersized child, but these were often kept from joining in with garrulous ward society by the haunted, hostile presence of their families. Jamie once slipped into a woman's room to return a video of *Come Into My Parlour* she had lent him. Her relatives were gathered around her bed in a premature wake. The stares with which they answered his polite greeting were so heavy with blame that he found himself shaking uncontrollably on his way back to his bed.

50

Christmas in Marrackech had not provided the restful break Edward had expected. Certainly the weather was delightful – like a warm, English spring – and the house Heini had borrowed was a lovely affair. It had big white and blue rooms built around a succession of miraculously quiet pools, gardens and courtyards where one could pass whole days oblivious to the grime and bustle in the alleyways beyond the high walls. Heini had not explained, however, that the house belonged to one of his more outrageous friends, an aristocrat who had put the respectable responsibilities of England behind him to seek as it were the wilder shores of love. The house was a temple to homoerotica. Thomas, of course, had possessed several such pieces, but had always camouflaged them among images of more conventional couplings. Here, wherever Edward's eye or hand came to rest, there seemed to be a rippling Greek torso or willowy Hylas. Even in his bedroom, especially selected for him at Heini's assurance that it held the calmest decor, the pretty watercolours proved on closer inspection to be of two-headed Cornish lads diving off rocks and romping by waterholes. Everything was in exquisite taste but the whole was so overtly thematic as to be oppressive to the unpersuaded mind. When, during dinner on the first evening, Heini began to tell a woman friend about his unexpected encounter with Edward's grandson at a ball and how charming his young friend Sam had turned out to be, Edward flared up saying he thought the pair of them had behaved dreadfully, flaunting themselves in public. He also confessed he had not spoken to Jamie since. He had made a foolish spectacle of himself, not only bringing a jarring note into the festive proceedings but drawing on himself the woman's only slightly indignant curiosity. She mocked him all evening as an interesting specimen of antiquated attitudes which was doubly galling for his sensing that she was right. For his part, Heini had seemed disappointed, even hurt, by his outburst. Edward saw why in the days that followed.

Heini began spending an inordinate amount of time with Mustapha, their host's servant. Edward did his utmost not to notice and not to mind, passing peaceful days swimming and reading, but Heini's clumsily disguised dalliance became a teasing presence forever on the edge of his vision. He had always known Heini was not the marrying sort, but whatever Heini did for pleasure, he had always done in secret and it was something he had had the good grace never to discuss. Now that an occasion patently had arrived where it needed at least acknowledging, Edward found himself tongue-tied. As the holiday progressed and Heini's subterfuges – sudden 'shopping' excursions, 'tedious' visits to Mustapha's family farm – came to seem increasingly pathetic, Edward caught himself wondering whether there might not be courage and even courtesy in the more honest approach Jamie had tried to take with him. He made several false starts on a letter to his grandson, tearing each one up when he felt it began to betray too much the struggle between his revulsion and his love. He saw no way out. As with Heini, what had been acceptable as a mere idea had become far harder to stomach when fleshed out and paraded beneath his gaze.

When his stay reached an end, he left Heini to enjoy a further week alone with Mustapha and his liberal women friends and flew back to Heathrow determined to do *something* to make his peace with his grandson, but had no clear idea what form this should take. He had bought Jamie a late Christmas present of a Moroccan bowl with a deep blue glaze and a crude brass rim. The fact that this was bought in Mustapha's brother's shop made this single purchase a sop to two guilts. He believed that the present would at least provide an excuse for he and Jamie to meet.

He wheeled his trolley out through customs and past

the usual faintly accusatory line-up of chauffeurs holding hand-painted signs for passengers they had never met, and was startled to find Alison waiting for him. She tried to ask him how his trip had gone and said something about having left her car somewhere illegal and then, quite unexpectedly threw her arms round him and wept where they stood on the crowded concourse. Passers-by paid them little heed, hot displays of emotion and tearful reunions being idiomatic to so multicultural and nervous a setting. When she had regained enough control to blurt out why she was there and where she was about to drive him, he felt suddenly that they must be as glaring a presence in the crowd as a towering pair of naked Masai.

As she drove him into town, he asked her over and over the same bald questions, unable to digest her calm replies. She led him as far as the nursing station on Jamie's ward then pointed the way and said, 'I think it's better if you go the rest of the way on your own and take your time. I'll wait downstairs.'

He walked slowly along the gaudily decorated corridor. When a nurse asked if she could help him he was aware that he was still clutching some luggage and she had assumed him to be a newly arrived patient.

'Yes,' he said. 'Could you tell me where I can find my grandson, James? Jamie. Jamie Pepper, that is.'

The tinsel and paperchains still strung about the place in wilful profusion highlit rather than disguised the wretched atmosphere. Recalling other hospitals – visits to his sister with her ruined mind, his old friend Thomas devoured by cancer, his parents-in-law wide-eyed with fear and his own imprisonment – he remembered asking similar questions and vainly entertained an irrational hope that she would deny all knowledge of the names he gave and send him cheerfully back to a life unscarred by alteration.

'Of course,' she said. 'He's down here past the Christmas tree. He'll be so pleased you came.'

51

Sandy was passing on an especially satisfactory piece of scandal concerning a cabinet member who had been sounding forth against single mothers, when the door opened and his grandfather stood there, tanned and clutching a suitcase.

'I came straight from the airport,' he said.

'Grandpa!' Jamie was staggered. 'I don't think you've met. Sandy. My grandfather. Edward.'

'Pleased to meet you.' Sandy shook his grandfather's hand. He nodded, eyes darting to the curious braids in what remained of her hair and down to her multiply pierced ear. 'Er. I should be going,' she added over her shoulder.

'Don't you want tea?' Jamie asked her, not wanting to be left alone with his grandfather just yet having had so little time to prepare himself. 'The trolley comes around soon.'

'No. Honestly.' She picked up her bag. 'I promised I'd see Shirley too. I'll grab a cup in her room.'

She kissed him swiftly on the lips, flashed a nervous smile at his grandfather as she left and all but curtsied. He suddenly seemed very tall, his hair very white and flowing as he loomed in the corner by the bathroom door, staring like an Old Testament patriarch. Remembering the change in his appearance since their last meeting, Jamie realised how great a shock his weight-loss must be, and tried to establish a light atmosphere.

'Yes,' he said, as his grandfather remained silent, 'I've lost a lot of weight and I look like Death itself. You'd better sit down and get used to it.'

His grandfather stepped forward and sank into the armchair nearer the bed, never taking his eyes off Jamie.

'How was your holiday?' Jamie asked.

'Fine. I brought you this.'

He unwrapped a glistening blue bowl and set it on the windowsill, far from Jamie's reach.

'Thanks,' Jamie told him. 'It's lovely. You look well. Bet you had a better Christmas than us.'

'Did you catch it from your . . . from Sam?'

'No. I haven't known him long enough and anyway, he's testing negative.'

'Who then?'

Jamie shrugged.

'Who wants to know?' he asked.

'I'll break their neck,' his grandfather said gravely.

Jamie laughed softly at him.

'Honestly! It isn't like that. It takes time to show up. It's hard to pinpoint.'

His grandfather raised a hand as though to strike someone, but let it fall back on the chair arm as the spasm of impotent fury passed.

'Damn,' he hissed. 'You're so young still.'

'Yes. But I'm not dead yet and I'm not dying.' Jamie's tone was studiedly calm. The anger he had always planned to show once they met again had been usurped by a need to reassure and shield. 'I'll be out of here in a few days, then I'll get my energy back and get on with life again.'

'I could kill him. Whoever he is.'

'Grandpa, *stop* it!' Jamie begged, his laughter a little forced now. After days of good behaviour from his visitors, even Sandy, the old man's naked emotion left him no time to armour his vulnerability. 'You sound like someone whose teenage daughter's got pregnant. But of course. She did. She was here this morning, in fact. She'll be sorry she missed you.' Jamie's tone was mocking, and yet the image had often occurred to him, that someone had impregnated him with this vile offspring, with its long gestation period and monstrous ability to use its host to sire progeny in others even before it had made its presence felt.

'Sorry. I'm sorry. I –' His grandfather broke off, dropping his face and briefly touching his right temple before pulling a hand through his shock of hair. When he looked up he seemed younger, almost boisterously healthy, his African tan flushed pink by emotion and the heat of the room. It was easy, for a few seconds, to see how he must have looked at Jamie's age, just as it was easy, in Jamie's sickness to see how *he* would look were he allowed to age to his sixties and beyond.

'Is your friend ill too?'

'No. I told you. He's still testing negative. We've been careful.'

'And he's still . . . around?'

'Yes. He's on a new site, in Wandsworth. He comes in every night.'

'He must love you, then.' His grandfather spoke as though the possibility were fresh to his understanding.

'I suppose he must.'

'Do you love him?'

'Yes.'

His grandfather absorbed this.

'I don't understand,' he said. 'I'm sorry.'

'No-one expects you to.'

'Maybe it's age.'

'Maybe.'

'I think –' His grandfather sighed deeply, looking out of the window where rain was lashing the glass. For an awful moment Jamie thought he was going to break down or start shouting again, but he merely took a breath and looked back to the bed. 'I think Sally would have understood. Your grandmother was entirely *open* to new things. She had no prejudice.'

Jamie only nodded. He pictured the old man driving back to his empty flat or out of London to his empty studio beside The Roundel. Normally he imagined his grandfather in a shifting crowd of old friends, admirers, colleagues, musicians, concert agents. He imagined him grateful for the odd day of solitude. Now he received a new, sharp sensation of a kind of bustling loneliness within him, a loneliness grown adept, with the years, at covering its own tracks.

'Your friend Miss Toye has quite a fan club here,' he joked. 'When *Mulroney Park* comes on, they practically take the phones off the hook. They were very impressed that my grandfather had had an affair with the woman. It made me quite proud of you.'

His grandfather gave a strained smile and promptly changed tack.

'You say you'll be out in a few days?' he asked.

'Yes. They need the bed. I'll be very weak for a bit. I had to give up my job in the record shop. They'd have me back, I think – they, er, they have no prejudices either – but I'll need the rest. I sleep for hours. I'd probably nod off behind the counter.'

'You must come home to The Roundel. Be quiet there. Your flat is no good. You need to get out of the city. I think The Roundel's special . . . It's a healing place. I've nothing much on. Nothing I can't postpone or cancel.'

'Grandpa, I –'

'I can take care of you, Jamie.'

'Are you *rescuing* me, then?'

'Yes.' The old man smiled at last, surprised at the unexpected truth. His tone was wry, as though making a sly reference to an old family joke. 'Yes. I will rescue you.'

'I'll . . . I'll have to talk to Sam about it this evening.'

'Oh. Of course. I'd forgotten. Talk to him by all means. Perhaps he has plans for you.'

'Can I call you tomorrow?'

He nodded. On rising he still made no move to touch Jamie or embrace him. Why should he? Theirs had never been a relationship of touch and a sudden change now, even after their recent estrangement, would ring false. But he held him with his big, dreamer's eyes for a moment and Jamie once again pictured him as a young man, resolute, passionate, fighting against the degradation thrust upon him by foreigners and against the insidious bacillus in his lungs.

Shattered from the unexpected encounter, he slid into a deep sleep where he sat, upright against the pillows. He dreamed of water again but this time it was a river. He was lying back on cushions in a shallow boat and a young, dark-haired man he knew to be his grandfather was vigorously punting them upstream in dazzling summer sunshine. He felt very tired in the boat but utterly safe, utterly trusting.

Influenced perhaps by the afterglow of the dream, he had expected Sam to feel jealous of his grandfather's suggested intervention. He had forgotten Sam's earlier enthusiasm for the house and his suggestion that they all go to live there.

'Fine,' Sam said at once. 'I've a couple of weeks to go on site. Alison and I were worried about you being at home on your own. Go. Will it be warm enough?'

'Sure,' Jamie nodded. 'There's central heating. If the house gets cold I can always go and sleep in the studio. He's got a sofa-bed in the main room over there.'

So it was decided. Jamie left the hospital and was driven home by a hospital volunteer. He spent a shattering afternoon packing a suitcase, amazed and furious at how long it took him. Then he allowed his grandfather to rescue him from urban temptation and unwholesomeness. Alison ascertained there was a clinic in Rexbridge he could attend as an outpatient and had the ward sister contact it to send on his details. Sandy made relevant enquiries to check that the local GP, should Jamie need him, was not on any blacklists. Miriam, meanwhile, having got so into the swing of visiting the ward every morning, applied to the volunteer coordinator and was delighted to be asked if she would give watercolour classes to any patients who had a yen to learn.

Rather than making do with teenage leftovers, Jamie was to establish himself at The Roundel for the first time in his adult life, surrounding himself with his favourite clothes and discs and books. He was no sooner over the threshold than he realised he was going to be there for longer than the fortnight agreed with Sam. The old house claimed him. His grandfather's cleaner had been in. The place was sweet with the lavender and petrol smell of furniture wax, its air still tangy with glass cleaner. Rugs bore the satisfying marks of recent hoovering. Woodwork glowed.

Tired after the drive, weary too of his grandfather's watchfulness, Jamie made himself a cup of tea then took himself off to bed with the radio and a new copy of *Hello*. He unpacked the idol from the suitcase and set her in the middle of the bedroom mantel-shelf so she could command the room. The bed was made up with fresh sheets that smelled of soap. There was a small pile of mail at the bedside. He set the magazine aside and opened the envelopes. Several contained get-well cards from local acquaintances who doubtless knew he had been ill but had no idea what with. Alison might, he reflected, have allowed it to be assumed that the pneumonia was a result of weak lungs inherited from his grandfather. There were the usual sorts of stale letters addressed to one's childhood home – school newsletters appealing for retirement presents and contributions to building funds, a flier advertising reductions in the Rexbridge store where he had bought his pinstripe suit.

He saved the most interesting-looking envelope until last. The stamp was German and, as he tore out the thin sheet of paper, he inevitably fell to thinking of Germans he had been to bed with and to whom he might rashly have granted his address in younger and less guarded times. Prepared for unconvincing expressions of enduring affection or roundabout requests for invitations to stay, he was nonetheless disappointed to find a formal, typewritten note on official paper. The notepaper bore the name of the hospital where he had been taken for his leg to be mended after his skiing accident. He remembered sleepless nights in a half-empty ward, an awkward visit from a representative of his holiday insurance company and one from the friends he had been skiing with, who were embarrassed at being obliged to return home without him. He remembered the very specific pain and then the intolerable itching of the stitched gash in his calf, encased in plaster. His tourist's German had improved a little during his recuperation – forced as he was to resort to German gossip magazines for his entertainment in lieu of further visitors or anything to read in English – but it was insufficient to master the formal sentences in the letter. He understood *We regret, dear sir, it is our duty to inform you* and *blood* and a reference to a firm of lawyers in Bonn. Assuming it was some tedious technicality arising from his long since settled insurance claim, he placed it on one side and returned to reading an article about the health minister's daughter and her plans for transforming

Godfreys's mansion once they returned from their Jamaican honeymoon.

It was only the next morning that, feeling stronger, buoyed up by a change of scene, he tracked down Alison's old German dictionary and began to piece the sense of the letter together. It had nothing to do with holiday insurance. He was being respectfully informed that, in the wake of a national scare, residual supplies of HIV-infected blood had been traced to the hospital's bank, dating from before the period in which he had been admitted to its casualty department. They saw from their records that he had received a transfusion following severe loss of blood during his accident and subsequent operation to repair the bone. It was thus faintly possible that he had been placed at risk of accidental infection. They would strongly advise his applying for an HIV test at once. They added, in an elliptical slur on his nature, that it was, of course, so long ago now that any unfortunate infection showing up in his blood could most probably be traced to more than one possible source. While the hospital was declaring itself immune from legal blame, having since been closed down, re-opened and privatised with new staff, any enquiries of a legal nature might be referred to a firm in Bonn who were representing the government department directly responsible for the testing of blood supplies. Et cetera.

Jamie read and reread the letter, in whose margins he had scribbled his stumbling translation, astonished that it could say so much in so few words and with so little attempt to dress up its message in softening conditional clauses or sympathetic expressions. Then he took it to the fireplace and set fire to it in the grate, watched by the inscrutable idol. He thought about this news when Alison rang during a quiet moment in her office in the afternoon, thought about it again when Sam rang sweetly to say nothing in particular after work. He thought about it especially when, with the utmost caution and deliberation, his grandfather asked him over supper whether there was any chance that he might have passed the virus on to anybody he knew. He decided, however, to tell nobody. Not Sam. Not anyone.

There had been much talk of innocent victims. Iniquitous

talk implying, by its choice of epithets, that the majority of people were, on the contrary, entirely to blame for their HIV infections or, worse, entirely deserving of them. Jamie knew with a strong, irrational certainty, that his infection *had* come from the blood transfusion, but far from feeling the helplessness of outraged innocence, he felt the anger and shame of betrayed trust. He was indignant at the letter's implications, feeling like a soldier coming round in a field hospital to find he had been bayonetted ignominiously in the back while fleeing a battleground. To die from such a cause – and he was dying, he knew, despite the talk of living and continuance he felt obliged to offer Alison and Sandy – to die thus was somehow more painful, futile and less *honourable* than to die from an old-fashioned sexual infection. He did not want to become like the women and children on the ward, surrounded by vengeful kin, isolated by his new blamelessness from the one thing that might give his death a value.

Putting some of his new books on the shelves in his room, he fell eagerly on an old address book of his dating from around his sixteenth birthday, long since discarded as being too painfully in need of editing. He flicked through the pages for what seemed like hours, hungrily scanning his younger handwriting for names of men who might have done the deed, desperate now that his fate be born of human choice, not of a mere crime of hospital inefficiency.

52

Sandy was throwing a birthday party and Alison was in no mood to go. After six months in a wheelchair, her old journalist friend, Guy, whom she had barely seen since the Gay Pride march, had finally been swept away by an attack of MAI, a rare form of tuberculosis.

'So typical,' he had croaked mirthlessly, as she sat at his bedside in the ward Jamie had recently left. 'We spend our lives trying to be different – eating and wearing things nobody else would dream of, decorating our houses in unheard of ways – and now what? Now we manage to be chic and rarefied even in death. TB? Nothing so *du peuple*! We even manage to suffer from the virus in different ways from each other. This is *customised* lurgy . . .'

He had died on Monday and was cremated on Thursday, too late for Sandy to cancel Saturday's party.

'It's my birthday,' she declared a few hours before, when Alison rang her ostensibly to discuss helpline rotas but actually to see whether she could find the courage to excuse herself from going. 'And I shan't have it turned into a wake. You dress up, girl, get yourself a lift so you can drink yourself stupid, and you *party*! And no black. *Schwarz* is absolutely *verboten*. The only black Guy would have allowed is underwear.'

By the time Bald Billy drove over from Greenwich to pick her up, Alison had tried on and rejected some five outfits. She answered the door to Billy in an old school suit of Jamie's she had tarted up with a red silk scarf and a flashy diamanté clip.

'Well? What do you think?' she asked him warily, sensing he was about to pass judgement anyway. Billy's window-dressing had won prizes. Tonight he had come out entirely in Hare Krishna orange. He had even found the time to dye some plimsolls tangerine.

'No,' he said after a moment's consideration.

'You no like? *Tell* me, Billy!'

'You're a girl, Alison. Wear that lot and you give out *quite* the wrong signals.'

'I thought it was sort of Barbara Stanwyck.'

'Precisely.' Billy stole a mandarin from the fruitbowl and began peeling it.

'Okay,' Alison sighed. 'Have we got time?'

He nodded.

'Right,' she said, returning to her bedroom and throwing off the suit. 'I'm a girl. I'm a girl. Damn it, I *am*!'

She snatched up a little red dress with skinny shoulder straps, pulled it over her head and cinched in her waist with a black belt. Then she put on lipstick to match.

'Lose the belt,' Billy told her in the hall.

'But –'

'Simplicity is all and anyway it makes you look like a centaur from behind. But the dress is good.' He stood back. 'Here,' he said, taking a heavy steel chain from his neck and fastening it round hers. 'I've taken the chill off it for you. Now *that* looks fabulous!'

'You're sure? I feel like a fire extinguisher. Billy, can't we stay in and watch TV? I'll cook.'

Billy rejected one of her coats with a little mutter of shocked distaste and grabbed another one for her.

'Do you know how long it took to get these shoes the right colour?' he asked her wearily.

Sandy shared a big, battered house in the considerable shadow of Arsenal football stadium with three other women. She had bought it in her earning days as a solicitor and, now that she earned nothing, needed lodgers to help her pay the mortgage. The lodgers changed regularly, so, assuming they had friends, there was always a good chance of meeting new faces at Sandy's parties. The fact that Alison usually found herself in the basement kitchen with the same old crowd, hiding from all the new people upstairs, did not stop her, even tonight, from entering the house with a certain sense of anticipation.

As a gesture to mourning, an old photograph of Guy puffing a drunken kiss at the camera over a birthday cake had been blown up to poster size and coloured, *à la* Warhol, with vibrant crayons. Glued on the hall wall above a table draped with a pseudo altar cloth and cluttered with Mexican prayer candles, it was already fluttering with tokens of remembrance people had pinned to it. There were red ribbons, inevitably, but also chocolate wrappers, a condom full of Smarties, a rubber snake, a pink carnation, a sombre polaroid snapshot taken during the picnic at the last Gay Pride, with Guy in his OUR DEATHS YOUR SHAME baseball cap, and a gaudy postcard of Plymouth Hoe.

Sandy ran out to greet them, a bottle in either hand, already in bare feet because she had been dancing.

'Damn you!' she shouted over the music, after duly admiring Billy's plimsolls and snatching his exquisitely wrapped birthday parcel. 'I wanted *me* to be the only one in a dress. Look at you!'

'Ah but I'm a girl,' Alison said.

'I know, babe. I *know*!'

'Well look at *you*. It's so . . .' Words failed Alison.

'Like it?' Sandy revolved on the spot to show off her incongruous blue satin ball gown. 'Found it in Help the Aged. I've come as your mother, incidentally.' Alison gave her a playful slap and received a kiss in return. 'No Boys?' Sandy asked.

Alison shook her head.

'Nothing can winkle Jamie out of the fens so Sam's gone up to join him there.'

'Jamie sent me a card, though.'

'You're honoured. I never get one.'

Sandy was distracted by the arrival of a recent ex of hers, new girlfriend in tow. Bald Billy was already in the living room, showing off his plimsolls, so Alison slipped downstairs to the kitchen. The grimy basement had been transformed like the rest of the house by a quantity of candles burning in jam jars and flower pots. It would be quite in character for a Sandy party for the evening to end with someone spectacularly catching fire and having to be rushed to casualty. Someone nobody had ever liked much. Sure enough, the gang were all in the kitchen, eating the cocktail sausages and mustard dip that no-one could be bothered to pass around upstairs. Sean and Nick stood, shyly entwined, by the door, inseparable even before anyone had found time to get drunk and predatory. Guy's widowed Buddy, Steve, looking incomplete without the wheelchair to push, was chatting to several colleagues from the helpline and Belgian Agnes. Belgian Agnes had brought along yet another man she had found at the Islamic Institute. He stared about him and clung to her as to a life raft. As Alison came in there were hugs all round because Guy's funeral was still fresh in their minds and, without anyone saying as much, they all knew she was in need of hugging and suspected Jamie's would be next.

Although she had made a point of still speaking to him every day and had sent him a couple of Red Cross parcels of magazines, books and chocolates, she had not seen Jamie since he left hospital. His departure to The Roundel had brought a temporary alleviation of pressure, allowing her to flex her spirit and check for sprains. She was shocked to find herself suffering a kind of revulsion with his sickness or, more accurately, a kind of dissatisfaction with its progress. Daring, now there was distance between them, to stand back mentally from their situation and examine her reactions, she found that his recovery had cheated her of something, and the long months ahead, months of checking he was still relatively well and of waiting for him to decline again, were a deadening prospect. Of course this reaction appalled her. She was grateful, truly, for his rescue from death's jaws, which according to the doctors had been a very close thing. She prayed, moreover, with honest selfishness, that he might be spared for another year, two years even. His so nearly dying had been a kind of rehearsal. She saw that now. It gave them all a chance to test their love for him like so many unfinished ships in a dock.

What disturbed her most was her being forced to accept that his death, whenever it came, would not destroy her. She would survive. She had already found ways of coping. He had been close as a limb to her for as long as she could remember, but nobody died of amputation these days. With careful deployment of what fate left her, the healing stump might not even show too much. Like the sensible widow, she would make new friends who had never known what she had lost and would accept her as she was, brotherless. Brotherlessness; that, she knew now, would hurt. Sometimes she dared to hope that Sam might stay around, play a brotherly role, but most of the time she knew the hope was vain. In both senses. With Jamie gone, the tentative roots Sam had put down would be groundless and he would be swept away from her by the same mysterious urban current that had first washed him into her path.

Alison began to find the considerate tone of friends hard to bear. She extricated herself from Nick and Sean's little pool of sweetness and, taking a washing-up bowl of crisps, went in search of oblivious strangers. She offered them to acrid solicitors who envied Sandy her freedom even as they decried her folly in giving up her legal career. She offered them to the lodgers, but found they were discussing the validity of the class struggle and moved on when one of them gave her a look that dismissed her as the Snack-bearing Bourgeoise from Hell. She offered them to some men downing quantities of fruit juice, flushed from dancing, then she realised the men were boys, young enough to have been brought by their parents. Finally she saw that the same man had put his hand in the crisp bowl in each group, and that he was still following her.

'Here,' she said. 'You take them. You're obviously hungry and they're getting heavy,' and she looked at him properly for the first time.

'Hi,' he said. He nodded slowly as though the mere fact of her speaking to him at last represented an opinion with which he was in fulsome agreement. 'Bruce,' he added.

She saw a long, Greek nose, dark eyes, and unkempt blond hair that looked almost yellow against his tan. Late twenties. Early thirties allowing for the candles' flattery.

'Alison,' she said, not offering her hand because his were now full.

'You a friend of the hostess?'

'Yes,' she said. 'But I'm a girl.'

'Oh. Thank God.'

He was American. Judging from the depth of his tan he was fresh from somewhere hotter than Finsbury Park.

'Why haven't I met you before?' she asked.

'I don't know anyone here.'

'No?'

'I'm a friend of Abby's. We arranged to meet here.'

'Oh.'

'But you guys haven't met yet, I guess.'

'Sorry. I wouldn't know her from Adam.' Sandy was passing. Alison broke off to catch at her sleeve. 'Bruce wants to know if Abby's here,' she shouted.

'Who?' Sandy laughed.

'Abby. I don't know her either.'

Sandy turned to Bruce, glanced back at Alison then said, as she was drawn away again, 'Stick with Alison. I'm sure she's a *much* better lay.'

Alison felt herself grin foolishly.

'With friends like her –' she began. 'Listen. Don't you want to try phoning this Abby to see if she's all right?'

What's come over me? she thought as she spoke. *Why must I treat everybody nowadays as if they're in a state of incipient social trauma? The poor woman's probably two-timing him with his best friend or skiving off for a quiet night in with the cat and a tin of chocolate brownies.*

'No,' Bruce said, bringing his mouth close to her ear to be heard over the music. She felt the warmth of him. 'But I would like to get somewhere quiet so we can talk properly.'

He steered her out through the crowd, then she led the way up to the landing where there was a sofa buried beneath discarded coats and yet another dangerous clutch of guttering candles. Clearing the coats onto the floor so they could sit, she uncovered a bottle of wine. Bruce opened it with a Swiss Army penknife and refilled their glasses. He had passed the crisps to someone else along the way.

'Geeze this is so embarrassing,' he said, after they had raised glasses and pulled simultaneous faces at the nastiness of the wine. 'I feel like some lousy gate-crasher.'

'That doesn't matter. Sandy encourages gate-crashers, as long as they bring bottles. One of her best friends began life as a gate-crasher in this very house.'

'You?'

She nodded.

'My brother and I had just been to a terrible wedding. God, I hate weddings! Don't you?'

He nodded. So far so good.

'Anyway,' she went on. 'We were passing and the party was going with a swing and we were both pretty drunk so Jamie – that's my brother – Jamie dragged me back to an off-licence and in we came, armed with bottles. I only found out afterwards he was after one of the blokes we'd just seen coming in here.' Bruce laughed uncertainly. 'He's like that,' she added. 'Impulsive. I hate parties. I didn't want to come out tonight in fact. I was all set to stay in with the cat and a tin of chocolate brownies. Actually I don't have a cat but you get the idea.'

Christ! she thought. *Doesn't this harpy* ever *draw breath?*

The trouble with straight men, she was remembering, was that unless they were lecherous bastards, they lacked small talk and, even the lecherous ones lacked finesse. Bald Billy, Sugary Sean, Nice Nick, even poor Guy, were never lost for an answer or a quip. Jamie didn't even allow the painful taking of a blood sample to stem conversational flow.

What the hell, she thought. *We're both adults. We know what we want.*

'So this Abby, is she your fiancée, your mother or what?' she demanded.

He displayed that phased slowness she found appealing in some Americans, a kind of daddish social clumsiness in the face of anything too witty or too blunt.

'Er . . .' He chuckled slowly, finally catching up with her. 'Er. He was my old college roomie. His real name's Peter. Peter Abrams.'

'Oh. *Oh!* Well isn't that nice.'

'He's a lawyer. I'm staying at his place. I only got here this morning and we still haven't met up. He left a note for me about meeting at the party. He's off to Japan tomorrow early so I guess we won't meet after all.'

'Are you sure you got the right party? I don't think Sandy knows the kind of people who can afford to go to Japan.'

'I've got his note.' He dug in the pocket of his big check shirt. 'Here.'

It was the wrong address.

'He'll be waiting for you over the road,' she said.

'Oh well.' He shrugged, grinned, topped up her wine. 'It sounded kinda quiet and tasteful over there, didn't you think?'

'I really didn't notice.'

'It was quiet.' He assured her. 'You won't tell Sandy?'

'Promise. But what do you care?' She smiled and he smiled and suddenly his pretty face seemed several inches closer than it had been.

'You have the most amazing eyes,' he told her.

'Oh phooey.'

'You do. Sorry. You don't like compliments.' He looked down at his glass, drank some more. His lips were wine-darkened, eminently kissable. He grinned. 'But you do, you know. Amazing ones.'

When did he start chatting her up? No-one had chatted her up in years. Not even the editorial assistant, and *he* had nursed an ulterior motive. It felt delightful. English men just stopped talking and pounced, however confusing and violent a subject change the pouncing constituted. The approach was one of stealthy surprise-taking; talk to her about politics, your rent rebate, motorway toll systems, then, just when her eyes are glazing over, pounce.

'Sorry,' he was saying. 'Does this sort of thing make you mad?'

'Not at all.'

'If I feel something I just come right out and say it. It saves time. I'm not very good at English reserve.'

'It's all a con.'

'What is?'

'English reserve,' she told him. 'We fuck like ferrets given the chance.'

'Really?' He rounded his big eyes and leaned fractionally towards her. 'You'll have to forgive me,' he said. 'I'm kinda jet-lagged. I'm still out on Planet TWA.'

'You look fine from down here,' she said, feeling his breath on her cheek.

'How about closer to?' he asked.

'Well . . .' She felt her heart race like a schoolgirl's. This was wildly irresponsible. She should go downstairs and mingle with the grown-ups. 'You've got wine stains on your lip,' she told him.'

'Where?'

'Just . . . there.' She touched his upper lip with her forefinger, exposing expensive teeth and a big, stirring tongue. He kissed her finger then the palm of her hand then, so slowly she felt steam should be hissing from her ears, he cupped her face in his hands and kissed her on the mouth. Comprehensively.

Pouring them both the remains of the nasty wine, he hummed along to the song booming out of the living room below them, perkily confident, now he knew that she wanted what he wanted. A queue had begun to form outside the bathroom and Alison felt the landing sofa was fast losing its appeal.

'Do you like dancing?' she asked. 'I love this song too.'

'I can think of other things I'd rather do,' he said slowly.

'Oh?' She smiled. He was hers for the taking.

'We could go back to Abby's place,' he said. 'But he'll be there later and I don't know about you but *I* like to make a lot of noise when I come.'

'Oh lord,' she said. 'Well I live way out in Bow. I'd hate you to go off the boil before we got there.'

'No danger of that,' he said, running a teasing finger under a shoulder strap on her dress and across her collar bone. 'Do you have anything planned for tomorrow?'

'I thought perhaps a day in bed.'

'Oh. Well *good*.'

They retrieved their coats from the pile and headed for the street. They kissed so heavily in the back of the taxi home that she found herself letting Bruce pay for it while she loitered on the pavement, shifty and exposed in the lamplight and the cab-driver's gaze. As she was fumbling on the doorstep for her key and Bruce was fumbling for her, the Vicar and his lodger got out of their battered Saab.

'Good evening to you, Miss Pepper,' he called out, mockingly, as she dropped her keys in the dark and Bruce stooped to her ankles to retrieve them.

'Rot in hell,' she called amiably back and took the couple's laughter as a benediction.

Bruce kissed her again once they were inside the hall. The new bony coldness of him excited her and she led him urgently to the bedroom – no dishonest footling around with cafetières or whisky. They fell to lovemaking with the self-conscious athleticism of film actors performing a sex scene, neither daring, by a momentary gesture or out of place smile, to deny the vital reality of what was taking place. They tugged one another's clothes off with stern concentration. She pushed his face back on to the mattress by his hair and bit at his neck. He rolled her off him and pinned her hands at her side to work gravely at her nipples with mouth, nose, stubbled cheek. She slid down beneath him to rub her face in the mustiness of his heavy balls. Manhandling her like a dead thing, he swung her up on to her knees and, clasping her from behind with an arm across her neck, slid his other hand between the cheeks of her arse and down between her legs to cup the lips of her aching vagina in a hot, slightly trembling palm. He was firm and smooth and she liked the weightiness of him about her, wanted it to crush her into untroubled silence.

When he reached for the light, she grasped his hand back, pulled his mouth on to hers before he could protest.

'Rubbers,' he managed to hiss in her ear at last. 'Do you have any?'

'What?'

'Condoms.'

'Oh yes. I think so. In the drawer.'

Again he fumbled. Something fell over.

'It's no good. I can't do it in the dark,' he said.

Blinking in the sudden light, she watched him tug open

the little drawer and find a foil packet. Something chilled her in the way he paused to check the thing's use-by date. Something chilled her too in the way he worked his cock with his fist while she opened the packet for him. Protected now, he turned out the light, kissed her again and entered her. Now, however, she found she could only lie there beneath him, inert. He continued to thrust away at her for several minutes, maintaining the sex scene script single-handed as best he could, but it took two to sustain the passionate illusion and he slid to a halt, still throbbing inside her.

'What's up?' he asked, stroking her cheek. 'Did I say something wrong? Was it the light? Listen. I can't see you now. You can't see me. I could be anybody. Get that? I could be *anybody* fucking you here.' She had to hand him marks for effort.

'Sorry,' she said. 'It's not you. It's me.'

'Hey,' he breathed. 'Ssh. It's okay. When you're ready, okay?'

He slipped out of her, held her close, stroked her breasts, her abdomen, her thighs. Breathing heavily, his hair brushing her stomach, he did his best to excite her, instead, with his fingers. His relentless massage of her clitoris, however, was somehow too educated, evoking all too vividly the impatient instructions of other women, and after a while she could not help but brush his hand aside. Undeterred, only concerned, he pulled the duvet up around them and held her in his arms.

'Is there someone else?' he asked.

'Yes,' she said, furious at herself for the way her mind filled with images of Sam and Jamie. 'In a way. Yes. Sorry. It's this guy I know. He –'

'Yes?'

'He's got sick.'

'Hey, I'm sorry.'

'Hey,' she echoed spitefully. 'It's AIDS.'

She couldn't resist it. Now it was his turn to freeze up; she knew he would assume that the 'guy' in question was an ex of hers.

'Wow,' he said and she fancied she heard the little rustle as his dick shrivelled into retreat, sloughing off its condom like an old skin. 'It's weird, you know,' he went on after a shocked interval. 'Because I'm from the Bay Area, right, where there are one fuck of a lot of cases, and still I don't know anybody who's got it.'

'Who does your hair?' she asked. 'A nun?'

'Geeze!' he nudged her. 'Honestly!' He was genuinely shocked at her irreverence – not for the Church or liberal etiquette but for mortality. She felt him grope between his legs for the derelict condom and drop it over the side of the bed. 'Hey,' he asked. 'I brought Abby over some dope – best Californian sensamilla – and it's still stuffed in the heel of my shoe. Would you like a joint?'

'You mean this is the alternative?'

'You never give up, do you?'

'Believe me,' she promised him, 'I've given up. Yes. A joint would be most satisfactory. Let's go the whole hog and light a candle while we're at it.'

She lit a candle while he rolled two joints. She observed him in the softer light and realised he was really very sexy.

'One *each*?' she gasped.

'Why not? I'm not going to get around to seeing Abby anyway.'

Coming on top of the cheap wine and interrupted coitus, the dope took swift and powerful effect. She laughed uncontrollably, as did he, as the bed seemed to float off the floor. Munching handfuls of Natural Crunch with freeze dried strawberry hunks straight from the box, they soon had one another convulsed over recitals of Bad Sex They Had Known, each seeking to outdo the other with stories which, in truth, were sadder than they were funny. Then she reached the point where she was so stoned she couldn't speak and he went upstairs to put on some music. He made the big mistake of putting on the Barber violin concerto, thus enabling her to round off a perfectly horrible evening by crying all over him. She cried about Jamie, and about all the men she had known who had died already and about all the men and, all too probably, women she was sure would die before she reached forty. One by one she cremated the party guests until only Belgian Agnes was keeping her sad company shovelling all the ash.

Whether he stayed the night, whether he slept even, after such a ghastly lullaby, she had no idea. He was gone when she woke on Sunday morning. There was a note on the kitchen table.

'Remember,' it said, 'There is nothing so bad that Positive Thinking cannot heal. Be cool. Stay well. Bruce.'

She had no address, no telephone number, no surname, not even an inkling of what he did while managing to live in San Francisco and remain untouched by the epidemic around him. Jamie would be proud of her.

53

In bringing his grandson back to recuperate in his care at The Roundel, Edward had acted with a rare impulsiveness that surprised him. During their drive from the airport, Alison had mentioned pneumonia, so he knew in part what to expect. The boy's painful shortness of breath, his evident weakness, was like a TB sufferer's. His obstinate graveyard humour and the effort laughter caused him, reminded Edward of long-stay unfortunates in the isolation hospital for whom there had been no hope of recovery. But nothing had prepared him for the emaciation. The shock of seeing Jamie hunched up against his pillows, distorted by weight loss, recalled the horrors of his first glimpse at pictures of liberated concentration camps. Only this was in colour and he could not look away and wait for it to pass.

On leaving the hospital, he had exchanged quiet words with the duty nurse, explaining his plans for Jamie, and confessing his ignorance of the disease's nature. The leaflets she had given him contained more disturbing parallels; along with the bloody sputum he had begun to cough up, night sweats and a dramatic loss of energy had been the symptoms which had finally drawn the attention of the internment camp doctors to his pulmonary TB all those years ago.

Back in the late 'fifties, his self-disgust following the end of his affair with Myra had pitched him headlong towards a second breakdown, only this time the tools of self-negation were alcohol, overwork and compulsive womanising. What began in a swaggering, I'll-show-her spirit swiftly achieved its own dangerous momentum. It had been Heini, of all people, then scarcely old enough to know much of suffering himself, who had intervened and diverted Edward towards the calm Kensington consulting room of Sonia Keppel. Over two long years, during which he had seen no-one and written nothing of worth, this small, enigmatic woman with her softly insistent voice and calculatedly self-effacing manner, had brought him to see how much misplaced guilt he had suppressed. With her guidance, he had come to a mature grieving and acceptance of the loss of his childhood as well as his family. She had led him, not to happiness exactly, but to an equilibrium based on self-knowledge rather than drugs or self-deluding denial.

'You'll never let this go, Edward-Eli,' she had warned him. 'You have this persistent sense of debt that's positively Wagnerian. We're both rational people so we don't believe in curses. The funny thing with curses, though, is the damage they continue to do even if we don't believe in them. Sometimes the only way to lift them is to suspend your rational dismissal and enter their crazy logic. Maybe all the months and money you've spent with me will get you nowhere and you'll never stop hurting yourself for having been saved, until you save someone else.'

Trapped in a Rexbridge cinema watching the shuffling black and white lines of hollow-eyed concentration camp prisoners, he had been besieged by feelings of guilt and helplessness. Faced with his grandson's living corpse however, he felt he *could* do something. Could this, he wondered, be his chance to lift the curse?

Having got the boy away, however, he saw immediately how futile was his impulse to 'rescue' him. Driving him out of London, the boy dozing in a blanket oblivious to their wintry surroundings, he was relentlessly reminded of Sally's mercy mission to snatch him from the Rexbridge psychiatric unit. He imagined that she had felt a similar sense of impulsive daring, a similar fear of risk-taking and of blindly smothering love. He could not save Jamie, however. The 'rescue' evinced only a naïve belief in the whole-some powers of the countryside over the perfidious influences of the city; the boy was as locked in his sickness as he was in his sickly perversion. Edward knew he spoke to his lover every day – he had occasionally stumbled in on their telephone calls. He was amazed, and sickened that, in full possession of the facts, the boy continued to cling to the very thing that was causing his death. He had initially thought that once they were alone together, he could set about getting to know Jamie properly as an adult, making up for lost time, wringing some meaning from the precious months left them. Instead he retreated to the musical territories they had shared during his grandson's early boyhood.

'I'm a coward,' he told Miriam during her first visit to see how Jamie was progressing. She had appeared with quantities of food which she was packing into the freezer in The Roundel's kitchen. Jamie was taking an after-lunch doze upstairs.

'Do you expect me to contradict you?' Her tone was suddenly abrasive.

Edward shrugged, opting for humour.

'It would be nice,' he said hopefully.

'Well forget it. You were the same about Uncle Thomas.'

'How do you mean? Thomas and I got on. I could *always* talk to Thomas.'

'Exactly. You talked *to* him, not *with* him. You always kept him at arm's length because of what he was and how he felt towards you. It embarrassed you.'

'Oh really,' Edward tried to wave her nonsense away with a hand and reach for his coffee. Miriam shut the freezer lid with a muffled bump.

'Thomas loved you,' she said. 'And you could never accept that.'

'Of course I accepted it. I mean, I couldn't *reciprocate* but –'

'You were relieved when he died and stopped making demands on you. You didn't even get me out of school for his funeral and he was a better father to me than you ever were.'

'Oh really?'

'Yes. Really. Thomas talked *with* me. He wanted to know what I wanted, what I thought about things, who I wanted to be.'

'And I didn't?'

'You never showed it if you did. You just wrote cheques, and waited for me to grow, like some impatient gardener.'

'Ah.' Edward smiled wearily at the table top.

'Don't laugh at me. You're always laughing at me!'

'I'm not laughing,' he assured her. She sat heavily in a chair opposite him looking momentarily, strangely, like his mother, her cheeks flushed with irritation, her plump hands restlessly picking at things. She had never looked like Sally. Only Alison looked like Sally. 'What does all this have to do with Jamie?' he asked.

'Everything,' she said. 'Your disgust, your fear, are neither here nor there. Just give him some space and show him some respect. I'm learning so much from all this and I think you could too if only you'd let yourself.'

'I think I'm a little old to start learning.'

'You haven't had a serious illness since your early twenties. You're strong as an ox. Right now, he's older than you are.'

'Don't bully me. You always bully me.'

'Somebody's got to.'

'I'm sorry,' he insisted. 'I can't change the way I feel. You . . . You don't like parsnips. I feel uncomfortable around homosexuals.'

'There's no comparison.'

'Of course there is. It's an irrational dislike. Maybe it's a race memory. Whatever it is, simple good will won't make it go away.'

'At least try. For me.'

'All right,' he sighed. 'For you. For my poor neglected daughter, I'll try.'

'Thank you.'

She smiled. He was fobbing her off. If he told of the churning revulsion he felt when he saw one man hold another's hand or confessed that no number of documentaries could rid him of the gut belief that this disease was a direct result of puerile self-indulgence, she would probably pack her son into her expensive car and drive him off to Essex. Coward or no, he badly wanted Jamie at The Roundel. For there were other things he could not tell her – for all his bluff dismissals, he did recognise that he had failed her as a father. He could not tell her that the bewildered, helpless love he felt for her children was the only chance he had to redeem that failure. He was a man, after all, with all a man's foolish, unfashionable pride.

Miriam became calmer. She poured herself a cup of coffee and reached into her shopping basket for a packet of chocolate biscuits which she opened between them.

'I meant to tell you at the time,' she said, 'But I was so het up. I never spoke to Venetia Peake. I mean, of course I spoke to her but I never told her all those silly things about alcoholic nannies and parcelling me off to school, truly I didn't. I think she got an Old Girls list from my year and tracked some people down. Josie Forbush or someone. Someone with a grudge.'

'I did wonder,' he confessed. 'It was kind of you to protect me.'

Miriam made a small, non-committal noise in her throat and ate another biscuit.

'She's called, you know. Myra,' he told her. 'She's called several times. I've only answered once.'

'What does she want?'

He thought a moment.

'I don't know. I think perhaps she's curious. She'd like to see me again. See how I've aged.'

'That would be a shock for her, given the way she looks.' Miriam looked across and saw that he was serious. 'Don't you want to see her?'

'I don't think so.'

'But it might be fun.'

'Miriam, you can't have it both ways. I thought Myra was meant to be the bugbear of your childhood dreams and a Hollywood monster.'

'She is. She was. But still, it might be fun.'

'I thought you found geriatric romance grotesque.'

'Who said anything about romance?' Miriam looked alarmed. 'You could just *see* her. That's all.'

'So you could brag to Francis's friends about meeting her?'

'Not at all. God you're so unfair sometimes! I wouldn't even want to be there. Of course I wouldn't. You could just meet for lunch, in London. She comes over to shop sometimes. I read it in a magazine. Now *she* could set you right on a few things; she does a lot of work for AIDS charities. Honestly, Dad, it might be fun. A trip down memory lane.'

'I don't think so.'

Edward trusted the glance he threw her was sufficiently withering.

54

As the recuperative fortnight at The Roundel turned into three weeks, then four, Jamie abandoned any pretence of an intention to return to London. After the crowded uneventfulness of his time in hospital, his days and nights in the old house were of a meditative monotony that soon became sweet to him. He rose when he felt ready – often not before mid-morning – took a long bath, went for a walk, lunched with his grandfather, slept again, read a book, ate supper with his grandfather and retired early. He spent hours just sitting. In his overcrowded childhood he had not appreciated how full the house was of good places to sit. He would begin to read or listen to a programme on the radio, find his attention drawn to the nearest window, and become peaceably transfixed by the unpeopled, unchanging view across ploughed fields silvered with frost, the river steaming slightly, or into the smaller landscape of the garden. Alone, or almost alone, for the first time in his life, he came to appreciate stillness and the space it gave for thought. Sitting in silence, he found that thoughts came to feel as distinct as speech so that sometimes, after sitting for a long while, he was not sure whether he had merely thought something or spoken it aloud to the empty room.

He did not spend hours with his grandfather. The knowledge that he was working in a room nearby was often company enough. The distant sounds of his synthesiser and sequencer, producing now the noise of a full symphony orchestra, now the intimate tones of a madrigal ensemble, was the aural equivalent of a comforting nightlight. When they were together, his grandfather often played them music rather than risk tiring Jamie with conversation. Jamie had not heard so much music since he was a teenager. They listened to whole operas at a sitting, whole cycles of string quartets. As in his childhood, music became their safe lingua franca.

Sam, Alison and Miriam paid visits. When Sam came, Jamie's grandfather acquired an unforeseen engagement in London and left the two of them to spend the weekend in bed and luxuriate in one another's company. When Alison came, she interrupted Jamie's routine with the brief imposition of her own habitual weekend behaviour – quantities of newsprint, coffee, convenience food, fitful attempts to tame the garden. Miriam worked in the garden too. She no sooner laid eyes on Jamie than emotions welled up in her she had to channel into practical action rather than give them voice. She would barely be through with hugging him in greeting before she was reaching for the gardening gloves or moaning that Alison had lost the secateurs again. Jamie was almost hurt by this. She did much the same on the telephone. She had no sooner got through and asked how he was before she started saying things like, 'Well, darling, I better go and feed Frank. You know how he is. I just wanted to hear your news . . .'

Worried, on her second visit, that Jamie was still not gaining weight, she began by riling his grandfather with an inquisition as to what the two of them had been eating. Then, seized by a sudden inspiration, she pulled on some gloves and marched with a hefty fork to the ruined greenhouse that leant against the wall in the most sheltered corner of the garden. She returned a while later with a big plant in her hand, its glossy leaves drooping and browned slightly with the effects of frost. It was a lone, self-sown survivor of the commune's long-lost marijuana crop, unspotted by the local constabulary, and spared Alison's occasional weeding forays, first by her ignorance and then by its authoritative size. Confident yet righteous, as though she were arranging flowers, Miriam dried its leaves off in a low oven, then donned an apron to bake the unappetising results into a double batch of gingerbread which had an aftertaste of bonfires. Packing half the batch into the deep freeze, she explained that her latest watercolouring pupil at the hospital had assured her the herb did wonders for suppressed appetites, while ginger counteracted nausea.

'It's not for fun,' she assured Jamie. 'It's strictly medicinal. Your sister's not to have any and you're to eat one a day. And you're not to tell your grandfather. He'd only be shocked.'

Jamie couldn't help noticing that his mother had slipped a handful of the leaves into her handbag and wondered if she were regressing or merely pursuing a small nostalgic indulgence. The gingerbread worked, up to a point, and he began to put on a little weight. Sometimes it made him so stoned that, far from giving him a hunger rush, he just sat for hours feeling other-worldly and forgot to eat altogether. Once he fed Sam a slice, thinking it might be fun to stay in control while Sam relaxed beside him, but Sam relaxed to the point where he started crying and couldn't stop.

When Sam's job on the Wandsworth site came to an end, he brought the Volkswagen down, filled with extra clothes and possessions from the flat.

'You don't want to go back there,' he asked. 'Do you?'

'Not much,' Jamie admitted. 'Do you mind?'

'I can't live there without you, that's all,' Sam said and it was understood that a new phase in their life together was beginning. After trying out various beds, they moved to a larger room that faced south. Jamie's old room, with its narrow bed and small, barred window, now had all the monastic connotations of a sick room, and he would only return there occasionally to lie alone when he was sleeping badly or wanted to nap in the daytime. He refused to let the flat. It was important to him to keep the possibility open that they could always jump in the car and drive up for a wild weekend if they felt like it. But they never did.

Sam hated to be idle for long. It made him restive and short-tempered. Tidying out the mess of dried-up paint tins and rotting boxes of carefully stored newspapers and jam jars so as to make room in the garage for Jamie's car alongside his grandfather's, he unearthed an old black motorbike, complete with mildewed side-car. It looked like a museum piece.

'It was Sally's,' Jamie's grandfather told him. 'My wife's. I thought we got rid of that years ago.' He touched the worn leather seat, ran a finger through the clogged cobwebs that had clouded the speedometer. 'You can tinker with it if you like but I doubt it still goes after all this time.'

Challenged, and glad of a project, Sam took the thing apart, made a few trips into Rexbridge for spares and tools and began lovingly to reassemble it. One of the bedrooms became briefly toxic with paint fumes. One end of the kitchen table, covered in newspaper, became littered with filthy engine parts he was gradually wirebrushing back to an approximation of their old glory. With the first days of spring, his work was finished. Jamie was staring out of an upstairs window at the daffodils that seemed to have coloured the garden's winter palette overnight, when he was startled by what sounded like a rook-scarer exploding followed by the revving of an engine. He came out of the front door just as his grandfather emerged from the studio, to find Sam performing a lap of honour around the house, grinning like a child with a new toy.

Touched at the trouble Sam had taken, Jamie's grandfather dismissed his suggestion of selling it off to a collector and said his efforts had as good as purchased it. He declined Sam's offer of a thank-you ride so Sam took Jamie out, covered in a rug and tucked down in the sidecar. Jamie would have felt safer riding pillion, wrapped around the driver, but the seat was far too small for two. Bouncing along, his head on a level with Sam's waist, convinced they would be stopped any minute for not wearing helmets, he was terrified the sidecar would become detached somehow and hurtle off into a dyke or a field below the road. Here, he thought, was yet another reason for respecting his dead kinswoman. Relieved to be returned home in one piece, he was afraid to hurt Sam's feelings by refusing to go out again. Sam divined his fear, however, and spared him, buzzing out on his own into Rexbridge or off around the fenland lanes whenever the unstirred atmosphere at The Roundel made him long for sensation or he felt himself beginning to brood.

'It goes faster with no-one else on board,' he enthused.

'I don't want to know,' said Jamie, and bought him a magnetic St Christopher to stick on the petrol tank. He also bought him a helmet and, for further protection, gave him his big leather jacket, bought in an ultra-macho biker store in New York but never previously worn on anything faster than the 31 bus to Earl's Court. Sam's excursions brought Jamie relief too, used as he had begun to grow again to the pleasures of solitude, but he liked it when Sam returned, cheeks pink and cold. The feel of him bulked up by the jacket occasionally stoked up his testosterone levels so depleted by drugs and infection.

Sam made enquiries around local building contractors but there was far less building going on there than in the city, and firms were far stricter about who they employed and the terms on which they employed them. Jamie's grandfather paid Sam to build him some new bookshelves then, satisfied with his handiwork, asked him to repair the studio's guttering. Miriam found him work next, repointing the walls of the older house.

'I know it's Alison's responsibility really,' she apologised, 'but poor Angel barely earns enough to buy clothes and food and it would be criminal to let the place fall apart.'

Sam was grateful for the money and happy to do work which didn't take him away from Jamie. Jamie viewed their intervention ambivalently, however. He felt sure they were only paying up so they could somehow negate the problem of Sam being his lover by turning him into a kind of estate handyman. When he shared his doubts, Alison told him not to be so paranoid.

'The work needs doing,' she said reasonably. 'It's nicer to pay somebody we know and love than have your peace and quiet invaded by a load of strangers with noisy radios and friends in the villages they can gossip to.'

'So you *are* embarrassed by us. You're trying to keep us quiet now!'

'Jamie. Think a little.' Alison sat on the arm of Jamie's chair and stroked his hair off his face. 'Does that honestly seem likely?'

'Suppose not,' he conceded, after a moment, but his doubts remained.

'As a matter of fact,' she went on, 'I'm not as poor as Ol' Big Hair seems to think. When she's paid for the repointing – which she should have paid for years ago in any case –

I'll see if I can get Sam to fix some of those rotten windows upstairs.'

Jamie was loath to admit it, but he was jealous sometimes of the place Sam had begun to carve, in his own right, in his family's heart. If he was dozing upstairs and Miriam or Alison rang, he would lie there listening to the bluff ease with which Sam now took their calls and chatted with them, resenting it and not knowing why. Now that his grandfather could no longer avoid Sam indefinitely, the two of them had begun to talk as well, sporadically. Their relations were not helped, however, by Sam reasserting his rights to much of Jamie's time his grandfather had been enjoying alone. Jamie's grandfather plainly resented the change, but could not voice his resentment without openly recognising the reason *why* Sam had a prior claim on Jamie's time. They were stiff with one another and uncomprehending. His grandfather affected to find Sam's Plymouth accent impenetrable, while Sam claimed the other's 'German' manner was forbidding.

'It's like being back in school,' he protested. 'I look at him and I don't know what to say.'

Sam's loving restoration of the motorbike, however, and the older man's subsequent gift of it, marked a turning-point between them. At first they had called each other nothing at all, contenting themselves with 'you' to one another's faces and with Grumps and Your Associate respectively behind one another's backs, but Jamie knew that he could not in all honesty continue to claim that his grandfather treated his lover as an employee once they were on first name terms. Sam was the only one of Jamie's friends ever to be allowed to refer to the great man as anything other than Mr Pepper. It happened quite suddenly. 'What's this then, Edward?' Sam asked one evening, when a piece of music had caught his attention. Jamie looked up, surprised, thinking a fourth person had walked into the room.

Sam would gaily broach the unbroachable subjects too: 'So you were too young to know any Nazis personally?' he asked, and, 'If you're Jewish, how come Jamie isn't?' and, another time which had really made Jamie cringe, 'So what did you do in the war, then, Edward?'

Sam and Edward talked as equals in a way that Jamie and his grandfather could never begin to do. Sam began to go over to the studio on his own and borrowed discs and tapes to play, listening to them with a perseverance that made Jamie suspect his grandfather of seriously undertaking his lover's musical education.

'Just don't start taking piano lessons from him,' he warned.

As well as telling him what to listen to or how to listen to it, his grandfather began to tell Sam things about Jamie. Jamie was, after all, their most solid common ground, however much the older man fought shy of understanding the younger ones' relations.

'You never said you sang,' Sam confronted Jamie after supper one evening.

'I don't.'

'But you *did*.'

'It's not important.'

'Sing for me, then.' Sam grinned, as though expecting tricks from a dog.

'I can't. Not any more. It would be embarrassing.'

'Edward thinks it would help strengthen your lungs again. He says he used to sing when he was getting over TB.' Jamie threw a glance across the hall to his grandfather who was frowning beneath a standard lamp over one of the glossy magazines Jamie was addicted to and which he found so shockingly superficial.

'Oh does he now?'

His grandfather nodded without looking up from his article.

'I was talking to Dr Marshall about it,' he said, turning a page. 'I think the regular breathing and controlled exhalation might help you overcome your shortness of breath.'

'I can do breathing exercises without singing,' Jamie snorted. 'I do them when I go for my walks.'

His grandfather and Sam exchanged a glance that spoke of private understanding and his grandfather shrugged patiently.

'As you see fit,' he sighed.

Jamie understood, then, what it was he so resented in Sam's slowly developing intimacy with his relatives. It was nothing as ordinary as jealousy – it had been in his power, after all, to keep Sam away from them and he had chosen not to. Rather, what upset him was that their behaviour implied that Sam was now easier to talk to than *he* was; he had become the sick person over whose bed and head and wheelchair people talked, and Sam had become the cheery nurse to whom visitors at the bedside preferred to direct their conversation.

This realisation was all it took to bring Jamie to a decision regarding his future, or lack of it. Without telling Sam, he contacted Geraint, the facilitator at the HIV support group he had been to in London, and asked to be sent the relevant forms for making both his will and his living will. In the one he left everything to Sam; car, flat, contents, everything, with the exception of some money and the idol, which he left to Alison. In the other, he made it quite clear that, in the event of his next life-threatening illness, he had no desire to receive treatment or medication beyond what was needed to make him comfortable. He still lacked the courage to stop taking the experimental drug he was currently prescribed, fearful of the mysterious symptoms that might replace side-effects which, however unpleasant, were at least a known and predictable evil. He intended to take the forms to a solicitor in Rexbridge and have his signatures witnessed by strangers. There was no need to trouble Sam with the matter before the relevant emergency arose.

One night he was sitting up in bed rereading the papers to make sure he had mentioned everything that was necessary. Sam was downstairs with his grandfather. The telephone rang. Sam answered and talked for a while, indistinctly, then hung up. Insidious as an outbreak of fire on a hearthside rug, an argument developed between the two men. Their words were indecipherable at first, with only a new aggressive punchiness in their phrasing betraying a change in mood, then their voices were raised and Jamie began to hear more clearly.

'Well what would *you* fucking call it?!' Sam suddenly shouted.

'Horror. Tragedy, by all means,' his grandfather shouted back. 'But only that.'

'*Only* that?'

'No-one is being murdered. A disease is not a murder.'

'It *is* when they sit on their arses and watch it spreading.'

'They? Always this mythical They.'

Jamie sat bolt upright, straining his ears and pushing the papers beneath a magazine. Even at this distance he could feel their anger as an electric stiffening of the air, and was relieved once he heard the front door slam. Even when he had tried to make him leave, all those months before, Sam had been angered but not this furious. Jamie had no doubt that if his grandfather had stayed in the house, Sam would have lashed out at him with something harder than words. In confirmation of his fears, he heard Sam kicking out at furniture, shouting to the empty hall.

'Fuck!' he yelled and Jamie heard something fly across the floor with a splintering sound. 'Fuck!' Glass smashed.

'Sam?' Jamie called out. 'Sam?'

Gone were the days when Jamie could spring out of bed. He set his feet carefully on the floor, shuffling them into the slippers Miriam had insisted he start wearing about the house, pulled his towelling gown about him and rolled forward into an uneasy standing position. Hardly waiting for the dizziness to pass, he made for the landing and, clutching the banister, headed downstairs.

It was only a bottle and the coffee table. Just as Jamie rounded the foot of the stairs, Sam muttered under his breath, lashing out at a big chunk of glass with his toe, sending it skittering across the floor through the puddle of red wine.

'Stupid old git,' he spat.

'Sam?'

'Fuck!' Sam kicked at the armchair, though less vigorously.

'What the hell happened? What did he say?' Jamie had to sit down. He sank on to the sofa, pulling his feet up out of the draught. Sam was muttering to himself, pacing. He began to clear up the glass.

'Leave that for a bit,' Jamie told him. 'The floor's stained already. It won't show.'

'Someone'll cut themselves,' Sam insisted crossly, then swore again, dropping a chunk of glass as he cut his finger.

'Leave it. Here. Come and tell me.'

The pain cut through Sam's temper. He stared down as blood oozed from his finger tip and splashed into the wine. He put his finger in his mouth and sucked.

'I nearly punched him,' he mumbled, his mouth full, finally making eye contact.

'I'm glad you didn't.' Jamie patted the sofa beside him. Shamed now, Sam came to sit.

'Hug,' Jamie told him. Sam hugged him.

'You'll get cold,' he said.

'No I won't. What happened?'

Sam sighed, exasperated at the memory.

'Well that was Alison who rang earlier. I thought you were asleep. Sorry.'

'That's okay.'

Sam pulled Jamie to lean against his chest, hugging him with his legs for warmth as he talked.

'She was in a right state. She's just had Sandy on the phone. The lease is up for renewal on the helpline office and the rent's going up by nearly double. They're forcing them out on the street.'

'Shit. But they knew that was going to happen.'

'Yeah but they've just heard their local authority grant's been cut to about two hundred quid, haven't they?'

'*What?*' Jamie was incredulous. 'Why?'

'There's been some fucking report wheeling out a load of statistics that say there's never going to be a hetero epidemic.'

'So? There's no need for a helpline? Other lives don't count? What about the worried well? What about rape victims?'

'That's what I said. When I hung up I explained to that old git and I said it was a fucking holocaust.'

'Ah.'

'And *he* flew off the handle then. I didn't understand at first. Thought he was agreeing with me and was just pissed off about the grant. Then I realised he was saying there was no comparison. I said . . . You don't want to hear this.' He ruffled Jamie's hair.

'*Sam*! Tell me.'

'I said that cutting the grant was no different to sending Jews to ovens. It was discarding a whole bunch of innocent people who just happened to be in the minority. Then that . . . that stupid old *wanker* –'

'Steady.'

'Well he is.'

'What did he say?'

'He said,' Sam assumed a parodic German accent. '"Zere is a vorld of difference between a religious culture and vhere deviants like you choose to put your dicks."'

Jamie was silenced a moment, shocked.

'He doesn't talk like that,' he said at last. 'You know he doesn't.'

'I know,' Sam admitted. 'But that's the way I heard it. Fucking Kraut.'

'He's as English as you or me.'

'Yeah, but –'

'Yeah but nothing. He was upset, Sam.'

'So was I upset.'

'He lost his parents in a death camp, for God's sake. His only sister –'

'You're joking.'

'Hardly. She was experimented on.'

'You never told me.'

'It's not the kind of thing that naturally comes up in a conversation. Anyway, I assumed Alison had told you.'

'She hadn't. Christ.'

Jamie hugged Sam's legs, twisted his head back against Sam's chest to reassure him. 'You needed to get angry and so did he,' he said softly. 'Come on. Let's get to bed.'

But Sam insisted on mopping up the spilled wine and sweeping away the glass first. Jamie sat on the sofa, yawning, hugging a cushion to himself for warmth and watching. Sam worked in silence but the argument was evidently still repeating itself in his head because he abruptly stood up, clutching the dust pan and the brush, which was now stained red with wine, and said, 'It wasn't just Jews they sent to the ovens, you know. It was people like us, too.'

'I *know*. I'm sure he does too.'

Sam was about to reply but he paused a moment. He looked down at the panful of green, jagged edges.

'Only . . . I'm not really like that. You know that, don't you?' he said, almost apologetically.

'I know.'

'I'm . . . I am with you but I'm not interested in other blokes.'

'I *know*, Sam. It's all right. I'm honoured.'

Sam walked away to the kitchen.

'Just thought you should know, that's all,' he said softly.

The following day, while Sam was at work on the repointing, Jamie walked over with a jug of coffee to find his grandfather in the studio. An old acquaintance, guilty at not visiting the hospital, had sent him a packet of Blue Mountain beans, so the luxurious brew was by way of a peace offering.

'Made us some special coffee,' he said. 'Sorry. Are you working?'

'No.' His grandfather swung around on the piano stool. 'Not really.' He carefully set a pencil back in the jam jar to the left of his keyboard while Jamie poured them each a cupful.

'I've been invited to stand in as conductor for some concerts in Stuttgart,' his grandfather announced. 'I think I'll go. I'll have to leave in a couple of days, so I'll probably go up to London tomorrow to sort a few things out with the record company. But I think you two can manage now.' He paused. 'If I made a reservation for dinner in Rexbridge tonight, would your appetite be up to it? My treat. A reservation for the three of us, that is?'

'Yes,' Jamie smiled. 'That would be great. Thank you. Er. Grandpa?'

'Yes?'

'Don't expect Sam to apologise for what he said last night. He won't. Because he meant it. And, well, you know, he's hurting quite badly right now.'

'That makes two of us,' his grandfather observed quietly. He was wearing a green suede waistcoat Jamie had always liked.

'I like that,' Jamie pointed. 'Very smart. Will you leave it to me in your will?'

'Of course.' Feeling unable to reach out to his grandson, Edward touched the waistcoat instead, smoothing the nap of the suede.

'So,' Jamie said. 'Since you're about to disappear again, what about my therapeutic singing lesson?'

'Are you quite sure?' His grandfather frowned. Jamie nodded, going to lean on the piano's flank.

'But there are probably spiders down there it's been so long,' he said.

'Well in that case . . . I think something simple, in the middle of the voice but,' his grandfather stretched up to take a book from the shelf beside him, 'We need something with long phrases to stretch you nicely. Fauré?'

'Fine,' Jamie shrugged. 'My French is terrible, though.'

'Yes.' The old man raised an eyebrow. 'I remember. *Après un Rêve*. I'll take it quite slowly. Stand up straight. Shoulders back. Legs apart.'

'I remember.'

It was only later, when they were dressing up for dinner and Sam confessed to having heard his singing from the top of a ladder, that Jamie realised his grandfather had taken care to choose a song he had already heard his lover admire.

'Well that's as near to an understanding as I think we'll get,' he said wistfully.

'How do you mean?' Sam asked, abandoning the tie he had been struggling with. 'Do I really have to wear this fucking thing? It's like a noose.'

'No.' Jamie shook his head, smiling.

'So how do you mean, "understanding"?'

'Oh. Nothing,' Jamie answered briskly. 'Just being sentimental. Shall I wear the red shirt or the green?'

55

'Where does it ache?' Alison asked. 'Here?'

'Left a bit. That's it. Oh! Oh yes! Oh God, that's good. You can press harder if you like. Oh yes. God!'

'*Now* I know what you sound like in bed!'

'Shut up and rub.'

Jamie was recovering from a four-week infection of cryptosporidiosis. Chronic attacks of diarrhoea four or more times a day stripped him of the proteins and calories the hash gingerbread had helped him regain and his weight had plummeted to an all-time low. The top of the fridge was laden with an assortment of high calorie body-building drinks and liquid foods he took several times a day – Complan, Bengers, Horlicks, Lucozade, Dunns River – drinks for little old ladies or hulking athletes, and his pockets rattled with vitamin bottles. Alison felt sure that left to his own devices he would not have bothered, but he saw how the weight loss worried them all. He carried a kitchen timer clipped to his shirt front whose beeping reminded him when it was time for more drugs. She noticed that he always sat on a cushion now to shield his protuberant bones. He felt the cold too. There was not a breath of wind and they were out in full sunshine that was truly warm. Alison had only a tee-shirt and flimsy skirt on but Jamie wore a thick cardigan, its collar turned up to warm his neck. Massaging away an ache in his shoulders, she could feel his bones even through the layer of chunky wool. It was like stroking a greyhound. Tension caused by the cold he felt seemed in turn to bring on muscular aches and pains. Both she and Sam had offered to drive him to the clinic in Rexbridge for a course of aromatherapeutic massage and reflexology but the very thought of travel left him too sleepy to move.

Sam was high up on a ladder, scraping old paint off a window frame. With the easy assurance of an acrobat, he turned around on his rung so that he was leaning towards the house, tugged his shirt off, let it fall and returned to his scraping, entirely unaware of his audience below. Stunned, for all that she was now as familiar with his body as any workmate, Alison had frozen to watch.

'It's so unfair,' she said, remembering herself and beginning to massage the back of Jamie's neck with her thumbs and forefingers.

'What is?'

'Why couldn't *I* have been a man?'

'Not *that* again. You could have an operation you know. It's very sophisticated nowadays, apparently. No more turning aside at the moment of passion to slip in icky silicone rods. Now they let you puff the thing up with a little pump disguised as one of your balls.'

'Oh *please*!' She cuffed him on the hair and flopped into a deck-chair beside him. If she massaged him much longer, he'd start to bruise. 'You know what I mean. Just look at him.'

'I am. I am.'

'He's so assured. So easy. If a woman took off her shirt like that it would be a statement. When he does it, it's . . . He . . . He just does it.'

'He never used to strip off on site. He's very shy really. Anyway, there are plenty of fat slobs who take their shirts off too. You wouldn't want to be one of them.'

'Those awful ones with that sort of bristly cleavage where their jeans are slipping down!'

'So what sort of man would you have liked to be?' Jamie looked at her quizzically, shading his eyes from the sun.

'Oh. I dunno,' she said. 'Handsome. Clever. Self-contained. I'd have liked very dark thick eyebrows and blue eyes and a nose like Paul Newman's. And I'd like to have been a really good jazz pianist. How about you? Haven't you ever wondered what kind of girl you'd have been?'

'I've always been quite happy being male,' he said.

'Yes, but.'

'Well presumably I'd have been you.'

She laughed; the thought was so very strange. She imagined him looking at her with her face.

'It could have happened so easily,' she said. 'Would you have minded?'

'Not a bit.' He grinned. 'Normality has its compensations.'

'Don't you call me normal.'

'You know what I mean.' He stretched luxuriously at the thought. 'But if I'd been a woman I'd have had lots of babies.'

'Really?' she asked. He had never discussed children with her before; none of their close friends had any as yet.

'I'd surround myself,' he went on. 'I'd found a tribe. I'd have a huge nurturing bosom – like Liz Taylor in the early 'seventies or some whore out of Fellini – and I'd have masses of hair. The children wouldn't be very clean but they'd be well fed and loved and happy.'

'Who would you want to father them?' she asked, smiling, guessing his answer.

'Who do you think?' Jamie glanced up at Sam. 'He'd have to marry me first, though. Make an honest woman of me. He'd probably stray, you know, start sleeping around, because I'd take a kind of perverse delight in losing my spectacular figure. But he'd always come back and I'd always forgive him and our makings-up would be sure to make me pregnant again.'

'I can't believe you're saying all this.'

'Neither can I. Maybe it's the drugs talking.'

'Why *do* male-to-female transsexuals have such pre-war attitudes? Roberta at the helpline wants to have her bottom pinched and be propositioned by married men during train journeys.'

'It's because gender matters so much to them and it's hurt them so badly. They want certainty. They want men to be men, and women to be subservient. Why don't *you* have babies?' he added abruptly.

'*Jamie!*' She laughed, shocked. 'Babies need time and money and responsibility and . . . and a suitable father.'

'So?' He glanced up at the ladder then back at her. 'Have babies with him.' He made it sound the most natural thing in the world. Which of course, she reflected, it could be.

'Sssh,' she said.

'He can't hear us. He's got the blow torch going.'

'Don't Jamie. This is silly.'

'No it isn't. I'm breaking Pepper's Law and plotting our destinies. Since I can't have his babies, why shouldn't you?'

'He's gay, for one thing.'

'No he isn't.'

'Whatever. He's not . . .' She broke off as the full significance of what he had said sank in, then pushed it aside with instinctive anger. 'Just stop it, Jamie.'

'*He*'d want to. He loves children. He's a big softy. I used to catch him looking enviously at young fathers in the park.'

'Are you sure he was only envious?'

He looked up at Sam, refusing to acknowledge her jibe.

'Yes,' he said. 'I'm sure he was. He looked as though he wanted to push a child on a swing, teach it football, carry it on his shoulders.'

'Oh please. What's come over you?'

'You really don't understand, do you?' he asked.

'Yes I do,' she insisted. 'You want me to make babies for the Fatherland.'

'I want you to make babies for me. Just one would do.'

'Well that's big of you.'

'Having a baby and breastfeeding it would reduce your risk of getting cancer. Everyone says so. And we do have a family history. Granny Sally's mother died of it and Miriam had that bump taken off last year.'

'Can't I just get a puppy? They're far cheaper.'

'But I think you *should*.'

'Have a puppy?'

'A *baby*.'

'Jamie please. Let's drop it, okay?' She stood impatiently. He was stabbing at a still bruised area of desire and there was something manic in his persistence. She hated the way he had taken to ranting sometimes. He caught her eye and saw she was in earnest.

'Okay,' he said.

'Come on.' She glanced at her watch and held out a hand to help him out of the deckchair.

'Time, hon,' he called up to Sam, and followed her in, clutching his cushion.

Alison had never been a great watcher of television beyond the occasional old film or arts documentary relevant to her work. Since the revelation of their grandfather's relationship with Myra Toye, however, she had become a guiltily faithful watcher of *Mulroney Park*. Its storylines were wilfully melodramatic, unconsciously absurd, its costumes grotesque, its standards of acting miserable, but it exerted a horrible fascination. The characters were uniformly unpleasant – grasping, lecherous, unprincipled. Even the acknowledged hero and heroine were capable only of self-justifying serial fidelity. Myra's performance – in common with the rest of the country, they all referred to her by her Christian name, sure of being understood – Myra's performance stood out among the dross; an over-blown bloom of Old Hollywood, transplanted into a cultural desert of lip-gloss and collagen implants.

Sam stepped into the room just as the title sequence was finishing, dusting off his hands on his trousers, his shirt draped over one naked shoulder. He sat on the rug, leaning against the sofa between their legs, instantly rapt in the observance of a weekly ritual. Even as she watched, Alison was aware of the strong scent of burnt paint and hot body he was giving off. She found herself staring at the screen without taking in what was happening, Jamie's words about Sam revolving in her head. The telephone rang and all three of them ignored it.

Myra's character – Louella – was overreaching herself as usual. She was blackmailing her former husband with a compromising photograph sold her by her private detective, she was pursuing a court case for custody of the children from her second marriage and, unable to help herself, putting herself in the hands of blackmailers by cheating on her third husband with the preposterously well-constructed tennis coach she had bribed from the bed of her vindictive but currently comatose daughter. Her steps were also being dogged by the son of her first marriage, crazed after a brain-washing at the hands of the desert sect he had joined when she had disowned him for being gay. None of this was out of the ordinary. Louella was trouble and incapable of opening her mouth without making mischief. But she had a god-like capacity for transformation and last-ditch escapes. She had outwitted hijackers before now, and a maniacal scalpel-wielding beautician. They all knew she would brush her plague of husbands from her like so many fruit flies and tire of the tennis coach too before the current series was done.

When the climactic scene, at a big anniversary party, came to a sudden end with Louella pumped full of bullets, marbling the waters of her vast swimming pool a shocking vermilion, it was as unexpected and shocking as if the actress's own assassination had been broadcast live. Alison laughed at the bravura of the scene. She assumed that Myra had tired of the series and been offered a more exciting role elsewhere. Jamie, however, reacted as though to a personal affront.

'How could they do that?' he gasped.

'Maybe she's not dead,' Sam suggested, softly concerned. 'She wasn't last time.'

'Of course she's dead. Look!' Jamie pointed to the screen where, as the titles finished rolling, the traditional post-title shot – always the curtain-raiser to the next week's episode – revealed a huge marble grave laden with orchids and chrysanthemum wreaths. 'She's dead.' He zapped the television into silence with the remote control unit. 'I'm never watching it again.'

'Who do you think killed her?' Sam asked.

'I don't care.' Jamie was breathing fast, almost hyperventilating in his distress.

'It's not the end of the world, Jamie,' he reasoned. 'She'll do something else. Something better maybe.'

'She *was Mulroney Park*. It'll be nothing without her. How could they? Louella was just about to buy out Warnerco. I could tell she was. And I'm sure she was getting back together with Rex.'

'Not now she isn't.'

'He still loves her, you know.'

'Sure he does.'

Alison realised Sam was humouring him as one might a lunatic.

'They cut her down in her prime,' Jamie went on. He was ranting now. 'Bastards.'

'Don't worry, Jamie,' she was about to say. 'It's only television.'

The words died in her throat, however, because she feared his angry reply. The three of them sat in stunned silence, staring at the black screen, and she began to feel something of his horror at the arbitrary slaying. The weekly instalments of the series had been a discreet way of mapping out a future. Jamie's refusal to follow it further inevitably carried fatalistic overtones.

In all these months she had seen him rage at the indignities of illness and joke hollowly about the accelerated pace at which he was now ageing, but he had never let her see him panic. The approaching certainty of his death was not something they had discussed, but she had begun to assume that he was confronting it with a kind of equanimity, a mournful acceptance. Now she was not so sure. They had all been so careful, but the television, in all its casual vulgarity, had provided an open window through which dread had slithered into the house.

56

Jamie couldn't sleep. The day had been hot and from late afternoon the sky had hazed over and the atmosphere had thickened with a tension that only rain could ease. Though night had long since fallen, he found the charge on the air so tangible that the darkness enveloping the house was as unconvincing as a stage effect. His mind was as active, his body as restless, as if it were high noon. Slowly he rose from the bed, pulled his dressing gown about him and went to push aside the curtain. There was no moon. No stars shone. They had come to bed without remembering to turn out all of the lights, so a thin glow spilled from the kitchen windows down below picking out a few glossy rose leaves and the outline of a garden chair. Jamie opened the window. It had seized up slightly where Sam had painted it and the sash-weights knocked in their channels as it suddenly gave way. Sam stirred on the bed as he often did during the night. He mumbled, reached out an arm, rolled over, tugged the bedding newly about him then subsided back into sleep. Jamie could not remember when Sam had last done more than press a kiss to his cheek or hold him in his arms. He had liked to be held in Sam's arms, had liked to fall asleep that way, in the happier months before he started dozing his days away, when he had still been sleepy at bedtime. Now however the somnolent weight of Sam's arm across him felt less a secure embrace, more a securing restraint.

'Be still,' it said. 'Thus far and no further. Sleep now,' it said, when sleep was the last pleasure on Jamie's mind.

As Sam treated him increasingly like a restive, fractious

child to be stilled with soft words and the reassuring pressure of an unshifting hand, Jamie was increasingly reduced to enjoying Sam's nightly company as one might that of a faithful hound – comforted by its neighbourly warmth, reassured by the occasional sounds of it stretching and resettling in the darkness.

He returned to the bed but, rather than lie down again, he sat at the opposite end from the pillows, leaning against the old quilt draped over the endboard by Sam's feet. His eyes accustomed to the darkness, he could just make out where Sam lay, saw his head and shoulders as a thicker patch of black against the deep grey of sheets and pillows. He knew his lips would be slightly parted, his hands spread, loose-fingered, where they lay, his legs stretched out to the mattress's limits. Jamie replayed scenes of their lovemaking in his mind; Sam carrying him across the room to the windowsill, gasping slightly under the strain but determined to make it; Sam pulling a shirt off him so eagerly that buttons were sent skittering across the floorboards; Sam kissing him as though he would suck the life from his body and pressing a hot fist in the hollow behind his balls as though he would reach up through his bowels and clutch at his heart. He remembered desire in its seeming unquenchability and rude, spontaneous demands. He remembered as though Sam were gone from him forever and not lying mere inches away.

At last a sheet of lightning transfixed the night. Like a brutal camera flash, it drove the image of Sam and the disordered bed-clothes onto Jamie's brain in a fraction of a second, then left him blind in darkness that seemed denser than a moment before. There was a low rumble of thunder – nothing very dramatic. Trained by his grandfather, Jamie had automatically counted off the seconds between the two phenomena and judged the storm to be centred over the spires and domes of Rexbridge. The atmosphere felt more charged than ever, sending a creeping sensation over his scalp. He wanted to scratch, but a lesion had recently appeared under his hairline and he was fearful of what might happen if he broke its surface. There was another flash and again thunder sounded, closer this time. Untroubled by the first outburst,

Sam stirred this time. Jamie felt him sit up just as rain began to fall on the roof.

'What . . . ?' Sam murmured.

'Listen,' Jamie said, taking one of Sam's feet in his hand.

The rain fell faster and harder forming a noisy cascade on the wall outside where Sam had yet to finish mending some guttering. The temperature fell. A breeze stirred the curtains, bringing a scent of moistened earth into the room. Jamie shivered and manoeuvred himself back to lying with his head on the pillows, wincing because leaning against the endboard, even with the quilt to soften it, had made his back sore. Sam reached out to extend the bedding over him and Jamie smelled the warm night scents of his body.

'I love that sound,' Jamie said as the summer downpour drummed on the tiles overhead. 'Don't you love that sound?'

'Mmm,' said Sam, pillow-muffled. 'Sleepy.'

And the restraining arm slipped over what remained of Jamie's chest, commanding sleep and silence. Jamie held on to it with both hands, feeling hair, sinew, heat, the metallic shock of Sam's watchstrap. He was wider awake than ever.

'Kiss me,' he said.

'Mmm,' said Sam and hoisted himself just far enough across the pillows to kiss him on the nearest part, which happened to be Jamie's ear.

'No,' Jamie said and turned to intercept Sam's mouth before it could be withdrawn again. He kissed it, once, twice, nuzzled it with his nose, then prised Sam's teeth apart with an insistent tongue and, taking his head between his hands, drew him to him.

With small sounds of drowsy resistance, Sam began to wake to the matter in hand. His tongue stirred and slid across Jamie's own. He brought a hand behind Jamie's shoulders and, as he slid one of his thighs up between Jamie's legs, Jamie felt his cock stiffen for the first time in weeks at the first touch of Sam's. Then Sam pulled back suddenly.

'You've been crying,' he said.

'No I haven't.'

Jamie tried to kiss him again but Sam was touching fingers to his cheek.

'Yes you have,' he said, almost accusingly. 'Your cheek's still wet.' He brushed the tears tenderly with his mouth, kissed Jamie on each of his eyelids. 'Why were you crying?'

'Nothing,' Jamie protested in all honesty. 'I didn't even know I had been. Don't talk. Stop being all nice. I want you. Come on. I want you.'

With a nervous chuckle, Sam stopped stroking his face and brought his hand down to Jamie's hard-on.

'So you do,' he breathed and lent to kiss then, fleetingly, bite one of Jamie's nipples.

For a few minutes it really felt as though they were going to have what Sandy, with hundred-weight irony, called 'good, old-fashioned sex'. For a few moments, Sam threw off the torpor of sleep, Jamie, the patient's melancholy. They were two bodies, ravenous for satisfaction from each other, nothing more. There was no kind pretence, no well-meaning effort. Then, tearing away from Sam's mouth, Jamie slid down his body to taste his cock and felt it swiftly buckle and deflate between his lips.

'I'm sorry,' Sam muttered. 'Don't mind me.'

He pulled Jamie back up beside him – easily done, now that Jamie was so light – and began to bring him off with his hand. But he was at the wrong angle to do it properly and Jamie ended up by brushing his hand aside and doing it for himself. Sam did his best. He held an arm between Jamie's thighs, even held Jamie back against the pillow by his hair, which he knew he liked, but Jamie, as he brought himself to a juddering, pleasureless climax, had rarely felt more alone in another's presence.

He wiped himself dry on the tee-shirt he had been wearing earlier, then went to close the window because the rain was coming in and staining the floor and the room was growing cold. He had taken to keeping a candle on the bedside table to read by when he couldn't sleep at night, because he found it less likely to disturb Sam than the reading light or a torch. He lit it now. Sam already had his face back in the pillows, sliding back into sleep.

'Going to read a bit?' he mumbled.

'No,' Jamie said. 'I want to ask you something and I need to see your face while I do it. Sorry. It won't take long.'

'That's all right.' Sam turned slightly and thrust an arm over Jamie's waist, pulling him closer. 'Sorry about just now,' he said. 'I don't know what happened. I – I really wanted you and then I –'

'And then you didn't.'

'No. Fuck. Listen. I –'

'It's okay, Sam. It doesn't matter.' Jamie stroked Sam's hair, now so much thicker than his own, which was laid waste by drugs and illness. 'You wanted to want me.' Sam briefly tightened his grip across Jamie's belly as confirmation. The rain stopped abruptly.

Fingers still meshed in Sam's hair, Jamie turned to watch the candle flame. His breath made it waver about the wick.

'When things get really bad,' he began, then faltered. 'Christ. It's amazing how long you can keep moving the goalposts. A year ago I'd have thought losing my hair by the handful was really bad, or having to get up in the night to change the sheets because I shat all over them; now really bad is something else. There's always something else.'

'Jamie.'

'What?'

'It's the middle of the night. You're rabbiting. What are you trying to say?'

'Sorry.' Jamie took a breath, stilling his mind into focus. 'When things get really bad, I want you to kill me.' He felt Sam's hand flinch involuntarily. 'Will you do that?'

Sam withdrew his hand.

'You've got to be joking,' he protested.

'It wouldn't be hard. You'd know I wanted it. You'd just have to switch off my life-support system or turn off my drip or something. You could just hold a pillow over my face. It would be a kind of love thing. Our last sex.'

'Fuck you're getting weird. Shut up. I don't want to hear this.'

'Sam it's not a big deal.'

Sam sat up now, staring at him incredulously.

'Oh no. I just top you, right? How do you expect me to live with that on my mind?'

Jamie had not meant to discuss this at all. He knew such decisions would be easier to take if he were no longer available for discussion. Now that he had started, he had to continue however. He paused, trying to screw his mind to the right words. Sam lay back on the pillows, frowning, watching him.

'Listen,' Jamie explained gently. 'A good death is a basic human right. We don't ask to be born, we don't get to choose how or where. The very least we should be allowed is to choose to die when we're ready. Look.' He touched Sam's shoulder. 'Forget pillows. Forget drips. I shouldn't have said any of that.'

'Quite right you shouldn't.'

'I wasn't thinking. All I want is for you to promise that when I next get ill you won't let them try to cure me.'

'But what if –?'

'I'm ready, Sam. I've had enough. Haven't you?'

'No. I – I want –' Sam broke off. He looked down at his hands on the sheets then out and away into the pool of darkness on which the bed now floated.

'What do you want?' Jamie demanded. 'Tell me, Sam. You never tell me anything nowadays. You've become such a fucking nurse. Tell me.'

Sam looked back at him defiantly.

'I want you to get well again,' he said, choked now.

'Well I won't. You know that now. You've got to accept it. Oh they can fix me up, one thing at a time. But it's like a computer game; them against the aliens. The more they shoot down, the faster they pop up. It's wearing me out. It's worn me down. Look at me, for fuck's sake.'

'I'm looking.'

'*Look* at me, Sam. Really look. How much further do you want it to go. My eyes? My legs. If you like I can get rheumatoid arthritis in all my joints, like Guy did. You can push me in a wheelchair then, listen to me cry with pain when I try to get dressed.'

'Shut up.'

'Or maybe you want to see me covered in these.' Jamie grabbed Sam's hand and pressed it to the lesion on his scalp and the new one on his thigh. 'If we wait a bit longer I can turn into Ribena Boy for you.'

Sam tore away his hand defensively, furious.

'I never said I –'

'Or what about the brain? Some of us really start raving. My brain could go really doolally. In fact I reckon it's already on the way.'

'Okay I promise,' Sam grunted.

'How can I be sure?'

'I said I promise, okay?'

Jamie was astonished at the anger he was feeling. It felt hot on his face. It churned in his chest. Directionless anger. Almost a pain.

'No more treatments?' he asked, teeth chattering. 'No more chemo?'

'No more nothing.'

'They can give me morphine. That's all I'll need. Apparently it gives you amazing dreams. Nightmares too sometimes. The trip of all trips, Sandy said –'

Sam had rolled over, turning his back.

'I'm sorry,' he muttered, 'but it's really late and I'm fucking tired and I'm going to sleep.'

Jamie stared at him, trembling as the anger drained from his face.

'Sam?' he asked, softly. 'Sam, I –'

But he felt Sam's determination and fell silent. He turned and blew out the candle, lay back on the pillows and pulled the bedding up over his shoulders again. Sam was retreating from him into a stony emotionless silence. Sam – who was always so free in his body, so easy to touch, so swift with his reactions – was becoming inhibited by the inability to express his rage and horror.

I've lost him, Jamie thought to himself, voicing the simple statement in his head to see how it felt. *I've lost him*. All he could really feel, however, was a sense of fierce, playground triumph at having wrested the all-important promise from him.

57

That summer was one of the most consistently glorious in Alison's memory. There was a succession of terrific June storms, which battered the plants and brought slugs and snails out of hiding, then there was no more rain until the autumn. The sun shone for week after blistering week. Lawns turned yellow, water was rationed, in some areas householders even had to fetch their water from stand-pipes in the street. There were daily warnings on radio and television about skin cancer and the dangers of sunbathing, but only the bed-ridden stayed pale. Even Alison, whose complexion rarely did more than turn an angry pink in the sun, or produce freckles, acquired a shade somewhere between honey and sand. People talked nostalgically of drizzle and hot meals. And yet for her, the summer was no more than one prolonged medical crisis.

It began when Sam surprised her by driving up to London to meet her for lunch near the office. He took a while to come to the point but finally, haltingly, confessed that he was having trouble managing on his own and wondered if she had been serious when she had offered to take a compassionate leave from the office.

'Of course,' she said with blind certainty.

There is no such thing as a fallow season in publishing – the summer lull is largely illusory, and the autumn ushers in another round of prizes, sales conferences and book fairs. She had never really thought through the logistics of leaving the office. She had vaguely planned to take a car-load of editorial work away with her and drop back in to Pharos once a week, but as soon as she started to outline the idea to some of the other staff, she saw how unfeasible the plan was. Her telephone rarely stopped ringing; there were queries from the production department, the publicity department, authors, agents, other editors. For every book at the calm, copy-editing stage, there was another in the frantic process of being launched upon an over-sated public. Raising the problem at an editorial meeting, she did not spell out the precise nature of Jamie's illness at first.

'He's sick,' she said simply. 'I need to be with him. Visits aren't enough. I'm owed about a fortnight's holiday but I'm going to need double that. Maybe longer.'

Cynthia started to raise objections. Could she not hire a nurse? Could she not simply move him up to London so she could see him every evening? Cornered, Alison realised that she was being called upon to weigh up her priorities, and that there was no question which came first. So she played the fear card and tossed the dread acronym onto the board table between them. The reaction was instantaneous. Oh my god. Her brother's actually *dying*. As they speedily agreed to let her take a month's compassionate leave, after which the situation would be reviewed, she sensed something distasteful in her colleagues' sudden eagerness to oblige. There was prurience, naturally. They asked if there was anything they could do to help on a practical level, she knew they were wondering just *how* was he sick? Where? Which bits? Cynthia sweetly suggested that this might be the opportunity for Alison to do some writing of her own that she had always talked about, and Alison heard the commercial calculation in her voice. Jamie's illness was a profoundly fashionable horror, after all, and there might conceivably be a non-fiction weepie in the making.

As she hurried from the board room to see how swiftly she could clear her desk and cancel her appointments, the young protégé she had manoeuvred into an editorship all those months before gave her a hug. He looked closely at her with as much soulfulness as his cold blue eyes could muster. When he said it must be so awful and to let him know if there was anything he could do, anything at all, she realised that he would take advantage of her absence to poach her authors and her position.

She rode home in a taxi with several bags of paper and, by the time she had emptied the fridge of perishables, turned off the boiler, packed in a cursing rush and set off for the motorway in a car loaded to the roof, her revulsion at her colleagues' reactions was great enough to give her pause for serious thought as to whether she would ever return to Pharos. Within days of her arrival at The Roundel, however, all thoughts of office politics had been swept aside by her concern for Jamie. As the hot days melted into one long, terrible blur, the bags of unpublished fiction stacked in a corner of her bedroom came to represent a little harbour of normality, slipping ever nearer the margin of her vision. Formerly an advocate of the psychological realists in the field, she now learned the true value of fictive escapism. Her daily phone call to the office, always in mid-afternoon, when Jamie was taking a nap, assumed all the spiritual importance of a religious observance; some people prayed, Alison rang her secretary.

Jamie now spent most of his time asleep, either in bed or in a drugged doze, pale from pain, beneath a rug on a sofa or garden chair. Alison spent more hours alone with Sam than she had in the brief time he was her lodger. She noticed the changes in him. He was more confident about the house, knowing where everything was, easy in his use of the objects of her childhood. Sometimes it was as though she were the visitor, he the host. She realised now how superior her old attitude to him must have been when she had regarded him as a safe, doglike presence. Either that or he had been on best behaviour, in deference to her hospitality or gender. He had become the dominant presence in a male household. He peed without closing the bathroom door, and it seemed she was forever lowering lavatory seats. The fridge was full of beer, which he drank straight from the can with appreciative burps. He cooked them large, uncompromisingly meaty meals on a barbecue he had built outside the kitchen windows.

Under stress, he lost his temper often now, usually with blameless, inanimate objects – the motorbike, the lawn mower, the television's remote control unit – occasionally with her grandfather or Jamie. He was furious having cooked a large, rich brew of *chili con carne*, only to find Jamie unable to cope with its spiciness, and hurled the mixture, pan and all, into the kitchen dustbin. He yelled at her grandfather for having forgotten to buy some blank video cassettes on a trip into town. He never shouted at Alison however, although she often expected it of him. There was something impressive about his sudden rages. Their pretexts were often so slight that it was easy to feel he was merely venting the impotent anger the rest of them were bottling up. She often kept out of his way when she felt vulnerable or sensed one of his storms approaching, but whenever, instead of shouting at someone or smashing a plate on the floor, he sped off on the motorbike for a few hours, she felt cheated. She began to feel his absences keenly. On the worst days it was only his unruly presence which saved the place from feeling too much a nursing home, too little a house.

Jamie refused to return to hospital. He refused all medication beyond what was necessary to spare himself pain. While Alison respected his courage in this, she hated the way it made the rest of them feel so powerless. It was like watching a slow-motion suicide through thick glass. He developed more and more Kaposi's sarcomas; on his chest, his arms, his legs and on his face. This last, which she had been dreading, finally sapped Alison's hope of his recovery. Appalled at the way he now looked, Miriam insisted he be taken to hospital to have the cancer treated and tried to enlist their support against the tyranny of the Living Will he had drawn up. Worn down, Alison was all for acceding to her mother's fresh strength and suspected her grandfather would agree, were he ever there. Sam shamed her, however, by standing up to Miriam.

'A good death is a basic human right,' he told her, and Alison sensed he was quoting Jamie. 'This is the way he wants it. He told me. He made me promise.'

'Oh. And who do you think you are to be deciding these things?' Miriam had snapped.

'Closer to him than you,' Sam had stated quite calmly. Miriam had crumpled, wept, apologised and then left after retrieving a last batch of doped gingerbread from the freezer. The violent little scene, played out across the kitchen table while Jamie slept upstairs constituted a black kind of marriage, leaving behind the sense that Sam was now irreducibly 'family'.

Alison's birthday stole up with no great expectation on her part. No-one asked her what she wanted or even talked about it so she assumed they had forgotten or, more depressingly, that they imagined she was reaching an age where she preferred the occasion to be marked as discreetly as possible. The day arrived with the expected small flutter of cards and presents – a book, some seeds for her garden, a diary, a sensible yellow cotton jersey. Miriam had already rung with her greetings, but she drove up unexpectedly during the late afternoon and it turned out that Jamie had invited her so as to give Sam and Alison the evening off. Having insisted they set out for Rexbridge remarkably early 'for a look around before the shops close', Sam did not stop but drove them straight out onto the London motorway and announced that Jamie had bought them tickets to a show and even supplied a wad of cash to pay for dinner afterwards.

The show was a dazzlingly inane musical revival, with a candy-floss love story, lines of chorines stamping gold-spangled tap shoes and astonishingly mobile sets. They were neither of them musical devotees and there was a certain tension between them as they arrived at the theatre lest the present backfire. But it had been a cunning choice on Jamie's part. The undiluted escapism was just what they both needed, enabling them to laugh and smile at nothing in particular, to stop thinking, in fact, for two merciful hours.

Jamie had booked them a table at a restaurant nearby. The air was lively with conversation and delicious smells but they were no sooner seated than Alison began to feel uncomfortable amid so much luxurious jollity.

'Are you hungry?' she asked Sam.

'Very,' he admitted. 'Why?'

'I'm not sure I can face all this. Why don't we get a really good takeaway and go home with it?'

He agreed, with something like relief, so they went to one of Jamie's favourite Chinese restaurants, then drove, with their portable dinner, out to Bow. It was a perfect evening, warm enough to drive with all the windows open. The sun had barely set, the pavements were crowded; it was one of those rare nights when London felt summery in the *soignée* European manner rather than the more usual hot and bothered English one. As the car filled with tantalising scents from the bags between her knees and Sam flicked between radio channels, Alison gazed out at the passing scenery and regained some of the mindless euphoria she had felt in the theatre.

After the warmth outside her house felt clammily unlived-in. There was something deadening about arriving to a heap of freebie local newspapers, irrelevant mail and a silent, unplugged fridge. Sam divined her mood, however and, making himself as at home there as at The Roundel he threw open the windows and used the junk mail to start an unseasonal fire in the living room grate. They ate the takeaway sprawled across the floor surrounded by the food cartons, washing it down with some red wine she had set by for a special occasion. But then she found herself wondering, *Now what?*

Conditioned by late nights at The Roundel, they were both far too awake with food and freedom to go straight to bed. There was always music or the television, but the fire had established an atmosphere either of these would vandalise. Hunched up on the floor against the sofa, Sam prodded the coals with the poker, his long face decorated by the firelight.

If he dares belch, she thought, *we can watch television.*

He sighed heavily, however, looked at her with a sigh of bitter amusement then looked down at his hands, pretending to adjust his watchstrap.

'What?' she asked.

'Nothing,' he said.

'No. What?' she insisted, but he only shook his head. 'Thanks for a lovely evening,' she went on. 'I needed it. I think you did too.'

'Don't thank me. Thank Jamie.'

'You never talk about him, Sam. You're going through so much, it might help you cope.'

'I'm not going to one of those bleeding groups you made him go to.'

'I'm not saying that but –'

'I talk to Jamie, all right?'

'Yes. Of course you do. So do I. But you can't tell him everything you feel any more, can you?'

'Yes I can.'

'You're too busy protecting him.'

'What would you know?' he asked flatly, his temper flaring. The hurt must have shown on her face because he made a blunt apology immediately.

'Don't be silly,' she said. 'I was talking out of turn.'

'You spend so much time around queers, you probably know more than I do,' he added. 'Why do you?'

'I don't mean to. It just happened that way. That's who my friends are.'

'Haven't you ever had, well, you know . . . ?'

She grinned.

'A lover? Well of course I have. Only a couple of months ago there was . . . Well. No. I mean.' She felt her cheeks grow hot and moved away from the fire a little, was glad of the shadows on her face. She had not blushed in years. 'I had boyfriends when I was a student and since then – Jamie must have told you.'

'Yes. He did a bit,' Sam allowed.

'I never lived with any of them, though. I'm not very good at domestic stuff. I get bored too easily.' She was going to say that she thought the jump from passion to buying cat litter came all too easily once two lovers shared a roof, but stopped herself, remembering how cruelly Sam's experience of the cat litter phase had been cut short.

'Who was the most recent, then? Have I met him?'

'Sam! This is most unlike you.'

'Sorry.'

'No. It's all right. I tell Jamie everything normally but I didn't tell him about this one. I couldn't.'

'Why not.'

'Oh. I dunno.' She looked up at Sam. 'He was just a gatecrasher at Sandy's birthday party. An American. Cute.'

'Oh yes?' Sam smiled, anticipating a sexy story. Alison sighed, sipped her wine.

'It started well enough but then I found I couldn't stop thinking about Jamie and it sort of killed it for me. I felt such an idiot.'

'Know the feeling.'

'Really?' She looked up again, surprised.

'Well of course I do. I'm fucking in bed with the bloke.'

'Sorry, that was crass of me –'

'I mean. I'm fucking in bed with the bloke. And not fucking.'

'Sam, I'm so sorry.'

'Stop apologising.' He raised his voice. 'It's not your fault, is it? The stupid thing is he wants to. I still get horny too, but I can't go through with it and that makes me feel such a shit, you know?'

He was obviously upset, and as he lurched towards her across the carpet she took him easily in her arms. She thought he was going to break down and cry on her shoulder, but instead she felt him kissing the side of her neck, then kissing her mouth and, as he held her harder than she had been holding him, she kissed him back. There was so much of him suddenly, a hard, controlling force. The taste of his skin, his warm scent, the hard chill of his earring against her neck, the feel of him beneath his clothes was, for a few seconds, so precisely what she wanted of him that she was consumed by speechless hunger. Then, as he began to fumble with her shirt buttons, she tried to hold him off.

'No,' she said, trying to laugh. 'Sam? Stop! This is . . . no.'

'Please,' he moaned. '*Please.*'

And she remembered Jamie trying to explain, 'He just took over. I didn't have any will any more.'

She froze. For what seemed like a full minute she was frightened, very frightened, aware only of Sam's strength, of his potential for violence, of the danger of resistance. Then he tugged his tee-shirt over his head and crouched over her to nuzzle at her belly and she found herself hungry for him again.

It should not have been erotic. It was, after all, a kind of assault – battery of a soft target. But she could not pretend, whatever the politics and morality of the deed, that a part of her was not eager for what was happening. As he began to enter her, she gabbled something about condoms in her bedside drawer but some crazed delicacy caused her to make her suggestion so enigmatic that it passed him by entirely and he was already in her and thrusting.

'I'll pull out,' he gasped. 'It's okay. I'll pull out in a second, before I –'

But desperation overrode prudence. She wrapped her legs about him to pull him in more deeply, just as he juddered to an unpostponable climax, and came with a defiant curse. Her belly, breasts and cheeks on fire, she held him so deep within her she actually felt his cum pumping into the neck of her womb.

Too stunned to talk, they drank the rest of the wine in silence, then lay entwined and sweating in front of the dying fire until Alison started to feel cold. Sam followed her to her bed where they escaped into almost immediate sleep, his chest pressed into her back beneath chilly, unaired bedding.

When she woke he had already dressed and been out to buy them breakfast. Hastily bathed and dressed, she sat across the table from him, obediently munching the toast he had made.

'Listen, Sam,' she said at last, unable to cope with another minute of monosyllables. 'We can't pretend last night didn't happen.'

'Well what else do you expect us to do?' he asked angrily. 'Tell Jamie? You think we can waltz home and tell him all about it?'

'No. No of course not. I'm just saying we can't undo what we have done. It won't go away just because we don't think about it.'

'Yes it will,' he said. 'It's *got* to.'

'Okay,' she said. 'If that's what you want.'

She toyed with the possibility of letting him go back without her, then sensed that would raise suspicions. They had the radio on as he drove them home again. It played bright, frenetic dance music and they managed eventually to talk about things, other things.

After running upstairs to check on Jamie, Sam drove off

swiftly again on the pretext of buying groceries. Miriam was having a last chat with her son before returning home. Jamie wore the love beads Alison had bought him on the march the previous summer. They were gaudy against his white pyjamas. She found it easy enough to kiss brother and mother on the cheek and enthuse about the show. She had enjoyed it after all.

'And how was the restaurant afterwards?' Miriam asked.

'We didn't go,' she said. 'Well. We did, then we thought a takeaway was more fun because it was such a lovely evening.'

'A *takeaway*?' Jamie sounded disgusted.

'From Fou Tsong,' Alison added.

'Ah,' he said, more approving. 'Fou Tsong. Well *that*'s all right. Happy birthday.'

He sounded exhausted although he had barely woken. He patted her hand, yawned and closed his eyes, falling asleep again as suddenly as a kitten. She left the room quietly and saw her mother off. There would be no more questions about her evening. Her guilt weighed heavily enough to merit an inquisition, but there would be none. What she and Sam had done was so unthinkable, she realised, as to leave them above suspicion. Incest was that easy. When Sam returned with the shopping, she caught him before he had a chance to speak to Jamie.

'I told him we enjoyed the show and bought ourselves a takeaway,' she said quickly. 'That's all. There's no need to lie.'

'Right,' he said, standing awkwardly on the kitchen stairs below her. 'Look. About this morning. I'm sorry if . . . well . . . You know.'

'I know,' she said. 'Don't worry. It happens all the time.'

She had meant to follow him to the kitchen, reassure him by offering the sisterly companionship of helping unpack groceries and making coffee, but bitterness rose up in her like bile and she had to turn away from him.

'Got to call the office,' she muttered.

His steps sounded lighter than usual as he carried on down; the steps of a man pardoned.

Over the following days her 'birthday treat' as she wryly christened it, continued to rise, an unacknowledged spectre, whenever their paths crossed. This was not entirely a new experience for her. There had been inconvenient indiscretions before – like the young editor at Pharos – but before, if she had regretted an encounter, it was because of her embarrassment at a lapse in taste. Her night with Sam only left her wanting him more. She sought self-disgust but instead found herself recalling the feel of his hands. She helped him turn Jamie's mattress and watched the flexing of his forearms. He brushed past her on the staircase and her skin seemed to buzz. For once, she did not confide in Sandy. Telling would only grant oxygen to a fire best stifled.

Jamie's condition suddenly began to worsen. It was astonishing that a body could withstand such an assault. He developed a kind of arthritis. Thanks to Kaposi's sarcoma lesions forming inside his bowel, he suffered another plague of chronic diarrhoea. Spasms seized his agonized bowels up to four times in just half an hour. He lost his sight courtesy of cytomegalovirus and then, mercifully Alison felt, he was struck by encephalopathy which clouded his thinking. Like someone enfeebled by senility, he forgot names, forgot what he was saying half-way through a sentence and occasionally stirred from a doze to produce a sentence of perfectly grammatical nonsense. Returning from Germany, where he had spent far longer than originally planned, Edward took one look at Jamie, one at Alison and Sam's exhausted faces and insisted on paying for a night nurse. A nurse arrived every evening at six and left early the following morning. Used to patients in Jamie's position who wanted to remain at home for their last weeks, the Rexbridge AIDS clinic cooperated by lending equipment – a wheelchair, a drip feed and so on – and supervised the administration of oxygen and morphine.

Jamie's deterioration accelerated so fast that several weeks passed before Alison realised she had missed a period.

It's stress, she told herself. *Just a common symptom of stress. I've read about it.*

And still she told no-one. The Cynthia in her wanted to

announce it at the supper table, the Good Child knew that the last thing Sam needed now was to be worried with the news, only to have it prove a false alarm.

One evening Miriam finally paid a visit with Francis. Any new face in the house, any new witness to what they were all undergoing, was welcome by this stage. Alison saw shock at the sight of Jamie's body turn him grey and, feeling sorry for him, led him out of the sickroom on the pretext of asking for advice on the sorting out of some papers to do with Jamie's various savings and bank accounts. Suddenly there was a terrific shout from upstairs that made Francis start as though a gun had gone off. There was another shout. It was Jamie. Alison jumped up.

'Stay here,' she told Francis, who looked immediately grateful. 'I'm sure it's nothing. He may need more morphine or something.'

Closing the door behind her, she ran out into the hall just as Sam appeared from the kitchen where he was making fillings for baked potatoes – their principal diet at the time. She followed him upstairs and around the landing to Jamie's room. They had moved him back to the little room with the barred window once it became obvious that he and Sam could no longer share a bed.

Miriam was sitting at his side, her back to the door, holding one of Jamie's skeletal hands in both of hers. She was stroking it and making little soothing, urging noises. They froze at the end of the bed as Jamie shouted again. As he shouted, he threw back his head and arched his back, pressing down on the mattress with his feet. Then he subsided, panting. Alison ran forward.

'Jamie? What is it? I'm here. Sam's here. Jamie?'

Again he yelled. Again he threw back his head and arched his back.

'Jesus!' Sam whispered, stepping forward.

'Where's the bloody nurse?' Alison asked. 'She should be here by now. Sam, shall I call a doctor?'

'It's all right,' Miriam said quietly.

'How can you say that?' Alison shouted at her over another yell from the bed. Still holding Jamie's hand, Miriam turned to face them. Her face was wet with tears but her voice was still and curiously dignified.

'He's having some kind of fit,' Sam said, his voice calm but his face appalled.

'He isn't,' Miriam said. 'He thinks he's having a baby.'

The dismissive retort dried on Alison's lips as Jamie shouted again, drawing all their eyes back onto him as he arched and subsided under the sheet, his pyjamas dark with sweat. There were footsteps on the stairs and Francis came in with her grandfather.

They all watched, Miriam with her round, soft face still washed in tears, as Jamie yelled and collapsed, yelled and collapsed in what was now a discernibly accelerating rhythm. Alison fought down an impulse to yell encouragement to him in his labour.

'Push,' she wanted to shout. 'Breathe. Breathe! Now push again. Nearly there. We can see the head now. Push, Jamie!'

The nurse hurried in, walked to the bedside and checked his pulse and temperature before administering more morphine. After three or four further spasms, silent now, Jamie collapsed back on to the mattress into a sleep that was calm rather than merely drugged. It seemed queer not to hear his yells replaced by the furious squalling of the new-born, not to see the sheet gaudy with blood. Francis came to Miriam's side and touched her shoulder tenderly.

'Look,' she said, half turning but keeping her eyes on Jamie's sleeping face. 'He's smiling. He's happy! Oh darling, I'm so *glad*!'

Embarrassed, Francis passed her the handkerchief from the breast pocket of his suit and she mopped her face and blew her nose, breaking the spell that had held them all. Alison suddenly realised that she had been clutching Sam's hand, or he had been clutching hers – it was impossible to say which. She released him with a little squeeze and hurried past the others, profoundly shaken, to lose herself in the swift making of a salad and laying of the table.

58

As a boy, Jamie had imagined his death often enough, usually at those times when the adult world had crossed or slighted him. There would be recriminations around his coffin.

'If only we had known!' people would cry. 'He was so good to us all and we never knew!'

The dubious pleasure of knowing that one's sudden departure left lives shattered depended, however, on a belief that one would still be around, in some form, to bear witness. Even when he had rebelliously had himself confirmed as a Christian at thirteen he had been beginning to harbour doubts concerning the plausibility of an afterlife, doubts which increased in direct proportion to his body's output of adult hormones. His powers of imagination dwindled just as his store of painful knowledge was swelled. Death, he came to realise, could bring nothing worse than life could present. As the virus sabotaged his body's defences, death came to seem no more than the ultimate painkiller.

The process seemed inordinately long. At around the time they started giving him small doses of morphine to deaden the agony in his joints, he became aware that his mind was going. He saw no hallucinations – nothing so frightening as his experience at Godfreys's party. Rather, the decay registered as a progressive dismantling of grammar; small but essential syntactical bolts seemed to slip out of place overnight so that speech became a defective construction toy too wearisome and distressing to bother with. He saw the poorly disguised perplexity in their faces when he failed to make sense. He tried to apologise to Sam when he shat all over the bed, but found he could only shout at him incoherently. Then his vision clouded over, something he could only communicate to them by his inability to feed himself or find the bedside lightswitch without knocking things over.

After that he began to drift in and out of consciousness. At times it felt as though he had withdrawn inside his upper body and was no longer in control. It was like a grotesque cartoon he remembered from a childhood comic – *Beano* perhaps, or *Dandy* – with the interior of a character's head pictured as the command deck of some monstrous war engine in which helpless, indignant subsidiary characters darted to and fro, peering out of the eyes, listening at loudspeakers connected to the ears, pulling at huge inefficient cranks labelled Sit, Eat, Smile, Swallow, Concentrate. Sometimes he could hear quite clearly and his tongue and brain would miraculously connect. Sometimes, more often, he could hear someone shouting or mumbling and it was minutes before he realised the mouth at work was his own. Sometimes, he could hear people talking to him. He was powerless to do much more than nod, or, with sudden rediscovery of ability, smile. He felt them hold his hands, kiss his cheek. He always knew when Sam was at the bedside on his own because he felt his hand slip between the buttons on his pyjama jacket and rest, heavy and cool against his heart as he talked. Alison used to brush his hair very gently, as one might a baby's. Miriam cut his nails for him. His grandfather was the only one not to touch him while he talked. His voice would just arrive out of the air, bodiless and unheralded, like the voice of God. He played music.

The whole experience was quite unlike the morbid imaginings of his boyhood. No-one unburdened themselves. Not even Sam. Their talk was strenuously matter of fact; a passing on of information. Still no rain. A cactus unexpectedly flowering on a downstairs windowsill. The results of the women's final at Wimbledon. Myra Toye's return to London in the wake of her axing from *Mulroney Park* to appear in a Bernard Shaw revival. A scandal involving the minister for health and an American pharmaceuticals giant. Sometimes their talk began nervously and he knew that he must have been scaring them by going out of his mind. *Out of his mind*; the little idiom, so commonplace before, now seemed astonishingly precise, as did that other, *beside oneself*.

Then there were the nurses. Always rather formal. Quite unlike the boisterous ones in the hospital. Politely aware of his blindness they would reintroduce themselves:

'Good evening, Mr Pepper. I'm Kathy.'

'Hello, Jamie. It's me again. Pru. Kathy's off with a bug so I'm doing two nights in a row.'

If he woke with a start, they'd be there again:

'It's all right, Mr Pepper. It's me. Kathy. Try to sleep. Here. Your pillow's fallen. That's better. Try to sleep.'

The nurses replaced the moonlight. It was only their soft, rustling presences at his bedside, their cooler touches, more reserved than those of his family, that told him another night had fallen.

One night he came to after what felt like a long spell in the depths. There was a delectable coolness about him and he guessed that his sheets had just been changed. The house was utterly silent and there was no birdsong so he knew it was night. Someone was in the room with him. He sensed rather than heard their movement towards him.

'Nurse?' he asked. There was no reply. 'Kathy?' Still nothing. He felt a hand briefly press his brow. 'Alison?' he asked. She smelled, very faintly, of vanilla, as though she had been making biscuits.

'It's Sally,' she said. 'It's time you were up.'

'I don't remember. Are you new?'

She laughed softly.

'I'm old as the hills. It's time you were up.'

'Why?'

'Come on.'

There was a firmness in her voice, an air of command.

'I'm sorry,' he said. 'I'm not sure I can.'

'I'll help you,' she said. 'Take my hands.'

59

'How much is a gill, for pity's sake?' Miriam asked, poised over the electric mixer with a bottle of milk and a measuring jug.

'A tablespoon?' Alison suggested weakly. 'Two? Why don't you just add enough to make it all join up in a lump? Otherwise I think there's a table of measurements and equivalents in the back of that old pink book.'

Miriam pointed with a floury hand to the shelf of cookery books. 'This one?' she asked.

'No. The one with all the cocoa and stuff on it.'

Miriam winced and took out the book. Alison turned back to the task of trying to cream butter and sugar with too small a wooden spoon. The lumps of butter were simply swishing around spilling sugar over the edges of the bowl occasionally, but she would not give up. She could not. They had started cooking things two hours before. It was still hot outside, and the kitchen, normally a haven of cool from the sunshine, was sweltering with the heat from the oven. Alison had protested that surely only a handful of people would be able to come out to East Anglia for a mid-week funeral.

'You'd be surprised,' Miriam had said. 'When Reefer's sister, Polly, managed to OD out at that farm in Wales the place was over-run. It was hell. There wasn't a thing to eat, so everyone just got blind drunk. If we make it tea rather than lunch, you can freeze anything that's left over and we won't need loads of cutlery or plates and things. I can probably borrow a couple of boxes of mugs from the Red Cross and some big teapots. You make some fruit cakes and I'll do a load of scones. Okay?'

It had all seemed utterly unnecessary to Alison. She saw no reason why people would want to eat after a funeral – still less have the indelicacy to expect the chief mourners to feed them – but once she started she realised she was grateful for the activity. Weighing sultanas, washing the sticky syrup off glacé cherries, rooting in the larder for spices none of them ever normally used, she found herself remembering girlhood domestic science lessons. She remembered that cherries rolled in self-raising flour before being folded into the mixture were less likely to sink during baking, and that a circle of greaseproof paper lightly pressed onto the surface of the fruit cake before baking stopped it forming a crust too swiftly. The air was perfumed with cinnamon, allspice and hot sugar. Miriam had turned the radio to a rock channel and Alison was amused to hear that her unpredictable mother had found time to learn the words to songs by teenage bands of which *she* was blithely unaware.

'It feels like Christmas,' she said.

'Bloody Australian sort of Christmas in this heat.' Miriam used a clean tea towel to tie the hair up out of her hot face, then turned on the mixer.

Alison felt the strangest thing about Jamie's death was his physical absence. The sudden lack of him was as brutal and shocking as vandalism. She had found him. She was grateful for that; it meant that she didn't have to have the news broken to her. He was lying in an almost orderly fashion, his arms stretched out on top of the covers as though he had reached out for something, then grown tired in the attempt. His eyes, mercifully, were closed. The night nurse usually left at about seven and it was only nine when Alison found him, so he could not have been dead for long. She sat with him for a while, had a brief cry, then remembered to telephone to stop the night nurse coming back. She called the doctor to register the death, and called the gay funeral directors Sandy had tracked down. She cried again, briefly, blew her nose and called Miriam. Luckily it was Francis who answered. It was easier telling him. Then she steeled herself and went to wake Sam.

His room was still fuggy with sleep, his breathing heavy. She drew the curtains a little to let some light in, then sat on the edge of the bed as he stirred.

'Sam?'

'What time is it?' he asked. 'Didn't get to sleep until about two.'

'Half-past. Half-past nine. Sam, I'm sorry. Jamie's gone. I just found him. I've called the doctor and Miriam and everything. I haven't told Grandpa yet.'

He said nothing, just stared at her for a few seconds, ascertaining the truth of what she had said, then he threw back the sheet that covered him, walked, naked, into Jamie's room and closed the door. It was a shock to see him naked in daylight. His legs bristled with thick black hair, stockings of hair almost, which stopped neatly below the pallid muscles of his buttocks. He stayed with Jamie for nearly half an hour while she remained sitting on the edge of his bed, waiting and listening. There was no sound. She imagined him standing, staring, at the bed's end then climbing on to share its narrow mattress, folding Jamie in his arms. She pictured pink hands against pale, warm lips against cold. When he emerged, he had wrapped himself in Jamie's green towelling robe, which stopped short of his knees. She left the room to let him dress.

The studio door was propped open with a wooden chair. Her grandfather had already been up for hours, working at his sequencer. The studio was buzzing with electronic string tremolo and a high, superhumanly high, it seemed, electronic voice.

'Yeats,' he said, not turning but sensing she was standing in the doorway. 'I thought something by Yeats might be good for the San Francisco commission. I've never set any before. One of the late, mystical pieces, I thought.'

'Grandpa?'

He turned then, saw her and understood at once. The sequencer continued to buzz for a few seconds, then he reached up and turned it off.

'When did he go?' he asked.

'It must have been this morning, after the night nurse left. I've called Miriam. She'll be driving here now.'

He walked over to her and gave her a hug, stroking her hair with his bony fingers. He smelled of coffee and burnt toast. Walking back to The Roundel with her, he kept a hand on her shoulder and gave her another hug, for himself this time, as they reached the top of the steps.

'Do you want to go up and see him?' she asked. 'He looks sweet. Rested.'

He shook his head vigorously.

'No,' he said, a catch in his voice. 'I don't think I could face it. Not just yet. Maybe later. Give me something to do, Angel. I can't work. Not now. There must be something that needs doing.'

The door swung open beside them and Sam came out in his leather jacket.

'Sam,' her grandfather began. 'I'm so –'

'Thanks, Edward.' Sam cut him short. He turned to Alison. 'I'm going out on the bike. I'll be gone some time. Tonight, maybe. When they've taken him away. Okay?'

'Fine,' she nodded. 'Sam are you . . . ?' Terrible thoughts entered her head. She thought of twisted metal, outraged flesh and of the period she still had not begun. 'You're not going to –'

'I'll be back,' he silenced her. 'Tell Miriam I said hi.'

Moments later they heard him rev the bike down the drive.

'You were going to give me something to do,' her grandfather prompted her.

'Oh. Yes.' Slowly she came to herself. 'There are loads of people to call. Friends. People he used to work with. It would be easier for you because you don't know any of them and you can just play secretary without getting into long conversations.'

'Fine. Is there an address book?' he asked.

She found Jamie's little black book by the hall telephone.

'I'll take it over the way with me,' he said. 'To leave you and your mother in peace. Angel, are you sure this is all I can do?'

'Grandpa it's quite enough,' she laughed. 'There are a lot of names in there and as I'm not sure who the important ones might be, you'd better call them all.'

He was gone for a couple of hours at least. Miriam arrived, shortly followed by the funeral directors – solemn, courteous women in grey suits. Miriam insisted on staying in the bedroom with them as they worked, breaking down when they loaded him into a white plastic body box and carried him out to their van. They understood exactly when Alison said they'd want everything as plain as possible; no flowers, the cheapest coffin. She assumed he would be cremated but Miriam surprised her by announcing that there was a family plot in the local church.

'Dad bought it when Sally died,' she explained. 'Francis and I will pay for a stone.' Then she laughed. 'Don't worry, Angel. There's still room in there for the rest of us.'

Guessing that Sam would not wish to be involved in the laying of plans, Alison plumped for a funeral as soon as possible. The suited women consulted their diary and offered Thursday afternoon. Miriam went upstairs to strip Jamie's bed and air the room, taking an armful of big, late-summer daisies to arrange in a vase on his windowsill.

Alison called a couple of newspapers to put notices into the next day's editions, then slipped over to the studio to tell her grandfather the date and time for the funeral, to pass on to the people he was ringing. Seeing him at his desk, little black book in hand, telling somebody, 'Yes. Jamie. Jamie Pepper. I'm his grandfather. No. He'd been ill some time. That's right. A merciful release', she realised that he was probably calling not just friends but all manner of startled married men or fleeting holiday contacts for whom her brother represented only an hour of passionate release, and maybe even less, men who had long since forgotten his name, men who had died. She let him carry on calling, however, working his way solemnly through from A to Z, calling even the ones who were only entered as Christian names and a number. It would have amused Jamie enormously, and might make the funeral less stifling, if the little country church were filled with a wildly heterogeneous crowd all asking one another, 'So how did *you* know him?'

In no time, her grandfather's calls generated others and The Roundel telephone began to ring. Sandy was among the first, announcing she had already hired a coach to bring friends to the funeral 'because everyone's going to want to drink', then Belgian Agnes called and cried so much that Alison had to hang up on her because tears had become infectious as sneezes. Her grandfather finished his task, and came over to the kitchen. He sat on a stool at one end of the table drinking coffee and watching the great bake-in. Slowly, automatically, he and Miriam began to bicker. He asked where Francis was and sniped at him for not managing to take the day off to be with her. She countered with a squib aimed across his bows at Myra Toye.

'She was on some chat show last night. A wreck of a woman really. Of course she has no pride since she lost her job on that series. Trust her to come back to London with her tail between her legs.'

'As a matter of fact,' he countered deliberately, 'I had heard that she lost the job because the actors she had to kiss didn't like her doing so much work for AIDS charities or the fact that one of her husbands was a promiscuous bisexual.'

Alison looked up, startled that this first mention of Myra Toye by him in months should be favourable. Miriam, startled merely at the sudden, bald mention of the virus, and worn out by the effort of sustaining bright, ordinary behaviour for the last few hours, had a fit of the shakes and dropped the bottle of vanilla essence she had been holding.

'Shit!' she hissed. 'Now look what you've made me do! And look, it's gone on my shoes too!'

The thick, beige syrup began to spread out from the puddle on the tiles where the bottle had shattered. The room swiftly grew sickly with vanilla. Nauseated at the strength of the smell, Alison plunged a cloth into hot water to mop it up. Miriam stepped daintily away from the broken glass in her stockinged feet, dabbing at her precious suede shoes with a piece of paper towel.

'Ruined,' she muttered. 'It's bound to stain because I hadn't got around to Scotchguarding them yet.'

A harsh sound broke from her father, causing them both to look up from what they were doing. Still clutching his coffee in a shaking grip, his whole body was tight with despair, his face grotesque with grief. For a moment they just watched him. Then he let out another sob. Alison dropped the cloth and darted forward to take the coffee from him before he dropped it.

'Don't,' she said. 'It doesn't matter. Don't.'

She touched his shoulder but he swept her hand aside with the sudden violence of a furious child. Her bones ached from the blow. Then, to her amazement, he reached out his arms towards Miriam. No less surprised, Miriam lurched towards him, still holding her shoes, her face becoming a reflection of his, and they fell into each other's grasp with such violence that his stool rocked beneath him.

'It's not right,' he kept saying, 'I shouldn't be here any more. Both of them. I shouldn't be here.'

Lingering clumsily beyond the knot they formed, Alison sipped the coffee in her hand and found it stone cold. She saw blood seeping out through Miriam's stocking where she had cut herself, then suddenly was aware of a familiar dragging sensation in her loins and lower back, like the withdrawal of a relentless, surgical fist. Sickened by the vanilla, then dizzy, she reached to steady herself on the back of a chair then heard, rather than felt, herself crash to the floor.

Emerging from oblivion, she was aware of a sharp pain beyond her nausea. She opened her eyes and raised her head, saw the great, red-brown stain on her skirt-front before she blanked out again.

How they got her to bed was a mystery but there she was, sheets comfortingly tucked up to her chin, Miriam at her side.

Her mother stroked her hair. She looked tragic.

'What?' Alison asked her suspiciously.

'Angel you'll feel woozy because they had to give you a shot to kill the pain.'

'Did I lose it?'

'What?'

Brought up short by her mother's confusion, Alison forced her mind to focus.

'Sorry. What happened?'

'You fainted and fell on to your broken coffee cup, which

cut through the top of your thigh. You bled like mad. It was really scary. We thought you'd cut into an artery or something. Gramps called Dr Marshall who gave you some stitches and the shot.' Miriam laughed softly. 'He gave me some sedatives too and they're *really* strong.' She began to cry spasmodically then managed to control herself enough to ask. 'What do you mean *lose it*?'

Alison paused for a moment.

'I'd have thought that was obvious,' she muttered.

Miriam stared, gave a little gasp then hugged her and started to cry again.

'You're not to tell anyone,' Alison said. 'Not yet. I will when I'm ready, okay?'

Miriam sniffed, pulled back and looked at her again.

'How long has it been?' she asked.

'Weeks,' Alison admitted. 'Six. Eight. I was well overdue. When I saw the blood I thought – you know how shock can do it sometimes . . . For a moment I thought, "Thank God".'

'Oh *poor* Angel. And you kept it so quiet. Whose is it? Have you told him yet?'

Alison shook her head firmly.

'You needn't know,' she said. 'It's no-one you know. Someone very nice but no-one who matters. Don't worry. I'm just following the family tradition. I'll be fine.'

Her mother smiled, a little smile flat and caved-in from trying to express too many things simultaneously. Eager to be rid of her, Alison had no difficulty closing her eyes and feigning exhausted slumber.

60

Edward clicked a few buttons on his computer, scanned a menu on the screen, then selected the latest entry and pressed Play. The studio filled with the sounds he had assembled for the Yeats setting; lower strings – no violins – coloratura soprano and a great bank of metal percussion instruments. A melody had been circling in his head over the days since the chaotic, crowded funeral, and this was his first chance to sit down at a keyboard to try it out.

He cleared all the sounds save the weird electronic 'soprano', then swung his chair around to face the keyboard and, after two false starts, fed the melody in. He pressed Play again, then got up and walked the length of the long, high room listening critically. He smiled, suddenly recognising the melody. It bore more than a passing resemblance to *Dancing in the Dark*, a song he had used to dance to with Sally. For a moment he sang along with the electronic voice in his hoarse baritone, rediscovering preposterous words he had not heard in years.

'We're waltzing in the wonder of why we're here. Love passes by. It's here and gone.'

Could those be the words? Sally had preferred more vigorous dances, but she had allowed him his weakness for romance. He walked back to the computer, stopped the sounds and altered the melody on the keyboard, changing its rhythm entirely but retaining its restless, yearning quality. Then he reprogrammed the sequencer, scrapping the coloratura soprano in favour of a counter tenor. The piece was becoming his memorial to Jamie, he realised. Miriam and Francis were giving a headstone, he would give this.

It was all over now. The boy was dead and buried under a mound of peaty soil and already rotting flowers. A solicitor had called to go over the will. Jamie had left everything to Sam except for some money he had set aside for his sister. Sam had seemed shocked at the sudden change in his fortunes. What had he expected, Edward wondered, to be cast out on the street? Now it was all over. Having shown she had some depth of feeling after all, Miriam had done the disappointing inevitable and gone back to her husband. Alison had driven back to London abruptly, as soon as the funeral gathering had gone. When Edward asked her if everything was all right, she claimed she needed to spend a weekend putting her life in order before returning to the office on Monday, but he sensed she was troubled by something she preferred not to discuss. He found he loved her more than he was able ever to show, she looked so painfully like Sally, particularly over these last weeks. Her collapse in the kitchen had scared him. At the sight of the blood on her dress, he had dithered hopelessly and had to be shouted at by Miriam into helping carry the poor girl to bed.

Myra had sent flowers too. Not to the funeral but to him, Edward, personally. They stood in a vase on the piano, a great spray of yellow against the varnished black. He had read and reread the card, retrieved it from the bin that morning to read it again.

Teddy, dear Teddy,

I saw it in the papers yesterday. I'm so sorry. These are for you. I won't bother you by ringing, but it would be great to meet. At Claridge's still but thinking of renting a flat somewhere. Now that the Shaw is over, I find I'm reluctant to go home. Is that strange? Have you still got that place by the Albert Hall? (Don't want to rent it. Just curious.) Call me whenever. The old broad is suddenly not so busy.

Love M.T.

Looking at these initials in the habitual violet-blue ink she used to joke matched her eyes, he remembered his bitter loathing of her after she had shucked him off with such apparent painlessness – whatever that biography had made out – and remembered the childish triumph with which he had noticed that M.T. said aloud sounded the same as Empty. He would not call her, now or whenever. What was there to talk about? How old they had both grown? How rich?

With time he had comfortably convinced himself that he had never loved her, that she was indeed too dreadfully empty to have inspired more than a feverish lust in him. A lust which would have died a natural death had she not chosen to murder it first, endowing their relationship with a tragic importance it never merited, an importance her biographer had now rendered official. Their relationship had become, he now liked to think, no more than an efficacious way of lancing his grief for Sally. As a drinking, rutting partner Myra had been a way of blotting out the guilt of his survival, nothing more. The last thing he needed was to do anything that might overturn these certainties. He felt too old. The balance of his life – which, all these years after Sally's death, he still thought of as his 'new' life – remained too precarious.

There. He reintroduced the shimmering string texture in a repeating series of twelve chords that slowly tightened in on themselves and expanded out again, a fragile harmonic lung. Then he added the percussion sequences he had figured; gongs, bells – including the little ones Heini had found for him in Benares, whose high, pure sound he had already taped and programmed in – and the triangle, that most basic yet penetrating of all orchestral timbres. He tried the mixture out, listened, frowned, scrapped the triangle and replaced it with a stick-struck cymbal. At once the atmosphere was rendered darker, more mysterious. Now he locked the new, high male voice into place with its altered melody, and watched the notes flash, beat by beat, on the 'manuscript' sheet on the screen before him. He pressed Play and stood back, thumbs tucked into waistcoat pockets to listen. He smiled. He had his first twelve bars. He doubted whether anyone would spot *Dancing in the Dark* now. If they did, they would think it one of those melodic accidents or, better still, read it as some encoded personal reference.

He turned to look out of the big window behind him,

hearing a thud of wood on sill. After days of airing, someone was closing the sickroom window, acknowledging a complete departure. He came closer to the glass, turning his gaze upwards, thinking to see Sam up there. But instead he saw Sally. Breathing heavily, dizzy with shock, he leant with both hands pressed against the pane. It could only be her. She was standing the way she always did at a window, with her head slightly to one side. He saw her hair, her dark gaze, her hand rising in a gesture like a quick, sharp wave. Then she vanished behind a drawn curtain.

Seized with a fear that left no time for reason, he left his music to repeat itself and hurried out of the door, across the garden and into the house.

'Sam?' he called out. 'Sam?'

The house was silent. Perhaps Sam had already left for London too. The Volkswagen was still outside. Edward had been on the telephone so had not seen Alison leave. Perhaps Sam had gone with her.

'Sam?'

Some late lilies, left by a consoling neighbour perhaps, lay on the kitchen table, still wrapped and unwatered. There was a sour smell, of old cigarette smoke and spilled red wine.

Edward was not easily frightened. He sometimes thought he must lack imagination. He was not afraid of the dark, tending rather to welcome its embrace. People frightened him, not places. Friends who had come to stay had claimed they found the old house unnerving in some way, and even stolid, realistic Alison, who loved the place, tended to keep more lights burning than was necessary when she was there alone. At first it was love for Sally which had kept him there, then it was simple love of the spot and the tranquillity of mind it fostered in him. When Miriam had become pregnant, left art school and taken over the house, he had thought seriously about moving far away, to California, perhaps, or Italy, but found he was rooted there. So he had stayed, building himself the studio close enough to remain under the influence of the old bricks and secretive windows.

Now, however, as he left the kitchen, walked out across the hall, listened again and slowly began to climb the stairs, something about The Roundel repelled him. The atmosphere felt cloying, thick with decades of dust and heavy sighs and he longed to be back outside, his feet on grass, somewhere he could inhale what little freshness the overcast day could afford. His reactions perplexed him. He had no time for the comfort of a belief in ghosts and felt sure that there was a rational explanation for the face he thought he had just seen at the window; a trick of the light, perhaps, or a visitor from the village come to help with cleaning. If he did believe in ghosts, surely the prospect of seeing Sally again would fill him with joy, not this sick fear?

He stopped as he stepped from the stairs out onto the landing.

'Hello?' he said. 'Is someone there?' Then, hearing the fear in his own voice, he was disgusted at himself for being so childish. Determined now, he marched swiftly around the landing and threw open the sickroom door. He saw the drawn curtain, the bare striped mattress on the narrow bed and, on a chair in the shadows, Sam, surprised in the act of shaking the contents of a pill bottle into his palm.

'Fuck,' Sam said softly. 'Edward.'

'I saw . . . I thought I saw her at the window,' Edward said.

'Who?'

'Sally. Don't.'

Edward stepped forward and made to take the pill bottle but Sam jumped up and elbowed him roughly out of the way as he headed back on to the landing. Winded, Edward slumped, gasping, onto the mattress. He tried to stand to follow Sam but found he couldn't. He heard the lavatory flush.

'Shit, Eddy, I'm sorry.' Sam had reappeared in the doorway, hands empty. 'I didn't mean to –' He hurried over. 'Are you okay?'

'Yes,' Edward breathed, managing to sit up. His eyes were watering. He fumbled for a handkerchief and dabbed at them. Some coins fell onto the floor. Sam stooped and retrieved them for him.

'Thanks,' Edward said.

'Are you sure you're okay?'

Edward nodded.

'Just winded,' he said. 'I thought you were –'

'I was. I mean, I thought about it. There were enough there. I couldn't though. Fucking couldn't.'

The bedsprings squeaked and Edward was almost pitched over as Sam sat heavily beside him, turning the empty pill bottle over in his hands, screwing and unscrewing the lid. The sinister idol was still perched on the mantelshelf. Edward was not surprised that Alison had preferred to leave it where it was. He had always detested the malignant thing.

'I didn't want his fucking flat,' Sam said, after a moment. 'I wanted him.'

'I know. We all knew that.'

'Did you?' Sam glanced up then looked back to the pill bottle, repulsed by something he saw in Edward's eyes. 'So why?' he asked. 'Why's it okay to help someone to die but wrong to help ourselves?'

Edward thought, cursing the pain in his chest, racking his brains for an answer to give this boy who reminded him so much of the bullies he had encountered at school. He remembered a fat woman in a hospital bed, a bathroom floor slippery-vivid with blood.

'Because . . .' He faltered. He touched the scars on his wrists, barely discernible now among wrinkles. 'Because we're strong enough to survive?' he suggested. 'Maybe because there's more richness in your memories than there is misery in your present? Have you thought about that?'

'I've thought,' Sam said.

'What will you do?' Edward asked. 'Go back to London? I know you didn't want it, but it is a nice flat.'

'I didn't want his fucking flat,' Sam said again.

'I know. We all knew.'

'Stop saying that.'

'Sorry. What about your family? Might you go back to Plymouth?'

Sam shook his head.

'There's nothing for me there now.'

'But maybe your mother –'

'Would you move back to Germany now?'

'No, but –'

'It's the same thing.'

'No it isn't. I don't have any family there any more,' Edward insisted. 'No roots to hold me.'

'Me neither. I wasn't made redundant, you know,' Sam said. 'I told you a lie.'

'I'm sure you had your reasons.' Embarrassed, Edward began to rise. 'You don't have to tell –'

'Just shut up,' Sam shouted. Edward flinched and sat back on the bed. Sam towered over him for a moment. Edward noticed the young man's fist was trembling. 'What is it with you lot?' Sam asked incredulously. 'I don't talk much but I'd have thought that was all the more reason for you to listen when I've got something to say.'

'Tell me,' Edward said, frightened, but Sam ploughed on, self-absorbed in his anger, smacking out at the bedstead with the flat of a meaty palm.

'Every time I've tried to tell one of you, and it's not easy to say, believe me, every *fucking* time you just witter on like it embarrasses you or something.'

'I'm listening, Sam.'

'What?'

'I said I'm listening.'

'Oh. Well, good.' Sam seemed slightly deflated, crestfallen even. He frowned. 'Sorry. I shouldn't shout like that. Jamie was always telling me. I just . . . I get angry and it comes out. Sorry, Eds. It's nothing personal.'

'I know. Tell me your story.'

'Don't patronise.'

'Tell me. I want to hear. Sit.'

'No.' Sam paced around as he began his tale, then unconsciously did as Edward suggested and sank on to the bed so that the mattress buckled and the bedsteads leaned in towards each other.

'It was in Plymouth, right? There's a lido facing the Sound. Below the Hoe.'

'A lido? You mean a beach?'

'No. A lido. Concrete. Little paths and huts people rent and cafés and salt-water swimming pools. Diving boards.

You *know*; a lido. Packed out in the summer. Anyway, at night it's where, you know, men go to find each other. I'd heard. Everyone had. I'd known since I was at school. We used to joke about it. Anyway, I'd been having a drink with my mates down at the Barbican, in the Navy – that's a pub – and I was walking back up over the Hoe to get home. It was late but it wasn't that dark because there are lights around and there was a moon out. Anyway I was walking and I saw this bloke. He was leaning on the railings, you know? One leg up. Having a smoke. And as I came up he looked at me hard for a second or two then went down the steps into the lido. And I followed him.'

Sam broke off and fell silent for a moment as though reliving the scene, breathing heavily, his eyes focused on the bedroom rug.

'Sam, I really don't think –' Edward began but Sam turned on him.

'You said you'd listen.'

'Sorry.'

Sam sighed, picking up the thread again.

'I'd never been in there before. Never done anything like that before. I just – I don't expect you to understand this. It just felt like something I had to do, suddenly, natural as taking a piss or something. So I followed him down two flights of steps to a kind of walkway built in under the pavement where it was darker. I didn't know what I really expected. I . . . I suppose I was a bit scared. Anyway, he started to touch me and suddenly I didn't want him to and I hit him.' He looked at Edward close to as he spoke, his hands were shaking violently in his lap, his brow shone. Edward felt hot breath in his face.

'I hit him again and again. I don't know what came over me. I still don't. And when he was down I kicked him in the face. Some blokes came running down behind us and pulled me off and got me down on the ground. Then it was their turn to start kicking me. It was the police. *He* was a policeman. He thought I was a fucking queer.' Sam paused a moment. He looked down at his hands, saw how they were shaking and clasped them over his knees to still them.

'And weren't you?' Edward asked.

'No!' Sam yelled, pushing him away and jumping up. 'No!' He ran out onto the landing and down the stairs. Edward hesitated a moment, breathless and uncertain, then went after him. He found him slumped on the bottom step, his great, bully's body shaking with unmasterable sobs. He had not cried once to Edward's knowledge, not once in all those last terrible months. It was as though all the anguish had come at once, with such velocity as to knock him, crippled, to the floor. He did not look up as Edward approached and lowered himself stiffly in the narrow stairwell to sit beside him, neither did he flinch when Edward briefly laid a hand on his juddering shoulder.

Edward swallowed, finding his own throat constricted with emotions he did not understand. He had to speak if he were to maintain control. He spoke the first words that came to mind.

'It was not a punishment. Miriam was right. It was just a disease. We love people and sometimes they're taken from us, sometimes not. He died but it wasn't a punishment. Not for him. Not for you. Now, tell me what happened.'

'No,' Sam groaned.

'Finish your story, Sam.'

Sam sniffed. He wiped his nose on the back of his hand. Edward pulled out a handkerchief and handed it to him but Sam merely clasped it, unused.

'I kicked him harder than I thought. He went deaf in one ear.'

'God.'

'And one of his eyes was damaged. They stitched me up, of course. Said I'd tried to pick him up then turned nasty when I saw his ID card. My word against theirs, three against one. Even my fucking parents believed them. And my mates. It was in the local paper. My solicitor appealed and I got let out after four years for good behaviour. End of story. Thanks for listening.'

He stood abruptly, dropping the handkerchief and making for the front door, unable to meet Edward's eye.

'Wait,' Edward called, having difficulty getting up as fast from such a low position.

'What?' Sam paused, half turning, eager to be off.

Only inches away, Sam seemed to be sliding down into a cold pool of isolation. Edward hated himself for his inability to reach out to him.

'You served your sentence,' he said. 'You had your punishment, however unjust the means. Don't punish yourself again. You're not alone. We all have bad things behind us. All of us.'

'*I actually killed someone*,' he wanted to tell him. '*I smothered her with a pillow*.'

'What would you have done,' he asked instead, 'if . . . if Jamie hadn't just got the doctors to take him off medication? If he hadn't been able to. If he'd been in a coma. What would you have done?'

'Pulled out the plug,' Sam said. 'Or whatever. Whatever it took. He asked me to kill him towards the end. I couldn't.'

'But it wouldn't really be killing.'

'Yes it would.' Sam turned sore eyes upon him. 'It *would* but it wouldn't be murder. I'd like to have had the chance, in a way. I wouldn't have felt so useless then.'

'You couldn't have done more than you did. You stopped Miriam taking him back into hospital. That was enough.'

'But it was cruel to leave it so late. Fucking cruel. Do you know what he said?'

'Tell me.'

Sam smiled to himself, evidently remembering.

'Jesus he said some stupid things sometimes. Weird things. Especially towards the end.'

'What did he say?'

'He said that killing him when he was ready to go would be "an act of love".'

Edward looked away, afraid of how much his expression might betray. He had received these words from beyond the grave as hungrily as any widow at a séance.

'Are you busy with something?' Sam asked at last.

'Yes. No. Not really. Why do you ask?'

'I could do with a drink.' His laugh was half a shudder, an aftershock of what had at last been drawn from him. 'Come out in the sidecar for a bit. I'll drive us to the Lamb and Flag for a pie and a pint before I set off.'

'All right,' said Edward, eager once more to be out of the house. 'Why not?'

Bouncing along in Sally's old sidecar, wrapped in a tartan rug, his hair blowing in the cold autumn air, he felt no fear, only the giddiness of late reprieve.

61

During Alison's absence, her secretary's services seemed to have been borrowed so often by her colleagues that he now regarded himself as some kind of editorial trainee. He did not bring her coffee when she arrived, and when she asked him to find her some files, seemed faintly surprised that she could not fetch them herself. Her desk had disappeared beneath an untidy pile of post and memos, several of which, she swiftly saw, had needed action taking on them within hours not days of receipt. A year ago she would have called him in at once for a summary scolding. Now she merely sat at her desk and worked her way though the pile herself, aware that people peered in at her as they passed the open door, checking for dramatic evidence of bereavement. She was ruthless, binning half the mail, answering the rest with speedy phone calls, but all the while her mind was elsewhere. The last outstanding task was the copy for a dust-jacket, required by the printers three days before. Half-way through checking it she became aware that her eyes were merely scanning the words, blind to error. She reached for the telephone again and called Sandy.

'Hi,' she said. 'I'm back in the land of the living. How are things? Did you sort out the lease problem?'

'Nope.' Sandy's tone was cheerful but resigned to the worst. 'And the council turned down our appeal against the grant cut. We've got until Friday, then we're out.'

'But can't you run it from home? As a temporary measure?'

'In theory, yes, of course. It's my home after all. But the girls have been having kitchen table conferences behind my back and they've all voted to move out if the helpline moves in. I need their rent, Alison. I dunno. Maybe I've done enough now. Maybe it's someone else's turn.'

Alison pushed the jacket proof to one side and brought out the notebook she had been scribbling in on her way to the office.

'Don't scream at me,' she began, 'but I think I might have a solution.'

'You've found us a squat?'

'Not exactly.'

'Is it legal?'

'Perfectly. There's a peppercorn rent. There's even a garden. And there's all the space you need to go on with your idea of a drop-in centre. Only . . . Sandy what do you think about a kind of holiday place for people affected by the virus? Not just PWAs, but everybody. Doctors. Nurses. Carers. Sisters.'

There was a pause as Sandy took this in.

'I think it sounds suspiciously wonderful. What's the catch?'

'Well the helpline wouldn't be a problem, but it might be a bit remote for people to just drop in. I think they'd *have* to come and stay.'

Alison made more calls; to her grandfather, to the bank, to her building society, to the Rexbridge Area Health Authority. Still on a roll, she dialled a number from memory, hoping to catch Sam at the flat. A stranger answered, a man.

'Hello?'

'Oh. Hello.'

'Sophie?'

'Er. No. It's Alison. I think I must have the wrong number.' Suddenly the man was apologetic.

'Oh. No. You haven't. He's gone out for a moment. Sorry. I only answered because I'm expecting a call from my secretary. I'm just measuring up for the details.'

'Sorry. I don't quite understand.'

'Colin Liddell. Tuckett and Hood estate agents?'

'Oh. Oh I see. Well, when he gets back, could you tell him Alison rang and she's coming over right away?'

'Of course. He shouldn't be long. I'll tell him.'

She threw a few things she wanted back in her bag, including the notepad which she had now covered with telephone numbers, facts and figures.

'You aren't going out already?' her secretary asked.

'Yes, Toby. I am.'

'But you've a meeting with Cynthia at twelve.'

'Well you should have done your job and reminded me about it before, shouldn't you? I can't think of everything. You'll just have to make my excuses and rejig it for tomorrow. I'll be back tomorrow. Say I'm wild with grief. And while you're at it, pull your finger out and answer some letters for me. That's what you're paid for. I've made piles; yesses on the right, noes on the left. And check that jacket proof through for me. It should have been faxed back last week. It's not good enough, Toby.'

'Sorry, Alison. Is everything else . . . all right?'

'Yes, thank you,' she said firmly. 'It's all lovely. I just have to go out.'

She made her taxi driver take the fast route, plunging down south of the river early on rather than trailing along the Embankment through Westminster. She tipped him precisely and waited for every penny of her change; she was about to join Sandy on a permanent economy drive. She ran to the bank of doorbells and Sam buzzed her in. There was a handful of post in the hall addressed to Jamie which he had ignored. She snatched it up and threw herself up the stairs two at a time. Arriving, breathless, at the open door, she walked in to find Sam alone again, packing a suitcase.

'Hi,' he said, still packing.

'Hi.' She put the letters on the kitchen worktop. 'You got my message.'

'Yes.'

'Are you letting this out?'

'Selling it.'

This was more than she had expected. Her mind was racing with possibilities. Her first thought, when she heard the estate agent's voice, was that he had found someone new. It was right that he should, of course. He would have to, sooner or later, she supposed. Some man or some woman. But the brief misconception had rattled her. And now the flat. She understood his wish to sell it, it was so irredeemably Jamie's, and the proceeds from the sale would change his life entirely. It was only that his action seemed abrupt, even dishonouring. She sat on the sofa, watching the man who had come to her with only two shirts in his possession, carefully fold away a whole colourful heap of clothes.

'What's wrong?' he asked, sensing her watching him.

'I – Where are you going, Sam?'

'I had a long talk with Edward. I've decided to go back home. To Plymouth. I need to see my mum, my brother, sort things out, lay a few ghosts. Maybe there'll be some work for me. I dunno. I might end up renting a place out in the country somewhere.' He sighed. 'You lot have given me a taste for that now. It feels wrong being back in a city.'

'Don't go, Sam.'

'What?'

'I don't want you to go.'

'Oh. Well.' He shrugged. 'I'm sorry. I don't want this flat, Alison. I never wanted it. You can have the money. Give it to your precious helpline or something.'

'Didn't you want to stay on with us?'

'Yes. Sure I did. But you've got your life to lead and so's Edward. We can't all just sit around missing Jamie.'

'Who says we'd sit around?'

'Well, *I'd* sit around. It was different when Jamie was down there. Now, well, I feel like a bit of a third leg. Edward's got work that's always taking him away. You've got your job up here. I'd go out of my box down there on my own with nothing to do.'

She was mad to have come here. Hearing the measured coolness of his words, watching him going about his business, reawakened the inappropriate anger she had felt in the days before the funeral. He had known about her fainting and cutting herself, how could he not with a lachrymose Miriam on the premises, yet he had said nothing. If anything, he had seemed resolutely colder towards her, not touching her, not meeting her eye, saying nothing more than occasion demanded of him. She had rushed over to see him on nothing more than the wings of infatuation, eagerly laying herself open to abuse. She would have to tell Sandy, she realised now, to make her feelings for him a thing apart from herself, something they could pick over and be appalled and eventually amused at. Anger at him and at herself coloured her voice with a tremble as she said. 'I'm not sure I've got a job any more.'

He left the suitcase, turning to her, all attention now. He cared on some level, at least.

'They haven't *sacked* you?'

'No. And I haven't handed in my notice. But I might later on today or tomorrow. Oh Sam, listen. Please listen. I –'

'Hey. Calm down.' He chuckled, briefly his old self. He sat on the other end of the sofa, up on the arm, his big shoeless feet pressing into the cushions. 'There,' he said, holding wide his palms, 'I'm listening.'

'A respite centre,' she said, uncertain how to start, so plunging straight to the heart of her idea. She would let this alone sway or lose him – if he was interested in the project she knew he could make a valuable contribution and her own untrustworthy feelings would simply have to be subordinated to the common good. 'An AIDS and HIV respite centre,' she said. 'We turn The Roundel into one. Not a hospice. We can't provide any medical care or drugs or anything, but we *can* have people to stay when they need a break and can't face an ordinary hotel full of healthy people and noisy children.'

'How do you pay for it?'

'I made a few calls, just theoretical ones, to see how people would react to it in principle, and I reckon we could persuade local health authorities to pay for people from their area to travel down and pay for their board and lodging. We'd have to get care workers to make referrals and so on. I mean the whole thing obviously needs looking into closely, but I think it could work. Sandy's always been saying the helpline could do more. Well now it can. We can base the helpline there – they're about to lose their space in any case.'

'Is that it?'

'That's it.'

He thought for a moment.

'Jamie was very happy there. Before he got sick, I mean. He

said it helped him. Old Eds is always saying he thinks it's a healing place.' He paused, sighed. 'I think it's a good idea. But why do you need to tell *me*? Is it the flat? I've already said you can have the money. It would help with all the improvements you'd have to make; new bathrooms and stuff.'

'Sam. Sam! It's you. We need *you*. I'd need your help.' Why was she persuading him? Had she no pride? Evidently not. 'You know the house,' she went on. 'You know about building.'

'I'm not an architect.'

'So? We get an architect if we need one. And we'll have to talk to planners too, over change of use and so on. But you can build. You could choose your own workmen and oversee the work. And then, if you were happy to, you could stay on and help in other ways. Jesus, you've just had more experience than most volunteers ever get.'

'I'm not sure I could go through all that again. Even with strangers.'

'But you'd help with the building?'

'I dunno.'

He stood, restless, nervously shaking out his long limbs as he walked over to the window and its view of the grey-brown river. She jumped up to follow him.

'Please,' she said, reaching up to touch his shoulder. 'Having you would mean more than having the money.'

'Well *that*'s a lie for a start,' he laughed bitterly.

'Okay. So we'll need every pound we can beg and borrow. But the sentiment's true. We'll need you too. Please, Sam.' She took a deep breath. 'This has nothing to do with what happened on my birthday. I promise. It's because you're family.'

He sighed wearily, staring at the river.

'I'll help you,' he said, 'but only if you take some of the money from the flat as well.'

'Oh Sam.' She hugged him hard, her face in his chest. 'Oh. Oh I'm so glad. You're family now. You really are. You can't go!' She laughed, close to tears in her relief. Then she realised he was holding her as hard as she was holding him. She leant back in his arms to look up at him. 'Thank you,' she said.

'If you're going to leave your job,' he said, rocking her slightly, 'maybe now is the time for you to have a baby.'

She gasped, on the brink of indignation, then perceived that, from some old-fashioned delicacy, Miriam had refrained from even mentioning the fainting. Relieved that his silence had not been coldness, she kept her counsel and forced hilarity.

'That was what Jamie kept on saying!' she exclaimed. 'He even suggested you could be the father, I really didn't know what to –'

'It's okay,' he said, still holding her. 'He was on and on at *me* about it too. Sometimes it got me so pissed off I was tempted to call his bluff, you know? Threaten to move into your room just to see what he'd do. After . . . you know. After your birthday, I even thought he knew what had happened, as if he'd set the whole thing up.'

She laughed, then bit her lip, remembering a conversation with Jamie in the garden and feeling tearful at the upsurge of emotions she had begun to tamp down.

'He was very conventional, in his way,' she stammered. 'Roses round the door, babies in the nursery. If he'd been my sister, he'd have been insufferable. Dear Jamie. I miss him so much it's like a physical pain. I keep wanting to ring him up.'

'I dreamed I did,' he said, slipping his arms down to hold her around the small of her back, gazing sideways at the river again. 'At least, I dreamed he called me. He was banging on and on – you know how he did.'

'I know.' She knew. She knew too that he was utterly oblivious to the effect he had on her. She knew he managed to see her 'birthday treat' purely in terms of his having taken advantage, with no breath of encouragement from her.

'And then he said he had to go and hung up, and I realised I'd forgotten to ask what his new number was. It's going to take so much time,' he went on. 'I can't imagine how much.'

'But it's okay,' she said, hoping she did not sound bitter. 'You'll survive.'

'You too,' he said. 'With a little help from your friends.'

He kissed her once, on the lips, before releasing her. It was not a brother's kiss but neither was it that of a lover; it was more like the kiss of a new, interested acquaintance.

'I'll drive down to Plymouth this afternoon,' he said. 'I have to. I've got things I never finished down there.'

'But you'll come back?'

'I promise,' he said. 'Maybe even before the end of the week. For all I know they'll have moved away somewhere and I won't be able to find them.'

She shivered, then pulled on an old jersey of Jamie's. It smelled faintly of him; the sweet, slightly buttery smell he gave off when he was hot. She would take it away with her to wear in bed. She pulled her feet up on to the sofa cushions and hugged herself. Watching Sam finish packing, she knew she was probably allowing her mind to chase mere possibilities down a path to certain pain, but what else could she do? As she had insisted earlier, he was family now. As for the child she was carrying within her, she had come with half a mind to tell him about it – partly because she felt he had a right to know, partly because it might have proved a means of holding him by her, however low. She knew now she would never tell him. If he stayed he would stay for her, not out of a misplaced sense of duty that would only sour his feelings towards her. For the child, she could pretend its father was in San Francisco; a lie that lay, after all, a hair's breadth from probability. Many people had seen her leave Sandy's party with – what was his name? – with Bruce. None of them knew him, none of them were to know she had not carried on seeing him for a while . . . .

An unfamiliar warmth began to well up inside her; a painless contraction of excitement. In deciding not to tell him she had at last smothered the Good Child within. She had achieved a pleasure, a secret treasure, entirely for herself. She might tell her conscience she was keeping silent because it was unfair to burden Sam and unfair to their unborn child to foist an unwilling father on it, but her primary impulse was richly, giddily self-serving.

Sam looked up from his shirt-folding, saw her face and smiled hesitantly. She sensed with a start that she had been sitting there beaming to herself like a crazy woman. She recalled that she still had a series of HIV tests to take, and held the thought as her anchor on unromantic reality.

62

The mezzo singing Keziah began a slow dance across the front of the stage in front of Job's throne.

'The lord taketh and he giveth away,' she sang. *'Blessed be the name of the Lord.'*

The choreographer had cleverly given her over-head hand-claps to point up the increasingly frenetic cross-rhythms of the finale.

Leaning on the rail at the front of the dress circle, Edward marvelled that she could produce such a bell-like tone while clapping and actually dance rather well at the same time. Like most of the younger generation of singers, she seemed to have been taking acting lessons too; something considered way above and beyond the call of duty among the student singers who had first performed the piece.

The soprano Jemima began to mimic Keziah's movements precisely. *'He wounds but he binds up,'* she sang. *'He smites but his hands heal.'*

Then the contralto joined them. Edward had met her in the coffee break earlier. She was a young black American. Elegant and thin – something contraltos never were in his day – her voice was so exciting, even when she was merely speaking, that he found himself wishing there had been time to rewrite her meagre role. This would have been impossible, of course, now that Thomas was no longer around to expand the libretto. Watching her glide across the stage, kicking out the golden fabric of her costume and upstaging the other two with imperious hand-claps that must have been deafening at close range, he wondered whether she would be available to sing the Chicago première of his Yeats setting in place of the counter tenor. Jamie would have appreciated her, he knew. She had the nebulous but instantly recognisable quality he had called camp.

He glanced at his watch. Sandy was late. Suddenly he realised the music had stopped and everyone was looking up at him.

'Edward?' the conductor was calling. 'Was the balance any better that time?'

'Much,' Edward called back, miming a hand-clap over his head then making a thumb's up sign before sitting back down. The three daughters now took a rest so the orchestra could run back over the fiendish passage during one of Job's curses. The baritone, not one of Edward's favourites, stood on the lip of the stage, arms folded.

'*Let the stars of his dawn be dark,*' he sang, saving his voice on the high A. '*Let it hope for light but have none, nor see the eyelids of the morning; because it did not shut the doors of my mother's womb nor hide trouble from my eyes!*'

The baritone broke off, dragging the orchestra with him, troubled by a disturbance at one of the doors in the stalls as some fool made an noisy entrance. Edward squinted downstairs into the gloom and recognised Sandy, following a small woman in a headscarf and dark glasses. He waved to her to come upstairs and the two women disappeared back through the door.

'From the top again, please, Anthony,' the conductor called, pointedly adding, 'Quiet *please*, everyone. Time is short. The dress has to start at two-thirty sharp.'

He had brought *Job* out of hiding and made Alison a present of it. This was partly inspired by his conversation with Sam in the sickroom back in the autumn, partly by Alison's extraordinary decision to jack in her career in order, as she put it, to 'do something useful'. All the royalties from its performances around the world and its imminent recording were to be hers and Sandy's, to spend on The Roundel as they saw fit.

He had been astonished at the swift reaction to the few phone calls he had asked his agent to make. Covent Garden,

San Francisco and Amsterdam had raced the little work into their schedules, the London opera house actually shelving several performances of an undersubscribed Bellini revival to make way for it. At first he cynically assumed this haste had something to do with the fashionable AIDS charity tag that came with the piece, but as he set about some speedy reorchestrations to allow for performances in auditoria larger than a mere college dining hall, he was forced to reasses the vigour of what he had always thought of as his sick child. Watching these last, slightly edgy rehearsals, he was surprised to feel so unembarrassed. Certainly the director and choreographer had dressed the piece up in the most flattering fashion. Dance now played an almost continuous part, dancers being used on a huge, empty stage to form breathing, shifting scenery about the singers. The costumes had been designed by a sympathetic young couturier, who had lent his services for the good cause, and the producer presented the story less as a faithful rendition of a biblical book than as a haunting dream-sequence. Time had also transformed the music. Compared to much of what was being written now, not least by himself, the music he remembered as being violent to no purpose had an almost Straussian lushness in parts, and an intoxicated, youthful brashness in others. Listening, he felt profound regret at the impossibility of Sally's being able to hear it, and felt Thomas's absence keenly too. Miriam's harsh words about his attitude towards Thomas had struck home, although he was too proud to let her see it. Reading the libretto afresh made a circle of time and rendered the memory of its witty and loving author as sharp as recollections of recent weeks. The climactic moment when Job's daughters were restored to him from the grave had, needless to say, acquired overtones that were hard for its composer to bear.

Inevitably the press and publicity office had been busy. Much was being made in profiles and articles of the arbitrary cruelty with which Sally had been taken from him and of the recent death of his beloved grandson. One, headed *The Great Survivor*, had crassly given equal weight to the deaths of his parents-in-law and Thomas, when, if he were frank, they had scarcely touched him at all. Several interviewers had surprised him by asking what seemed to him unpardonably intrusive questions concerning his attitude to both Thomas's and Jamie's sexuality. They were raking up his time in hospital too, looking through *Job* for signs of incipient breakdown and references to Judaism and the Holocaust.

The first night was to be a typically showy affair with people eager to pay extra so as to be seen to be patronising a charity while hobnobbing with celebrities. At least one member of the royal family was to attend, to Miriam's great excitement, as was the Israeli prime minister and the new health minister, her predecessor having been disgraced after a lengthy trial-by-press. Rumour had it that there was to be a demonstration by AIDS activists in the foyer, but Sandy had promised to use her contacts to persuade them to keep it on the picturesque side of disruptive, with nothing noisier than a die-in.

Sandy had come along to introduce him to the charity's honorary chairwoman who was keen to meet him. He expected at best a more discreet lesbian than herself, at worst, some tiresome society do-gooder of the species he had all too often encountered in America, with a wealthy husband and too much free time. At first glance, however, the thickly befurred creature she beckoned him up the aisle to meet put him more in mind of Dr Pertwee, she seemed so small and birdlike. At second glance, she was younger and considerably more glamorous. Her skin was pale to the point of whiteness against her dark glasses and sable coat. Smiling slightly without showing her teeth, she slipped off her blue silk headscarf, which seemed like a tablecloth in her tiny, jewelled hands. She revealed blonde hair that was no less amazing for being so patently unreal for someone of her age. Gold glistened at both her ears, around her neck and on her fingers.

The orchestra and singers were breaking up for lunch. Suddenly the place was noisy with unmusical operations and yelled instructions among the technical crew.

'How do you do?' he said, offering his hand in the half-light. 'Edward Pepper.'

'Oh my God,' the woman drawled to Sandy, with whom she had clearly already struck up one of those instantly conspiratorial understandings at which American women so excelled. 'He doesn't recognise me.'

'Mr Pepper,' Sandy explained with a proud grin, 'This is our honorary chairwoman, Miss Toye.'

Edward looked again at the blonde coiffure, the thin, vermilion lips. It was her.

'Myra?' he stammered.

She took off her glasses and was instantly recognisable, though only as the woman she had made herself, not as the woman he remembered.

'Who did you *think* it was?' she asked. 'Her mother? Give me a kiss darling. It's been too long.'

He kissed her cheek. Her laugh as he did so and the extraordinary resilience of her flesh were those of a younger woman, but the way she rested a hand lightly on his shoulder spoke of her true age and reassured him.

'You look stunning,' he said.

'Well thank you. And so do you. Doesn't he look good, Sandy? Your hair's gone white.'

'So, I would imagine, has yours.'

She laughed again, and lost her dark glasses somewhere in the folds of her coat.

'Don't worry, honey,' she told Sandy. 'This is entirely fake. It never suffered, but they charged just as much for it as the real thing, so *I* did.'

He kissed her again, still amazed.

'I can't believe you're here,' he said. 'Why didn't anyone tell me?'

'I was going to,' Sandy explained, 'but Miss Toye told me you'd disappear at the very mention of her name.'

Something in the way she said 'Miss Toye' spoke of hopeless enslavement.

'You must let me buy us lunch,' he said, leading them back through the bar and on to the mirrored staircase. 'The dress rehearsal doesn't start until two-thirty.'

'My treat,' Myra insisted.

'Let's go Dutch,' he countered, 'and both treat Sandy.'

'Er . . . I'd love to, but I've got a few things to sort out with the publicity people,' Sandy said quickly. He knew what this lie was costing her and made a mental note to return the favour.

Those of his friends Edward thought of as famous were well-known only in the households of the intelligentsia. Myra's fame was on quite another plane. As he led her the short distance from the opera house to an Italian restaurant where he often took lunch, pedestrians turned to stare, taxi drivers would down their windows to call greetings and he was given the impression that if they stood still, the street would soon be choked with people pressing forward simply to gawp. The restaurant was fairly expensive, its clientele studiously blasé, and yet even in there Myra's arrival caused a flurry and the head waiter led them immediately to the corner table Edward had never succeeded in booking before. He suspected he would have no such trouble in future. As champagne was brought to them with the manager's compliments and an admirer who had glimpsed her out in the street sent in some flowers Myra remained apparently impervious. At last, when the fuss had died down and they had both placed their orders – she for a spartan salad that appeared nowhere on the menu – she slipped her headscarf off on to the back of her chair and removed her dark glasses. She narrowed her eyes slightly at him in a near-smile that felt far more intimate than her laughter when Sandy had been with them.

'Does this often happen to you?' he asked. 'It never used to.'

'Television,' she sighed. 'It's huge. It is to cinema what cinema is to books.' She raised her champagne flute. 'Old times,' she said.

'Hmm,' he said, less certainly.

'You don't sound too convinced.'

'I mistrust nostalgia.'

She arranged her scarf across her shoulders, detecting a draught and smiled dryly at the young waiter who brought their food. He noticed the waiter's hand shake as he topped up her champagne and wondered whether she had a lover at the moment, since she was clearly defying age and ageing anything but quietly.

'How did Alison get hold of you?' he asked. 'Or was it Sandy?'

'I think it was a combined effort. It didn't take a detective to find out where I was staying – the papers were full of it. Anyway, I told you I was at Claridge's in that note I sent with the flowers.'

'Thank you for those,' he said. 'I was touched that you bothered.'

She waved away his thanks with an impatient gesture that recalled her younger self.

'I'm surprised at you wanting to get involved in all this,' he said.

'Are you?'

'After the book,' he explained. 'I thought you might be angry at the things I told your biographer.'

'But who do you think sent her to see you? Venetia Peake is many things to many men, but she's not a mind-reader. I admit I didn't think you'd show her *all* the letters but then again I thought it was rather sweet of you to have kept them so long.'

'You'd kept some of mine too.'

'Sorry, darling. I hadn't, actually. The whole lot turned up in the library of some university in Texas. God knows how. Some maid must have stolen them and sold them. Don't be hurt. It happens all the time.'

'Really?'

'Really. I even got a letter the other day from some drag queen in New York who had one of my old Balmain frocks and wanted to check which shoes I'd have worn with it.'

As she laughed she patted the back of one of his hands; another gesture he remembered. Image by image, the past Myra was reassembling herself before him.

'You've hardly changed at all really,' she said after a moment. 'And you're a much nattier dresser than you used to be.'

'I'm much richer than I used to be.'

'Money has nothing to do with it. Don't let anyone cut your hair by the way. It looks great that length. Manly. Do I sound terribly American now? I've been talking to a few producers over here and I'm worried they think I can't play British any more. Do I?'

'Only now and then. I like it. It makes you sound more relaxed.'

'As opposed to my old voice, you mean? Do you remember? I can still do it. Listen!' She assumed the stilted, clipped tone she would have used to play one of her romantic heroines in the 'forties. 'Oh darling. I'm so terribly *terribly* happy.' He laughed. Encouraged, she went on. He wondered if she were quoting an actual script or making it up as she went along. 'Sometimes, when I'm all alone here, with the wind in the trees and all those terrible shadows on the stairs, I get so frightened but then I remember there's you and I feel alright again. Oh *darling*.'

'It's good. Really good,' he chuckled. 'You should stop doing all that nonsense and start playing some comedy, on stage.'

'Night after night? It would kill me. The Shaw was only a short run and that was purgatory. And my voice goes nowhere in a big space. And what do you mean, nonsense?'

'Well . . . I –'

'It's all right. It was crap. I know. But it paid a lot of debts.' She sighed heavily. 'And Claridge's is very expensive nowadays.'

'Jamie used to watch it every week,' he told her.

'You're kidding.'

'I'm not. And his – And Sam. They watched it every week. Nothing got in the way of it. Jamie was furious when they wrote you out of the series. In a strange way he seemed to give up trying to stay well after that.'

'Was it very hard?' She touched his hand again but this time she left her fingers there for a moment or two. 'What am I saying?' She took her hand back. 'Of course it was hard. It must have been hell. Was he sick a long time? My dresser died of it last year. He took four years from start to finish. Four years. Jesus.'

'I suppose Jamie was lucky,' Edward said. 'Alison said he went very fast compared to most people but then, he asked to be taken off medication.'

Myra creased her face in sympathy.

'I suppose he might have gone on a lot longer than that otherwise. But you don't want to talk about this.'

'Yes I do,' he insisted. 'I brought the subject up, remember?'

He broke off a piece of bread to mop up his sauce. She had finished with her salad and pushed it to one side.

'I keep remembering how he looked at the end,' he told her. 'It's like after Sally was killed. I remember him in dreams. He got so thin, Myra! It changed his character, to look at him. I mean, he was never perfection. His feet were too big and he'd built up his muscles out of all proportion to his build –'

'Boys will be boys.'

'But he always, oh, I don't know. He always exuded well-being. His skin was golden rather than white, olive really, like my mother's, and he had thick hair –'

'Like you.'

'Yes.' Edward touched his own. 'Yes. I suppose so. And he had the kind of voice that carried across the most crowded rooms it was so full and confident. But the last time I went into his room he was wasted. Alison was washing him, I remember, and when I came in through the door he looked like some limp Christ in a Spanish *Deposition*.'

'A what?'

'You know; where they show Jesus being made ready for the grave. His hair had got all dull and thin, his cheeks had sunk in, his lips were cracked. They always seemed to have this kind of off-white spume on them at the end. His lower ribs stuck out so much it looked like he had four bony breasts.'

'Don't.'

'Sorry. I'll shut up.'

'No.'

'Let's talk about something else.'

'No.'

'Please.'

'Okay.'

They were plunged into silence, trying to clear their minds of the unappetising image he had conjured up between them.

Their waiter returned to clear the table and offer them dessert menus. He ordered coffee, she a mint infusion.

'So,' she said at last, 'your opera. You must be very proud of all the fuss.'

He shrugged.

'People like to make a fuss. But yes, I'm pleased. It's strange. I don't think it's any better than I remember it, not really, but time's moved on. So much has happened since I wrote it. First time around it was like an amateur dramatic passion play.'

'And now?'

'Now it's as if the story's got a new meaning.'

'It's about Job, right?'

'Yes. Only now it seems to be about survival not disaster.'

'It's you that's changed. Losing your wife and children doesn't seem so appalling when you get older because it's the sort of thing older people expect. Kids expect everyone to live forever. We were so young, you know. Back then.' She smiled sadly. 'I thought I was ancient when I got involved with you. I was barely thirty, for God's sake!'

'But the thing with Job,' he said, 'is the ending. They all come back to life again at the end. I used to think that was so cynical. God gives him this terrible trial then just says, oh what the hell, live to be an old old man and have all your kids and wealth back twofold. I used to think that was so cynical. Now I'm not so sure.'

'Teddy Pepper! Have you become a romantic?'

'Hardly that,' he laughed. 'But. Well. I think I might be opening up to possibilities.'

She nodded, an actress playing a wise old woman.

'Will you come to the dress rehearsal?' he asked. 'We could sit together.'

'And sit through it all again tonight? Darling, try to remember, I'm a philistine. Tonight will be lovely, though.'

'You'll sit with me?'

'If you don't mind people talking. They will talk, you know, Edward. They'll say you're my reason for staying on in England.'

He shrugged. He was uneasy of saying anything in reply, being uncertain just what he thought as yet.

'Anyway,' she went on easily, slipping a gold credit card onto the bill and back into the waiter's hand before he even noticed what she was doing, 'I couldn't come this afternoon, even if I wanted to, because I've got a fitting at Tobit Hart's. Quite a coup, don't you think, wearing a gown by the boy who's dressed the divas *and* the Princess.'

'I wouldn't know,' he said.

'Well take it from one who knows; it's a coup. Poor boy.'

'Why? What's wrong with him.'

'The usual,' she sighed. 'I mean, he's up and about and working, but he's several stone lighter than his photograph in September's *Vogue* and nobody diets that successfully. That must be why he's designed your costumes for nothing.'

'You think dying makes people charitable?'

'No, my sweet, but I think it can make them superstitious. Have a few thousand dollars' worth of frocks, God, and spare me for another year or two. Do you pray, Teddy?'

'No,' he said. 'I never did. You?'

'No time,' she said. 'I tried chanting for a bit but it did nothing for me. I've been to synagogue a few times since I've been back here, though, and I love it.'

'But you're not Jewish.'

'Says who?'

'Your authorised biography for one.'

'It just said I grew up in Bethnal Green, it said nothing about religion. Unlike you, I wasn't prepared to tell Ms Peake everything.'

'Why not?'

'I have a career to think of. What remains of it. Let them know you're Jewish at my age and there are even fewer parts left for you. Bang go the gracious old lady roles.' She sipped her tea. 'I told your granddaughter I could come to this party of hers at the weekend. Do you mind?'

'Why should I mind?' he asked. Alison was following up the première with a fund-raising barn dance at The Roundel.

'Oh,' Myra fiddled with her dark glasses, eyes downcast. 'You know. Having me trespass on your private space finally.'

'You've never been there?'

'You *know* I never went there!' Her flare of anger was only partly playful. 'I only ever came to that damned flat behind the Albert bloody Hall.'

He smiled.

'Of course I don't mind you coming. You could stay the weekend, enjoy some peace and quiet after everybody's gone. I don't live in the main house any more. I moved out long ago, when Miriam grew up.'

'Ah yes. Miriam. What a lot we have to discuss. I must be going now, though. And so must you, Teddy. Weren't you due back at two-thirty? It's nearly that now.'

'I was enjoying myself.'

'Me too.'

She allowed him another little narrowing of the eyes, her smile for intimates.

As she stood he took her furs from the waiter who had sprung forward, and helped her on with them. They were so heavy he was sure they were not truly fake. Once again there was a flurry in her wake. By the time they had reached the street she had once more assumed her wafer-thin public disguise of headscarf and dark glasses. She lifted a palm and a choice of taxis squealed to a halt. Resting a little hand on his shoulder she kissed him, on the lips this time.

'*Hasta la vista*, Teddy,' she said and, for all the glamour of her gestures and her perfume that lingered about him, there was something small and vulnerable about the sight of her stooping into a taxi and raising fingers in farewell through the back window, and it made his heart lurch in its moorings.

Sandy and the press officer were waiting for him in the foyer with a list of last-minute arrangements to discuss on their way up to the dress rehearsal.

'My granddaughter and Miss Toye will be sitting by me,' he told the press officer, 'and I think Sandy should be placed on the other side of Miss Toye. Would that be all right, Sandy?'

Sandy's gasp and swift acceptance allowed him to believe that the pleasure in the arrangement was entirely hers.

Epilogue

Myra had learned relatively early in life that it was a delusion to believe that age was entirely chronological. Stasis was ageing, as was too much belief in duty or one's own importance to others. Having children was ageing also, presumably because it demanded all three. After her years in California, the English felt old to her. This was not just because they put less faith than Angelenos in plastic surgery. There was a certain immobility about them, and a horror of change. She disliked the phrase 'You're as old as you feel' – which seemed bossy and judgemental – but she had long since bitten through to its kernel of truth. She had stayed young because she had never held on to anything, not even to her nationality. With each divorce she had lost friends. With each marriage she had found new ones. She had been burgled times without number. Jewellery, jobs, religions, houses, men and telephone numbers; they all slipped through her fingers with time. She enjoyed what she had when she had it, but she would no more try to keep it by her side than she would think to live on only one lungful of air. She had never sunbathed, she drank at least a litre of water a day, she had never given birth and she always slept eight hours in every twenty-four, without a pillow. The only plastic surgery she had purchased, beyond a few little tucks around the eyes that she regarded as no more than routine maintenance, had been breast implants after the humiliation of her third divorce, and these had caused such an uplift in her popularity among casting directors and public alike that she had never regretted them.

Myra took upheaval as the opening, not the slamming shut,

of a cosmic door. Her last-minute excision from the series had been a shock, a horrendous betrayal, but where some of her contemporary rivals might have let it drive them into a downward spiral to the detox clinic, here she was forming her own production company. She had recently camped her way through new recordings of *Peter and the Wolf* and *Façade*. Now she was negotiating with a sweet pair of pop musicians, young enough to be her grandchildren, to perform a sultry speaking role on their new hit single and appear in its promotional video.

Seeing Edward again, however, had proved a rudely chronological jolt to her survivalist philosophy. For a start, his participation in the research for her biography had surprised her. She had given him little thought over the years beyond what was required to remember his birthdays. She had always recalled their affair with a vague fondness as she imagined he did. She assumed that he, too, would have passed on to pastures new by now. She had no idea that he would still feel rancour towards her, much less that he would have hoarded her every scribbled *billet doux* to keep the emotion alive. The revelation of the affair had brought her a new distinction. The other members of what she privately referred to as The Dino Club – as in Palaeontology, not Dean Martin – had only affairs with athletes and other actors to boast of, or the occasional president or minor royal. Composers, like painters, were in a different league. To be an acknowledged muse was to gain a more exalted immortality than that of the commonplace, celluloid variety. Her agent had been extremely impressed by the new angle, and had been all for hiring a publicist to hatch up stories of a romantic rekindling of the now prestigious flame. She had scotched that idea, of course, and coolly defused any rumours she found circulating among her neighbours up on Mulholland Drive. But her surprise at the importance with which Teddy still invested her, albeit as a monster in his past, made her newly interested in him. She listened to the discs of his new music, not always with understanding, but not without pleasure either. She read profiles of him. She tried, without success, to catch him on the telephone and found that her failures – polite conversations with his granddaughter and the tantalisingly brief sound of his voice on his answering machine – only fed her curiosity. Several months after her return to London, she was shyly approached by his obviously pregnant granddaughter at an AIDS benefit in a West End theatre, any hesitancy she displayed about the honorary chairwomanship was feigned with difficulty.

Teddy had aged far more obviously than she, but she expected this, indeed welcomed it, in a man. When she had first known him, she had felt very much the older, more sophisticated lover, at pains to hide her vulnerability to the casual promptness of his lust. Even had her career not demanded it, she would have had to make the break with him sooner or later; if she had waited for him to tire of her, it would have left the kind of wound that never would have healed. Now, curiously, she knew the situation to be reversed, now that they had sat face to face across a restaurant table, now that she had felt him hand her, once again, into a London taxi. He was spry, dapper even, but it was obvious he felt himself the older of the two, and she was attracted by her power to enchant, indeed to wound him.

But wounding was the last thing on her mind. What had bothered her throughout her fitting, her second meeting with her agent and the young pop stars, and an incognito visit to her parents' graves in North London, and what had struck her afresh as she had made her entrance into the Opera House foyer and let him lead her to sit beside him, was that he made her *want* to age at last. He made her want to let go, stop making the effort, put down roots. He made her want to become an Englishwoman again.

'I wonder,' she found herself saying aloud, as the hairdresser worked on her in her hotel room in preparation for the fundraising party at The Roundel, 'should I let the blonde go finally? Let the white come through? What do you think?'

'If we did it very, very gradually,' he said judiciously, standing behind her shoulder to look at her face in the looking glass, 'it could be very stylish, even flattering. We could leave the cut exactly as it is, but just let in a long streak, like so.'

'Not just yet, though,' she added hastily. 'Maybe next month.'

She had pulled herself back, but the brink was closer now, she had peered over the edge and she suspected that the fall would be sweet and relaxing, like the long silent falling that recurred in her dreams.

Ordinarily she would have used her driver for the evening, maybe even paid her dresser to travel with her, but Teddy had suggested she stay beyond the party, for the whole weekend, and she wanted to keep her options open. She was late leaving London. The only half-way decent car available had a stick-shift gearbox and she had some difficulty remembering how to drive with such a thing. Alison's invitation gave crystal clear directions for finding the house, however, and a little map, so at least Myra was spared the indignity of having to stop to ask for directions and end up autographing road atlases.

She left the motorway at the first exit after Rexbridge, and soon found herself out in the eerie fenland landscape driving along a thin road perched high on a bank with a dark waterway lying to the right and a system of huge fields just as deep to the left. She shivered, thinking, for the first time in years, of his wife's hideous death. It was early evening and the sun was low over the horizon behind her so that shadows of the sparse trees, the car and the telegraph poles were stretched out for yards and yards across the chill, ploughed earth. She passed a clutch of houses, the village. She passed the quaint old church, whose tower had been visible for miles. She thought of his wife and grandson mouldering in its shadow. She remembered reading how severe floods caused newly dug graves to give up their dead. She shivered again, turned up the heating and cursed the self-consciously eccentric English habit of throwing outdoor parties in mid-winter.

Then she saw what could only be The Roundel, perched on a slight rise above the harsh landscape, pretty and incongruous as a single, perfect breast. All its windows were brightly lit and long strings of coloured lights looped through the trees marked a path from the house to a big barn a couple of hundred yards away across the road. Even through the closed car windows, Myra could hear loud cries and rough fiddle playing. She drove on a little way to where several rows of cars were already neatly arranged in a field. A tall man in a hat and scarf waved her in. She parked, checked her make-up, then stepped out into the cold evening air. The tall man was walking over to meet her.

'Sorry,' she said, 'is this the right place for the barn dance?'

'Yes,' he said, pulling off his hat. 'Miss Toye?'

He towered over her. The last of the sun caught the side of his face and hat-messed hair, glinting in his earring, and she saw that he was beautiful.

'Yes,' she said.

'I'm Sam,' he said.

'I'd guessed,' she told him. He shook her hand with a big man's gentleness. 'They've all talked about you so much,' she said. 'I reckon I could have drawn your picture. I gather you're the one that holds this place together.'

'Well,' he looked down at his feet. 'I wouldn't say that. Erm. I came out to wait for you in case you got here after dark. The ground's a bit rough and it's easy to trip up on the ridges. They'll be glad you're here. I think Alison was afraid you weren't coming.'

'I thought she said it was informal.'

'It is,' he said, leading the way, 'but you're still the guest of honour.' He grinned a bashful fan's smile and she knew him for an ally. She slipped a hand through his arm, pretending to be colder than she was.

'She expects us to spend the whole night in that barn?' she asked. 'We'll *die* of cold.'

'It's only for the dancing,' he explained. 'Once all the food's out and ready, we'll all go up to the house to eat. Then we can come back and dance some more after supper.'

'Oh yes?' she said, uncertainly.

'It's American. You'll love it.'

'But I'm not American!'

'Aren't you?'

'Do I sound it?' she asked.

'Well,' he hesitated and she knew she would have to work on her accent some more. 'You do a bit.'

'I was born in Bethnal Green,' she told him. 'But you're

probably far too young to remember any of my British films, the black and white ones.'

'I've watched some of them,' he confessed shyly. 'They show them in the afternoons sometimes.'

'How very good of them,' she sighed. They were nearing the barn. She heard hand-claps, stamping feet, whoops of excitement and the frantic sawing of a fiddle player. There seemed to be a caller too, just like in America, his voice booming out over a rudimentary PA system.

'And swing her around and doh-see-doh her left and doh-see-doh his right and down the end and up the middle –'

'So who's here?' she asked. 'There were a lot of cars.'

'Everyone who's helped, or given money,' Sam explained. 'There are lots of people from the village and old friends of Eddy's from Rexbridge and London and places.'

'Uh-huh.'

'And then there are all the helpline people. And friends of Alison's of course.'

'So what about friends of *you*?'

'Oh,' he had to unwind his arm from her hand to tug open the barn door. 'I don't have many, really.'

'Or do you know when you've got enough?'

'Something like that,' he said, catching her eye.

She had grown accustomed to the fading dusk light, so when he opened a huge wooden door she was momentarily dazzled by the glare from inside. Behind her it was suddenly night-time.

'Drink?' he suggested.

'Sure,' she said. 'Thanks. Get me some fizzy water with a bit of something white in it.'

As he strode over to a trestle table that was bent in the middle from the weight of bottles and barrels, Myra looked about her and began to suspect she was going to enjoy herself. Like most stars, she knew that the only way of being guaranteed a pleasant evening free from autograph hunters and columnists was to call round a few friends and have a girls' night in. Sometimes she had accepted an invitation to some 'informal' affair, only to find herself awkwardly underdressed in a crowd who had put on their most glamorous clothes the second they heard that she was coming and who interpreted informality as a licence to smother. Sometimes even friends could betray, luring her round to an 'intimates only' evening, merely to spring some hideous surprise like an ex-husband or pushy, chiropodist-to-the-stars type.

From the moment she saw two boys whirling each other around on the hay-strewn floor and was offered a hot sausage roll by a duffel-coated woman who politely called her Mrs Toye and refrained from prattling, Myra knew she was back among the civilised. She leant against a pile of hay bales and concentrated on blending in, glad she had been brave enough to wear flatties and come without her big jewellery.

There was applause as the dance finished and, just as Sam brought her a drink in a plastic cup, Alison and Teddy emerged from the crowd to greet her. Alison shook her hand and blushed when Myra kissed her cheek. Teddy, slightly breathless and pink-cheeked from dancing, grasped both her hands.

'You came!' he exclaimed.

'Looks like it,' she said.

'I'm hot,' he warned her.

'So?' she said, and kissed him, surprised at the heat he gave off when she held him close. In fact the whole place felt warm, from no source other than the bodies drinking and dancing, and the glitter of the lanterns slung from the beams overhead.

'Did you have a good drive down?' Alison asked. 'We were worried your driver might get lost.'

'My driver?' Myra laughed. 'I drove myself. I didn't want some boy in uniform cramping my style.'

'So you can stay the weekend?'

'If you'll still have me, and only if you promise I get to have a lie-in tomorrow.'

She took their laughter as assent and gestured to the prominent bulge beneath Alison's tent-like dress.

'Don't tell me you've been dancing in that condition,' she said.

'Only the slow ones. We did the waltz.' Alison patted the mound. 'Just the two of us, and it kicked a lot so I think it'll have its great-grandmother's fondness for dance halls.'

She broke off, looking up warmly as Sam came over to murmur that supper was now ready.

'Oh,' said Alison turning back to her. 'Do you mind if we eat so soon?'

'Not at all.'

'I'll tell the band to take a break.'

For a second Myra fancied there had been something faintly aggressive, territorial even, in the girl's mention of her grandmother. Teddy seemed to have sensed it too because he moved protectively closer to Myra's side and chipped in. 'The Guest of Honour should have a dance first.'

'Oh but –' Myra began to protest.

'Just to warm you up,' Teddy said, offering his hand. 'I remember what you're like. You'll get up to the house, toy with a lettuce leaf then come over all tired and we won't see you again until lunch-time tomorrow.'

'Nobody calls me a party pooper and gets away with it,' Myra told him. 'One more number,' she said to Alison, 'and tell them to make it a *fast* one.'

There was a little flutter of applause as she let Teddy lead her to the head of the dance area, just beneath the wagon where the band were perched.

'Two long lines,' shouted the caller. 'Boys on the left and girls on the right.' The lines began to form, running down the barn away from where she stood opposite Teddy. 'Or whatever,' the caller added, raising a laugh, since in several places along the lines man faced man, and woman faced woman. The band struck up a chord for a little quiet, then the caller made the lines split up into smaller units of eight, and talked them through the first set of the dance, stage by stage, making the first couple of each unit go through the motions at a walking pace. 'Are we ready?' he called and, in answer to the yell of affirmation, the fiddler began to play.

Way back, when she had been a swan-necked, puppy-fatted protegée of Jerry Liebermann's studio charm school, Myra had been forced to learn Scottish country dancing and accompany carefully groomed suitors to country house balls. In view of her pale complexion it had been decided to dye her hair auburn and launch her on the public as Myra Toye, chirpy Scots Lassie. The image failed, as did Myra's attempts at a soft, Wigtownshire accent. She was relaunched as the latest chemical blonde, but not before she had developed a hearty dislike of organised country dancing. At the balls she had been to everyone seemed to take it far too seriously, bossing one another around in a thoroughly unromantic fashion and dancing with a po-faced glower of concentration which defeated the object of the exercise.

The dancing here was quite different, for all the familiarity of the movements. Onlookers and those waiting to dance clapped and stamped vigorously to the beat, urging on those hurrying down the lines before them. Far from daintily hooking elbows to perform gently skipping circles, dancers locked hands, thumbs up, wrist over wrist, and whirled each other so swiftly that they could lean giddily outwards against their partner's weight. Instead of staying politely with the partner of one's choice, the choreography seemed to require everyone to dance at least once with everybody else. Myra mischievously waved goodbye to Teddy as she was passed down the line, swung on the arms of a succession of men, boys and mannish women, ending with Sam. Then she had to wait, panting and laughing to watch Teddy do the same along the line of women, girls and wilfully feminine men. It was impossible to retain dignity, or reserve a hint of self-consciousness. She was soon as warm as her neighbours and tossed her cashmere coat off on to the nearest hay bale and her silk scarf after it. There was something hugely pleasing in simply being involved in the gradual working out of the dance's mechanics. As two women spun past and she recognised one as Alison's colleague, the transparently doting Sandy, she found herself clapping and whooping like a cowgirl. Someone took a photograph but she didn't care if she was plastered across the *National Enquirer*. A shout from the caller sent them linking hands with whoever they happened to have ended up beside, and they formed three big concentric circles, each dancing round in an opposite direction to the next. Myra found herself on the outside, in the circle which had to move faster than either of the others in order to keep up. The tough-handed men on either side of her, who sounded like locals, danced in great strides so that she found her own feet barely touching the ground before she was tugged on. She nearly lost a shoe.

When the music, which she was sure had been insidiously speeding up, finally lurched to a halt with a boisterous flourish, people clapped the band and dropped mock curtsies to their partners.

'Thank you,' Myra laughed breathlessly to the men on either side of her. 'Thank you!'

They just smiled shyly, as though whirling women of a certain age around a barn were something they did every day, and went off to find more beer. Teddy made his way through the crowd towards her, mopping his brow with a green, spotted handkerchief.

'Hard work,' he gasped.

'Wonderful,' she said. 'It was wonderful. How was I, for an old broad?'

'Better than me,' he said, touching the small of her back. 'I lost you.'

'I think that was the idea. Shall we go eat? I mean, is it time for supper now?'

He smiled at her hasty correction of her Americanism.

'Yes,' he said. 'Let's go eat.'

He retrieved her coat and scarf for her, brushing off any straw which clung to them. With the opening of the door, the night air had slipped in with an extra chill about their overheated bodies and she gratefully took his arm after wrapping herself up again.

'Stars,' she said, as they emerged with the others into the darkness.

'What?'

'Stars. You can hardly see them in London. It's never dark enough. Look at that!' She pointed overhead to where the bright points of light spangled the dark outline of a leafless tree.

'Do you remember that night you made us leave the flat

and walk all the way through Hyde Park in the dark to try to find a bit dark enough to see some?'

'Enough of that,' she said. 'I hate playing Do You Remember nowadays, in case I come across something important I've forgotten.'

'All right,' he said. 'Truce.' They walked towards the house under the swinging ropes of coloured bulbs.

'Jamie liked the stars too,' he said. 'He liked to sit in that window high up under the roof, with all the lights off, and try to spot a shooting one.'

'This party,' she began.

'Yes?'

'I mean, I know it's for The Roundel and everything but, well, it's sort of a delayed memorial as well, isn't it?'

'I suppose so. Nobody's said as much but yes. I suppose it is.'

She squeezed his arm. She tried to imagine her friends and colleagues throwing a barn dance in *her* memory, whirling around her pool, stamping out their cares in a giddy loss of control. The effort defeated her. She would be doomed to go like everyone else; a gloomy lying-in-state in a chapel of rest, a crowded burial, all schmaltz, TV crews and lilied trumpery, in Forest Lawn – where her last late husband had reserved her an uneasy eternity in a plot beside his – then the surviving members of Dino's Club would probably spend a long evening getting discreetly pissed in somebody's garden, remembering various insults and betrayals she had dealt them over the years.

'It's a beautiful house,' she told him.

'Yes.'

'I always knew it would be. Do we have to go inside straight away?'

'Of course not. Let's walk around the side. There are more lights in the garden.'

'Is there a way in from the other side?' she asked.

'Yes,' he nodded, patting her arm and she knew he had guessed she wanted to avoid making anything that might be mistaken for an entrance.

They walked on, skirting the house, stepping in and out

of the pools of light thrown from its small Gothic windows. It looked like an illustration to Hansel and Gretel. When she woke the next day she would be able to enjoy exploring it without all the crowds.

'This is so strange,' she said.

'What?' The house?'

'No. Being here. I often thought about it. I know you think I was always wrapped up in myself.'

'I don't.'

'You do, but it doesn't matter. But I did think about it. Even before . . . You know? When I first ran into you a few times on the set of *Desire*, I asked Heini about you.'

'I don't believe it.'

'I did. And he told me all about this place, and how your wife was a doctor and about how you'd lost your parents and sister and, well, it just made me think. I used to see you about the place and I'd wonder about your home. You weren't the only one. I wondered about Fred's home too, and Benny's. I think it must have been because I was already so rootless by then. I seemed to live in trailers and rented flats and hotels from one year to the next. I don't know how I stood it.'

'But you're rooted now,' he said.

'Not really,' she admitted. 'I'm more rooted than I was but, well, people in LA are always moving on somewhere. And now the earthquakes have *really* loosened their ties to the place.'

'I thought you loved your gypsy existence.'

'I did. I still do. Sometimes. Don't tell a soul, Teddy, but I think I might be starting to feel my age.'

'That'll be the day.'

She stopped, turning in the patchy darkness, trying to gauge his expression.

'Do you despise me so much?'

'Not at all. Why do you –'

'I don't know. There was something in your tone just then. I – I suppose I'm as insecure as ever. Teddy, it's very kind of you to have me down like this.'

'It's very kind of you to support The Roundel.'

'Stop it!'

'What?'

'Just stop it. You know that's not what I meant.'

'And what did you mean?'

He was right. What *was* coming over her? Her mood was see-sawing. It was this place. Or perhaps she was hungry. She sat on a bench, drawing him down beside her, and made a fresh start.

'You know I was serious when I said you could come and stay out in California for a while.'

'Were you?'

'Stop answering me with questions. You always used to do that and I'd forgotten how much it irritated me.'

'Did it? Sorry.' He chuckled under his breath.

'Are you laughing at me?' she asked.

'No. No,' he assured her. 'I'm just laughing.'

'It's a big house. With a view.'

'I can imagine.'

'You could have a whole suite of rooms to yourself. There's room for your piano and anything else you'd need. There's a pool. You could use one of the cars whenever you needed. This place is going to get pretty hectic once it takes off. It won't be exactly restful any more.'

'I know. I confess I was worrying about that.'

'You could come and go as you pleased. I mean, LA can be kind of nightmarish, but there's always the beach house outside San Francisco if you wanted a change of scenery. I've often thought of getting rid of Mulholland Drive and moving up there altogether. The people are a bit more civilised, only it gets kind of damp and cold in winter, not that you'd notice after living here.' She fell silent, worried she had said too much already, worried she was rushing him. He waited a moment, mulling her words over.

'Is this a proposition?' he asked at last.

'No,' she insisted. 'Only in a way. I mean. It could be. If you wanted it to. Damn!'

'What?' he touched her hand.

'I hadn't planned it this way at all.'

'Oh?'

'I'd planned on – well, never mind.'

'We should go in,' he said, 'and find you something to eat. You're getting cold.'

'So are you.'

They stood to go in, and she assumed that this was his way of brushing her proposal aside without subjecting her to the insult of a direct refusal. But then he turned and brushed her face with his hand and kissed her, and suddenly they were sitting down again. At least, he was sitting down, and she was sort of crouched across him. She had kissed numerous men during the course of her stint on *Mulroney Park,* many of them tanned, rock-bodied creatures nearly twenty years her junior. If the opinion polls were any indication, she had kissed and fondled some of the most desired men in America, and yet those kisses had meant nothing. The men were always worried about their hair, she about her camera angles, and they were always watched by some forty crew members. Sprawled on a bench, in the cold, necking, unobserved, with a man who, however slender, looked every year of his considerable age, she felt a real, keen excitement. So, decades of practice informed her, did he. She thanked God for HRT.

'My studio's just over there,' he murmured, holding the back of her neck, sliding his other hand up beneath her coat. 'That's where you'll be sleeping.'

'Mm,' she managed. 'Good.'

'We could go there now. Just take a look.'

'Mm. No. Teddy!'

Remembering where she was and why, she slid off him and stood up, shaking out her coat and frantically tidying her hair. She seemed to have lost her scarf somewhere.

'Please.'

He stood close to her, hands encircling her waist.

'Later,' she said. 'Later, Edward!'

She took his hands from her waist and slipped her arm firmly through his.

'Edward. Eds. Teddy. Grandpa. Eddy. Dad,' he said. 'No-one ever calls me by my real name.'

'Do you mind?'

'No. Of course I don't. It hasn't been my name since I was

a child. It just struck me how funny it was that instead of one name I've ended up with six.'

Myra tugged on his arm.

'I'm famished, Eli,' she said. 'And poor Alison will be wondering where we've got to. Feed me.'

The next hour or so were blurred by her anticipation of pleasure. She ate, drank, joined in conversations, was introduced to countless people, but all the time she was thinking about where he was in the room, whether he could see her, whether he was coming back to her side. The blurring made her task easier, somehow. She was every inch the charming, modest patron of the charity. She wowed the impressionable locals with her finely judged blend of glamour and normality. She listened to sweet old ladies' memories of films of hers she remembered in less detail than they seemed to. She camped it up with groups of boys and queened it among leather-jacketed girls, allowing them to fetch her drinks and light her cigarettes. For the first time in years she drank wine without water.

Alison introduced her to her mother, Miriam, who she knew full well had always detested her, and Myra turned the full wattage of her attention upon her, watching her melt. She wondered what the uneasily respectable woman would say if she had chanced upon the little tableau her elders and betters had presented on the garden bench earlier. Passing behind her later, it amused her to hear Miriam commenting, 'Oh but I think she's *beautiful* for her age. And you get no idea from seeing her on screen that she'll be so *little*! Frankly I'd expected to be terrified, seeing her after all this time, but I wasn't frightened at all!'

She met Miriam's husband too. His eyes kept starting from his head at things he saw in the crowd around him. Evidently drinking heavily so as to cope with it all, he had had enough to become gushing and indiscreet. Swaying slightly as he talked, and spraying her lightly with crumbs of the vol-au-vent he was eating, he confided that Miriam faithfully watched her every film and series episode when she knew there was no-one but him in the house to catch her at it.

'Recently she's even started boasting about the times you

came with Edward to visit her in boarding school. But you never did, did you?'

'Whatever helps her through the night,' Myra replied lightly and, after a moment's pause, he laughed.

What she saw of the house was bizarre; a big almost perfectly circular double height hall with a landing running around outside the first floor rooms to form a gallery and, high overhead, a glass dome. She saw no more than this because one of the first laws of saving energy while party going, she had learned long before, was to remain in one area and let other people do all the walking. Paper streamers had been looped through the old wooden banisters and waved to and fro in the warm air rising from the guests. A log fire was burning in a big grate. She saw Sam standing alone, staring out of a window on to the darkness and watched Alison approach with a pregnant woman's rolling gait, touch his arm and offer him a drink. He shook his head, she touched his arm again and walked away but as she left his side, he gravely gazed after her for a few seconds before another guest approached, with Sandy, and drew him back into conversation. As Alison climbed gingerly on to a stool above everyone's heads and clapped her hands for silence, Myra found Teddy at her side again. Under cover of the people pressing forward about them to listen, he took her hand, squeezed and released it, all without catching her eye. She had only recently seen photographs of Sally when the biography had gone to press, but they had been amateur, unrevealing snaps. Teddy had said, however, that Alison strongly resembled her. Listening, Myra studied the girl, looking for the dead doctor who had never really been her rival yet, in a sense, would always be. Alison was thin, long-legged. She was not beautiful, certainly, but there was luminosity about her and a set to her brow and chin that suggested bravery and determination. Wrapping her in imaginary chain mail, picturing a wind-flapped banner in one of her arms and a golden sword in the other, Myra saw her as Saint Joan. She was not a born public speaker – her voice wavered with nerves and she tended to swallow the ends of her sentences – but she would learn, simply because she now had to.

'Ladies and gentlemen,' Alison said. 'Friends. I won't bang on, because this is meant to be a party, not a rally. Just two things. I'd like to extend a warm welcome to Myra Toye, our honorary chairwoman and, to quote this morning's *Guardian*, our *dea ex machina*.' She was briefly interrupted by loud cheers and whistles. 'Miss Toye may not realise it, but simply having her name on our letterhead, quite apart from her widely publicised presence at the performance of *Job* the other night, is already doing wonders for the seriousness with which the various health authorities and our larger sister charities are taking us. *Mulroney Park*'s foolish loss is our priceless gain. There's now no question that, along with the money from the sale of Jamie's Saxon statue to the Sadlerian, we've raised enough capital for the builders and decorators to move in and start work next week.' More cheers. 'Our first guests have clearly already started spreading the word among their local social services networks, even though they were staying here under pretty rough and ready circumstances, and we now have booking requests stretching as far away as next Easter. The problem now, of course, is manpower.'

'So try womanpower!' somebody shouted and there was laughter.

'Whatever,' Alison said with a smile to the shouter. 'We're going to need more volunteers. The more volunteers we have, even for mundane things like picking guests up from the station, ironing pillowcases or helping in the garden, the more flexibility we will be able to offer. We're not rich. We can't afford to pay anyone beyond the skeleton staff we already have. So if you live in the area, do, please, spread the word. Now. Enough speechifying. Thank you, thank you for all your work and support and MONEY, and thank you, Grandpa, for giving us *Job* –'

'And thank you *Jamie*!' a boy called out.

Shocked, Myra touched Teddy's hand again. Alison faltered, blanched, but used the interruption brilliantly.

'Yes,' she said, nodding, the catch in her voice clearly genuine. She drew a breath, unconsciously clasping a hand to her unborn child. 'Yes. *Thank* you, Jamie.'

She was helped down off her stool amid warm applause,

then clambered back on to it to add, 'Oh. Yes. Mrs Sheldon says to add that more coffee's on its way for those that want it, and the bar has moved back to the barn where the band is waiting for you to start dancing again, now that you've all learned how it's done!'

There was a short flurry of autograph hunters after all. Teddy watched, with wry amusement in his eyes, as Myra borrowed a pen and signed the scraps of paper held out to her.

'I had no idea it was really you,' one woman exclaimed. 'I thought my husband was pulling my leg.'

'Didn't recognise me without the gold lamé, huh?' Myra cackled, briefly donning her *Mulroney Park* character and raising a little ripple of pleasure from her devotees.

'What are you going to do now?' asked the parson, who had earlier confessed to being a closet authority on British costume dramas from the 'forties and 'fifties.

'My dear,' Myra told him, mockingly stooping her shoulders, 'I'm going to plant vegetables somewhere and grow old with dignity.'

She stepped graciously away towards Teddy and the fans knew better than to follow.

'Good speech,' she told him. 'But what the hell's a *dea ex machina*?'

'A good fairy,' he said, relieving her of her empty coffee cup. 'Properly speaking, it's the goddess who intervened at the end of some Greek dramas to make everything right. Like Athena at the end of the *Oresteia*.'

'I wish I hadn't asked.'

'Are you going to fade out on us now to get your beauty sleep?'

'Are you mad? I want to dance!'

'Oh good.'

The hall was emptying rapidly as guests hurried out, exclaiming against the cold breeze, eager to return to the fun in the barn. Myra held him back with a gentle pressure on his sleeve.

'Teddy I'm not really a goddess, you know. This face is held together by little more than good will, and I get ladders in my stockings like everyone else.'

'I know.' He smiled. 'I remember.'

'You remember too much,' she told him.

'Where are you going?' he asked, seeing her turning back.

'I left my coat,' she said. 'Go on. I'll catch you up. Go dance with Alison.'

'Myra Toye, I love you.'

'Oh poo. Go on.'

She pushed him gently out of the door and walked back across the hall. She had seen, Teddy had not noticed, the boy, Sam, standing alone back at the window where she had watched him earlier, half hidden behind the curtain. His forehead was leant against the glass. He watched the last few guests, Teddy among them, walk down the short gravel drive, out of the gateway and across the road to the barn. The wind was lifting. A gust caused the coloured lightbulbs to swing quite violently between the trees. The house was quiet now, though hot and airless from the recent crush. Water splashed into a sink and some helpers talked brightly as they stacked plates down in the kitchen.

'Aren't you coming to dance again?' Myra asked.

He stayed exactly where he was, only shook his head slightly.

'You were good at it.'

'Not really my thing,' he muttered.

'But you *seemed* to be enjoying it.'

He waited a moment or two then said, 'I hadn't meant to.'

She stepped up beside him, pushing aside the curtain a little so that she too could look out at the night.

'God these stars!' she exclaimed softly. 'Enough to break your heart.'

'And don't tell me the pain doesn't last for ever,' he said suddenly, pursuing his own track of thought. 'Because I know.'

Myra turned, leaning her back on the window to face into the room, as though guarding him from sudden approaches. She wondered whether to tell him Alison loved him, but bit her tongue. There was time enough for him to notice. Time enough for matchmakers to interfere once the mysterious child was born. There was always time.

'When my third husband died – George – I didn't want the pain to stop,' she said thoughtfully. 'It was as though if I stopped hurting I would have stopped loving him.'

'I thought he was queer,' Sam said, and she heard an edge of cruelty in his voice. 'I read the book,' he added.

'He liked it both ways,' she said. 'He had a lot to give. I knew about the others. It didn't touch me. He loved me too. He loved me so it hurt when I looked at him. The pain's gone now but I swear if he walked through that door now I'd still crumple at the knees. I never loved anybody as much.'

'Not Eddy?'

She stopped to think.

'No,' she admitted. 'Not even Eddy.'

'Look,' he said. 'He's down there now. Waiting for you.'

'Where?' She turned and Sam pointed to where Teddy was standing outside the barn, caught in the light spilling through its half-open door.

'He'll catch his death out there,' she said. 'The idiot.'

'He doesn't want to dance without you,' he told her. 'You'd better go and rescue him.'

She stood there, feeling the cold radiate from the windowpanes, watching Teddy stamp his feet and rub his hands together. Then her breath misted the glass and hid him from view.

Patrick Gale

Facing the Tank

A writer visits a quaint English Cathedral town and discovers its goings-on are stranger than fiction.

When Evan J. Kirby, an eminent American expert on Heaven and Hell, arrives in Barrowcester to do some research, he finds the community in a less than blissful state. There is the bishop sharing his doubts with the confirmation class, while his mother feeds marijuana cookies to Evan's landlady to unleash her psychic powers. Then there is Emma lurking in her father's study waiting for love; Dawn sitting naked in a deckchair at midnight waiting for the Devil, and Madeline seeking refuge from a carnally inclined Cardinal. When Evan delves into the true origins of the local saint, a macabre and romantic sequence of events begins to unfold.

'The sheer funniness of *Facing the Tank* made me laugh out loud.' *Sunday Times*

'The close world of The Close is tea-cosy warm. But not for long, as Patrick Gale speedily unleashes his merrily black mischief. The uncovering of the sadness behind the doilies and twinsets is in the best traditions of black humour.'

Observer

'Original and amusing, Patrick Gale is an elegant, witty writer with an engagingly bizarre imagination.'

Sunday Telegraph

'A commendably intelligent, entertaining and, at times, moving novel.' *Times Literary Supplement*

ISBN: 0 00 654545 9

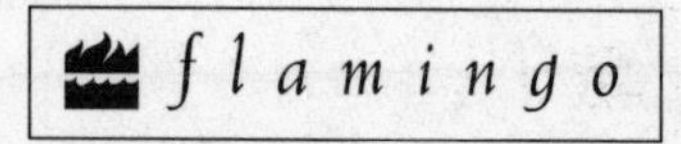

Patrick Gale

Aerodynamics of Pork

Patrick Gale's first novel is suffused with heady wish-fulfilment as two contrasting love stories entwine in the space of one simmering summer week.

Mo, a lesbian cop, is surprised with subversive lust while investigating a series of violent attacks on newspaper astrologers in London. Meanwhile in Cornwall, the Peakes are conducting their annual music festival, the cue for their two children – Seth, a young violin prodigy, and Venetia, a highly-strung scholar – to embark upon a voyage of self-discovery. As Seth sets out in hot pursuit of unconventional romance on the cliff-tops, the virginal Venetia displays every symptom of an Immaculate Conception.

'It is packed with arch dialogue, affectionate caricatures and the feigned good humour more commonly found in memoirs written by chauffeurs of the famous.' *Observer*

'Gale's concoction is irresistible: modern relationships sketched with period charm. I couldn't have liked it more.'
ARMISTEAD MAUPIN

'A sad, funny and deeply searching novel. Plotting, characterisation and dialogue quicken the reader's pace, just as the delicacy of the unfolding love stories quickens the heart.'
Publishers Weekly

ISBN: 0 586 09146 7

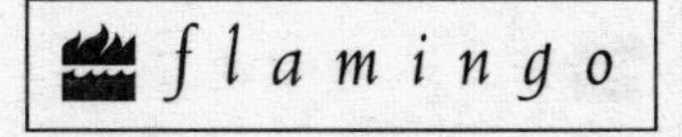

Patrick Gale

Ease

A novel about downsizing from a life of ease and upgrading to one of sleaze.

Many people would kill to be Domina Tey. She's one of life's successes: an award-winning playwright living in a beautiful house with an equally celebrated writer. A lucky woman. And she knows and appreciates it. But she isn't happy. Life is too easy. It's becoming stultifying, negating her creative force.

Domina decides upon a spell of sleazy living to give both her work and her soul a spring-clean – and elopes with her typewriter in search of just a hint of degradation. She finds it in Bayswater. Safe in bedsit land, she immediately sets about getting to know her neighbour, a candidate for the priesthood half her age.

'Patrick Gale writes with the understated fluency that is the hallmark of contemporary British fiction, and with the irony that usually accompanies it. Like William Boyd and Martin Amis, he skilfully blends the light and the dark, moving unobtrusively from comedy to drama without losing narrative momentum or integrity.' Book World, US

ISBN: 0 586 09147 5

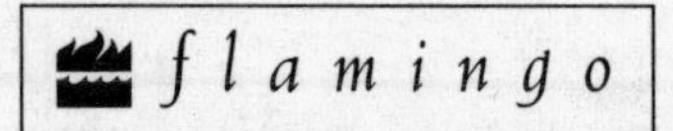